Scoundrel in the Thick

SCOUNDREL *in the* THICK

Vol. #1
The Life & Times
of
Colonel Thomas Edward Scoundrel, USA, Ret.

B.R. O'HAGAN

Pedee Creek Press
Hilton Head Island• South Carolina

Scoundrel in the Thick is a work of historical fiction. Apart from the well-known actual people, events, and locales that figure in the narrative, all names, characters, places and incidents are the products of the author's imagination or are used fictitiously. Any resemblance to current events or locales, or to living persons, is entirely coincidental.

Printed in the United States of America
ISBN: 9781734226331

For inquiries about volume orders please contact:
admin@brohagan.com

Cover Illustration
Thomas Scoundrel in the Rockies
by Tyler Jacobson

www.brohagan.com
info@brohagan.com

For Lesli, my wife, best friend, and partner in the grand adventure.

Thomas,

There comes a time in the life of each man, in the face of the wind, in the gut of the fight, when he has but an instant to make his most important decision; will I die as small as I have lived, or, will I live large, without hesitation or reservation.

I have tended to your fevers and watched you heal. I see a boy who has become a man and who has made a damn fine, shining decision. Give me the splendid, silent sun with all his beams full-dazzling, I hear you say.

Good on you, Thomas Scoundrel. You must habit yourself to the dazzle of the light and of every moment of your life.

Do anything, lad,but let it produce joy.

Walt Whitman
16 April 1865
Meridian Hill

Darrow, Lesli J: "In the Care of Poet and Nurse Walt Whitman, April 2-19, 1865, Mt. Pleasant Hospital Washington, D.C.," *The Annotated Journals of Colonel Thomas E. Scoundrel, USA.* Volume I (Independence, OR, TES Press, 2012)

PROLOGUE

Cuernavaca, Mexico, June 1882

The first shot tore through the bedroom door, shredding the hand-carved cherub on the headboard above Diego's pillow. The second shot severed the beeswax candle on the nightstand that he had blown out only a moment earlier.

He did not wait for a third shot. He threw back the covers, rolled onto the cold tile floor and scurried on his hands and knees over to the chair where the trousers and jacket he wore to the engagement party were folded. Out of habit he reached for the holstered Schofield revolver he kept on the arm of his bedroom chair. But, as he shook off the last remnants of sleep, Diego remembered that he was not in his own home, but in a second-floor guest room in the lakeside villa of Don Eduardo Verján, who was both the father of his fiancée Rosalilia, as well as the Minister of the Interior for Mexico, and the leading citizen of the city of Cuernavaca.

More shots rang out. Diego slipped into his trousers and went to the door. He took a deep breath, pulled the handle, and stepped out into the chaos.

His room was at the end of a rectangular gallery that ran the length of the villa, above a flower-filled courtyard. Candles flickered in gargoyle-faced wall sconces mounted outside each guest room door, providing just enough light for Diego to make out figures running through the smoke that was billowing up from a fire somewhere below.

Doors began flying open along both sides of the gallery, and he saw people rush towards the stairs in their nightgowns and robes. They were some of the two hundred guests who had gathered earlier under a starched cotton pavilion on the Verján's sun-drenched patio as Bishop Orozco joined Rosalilia's hand to Diego's with a satin ribbon to seal their formal engagement.

Then they moved to the terraced gardens, where dozens of wicker baskets filled with fresh-cut flowers were scattered among blossoming orange trees and lavender-colored bougainvillea vines. A dozen tables were piled high with platters of grilled beef, lamb, fresh shrimp, melons, savory tamales, roasted peppers and tomatoes, chilled sea bass, and all kinds of cakes and pastries. The smell of jasmine and honeysuckle intermingled with the elegant strains of a string quartet in the soft June air all that afternoon. Now, the sour odor of burnt gunpowder and roiling smoke nearly overwhelmed Diego's senses.

A pistol ball suddenly shattered a flowerpot on the gallery railing, and one of the guests stumbled over the clay shards and fell to the ground. Diego stooped to help the man up as another bedroom door swung open right in front of him. It was the room in which Rosalilia's widowed aunt was staying, but it was not the widow who raced out into the corridor. Instead, the portly Bishop of the city huffed into the crowded passage, tugging his nightshirt down over his pendulous belly. Behind the Bishop, also pulling on her nightgown, was the widow. They joined the crowd running for the stairs, oblivious for the moment that had they been seen like this in any other kind of social setting the scandal would have been the talk of the tight-knit aristocratic community of Cuernavaca for years.

Diego would normally have savored the sight of the famously officious Bishop caught in such a compromising position, but he could only think of getting through the hail of bullets careening around the gallery, down the smoke-filled staircase and into Rosalilia's room.

As for who was doing the shooting–and why–that question would have to wait. Diego knew that Don Verján's home was patrolled by private *soldados* who were paid to keep watch over the homes of the city's wealthiest residents. He hoped that some of the gunfire he was hearing was coming from those guards fighting back against the intruders.

Diego leapt down the stairs, pushing his way through the crush of guests trying to get to safety. When he reached the stair landing, he saw that the massive oak doors that separated the outer courtyard from the inner garden space had been blown off their hinges. It would take a cannon to do that, he thought. At the foot of the stairs a man in dark clothing with a black scarf tied around his face appeared out of the smoke directly in front of him. He seemed to recognize Diegoand raised his revolver to shoot. But before he could pull the trigger, a dark object slammed into the side of the intruder's head, and he fell wordlessly to the ground.

Itzcoatl raised his war club and smashed it into the fallen attacker's head once more for good measure. The ancient Aztec weapon was studded with razor-sharp volcanic glass that was embedded into the wood. Diego knew the man would not be getting up.

The old warrior had been roused from his sleep in a warm corner of the estate's great kitchen by the sounds of gunfire, and he had immediately raced to find Diego, whom he had instructed and watched over since the boy was born. Now, Itzcoatl motioned for his ward to follow him outside to safety.

"No," shouted Diego above the din of shouts, breaking glass and gun shots. "First, we find Rosalilia!"

The two men shouldered their way through the crowd of people streaming down the stairs and into the courtyard. Diego had to leap to avoid tripping over one panicked man who lost his footing and slipped into the fountain. There was no time to help him. He sprinted down the hallway and through the open door of Rosalilia's room, where candles flickered on the oak sideboard and the smell of night-blooming moonflowers and sulphur drifted through the broken window. The covers had been pulled off the ornate four-poster bed and were strewn around the floor. On a pillow at the head of the bed, the leather-bound volume of poems by John Keats he gave Rosalilia at dinner was open to the page she had been reading when she was taken.

"*Tecolote*," called Itzcoatl from the doorway, using the Nahuatl word for "little owl" that he called Diego as a child. "Come with me, now."

Diego turned from the bed and went across the hall to Rosalilia's parents' room. A fight had raged here. Two chairs were knocked over, the mirror behind the oak dresser was shattered, and a tall armoire had toppled over. One of the window curtains was burning. Itzcoatl pulled it down and stamped out the flame.

The bed sat on an elevated platform in the center of the room, beneath a large oil painting of the Battle of Chapultepec Castle. That was where the young Lieutenant Verján and five of his military cadets held off repeated assaults by a company of American soldiers commanded by Captain Robert E. Lee during the Mexican American War, thirty-five years earlier.

Diego approached the bed. The lifeless body of his fiancée's father lay flat on his back, his arms splayed wide. His right hand still gripped the cavalry sabre he had pulled from the scabbard beside his bed to fight off the attackers.

Diego rested his hand on Verján's shoulder. Rosalilia's mother was not in the room. She and her daughter must be together. He motioned to Itzcoatl, and they climbed out the open bedroom window and into the flame-lit garden to join the fight.

Several dozen people were running through the moonlit garden in the direction of the lake. Diego watched as one of the estate guards knelt and fired at a dark-clad man who was clutching a silver candelabra he had ripped from the dining room ceiling. The .50 caliber bullet caught the robber square in the back, flinging him forward and slamming his body into the high garden wall.

Then, Rosalilia's aunt appeared at his side. She took his arm. "Do you know where my sister is?" she cried.

He shook his head and called out to one of the Verján servants who was rushing past. "Get the Señora to the lake," he told the man.

Then, a shout. Diego turned to see Itzcoatl on the other side of the fountain. One of his boots was pressed hard into the back of a man lying face down on the ground. His war club was raised high, ready to take another blow if the idiot was foolish enough to try to get up.

Diego splashed through the lily pads in the fountain pool and joined Itzcoatl.

"This one will speak, now," said Itzcoatl, "or he will die."

A pool of blood was spreading on the ground around the intruder's head. If he was going to speak, it had better be quickly.

"Who are you?" shouted Diego. "Why are you here, and where have you taken the mistress of the villa and her daughter?"

The man raised his head a few inches off the ground and turned in the direction of Diego's voice. He defiantly spat out a mouthful of blood and teeth, grunted, and turned his head away.

Diego looked around at the scene unfolding in the smoky garden courtyard. Most of the guests had made their way out of the villa grounds and were being guided to safety down the lake shore by four of the private *soldados*. An outbuilding next to the villa was fully engulfed in flames, and two of Casa Verján's defenders lay dead on the stone porch at the main entrance.

Then he saw the intruders: a dozen or more men in black woolen ponchos who were loading stolen valuables into three horse-drawn freight wagons outside the main gate. A tall man in a buckskin fringe jacket and wide-brimmed hat stood on the seat of the lead buckboard, barking instructions to the men loading the wagons. Diego noticed that his wagon, the only one backed up under the arch, had a small, swivel-mounted cannon clamped onto the tail board. That explained how the doors had been blown off their hinges.

What he saw next made Diego go cold. Two men were lifting a struggling woman dressed in nightclothes over the siderails of the middle wagon. A cloud slipped past the full yellow moon, and in the pale light Diego was able to make out Rosalilia's terrified expression as the men dropped her into the wagon and then tossed a heavy blanket on top of her.

Itzcoatl saw it at the same moment. He delivered a final blow to the intruder on the ground and came up alongside Diego. The old man was descended from Aztec royalty. He wore his hair in the fashion of Motecuzuma, the ruler of Tenochtitlán who was killed by Hernán Cortés in the early days of the Spanish conquest of Mexico in 1520.

Itzcoatl was as proud as he was stoic; he alone had taught the young aristocrat Diego Antonio de San Martín to ride, shoot, hunt and most importantly, to live as he should also be prepared to die: with honor.

Itzcoatl immediately understood what Diego was contemplating. Though they had only one weapon between them, Diego was going to charge the wagon in which his fiancée was held captive. They would probably die, Itzcoatl thought. He looked down at the heavy club in his left hand. Only one weapon, yes, but it was a weapon of kings. He would take many of the intruders to the afterlife with him.

For his part, Diego also knew what his mentor had in mind. He put his hands on Itzcoatl's shoulders. "You don't have to do this," he said softly.

"I have to do this as much as I have to breathe," Itzcoatl replied.

Diego nodded and began to move towards the wagon where Rosalilia lay covered. Smoke swirled everywhere, and the horses in the stable began frantically kicking at their stall doors. Suddenly, one wall of the outbuilding collapsed in a shower of sparks and flaming timbers right beside them.

Itzcoatl grasped his war club in both hands, and together the two men rushed towards the wagon. A black-clad intruder spotted them, raced forward, and fired his rifle at close range. The bullet hit Diego in the thigh, glanced off bone, and passed through the back of his leg. He spun to the ground, then righted himself and charged on. Itzcoatl's glass-studded club flashed in the firelight, and the shooter dropped. Then, a second intruder fired. This bullet pierced Diego's abdomen and knocked him hard back into Itzcoatl. Both men fell to the ground. Itzcoatl leapt back to his feet, but Diego was unable to stand.

He was losing a lot of blood and knew he would not remain conscious for long. He pulled himself up on one elbow, and, just as the last attackers clambered over the sides of the moving wagons, he saw the man in buckskins grab the reins of his buckboard and snap his horses into motion. Then, the man swung his head in his direction. Diego struggled to see through the fog of smoke and pain that was enveloping him.

The leader made brief eye contact with Diego and smiled. He slapped the reins again, and his wagon lurched away from the gate and toward the town road that ran along the lake shore.

"Him!" Diego's mind raged. "How could it be *him*?" Then he fell back to the ground at Itzcoatl's feet.

The Aztec held his bloodied war club high above his head and straddled Diego's body protectively until the wagons were out of sight. Then he knelt and cradled Diego's head on his lap. He clutched the war club in one hand and reached down with his other hand to staunch the flow of blood from Diego's stomach wound.

"Tecolote," he said tenderly.

The wagons carrying Rosalilia and the Verján family treasures hurtled down the cobbled drive, away from the fires and choking smoke that were engulfing the villa. A moment later they passed a troop of soldiers from the Cuernavaca garrison galloping up the lakefront road towards the scene of the battle. They could not have known about the men in the wagons. But Diego knew.

Just before he passed out, he lifted his head.

"Find Thomas," he said to Itzcoatl. "Thomas will know what to do."

ONE

New York City, June 1882

Thomas knew exactly what to do. He gripped the heavy bottle of Maison Clicquot champagne tightly in his left hand, and, without diverting his gaze from his target for a second, swiftly tore the wire wrapping from the cork with his right hand and let it fall on the linen tablecloth.

The next part was especially tricky. His dinner companion, Mademoiselle Annette Lescoux, was chattering on about the Gilbert & Sullivan operetta, *Iolanthe*, which they had attended earlier that evening at the Standard Theatre. It was the first electrically lit musical event ever held in the nation, and the mayor of New York had been on hand to introduce Thomas Edison, the inventor and businessman whose electrification process was transforming the city.

"It's not that I have any special affection for illumination from oil lamps and candles," Mademoiselle was saying, "but I do wonder if there is any part of our lives that electricity will not change, and not always for the better. Don't you agree, Thomas?"

"Some things in this world are in great need of change," he replied, even as his brain raced to complete the speed, distance and trajectory calculations that had occupied his mind since the Maître d'hôtel had seated them in Delmonico's quietest alcove.

He raised his eyes from the champagne bottle. "But not you, Annette. Some kinds of beauty are eternal, and I'd wager that there will never be an invention– not from Mr. Edison or anyone else that will ever change the sense of absolute exhilaration a man experiences while in your company."

Thomas's reply elicited two physical responses, each of which he believed was a sign that his campaign to persuade Mlle. Lescoux to join him for an *escapade romantique* at his friend's quiet country home was advancing nicely.

The first reaction was a subtle blush that began at Annette's cheeks and spread down her neck before blooming across the spectacular décolletage that was framed so magnificently by her blue velvet dress. The second reaction was a brief, lilting laugh, accompanied by a heightened sparkling in her forest green eyes.

This romance was budding slowly, and, after three dinners and tonight's operetta, both his affection and his bank account were beginning to wane in the face of unrealized returns on his emotional and financial investment. He genuinely cared for Annette. She was intelligent, independent, witty and accomplished, and the daughter of one of the city's most successful merchants.

All things being equal, his pedigree simply did not match hers. He was a newly hired junior manager at a mid-size bank with neither family nor social connections. He had kicked around the country–the world, in fact for fifteen years after the Civil War. His main source of income before taking the bank job was the pension he received from the War Department after separating out of the Union Army at the rank of colonel. That he was the youngest full colonel in the history of the army, as well as the acclaimed hero of one of the War's final great battles, probably explained why Annette's family had accepted him as a suitor for their twenty-four-year-old daughter. Fame had opened many doors for Thomas. This weekend, he hoped, it might just open one more.

❈

Annette prattled on about the operetta and even hummed the melody from one of its most popular tunes, *"Tripping Hither, Tripping Thither."* Thomas continued his work with the champagne cork as the waiter prepared their dessert of caramelized bread pudding with bourbon crème anglaise and butter pecan ice cream on a cart next to their table.

The waiter had been a bit put out when Thomas insisted on de-corking the champagne himself. He had also been surprised that someone as slender (albeit splendidly endowed) as Mademoiselle could consume so many of the rich dishes from the Delmonico menu. She had opened with a bowl of chilled berry soup before sallying on to a plate of satiny Blue Point oysters smothered in smoked bacon and crème. Next came pan-seared dayboat scallops sautéed in lemon, butter, and Marsala wine, followed by a green salad with asparagus tips. Two bottles of Château Gruaud-Larose Bordeaux from St. Julien preceded champagne and dessert, by which time the waiter found it difficult to believe that the young lady was capable of remaining upright. He sighed, completed their desserts, and spooned them into silver bowls before leaving to attend to other customers.

Thomas had pulled and twisted the champagne cork nearly to the top of the bottle. This was the difficult part. He had to let off enough of the bottle's inner pressure to make sure it did not fly out across the room, while keeping just enough pressure under the cork for it to perform exactly as he wanted when he removed his hand and let it take flight.

As Annette lifted the first taste of bread pudding to her mouth, he concluded that the force being exerted by the champagne's carbonation was exactly right. He smiled at Annette and then removed his thumb from the top of the cork. It took three seconds for the power of the gas to overcome the pressure holding the cork in the neck of the bottle, and as he waited for the explosion, he surveyed the dark-paneled dining room and its well-dressed inhabitants. Animated conversation mixed with the tinkle of crystal and stemware. Ornate gas-lit chandeliers cast a golden glow around the room (one of the romantic qualities electric light would no doubt destroy, he thought), and waiters, table captains and kitchen helpers scurried along the narrow aisles between the long rows of tables.

Then, a soft "pop," and the cork missile was expelled from the heavy Clicquot bottle. He expected the cork to travel a foot or two into the air before alighting gently in the center of the table, just as it had done every other time he had performed the trick. A bit showy, of course, but he knew it was the kind of effort that would please Annette.

Unfortunately, while practice can make perfect, he should have paid more attention to the mathematical aspect of trajectory science than to his seat-of-the-pants formula for the behavior of gasses trapped inside a glass vessel. The cork, it seemed, had its own plan.

❖

A Chinese philosopher once proposed that the outcome of a battle could be decided by something as innocuous as the flutter of a sparrow's wing on the other side of the world. If true, then certainly the likelihood that a lover's tryst might come to pass in a weekend country house could be determined by the flight of an errant champagne cork. But in war, as in romance, chance also plays its part. Thomas knew instantly that both his timing and his aim were off. Once the cork was in motion, however, no power on earth could have prevented what was about to happen.

Annette's spoon was just touching her lips when the cork took flight. He watched in horror as it exploded outward at four or five times the speed he had expected. In that instant he knew that the only question remaining was whether it would hit Annette in the face with enough force to break her nose or chip a tooth, or if it would mercifully bypass her and wing its way across the room to smash some other innocent diner in the head.

The cork picked a third way: it shot directly across the table and lodged securely in Annette's cleavage.

It could have been the sound of Annette's fork hitting her plate that caught the bellboy's attention, or the squeal that escaped her lips as the cork plowed into her bosom. The desk captain had given him an urgent telegram to deliver to a Colonel T. Scoundrel in the main dining room ten minutes earlier. He had a description of the Colonel, and a stick-mounted placard with 'Col. T. Scoundrel' written in grease pencil on it that he had been holding high in the air as he made his way in and around the tables in the crowded restaurant. He was about to give up his search when he heard a commotion in a far corner of the room.

The boy swung his head in the direction of the sound and saw a beautiful young woman in a revealing dress staring in horror at the cork that was wedged incongruously between her ample breasts. Seated across from her was a tall gentleman whose back was turned to the boy. The bellboy grinned inwardly; he did not need to see the man's face to know that he had found Colonel Scoundrel.

The clattering fork and Annette's yelp startled Thomas into action. He pulled off the linen napkin that had encased the champagne bottle and tossed it across the table to her. Then he jumped up into the aisle to block her from the view of the dozens of diners and staff who were craning their necks to find the source of the hubbub. Annette held the napkin against her chest and discreetly withdrew the cork from its tender resting place. By the time the waiter raced to their table a few seconds later Annette was already composing herself, and Thomas was pouring her a very full glass of the excellent champagne.

Then he poured a glass for himself and settled back into his chair. In any other circumstance, he would have allowed himself to concentrate on the superb crispness and slightly spicy flavor of the dry Clicquot Brut. He would have told Annette how the champagne's blend of two-thirds Pinot Noir and Pinot Meunier black grapes gave it body, while the addition of Chardonnay grapes for the other third gave it an unmatched elegance defined by hints of apple, citrus and caramel. And if he was being completely honest, he would also have told her that as much as he enjoyed such a fine wine, he was seldom able to afford it. The pyrotechnics of the past few moments dissuaded him from going down that conversational path, however.

Only moments before he had high hopes that tonight's dinner was leading to a moonlit carriage ride to the country, where a crackling fire, snifters of cognac and a feather bed the size of a playing field was waiting. How *was* Annette going to react to being so indelicately harpooned by the champagne cork? To be sure, in choosing to wear such a low-cut dress she had to know that a good portion of her bust was going to be on display. On the other hand, Thomas could not conceive of any situation in which a woman would think it acceptable to have her cleavage assaulted as hers had just been.

Had his chance for a country getaway with Annette just been popped by that damn cork? It was time to find out. Annette drained her glass, and Thomas filled it again. As the restaurant returned to normal around them, he cleared his throat and prepared to speak, but Annette beat him to it.

She took a deep breathe, and said, "That was...."

"A stupid and thoughtless action on my part?" he finished, doing his best to hold back a sheepish grin.

Annette put her hand across her mouth to suppress her own smile.

"I was about to say that was perhaps the funniest thing that has ever happened to me, or more correctly," she added in a whisper, "to my breasts."

Thomas tilted his head back and let out a great laugh, and Annette clapped her hand over her mouth and nose in an effort to at least appear calm. Her attempt failed, however, and she let fly with a short, snorting chortle that caused him to burst into laughter again. Their waiter, who was returning at that moment to make sure all was well, threw his arms in the air in a sign of exasperated disbelief and marched off to deal with the first well-mannered table he could find. Barbarians!

For his part, Thomas began to relax. There was no doubt as to the meaning of the transformation that the well-aimed cork had brought to Annette's appearance. Her eyes were shining, her cheeks were flushed, and the very same bosom that only moments before had been unceremoniously pelted by the champagne stopper looked to Thomas to be rising and falling faster and faster in time with her laughter.

There would not be a better moment than this to broach the idea of going to the country for the weekend. He reached across the table and took her hand in his. She looked down for a moment, then slowly raised her head, tilted it just so, and looked deep into his eyes. Her message was unmistakable.

Unfortunately, so was the bellboy's. He had made his way across the crowded restaurant and planted himself in the aisle next to Thomas.

"Colonel T. Scoundrel?" asked the boy.

Without turning his head from Annette's face, Thomas nodded.

"I have a telegram for you, sir. It's marked urgent."

He turned to the boy, took the envelope, and reached into his pocket for a dime. The boy happily accepted the gratuity, tipped his hat, and after a fleeting glance back to the exact spot where he had last seen the cork, vanished into the main dining room.

"Would that be work?" asked Annette.

"Not possible," replied Thomas as he tore open the envelope, "they wouldn't know I am here."

The routing history at the top of the yellow paper showed that the telegram had taken three days to shuttle from Cuernavaca to Mexico City, from there to El Paso, then Atlanta, and finally on to his hotel in New York City, where the manager had scribbled a note suggesting they deliver it to Delmonico's.

The message consisted of three short sentences, and in the moment it took Thomas to read them, Annette saw his expression transform from a lover's playful, passionate expectation, to the steely-cold resolve of a battlefield commander.

"Diego seriously wounded," the telegram began. "*Rosalilia kidnapped, taken to Colorado. Meet me in Trinidad, CO, your earliest possibility."*

Itzcoatl

❖

TWO

Outside Denver, Colorado

"He is lower than quail shit in a wagon rut, that's what he is," grumbled the driver as he crawled out from under the rig the senator had rented that morning in Denver. "All's he's got to do is slap him a pint of grease on an axle when the damn thing starts to grinding. Just that one thing and we wouldn't a gone all busted up out here in the damn middle of nowhere." For good measure, he spit a gob of wet chew against the spoked wheel he was repairing.

Senator Mack pulled a cheroot and matches from his jacket and leaned back against the rock he had been standing near as the driver labored. This might be the damn middle of nowhere, but it was a sight handsomer than the humid, low-lying swampland he left in Washington, D.C. last week.

The wheel slipped off its axle two hours out of town on a bend in the dirt road where it followed a mountain stream. Meadows thick with lemon grass and sage bordered the creek, spreading gently to the north and south. Mack had seen a bull elk with its harem a few miles back, munching contentedly and without fear in a field dotted with wildflowers. The pine forests that swept up the mountains on either side of the little valley were teeming with game, and he knew the still pools that formed in pockets where the stream twisted and turned would be boiling with cutthroat trout.

They had been traveling since dawn and were still three hours out from the Claybourne ranch house, but they had been traveling on his land almost since the minute they left town. Every stick of timber, every beef cow, sawmill, range shack, fence post, well-head, and lean-to for thirty-five miles in each direction were Claybourne's, and God help the man who–innocently or not– wandered on to this land to hunt, fish, or camp without permission.

The driver slipped the wheel back on its freshly greased axle and slammed home the hold rod. Then he fetched the horses from the other side of the road and hitched them back into their harness.

"We're ready to be going, Mr. Senator," he said.

A thick puddle of axle grease had spilled across the passenger seat, so Mack reluctantly climbed up front beside the driver. He felt the complaint of the heavy spring under the seat as he stretched his legs out to the toe board. It was going to be a long journey.

The driver pulled another plug of tobacco from his shirt pocket and released the brake. Then he wrapped a leather rein around each wrist and called to his team. The wagon lurched forward.

"You been out to the Claybourne place before?" asked the driver as the wagon settled into a slow, rhythmic trot.

Senator Mack would normally have ignored–or even punished the impertinence of –a hired hand for being so familiar as to think he could engage a United States Senator in casual social conversation. But, as the wagon swung around what seemed like the hundredth boulder in the road they had encountered since daybreak, he decided that a little talk might help to break the monotony of the drive. Damn, why couldn't Claybourne move closer to town?

"Many times," he replied. "When we became a state six years ago, Mr. Claybourne hosted a weekend gathering of business leaders and political folk from all across the state to talk about Colorado's future."

Out of respect for his passenger, the driver gauged the breeze before letting fly with his next cheek full of chaw juice. "It true he owns his very own private railroad car?" he asked.

The Senator nodded. "And the finest wine cellar between St. Louis and San Francisco, and the best stud bulls, too." Not to mention a stable of politicians, judges and municipal officials, he mused to himself.

Present company included.

"He an English feller?"

"He was born in England to a British father, but his mother was an American," Mack answered, just as an osprey appeared from nowhere to swoop down to the stream and snag a small cutthroat that had made the mistake of gliding a little too close to the surface.

"His father, was, I believe, the fifth son of an English baronet, which meant he could not inherit any of his family estate. He was sent to America with just enough of a stipend to purchase some land and build a home. Claybourne was just a boy. They settled in Ohio for a few years and then came out to Denver in '59. Same year I arrived. The town plat had just been laid out, and as quick as they settled in, Claybourne's father got himself engaged in property development. Turned out he had a real head for it, and by the end of the war he was one of the wealthiest men in the territory."

"Don't believe I ever heard about him," said the driver, "Not in all the years I been here. Kinda strange."

Mack relit his cheroot and adjusted his legs to find a little comfort in the ceaseless fight between the unforgiving springs under the seat and the endless ruts and potholes that covered the red dirt road.

"Claybourne's father had a head for business," Mack continued, "but he liked his liquor, and he couldn't walk past a card table without sitting down for a hand or two. Real estate he was good at, but gaming, well, let's say that the cards never much favored him."

The driver nodded somberly. Business and politics were complete mysteries to the likes of him. But liquor and cards? That's where the barriers between the classes evaporated. He indulged in both, but by the grace of the God who watched over the foolhardy, he had never had enough money in his pocket to be able to piss away much more than a dollar every now and then.

"Claybourne's mother died of the typhus the year they came to Colorado, and his father pitched himself down the stairs of a Market Street sporting house a couple of years after the war. Broke his neck."

"So, the young Mr. Claybourne inherited the boodle," surmised the driver. He waved one arm towards the horizon. "And all this."

"More like inherited the whirlwind," Mack said. "The day the guns went silent after Appomattox, his father was worth a fortune. When he died two years later, he was fighting off bankruptcy creditors. He fell far and fast."

The driver couldn't hold back a chuckle. "Right down them stairs," he said. "Course it sounds like he took himself a little ride with one of them sporty gals first. A man could do worse than to die like that."

Senator Mack did not reply. He had known the senior Claybourne quite well. In fact, he had done some legal work for him when he was fresh out of school.

Father and son shared a remarkable affinity for business, but in all other habits and characteristics they were as different as two men could be. The younger Claybourne, Noah, was possibly the most disciplined individual Mack had ever known.

As far as he knew, Noah did not indulge to excess in anything: not drink, or women, nor gambling. That was not to say that he did not take a dip into the vices of the flesh from time to time; but, for him, participating in such activities were more like scratching an itch than luxuriating in the experience. Once the itch subsided, Noah Claybourne went on about his business without regret or any need for self-reflection or recrimination. And he never, not for a moment, lost control of himself or his circumstances. If there was anything remotely resembling a sliver of warmth and compassion within his soul it was evidenced only by his love for his daughter, Hyacinth, whose mother died giving her birth.

Mack knew as much about vice as he did about all the other human frailties that people work so hard to hide, or at least to keep muffled away from public view. He relied heavily on his ability to exploit those frailties to break the will and ultimately dominate the lives of the men and women he had used to vault to political power; first in the rough and tumble days when Colorado was still a territory, then as a force in helping Colorado to achieve statehood, and now, in his role as an acknowledged power broker in the Senate. That Mack himself had ended up being played by and ensnared in Claybourne's complex web of empire building and political misfeasance was the highest compliment that one corrupt man could pay to another.

They began a slow plod up a long, low hill, and Mack pulled another cheroot from his pocket. The driver struck a match on the side of the wagon and gave him a light.

The senator had given a lot of thought to the nature of Noah Claybourne's character over the years, especially in the last several weeks leading up to tomorrow's meeting at the ranch. Mack had never put anything he seriously valued on the line for anyone's dreams but his own. He attributed his success in politics to that credo. He was sure that none of the others who would be in attendance tomorrow had done so either. On the other hand, he had never known anyone who dreamed as big as Claybourne, including the colossally wealthy railroad tycoons and industrialists with whom he interacted in the halls of Congress and salons of New York City. Noah Claybourne was the only man the senator knew who had the balls and the brains and the money to pull off the scheme they were about to undertake.

On the face of it, no rational person would entrust Claybourne with the power to make or break their future so completely and totally. Mack knew that Noah was more than happy to stand idly by as his associates indulged in all manner of depraved behavior, from kidnapping, to murder, to theft of money and property on the grandest and most outrageous scale. More precisely, Mack thought, he was happy to stand back if the crimes committed by his associates helped him to advance his own circumstances to the next level. The man was a complete cynic and fatalist. He was also supremely self-confident, the true architect of every corner of the world he inhabited.

After dinner at a private club in Philadelphia the year before, the senator and others who would soon be gathering at the ranch sat quietly as Noah expounded on the personal philosophy that underlay the breathtaking scheme they were about to set in motion.

"Romanticism is a fool's dream, love is an addiction, and compassion is a disease," Claybourne began, as waiters poured a rare Sandeman port and handed out Tabacalera cigars from Madrid. "The purpose of life is to expand, to possess, and to control. Any activity not directly tied to one of those objectives is not simply a waste of time, but, in my belief, a sin."

The senator was not a religious man, but when it came to the topic of sin, he knew himself to be an expert. He had done his best to practice at it nearly every day of his adult life.

❖

The wagon reached the crest of the hill, where the driver reined the horses to a stop so that they could take in the full breadth of the panorama below. They had been traveling east-northeast for nearly five hours, and for most of that distance the rutted path had been gently sloping upwards. Mack estimated they had gained 1,200 to 1,500 feet in elevation. Behind them, to the west, lay Denver and beyond that the Front Range. The road before them pointed east, beginning a descent equal to the elevation they had climbed all day until it spilled into a broad, open valley bounded on the north by a wide creek dotted with stands of plains cottonwoods. As far as Mack could see, rolling grasslands bisected by a multitude of creeks covered the landscape, stretching for hundreds of miles through the region divided by the South Platte and Arkansas Rivers until they melded farther east into the vast expanses of the Great Plains.

Claybourne ranch sat at the far edge of the bountiful rainfall region; the land to the east beyond his estates became quickly and increasingly arid with each passing mile. It was a perfect place to farm, harvest timber, or raise beef cattle. Noah Claybourne had chosen well.

"Langton Hall," he murmured.

"Beg pardon?" asked the driver.

"Langton is the village in Yorkshire where the ancestral Claybournes lived for centuries," replied the senator. "He named his house in its memory, but I'm fairly certain there are no houses like that in its namesake village." He looked down on the house and outbuildings scattered below. No, he thought to himself, not in Yorkshire and maybe not anywhere.

The road wound down to the gated entry to Langton Hall, still about a half mile distant. Two massive trees had been felled and trimmed, and their bark had been scraped off. They were planted upright about thirty feet apart. A professionally painted signboard stretched from one pillar to the other, with *Claybourne Ranch* painted in three-foot high dark blue letters that were outlined with gold gilding. The closer Mack's wagon got to the house, the more dramatic and architecturally appealing the whole effect became. The barn and stables off to the left were designed in the same style as the main house, and behind them was a brick smokehouse with a metal roof. The two-story bunkhouse for the ranch hands sat one hundred yards to the east of the main house, and next to it was another stable and a wood and post remuda for their horses. Running from north to south behind the bunkhouse was a low ridge beyond which were pens for calving and branding cattle.

Seeing the entire property spread out across dozens of acres when you came over the rise from the Denver road was a sight that visitors never forgot. The senator knew that was exactly the effect that Claybourne intended.

❖

The sun was arcing high overhead as the senator and his driver finished their individual appreciations of the ranch from their wagon seat. Then the driver hopped down and moved over by a tree to do his necessaries. He returned a moment later and wadded one final plug of tobacco into his cheek.

Mack stretched his legs and asked himself for the hundredth time if he was sure about what he was doing. There could be no halfway results once he joined forces with Claybourne; it would be win or lose. There would be no draws. Even if Claybourne's plans were executed flawlessly, innocent people would die, two small towns would be burnt to the ground, and governments would be shaken to their foundations.

There could be war, or revolution, or both. He flicked the stub of his cheroot to the ground as the driver climbed back up into his seat. Of course, he could also be rewarded with a staggering fortune and power the likes of which few people could imagine. The risk, he concluded for the last time, *was* worth it.

As the wagon began the descent to the valley floor and the house beyond, a line from Shakespeare's *Julius Caesar* echoed in his mind:

"There is a tide in the affairs of men which, taken at the flood, leads on to fortune; omitted, all the voyage of their life is bound in shallows and in miseries."

The United States senator from the new state of Colorado was going to catch that tide.

THREE

Trinidad, Colorado

The southbound Santa Fe steamed into the Trinidad depot a half hour late. Its locomotive braked to a halt twenty feet from the telegraph office, where newly appointed city marshal Bat Masterson was half-asleep in a wooden rocker on the deck next to the track.

The town of 6,000 had been quiet the night before, so Masterson took advantage of the unusually civil behavior by the cowhands, miners, professional gamblers, drunks, prostitutes and others who typically packed the saloons and gambling halls lining Main Street. Instead of arresting brawlers or tossing drunks out into the street, he settled into his usual table at the Imperial for a long night of faro, before walking down to meet the noon train from Wichita.

Bat was counting the peaks in the snow-dusted Sangre de Cristo Mountain range while he waited for the train. Tall and rugged and narrow, they formed an unbroken line of summits and ridges that dominated the horizon from north to south. Most of the other mountains he had observed in his travels rose gradually from valley floors, beginning as low foothills that swept higher and higher for miles before they became real mountains. This stretch of the Rockies was different; there were no foothills at all. Instead, the solid rock mass of the Sangres pushed straight up more than 7,000 feet above the valleys and plains. The dramatic mountain vista was one of the features that attracted the twenty-nine-year-old lawman to the city, along with the temperate, semi-arid climate. The booming gambling scene was a plus, too.

He had never settled in one place for very long, but if he were to put down roots, Masterson thought, Trinidad might be it.

❖

The engineer climbed down from the locomotive, and Pullman attendants swung open the passenger car doors and unfolded their steps. In a minute the platform would be a beehive of activity with porters offloading luggage, passengers disembarking, and barkers from the local hotels and saloons shouting out invitations for the tired, thirsty travelers to visit their establishments.

Masterson frequently met trains coming into town, as much out of curiosity about who was visiting as it was a professional duty to look out for anyone whose preferred brand of trouble might be more than even a wide-open town like Trinidad would care to welcome. The engineer had learned not to pull out of the depot towards the coaling site until the marshal signaled that none of his passengers were going to be ordered back onto the train before their luggage made it to the platform.

It was a telegram he'd received from his counterpart in Wichita about one of today's passengers that prompted the marshal to pay extra attention to the folks who were about to disembark. The Kansas lawman explained that he had engaged a questionable-looking man in conversation at the station and said the passenger had introduced himself as a retired Army Colonel. A damn sight too young for that, wrote Masterson's associate. Looked to be in his early 30s. As for the name the passenger gave, Thomas E. Scoundrel, what the hell was that all about?

"Bat," the marshal wired, *"I believe you have an accomplished confidence man headed your way. If he was landing in my jurisdiction, I'd tell him to pack it back on the train, and head elsewhere."*

Masterson smiled to himself as he read the telegram. He did know Colonel Scoundrel's name, and something of his reputation. The story of his heroics at the battle of Pebble Creek Ridge was well known, and the marshal had also heard about a duel of honor in New Orleans that resulted in the death of a wealthy businessman, and a South Seas venture gone bad that culminated in a shootout with a gang of Pacific Island natives in, of all places, an uptown New York City art gallery. Confidence man or not, Colonel Scoundrel was someone Masterson wanted to meet.

The first passenger onto the platform was Felipe Baca, whose family had founded the town just over a decade ago. No one–especially Baca–had expected the tiny settlement to grow the way it had. Masterson tipped his bowler hat to Baca, who smiled and waved in return. Several members of Baca's family came down the steps, followed by an oily-looking man accompanied by two young women who Bat expected would be looking for employment in one of the half-dozen bordellos that fronted Main Street. No law against that, of course, but the man would bear some watching.

Several more locals debarked the passenger cars. Then, a tall, lean man with broad shoulders and wavy brown hair stepped onto the platform, just a few feet from Masterson. He had hazel eyes, a tanned, open face, high cheekbones and a determined jaw. He set down a well-worn leather valise, looked around the platform, and immediately realized he was the object of Masterson's scrutiny. Instead of turning away, he smiled, and nodded in the city marshal's direction. Bat pulled back his coat so that the silver badge pinned on his vest would be visible. This was a test; Masterson could tell a great deal about a person by the way they reacted when they discovered that the compact man in the fashionable bowler hat and three-piece suit was the law.

Colonel Thomas E. Scoundrel took note of the display of authority. He grinned, touched his finger to his forelock, and then turned to fetch the rest of his luggage from the porter.

The marshal approached and said, "Would you like me to hail a hansom cab, Colonel Scoundrel? It's a bit of a walk to the hotels."

Thomas wasn't surprised that the marshal recognized him. Doing his job, he supposed. "That's kind of you, thanks, marshal..."

"Masterson," Bat answered. He waved to a driver who was standing by his horse and cab alongside the depot. The driver gathered up

Thomas' bags and swung them up into the hansom.

"Where will you be staying?" Masterson asked.

"I'm meeting a friend tomorrow at the Grand Union Hotel, and from there, on to Denver."

"Fine restaurant at the Grand," volunteered Masterson. "Somehow they managed to steal a French chef from a hotel in New York City. I can vouch for his seared elk back-strap in a Bordeaux glaze. Nothing like it anywhere."

Thomas made a mental note to try the specialty. Then he extended his hand to Masterson. "Perhaps we will meet again while I am here," he said.

"I'm sure we will."

Thomas stepped up through the folding wooden door and into the cab. He instructed the driver about the hotel and settled back in his seat. Then, a tap at the window. He cranked the glass down.

"I should have mentioned," said Masterson. "If you favor a game of faro, the tables at the Imperial are honest, and their wine cellar is first-rate." He raised his hand goodbye and nodded to the driver. Thomas raised his hand in return, and the cab trotted away from the depot.

❖

It was difficult to believe that Trinidad was little more than a wind-blown way station on the Santa Fe Trail between Missouri and New Mexico until a few years ago. Today, dozens of handsome multi-story buildings, many built with locally quarried stone, stretched for blocks along Main Street. At the edge of town was Webster Brown's General Livery & Sale Stables, next to Tony's Market and Steam Sausage Factory. Moving into town, Thomas saw the signs for Mather's Druggists, and, pleasantly, H. Detmers & Co. Wine Merchants & Purveyor of Fine Kentucky Whiskies. The cab trotted past butcher shops, sash and door retailers, physician offices and bakeries. Midway down the street the lineup of saloons and gambling houses began in earnest. Tim Carney's establishment boasted louvered bat-wing doors topped by a sign that said, *"These doors never close."* Next door was the Tivoli Saloon, with a colorful banner promoting *"Handsome and Orderly Club Rooms,"* followed by Jake's Brunswick Saloon, Mac's Place, The Boss Club, Collier & Gillmans, and, as promised by the marshal, the Imperial Saloon.

By the time the cab reached the Grand Union Hotel, he estimated they had passed nearly two dozen saloons and gambling houses, plus an unknown number of shadier businesses who knew better than to advertise their wares in a town that was clearly on the cusp of becoming civilized.

The Grand sat at the intersection of Commercial and Main, and boasted a three-story dun-colored stone façade that covered most of the block. Four dark green canvas awnings stretched out over retail display windows, and the main entrance to the saloon at the front corner sported fluted stone pillars that rose above the rooftop to a crowning sculpture of an eagle, above which flew the American flag. The hotel entrance on Commercial Street featured three cobbled stone columns supporting a second-floor balcony. At the top of the columns was a twenty-foot-wide signboard topped by another flagpole, this one bearing the scarlet red standard of John Conkle, the hotel's owner.

He paid the hansom driver and handed his bags to a hotel doorman. Inside, fans in the high-ceilinged marble and walnut lobby pushed a cooling breeze around the room. To the left of the reception desk were frosted glass doors leading to the bar, while the entry to the hotel restaurant was to the right. The bar doors swung open just long enough for the aromas of cigar smoke, fresh sawdust, and spilled beer to drift into the lobby.

The doorman deposited his bags at the desk, where a middle-aged clerk was making notations in a ledger. His empty left sleeve was pinned to the side of his coat, a sight Thomas had seen a hundred times since the end of the war. His friends in the regiment used to say–only half-jokingly–that if a flea bit you on the ass in the presence of an army surgeon, you'd never fill out the backside of a pair of trousers again after the doc was done treating you. The truth was almost that gruesome; doctors had no way to prevent wound infections like sepsis or gangrene, so preventative amputations were the order of the day on the battlefield.

The clerk greeted him and swung the registry around. He wrote his name and New York hotel address under the clerk's watchful gaze.

"Colonel?" asked the clerk in a thick southern accent. "Yankee colonel?"

"Battlefield commission, northern Virginia, last week of the war."

The clerk pointed to where his left arm should have been. "Chickamauga, southeastern Tennessee, '63." He chuckled. "The history books say we whupped you boys, the best damn victory the Confederacy enjoyed in the West. Course, 18,000 of us butternuts ended up wounded or dead to pull that little miracle off. I don't remember any of us dancing the jig when your General Rosecrans and the Army of the Cumberland called it a day, that's for damn sure."

Thomas smiled. "Victory is a funny thing. On that we agree."

He paid for two nights in advance and followed the bellboy up a single flight of dark tile stairs to a second-floor room where he unpacked his two sets of clothing–his only sets, he reminded himself–before going over to the window and pulling the curtain aside. With all the carriages, buckboards, horses, and pedestrians streaming up and down Trinidad's main street, he could very well have been in St. Louis or Chicago, not in a dusty corner of the high desert in the middle of the vast American west. Itzcoatl would find him soon. He would get news about Diego and learn why Rosalilia had been kidnapped and spirited away to Colorado.

He pulled his revolver from the valise, checked the action, and gave the empty cylinder a spin before pulling out a box of cartridges and loading them into the gun, one by one. Then he put the pistol back into his bag and set it on a side table next to the bed.

He slid a chair over to the window and closed the curtain halfway. Then he poured a glass of water from the nightstand carafe and sat at the window to watch and wait.

Victory *was* a funny thing. His whole life was proof of that.

❖

FOUR

Dinwiddie County, Virginia, March 1865

Brigadier General Horatio Yoke was having none of it. No, by God, not a bit. Not after what it had taken for him to keep his regiment out of the shadow of harm's way for nearly three years. Those preening West Point battlefield commanders were welcome to their shiny campaign medals. For Yoke, every day that passed without the sound of a single shot being fired was what real victory looked like. And now this.

"Say that again sergeant?"

"General Sheridan sends his compliments, sir," said the messenger, "and directs that you decamp with all due haste. You are to move your infantry units up to the line, double quick, and join up with General Merritt's Third Division, right here."

The sergeant handed General Yoke an official dispatch envelope, and then pointed to a spot on the map he had unfurled on the General's camp table. "The junction at Five Forks. Your regiment will support the cavalry assault on the rebs right flank. You will secure and hold this section of the South Side railroad. That will close the rebs supply line and choke off their only evacuation route."

"The early reports I got this morning about the action at Dinwiddie Court House suggested we had Pickett's men on the run," said Yoke. "And with Petersburg surrendered, I expected Lee would be ready to lay it down."

"Sir, when I left the lines five hours ago, General Sheridan's forces were fighting delaying actions and doing their best to push Pickett back towards Five Forks. They're advancing on his flank. General Warren's V corps have arrived to reinforce, and you will be a part of that action."

Yoke ran his hand through his hair and barked at his adjutant, Captain Morrison for a cigar.

"Sergeant, you have delivered your message. Now, please inform General Sheridan that the 109th Ohio will do its part, as we always do." He lowered his head in thought before continuing. "And please tell his aide, Colonel Brandman, that I will personally see to it that his son will be on the tip of the spear that we ram down Johnnie Reb's throat. Oh, and sergeant," added Yoke. "Stop by the mess tent and get something to eat. Then have them send someone to clean up my dinner dishes."

The sergeant saluted, pulled the tent flap aside, and stepped out into the bright afternoon sunshine. Major Rolande set down his cigar and brandy and stood up from the table where he and Yoke had been making plans for their respective returns to civilian life when the war ended–any day now, if the rumors were true.

"Sheridan has 20,000 men he can throw at Lee and Pickett," he said, almost to himself. "What the hell does he need with us? We've never had a full regimental complement of ten companies, and not one of the six companies we do have is at full strength. We have maybe six hundred men in this whole command."

"Five-hundred-eighty-four as of yesterday," replied Yoke. "And fewer than one hundred who can lace their boots by themselves, let alone load and fire a weapon. The question is, what is Sheridan playing at? He may not know the reason I organized this regiment in '63, but his commanders sure as hell do, considering we have been hiding many of their sons from battle for years."

Rolande looked down at the location on the map where Sheridan had ordered them to march at double speed. Unlike General Yoke, he had been in combat. He knew the smells and the sounds and the otherworldly horrors that brew in the belly of pitched battle. He had stepped over the charred and twisted bodies of soldiers so maimed and disfigured that it was impossible to tell if they belonged to Union or Confederate forces. It had only taken a few days on the front lines for him to conclude that what mattered was not if you wore blue or gray, or supported this line of politics or that one; what mattered was survival.

When he heard the stories two years ago about a ghost regiment that had been organized to protect the sons of politicians, judges, bankers, and industrialists who had been so unfortunate as not to be able to buy their way out of service, Rolande determined to find it. He was not a coward, he told himself. Far from it. Instead, he was a man who was determined to survive this damn war.

He found Yoke and his loosely organized regiment a few weeks later. They were waiting in reserve behind Major Benjamin Butler's 33,000-man Army of the James as it launched the Bermuda Hundred Campaign to disperse the Confederate government at Richmond. The campaign went on to fail, but Rolande found the home he had been looking for.

Yoke kept ahead of the game by virtue of being privy to intelligence that only the most senior commanders received. In fact, if President Lincoln decided where to commit an army to battle, Yoke usually found out about the plans even before Grant or Sheridan were officially informed. That was the benefit of being the protector of the powerful. Civilian and military aides to the President and the Secretary of War had a vested interest in seeing to it that Yoke remained far from harm's way, and they paid handsomely for the protection Yoke provided their sons.

For the past two years Yoke's regiment had been in constant motion, always in such a way as to mask the fact that their primary momentum was always away from battle, not towards it. The 109th would march to within a mile or two of a major engagement and sometimes commit a single company of one hundred battle seasoned men to participate in a few small skirmishes. Those men's families, of course, were not wealthy enough to pay for their boys to be hidden away.

Then, using the information he had been secretly given about the strategy conceived by field commanders for that battle, Yoke would recall his company from action and wheel his regiment well to the rear of whatever regiments or brigades were about to be thrown into the thick of the conflict. The fact that after action reports consistently mentioned that the 109th Ohio had been kept in reserve yet again during battle did not raise eyebrows in the field command tents, or in the offices at the War Department. That is exactly where they were supposed to be.

"The order for us to move up to the lines comes from Sheridan himself," said Rolande. "If he asked for us specifically, it was for a reason. And if we don't show up and engage as ordered, he will know, and we could be looking at courts martial, and years behind bars in federal prison. Can Colonel Brandman do anything about it?"

"He will get the message about his son," replied Yoke, "and he will cover us in whatever way he can. But you are right that if Sheridan himself made it clear that he wants the 109th at the front, a lot of people will be watching what we do." He was certain that there were some officers who knew of his game and who would have loved nothing more than to find a way to force him onto a battlefield–preferably on horseback, leading the first bloody charge.

The general removed his jacket and hung it on a peg. He poured a brandy and stared glumly at the map.

"There might be a way," Rolande volunteered. "What if, just for the sake of argument, we are engaged by the rebs only an hour or so after we move out? Let's say a reb cavalry patrol finds us by chance, and attacks. We take defensive positions here, at this bend in Pebble Creek." He pointed to a spot on the map a quarter mile away. "When we send a company to flank them, our men report back that an entire reb infantry column and artillery company are only an hour behind the patrol…"

"Meaning we would have no choice but to swing far around them, miles around them, before we could make the march to Five Forks," Yoke finished.

"By which time, with any damn luck at all, the engagement would be over," said Rolande. "The after-action report would detail how we were slowed down by a couple of regiments but were able to finally fight our way out and double-time it to reinforce General Warren."

"Colonel Brandman would see to it that the report makes it clear that we fought like demons," chuckled Yoke. "Heroes, every damn one of us–especially his son."

The tent fell quiet. They understood, without saying it, that if they undertook this scheme only to see it fail, it wouldn't mean just a court martial. They would hang by the neck for treason.

"What we do in the next hour will make or break us," surmised Yoke. "There's no time to overthink. We've got to be quick about it and be ready to fill in the blanks later."

"Captain Morrison," said the general. "What do you see as the biggest obstacle to such a plan?"

"That would be figuring out a way to find the right rebs who we can invite to play along," replied Morrison. "Not exactly like extending an invitation to a cotillion dance."

"I don't know about that," said Rolande. "Every Johnnie Reb from here to Atlanta knows the war is over. All except for the ink on the surrender document. They want the same thing as we do: to get home with their sorry backsides in one piece. We just need to find a way to help a few of them do just that."

It was getting stuffy in the General's tent, but until their conversation was complete the heavy canvas door flap would have to remain closed.

Yoke emptied his glass and handed it to Morrison to refill. "What's that chaplain's name? The one who joined us after Petersburg; he stutters like the devil."

"Landston," said Major Rolande. "He bunks with Company H."

"Isn't his brother also a chaplain?"

"A reb chaplain, yes sir, he is. Probably with one of Pickett's regiments."

"Do you know if he is an honest man?" asked Yoke.

Rolande spit a little brandy back into his glass. "Well, if it runs in the family, he is probably one of those men of the cloth who like the cloth on their back to be made of silk. Landston sure does. So, even if his reb brother is $20 worth of honest, I expect that a few hundred Yankee greenbacks would probably help him see the higher light."

"Captain Morrison, find Landston," said General Yoke. "Ask him if he knows how to contact his brother, and if he can do it right now. Could be he is only a few hours ride from here."

"Have Landston tell his brother that if he can find a dozen–no, make it two dozen– rebs who would be willing to feint an attack on us at dawn tomorrow that we will pay each man jack of 'em $100 dollars in fresh Yankee green. Confederate dollars won't be worth a spoonful of warm spit in a couple weeks. They just have to ride over the ridge to the east of us, holler like hell, wave their battle flag and fire a few rounds into the air. They need to be seen and heard, that's all. 'Course," he added with a sly smile, "when the manure settles, and all this is over, we will dress up the report a little to make it look like we were under heavy and sustained fire during their attack."

Rolande shook his head. It was one hell of a risk. At the same time, the rebs surely knew that their cause was lost. One hundred dollars in Union cash would go a long way to getting a rebel soldier home, and in style. Better to end the war with a stomach full of food than one full of sawdust, or worse: grapeshot. Finding a few graybacks who might be amenable to such a practical arrangement shouldn't be so hard.

"And when the skirmishers ride away, our scouts will report that a whole god damn rebel brigade is coming right up behind them, headed straight for us," Yoke continued. "We'll pay our scouts to make that report and then keep their mouths shut until they sail through the gates of perdition. Every other man in the camp will only know that a reb attack really did come from over the ridge. They'll see it happen. And they'll see us repel Johnnie. Hell, I might lead that charge myself. Our men will believe what the scouts say about the advancing column, they will watch us throw the skirmishers back, and that's the tune they will sing for the rest of their lives."

Rolande and Morrison nodded in assent. It was as solid a plan as any other they could think of.

Yoke turned to Captain Morrison. "Requisition $500 from the paymaster for your parlay with Landston and make damn sure he understands that money is for his brother. He needs to leave within the hour, and make sure he has a solid mount. Get him a small white flag, too, in case he gets stopped by sentries. A few dollars to those boys, and he should pass through the lines without trouble. Then, get the clerk in here and tell him to bring the regimental record books for the past year. We've got some old tracks to cover and some new tracks to lay."

Morrison threw open the tent flap and hurried off to find the chaplain. Yoke and Rolande turned back to the map. There was a lot of planning to be done.

A moment later the sentry appeared in the open doorway. "Kitchen lad is here, sir," he said. He stepped aside for a tall, shaggy haired youth in a long cotton apron holding a canvas-sided dish collection tray.

"Private Scanddrél reporting," said the young man.

❖

FIVE

Dinwiddie County

Thomas gathered up the cups and dishes from General Yoke's tent and carried them through the camp to the open-air mess kitchen. The rain that had turned the path to mud was letting up and the soldiers of the 109th were coming out of their tents to sit on camp chairs, smoke, eat, write letters home, or just jawbone in the late afternoon light.

The mess boy had always liked this time of day, especially the way the sky transformed in the golden hour, just before dusk. Scrubbing out pots and pans and butchering chickens for Sunday dinner weren't his idea of real soldiering, of course. When he joined the army six months earlier, he had the usual romantic notions of war that most young men harbored when they heard the fife and drum, saw the glint of sunshine on brass uniform buttons, and watched the orderly march of troops as they filed down main street during Independence Day parades.

It took all of about a week after signing up at a federal depot outside of Cincinnati to disabuse the seventeen-year-old of any notion that he had joined King Arthur's Round Table in pursuit of some grand and glorious cause.

He had yet to hold–let alone fire–a rifle or pistol. He had been shooting on the farm since he was six, and pretty much everybody back home said that he could also ride a horse with the skill of a Comanche warrior. That was the army's loss, he figured. The fact that he hadn't been allowed to mount a horse, help move or fire artillery pieces, or even join in infantry drills pretty much rounded out his overall disappointment with military service.

and the night duty sentry poured steaming coffee from a porcelain pot.

Yoke took a cup and sat at the table. A moment later the tent flap parted, and Landston stepped in. The general had never had much use for the florid-faced pastor, but if the man had done his duty this day, it would be the perfect capstone to the 109th's story, or at least to the version of the story that Yoke hoped to sell to the War Department in the months ahead.

But the moment Yoke looked into the chaplain's eyes, he knew the man had failed. "Tell me," he growled.

"I made it past the pickets without trouble," began Landston. "As you said, a couple of dollars speaks loudly these days. One of them escorted me to the camp, which I swear looked like it went on for miles. Line after line of artillery pieces, a thousand or more tents, horses lined up farther than I could see."

Major Rolande shot the general a worried look.

"And then?" asked Yoke.

"We found my brother at the chaplain's station. He was more than a bit surprised to see me, of course. I laid out your offer right away. Five hundred dollars for him, $100 each for two dozen men who would make a false run along the ridge outside our camp, the whole thing."

"And how did he take it?" asked Rolande.

"He was subdued," said Landston, "I didn't expect that. In fact, he seemed downright perturbed. He stepped outside the tent and sent a passing soldier to fetch a major named Elijah. We caught up on family news for a few minutes, and then the major arrived."

The chaplain paused and pointed at the coffee pot before continuing. "Major Elijah got right to the point when I told him the purpose for my visit," he said, as the captain poured coffee for him. "I'll be taking that $500 off your hands,' was pretty much the first thing he said."

"Son of a bitch," muttered Rolande softly.

"And then?" asked Yoke.

"And then he surprised me. He said, 'Preacher, you have terrible timing. If you had come to me with this scheme a week ago, I'd have been on it like a fly on warm syrup. But that was before the fights at

White Oak Road and Dinwiddie Court House these past several days. We pushed your boys back, thousands of 'em. And now we are massing our forces at Five Forks, where, God willing, we will smash Sheridan and send him packing to hell, or at least force him to sit at the table to sign a peace treaty that is favorable to the Confederacy. We have the wind at our back, and our boys know it. I believe we are going to pull it off tomorrow. That's how I see it.'"

"But he still let you go," said Rolande. "Why?"

"He wanted me to bring you a message," replied the chaplain. "He said, his exact words were, 'Extend my compliments to General Yoke. Our scouts told us three days ago that y'all were camped at Pebble Creek, but given your reputation for fleeing instead of fighting, we didn't figure it merited our time to root you out. 'Course, if your plans still include a forced march to Five Forks to support the engagement there, I expect my commander will be inclined to go ahead and pay you a visit at first light.'"

General Yoke flung his coffee cup against the tent wall. Whatever he did now, he was in one hell of a pinch. If he stayed put, he would be facing off with a seasoned reb regiment, maybe two, in just a few hours. If he tried to flank their advance and join up with General Warren at Five Forks as per his original orders, the reb cavalry would know exactly where he was headed and run him down. And, if he turned tail and ran towards the relative safety of the eastern woods, he would be branded a traitor and a coward and face a general court martial for sure.

❖

Yoke sent the chaplain back to his company and asked Morrison to have the sentry wake up the clerk. Then he motioned to Morrison and Rolande to sit with him at the table.

"Gentlemen," said the general. "I know two things: first, there is always a way forward. Always. Second, there is a bank in Philadelphia that has been holding onto every payment made to us by the families of almost four hundred soldiers sleeping safely out there tonight like they have been every night since we organized this regiment. I have no intention of giving that money up."

The other two officers nodded in agreement. It was everything or nothing from this moment on.

"Your thoughts?" asked the general.

Captain Morrison had an idea. "Running away means prison and financial ruin," he said. "But trying to outflank a rebel cavalry regiment means capture or death. That leaves us with only one choice: we make a stand."

He began pacing around the tent as he talked. "Now, we know that most of the linen-breeches boys out there aren't strong enough to wring so much as a single drop out of a milk cow's teat. They will be of no use in battle. At the same time, we cannot allow them to be captured, not this late in the day. They are our fortunes, and that's how it is. There is only one course of action regarding our charges: we must get them organized and get them the hell out of here. Towards the east and safety. Right now."

He paused, took a last drink of coffee, and then poured brandy into the cup. Yoke and Rolande held out their cups, and the captain filled them to the rim.

"My thinking goes this way: we send our charges to safety, and we pick a rendezvous spot a couple days east and tell them to wait until we arrive."

"And we do what?" asked Yoke. "The three of us lead the one company of fighting men we actually have against a full regiment of reb cavalry and infantry? Where's the profit in that?"

Morrison smiled. "Oh, there will be an attack, alright. And our best men will be in it, right up to the end. But you won't lead that attack, General. And neither will you Major, nor will I. No, gentlemen, the attack will be led by our regimental colonel."

Yoke shook his head. "We have no colonel, and there sure as hell isn't time to get approval from Sheridan to get one transferred here."

"Granted, sir. But we don't have to borrow one from another brigade. We can make our own goddamn colonel, here, right from inside our own ranks. A battlefield promotion."

Yoke and Rolande were silent. Then Rolande said, "Assuming we get that colonel....and I don't know that any man above the rank of private would be stupid enough to agree to the job, but assuming we do, and further, if he leads a charge right into the teeth of the advancing rebs, how the hell is that going to help the three of us? Anyway, what chance would our men have of getting out of there alive, let alone of winning the day?"

General Yoke chuckled softly. "But that's the point, isn't it captain? They're not supposed to get out alive. They're supposed to die, every one of them. In fact, for this to work, they have to die."

Morrison nodded, his face dark and solemn in the pale lamp light.

"And when they ride over that ridge to attack the rebel force, the three of us will watch safely from the tree line two hundred yards to the east until it's over and done. Shouldn't take but a few minutes if what Landston's brother said is true and half the Army of Northern Virginia is on their way to stomp us out," he said.

Rolande picked up the thought. "When it's over, we can bruise ourselves up a bit and tear our uniforms to look like we have been in a big fight. Then we work out the details of whatever story we are going to tell while we ride to join the rest of our regiment waiting in the hills to the east."

"We'll be heroes," said Yoke in a hushed voice. He set his cup softly on the table. "One hundred men will die so we can have that title," he whispered in a voice that was almost tinged with regret. But only almost. Then he raised his cup into the air.

"Here's to the heroes of the 109th Ohio," he said in a strong, clear voice. The three men emptied their cups.

"Now, let's find our new colonel."

❖

SIX

Trinidad, Colorado, June 1882

The summer breezes that flow down the icy ridges of the snow-capped Sangre de Cristos and across the Purgatoire River valley in the afternoons are gifts to the people of Trinidad. These *brisas* blunt the withering heat that builds up on the Great Plains to the east and the deserts to the south, cooling the hot city streets each evening when the sun goes down.

Thomas had nodded off in his chair by the window in the muggy hotel room. Then, right on time, a gentle wind began to drift through the curtains. It was nearly spent from its long journey off the mountains but still carried enough alpine frost on its breath to rouse him from his sleep.

He pulled his watch from his waistcoat pocket and saw he had been napping for nearly two hours. He pulled the curtain aside and looked down on the busy street. Despite what he had told Marshal Masterson, Thomas had no idea when Itzcoatl would be arriving, or if he was already in town. The telegram he received at Delmonico's five days ago simply said he should get to Trinidad as quickly as possible.

He had arranged for a cab to take a most disappointed Annette home from the restaurant before returning to his hotel. He penned a resignation note to the bank, then packed his few belongings into a single bag before taking the elevated line outside his hotel to the New York Central Railroad terminal to begin his journey west. The trip from New York to Chicago, on to Wichita and through to Trinidad took four and a half days. He assumed Itzcoatl would know that timeline. Now, he could only wait for Diego's man to make his appearance.

He washed his face in the nightstand basin, checked his wallet, and put on his coat. He would take dinner early and then walk along Main Street in hopes of encountering Itzcoatl among the throngs of people moving up and down the boardwalks. He stepped towards the door and then paused to do something quite uncharacteristic. He stood in front of the oval mirror above the dresser and took stock of the reflection peering back at him.

He had never been one to dwell on the past. He had made more than his share of mistakes, and he understood his own nature well enough to know that he would make plenty more. Even so, the dark hazel eyes that regarded him from the mirror showed no hint of any sense of contrition for anything he had done in his life, including the men he had killed or the women he had loved. He learned long ago to forgive himself–and most other people–for simply surrendering to the sins of the flesh to which all humans are heir by virtue of their primitive animal natures.

Diego once keenly observed to Rosalilia that Thomas could be counted on for only two things: he would always be there to help a friend, and, in the pursuit of his next romantic entanglement he would toss common sense out of the lady's bedroom window the first time he climbed through it.

He was quick to take a bet, the first one to sit down at the gaming table, and the last to leave. The game was the thing to him–in cards, and in love. He was no fool, of course. He understood full well that the next petticoat chase and the one after that would end as they always did, just as he knew that his pockets would be nearly empty tomorrow when the morning sun streamed through the saloon doors, and the dealer called the last hand. It didn't matter. For Thomas Scoundrel, the sun was always going to rise on new opportunity. He was an adventurer and soldier, not a farmer or shopkeeper. And he was under no illusion that he would survive to a ripe old age.

He regarded himself in the mirror. Sixteen years had passed since he mustered out of the Union Army. In the span of a few days his name and age had been officially changed, his rank had skyrocketed from kitchen boy to colonel, and he had fought–and won-a decisive victory against rebel forces in which he was badly wounded. When he was discharged from the hospital in late April of 1865, he was a hero with no past, a military officer with no formal education, a wanderer with neither family nor friend to confide in.

He was also the beneficiary of a breathtaking criminal scheme concocted without his knowledge or approval; but, if he ever made public what he had learned about General Yoke and his co-conspirators at Pebble Creek, it would have meant the loss of his lifetime annuity and perhaps even prison. In the dangerous days following the assassination of President Lincoln, the revelation of how Yoke had kept the sons of so many prominent figures out of harm's way while hundreds of thousands of ordinary Americans were killed or maimed in battle would have torn deeply into the fabric of a nation that was already reeling from the loss of its great president.

He allowed himself a slight smile as he contemplated the face in the mirror. The crinkles around his eyes had deepened from years on horseback on the plains and prairies, and his nose had never fully healed after being smashed by the handle of Chief Varua's war axe in Tahiti. The rebel bullet that chipped his rib and tore through flesh and muscle still caused pain if he over-exerted his back, while fragments of the ball that shattered his left hip in a New Orleans duel six years ago could take his breath away when they pressed against the deep nerves, especially in winter. For a man in his early thirties, he thought, he had garnered quite an impressive catalogue of injuries.

He ran a hand through his hair, almost as if to push the moment of self-reflection back into the deep recesses of his mind. He picked up his revolver, then thought better of it and returned it to his bag. He locked the door and headed down to the lobby. He was hungry, and the wine-braised elk back-strap that Masterson had recommended sounded like a perfect meal.

The hotel lobby was busy, but the clerk was able to make eye contact with him through the line of people heading into the restaurant, and Thomas went over to the desk.

"Injun feller here for you a half hour ago," drawled the former reb in a tone that Thomas knew was meant to convey displeasure.

"Yes?"

"My boy was off delivering a bucket of beer, so I didn't have no way to let you know. And a'course, we don't let red men wander 'round the premises, if you know what I mean."

"The gentleman is Aztec," said Thomas. "Member of the royal family, in fact."

The clerk snorted. "Royalty? Well, I'll be, Colonel, that is a first for us. Mexican high muckety-muck right here in our little burg. Never seen one with a head of hair as white as his, that's for certain. He weren't gussied up like a king, I can tell you that. Couple weeks of road dust on his boots, too."

"Did he leave a message?"

"He did, yes sir, he did. Says to meet him at the Torobino. It's to your left out the door two blocks along."

"And what is a Torobino?'

"Well now," said the clerk, "that would be the one saloon in town that might be willin' to give an injun a sideways glance-if'n he came through the door for a drink and was smart enough to grease the barman's palm first. He'd have to take his drink out back, of course, what with there being no room inside for uncivilized folks."

"Something that would never be allowed to happen here."

"You can count on that fact, colonel, you sure can." He shrugged the shoulder to which his arm was once attached. "I don't aim to lose no more parts, and that goes special for my scalp."

Thomas headed out of the lobby. He turned left and joined dozens of people strolling along the wide boardwalk past shops, offices, and saloons. He crossed the street and walked to the end of the next block to where a freshly painted, false-fronted saloon featured a sign that said, *Torabino, Bongero & Co. General Merchandise & Saloon*. Inside, a long hallway ran the length of the building. To the left was the saloon, and to the right, two separate entrances to the general store. He went through the saloon doors where about a dozen people were seated at tables around the room. Clean sawdust had just been sprinkled on the floor, and the late afternoon light filtered through a row of windows high up along the west wall, casting long, finger like shadows. An inlaid counter with an impressive mirrored walnut backbar ran the length of the far wall, where a wide selection of liquors was on display. Most of the saloons he had visited in the west offered only two kinds of whiskey: bad, and slightly less awful, plus tepid beer, fiery mezcal and blue agave tequila. If this was Trinidad's low-rent saloon, he thought, he was looking forward to seeing its finest watering hole.

He scanned the patrons sitting at the small tables and the three men standing at the bar before he spotted Itzcoatl's shock of snow-white hair. The Aztec sat facing the street. He wore a blue cotton jacket over a high-collar shirt and pale brown trousers, and, as the hotel clerk had observed, his boots were crusted with dirt and dried mud. Without turning to look, Itzcoatl raised his glass of mezcal into the air in welcome. Thomas sat down, and Itzcoatl poured another glass from the half full bottle and slid it across the table. The old man had the bluest eyes he had ever seen. His brown, weathered face set them off like gleaming sapphires on black velvet cloth. The warrior was compact and lean, but his slight build had lulled many an enemy into a false sense of confidence.

Thomas had once traveled with Diego and Itzcoatl from Cuernavaca to Mexico City to purchase a buckskin Morgan stallion. One evening after dinner they took a walk past the lamp-lit market stalls and open-air cafes of the enormous Plaza del Zócalo. Itzcoatl was midway into a description of how the square had been the ceremonial center for the Aztec city of Tenochtitlan seven hundred years earlier when they were set upon by four dark-clothed bandits. One of the robbers knocked Diego to the ground, and while Thomas traded punches with a second bandit, Itzcoatl drew his double-edged *tecpatl* dagger from his waistband. He grabbed one of the bandits by his jacket and pulled him close. Then he thrust the obsidian knife blade up under the man's jaw, pushed it through the roof of his mouth, and plunged it into his brain. He withdrew the blade and swung the bandit's dead body into the path of the fourth robber, who was trying to help his companion tear Diego's wallet from his waist. The man was knocked off his feet but got quickly to his knees and prepared to lunge against Itzcoatl's legs to pull him down. Itzcoatl leapt over the bandit, spun quickly around, and dropped one knee onto the man's back. With his left hand, he grabbed the bandit's hair and jerked back his head, while with his right hand he sliced deep across the man's throat with the razor sharp *tecpatl.*

The sound of a pistol firing routed the bandit who was fighting Thomas, and the man fled into the darkened plaza. As onlookers gathered around and two officers of the 1st Military Police Brigade rushed over with rifles drawn, Diego pushed away the lifeless body of the bandit he had just dispatched with his pocket revolver.

It comforted Thomas to know that Diego's protector was a descendent of the legendary Aztec jaguar warriors.

❋

"Your journey was good?" Itzcoatl began as Thomas sat down.

He took a drink of the mezcal and nodded in reply. "Diego?"

"He is alive and is being cared for at his parents' home. He was shot twice; in the leg and here," Itzcoatl pointed to his side.

"What happened? Why Rosalilia? And why Colorado?"

"The day of their engagement was a good day, and the celebration lasted long into the night," Itzcoatl replied. "Many guests had traveled far, and so they stayed the night with the Verjáns.

"The attack came when the moon was high over the lake. Three wagons, at least a dozen men. They took down the main doors with a cannon and swarmed into the house. Some went for the silver, but most of the men went down the hall to the bedrooms. Senór Verján was able to get his saber, but he was overpowered and killed on his own bed. They took his wife, and they took Rosalilia."

A woman came out from the kitchen and asked Thomas and Itzcoatl if they wished to eat, and then the old warrior continued his story.

Sergeant O'Hanlon ran the mess and was as solid a regular army soldier as Thomas had met. When the big Irishman learned that Thomas could read and write, as well as speak fluent French and a smattering of Latin, he pulled the boy from kitchen duty for two hours every afternoon so that Thomas could write letters for the men in his company who had no education. That was most of them, he quickly learned.

The regiment never settled in one spot for more than a week, but each time they relocated, the layout of the new camp remained unchanged; seventy or eighty tents–including the regimental commander's–were lined up in two tight rows at one end of the camp. Then, a wall of horse corrals, freight wagons, artillery caissons and limbers, and assorted rolling stock were in such a way as to form a barrier between what O'Hanlon called "Fort Gentry" and the one hundred fighting men in Company B he called "The Pugilists."

"The gentry do get better chow and more frequent laundry," O'Hanlon told Thomas on the boy's first day. "But if ever this dandy regiment of ours should find itself going toe to toe with the rebs in a real donnybrook, you'll thank the livin' saints that you are bunked with boys who can fight, and not with them high-born, silk-waisted cockerels over there, not a one of whom could buy his way to the upstairs sportin' rooms of a New York whorehouse if'n he had a pocket full of gold eagles."

Rumors of the impending collapse of General Lee's army had been running through the camp for days. As Thomas loaded General Yoke's dirty dishes into the soapy water of one of the huge cauldrons that were kept simmering over wood fires laid in trenches, he found himself hoping that, for once, maybe the scuttlebutt was true. The war would be over, and with it, his dishwashing career. Someday.

❖

Captain Morrison roused the general at 2:00 a.m. "Landston's back from the rebel encampment," he said.

Yoke swung his legs off the cot and took his jacket from Morrison's outstretched hand. Major Rolande put a match to two more lanterns,

"Diego and I fought as best as we could. We had no guns. I had only my club."

Thomas had seen the Aztec war club with its volcanic glass shards. In the right hands, he knew it was every bit as effective as a revolver.

"They set fire to the outbuildings to cover their escape. Diego was shot trying to get to the wagon carrying Rosalilia away."

"And her mother?"

"They had no interest in her and let her go. The senóra made her way to the safety of the lake shore with the other guests. She is helping to care for Diego," Itzcoatl slid a leather wallet across the table, "and, she is doing this."

Thomas untied the band around the wallet and opened it. There must have been two or three thousand US dollars inside. He slid the wallet back. "I will not take money to help my friend. Please thank the señora but tell her it is my honor to stand with her family."

Twilight was approaching, and a kitchen boy began lighting the wall lamps that circled the room. Itzcoatl smiled and poured a little more mezcal into their glasses. "The money is not payment to you, my friend. It is for us to purchase weapons and horses and supplies, and for payment of *la mordida*–the bite–to anyone who can provide us with information about where we can find Rosalilia."

"That is what I don't understand. Why did they bring her here? Who brought her here?"

"As the last wagon pulled away from the gate, Diego was able to make out the leader's face in the light from the fires. He is well known in Mexico, an American mining engineer named Matthew Cord."

"An engineer? Murdering a senior government minister and kidnapping his daughter? That is insanity."

The woman returned from the kitchen and placed a bowl of fresh, warm tortillas in the center of the table along with a plate of sweet, sliced jicama. Then she handed each of them a stoneware plate heaped with pinto bean salad topped with roasted chiles alongside a pork chile verde stew.

Thomas asked her for coffee. "Much more of this mezcal, and I won't be of use to anyone. Now, tell me about Cord."

Itzcoatl talked as he ate. "He is an employee of an American named Noah Claybourne who lives on a ranch outside of Denver. He has interests in mining, railroads, cattle, timber, and land speculation. Cord is responsible for securing and exploiting mineral rights across much of northern Mexico, from the state of Sonora in the west, to Tamaulipas and the Gulf of Mexico in the east."

"One company wants to control mining in an area that huge?

Itzcoatl spooned some chile verde and jicama into a warm tortilla and handed it to Thomas. "Eat it this way," he said. "Claybourne thinks big. There are vast deposits of silver, gold, copper, and zinc spread across the region, which is about as big as the land area of Texas."

"And to secure the rights he would need a license from the Mexican government."

Itzcoatl nodded. "Many licenses, not only from the federal authorities, but also from each state where he wishes to mine."

"Which means he would have to get approvals from Rosalilia's father and the Ministry of the Interior," added Thomas.

"Something that Minister Verján had denied on three separate occasions. Cord is known to treat his local workers like slaves. He pays low wages, disrespects his suppliers, and drives smaller competitors out of business. Mexico is a poor country, Tomás, but we are proud, and we are patient. We will develop our own resources in our way and in our own time."

"And you believe that Cord kidnapped Rosalilia because…?"

"To send a clear message to the next Minister of the Interior. Grant the mining licenses now, or see your family destroyed."

They finished their meal, and the kitchen boy cleaned their table and brought more coffee. Thomas could not help but think about his own days working in the army kitchen, and he handed the boy a 50¢ tip–a good day's wages. "If Cord brought Rosalilia here to Colorado, it must mean that Claybourne is behind all of this."

"That is possible, but we are not certain," replied Itzcoatl. "Diego's family and the Verjáns have each made inquiries through a number of private channels. Claybourne is rich and influential, and he has a reputation for being a hard man of business, but to do something like this would be to expose himself to government investigations that would cause him great financial loss. More likely than not, Cord acted on his own."

"As a way of pleasing his boss?"

"And to get the job done, which to a *caudillo* like Claybourne is ultimately all that matters."

Itzcoatl pulled a cigar from his jacket, cut the end with his pen knife, and struck a match. Thomas did not smoke, but he called to the barman and asked for brandy to go with his coffee. It was nearly dark outside the Torabino, where the crowds had dulled to a handful of people moving briskly home along the boardwalk. Bat Masterson or not, Trinidad was not a safe place to walk at night. The brandy arrived, and Thomas poured some into his coffee. "Where do we go from here?" he asked.

"I will take the train south, to El Paso del Norte. People and information come cheap in border towns. I will continue to seek answers while I wait there for Diego to join me. It may be several weeks before he can travel. When he does, we will find you."

"And what will I be doing?"

"Many of the answers are already here in Colorado. Seek out Claybourne. Determine what he knows and find out if he is our friend or our enemy. Then, get word to me, and wait."

That is the one thing in the world that I am not good at, Thomas thought to himself.

As night gathered around them and the saloon began to come alive, the two old friends finished their drinks, each deep in his own thoughts.

❖

SEVEN

Trinidad, Colorado

When Thomas stepped through the doors of the Imperial Saloon he felt right at home. The high-ceilinged game floor was ablaze with light and noise. He counted three faro tables in the center of the room, two monte tables and a roulette wheel along one wall, plus more tables set up for Chuck-A-Luck, High Dice, and poker.

Dozens of men crowded the gaming tables with more lined up at the bar waiting their turns, bending their elbows with drink, or negotiating for the services of the upstairs ladies whose prices began at a dollar for a quick tickle and went up to $25 for half a night in a bed with clean sheets. He recognized Lou Rickabaugh, who had leased the gambling concession at the Oriental Saloon in Tombstone, and Bill Harris, the gaming boss from the Long Branch. Trinidad might be small, Thomas thought, but it boasted a first-rate gambling industry that would stack up to San Francisco or Denver.

An hour earlier, he had walked with Itzcoatl to the livery stable to collect his horse and gear. The old warrior would camp outside town and buy passage for himself and his horse on the morning train to El Paso Del Norte, four hundred miles to the south on the Texas-Mexico border. He would wait there for Diego.

Itzcoatl was not much for good-byes. He swung up into his saddle, touched his finger against his forehead, and gave Thomas the traditional Aztec salutation used for both hello and farewell: *"You have wearied yourself, troubled yourself in coming. This will not be forgotten."* Then he trotted off into the night, leaving Thomas to walk uptown to the Imperial to find a game.

He made his way past the piano player and headed for the bar. As he pushed his way past a boy who was going from table to table selling sandwiches out of a bucket, someone tapped his elbow. He turned to see Bat Masterson alone at a table.

"Marshal," he said.

"Sit down, Colonel; I can get you a drink faster than they can at the bar," said Masterson.

Bat tilted his head towards an aproned waiter a few tables over and pulled a chair out.

"Louis," Masterson asked the waiter, "do you have any of that special Madeira left, the bottles that came from the shipwreck?"

"We do, Marshal, four or five, I believe."

"Bring one, and a couple of those tall, thin glasses."

The waiter hustled off through the crowd, and Masterson sat back to light a cigar.

"Shipwrecked?" asked Thomas.

"1840, off the coast of Georgia. The good ship *Able.* All hands were saved, but the consignment of 1800 Madeira they were carrying went to the bottom. And now, this is the damndest thing: twenty-three years later, in 1863, a Confederate ironclad faced off against a Yankee frigate, the fifty-gun *Restoration*, I believe it was. The frigate pulled alongside the ironclad, and that old girl opened up with everything she had. Sustained cannon fire blasted that iron boat for ten minutes, but every shot bounced harmlessly off her hull and dropped into the sea.

"The Yankee captain grew exasperated as hell, and finally ordered the frigate to pull so close to the ironclad that the muzzles of their cannon were touching. He had two satchels of explosive charges prepared in waterproof oilskins to be dropped onto the ironclad's deck. Two minutes later, the satchels were tossed down. One exploded on the ironclad's deck, but the other slipped into the sea and exploded deep underwater. The ironclad was still afloat."

Louis returned with a dark, tulip-shaped bottle and two glasses. He left them on the table as Masterson finished his story.

"It was getting dark, and the ships withdrew so they could finish their match at first light. As they began to sail off, the reb captain sent two men on deck to survey the damage from the Yankee satchel charge. They were making notes of the damage when one of the men spotted a dozen or so wooden cases bobbing around in the water at their fantail. The Yankee ship was at a safe distance now, so the men called down to the ironclad's captain to come up and have a look-see. The captain was a might perplexed at the sight of the floating boxes, and he ordered a crewman to throw a gaff on one and haul it in.

They tore off the top of the case, and there inside were a dozen of these bottles, wrapped in cloth and packed in hay. Still dry after twenty years in the drink. Seems the satchel that missed the deck of the frigate blew a hole in the side of the *Able* sitting down there in the sand, and the force of the blast popped those boxes out of the hold, where they floated right up to the surface."

Masterson cut away the wax sealer that covered the cork. "The captain had all twenty-five cases hauled into the ironclad and figured he was set up with a supply of sipping port that would last him for the rest of his natural life. That much was true, but as fate would have it, his natural life ended a year later when a boom line caught him square in the neck during a squall and snapped it like a twig. Somehow, God only knows how, the owner of the Imperial got his hand on five of the cases from the captain's family a couple of years ago. And here we are."

The marshal withdrew the cork, which prompted a soft groan from Thomas.

"Bad meal?" asked Masterson.

"Bad memory," replied Thomas as he thought about Annette and the untested feather bed.

Bat poured two glasses of the fortified wine. Thomas noticed pronounced aromas of caramel and coffee in the deep ruby liquid, and the first sip was true to the sweet and spicy flavor that was characteristic of Malmsey style Madeiras.

He raised his glass to the marshal. "A fine choice, thank you."

Masterson topped both glasses off and then stood for a moment to survey the action ongoing in the room around them. The Las Animas

County deputies were on duty in the streets tonight, and so was Bat's brother Jim, who was working for the marshal's office when Bat first arrived in town. With any luck, the marshal would be able to settle into one of the faro games for the night.

"This is quite an establishment," Thomas said when Masterson sat down. "A man could hang his hat here a while."

"It is, and Rickabaugh and Harris pay the owner $7,000 a month for the rights to run the gaming here, so he'd better keep it that way."

Thomas raised his eyebrows, and Masterson laughed. "The same set up in San Francisco would cost them $10,000 per month, and even then, it would be worth every copper penny. Where else in the world do you get paid to have men standing in line to hand over every bit of their hard-earned money to you, night after night?"

"You said the tables were fair here. Doesn't the house ever lose?"

The marshal refilled their glasses. "Let's just say the house doesn't lose very often. I usually break even at the faro table, but some of my luck might be decided by dealers who would rather I didn't run them in for running a stacked bank. But don't worry; every jack one of them saw you sit down with me. You will get straight deals and honest counting."

It had been several weeks since Thomas had set foot inside a gambling establishment. New York City had some fine gaming parlors, at least if you liked overstuffed chairs, overdressed patrons, and overpriced liquor. He had always found that the gentility of east coast gambling to be a stifling experience; for Thomas, the hallmark of real gaming was in its ability to heighten and focus all your senses, especially your sense of survival. The banker playing opposite you in Newport, Rhode Island, was unlikely to try to settle a dispute with you over how a hand was dealt by jamming his twelve-inch Bowie knife into your gut right up to the cross guard. He might pay the doorman to toss you out into the street or ask the manager to revoke your gaming privileges, but you didn't have to worry that your balls might be sliced off and tossed to a hungry cow dog, as Thomas once saw happen to an unfortunate card shark at the poorly named Harmony Saloon in Abilene.

Guns were forbidden anywhere on Main Street, but the cowhands, teamsters, miners, and ranchers tossing their dollars on the green baize cloth of the tables at the Imperial all carried a weapon of some kind, and everyone knew that a simple argument could escalate into a bone-crunching, sinew-snapping, knife-slashing brawl with the turn of a single card. Thomas didn't envy Masterson his job.

"Are you still lined up to meet your man tomorrow?" asked Masterson.

Thomas figured that the marshal probably already knew the answer to that question. It made sense to answer honestly, and in any event, he was beginning to take a bit of a shine to the lawman.

"In fact, he arrived early, and we met this afternoon at the Torobino. He's headed south, and I'll be on the afternoon train to Denver tomorrow."

"You know, about that," began the marshal, "I've wanted to ask you...."

Masterson was cut off in mid-sentence by a young woman who had either slipped or been pushed into his lap. He pulled his chair back to help right her, and Thomas jumped up to assist. The marshal recognized her as one of the women who got off the train from Wichita that morning. She was only a kid, but her pimp had wasted no time in finding a place to ply her trade.

"I am so very sorry," she said in a pronounced British accent before checking her hair and smoothing her dress. "That boy..." she pointed to a young cowhand in a checked shirt and black jeans standing a few feet away, "...has been on me for the past fifteen minutes."

Bat handed her his glass of Madeira. "Can't negotiate a satisfactory arrangement?" he asked.

She took a sip, and Thomas sat back down.

"He should have been my first for the night," she said, "but when he opened his mouth, I realized he was an Irishman. I cannot abide their lot."

"And you need to *abide* the gentlemen you go upstairs with?" asked the incredulous marshal. "That's a new one to me."

"Well, look at the tout." She took another drink. "Would you go upstairs with the like of him?"

"You've got us there, that's the truth," said Thomas. "I don't believe that the marshal or I would look forward to that trip, though you should also know that my mother was Irish, God bless her soul."

"But you are a gentleman," said the girl with an air of coyness that surprised him. She *was* new at her job. "And you are the marshal?" she said to Bat. "Dear…am I in trouble?"

"You may be with your manager for turning away a paying customer, but that is between the two of you and is not the concern of the law."

The girl set down her glass and smiled at Thomas and Bat. "Thank you for the drink," she said to Masterson. "And thank you, sir, for your kindness." She touched Thomas lightly on the arm and walked away.

"You make friends easily, Colonel," said the marshal.

Thomas was about to reply when a woman shouted, and people began to scramble away from the bar. He turned in the direction of the commotion and saw the Irish cowhand standing behind the woman they had just been speaking with. He had one arm tightly wrapped around her neck, while in the other hand he held a buffalo skinning knife to her throat.

Before the marshal could draw his revolver, Thomas bolted out of his chair and advanced to within a few feet of the terrified young woman.

The Irishman snarled at Thomas. "Back off now, you tinhorn, you. I have first call on this whore, and you can wait for whatever is left of her when I'm done."

Thomas stopped in his tracks. The cowboy kept his grip on the girl and backed up against the bar. The other customers pulled back even further. He sensed Masterson standing right behind him.

"I can't shoot him when he's holding the knife like that," the marshal said in a low, calm voice.

Thomas half-turned his head and nodded. "Maybe I can have a talk with our friend."

He took a couple of steps closer to the bar. The cowhand shuffled to the left and adjusted his hold on the young woman.

"I have no problem waiting my turn," he said to the Irishman. "But I sure as hell wouldn't want to have to mount a damaged filly. Where's the fun in that?"

His conversation confused the cowhand, who shook his head wildly back and forth before bringing the knife up to the girl's face and pressing it on her cheek, just under her right eye.

"It's her eye I'll be taking, not her poke-basket," said the Irishman. "Next time she sees the likes of me with her one good eye, she'll think twice about ever turning down a son of Dublin again."

"He means it," whispered Masterson.

"Have your revolver ready," Thomas replied.

The girl's eyes went wide with fear as Thomas took two steps towards a table where an elderly man was sitting with a walking cane resting on his lap. Thomas snatched the cane off the startled man's legs and advanced towards the Irishman and the girl.

The cowboy pulled the knife away from the girl's face and pointed it straight out at Thomas, while tightening his grip on the girl's throat with his other arm.

Thomas did not slow down. He walked to within a few inches of the girl, then flipped the cane from his left hand to his right and raised it high in the air above her head. The cowhand's eyes followed the movement of the cane, and Thomas took that instant of distraction to reach forward with his left hand, grab the inside of the Irishman's right wrist, and twist it backwards.

He pushed down hard on the wrist while stepping into a position that put him perpendicular to the cowboy's body, all the while applying more pressure. The move caused the Irishman's right shoulder to pitch forward, and with it, the girl's body, at which point Thomas immediately thrust the cane between them, pushed it behind the cowboy's extended elbow, under his side, and against his chest.

Then, he pulled the Irishman's knife hand high at the wrist and pulled the cane down towards the floor with all his strength. The cane acted as a lever where it was wedged between the cowboy's elbow and chest, and he and the girl tumbled to the ground. The entire series of moves took less than five seconds.

Masterson stepped around them and grabbed the knife from the Irishman's broken hand, and, while Thomas kept the pressure on the cane, the girl pulled herself out from under the cowboy. The barman helped her to stand and sat her down at a table.

The marshal's brother and a county deputy pushed through the crowd to help haul the cowhand to jail, and Thomas returned the cane to its quite delighted owner before sitting down with Bat, who had a grin a country mile wide on his face. "You spend a lot of time sticking your neck out for strangers?" he asked, as he poured two more glasses of the excellent Madeira.

Thomas shook his head. "It just came on me. Maybe I just didn't like to see a fellow Irishman make such a public spectacle of himself."

"Or maybe that little sportin' gal got you thinking you might not mind making a trip upstairs yourself. Looks to me like she's the pick of the litter tonight."

Thomas looked across the bar to where the English girl was talking excitedly with two of the other ladies. She caught his eye and raised a glass of medicinal brandy in his direction.

"Another time, perhaps," Thomas said. "It had been my intention to sit at faro for a few hours, but the festivities have dispelled me of that particular desire for the moment."

The gaming boss came up to their table, and Masterson turned to speak with him. When he turned back, he spilled a handful of chips on the table.

"Compliments of the Imperial, with thanks for keeping the bloodshed to a minimum tonight. That would be the girl's blood, by the way. There's more cowhands than prairie dogs around here, but a first-rate upstairs lady is a rare commodity."

Thomas sighed; he was going to have to forgo two of his favorite pleasures tonight. He wanted to think through everything he had learned from Itzcoatl and get prepared for his journey north to Denver.

"Can I ask you a question, Marshal, without having to provide too much in the way of an explanation for my inquiry?"

Bat re-lit his cigar and waved to someone walking by. "I'm sure you can, Colonel, if you will do me the reciprocal favor of answering one of my own."

"Fair's fair." He thought for a moment about how to best to begin his question before lowering his voice and simply asking, "What can you tell me about Noah Claybourne?"

Masterson's eyes narrowed. "I'm going to assume that this isn't idle curiosity speaking?"

Thomas shook his head.

"You plan on gunning him down or doing anything else to him a fella in my business might have a problem with?"

"Someone who works for him has done great harm to the family of my best friend. I need to find out what Claybourne knows-and also if he had anything to do with it."

"Which is where that whole 'gunning down' question pops back up, wouldn't you agree?"

Thomas shrugged. "The general thinking is that Claybourne's man was acting on his own. But the thing is..." he hesitated. To go any further was to invite the possibility that Claybourne could be alerted to his mission. That could result in Rosalilia's death. He looked into Masterson's eyes. He trusted the man, dammed if he didn't. He couldn't say why, for certain. He just did.

"My friend's fiancée was kidnapped in Cuernavaca eight days ago. Her father, who was a senior political figure in Mexico, was murdered. My friend was badly wounded trying to rescue her. I owe him more than my life. He has reason to believe that Claybourne's people organized the kidnapping and murder. And they are sure that his fiancée was brought here to Colorado."

The marshal leaned back in his chair. Across the room his deputy stood a drunk cowboy up and walked him to the door, and the piano player got back to work after the fracas with the Irishman.

"And so, you've come all the way from New York to figure it out, and just maybe to find your friend's fiancée, not to mention stirring up a hornet's nest with the most powerful businessman in the state."

"That's pretty much the picture."

Masterson poured the last of the shipwrecked wine into their glasses.

"My job is pretty easy, Colonel. I keep the peace. The trail hands spend their money on liquor and whores, the miners and ranchers drink and make deals, and the gamblers pray for a run of luck that will get them the hell out of here and off to Chicago or San Francisco. The job is messy, but it isn't complicated. Pays $70 a month and a small house. I like it. And I'd like to keep it a while. So now, here you show up, asking me to help you to stick your nose into the business of a man who plays cards with the President of these United States. And I'm supposed to do you that favor?"

Thomas smiled. "Sometimes, doing the right thing is enough. All by itself."

"I promise you that whoever said that in the morning was dead before dark," replied Masterson. He finished off his Madeira and waved to the waiter to bring food.

The men sat quietly for a moment listening to the sounds of roulette wheels, laughter, banging kitchen pans, and beer glasses slamming on tabletops. Then, the marshal made up his mind. "Claybourne is a bona fide son of a bitch," he suddenly said. "Owns pretty much everything and everybody in and around Denver. No scruples, no charm. He is relentless: he has railroads, sawmills, freight companies, mines. Hell, he even makes his own dynamite.

"You ever had California wines?" he continued."Krug and Niebaum make some of the best, but Claybourne owns the biggest vineyards and the most profitable cellars in the state. He sold munitions through his European companies to both sides in the Serbian-Ottoman War in '76, and when the Russians and the Turks went at it in '77, he sold to them both. His hands are dipped in pretty much anything that can make a dollar."

"Does the list include mines in Mexico?"

"It does, though I hear that the going is tough on the political side. It seems that too many Mexicans would like to keep their minerals on their side of the Rio Grande. Is it mining that your friend is involved with?"

"His fiancées father was in a position to deny Claybourne's companies the licenses they need to expand operations. With him dead and his daughter kidnapped, those permits will probably be granted."

The waiter returned with two stoneware crocks of cold beer, along with a plate of cheese, bread, and apples. Thomas was surprised at how hungry he was after the dance with the Irish cowboy.

"German fella name of Coors makes this beer outside Denver, in a town called Golden," said Masterson. "It's delivered fresh twice a week by train. You'll like it."

Thomas drank deeply and then tore into the bread and cheese. He wasn't used to drinking beer cold. It was quite good.

"You'll want to be visiting Golden to get outfitted," Bat said. "Major T.R. Rhine has a place just outside city limits where the river forks. Everybody knows him. He used to command a federal armory, and he stayed in the supply business after the war. He provides horses and tack to the cavalry, but mostly he sells guns, grub, and anything you might need out on the prairie, from your tent to your toothbrush. Has a special-built freight wagon that he rides up into the mining towns with. He is a gunsmith, too. A real artist. Rhine is as solid as they come. If you build trust with him, you will have a valuable ally, no matter what kind of nitroglycerine-soaked manure pile you find yourself in." Masterson clanged his stoneware crock against Thomas'. "And, friend, if you are even remotely considering putting the hurt on Noah Claybourne, you are going to need T.R. in your corner."

Thomas finished his meal in silence, oblivious to the singsong chattering of the dealers, the out of tune piano, and the catcalls from cowboys shouting at friends who were heading upstairs to take their rides. Bat Masterson finished his beer, lit a fresh cigar, and asked the waiter to bring coffee and brandy.

"And now, it's my turn. So, just how in the bloody hell did you become a full colonel in the United States Army when you were just….?"

He had trusted only one other person in the world with the answer to that question. He looked Masterson directly in the eyes.

"Seventeen."

❖

EIGHT

Dinwiddie County, Virginia, April 1, 1865

Camp was breaking up. Thomas could feel it in his sleep even before he heard horses being hitched to freight wagons and sergeants calling to their men to strike tents and load their gear. He threw off his wool blanket and was pulling on his trousers when O'Hanlon's enormous form appeared in front of the small canvas tent.

The sergeant anticipated his question: "Four o'clock, boyo. Two hours 'til daybreak, and not a drop of rain to spoil the morn. It's salt pork and hardtack for the lot of 'em, and barely warmed, at that. Get yer boots on, we've got a kitchen to move."

O'Hanlon disappeared into the blackness and Thomas finished dressing, folded his cot and blanket, and threw his few personal possessions into a haversack. Then he piled them outside and then pulled his tent down, rolled it tight, and lashed it with leather ties before slinging the haversack over his shoulder and tossing the cot and tent into a wagon with "Company M" painted on the side. With that complete, he trotted over to where three soldiers were loading the field kitchen into covered wagons by the light of coal oil lanterns.

He was pulling down a row of five-gallon pots that were strung over a smoldering cooking trench when O'Hanlon and Captain Morrison approached.

"This is Scanddrél," said the sergeant, nodding in Thomas's direction.

Thomas set down the pot he had just unhooked and saluted the officer.

"And you say he can read and write-and speak French?" Morrison asked O'Hanlon.

"Aye, that he can, sir. And he's good with sums too."

Captain Morrison looked Thomas over. "You might just do," he said, almost to himself.

Thomas shot O'Hanlon a questioning glance, but the sergeant could only shrug and shake his head in return.

"Sergeant, I want this man at General Yoke's tent in five minutes," said the captain. "Have him bring his personal things." Then he turned and walked swiftly off into the darkness.

"What kind of trouble have you gotten yourself into laddie?" wondered O'Hanlon aloud.

This time it was Thomas' turn to shrug.

❖

The 109th Ohio Regiment had been camped at the base of a long, narrow ridge near Pebble Creek for five days. Now, in the pre-dawn chill, nearly five hundred men, horses, and wagons were making ready to move to a heavily forested area about eleven miles to the east. B Company, with eighty-seven men, three sergeants, one lieutenant, and the regiment's only battle-seasoned captain had been ordered to hold and await orders.

Thomas wound his way along the crowded, dimly lit path towards the command tent. Soldiers streamed past him in the opposite direction, their rifles slung, packs full, and bellies rumbling for the coffee, bacon, and biscuits that the kitchen staff would normally be preparing at this hour. Grumbling had been the lot of the common soldier since Caesar's legions invaded Britain nineteen hundred years ago, and Thomas heard plenty of that from the soldiers marching past him.

But, for the first time in weeks, he heard something else too; the dull booming of massed artillery fire off to the west. He had heard this cannonade sound only once before, outside the ramparts of Petersburg. O'Hanlon told him it was a Confederate *Canon obusier de 12*, also known as the "Canon de l'Empereur" or Napoleon, a French designed smooth bore cannon that could fire either shells, solid cast-iron balls or grapeshot. The Napoleon's range was up to a mile, and Thomas estimated from the sound that the Confederate guns must be fifteen to twenty miles from the camp. One more thing to worry about as he hurried through the lines of horses, soldiers and wagons heading east.

General Yoke's tent was the only one still standing. Lanterns blazed in front of the entrance, where several men were feeding and saddling a line of horses, including the general's personal Morgan-Thoroughbred cross, a huge, coal-black beast named Cornwall.

Thomas identified himself to the sentry and was told to wait. The sentry entered the tent, and a moment later Captain Morrison emerged and waved the bewildered kitchen boy into the general's presence. He stepped into the well-lit tent and stood at attention. General Yoke and Major Rolande were seated at a table on which Thomas noticed a plate of fresh biscuits and a pot of coffee. He wondered who had prepared them, since his kitchen crew had doused their cooking fires almost an hour ago.

At the back of the tent, a gray-haired clerk sat at a small folding table, scribbling furiously across the pages of a thick, leather-bound book.

The three officers looked Thomas over.

"Can he pass for twenty-two?" asked Yoke.

"I would believe that, yes," replied Rolande.

"And you're sure he can speak like an educated man?" continued the general.

"Including, I am told, in the French language," added Captain Morrison.

"That true, can you parley-vous, boy?" asked Yoke.

"Yes, sir. My father was French, and I have spoken it since I was a boy," said Thomas.

"And your father, where is he today?" Rolande asked.

"He is dead, sir."

"And your mother?"

"Also dead, just before I signed up."

"Brothers or sisters?" asked Morrison.

Thomas shook his head. "Just me," he replied.

Rolande nodded to the general. This boy was by far the best candidate they had interviewed in the past hour. No family, no real profile in the regiment, as empty a slate as they could have hoped to find. And, if he wasn't fully up to the job, so be it, the major thought. They were out of time. He would have to do.

"Who is his sergeant?" Rolande asked Captain Morrison.

"O'Hanlon, kitchen company. They should be moving out right now."

The major turned to the clerk. He knew that the one person in the regiment who knew much at all about Private Scanddrél would have to be re-located before today's business was done. "Write a transfer order. O'Hanlon to the 112th Ohio, effective immediately."

"And now boy," Rolande said to Thomas, "you'd probably like to know why you are here."

Morrison pulled a camp chair over in front of the table and motioned for Thomas to sit down. At the same time, the tent flap opened, and the regimental barber stepped in. He looked as mystified as Thomas had been only moments before.

"Clean this boy up," Rolande ordered. "Give him a fresh out of West Point cut and be quick about it."

The barber stood behind Thomas' chair, pulled out a comb and scissors, and set to work. Morrison sat down at the table with Yoke and Rolande and slid the plate of biscuits over to Thomas.

"Take one, boy, and some coffee," said the captain, "and listen carefully."

Thomas accepted a biscuit and slowly raised it to his lips. He was completely baffled by the events of the past few minutes. Yanked from sleep, ordered to the commanding general's tent with no explanation, and for what? Breakfast and a haircut? War was a damn strange affair. Damn strange.

General Yoke loosened his collar, leaned forward, and began to talk in a soft, almost fatherly voice. "When a conflict as mighty as the one we have been engaged in against the rebs is in its final days, as we hope to God it is, "he said to Thomas, "the path to the surrender table can go in a smooth, straight line, or it can take a lot of twists and turns. A commander has to be ready for either eventuality." He sat back in his chair and placed both of his hands flat on the table. For emphasis, Thomas thought.

"This morning the path to Union victory is looking closer and more promising than ever," Yoke continued, "but, even as we bear down on these rebel bastards for the last time, there is always the possibility–small, but real-that something unexpected can happen at the last minute that can take the wind out of the sails just enough to turn the tide against us. This is one of those moments. And so, today I have been called upon to make some command decisions that to some might look, let's say, a little strange."

Major Rolande could not help sharing a smile with Captain Morrison, who, in turn, continued to fiddle nervously with his handlebar moustache.

General Yoke pushed the plate of biscuits back across to Thomas. "And that brings us to this meeting and to the reason you are here, Private...I'm sorry, Private...?"

"Scanddrél," replied Thomas as he scooped up his second biscuit.

"Scandrel. That a European name?" the general asked, ignoring Thomas's careful pronunciation.

"With two ds. And an accent for emphasis on the last syllable," said Thomas. "It's French."

"Ah, French," said Yoke. Then, the general turned his head to the clerk at the table behind him and in a loud voice asked, "Are you getting this, Sergeant?"

The elderly scribe kept his head down and simply nodded in assent, writing faster than ever on one page, and then flipping to another to continue writing.

"Damn fine clerk," said the general to no one in particular. "But he couldn't hear a grizzly bear break wind if they were sharing the same cot."

Thomas didn't join Morrison and Rolande when they laughed at the general's joke. He wasn't sure what he was supposed to do. So, he finished his biscuit and took another drink of coffee, which, he thought, was a hell of a lot tastier than the swill made from chicory and used grounds that the enlisted men were served.

The darkness outside the tent was softening, and Thomas noticed that the sounds of soldiers and wagons departing the camp was also fading. Daybreak was less than an hour away. While he had no idea why he had been called before the regimental commanders, he did know that whatever was waiting for him when the sun finally peeked over Pebble Creek Ridge, this was not going to be an ordinary day.

❖

The barber finished cutting Thomas' hair and left the tent, and Captain Morrison stepped outside to check the progress of the regimental move-out as General Yoke continued to talk.

"I have never been one for secret, behind the lines shenanigans, or for using agents and spies," he said. "But yesterday, a rebel patrol under a white flag approached our outer sentries and requested a meeting. Those boys were tired and hungry, and there wasn't a pair of decent boots between the six of them. Ragged is what they were, right Major?"

Rolande nodded. "Ragged *and* desperate, sir."

"Desperate, yes, that's the perfect description. They wanted to surrender, and I was inclined at first to accept their offer and have them marched under guard over to Warren's command. On reflection, I decided to take a different course of action. I had the sentries take the rebs to get a hot meal, and I proposed a plan to my commanders designed to take advantage of the circumstance in such a way as to bring us one step closer to an assurance of victory."

"I don't expect you to understand how battle strategy is constructed, son, nor do I intend now to burden you with much detail on how this plan came about, or how exactly it will play out to the benefit of President Lincoln, General Grant, and the entire Union war effort."

Or to *our* benefit, thought Major Rolande.

"Private Scandrel, when you signed your enlistment papers, did you hope, as I believe all young men do, that your exertions in battle might one day bring honor and glory to your regiment, and even to yourself?" asked Yoke.

Thomas perked up. "Sir, yes, I certainly did. I still do."

Captain Morrison came back into the tent. "We have only a half hour, General," he said.

"Then let me get right to it, Private," said the general. "After we fed the reb patrol, we sat them down and made them an offer. If they would gather two dozen of their fellows on horseback an hour after sunrise this morning and feint an attack against us from over the ridge, we would agree to take them into safe custody. They must send one member of the patrol back to their HQ to report that they encountered heavy Federal resistance, and most of the patrol was killed or captured. In exchange, we would provide medical care, food, clothing, and safe passage home for every member of the reb patrol, and even put a few dollars in their pockets. The outrider they sent back to the reb commanders would be allowed to surrender to us later and get the same deal. At this juncture in the war, with the tide of events turning so completely against the Confederacy, it was an offer they were more than happy to take."

The general was certainly right about one thing, Thomas thought; he could not conceive of any battlefield strategy in which such a wild sounding scheme made sense. On the other hand, his only battle experience to date had been completely culinary in nature. Whatever it was the general had in mind for him, he was certain that it was his duty to obey.

"I can only tell you that the larger plan is for us to make Pickett's whole reb army believe that when their patrol rides over that ridge this morning they are coming face to face with an entire regiment of first-rate infantry and cavalry. That will give the rebs pause and perhaps provide General Warren's troops at Five Forks with a bit of a respite from rebel counterattacks. As for us, while the rebs are deciding what to do about our regiment, we will be quietly marching and regrouping to the west along their weak flank. When Warren attacks them from Five

Forks, we will support him and surprise the rebs by crawling right up their backsides while they think we are still assembled and waiting in reserve right here."

General Yoke was almost impressed by his own completely fabricated little speech. In a different time and a different war, he was convinced that he would have been a stellar battlefield commander.

Yoke stood up and walked over towards the clerk. "Major Rolande, please explain the private's orders."

"Private Scandrel, you are about to be given a once-in-a-lifetime opportunity to serve your country. We need an officer, someone not known to the rebs, to ride up along the ridge this morning to meet the rebel incursion that we planned yesterday. You are going to be that officer."

Thomas was stunned. An officer? At seventeen? With no battlefield experience, no training, and no command experience? O'Hanlon was right: what *had* he gotten himself in to?

Rolande read the boy's facial expression. He smiled reassuringly and said, "We make battlefield promotions all the time, Private. I myself began the war as a lieutenant, and Captain Morrison was a sergeant. George Custer, with whom I attended the academy, was brevetted brigadier general at the age of twenty-three. You are part of a long line of soldiers whose rank has been advanced in wartime for any number of reasons. When your tasks are complete and the war is over, you will be reduced back in rank, but, as our way of thanking you for your heroic effort, General Yoke has agreed that you will muster out of the 109th at the rank of 1st Sergeant. Isn't that right, General?"

"That's right, boy," replied Yoke, "and you can expect enough mustering out pay from the War Department to get a new start back home."

"And what rank am I to be elevated to with this temporary advancement?" asked Thomas.

General Yoke looked down at the clerk. "Where are you with this?" he asked.

"I have made new entries going back three and a half years," he said in a halting voice. "In all I have made eighteen entries for him in the regimental record. The lad came to us at nineteen, a transfer with the rank of sergeant from the 121st. One year later he was brevetted lieutenant, the year after that, captain. After his distinguished performance at Petersburg, you elevated him to major. And, six months ago, due to a combination of regimental organization requirements for officer staffing, and there not being any other officer qualified for the position, you promoted him to the rank of full colonel."

Rolande could not help feeling a bit of a twinge at the comment about there not being any other officer qualified for the brevet. Ruse or not, he had his pride.

For his part, Thomas could only lean forward on his chair, wide-eyed and open-mouthed. Colonel? Good god almighty, what was happening?

The clerk wasn't finished. "Official approval of his rank of colonel in wartime requires the signature of General Grant, of course, just as it would require the President's in time of peace. I have made a journal entry showing that your promotion request was sent to Grant in proper form and time frame four months ago, by courier." The clerk smiled. "Of course, like so many other communications, yours was no doubt lost in the chaos of battle. One of many thousands of dispatches that the War Department will be sorting out for years, I assure you."

A sentry opened the tent flap just as the first gray streaks of morning light began to pierce the darkness. Then the clerk handed General Yoke a sheaf of papers and asked him to sign each of them. The sentry waited for Yoke to finish, and then said, "It's time, General."

Yoke nodded and handed the signed paperwork to Major Rolande, who flipped through it page by page. "And these dates and circumstances replicate what you have put into the regimental record?" he asked the clerk.

"They do, exactly" replied the clerk. "The entries are as complete as you will find in anyone's service records anywhere. Best of all, there is this."

He handed a sheet of thick, oversized parchment to the general for his signature. "It is the most important document of all," continued the clerk in a tone that indicated he was most pleased with this morning's work. "Regimental stationary, certified watermark, everything."

Yoke signed the paper and handed it back to the clerk. "Sirs," the clerk said to the assembled officers with an almost courtly flourish, "I hereby declare that one Thomas Edward Scoundrel is hereby brevetted colonel of the 109th Ohio Regiment of the Army of the United States of America."

The tent went silent. Thomas felt his eyes water and his throat parch. For a moment, he even forgot to breathe. Yoke, Rolande, and Morrsion were quiet too, but more out a sense of relief that their scheme was moving ahead as planned.

At last, Thomas found his voice. He cleared his throat, raised his head, and in a quavering voice just above a whisper said, "But, my name is not Scoundrel."

General Yoke grabbed the certificate he had just signed. A scowl darkened his face, he slammed the document on the desk, and balled his fists at his side. Rolande spread the pile of newly created records on the table and scanned through them quickly. He looked at Yoke and shook his head.

Yoke exploded. "*Scoundrel?* You wrote his last name as Scoundrel on every damn one of these? And in the regimental record book as well? What the bloody hell is wrong with you? Who on earth is named Scoundrel, for the sweet love of God? You might as well have called him Colonel Piss-Ant!"

For the first time in his life, the terrified clerk found himself wishing that he was completely deaf, not simply hard of hearing. He could only nod and say, "I am sorry General. It's what I thought I heard."

"How much time would it take to redo the records and documents?" Captain Morrison asked of the clerk who he suspected would be exiled to the West to fight the Apaches before this day was done.

"Several hours, at least," said the old man. "But I cannot duplicate the formal notice. I have no more parchment stationary." With that, the clerk retreated into a darkened corner.

"We don't have minutes, let alone hours," said Major Rolande.

He and Morrison looked at General Yoke. The general shook his head and sighed. Once again it was up to him to chart a solution to the mess. At this juncture, there was only one thing he could do.

"War asks many sacrifices of each of us, lad," he said to Thomas. "Today, you give up your name, but in turn you gain five years in age, your rank is advanced, and you are the beneficiary of our respect, our undying gratitude, and the thanks of a grateful country."

"Stand up and raise your right hand, boy," he ordered, "and repeat after me."

Thomas stood and raised his hand. The blood was pounding so loudly in his ears that he could barely make out the words of the oath that he was repeating. He did his best to speak coherently, but he could not be sure that the words tumbling out of his mouth made any sense at all.

"Solemnly…swear…faithfully discharge…constitution…support and defend…so help me…"

Then, it was over. Captain Morrison and Major Rolande faced him and, in unison slowly raised their hands in salute.

To me, thought Thomas, my god they are saluting me.

"Colonel Scoundrel," said Yoke, "by virtue of my command authority, and on behalf of the President of the United States and General Ulysses S. Grant, I congratulate you. May the blessings of almighty God follow you all the days of your life."

Thomas's vision blurred, and he dropped to the dirt floor like a stone.

"Sentry," said Yoke, "pick the colonel up and splash cold water on his face. It's time for him to meet his destiny."

❈

NINE

Pebble Creek, Virginia, April 1, 1865

Thomas shook off the water and scrambled to his feet. General Yoke, his officers, and the regiment's quartermaster sergeant were standing in a semi-circle around him. Folded over the quartermaster's arms were several long, dark blue coats with silver buttons down their fronts.

"Turn around, boy…I mean, Colonel," he growled.

Thomas obeyed, still in a daze at whatever madness was unfolding around him. The quartermaster slipped one of the coats onto his arms, then pulled it off, and slipped on another. "This one will do," he said.

"Shoulder straps?" asked Major Rolande.

The sergeant held up two rectangular strips of dark blue wool, each about two inches by four inches, framed in gold braid. Each was embroidered with a silver American eagle holding an olive branch in one talon and a sheaf of arrows in the other. It was the insignia of a full colonel. "Have them sewn on immediately," Rolande told the quartermaster. "And find him some officer's trousers."

"He needs the right hat," added Captain Morrison.

General Yoke reached over and took Morrison's hat from his head. "Yours will be just right."

Morrison grimaced. Hardees were expensive. His sported a badge in the shape of a brass bugle that was affixed to the front with a woolen cord in cavalry gold wrapped around the crown to form two tassels. The right side of the brim was folded up and pinned to the crown by a brass eagle badge, and on the left, a black feather plume poked above the crown at a rakish angle. Fortunes of war, thought Morrison, as Yoke stepped forward and planted his hat on Thomas' head.

Outside the tent, the sky was turning from black to dark gray. A sentry carried the last boxes from the tent to a waiting buckboard and climbed up onto the seat. Except for the ninety-two men of B Company and those in Yoke's command tent, the camp was empty.

It took only a minute for the shoulder straps to be sewn onto Thomas' new coat. He slipped on the trousers handed to him by the quartermaster–the best he had ever worn–followed by a pair of slightly worn boots. Someone handed him a belt, and then Yoke himself gave Thomas a light cavalry saber in a metal sheath.

"Can you shoot?" asked the quartermaster.

Under any other circumstances, Thomas would have been thrilled to answer that question. He had yet to even hold a gun in this war.

"I can shoot," he answered, "and ride."

The sergeant drew a holstered revolver from an oilcloth sack. "This is the Remington six-shot percussion, .44 caliber, with paper cartridges. Do you know how to load and fire this model?"

"I do."

"Strap it on, Colonel. And here's a supply pouch."

The quartermaster handed Thomas a small canvas bag and then stepped back so that everyone in the tent could take stock of their creation. The overall effect of the uniform, hat, and sidearms on the former kitchen boy was impressive.

Hell thought Major Rolande, this boy could pass for twenty-five. No worries on that count. "Just two things now, sir," he said to the general. "His signed orders and a mount."

General Yoke pulled a folded piece of paper from his coat pocket. "Your orders are simple. You will take command of B Company at first light this morning and proceed immediately to reconnoiter along Pebble Creek Ridge from the crossroads on the south to the creek on the north. Do not engage the enemy unless engaged. Send a rider to report the enemy troop disposition to me at my field HQ at Turner, three miles due north of this camp. Do you understand your orders?"

He took a deep breath. One part of his brain was reeling in panic. He understood the orders, but he had no idea how he was going to carry them out. Take command? Reconnoiter? Report back? Yesterday he was cleaning slop buckets and making coffee for five hundred men. Today he would be leading nearly one hundred of them in a complicated scheme that just might get them all killed.

At the same time, he thought, what an opportunity he had just been presented. Yoke assured him that the fix was in; the Johnnie patrol would meekly surrender, he would place them under guard and lead them to Yoke, and that would be it. The war was ending, and he would muster out with the rank of First Sergeant. He would go back to Ohio having accomplished something for the Union, and with a small pension to boot.

"I understand them, sir."

The general handed him the orders. "One last thing, Colonel Scoundrel. To make a suitable impression, you will need the right mount. You will take Cornwall, my personal horse."

Major Rolande and Captain Morrison shared a surprised look. The stallion was like a family member to the general. Surely, he knew that if everything went as it had to, Cornwall would likely not survive the morning. It was clear that General Yoke was looking ahead to the post-war investigation that would look back at this day's events and determine if he had acted properly and in accordance with military law. Only hours earlier he had been ordered to march his regiment to the west to support General Merritt at Five Forks. Instead, he sent most of his command to safety in the east, miles away from the impending battle.

For Yoke's story to be believed at the War Department, every detail surrounding the supposed attack against his regiment by a full rebel brigade, including his decision to swing around to the east instead of making a forced march to the west, had to be militarily sound. Making sure the new regimental colonel wasn't found dead alongside some old farm plug was one of those details. Colonels rode thoroughbreds, like Cornwall. Yoke loved that horse, but he loved his own hide and the fortune that was waiting for him in Philadelphia even more. The general had done everything possible to cover his tracks. He was leaving nothing to chance; the boy had to die on that ridge, and so did every soldier in B Company.

Yoke motioned for everyone to leave the tent. There was no time to strike it; dawn was fast approaching, and with the first sunlight, the rebs would come boiling over Pebble Creek Ridge. Morrison, Rolande, and the quartermaster climbed into their saddles and waited while Yoke walked Thomas over to where Cornwall stood saddled and waiting.

The general stroked his horse's muzzle. "This is a war horse. Be good to him and bring him back to me."

"I will, sir."

"Captain Hayden and B Company will be along momentarily," continued the general. "Morrison has told them that we have a new regimental colonel. They won't recognize you, and they won't be happy to have a new commander dumped on them like this without notice, but they will respect your rank and obey your orders."

"Let Hayden take the lead up to the ridge. He is a fine officer, and he has faced enemy fire many times. Remember that he is not aware of our agreement with the rebs; there is no need for him to know. He will be ready for a fight, but he will be pleased when the patrol hauls out the white flag and drops their arms. When he asks what is to be done with the prisoners, tell him they are to be taken to me. Are we clear?"

Thomas could only nod. His mind was racing. But he also felt a growing certainty that he could carry this off. Seventeen or not, he knew he was at a crossroad. His Irish mother had sometimes talked about how lightning could strike you without warning, anytime, anywhere, and in any weather. It could kill you, or it could light your way to glory. God willing–and you jump quickly enough–she would say, you could ride that lightning bolt instead of being consumed by its flame.

What took place in the next few hours would affect everything he did tomorrow and every day after that. For the first time in his life, Thomas Scanddrél–now Scoundrel–knew what it was like to take a hand in shaping his own destiny. He felt the weight of the saber and revolver at his waist and looked down at the silver eagles on his shoulders. Whatever played out on that ridge this morning was going to define his life. And he was fine with that.

General Yoke handed Cornwall's reins to him. "Remember," he said softly, "the rebs are with us today. No one will be harmed. They will play their role, and you will play yours. It's a fine thing you are doing for the regiment and a fine thing for your country. I am proud of you. The President would be proud of you. Now, wait here for Captain Hayden, and do your job."

The general pivoted and walked to the buckboard. He got up on the front seat beside the driver and saluted Thomas. Then, the wagon rolled away into the graying morning.

Major Rolande reined his horse up alongside the wagon. "Brave boy," he said to General Yoke. "Shame he is going to die this morning."

Yoke was a little surprised at the major's tone. His condolence sounded sincere. "It is sad," he replied, "but thousands have died for far less gain in this damn war. At least his death will stand for something."

"Sir?"

The general lit his cigar. "His death will be in the service of all of those we have protected these past few years," he said. "You realize, major, that the men we sent to safety will lead this nation after the war. They will be the bankers, the industrialists, the politicians, and the judges. They will brush the red man and the deserts aside, and they will build the great cities that fulfill our manifest destiny. No, Major, that boy will die in the cause of something more noble and hallowed than he could ever imagine. A soldier could not ask for a better death."

I doubt if the boy would feel the same, mused Rolande. He looked ahead to where the men and horses of B Company were assembled in the light of a row of flickering torches. Scoundrel's death would stand for something, including the major's personal enrichment. He turned in his saddle and looked back at the kitchen boy in a colonel's uniform standing silently beside the general's horse. As for what his own life would stand for after today, thought Rolande in a momentary twinge of conscience, that remained to be seen.

❖

Thomas checked Cornwall's saddle cinches and bridle. He noticed the grain bag tied to his side, and he was pleased to see a rifle seated in the saddle scabbard. One of the few useful things he had learned from his father when the elder Scanddrél wasn't gambling, whoring, or concocting another seedy investment scheme, was the art of horsemanship. His father was an exceptional judge of horseflesh, and Morgan-Thoroughbreds were his preferred breed.

As the last echoes of General Yoke's buckboard faded into the approaching dawn, Thomas appraised his horse. Like the best of this kind, Cornwall had strong legs, a well arched neck, laid back shoulders, and a distinctly expressive head. The combination of the longer back, strongly muscled hindquarters and tall, graceful tail added to the impression of strength and robust power. No matter what lay ahead this morning, Thomas was glad to have such a horse under him.

A breeze picked up out of the west, and the eastern sky was light enough now for him to just make out the crest of the long, low ridge he was to reconnoiter. He mounted Cornwall and walked him several times around the command tent. The horse was quick and responsive, and he accepted him from the start. That was a good sign.

Captain Hayden and B Company would join him shortly, and the game would be underway. Could he fool a battle-hardened veteran like Hayden? Would he need to? Yoke's orders were to let the captain take the lead up the ridge. That was standard military protocol. Colonels normally commanded an entire regiment of ten companies, each of which would have its own experienced officer. Hayden would think nothing of Thomas instructing him to take the lead of the single company.

Sergeant O'Hanlon held Hayden in high regard, and that was sufficient for Thomas. The only thing he knew about the captain was that he had been a successful engineer in private life and that he had personally purchased new seven-shot Spencer repeating rifles for every man in B Company after General Yoke refused to requisition them. President Lincoln had approved the magazine-fed weapons, but senior commanders were reluctant to adopt them because of their cost, the massive amount of ammunition they went through, and the considerable amount of smoke they produced on already smoky battlefields.

Smoke or not, every private in the Union Army knew the story of Colonel John T. Wilder's 4,000-man Spencer-armed brigade. During the Battle of Hoover's Gap in Tennessee two years earlier, they held off 22,000 Confederate attackers with those rifles and suffered only twenty-seven losses against two hundred eighty-seven rebs killed. Thomas had enjoyed watching Hayden's men do field drills in their rifle-green coats with black Goodyear rubber buttons down the front. The odd-looking buttons were a favorite of snipers and sharpshooters because they didn't reflect light and give away their positions the way brass buttons did.

❖

Then, the sounds of voices, and horses approaching. Captain Hayden rode out of the darkness at the head of a mounted column of two dozen men, followed by fifty or sixty soldiers on foot. Thomas steeled himself for the performance and was almost surprised that he did not feel the least bit agitated or stressed.

Hayden rode up to him. He was razor thin, with a short beard and eyes that pierced the darkness like a wolf. The captain halted in front of Cornwall and saluted. As Thomas returned the captain's salute, he could tell that he was being given the once-over by someone who would know the difference between a senior officer and a kitchen boy. This was it.

"Colonel Scoundrel," Hayden finally said in a low, deliberate voice. "My men and I are pleased to meet you."

❖

TEN

Pebble Creek Ridge

In the moment it took for Captain Hayden to emerge out of the shadows and ride up beside him, Thomas formulated his plan. General Yoke had set the table, but it was his mother who made the meal. He could follow the general's orders to the letter and go quietly into an ordinary future, or he could alter the plans a bit and catch the lightning. Only one of those paths would lead to fortune and glory.

"Captain, it is my pleasure," he said. "General Yoke speaks highly of your company, and I am honored to ride with you this morning. I regret we have not had a chance to get to know one another, but I look forward to doing that at mess this evening." The sound and formality of his own voice surprised Thomas. All his life he had spoken with a hint of his mother's County Clare brogue. Now, he only heard northwest Ohio farm country.

Captain Hayden nodded. Nothing that happened in war was routine, but everything that was happening this morning was unusual. He appreciated that the colonel recognized the importance of establishing a solid relationship with his officers.

"Our orders, sir?" he asked.

Thomas was almost startled at being addressed as a superior officer, but he resisted the urge to burst out laughing.

"We are to reconnoiter the length of Pebble Creek Ridge from the southern crossroad to the northern creek, a distance of one and a half miles. General Yoke wants us to observe the presence of any rebel forces that may be marshaling on the eastern flank of the ridge and report any troop strength and configuration to him at his new headquarters at Turner."

Hayden looked skeptical. He patted the side of his horses' nose, and then said, "Begging the colonel's pardon, and with all due respect, but wouldn't that task be more suited to a patrol of six or seven mounted men, rather than a company of our size? A handful of men can fade into the brush and go about a reconnaissance pretty much undetected. Ninety men, well, again my pardon, but that's akin to trying to sneak an elephant into a convent shower room without being seen by the Mother Superior."

Thomas knew he should remain in character, and perhaps even admonish the captain for questioning the general's orders, but he could not suppress a chuckle at the vision created by the captain's imagery.

"Captain," he replied with a smile, "at this late stage in the war I confess I wouldn't be surprised to encounter your elephant anywhere; from the other side of that ridge to Robert E. Lee's washtub itself."

Now it was Hayden's turn to smile. Perhaps the new colonel wouldn't turn out to be a strutting martinet like General Yoke. This morning's events would tell.

Thomas asked Hayden to summon his lieutenant and sergeants. It was time to call up the lightning. Hayden called them forward, and the four men approached on horseback as the last of the darkness gave way to gray. It would be light in just a few minutes.

Captain Hayden introduced his men one by one. They regarded the new colonel warily; whether warriors lived or died at any moment in battle could come down to the degree to which they trusted their commander. They did not know this Colonel Scoundrel, and more importantly, they did not give their trust and respect to any man who had not earned it in the smoke and fire of battle.

Thomas sensed their reticence. He did not blame them, but he still had to convince them that what he was about to propose made sense.

"Gentlemen, today we have been thrown together under unusual circumstances, and I appreciate that you do not know me. Fairness being a mutual endeavor, it is also true that I do not know you. Time will resolve that matter, and I trust it will be to our mutual satisfactions."

Several men made cursory nods, and he continued. "Our orders are to ride up and along Pebble Creek Ridge from south to north, and to report any rebel activity we observe, in detail."

Echoing his captain, the lieutenant asked, "The entire company sir? Not just a patrol?"

"Those are General Yoke's orders. Of course, orders can be impacted by events as they unfold. With that in mind, I am going to make a small change to our orders, really more a delay than anything else."

The captain's ears pricked up. He leaned forward in his saddle and cast a quizzical glance at his lieutenant. It was damn unusual to make a change to a general officer's explicit orders, and that applied to a colonel just as much as to a private.

Thomas prepared to take the chance. His spur of the moment plan was based on two assumptions; first, that Yoke was correct, and the rebel patrol would abide by their deal and not fire a shot at the Union soldiers. They would surrender, and then come along quietly as the prisoners of B Company. The second assumption is where things got a bit dicey; if the rebs were set to surrender in any event, why wouldn't they surrender to a single officer just as readily as they would to an entire company of soldiers? There would be no glory if he simply waited at the base of the ridge as Hayden and his men rode up to the crest and accepted the rebel patrols surrender. But, if he rode up the ridge by himself, with no other union troops in sight, and the rebs surrendered to him alone, *en masse*... that would be a heroic action deserving of attention and accolades. A citation for bravery or perhaps even a medal could not help but improve his status and therefore his prospects after the war. His mother would have understood his thinking; this was exactly what she meant when she talked about riding the lightning.

Dawn would be upon them in a minute, and with the light, the rebel patrol would ride over the ridge to fulfill their agreement with Yoke. There was no time to waste. He let out a deep breath.

"Gentlemen, I will ride to the top of the ridge alone. I will make a preliminary observation and then signal to you with the Stars and Stripes, which I will carry up the hill. If I do not signal, you will remain here until I return. If I wave the flag back and forth slowly, you will advance as a unit up the ridge to my position. Should I wave the flag in a rapid motion, you will split into three units and get up to the top as fast as hell. Half the mounted riders to the left, half to the right, and the infantry in the middle. Is that clear?"

Hayden and his men understood what their new colonel had just said, but none of them had an inkling what it was about or why a colonel would expose himself like that to potential enemy fire. The captain looked at his men and raised his eyebrows in a half shrug. It was not his place–or theirs–to question the colonel's orders.

Hayden called to the trooper who was carrying the Union flag. The soldier rode forward, planted the flag in the ground next to the captain and then wheeled around and rejoined the line. Hayden pulled it from the ground and rode over to Thomas, who took the flagpole in his left hand.

The captain shook his head and allowed a smile to cross his lips. "You a gambling man, colonel?"

Thomas gripped the flag tightly and reined Cornwall back a bit, which caused the horse to lower and then raise his head. He loosened the strap holding his rifle in its scabbard and adjusted his holstered revolver.

"Not with my skin, and not with the skin of the men I command."

He saluted Captain Hayden, picked up his reins, and touched Cornwall's flanks with his boots. As he galloped away a soft corona of yellow light was edging over the top of the ridge.

※

Thomas rode out of camp towards the rising sun and Pebble Creek Ridge, about two hundred yards distant. Cornwall moved at a steady gait, picking his way effortlessly around fallen logs and small boulders. It took only a few minutes to cover that distance and begin the gently sloping climb up through low brush and stands of spring wildflowers. The crest of the ridge was no more than one hundred yards away now, and he held tightly to the flagpole as Cornwall wound his way up a narrow switchback trail that had been stamped out by deer moving up and down the ridge in search of leaves and berries.

The sky was clear and soft, but there were no indications of the rebel patrol that should be making its way up the other side of the ridge. As he went, he thought about how he would contact the patrol and what he should say. Yoke had promised them cash in exchange for their surrender, but he didn't give him any money. Would they be expecting payment right now? And if they didn't get it, what then? Would the deal be off, or had Yoke made it clear that they wouldn't be paid until they were taken to his headquarters? He cursed softly to himself. Why hadn't he asked for more information before he took off up this damn hill?

Cornwall swung around the tangled limbs and trunk of a fallen oak tree just as the sun crested the ridge. The horse stepped around a heavy branch, and they found themselves at the top of the hill. Running north to south as far as they could see was a path of grass, low scrub, and a sprinkling of trees and boulders about fifty yards wide. It was the perfect place to wait for the rebel patrol.

He had to squint his eyes against the rising sun. Then, the horse shook his head rapidly from side to side, and his ears flared back. He strained to see or hear anything out of the ordinary, but the only sounds traveling through the crisp morning air were being made by a pair of angry killdeers skittering along the path as they tried to protect their ground nest.

He patted Cornwall's head, and they headed over to the opposite side of the ridge top. Standing at the edge, he could see for miles across the valley to rows of purple and blue wooded hills that marched beyond the limits of his sight. Much of the valley floor below the ridge was shrouded in morning fog that rolled off the North Fork of the Shenandoah River. He knew that a great battle was brewing beyond the river at Five Forks, where he imagined that Union Generals Sheridan, Merritt, and Warren were probably completing their plans to deal the final defeat to the rebel army under George Pickett. He found some part of him wishing that he was there in the thick of a real battle with real commanders, instead of role-playing on this grassy ridge, miles from the action.

It was a short-lived daydream. Cornwall suddenly stamped his right hoof hard, three times, and then jerked his head back. He was about to rein back when he saw movement about a hundred yards down the slope. He sucked in his breath as a line of gray-coated Confederate cavalry burst out of the gray fog at a gallop, followed by at least three full companies of infantry advancing at a fast trot. This was not the small rebel patrol he had been told to expect. And the riders and foot soldiers were headed right for him.

Everything around Thomas froze; Cornwall stood stock still, the breeze ruffling the Union flag he was holding died away, and the killdeer ceased their piercing cries.

"God almighty," he said out loud. Cornwall responded by slowly backing away from the edge of the ridge without waiting for a command. Whatever deal the general had made, the Johnnies were having no part of it this morning. There were at least three dozen mounted cavalry fronting ten times that many foot soldiers surging up the hill. To add insult to the drama charging his way, he could just make out the insignia of a full colonel on the hat of the officer leading the charge. That saber wielding soldier, he realized, was a *real* colonel.

He wheeled Cornwall and galloped to the other side of the ridge. The rebs would be here in a matter of seconds, and he had few options. He couldn't outrun dozens of mounted soldiers, and he couldn't fight them either. He could surrender, but then he would have to watch helplessly as they swept down on Captain Hayden and the men of B Company, who would be outnumbered better than four to one.

He could also wave the flag, as he had told Hayden he would do. Damn, what were the signals? A slow wave for them to proceed up the hill at a steady pace, a fast wave to gallop? His mind raced as he clutched the flag; he had to do something right now.

The first rebel riders poured up over the top of the ridge about fifty yards to his right. They spotted him immediately and swung in his direction. Thomas reined Cornwall around and raced southward along the grassy path. The Union Flag he was holding unfurled and waved against the brightening sky as Cornwall ran in long, flowing strides and jumped over brush and rocks with ease.

He swung his head around and saw that five or six riders were closing on him. That's when he heard the first pistol shots. He could try to make it to the end of the ridge and into the forest beyond, but it was nearly a mile, and even with Cornwall's strength and speed, escape in that direction was unlikely. Straight ahead, a massive oak tree blocked his path. He pressed his right knee against Cornwall's flank, leaned hard, and pulled the reins to the left. The horse made a racing turn beneath the tree's outspread canopy, circled the trunk, and flew back in the opposite direction right past the startled rebels.

The rebs followed suit; they swung around the oak and followed close on Thomas' track. Seventy-five yards ahead a dozen more riders were strung out across the path, their rifles pointed right at him. To his left, a full company of rebel infantry soldiers were cresting the hill. In a matter of seconds, he would be surrounded by the enemy.

More shots rang out, and Thomas felt a punch to his lower back. He held tight to the reins with his left hand, while with his right hand, he held out the Union flag, waving it back and forth in the clear morning light. Then a hail of gunshots enveloped him, and his left thigh felt like it had been struck by a swarm of angry wasps.

He reined Cornwall to a halt, wheeled, and galloped straight towards the pursuing soldiers. His turn was executed so quickly and so close that he careened right between them before they could get off any more shots.

He sped south along the ridge, waving the Stars and Stripes furiously. He hoped that Hayden could see him, but he also knew that B Company would not make it up the hill in time to help him. Now, he heard rebel yells and the pounding of hooves right behind him, and for a moment, he thought he could feel hot breath spewing from the nostrils of the rebel horses. As he flew past the oak for the second time amid a barrage of bullets that tore into the trunk and showered him with bark chips, he was sure that his ride was about to come to an end.

In choosing to come up the hill alone, he had gambled that he could catch the lightning. Now all he could do was to ride it until the very end.

❖

Captain Hayden and his men watched as their new colonel headed up the ridge. When he was halfway to the summit, Hayden ordered his men to proceed to the base of the hill, in defiance of the colonel's orders to keep the company together until and unless he waved the flag. Hayden split the company into three sections, with half of the mounted soldiers on the right and half on the left. While the cavalry waited in the brightening morning light, Hayden ordered his infantry to begin making their way up the middle.

The men of B Company squinted against the rising sun and watched as the colonel slipped over the ridge and disappeared, only to re-appear a moment later at a full gallop, with a half dozen rebel cavalry in pursuit. Then Hayden's men heard gunshots and saw the colonel swing his horse around an oak tree and race back to the north.

At Hayden's command, two dozen mounted soldiers drew their Spencer rifles and tore off up the hill, followed by sixty-two infantry men running full out.

All eyes were on Colonel Scoundrel and Cornwall as they flew along the ridge. Hayden thought he saw the colonel hit by pistol fire at least once, and he urged his horse faster up the hill. That was when the men of B Company witnessed the grandest battle scene any of them could ever have imagined or would ever see again. They saw the disc of the sun break above the tree line, yellow and bright in the cloudless sky above Pebble Creek Ridge, and then they watched in astonishment as Colonel Scoundrel reined Cornwall to a stop amidst a fusillade of bullets from the Confederate riders.

He held the Union flag out at arm's length, raised it high above his head, and pulled on the reins. Cornwall reared back on his hind legs, and for a moment, horse and rider and waving flag were silhouetted against the sun in a tableau that was both magnificent and terrible.

Hayden watched the remarkable scene unfold as he breached the hill. Then, the Union soldiers racing to Colonel Scoundrel's defense saw their new commander topple slowly off his horse, fall into the folds of the Union flag, and drop to the ground. Cornwall took two steps forward, buckled to his front legs, and fell on his side beside his master.

❖

ELEVEN

Claybourne Ranch, June 1882

United States Senator Terrance Mack was the ninth and final conspirator to arrive at Langton Hall on the Claybourne Ranch. He had barely stepped out of the buckboard and brushed the road dust off his coat when Noah's housekeeper appeared on the porch to inform him that the rest of the guests were assembled in the dining room. He pulled a dandelion thistle off his trousers, hung his hat on a peg, and followed the housekeeper across the massive, open beam living room, past a stone fireplace large enough to spit a whole side of beef, and through an open set of sliding pocket doors.

"Mr. Claybourne will be along shortly," the housekeeper said. "There are refreshments on the sideboard."

Six men were seated around a hand-carved oak table that could easily accommodate a dozen diners. In a darkened corner near the head of the table, a man and a woman were engaged in a hushed but animated conversation. Including Claybourne, Mack thought to himself, that makes ten of us. Ten people with the vision–or the temerity, depending on your viewpoint– to bring the nation of Mexico to its knees and shake the government of the United States to its core.

Each of the men at the table nodded in Mack's direction before returning to their conversations. He poured a glass of port from a decanter, lit a cheroot, and took a chair at the far end of the table. An enormous map of northern Mexico and the southwestern United States and its territories hung from the wall to his left. At the head of table, next to Noah's empty chair, a pile of leather portfolios was stacked next to several bottles of mineral water. On the sideboard were bowls of fruit, foie gras on toast, cheese and bread, bottles of wine and liquor, and several cigar humidors. Paintings of Claybourne's ancestral English village lined one wainscoted wall, along with an oil portrait of his adult daughter, Hyacinth, by the impressionist artist Mary Cassatt.

The quick brushstroke styling and pastel color palettes of the portrait were not Mack's favorite technique. He preferred the Old-World masters with their somber coloring and realistic subject portrayal. Even so, he had to acknowledge that Cassatt had captured Hyacinth's exotic beauty exceedingly well. Her lustrous, curly hair and crème complexion set off her smoky violet eyes and full, vermillion lips in a way he found quite stimulating.

In the painting, Hyacinth was leaning back with her head turned slightly to the right, her arms resting comfortably on the chair arms. She was smiling, perhaps having just finished a private laugh at some suitor's witty repartee. Mack couldn't help but notice that, leaning back or not, *fille* Claybourne's breasts seemed poised to break out of her low-cut, black satin gown. The Senator knew fine art, and his impression of the combined effect of the lighting, color, attitude and figurative positioning in the painting suggested that had such a breakout occurred, the young lady would not have minded the exposure in the least.

He finished his port and turned his focus away from Miss Claybourne and her tumescence-inspiring charm. Perhaps he should make a visit to Madame Olivier's discreetly located house in Denver tomorrow to soothe his itch. He could arrange for another romp with the freckled Irish girl with the copper-hued mons Venus and her friend, a sultry, athletic South American with a perfect, pear-shaped backside. That international duo had fulfilled his randiest desires only a few weeks earlier.

Mack returned to the sideboard. He refilled his glass, helped himself to a Tabacalera cigar, and then lingered a moment to observe what was going on around the room. Army Major General Winston Greer was tapping his finger on the table as he spoke in earnest tones with his aide, Colonel Franklin Alphonse. Greer was fleshy and ill-mannered, but Mack knew that the senior US military commander in the West was smart, crafty and, if crossed, brutally unforgiving. If all went as planned with the Mexican Scheme, Greer would become the de-facto Military Governor of the new provinces, from the Gulf of California to the Gulf of Mexico.

Next to Greer sat the Assistant US Secretary of State, Wharton Geve, who was sketching something on paper for Congressman Titus Renton. Mack knew them to be consummate political operators whose ambitions far exceeded their abilities. Each was well-connected, however, and occupied positions that would be critical to the success of the plan. Geve felt Senator Mack's gaze and raised his glass in acknowledgment.

Across from the general sat two of the most important actors in today's event; Antonio Marquez Resposo, the former vice-president of Mexico under Porfirio Díaz, and Claybourne's enforcer, the engineer Matthew Cord. Resposo was born into an aristocratic family that had fallen on hard times and so was willing to betray his native country to turn his fortunes around, both financially and politically. The silver-haired patrician was flipping through a sheaf of maps with Cord, who was the only person in the room Mack knew well enough to truly fear. Cord had murdered dozens of people on Claybourne's behalf, including women and children whose only crimes were belonging to Claybourne's enemies. The engineer's sandy hair and lopsided, toothy grin were gross misrepresentations of the man's true character. He once slit open a cattle rustler's abdomen and pulled out a length of the man's intestines so quickly that when he tossed them into a crackling campfire, the poor fool was still alive to hear them sizzle when they hit the coals. Cord told the story again and again over the years, always pinching his nose in feigned disgust when he got to the part about the stench that arose when the rustler's lower bowel exploded its fetid contents in the flames, spraying one of Cord's own men with gobbets of hot, greasy, fecal matter. Mack himself was no innocent but being in Cord's presence made the hair on the back of his neck stand up.

Senator Mack took his seat as Noah Claybourne stepped into

the room. All conversation stopped, but Claybourne made no greeting to the group. He poured a glass of mineral water, stood behind his chair, and looked through a pile of papers until he found a particular document that held his attention.

While each of the conspirators in the room were individuals of some accomplishment, it was Claybourne who most fascinated the senator. From his imposing physical persona to his polished speaking style, Claybourne was the most compelling individual Mack had ever known–and the most dangerous.

As Noah continued studying the document, Mack reflected on what he knew about the man, both from personal observation and experience, and from the rumors that swirled around the halls of Congress. Everything about Claybourne was thin and long, a series of acute angles built one upon another. He was well over 6' tall, with almost abnormally long arms and equally long fingers. He wore his gray-flecked black hair almost to his shoulders, and he had uncommonly dark-blue eyes. His cleft chin, high forehead, thin nose, and fine lips fit his face perfectly. Claybourne could almost have been thought of as handsome, at least until one saw his lips curl back from his teeth in an almost lupine grimace that was his version of a smile.

Noah had a deep, milky baritone voice that was self-assured and comfortable issuing commands. He moved slowly and deliberately, but there was nothing lazy about his stride. It was purposeful and economical. Every step, every hand gesture, every turn of his head seemed planned out. And, despite his lanky build, Mack knew that Claybourne was an enormously strong man who was equally adept with a knife, saber, or pistol. Noah's emotional temperature did not slowly warm up from being mildly annoyed in each situation to becoming volcanically angry. His anger flashed instantaneously at full force and without warning. And if that happened, there would be a pistol shot, or a knife strike into the heart. Someone was going to die.

Claybourne did not clear his throat or rap his knuckle on the table to announce that he was ready to begin. He had no need of that; in this room he was the undisputed master. He simply set the paper down that he had been reading and began to speak. As he did, Mack noticed that the man and woman standing in half-shadow were remaining in their corner.

"For the past eighteen months," Noah began, "we have applied ourselves as instruments of a just and noble cause that will forever change the geography and politics of our great nation." Heads nodded around the table. Like Senator Mack, each of the individuals in the room today were risking imprisonment and financial ruin simply by virtue of attending this meeting. Claybourne understood that and knew that he owned the soul of every person who had signed onto his plan. "We are representatives of the worlds of politics, business, diplomacy, and the military," he said. He turned his head in the direction of the man and woman in the corner and added, "and some of you represent action of an even more proximate and consequential nature." Mack could only guess what that comment meant.

"Each of you has a great responsibility. Each of you has trained and planned and prepared for this moment," Noah continued. He turned to the detailed, hand-rendered map behind him. "The prize is within our grasp," he said, as he ran his hand across the map from Baja California on the west to Northern Mexico's eastern coast on the Gulf of Mexico. "In a matter of days, our raiding parties will begin their sorties against targets inside the New Mexico and Arizona territories. General Greer and Colonel Alphonse will coordinate the American response to the raids from their headquarters in Santa Fe. General?"

Greer pushed his chair back and walked up to the map. "The raiders will initially strike against two towns: in Arizona, here at Monteverde; and in New Mexico, here, at San Rafael. The first raid will likely be dismissed in Washington as an aberration on the part of bandit groups who routinely cross into American territory to steal cattle and horses. However, when the New Mexico raid takes place two weeks after Arizona is attacked, even the dullards at the War Department will take note that something serious is afoot. That will be especially true with the raid on Monteverde. Not a building will remain standing, and not a citizen or soldier or farm animal will be left alive. In the wake of such terrible destruction, Washington will be forced to respond aggressively. Absent a full declaration of war at that time, my command will undertake reprisals against Mexico per my authority as Military Commander in the West. And, if that doesn't move Washington, we will resume the raids against more border towns until they do act."

Greer returned to his seat, and Congressman Renton took his place at the map to pick up the narrative. "Americans in the Southwestern territories have grown increasingly frustrated with Washington's failure to stop the cattle raids and robberies over the years," he said. "These new attacks will only amplify calls for Congress to take serious action to squash the raids once and for all. No one will want a full-blown war between the US and Mexico, of course. At least not at first. They still remember that thirteen thousand Americans died in the 1847 conflict with Mexico…"

"Twenty-five thousand Mexicans perished as well, my friend," added Señor Marquez.

"To be sure," said Renton. He swept his hand across a wide swath of the map. "The end result of the war was that Mexico ceded over 900,000 square miles of land to America, including California, Nevada, Utah, most of New Mexico, Arizona and Colorado, and parts of Texas, the Oklahoma Indian Territory, plus Kansas and Wyoming. I would argue that thirteen thousand lives were a small price to pay for the acquisition of a land mass larger than Europe." Heads nodded around the room.

"Well, that and the fifteen million dollars the US paid my government," added Marquez. "I believe that worked out to a purchase price of 5¢ an acre. Quite a bargain."

"President Polk was bold to undertake that expansion," said State the Department functionary. "But he was not bold enough. Every inch of land we are preparing to take today should have been included in the Treaty of Guadalupe Hidalgo in 1848 while we had Mexico by the balls."

"Our *cojones* were never at risk, my friend," Marquez interjected angrily. "And had the war gone on for even a few more weeks, you would have seen the Mexican armies...."

Claybourne's laugh startled the assembled group and brought the argument to a halt. "Be that as it may, *Vicepresidente* Marquez, I assure you that at this moment, each of our coin purses are most distinctly in danger of being sheared off at the crotch." He turned in the direction of the woman standing behind him in half-shadow, acknowledging her presence for the first time. "Present company excepted, of course, my dear Demetria." He motioned for the woman and her companion room to step out of the shadows and join him at the map. Senator Mack recognized Geronimo Rivas, the half-breed Mescalero Apache who was one of the very bandits who had been raiding American settlements along the border for years. His long hair was pulled back and tied with a red and black kerchief, and a bandolier was slung sash-style over his shoulders, stuffed with ammunition from his chest to his middle. Rivas's eyes were coal black, and his facial expression was impassive. Mack had no doubt that the man was very good at his job.

The woman beside him, who Mack had never seen, was stunning. She was tall, with straight raven hair parted in the middle that fell below her shoulders. She had an olive complexion, emerald eyes, and naturally rose-colored lips. Her plain, long sleeve white cotton shirt had a Chinese collar that was partially unbuttoned at the top, just enough to show a hint of cleavage. She wore the shirt tucked into her belted, calf-length riding skirt, above hand-tooled leather boots. Demetria had a dancer's posture: shoulders back and head high, with full, firm breasts that strained against the buttons of her shirt. As his eyes soaked in her figure, Senator Mack realized he was holding his breath. A quick glance around the table showed him that every other man there was, too. Except for Claybourne. Mack saw that Noah was instead appraising the lust in each of the conspirator's eyes in the same way that a potential buyer for an expensive stud bull watches the beast's reactions around a heifer in heat.

When Mack saw Claybourne's mouth turn half upward in the barest hint of a smile, he knew that he and the others had been the subjects of another one of Claybourne's famous object lessons: this woman is my possession, just as the Rodin sculpture on my desk is, and the Cassatt painting on the wall, and the jewel-encrusted Fabergé egg in the domed case. You may gaze upon them with my permission, Claybourne's expression said, but you will never possess them. Mack shrugged inwardly at Claybourne's elitist gesture, but at the same time he felt a familiar wave of excitement surge through his body. That visit to *Mme* Olivier's sporting house could not come a moment too soon.

Claybourne brought the room back to the present business when he said, "As you were, gentlemen. Let me introduce Miss Demetria Carnál of Santa Fe, in the New Mexico Territory, some four hundred miles from here." Demetria nodded, and Claybourne continued. "You all know about Mr. Rivas's unique, ah, occupational skills." That would be murderer, rapist, thief, arsonist, and bank robber, Mack said to himself.

"Miss Carnál herself leads a group of several dozen of the finest *pistoleros* in the Southwest," said Claybourne. "Mr. Rivas will prosecute our actions in Arizona, while Miss Carnál will lead her associates against our objectives in New Mexico. As the effects of their actions become widely known, Senator Mack and Congressman Renton will lead the charge in Congress to punish Mexico for not stopping the raids, while Assistant Secretary Geve sells the State and War Departments on the idea that the actions are not simply those of random bandits, but an actual concerted effort on the part of the Mexican government to take back the territory they lost in the 1847 war. And while that is all bubbling, Señor Marquez will be garnering support from Mexican politicians who are still aggrieved at their country's loss of face and land to the Americans. The former *vicepresidente* will convince Mexico City that a fast, intense attack on American troops in the Southwest would bloody America's nose just enough to remind her that war is hell, and that further conflict should be avoided at all costs."

Everyone in the room knew the plan and the multiple political and military scenarios by heart, but they loved hearing how all of the pieces fit together.

"When Washington learns that Mexico is considering such an attack at the exact time that the town of Monteverde in Arizona is razed to the ground and all its inhabitants butchered," Claybourne continued, "President Arthur will have no option but to ask for a declaration of war. At General Greer's urging, the armies under his command will then march into Mexico and take possession of these territories for the protection of our southern border." He ran a finger across the northern Mexican states as he recited their names from west to east. "We will take Sonora," he said, "followed by Chihuahua, Coahuila, Nuevo Leon, and finally, taking us to the Gulf of Mexico, we will assume control of Tamaulipas." Claybourne turned back to the conspirators seated around the table. "In all, these states comprise 276,000 square miles. That is nearly the size of Texas. Add to that the vast mineral deposits, cattle, timber and farmlands, and, of course, a large work force who are used to being paid very, very little, and gentlemen, we will have achieved more than a simple victory. We will be realizing our greatest destiny."

For the first time since Senator Mack had known Noah Claybourne, he saw emotion register in his glistening eyes and flushed cheeks. That it took the promise of war and the death of hundreds, perhaps thousands of people, to elicit such a response, was a story unto itself.

A servant came into the room. She placed a crystal flute glass next to each of the conspirators and handed one to Noah, Rivas, and Demetria Carnál, who remained standing. Another servant wheeled in a cart on which sat a tub filled with bottles of Perrier-Jouët champagne on ice. As he filled the glasses, the doors from the kitchen opened, and more servants carried in platters of King Crab salad, garlic mashed potatoes, and roasted leg of boar with red wine marinade.

Noah Claybourne held his glass high. "Fortune favors the bold, my friends," he said to the hushed room. "We may die tomorrow, but tonight we have changed history. *Prost!*"

Senator Mack's eyes never left Demetria Carnál's breasts as he raised his glass and downed the exceptional champagne in a single gulp.

❋

TWELVE

Golden, Colorado

The afternoon coach from Denver to Golden left the train depot on time. Thomas slept during most of the seven-hour train ride up from Trinidad, and the moment he climbed into the crowded four-horse passenger coach for the eleven-mile trek, he missed the comfort and spaciousness of the Pullman rail car.

Bat Masterson walked him to the Trinidad depot at daybreak and provided him with directions to Major Rhine's ranch, along with an admonition to approach the house cautiously. "Rhine isn't just an ex-army provisioner and gunsmith," Masterson said. "He's done business with pretty much everybody in the state, and he is successful because he doesn't trust many people. Caution keeps him alive. Considering that he's got enough firepower stored at his place to equip a small army, that makes sense. A few folks have been stupid enough to try to help themselves to some of his stock over the years, but after the Major caught them in the act, there wasn't enough of them left for the sheriff to arrest."

Masterson handed him a revolver for Rhine to repair and send back to him. As Thomas stepped onto the stairs to the passenger car, Bat wished him well and added, "If you discover that Claybourne is behind this kidnapping, you best telegraph me. He owns the county sheriff, and the magistrates, and damn near every pistol-swinging cowboy this side of the Front Range."

Thomas nodded somberly in reply, but that wasn't enough for the marshal. When the trained steamed up and began to pull away from the platform, Bat said, "Don't try to do this yourself, Colonel. Find me. I'll be there."

He knew that Masterson meant what he said. "Thank you," he replied. Then he turned and vanished into the Pullman.

❖

The stagecoach rolled into Golden at sunset, two hours after it left the train depot. It trotted down Main Street and deposited the passengers in front of the Golden Hotel, where Thomas would spend the night before renting a horse for the ride to Major Rhine's.

He liked the little town the minute he saw it. Golden was nestled between low, rolling hills that were capped with dramatic limestone bluffs and intersected by creeks that wound among stands of blossoming cottonwoods. One of the passengers on the coach was a local banker who told him that the small town boasted three flour mills, five smelters, the only paper mill west of the Missouri, a brick works, and the first railroad into the Colorado mountains. All that, plus a genuine opera house, an engineering school, world-class food, and, as Masterson said, a brewery owned by the German immigrant, Adolf Coors.

A young woman was lighting wall lamps in the massive open-beam lobby when he checked in. The orange glow from the gas flames wrapped the mounted heads of buffalo, elk, bighorn sheep, bull moose, and antelope in eerie shadows that flickered down the brocade flocked wallpaper. It was cool for June, and a boy was loading fir and oak into the stone fireplace. He went to his room, deposited his valise, and headed down to the hotel restaurant. The captain seated him at a table against a walnut-paneled wall, beneath a romanticized painting of the Grand Canyon during a summer storm. A waiter appeared with a menu, and he was pleased to see that the selections of fresh local game and fish were as impressive as the banker had promised.

He started with a bottle of *Louis Roederer* champagne while he perused the menu and discussed the evening's offerings with his waiter. The hotel was unique, the waiter explained, in that everything they served, from vegetables to fish and game, were grown, caught, or hunted by hotel employees. As a new hire in the kitchen became more proficient at hunting, he could become a waiter, and, if he really excelled at that task, he might be trained to assist the chef. The seared prong-horn steaks on tonight's menu had been hunted by the chef himself.

After some discussion, he decided to open with mushroom-stuffed quail in truffle sauce, followed by a simple pan-fried trout with lemon butter and almonds, with sides of asparagus, wild rice, and a salad made with spinach, feta cheese and pine nuts. To accompany the trout, his waiter recommended *Königsbacher*, a drier German Riesling.

It had been nearly ten days since his last grand meal with Annette, and after three glasses of the elegant and lively *Roederer*, Thomas attacked the trout as if he hadn't eaten in days. Two hours after he sat down, he finished the last of the riesling, enjoyed a single cup of coffee, and then set off in search of the nosiest, brightest, fasted-paced gaming tables that Golden had to offer.

❋

The horse he rented at the livery stable the next morning was a bit of a plug, but it held easily to the narrow coach road that ran north-west out of Golden through fir covered hills and tall grass meadows. Masterson's directions were to ride until he came to the sign for Rhine's business, about ten miles from town.

He rode along creeks lined with box elders and chokecherry, passing an occasional ranch house set back off the dusty road. When he rode around a bend where the road forked in two directions, he saw a painted sign on a pole just beyond the north fork. As he got nearer, he could make out the lettering: *MAJ. T.R. Rhine, Provisioner & Smithy*. He swung his horse through the open gate and rode for a quarter mile along a brushy embankment until he reached the crest of a low rise. Below him were rows of low, undulating hills that spilled down to a clear, wide creek. A well-kept ranch house and several outbuildings were planted in a notch where three of the hills sloped down into a meadow blanketed with grass and wildflowers. Smoke was rising from the house and from the forge in the adjacent smithy. Three freight wagons were parked near the remuda in which about a dozen horses were lazing in the warm afternoon sunshine, but he saw no signs of Major Rhine.

He rode down to the corral and hitched his horse to a post, took Masterson's revolver from his saddle bag and stuck it in his belt, and walked over to the smithy. The forge was fired up beneath a row of blacksmith tools hanging on pegs. A set of iron tongs lay open on the enormous anvil and an ancient hound dog was curled up in a fresh bed of straw next to the dousing tub. He leaned down and scratched the dog behind one ear. "Hello, old boy," he said, just before he heard the familiar *clatch* of a revolver hammer being cocked. He raised his hands half-way above his head and turned around. Major Rhine was holding a bellows in one hand and an old 1860 Colt Dragoon .44 caliber revolver in the other.

He nodded in the direction of the gun. "I didn't know anybody carried those anymore. Is that the seven-and-a-half-inch barrel?"

Rhine didn't blink or lower the barrel that was aimed directly at Thomas's navel. "Eight inches, actually," he said in a calm, quiet voice. "Four and half pounds, blade front sight, notch rear sight, and at this distance the hole it would blow in your back after it tore out most of your innards would be the size of a grapefruit."

Thomas smiled and said, "I've never seen that particular fruit, but I will take your word for it."

"Most business callers come to the house," said Rhine. "And yet here you are poking around the forge, not fifty yards from my armory. Were you planning on having a look over there, too?"

"Saw your dog, and thought I'd say hello." He could tell Rhine was giving that comment some thought. The major was a compact, solidly built man in his mid 40s. He wore a heavy blacksmith apron and had dark hair, steel-blue eyes, and a wide, intelligent, friendly face. That is, he supposed, it was probably friendly when it wasn't concentrating on how best to blow your stomach out your backside.

"Can I…" Thomas asked, half lowering his arms.

"Slowly and keep them far away from your belt."

Thomas lowered his arms.

"What is your business here?" Rhine finally asked.

"Bat Masterson recommended that I pay you a visit. I'm in need of supplies. And a horse."

"From the looks of that glue pot you rode in on, I agree you need a new mount. Rental?"

"Livery in Golden."

"And the pistol in your belt? Is that for saying hello to my dog, too?"

"Bat sent it along. It has a bad ejector rod, and the main hammer spring needs replacing."

Rhine looked thoughtful. "Is he still sportin' that ugly Mex sombrero and beard when he's marshaling?"

Thomas grinned at the major's attempt to catch him in a lie. "Well, in my mind it is ugly, but it's a bowler, not a sombrero, and it kinda fits him. And he wears the dandiest moustache you ever saw, no beard. You know," Thomas continued, "Bat said you were a suspicious cuss."

"Did he, now?"

"Warned me I might get my ass shot off if I didn't mind my manners around you, in point of fact."

"And he was right," said Rhine. Then he turned and lay the bellow next to the forge. He slipped the Dragoon into his apron pocket and stuck out his hand. "T.R. Rhine," he said with a smile.

He shook the major's hand. "T.E. Scoundrel."

Rhine stroked his chin. "Would that be *Colonel* Thomas Scoundrel, late of the 109th Ohio and the Battle of Pebble Creek Ridge? And the hero of Wolf Mountain during the Sioux wars in '77?"

"I was called back to duty for a year for that one. Coldest, most miserable winter in my life."

"You remember that right. I was called up, too, first time since '65. Spent my time doling out dried beef, bullets, and beans to the cavalry in Montana. Witch's' teat cold, that's what it was. One morning it was so cold that when my horse backed up into a fence, his tail snapped right off." Rhine shook his head at the memory and said, "Let's go up to the house and get something to eat."

Thomas handed Masterson's revolver over by the butt and then followed Rhine across the yard to the covered front porch of the house. Rhine motioned for Thomas to sit down at a log table and then opened the front door and called to someone inside. A moment later a handsome Indian woman appeared with a clay pitcher and two glasses.

Rhine filled their glasses. "You'll like this."

Thomas drank deeply and was surprised that the beer was almost ice cold. But he wasn't surprised at the flavor.

"This from that Coors fellow?"

"You know about him? Masterson must have told you. I understand Coors ships the beer by rail to Trinidad."

"But it's the end of June...how the hell do you keep it so cold?"

"We have a full basement under the house, dug extra deep so it holds the frost from the ground. Every February we take two wagons down to the river and use saws to cut fifty-pound chunks of solid ice. Then we lay a foot of sawdust on the basement floor and start stacking the ice. We do one layer of ice after another, with a foot of sawdust between each layer until the basement is full. Last year we had ice through the end of August."

Thomas finished his beer, and Rhine refilled it from the pitcher. Then the door opened again, and the Indian woman brought out a platter with two bowls of savory venison stew, a loaf of fresh bread, and a bowl of butter. He watched the glance that Rhine and the woman exchanged, which told him that this was not a simple rancher-servant relationship. Whatever it was, it was no business of his. Men came to the West to get away from civilized prejudice and accepted rules of behavior. In any event, the company was good, and the stew was excellent. That was enough.

❖

They finished eating in the gathering twilight. Then Rhine lit a pipe, and suggested they take a walk and talk business. The old hound dog got up from his straw pallet and followed them down to the mossy bank of a deep green stream.

They stopped under the outstretched limb of an oak tree, and Rhine said, "Bat knows you can get outfitted anywhere. You sure didn't have to come all the way out to Golden."

Thomas nodded and watched a dragonfly skit along the surface of the creek. "It's complicated."

"I figured that from the minute you arrived," replied the Major. He pulled a silver flask from his back pocket and handed it to Thomas. "Brandy, just right for getting things out on the table."

He took a drink and told his story, from Rosalilia's kidnapping in Cuernavaca to his meeting with Itzcoatl in Trinidad, and the friendship he had forged with Bat Masterson over the past two days. When he finished, Rhine picked up a small stone and tossed it across the creek. Then he patted his dog and said, "If you mean everything you have just told me, and if you really do intend to confront Noah Claybourne in his own house, you'd be advised to take a company of infantry with you. His home is a fortress, and he is guarded at all times by a couple dozen heavily armed fellas who know how to fight."

"Like Matthew Cord, for instance?"

"Yes, like that first-rate sack of human offal. I don't know how he got elevated from the rank of hired killer to become a mining engineer but that is one deadly son of a bitch, and there's many a man taking his long dirt nap right now who didn't keep that fact in mind when they crossed him."

A barn owl swooped low across the creek in front of them, earning a low growl from the dog. "There won't be a company of soldiers with me, at least not yet," Thomas finally said. "If Claybourne is in this thing though, that time might come. First, I have to look him in the eyes and find out what he knows. No matter what, I'm going to knock on his front door and hear it from his own lips."

Rhine tapped his pipe against the oak and emptied out the last of the cold tobacco. "Then we've got a lot to do to get you ready," he said. "We'll put you up in the spare room tonight, and first thing in the morning, we'll line you out with everything you'll need." He grinned and finished with, "Except common sense, of course. That, Thomas my friend, I don't have enough of my own to spare."

As darkness fell, the two men navigated back to the house by the light of the porch lantern.

❖

The next morning Thomas and Major Rhine leaned against a fence under a warming sky, watching as a hired hand put a Morgan stallion through its paces. Their attention was diverted by an iron rod clanging on a horseshoe up at the house. Thomas turned to see the Indian woman standing by the door. She caught Rhine's eye and waved for them to come up to breakfast.

"Her name is Anaya," said Rhine as they walked towards the house. "Arapahoe. She has been with me for five years. I lost my wife to the fever eight years ago. It was good to have companionship again."

Thomas nodded. "It doesn't hurt that she cooks like a New York chef, either."

They sat at the log table while Anaya laid out a plate of thick buttered toast with honey, a couple rashers of bacon, and a bowl of scrambled eggs with onions and cilantro. Thomas noticed that she had placed a couple of wild strawberries on Rhine's plate.

"What do you think of the bay Morgan," asked Rhine. "Four years old, saddle and trail smart, and great endurance, too."

"I have always favored the Morgan-Thoroughbred cross, but I have to say your stallion has a fine cut about him."

"Where you're going the Morgan has some advantages over the cross. His slightly smaller size is compensated by muscling that makes him almost unstoppable on the gallop. They're an easy keep, too. This one is fresh-shod this week. I know you like the thoroughbred cross but given what you may be facing I'd advise that you pick the Morgan's endurance and strength."

"Done."

"Fine, now let's get you squared away on firepower. What are you carrying now?"

Thomas unholstered his Smith and Wesson Model 3 and handed it across to Rhine.

"Solid gun," said Rhine. "I see you have the model with Major Schofield's recent improvements." He rotated the cylinder and then broke open the top. "I always liked that feature," he said. "Faster reload than the Colt. That said, I'm recommending you go with a new seven-inch Colt single action. It's more robust, accurate, and easier to maintain than your Model 3. Better add a new holster and belt and two hundred rounds of .45, too."

Thomas felt a twinge of loss when the Major unloaded his beloved S&W and placed it in a box beside the table before pulling a new Colt from an oilcloth covering and placing it on the table. "We'll go down to the creek after dinner and run a few dozen rounds through it," said Rhine. "Now for your rifle."

He opened a long wooden box that was leaning against the porch railing behind his chair. "This is the Centennial Winchester '76. You familiar with it?"

"I had the '73. Gave my Spencer away for it. Fine rifle. Never gave me a lick of trouble."

"This is the thirty-two-inch musket version, the perfect tool for long-range shooting. The butt-stock and forend are walnut, it's got a casehardened forged steel frame, and all the parts are blued steel. This one is chambered for a full powered centerfire .45-.60, and the tube magazine will hold fifteen rounds. We will add a saddle scabbard and a cleaning kit and one hundred rounds to get you started."

Rhine handed the rifle to Thomas. He looked through the sights and worked the lever action. It was a heavy gun.

"Let's pick out a saddle and tack this afternoon," said Rhine. "Anaya will provision you with a week's food, and I'll set you up with everything else you will need, from your bedroll to a good compass. You can leave your valise here and pick it up on your return."

"You think of everything," said Thomas. He pulled the leather wallet from his bag and asked, "what's it all going to come to?"

Major Rhine jotted a few lines in pencil on the tabletop. "Let's call it $600 for everything. Horse and saddle, tack, guns, ammunition, provisions and gear. Sound fair?"

Thomas counted out the money and slid it across to Rhine. "That's more than fair."

The major pocketed the cash and asked, "Has anybody told you about Claybourne's fishing tournament?" Thomas shook his head. "Takes place around the first week of September, and it's the biggest shindig from Omaha to Carson City. Folks come from all around the world for three days of trout fishing in the lakes and streams on his ranch. Hundreds enter the competition, and even more pour onto his front lawn at night for the parties. Whoever piles up the greatest total weight in fish is the winner of a gold cup and $5,000 in cash, and everybody who passes for society in these parts will be there, along with a fair number of swells from the east and even Europe. The actress Lily Langtry herself will be there this year.

"This will be the tournament's fifth year," Rhine continued. Then he grinned, pulled the hammer back on Thomas's new Colt, and pointed it into the air. "At least it will be if you don't spoil everybody's good time by going off and shooting the host."

"Sounds like quite a soirée, but I plan on having this business concluded long before then."

Rhine raised his coffee cup and saluted Thomas. "You might want to think about what boxers say about climbing into the ring for Round 1: everybody's got a plan–right up until they get punched in the nose for the first time."

❖

THIRTEEN

The road to Denver

Dawn was breaking when Thomas rode through the gate of Major Rhine's ranch and turned north on the coach road. The fastest way to Claybourne's would have been to ride southeast to Denver, cut through town, and head due east towards the prairie.

"Noah doesn't know you're coming yet, but he will soon enough," Rhine said earlier as Anaya finished packing Thomas' saddlebags. "And when that happens, there isn't a one among Denver's 30,000 souls who wouldn't turn you over to him for a $20 gold piece."

He handed Thomas a map he had sketched on a small piece of paper. "Ride north and swing around Denver to the east. The trail follows the hills above town. There is a crossing here at the new canal," he pointed to the map, "and that is where you will turn southeast. Ride the post road down to the freight station at Fletcher and tell Mayburn that you work with me. He'll put you up for the night. From Fletcher you'll ride due east for sixteen miles. There is a bridge across Kiowa Creek, and from there it's about twelve miles out to Claybourne Ranch. Ulysses can cover a good four miles an hour through this kind of terrain, so you've got two pretty good days of riding ahead of you."

Thomas belted on his new Colt and checked the saddlebags. He patted the side of the horse's neck. "He didn't have a name yesterday."

"That's true, but I gave it to him before I wrote out the bill of sale, so you are going to have to live with it."

"And why Ulysses?"

Rhine's tone became serious. "Because he wandered the world for twenty years after the fall of Troy, chasing one adventure and one skirt after another until he finally reached his home on the island of Ithaca."

Thomas swung up into the saddle and adjusted his hat. "And when he made it home after all of that, were things the same?"

"I expect that you'll discover that for yourself." Rhine adjusted the rifle scabbard on the saddle and added, "Remember that the action on that Colt is lighter than your old Model 3. Squeeze that trigger easy. We'll see that your glue pot is returned to the livery and we'll store your valise until you need it." Then he wrapped his arm around Anaya's shoulders and watched as Thomas tapped his boot against Ulysses's flank and rode off into the sunrise over Clear Creek Canyon.

❋

At midday he staked Ulysses out to graze on a bluff above the South Platte River Valley and the sprawling city of Denver. He grabbed his canteen, unwrapped the venison sandwich that Anaya packed in his saddle bag, and sat on a rock to watch the world below move in slow motion.

He'd make Fletcher before dark, and if the weather held, he should be at Claybourne's by late afternoon tomorrow. And then? He was certain that Colorado's wealthiest man would grant him an audience; most people who were adults during the War were familiar with Thomas's name, after all. He typically did all he could to avoid the notoriety that came along with the fawning newspaper stories about Pebble Creek Ridge, but now, that little bit of fame might be the only thing that would pique Claybourne's interest enough to let him in the door.

He had never been good at disguising his emotions, except at the card table. When he finally came face to face with Claybourne he was not certain he would be able to restrain himself from skipping the conversation and moving right to pistol whipping the bastard–or worse. Rosalilia's father was dead, Diego was badly wounded, and it was quite possible that Rosalilia had also been murdered at Claybourne's direction. God help Claybourne and his men if that were true. Diego and Itzcoatl would not leave a blade of grass standing at Langton Hall when they exacted their revenge–and Thomas would be standing beside them with a match to start the fire.

He finished his meal and walked Ulysses over to a spring that flowed from the base of a granite outcropping. As the horse drank, Thomas steeled himself for the meeting. He would remain calm and focused-because he had to, for Diego and Rosalilia. What was it that Walt Whitman said to him that night at the hospital? He strained to remember. It was the night that Nurse Angela brought him a special dinner, the night he lost his virginity. How could he forget a single detail of that momentous evening?

Yes, that was it. Whitman had counseled him that for any circumstance in which high emotions were at play and everything was at stake, you should take care to replace your judgment with a sense of curiosity. Even if your initial judgment turned out to be true, Whitman said, by leading with curiosity you would become a part of a much more interesting tale.

He mounted Ulysses and returned to the dirt road. Curiosity first, he determined. He let his right-hand rest on the Colt revolver. And *then* judgment.

FOURTEEN

Mt. Pleasant Military Hospital, Washington DC, April 1865

On his seventh night in the hospital Thomas decided to live for at least one more day. On his twelfth night he found a reason to live for as many more years as he could.

He remembered nothing of the horse-drawn ambulance ride from Pebble Creek Ridge to the military hospital on the outskirts of the capitol. The first few days there were a blurry mix of pain, fever, and faces that floated in and out above his bed. He was certain that Captain Hayden of the 109th had visited, and Sergeant Hanlon, too. One night he thought he saw General Yoke and Major Rolande in hushed conversation at the foot of his bed, but he couldn't be sure. Between frequent administrations of tincture of opium, chloroform, and ether, he lost track of time and place. Only the endless fire in his gut and the searing pain he felt each time the doctors and nurses bandaged his right leg kept him grounded in reality.

On evening of the sixth day, he found himself fully awake for the first time. Moonlight was streaming through the window. He was in a metal frame bed in a long, narrow room with a wash basin in one corner, a small cabinet on the wall, and one chair near the door. His leg was elevated in some kind of harness and his abdomen was swathed in heavy bandages that smelled of camphor.

A middle-aged man with long hair, shaggy beard, and a thick moustache was seated on a chair next to him scribbling notes on a pad by lamplight. Thomas turned his head. "Where am I? Who are you?"

The man dropped the note pad on the floor and brought his face close to Thomas's. "Well, boy, you are back, and praise the saints for your return. Here, take this."

He held a glass of water to Thomas's lips. They were parched and swollen, but when he tried to drink deeply, the man pulled the glass back.

"Not yet, boy, you were gut shot, and you have been fighting infection. Too much water could finish the job those rebel bullets couldn't get done."

"Thank you. But how did I get here? What became of Captain Hayden and B Company, and where…?"

"Patience, lad, you can't drink all that information in any faster than you can the water. The world has been transformed since you arrived, and we'll get to it all. First, you are in the officer's ward at Mt. Pleasant Military Hospital. That silver eagle on your cap earned you your own room and a sight more attention than the lower ranks will ever see."

"And you are my doctor?"

The man laughed, which is when Thomas noticed that he had the palest blue-gray eyes he had ever seen.

"I am your nurse, boy. Volunteer corps. I am an army paymaster clerk by day and nurse by night. You've got me for three nights and then Angela is with you." He leaned down and retrieved his pad.

"Mostly though, in my singing heart and troubled soul, I am a poet. Damn fine one, too, if you want to know. My name is Walt Whitman."

Thomas smiled. "What happened to me?"

"You took a rebel bullet through the back. Tore through you from left to right. It blew through your muscles, pierced a bit of your liver, and clipped off a good chunk of your lower rib before exiting out your abdomen. Clean shot, through and through, as lucky and clean a wound as a fellow could hope to receive."

"Doesn't feel all that lucky." He nodded towards the water, and Whitman gave him another sip.

"Aye, but take my word for it, someone was watching over you on that ridge, boy. As for your leg, that is a different story."

Whitman checked the harness that held Thomas' leg at a 45-degree angle and then sat back down.

"One of them rebs hit you straight on in the center of your femur. Shattered the damn thing. First thing the surgeon wanted to do when they carried you in here was to amputate your leg just below your balls."

Thomas winced. "But it's still there…isn't it?"

"It is, boy, and I don't mind saying that it is still attached to your lucky arse because your resident poet here made a stink. I looked at you under those blankets, all bloodied and racked with fever, and I saw something the doctors missed. They only saw a leg that experience told them should probably come off before infection could set in and kill you."

"And you saw?"

"I saw a boy," replied Whitman in a tender voice. "The docs can never get past the insignia on the uniform. That drives everything they do. But I knew when I saw you that there was a big piece of the story missing. They were getting ready to treat a colonel. I wanted to save a boy. I asked them to give it one more day, and by the grace of God your fever broke, and no infection developed."

Thomas's eyes misted over. He was not used to anyone expressing this kind of concern for him. He could only nod in thanks.

"Time for your laudanum," said Whitman. "It keeps the edge off the pain." He poured a dose of thick, dark liquid into a spoon and placed it against Thomas' lips. He felt the warmth begin to spread through his body almost immediately.

Whitman leaned back in his chair and said, "I'll buy for the moment that by some miracle of prestidigitation you were transmogrified into a full colonel in the United States Army. How, why, and on whose orders I can only imagine. It might explain why more brass has been in to see you than any other patient I have ever cared for, though. That and the newspapers, of course."

So, thought Thomas. Perhaps it wasn't a dream, and Yoke really did come to see him. "Newspapers?"

"We'll get to that in a minute. First, tell me how old you really are. Your chart says twenty-five. I'd guess more like nineteen."

"I'm seventeen. And I was an officer for just one day. I'm really just a cook's assistant."

Whitman went to the door, looked out into the hall, and them came back to his chair.

"Listen to me,Thomas, and listen well. Robert E. Lee surrendered the Confederate armies at Appomattox Court House a week after your little set-to on that ridge. Wonderful news for our nation, but the truth is that the days following a war are every bit as dangerous as the war itself. That's when history gets written and a lot of old scores are settled. Somehow, for reasons I don't understand, you have been pulled into something portentous. See those newspapers?" He pointed to a pile on the floor. "You are front page news on every one of them." Whitman picked up the paper on top and read a headline: *"Last Hero of the War Fights for Life in DC Hospital."* Then he turned and grabbed another paper and continued reading: "This headline says, *'Colonel T.E. Scoundrel Rallies Federal Troops at Pebble Creek, Leads a Single Company in Defeat of Entire Rebel Regiment.'* There's dozens of them here, Thomas. You are a national hero. The president is going to pin a medal on you, and wherever you go from now on people are going to want to buy you a drink. Some will be sincere, but a lot of them will just be figuring out how to use your fame to their advantage."

Thomas couldn't begin to make sense of what he was hearing. He rode up that ridge at daybreak so that he could pretend to look heroic. He didn't deserve fame and accolades. If Captain Hayden and his men had truly rousted an entire rebel regiment, it was those men who deserved medals, not him.

The laudanum was taking hold and he felt himself drifting off. "I'm no hero," he said in a soft voice. "I don't want to be famous. I just want to go home." And then he fell asleep.

Walt Whitman straightened the bed covers and placed his hand gently on his patient's forehead. "Home is a place you will never visit again," he said in a sorrowful voice. "And more's the pity for that, lad."

❖

Thomas woke on the morning of his sixth day in the hospital more alert–and more miserable–than he could ever remember being in his life. He asked the morning nurse to stack all the newspapers on the bed and spent the day devouring every article about the Confederate surrender and the battle at Pebble Creek Ridge. As he read one breathless article after another about his *"selfless heroism in the face of certain death,"* and how he was found on the ridge with his horse and the bodies of dozens of dead rebels around him *"wrapped in the American flag, holding his saber high in the air even after falling unconscious,"* he was overtaken by a melancholy the likes of which had never imagined. He had almost no memory of the event from the time he felt the first bullet hit him. He did not recognize the person described in the newspapers, and further, he did not want to be that person.

He felt so low that when the doctor checked in on his progress, he lied about how much pain he was feeling so that he would be given an extra dose of laudanum. He slept well into the night and awakened to find Whitman back on duty.

Walt changed his abdominal bandage, washed the area, and slathered the wound with more camphor salve. Then he brought Thomas a bowl of soup and sat beside him as he ate.

When he finished eating Whitman closed the door and pulled his chair close to the bed. "I told you that in my day job I am an army paymaster," he began. "Today I went to the records bureau and examined the accounts of your regiment. I had heard rumors about an outfit that existed to hide the sons of wealthy and powerful people from battle, but until I read the 109th's pay records I didn't believe it. Hell, boy, half of the people on that list come from families who are household names."

Thomas was confused. "How does that affect me?"

"I don't know the whole story, but I'm going to guess that someone in your regiment was being paid to hide those boys. That's a military crime, a civilian crime, and by God, it is a crime against morality."

The door opened and an aide brought in fresh water for the washbasin. When he left, Whitman continued.

"I believe that you were used as a pawn in some kind of big scheme, and I also think it is safe to assume that your life depends on keeping the story buried. People who are powerful enough to do something like this are powerful enough to cover their tracks, whatever that may take."

"But I don't know anything. I never heard anyone talking about hidden soldiers or money being paid by families to protect their sons."

"And that just makes it all the more important for you to play along with the scheme for now. When you are discharged from here you will have to go to the War Department for your mustering out orders. Depending on the rank you keep on separation day, you should qualify for a pension. A colonel gets 65% of his base monthly pay for the rest of his life. I did a mustering out pension today for a colonel who was making $212 a month. His pension will be $137 monthly. Won't make you rich, but it will keep you in beans and bacon wherever you go. You can collect your pay at any army facility or post office."

"Thomas," Whitman continued in an earnest tone, "believe me when I tell you that whoever set you up would have had no qualms about finishing the job the rebs started on you."

"*Would* have had?"

"That's right, boy. They could toss a kitchen boy out a tower window and no one would give it a second thought. It's chaos out there, with the war ending and soldiers pouring into the city to get their going home papers. But no one, no matter how powerful, can murder a genuine, god damn hero, especially not one who was shot off his horse right into the arms of Old Glory. You're protected as long as you are that hero."

Whitman smiled and placed a hand on his arm. "Son, it's better to be a live hero than a dead kitchen hand."

Whitman's counsel was probably the best course of action for Thomas to follow, but he still could not shake the sense of depression and worthlessness that had taken hold of him. He slept fitfully, thinking over and over that the only real way out of this maelstrom would be for him to figure out a way to loop a roll of bandage around the frame holding his broken leg, tie the other end around his neck, and then throw himself off the bed. But not tonight. Not when the only person in the world who cared for him would be sitting right outside his door.

Tomorrow, Walt Whitman would be off duty. Tomorrow was a better day to die.

FIFTEEN

Mt. Pleasant Military Hospital

Nurse Angela hurried up the stairs to the officer's ward and bustled along the corridor towards Colonel Scoundrel's room. It was early evening, and with just nine patients to care for the ward would be quiet tonight. She nodded to a passing doctor, ignoring the way his eyes intentionally played over her breasts. In her three years of nursing she had become used to being undressed by stares like his. She was young, athletic, and attractive, and the tent-like covering of her hospital smock hid far more of her figure than it revealed. Not enough, however, to deter the openly lascivious glances of doctors, male nurses, and more than a few badly wounded patients. Her only defense was to become the best, most indispensable nurse in the hospital. She knew she had succeeded at that goal, and so did the hospital administrator. A small recompense, she acknowledged to herself, but one she was proud of.

Angela read the young Colonel's chart notes as soon as she arrived for her overnight shift. Nurse Whitman noted that he had regained consciousness, only to fall into deep depression. "*I am concerned for this lad,*" Whitman wrote, "*and for the harm he might do to himself. Watch him carefully.*"

She knocked on Thomas's door before entering. He was seated upright, and she saw that his injured right leg had been lowered back onto the bed after a week in traction. She had never seen him awake.

"You have green eyes," she was surprised to hear herself say.

"Sorry?" replied Thomas.

A blush crossed her face. She approached his bed and straightened the pillow. "No, I am the one who is sorry. It's just that I have been with you for four nights and this is the first time I have seen you when you weren't asleep. I didn't know you had green eyes. They are very nice."

He managed a half smile. Complimented by a young woman, and a highly attractive one at that; now it was his turn to blush.

Angela checked his leg and abdominal bandages before dipping a clean sponge into the wash basin. She carefully wiped Thomas' face, leaned him forward to sponge his back, and then set him back and gently cleaned his chest and stomach. Then she rinsed the sponge, pulled his gown up to his thighs and dabbed his feet and legs. Finally, she rinsed the sponge again, handed it to him, and said, "I will turn my back so you can finish."

"Finish? I don't understand."

Angela grinned, and he was certain her eyes were twinkling. "Washing your privates, Colonel."

She saw that he was embarrassed. "Every patient is bathed each day," she said in her most professional voice. "Privates and all."

He took the sponge and said, "But I have been here for a week. Who has been bathing me up until now?"

Angela replied with a sweet, low laugh. "I have bathed you, including your privates, three times now. You were not conscious, but I am a professional, after all."

The way she said it made him chuckle. She smiled and placed a hand on his shoulder. "How about this, Colonel. I will wash your privates again the next time you are shot, but as long as you are conscious how about we agree that you will do the washing down there?"

Almost any other male patient would have taken her little joke as an opportunity to make some crude reference in reply. He simply nodded and said, "Turn around then, and I will do my part."

Angela turned away, and he pulled his gown up and washed himself. Much to his dismay, however, he found himself enjoying the sight of her backside a bit too much. He finished quickly and yanked his gown back down before she noticed the evidence of his obvious physical consciousness.

"Done." Angela retrieved the sponge and said, "You'll be seeing more of me than usual tonight. There are only a handful of patients on the ward."

She left to attend to other patients, leaving him alone to think more about his plan. The idea that he would be forced to live a lie and pretend to be the hero he was not–even if that was the only way to save his hide-was more than he could bear. But if he went to the War Department with what he knew about Yoke and the secret regiment and his real actions at Pebble Creek Ridge, he would probably be imprisoned. Either choice was really no choice at all.

❖

The moon was low over the capitol dome when Thomas decided to act. He had spent hours running through every possible solution to his dilemma, but he simply could not find a path forward that did not end either in prison or personal ruin. So, he chose a third way.

When the hospital clock tower chimed 3:00 a.m he grabbed a roll of thick cotton bandaging from the table beside his bed and began twisting it into a knotted rope. When it was about eight feet long, he leaned forward and tied one end to the cross bar to which his leg had been tethered for the past week. Then he began wrapping the other end around his neck.

He tried not to let any other thought enter his mind. He was sorry for what Nurse Angela would have to see when she came to check on him, but as she herself had said, she was a medical professional. She knew what death looked like.

He finished wrapping the rope around his neck and prepared for the final step. He would pull himself fully upright and then fling his body off the bed as violently and as rapidly as he could. It should be enough to break his neck and end his troubles.

Waves of pain shot through his abdomen when he sat up. No matter, he thought. His pain was about to be gone for good. He sucked in his breath and prepared to plunge into the emptiness that was his only hope for salvation.

Then the door opened. Lamp light spilled in from the corridor, illuminating the form of Nurse Angela. She understood in a heartbeat what was happening. She rushed to the bed and began unwrapping the cord from around his neck. He struggled against her at first, but he was weak from his wounds and the laudanum and days on his back in bed. She overpowered him and unwound the rope from his neck. Then, as he began to softly cry, she lowered him back onto his pillow, wrapped her arms around him and held him tightly.

A few minutes later, Angela stood and went out into the corridor. She looked up and down the long hallway before locking the door and returning to his side. He lay quietly, but he was not asleep. He was racked by feelings of self-loathing, embarrassment, and a sense of total failure for not being able to do something as simple as hang himself.

Angela did not say a word. She belw out the lamp, and Thomas watched her pull her apron over her head and hang it on a peg beside the door. Then she came over to the bed and stood beside him, illuminated only by the silvery moonlight streaming through the high windows.

"Life is meant to be enjoyed," she said. "Even in war. We make choices, Thomas. Each one adds a little to your life, or it takes a little away. Only you can decide."

With that, Angela pulled her long sleeve blouse loose from her skirt waist. She reached up and slowly undid the top button. Her eyes never left his as she undid each button. She pulled the blouse off in a smooth, liquid motion and stood motionless in just her skirt and a silk chemise.

Time stopped. He was transfixed as Angela slowly lifted the chemise over her head and dropped it lightly on the bed. She stood straight with her shoulders back, and he watched warm moonlight wash over her full, creamy breasts.

Angela leaned in and kissed him on the lips, and he felt the warmth of her breasts brushing against his chest. Then she moved towards the head of the bed and let her breasts move softly back and forth across his lips for a moment before sliding back to sit on the edge of the bed. She took his hands and placed them on her breasts. Then she pulled his hospital gown up over his waist and began massaging him between his legs.

He had never experienced anything like this. Angela's auburn hair glowed in the moonlight, and her half-parted lips whispered things he had never heard a woman say. He ran his hands lightly over her face and her breasts as she moved her hand faster and faster between his legs.

After he exploded Angela lay down beside him and held him in her arms for a long time. They didn't speak. When she finally stood up to get dressed she went to the basin and came back with a soapy sponge.

"It seems I lied, dear Thomas. I didn't wait until the next time you were shot to wash your privates."

❋

That next week was the happiest time he had ever known. Angela was on duty for three nights after he had attempted to take his life, and each evening ended with her removing her blouse, sitting on the bed, and massaging him to new heights of delirium. Afterwards she would lay down beside him and talk for hours on end about art and music, food, literature, and the theater. He had never been in love, but as he lay back on his pillow in the softly lit room, listening to her animated descriptions of favorite books and music, watching her naked breasts rise and fall to the rhythm of her conversation, he was certain that love had found him. He would find a way to put his other problems behind him.There was nothing he wanted more than to spend the rest of his life with Angela.

Walt Whitman did his part. When he returned to duty after four nights off he shared everything he had learned about Yoke and the 109th regiment from the files in the Army paymaster's office.

"Yoke has officially mustered out," Whitman told him on the night of his return to the officer's ward. "He's one of few general officers who leaves at his full rank of Brigadier. Another is that damn fool George Custer, who was breveted to Major General a month before the surrender. God himself only knows how that strutting popinjay was able to retain his rank."

"What does Yoke's new circumstance mean for me?"

"It means that the politicians whose sons he hid from getting so much as a scratch on their lily-white butts are protecting him. They're all invested in making sure his scheme never comes to light. Too many would lose too much."

"Am I the only thing standing in their way?"

"Had you asked me that question yesterday, I would have said yes. You were the proverbial turd in the Sunday punch bowl, and I wouldn't have given a plug nickel for your chances once you were discharged from hospital."

Thomas looked glum. Whitman leaned over and slapped him on his thigh. "But that was yesterday, boy," he said with a great laugh. "Today, fortune has decided not to piss on your prospects." He pulled a sheet of paper from his notebook and handed it to Thomas. The insignia of the United States War Department was on the top, above the words, *'Recommendation for Award of the Congressional Medal of Honor to Col. T.E. Scoundrel, 109th Ohio, for His Actions at Pebble Creek Ridge, 1st April 1865, by Horatio Yoke, Brigadier.'*

"I don't follow."

"Your general is going to do everything he can to pave your way to a very bright future, Thomas. Very bright. Copies of that document went to the Secretary of War and the President himself this morning. It describes your heroic deeds at Pebble Creek Ridge…."

"Of which there were none!"

"Of which there were enough to assure that you can leave this rat-infested political sewer and go out there and have a real life, one where you die at a ripe old age in your own bed in the arms of a beautiful lady instead of being clubbed to death next week in some damn alley."

Whitman shook the document. "This is your ticket boy, and you are going to take it and you are going to ride with it for the next sixty years."

"But I don't deserve this…"

"And my brother George didn't deserve to be captured by the rebs and tossed into a hellhole prison, and my brother Andrew didn't deserve to die from consumption and alcoholism last December, and I sure as hell didn't deserve the sad duty of committing my brother Jesse to the Kings County Lunatic Asylum on Christmas Day!"

Whitman grew red-faced as he spoke, and Thomas wasn't sure if it was rage or frustration that was driving him.

"Bad things happen Thomas, to everybody, everywhere, and that goes equally for the prince as it does for the pauper. The measure of a man is not in what he makes happen but in how he deals with what happens to him."

Where have I heard that before, thought Thomas.

"I have been trying to get the world to embrace my volume of poems, called *Leaves of Grass,* for ten years. I can give up and let it wither by the side of the road; my family and plenty of other folks would like me to do that. But that is the way of the lamb, not the lion." He put his hands on Thomas' shoulders and gave him a good shake. "Time for you to be the lion, boy!"

"Yoke hopes to buy your silence and there are a lot of powerful people who are going to make sure that happens, one way or another. He can use his influence to get you the medal and probably to see that you muster out at the rank of colonel. But he doesn't own you, son. He can't adjust your sails and set your course. Only you can do that. Let Yoke and his kind live their pitiful lives. Choose to live your own life, in your own way, for your own reasons."

Thomas was overwhelmed. Between the exuberant physical and emotional passion he was sharing with Angela and the wisdom he was soaking in from Walt Whitman, he felt as if he had been away at university for several years.

"So, what now?" he asked the poet.

"Now we tend to the business of your exit from the army," Whitman replied. "I can help there. I will hand carry your paperwork personally from desk to desk. I will make certain that your pension is every bit as remunerative as it can be, and I will see to it that there are no limits on how long you can collect it. By the way, recipients of the Medal of Honor get a boost in their pensions."

He lay back exhausted, not knowing what to say. He owed the poet a debt of gratitude he would never be able to repay.

"I'm on to my other charges," said Whitman as he went to the door. "Think on these things, and we will talk again in a few hours."

❖

The next day, April 14th, marked the beginning of Thomas' third week at Mt. Pleasant. His abdominal wound was healing well and each day the bandages on his leg were getting smaller. Best of all, he received a letter from Captain Hayden about the events that transpired on Pebble Creek Ridge after he had been shot off Cornwall and lost consciousness. He sat up, placed his pillow in front of him, and unfolded the letter on top of it.

13 April 1865
John Hayden, Capt., CO. B, 109th Ohio

Colonel Thomas Scoundrel
Mt. Pleasant Military Hospital
Washington, DC

Colonel,

My men and I learned with great pleasure that you survived your wounds and are recovering in the capitol. We served with you for less than an hour, but I assure you it is an hour we will remember brightly and clearly for the rest of our lives. I have made a formal after-action report about the skirmish on Pebble Creek Ridge to the War Department and General Yoke but wanted to also personally recount to you what my men and I experienced that morning.

As you ascended the ridge, and I must confess, in partial contradiction of your orders, I broke my Company into three units, with mounted cavalry on the left and right, and infantry in the center. Almost as soon as we saw you crest the hill, we saw you being pursued along the ridge by a half dozen mounted rebels. I immediately ordered the eighty-six men in my command to go to your defense with all due haste.

I swung to the center in front of the infantry, and, with the other twenty-six mounted soldiers, drew my rifle and charged up the hill. In the moment or two it took for us to reach the top of the ridge, you had swung around an oak tree and doubled back on your pursuers. We saw you ride past them, and then, to our surprise we saw you turn back yet again and race past them once more.

Just as we were about to make the top, we saw your horse rear back, and we watched as you raised the flag high in one hand and your saber in the other. Colonel, with the rising sun behind you and the Stars and Stripes waving against that clear blue sky, it was the most magnificent thing I have ever witnessed. We cleared the ridge just as you fell from your horse, into the flag, and onto the ground. As distressed as we were at the sight, we were even more surprised by the number of Johnnies boiling up from the other side of the ridge. Two waves of cavalry swept towards us, followed by at least three or four infantry companies. As I rode towards you, I looked down into the valley and made a quick surmise that we were being attacked by a regiment of at least eight hundred men.

Four of my men joined me to form a semi-circle around you, and all of us on horseback opened fire at the rebs with our Spencers. Then our infantry made it to the top, and they joined in the fire, too. There were perhaps one hundred rebels on the ridge at this point, with hundreds more right behind them. I'm pretty sure this Johnnie regiment had never faced repeating rifles, and I could almost see shock on their faces as my men just kept firing and firing as they had to stop to reload.

Our initial volley pushed the rebs back halfway down the ridge. I had my men spread out along the ridge top, knowing full well that their commander was going to regroup and push ahead. By the time we were on the ground with rifles pointed down the valley, the rebs swarmed back up towards us. I sent our mounted soldiers to positions slightly north and south to look for anyone trying to flank us, but the rebs figured they could take us in a head on assault.

They came at us like hornets, Colonel. All those stories we were hearing about the South losing its fighting spirit must have passed these boys up. They came in waves up the hill, and we peppered them with everything we had. To be honest, they could probably have taken us if they'd kept at it. But after about fifteen minutes we heard the bugle, and they began trekking back down into their side of the valley. I didn't learn until a couple of days ago that their commander had been ordered to double-time it to support Lee at Five Forks, where the major action was taking place. We were just a gnat on their ass and beating us would have served no strategic purpose.

Our men fought like demons, Colonel. You should be very proud of them, especially Pvt. Malsom, who was the only man we lost that morning. Every last one of them told me that seeing you on your horse up there waving the flag in the face of the attacking rebels was the most inspiring sight they ever beheld. (By the way, you may not know this, but your horse did survive. I violated army regulations twice that day; once for heading up the hill sooner than ordered, and the second time for not putting down a horse that was wounded on a battlefield. That big beast deserved to live. He'd been grazed in the leg, and we walked him back here to the capitol where my cousin is an army vet at the Potomac Barracks. He says your horse will be good as new and ready for you when you are, but if you don't mind, I'd appreciate keeping that between us.)

I will be leaving the army to return home to Ohio soon. My family owns a small manufacturing business, and I am anxious to rejoin them and my wife and children. You will always be a welcome guest in our home.

With appreciation and admiration,
John Hayden

Tears welled in his eyes as he set the letter down and reached for a glass of water. His life had changed profoundly in the past two weeks. And now? He was sure of only one thing: tonight, he was going to ask Angela to marry him. Walt Whitman would be his best man. They could remain in the capitol, move to Ohio, or go anywhere she wanted. Where he went no longer mattered, as long as she was by his side.

❋

SIXTEEN

Mt. Pleasant Military Hospital

The day nurse changed Thomas's dressings and brought him supper. Then he slept until late evening so he would be fully awake when Angela came on duty at midnight. The hour came and went, but she did not appear in his doorway. As the clock tower chimed 2:00 a.m, the nurse came into his room.

"Something big is happening in the city," she said. "Troops are everywhere, and they have blocked off the road to the hospital. I'll be here until Nurse Angela arrives or we get this figured out."

He hadn't been out of bed for over two weeks, but he decided that if ever there was a time to get his feet back under him, this was it. When the nurse left his room, he sat up and swung his legs gingerly over the side of the bed. Then he slid the chair that Angela should have been sitting at over in front of him, turned it around and placed his hands on the back. He pushed the chair a few inches away from the bed and slid far enough forward that his toes were just touching the floor. Now he drew his breath, put his feet flat on the floor and pushed himself into a standing position behind the chair. It took every bit of his strength to stand upright. All he had to do now was use the chair as a balance while he shuffled across the room to the window.

A sharp pain shot through his leg with the first step. When he took his second step the chair came out from under his hands, and he collapsed on the floor. Before he had a chance to figure out his next move his door flew open and the nurse appeared.

She stood over him and said, "Colonel, just where did you think you were going?"

Even in his pain he realized the absurdity of the scene. He put one arm over the side of the downed chair and replied with a smile, "It seemed like a nice night to take a walk."

That earned him a laugh from the nurse. She bent down and helped him to get up into a sitting position on the edge of the bed. Then she checked his bandages for bleeding and packed two pillows behind him.

"If you are feeling good enough to stand up, perhaps we should be doing something about it." She left the room and returned a minute later with a pair of crutches in one hand and a silver flask in the other. "This first," she said as she handed him the brandy. He took a drink and felt a kick roll through his body.

The nurse handed him the crutches and showed him how to position them under his arms, lean forward, and let the crutches bear his weight as he stood up.

"You are really about a week early for doing this," she said, "but I see no reason you can't give it a try tonight."

She helped guide him into a standing position and showed him how far he could bend his injured leg without tearing the bandage.

"Do you feel dizzy?"

"A little, but I can do this."

The nurse stood in front of him as he took a tenuous first step, then another, and then another. Two steps later he was at the window.

He turned to the nurse and smiled. "Not bad for my first try."

"I'll give you five minutes at the window. Then it's back to bed."

She went to the door and then turned. "I'm sure Angela is fine, Colonel," she said in a most motherly voice. "She will be here as soon as she can."

He nodded his thanks and stared out the window. Did everyone in the hospital know about he and Angela?

The buildings and grounds around the hospital looked ghostly in the light of the waning gibbous moon. He could make out the water tower in the distance, the tall picket fence that separated the officer's ward from the canvas tents that housed enlisted men, and he could just see a line of trees about one hundred yards out that bordered the river. The dirt road from the city into the hospital grounds was muddy from the afternoon rain and he could clearly see the temporary barricades and sentries that his nurse told him about. But the South had surrendered, and the war was over. What could explain the presence of additional federal troops around the hospital? Had some rebel units refused to surrender, and were they trying to bring the renewed war to the capitol?

He hobbled back to his bed and leaned the crutches against the nightstand. All he could do was wait and wonder.

❖

He drifted in and out of sleep. At 7:00 a.m., the nurse came into his room with oatmeal and toast. Her face was streaked with tears.

Before he could ask, she said, "President Lincoln was shot last night while attending a play at Ford's Theatre. We don't know who did this awful thing, but he is alive, and we have hope he will recover."

He was stunned. How could anyone get close enough to the President to shoot him? And with the war over, why? He had a million questions, but the nurse knew nothing beyond the facts she had shared. It did explain why federal troops had sealed off the hospital, though; they were probably standing guard at every federal installation in the capitol in the event the attempt on the President's life was part of a much larger conspiracy.

He pushed his breakfast aside and sipped at his coffee. He desperately missed Angela, and he wished that Whitman were here to make sense of the terrible news. All in good time, he supposed.

It was almost 1:00 p.m. when Walt Whitman walked through his door. He had never seen the man in daylight; the poet looked equal parts rumpled and careworn. He clutched a note pad and book in one hand and in the other, a cane. He came over to the bed, sat down, and wrapped his arm around Thomas' shoulder.

"He is gone, boy, he is gone."

"The President?"

"Yes, this morning, around ten. His wounds were too grave for the doctors to manage. Mr. Lincoln saved our nation, but they could not save him."

Whitman took a deep breath and then exhaled the most agonized sigh that Thomas had ever heard.

"But, how? Why? What happens now?"

"No one can answer those questions yet. I'd wager that it will be weeks or months before we have answers. The city is filled with troops, there are rumors of the arrest of high officials for conspiracy and the only thing I can tell you for certain is that chaos is the rule everywhere you look."

"Thank you for coming, Mr. Whitman. I'm sure you have so many other responsibilities today."

"All federal offices are closed, and my boarding house is in a part of the city that is cordoned off. No one in, no one out. When I discovered that the paymaster's office was shuttered and I could not return to my home, this is the only place I had to go."

Whitman looked off into the distance, his eyes fixed on nothing. His shoulders sagged and he leaned forward on the edge of the bed and began to cry softly. Then he wiped his sleeve across his eyes, stood, and said, "I am sorry, boy. "

Thomas rested his hand on Whitman's arm. "My mother told me that at times like this we need to get back to what we do best as quickly as we can."

"Yes, I will be assisting in surgery today, cleaning bed pans, anything I can to be of help."

"That is good, but it isn't really what you do best, is it." He took up Whitman's writing pad and said, "This is what you do best, my friend. History is all around us today. Terrible history, but that is what it is. '*No one is lost to history who is remembered by great poetry,*' didn't you tell me that?

"Aye. I did."

"Perhaps writing when your pain is deepest will produce a thing of greatness. Emptying slop buckets sure won't."

Whitman smiled. He stood, reached out a hand and tousled Thomas's hair. "Good on you, boy. I really do think you have the heart of a lion."

The poet gathered his things and went to the door. "I will keep my eyes out for Nurse Angela. The three of us will see this thing through together."

❖

The nurse insisted on giving him an extra dose of laudanum after Whitman left the room. "That was a lot of exercise for a man with your injuries," she said, "and I don't want you moving for the next twelve hours." He didn't complain; the elixir would help him to rest and ease his worries about Angela.

He slipped into a deep sleep, waking hours later when it was dark outside. He sat up and was startled to see Whitman seated in the corner at a small table writing by the light of a coal oil lamp. Seven or eight wadded sheets of paper were scattered around the floor at his feet, the stub of a cigar was glowing softy in a dish, and a pint of whiskey was at his elbow. The poet was humming to himself as he scribbled across the paper.

"Hello?" said Thomas.

"Ah, you're awake, that's good. I am in need of company, and you need something to eat."

"What's the news?"

"That I cannot say. I spoke to the captain of the barracks several times today, and all he hears are rumors, and rumors about rumors. The city is under federal marshal law and a house-by-house search is taking place. Why, or for who, we do not know."

"Any word from Angela?"

"No, boy, and I wouldn't expect anything for a day or two at least." Thomas sighed and reached for a glass of water. He was certain she was simply locked in her home like the rest of Washington.

"What are you writing?"

"It's an elegy, a mourning poem. Your inspiration, Thomas. You were right, I could weep about all day, or clean the dunny for the hundredth time, or I could do what God almighty Himself put me on this earth to do." He held up the piece of paper on which he had been writing. "This is my fifth draft. It's only three stanzas and I think I have now re-written the first stanza to my satisfaction. Will you read the stanza to me? It helps me to hear the words spoken aloud."

Thomas stretched out his hand and took the sheet of paper.

"The title," said Whitman, taking a sip from the bottle, "Is '*O Captain! ...My Captain!*'"

Thomas cleared his throat and read the first stanza of Walt Whitman's poem about the fallen President in the poet's clean, flowing handwriting:

O Captain! My Captain! Our fearful trip is done,
The ship has weather'd every rack, the prize we sought is won,
The port is near, the bells I hear, the people all exulting,
While follow eyes the steady keel, the vessel grim and daring;
But O heart! heart! heart!
O the bleeding drops of red,
Where on the deck my Captain lies,
Fallen cold and dead.

He finished reading and then sat quietly, not knowing what to say. Whitman, too, was quiet, and his head was bowed, though whether it was in prayer or emotional exhaustion, Thomas could not say.

When Whitman raised his head his eyes were misty. "You have a fine voice, Thomas. I hear a touch of Ireland in its temper; your mother would be proud."

"It's beautiful," were the only words that Thomas could find.

"I will finish the rest tomorrow and send it to my friend, who is the editor of the *Harper's Weekly*. We should share our sorrows as we share our celebrations. Now, I'm off to get you something to eat. We don't want Angela to find you have wasted away in her absence."

Whitman left the room and he read the poem again and again before falling back to sleep.

❖

SEVENTEEN

Mt. Pleasant Military Hospital

Three days after the President's assassination the state of martial law was lifted in Washington, DC. The roadblocks were lifted, Federal troops were removed from street corners and public squares, and Angela was able to return to her duties at the hospital.

That same afternoon Walt Whitman paid Thomas an unexpected daytime visit. As promised, he had hand-walked Thomas's mustering out papers to every officer responsible for approving and signing pension documents in the paymaster's office. Thomas was seated in a chair by the window and Whitman dropped a leather portfolio onto his lap.

"Those are copies of all of your retirement documents. You will muster out at the rank of full colonel," he said. "I am told that General Yoke himself went to the Secretary of War to make the case for you keeping that rank." He winked, and added, "I am also sure that Yoke paved his way into the Secretary's office with a mountain of bribes to a small army of bureaucrats and political types. Yoke needs you happy and he needs you out of Washington. You are one of only a handful of brevet colonels who will retain his rank. Quite a coup, lad."

"Colonel," Thomas said in a half-whisper. "It's real? It can't be taken away?"

"Not now, boy, not after the Secretary of War himself has signed off. I squeezed every penny-pinching desk jockey in the accounting office to get you a pension of $175 per month too. Not a fortune, but it is enough to get a start in life, and even to live on if a man doesn't get eaten up with too much gambling and wenching."

Thomas could only shake his head in disbelief. Eight months ago, he was an ordinary Ohio farm boy. Oh, he could read and write and converse in two languages, but on his seventeenth birthday his greatest ambition was to return home and start a farm. Now, not yet eighteen, he was a retired senior army officer with a lifetime pension. How could he get his head around that?

"There are a few things you need to know," continued Whitman. "You can have your money deposited in any bank, or you can pick it up personally in the paymaster's office at any army outpost. You can also continue to use the title of Colonel in civilian life. I highly recommend that you do. It will open doors, clear paths when the going is tough, and I'd wager, it will get you the best tables in restaurants too."

Thomas chuckled. "It's so much to take in all at once."

"Aye, but there is something else you need to know: as a senior military officer you can be recalled to active duty in a time of emergency."

"But…I don't know how to be a colonel."

Whitman laughed. "You'll have plenty of time to learn, boy. If you get the call put on your uniform and then find the best damn active-duty officers to do the work. For now, you should be thinking about what you want to do with the rest of your life."

Thomas got up from his chair and began to pace around the room. The pain in his leg and abdomen was bearable now, and he felt ready to begin taking walks along the window-lined hospital corridors outside his room. Angela would be so surprised. And now that he had an income, he was much more confident about asking her to marry him.

"I have to return to my office," said Whitman. "Read those papers. Oh, and I hear that Angela will be back on duty tonight, not that you probably care."

Thomas could only grin. "Thank you, Walt, for everything. I don't know how I can ever repay your kindness."

Whitman embraced him. "You and I are of a kind, Thomas. We chafe under authority, and we prefer our own company to the oppression of crowds. Most of all, we crave adventure; for me, it's living the life of the mind through my poems. For you it will be the poetry of the open road with the sun on your back and a game of chance and a lovely woman waiting for you when the sun sinks below the purple mountains."

Whitman reached into his pocket and pulled out a small, cloth-bound book. He set it on the nightstand and went to the door. "We don't grow old until our regrets are bigger than our dreams, Thomas. Don't ever lose sight of that." The poet touched his hand to his heart, smiled, and left the room.

❖

At 9:00 p.m., three hours before she was scheduled to be on duty, Angela appeared in the open doorway. She was surprised to see him sitting in a chair by the window, and even more surprised that he was wearing a shirt and trousers instead of a hospital gown. He flew out of the chair and held her in a tight embrace.

"You can walk!" she exclaimed.

He pulled back from her and held her by the arms. "I can do so many things now, and I have so much news, and so many questions that I…."

Angela kissed him lightly on the lips. "One thing at a time, my darling. I have been down in the kitchen, and we need to eat before everything is cold."

She stepped back into the hall and returned with a wheeled cart. Then she pulled two chairs together and set up a small table before handing Thomas a bottle of Verdelho Madeira wine and a corkscrew. By the time he opened the bottle and poured two glasses the table was set, and a candle was burning. Angela uncovered the serving dishes and filled two plates with buttermilk fried chicken, German potato salad, and a mix of green onions and tomatoes in vinaigrette.

They toasted their reunion and sat quietly for a time, holding hands across the table and simply enjoying being together. The food was excellent, but he could barely taste anything. He was bursting to share his news and to lay the big question before her. Before he could,

Angela began talking about the shut-down of the city and about the fear that still gripped the country about a possible nation-wide conspiracy that could topple the government of President Andrew Johnson. So much had changed so quickly.

When they finished eating, Angela went to the door and locked it. "We won't be disturbed tonight, Thomas."

"That's good; there is so much I want to talk to you about."

She took him by the hands and led him to the center of the room. Then she put one finger against his lips and said, "Shush now, we will talk later. Right now, there is something else we are going to do."

With that she turned down the wall lamp and began to unbutton his shirt. She pulled it off him, kissed his chest, and lay the shirt on a chair. Then she knelt and undid his trousers. He had no shoes on, and she slipped his trousers and underwear off and piled them on top of his shirt. She raised herself slowly, showering his thighs, stomach, and chest with kiss after lingering kiss. "Stay here," she said in deep whisper. She went to the basin and came back with a washcloth and began cleansing every inch of his body. When she was done, she took a towel from the rack and dabbed the dampness away from his skin.

"Lay down now," she ordered. He did as he was told. He lay in the center of the bed, overwhelmed with physical excitement, ready for the massage that she had given him several times before.

But Angela did not simply remove her blouse and sit beside him in her skirt as she usually did. Instead, she stood at the foot of the bed and removed her blouse and chemise and then moved her hands to the side of her skirt. She smiled lovingly at him in the soft glow of the lamp as she slowly unfastened the stays. When they were undone, she stepped out of the skirt, and he saw that she was not wearing any undergarments.

She let her arms drop to her side and stood stock still. He feasted on the sight of her silken smooth breasts, her hourglass waist, and the inviting curves of her hips. His eyes were drawn to the triangular tuft of hair between her legs, and, for a moment, he thought he was not going to be able to contain himself from exploding. Then Angela slowly turned around, and he marveled at the long arc of her back and the magnificent pout of her perfect derrière.

She turned again and walked to the bed beside him. She took his outstretched hand, pulled it between her legs, and showed him how to caress her there. As he moved his fingers gently back and forth, Angela's head tilted back, and she began to moan softly. He watched spellbound as her countenance was transformed in the soft lamp light into a canvas of pure bliss.

After a moment she lowered her head and smiled at him with an expression that was a mix of love, passion, and mischief. It was the most beautiful sight he had ever beheld.

Angela pulled back from his touch and then gently pushed his head onto the pillow. She went to the table and brought the candle to the nightstand. "I want you to see everything, my love," she said.

Then she kissed him on the lips before letting her mouth trail down his chest, across his stomach, and around and onto his manhood. She stroked his thighs with her long hair and breasts and then, to his amazement, she raised herself up and straddled his body with her legs. She simply said, "Now my darling," and guided him deep inside her with her hand before starting to rock back and forth in a fluid, rhythmic motion.

Thomas put his arms around her hips and thrust up into her in time with her movements. He had never known a physical sensation as exquisite as this, a bonding so deep, or a passion so completely enveloping. It was like riding on the crest of a surging wave that was growing higher and higher as it neared the shore, billowing with raw energy, shot through with rapid-fire pinpricks of such intense delight that he could barely keep control of his senses.

Angela moved faster and faster. She pulled her hair back and cupped her breasts together, and he saw tiny beads of glistening moisture forming on her creamy skin. He raised his head up and covered her breasts with kisses as she raised herself ever more wildly up and down, faster and deeper. Then she placed both of her hands on his chest, thrust one final time, and collapsed onto him in a heap.

He didn't know what to do. After a moment Angela stirred, sat up, and began moving her hips slowly back and forth on him. She smiled and ran her hands through his hair. "It's your time, Thomas. Let yourself go."

He put his arms around her waist, thrust upwards, and felt the wave surge forward for a final time. It rocketed through every cell in his body in an explosive, rapturous burst that brought all his senses to a sudden, convulsive release.

Then he lay back, spent. Angela's warm body curled up beside him and he drifted off to sleep.

❋

He awoke with the first rays of morning light streaming through his window and turned to hold Angela, only to discover that she was gone. He slid the covered thunder mug out from under the bed and relieved himself, washed with cold water from the basin and got dressed. Then he picked up the book that Whitman had left for him on the nightstand. He was pleased to see a finely done woodcut illustration of a better-shorn and more respectably dressed Walt Whitman across from the title page: *Leaves of Grass*, Boston, Thayer & Eldridge, 1860-61. A thin red ribbon bookmark had been inserted into the text, and he flipped to the page. At the top, his friend had penned a short note: *"Thomas, let this be your song!* Walt."

Poem of The Road

AFOOT and light-hearted I take to the open road!
Healthy, free, the world before me!
The long brown path before me, leading wherever
I choose!

Before he could begin the second stanza the door opened. Angela was back in her crisp white apron, with her hair pulled back and her most professional no-nonsense nursing expression. She carried a pot of coffee over to the nightstand where she poured two cups and added fresh cream before pulling a chair next to his.

Thomas's heart was bursting with a mix of love, wonderment, and a flood of intoxicating memories of what they had shared only hours before. "How can you expect me to drink coffee right now?" he asked her. "In fact, how can you expect me to do anything except just sit here and drink you in?"

"You have been around that poet for too long, my dear. You are beginning to sound like him. As for what I expect, I expect you to eat your breakfast, and then I expect you to get out of this room for some exercise and fresh air."

He took a sip of the coffee and willed his heart to stop pounding so loudly. It made no sense to wait a moment longer. He would propose to her, right now, no matter what. He set his cup down, took a deep breath, and reached for Angela's hand. To his surprise she pulled back, clasped both of her hands tightly around her coffee cup and looked at him with a misty, faraway gaze whose meaning he could not interpret.

"Please listen to me, dear Thomas. I know what you want to ask, and I am beyond flattered that you would do so. I do love you, and I want only the best for you, so please hear what I must tell you."

A chill ran through him. The hospital clock tower began to chime, and the sound of the bells felt suddenly funereal. Somehow, he kept silent, simply nodding in reply even as his heart filled with dread.

Angela sat back in her chair. "I should have had this talk with you before last night. Last night was…it was magical and spectacular and heartbreaking, all at the same time."

Heartbreaking, he thought? Did I perform that badly?

As if she was reading his mind, Angela said, "You were tender and magnificent, my darling. You made me feel every intimate sensation a woman can experience with a man. I will cherish our evening for as long as I live."

He felt his stomach churn. There was no way that her last sentence could be followed by anything other than a swift and permanent kick in the ass.

"Go on," were the only words he could form.

"I have been a nurse for three years. I love my profession, and I feel like my work makes a difference. But I wasn't always a nurse, Thomas."

She leaned forward and took his hand. She looked deep into his eyes and said, "I was a wife. My husband was a businessman who joined the Army right after Fort Sumpter. He was a major, and he was killed on September 17, 1862, at the Battle of Antietam."

Tears welled up in his eyes. He had wondered how someone as lovely and bright and talented as Angela had remained unmarried. A wave of sorrow and shame washed over him. He had been thinking only of himself, of his needs and his desires.

"Oh, my sweet Angela," poured out of him like a teardrop. "I had no idea, no idea."

She ran her hand down the side of his face and said, "Three years is a long time, Thomas. The pain will never go away; it is always there, just below the surface. I have had many opportunities to take a husband–or, God knows, a lover–since my husband died. Until I met you, I hadn't so much as held a man's hand. Do you believe me?"

He sensed that she was asking a very important question; it wasn't really "do you believe I am telling you the truth?" as much as it was asking, "do you believe I am truly the person you believed me to be when you fell in love?"

He took both of her hands in his and said, "I believe you, Angela. And I believe *in* you." He cleared his throat and added, "I hope that you can forgive me. Had I known, had anyone told me about your husband, I would never have let any of this happen."

She smiled, and a single tear rolled slowly down her cheek. "Thomas, darling Thomas, you must never feel that way. I *wanted* this to happen. I *needed* this to happen. And so did you. We each needed to find a way to come back to life, my dear. To do that we needed to come together here, in this hospital, and…" she leaned over and patted the mattress, "in this bed."

He had never felt an emotion as powerful as the love he felt for Angela in that moment. As for what he should do about it, that was a mystery greater than his power of reason or comprehension. He sat in silence, staring at the floor. Then he raised his head, squeezed her hands, and asked, "And now?"

Angela bent forward and kissed him tenderly on the lips. "Now we live, my darling. You will seek out your best destiny, and I will seek mine. In my case, that means moving away to Boston with my mother. We are going to care for her sister, who has been ill for a long time. She has a home and an income, and we will want for nothing. For the time being that will be sufficient for me. I have had enough of death and dying these past several years. I'm actually looking forward to a bit of boredom."

Every living cell in his being wanted to shout in protest at what Angela had just told him. It's not what he wanted. He looked into her eyes, and saw her love, her longing, and her sorrow. He understood that this was every bit as difficult for her as it was for him. The only question now was did he love her as much as she loved him? Enough to let her go away, enough to be prepared to never see her again?

"I do," he suddenly blurted out, without thinking about what he was saying. It was so silly he almost laughed. That can't make sense to her, he thought. But it did. She lay her hands on his shoulders. "And I do, as well, my darling." They stood and wrapped themselves in a long embrace. Then Angela pulled away. She touched her fingers to her lips and pressed them against his mouth. She took several steps back, turned, and disappeared into the hospital.

He sat down on the edge of the bed. He could not cry, he could not think, he could only breathe. After a few minutes, he went over to the window and looked out across the sun-drenched hospital garden. A shimmer of his reflection stared emptily back at him in the glass.

As he stood there a deep resolve the likes of which he had never known began to rise in him until it was anchored in his mind like a steel pillar. A kitchen boy masquerading as a colonel had been carried unconscious into this hospital three weeks ago. Tomorrow, a colonel who had once been a kitchen boy would be leaving.

❖

EIGHTEEN

Dinosaur Bluff, Colorado, July 1882

The sun was beginning its descent into the west when the red dirt road out of Denver swept around an imposing limestone promontory. The distinctive formation was composed of layers of light gray, red, and greenish gray rock that felt out of place after the forested valleys and tall grass meadows Thomas had been riding through since dawn. The closer he got to the bluff the more it looked like it had been pushed up through the earth's crust and fresh-painted that morning.

His eyes followed a line of weathered, sparsely vegetated hills that spilled off the bottom of the crag before flattening out beside a creek that wound past the bluff and out into the grasslands. The road to Claybourne's ranch branched to the right, but Thomas wanted a closer look at the multicolored rocks, so he guided Ulysses to the left, towards the creek.

He picked his way along a thick copse of cattails that lined the stream bank, looking for a break where he could make his way across the shallow water and over to the bluff. As he pulled around a flowering cottonwood he suddenly heard a deep, muted *"whump,"* and to his astonishment, an enormous sandstone boulder the size of a stagecoach rose ten feet in the air just a few yards in front of him and then splashed down into the creek.

Ulysses instinctively wheeled hard and fast to the right, and Thomas was nearly thrown from his saddle. He righted himself and reined back.

That's when he noticed he had been showered with creek water and cattail dust. He took off his hat, and as he began brushing away the powdery brown and green granules, a voice called out to him.

"Hallo, my word! I am so very sorry. Are you alright?" The accent was distinctly German, but Thomas could not see who was speaking. Then a section of the cattails parted and a tall, blonde-haired man in a straw hat and spectacles stepped out of the brush. He wore suspenders over a long sleeve undershirt that was tucked into miner's tin pants, the kind that were impregnated with a mix of oil and wax that made the tightly woven cotton nearly indestructible. His rubber waders went up to his knees and a knife sheath hung from one side of his belt, with a holstered revolver on the other.

He was still shaking the dust off his vest as the man stepped closer and put a hand on Ulysses's bridle. He patted the side of the horse's neck and asked, "You are well? No harm to you or your horse?"

It took Thomas a moment to compose himself. He shook his head. "I seem to be fine," he finally replied. He pointed in the direction of the boulder that was now resting easily in the middle of the creek. "What the hell was that?"

"An experiment, and one that actually worked as I had hoped it would, not including your unfortunately timed and unplanned appearance, of course."

He pulled a whiskey flask from his back pocket and handed it up to Thomas, who took a long pull. "Thank you," he said. "So, what exactly are you doing tossing boulders around at passing strangers?"

The man laughed. "Tie your horse over there and let me show you."

He dismounted and walked Ulysses to a sapling tree. That's when he saw a burro loaded with heavy canvas bags munching contentedly on a thicket of grass at the creek's edge. A few feet away was a wooden box marked "DYNAMITE" next to a smaller open box in which he could see primer cord and blasting caps.

"You experiment with dynamite?"

"Among many other things." He removed his straw hat and extended his hand. "Peter Von Sievers, paleontologist. I am at your service, with regrets for almost blowing you and your fine horse to bits."

Thomas introduced himself and said, "A dinosaur scientist? Like that Cope fellow who brought those giant fossils to New York? I saw some of them on exhibit not six months ago."

"I haven't his style or his financial backing, alas, but yes, we are in the same field of study. He is working farther to the west in a part of the Morrison Formation that requires a team of laborers and horses to extract and transport his specimens. My team is comprised of my wife and a couple of burros, which explains my experiment today using Professor Nobel's loveliest contribution to humanity."

"I didn't know dinosaurs were extracted with dynamite. Isn't that a little hard on those old bones?"

Von Sievers laughed. "Let me show you." He led Thomas through an opening in the wall of cattails to the remains of the boulder he had just blown.

"The bluff over there was laid down over 150 million years ago; it is the products of eons of flooding and endless compression of dirt and silt. The colored bands you see running across the face of the bluff are made of mudstone, sandstone, siltstone, and limestone. The best fossils are found in the green siltstone and lower sandstone beds. Do you see those white flags there to your left, half-way up?"

He nodded, and Von Sievers said, "I have been working there for the better part of a year. A month ago, I hit an area that is rich in specimens. But I simply do not have the assistants or the equipment to dig by myself, and so…"

"And so, you cheat. I suppose a little nitroglycerin can do the work of a dozen men."

"I prefer to think of it as a creative application of explosive potential. I have been working on ways to apply just the right number of sticks at the optimal depth to remove surrounding rock without destroying the embedded fossils. In a few days I will load up my jenny," he pointed to the burro, "and plant my first garden. *Gott in Himmel* willing, I will reveal new specimens, and not bring the whole bluff crashing down on my head."

"And your wife is fine with this?"

"She did the calculations! If she turns out to be wrong and I am buried alongside my dinosaurs, well, a man's fate could be worse than to become a fossil in some museum collection a million years from now, don't you think?"

Thomas grinned; he liked the scientist and was glad he had wandered off the main road.

"So, where are you headed?" asked Von Sievers. "Not many people take this road. Almost everyone leaving east out of Denver takes the southern passage."

"I'm going to Claybourne Ranch, but as you see, not by the main road."

"Ah, a surreptitious visit? You have earned my curiosity, and that is not something I often feel about anything that has not been embedded in stone since the Jurassic Age."

"Let's just say I am a cautious man."

"Yes, you came up on my boulder most stealthily," laughed the scientist.

Thomas smiled and shook his head. "I'd best be going. I want to make Langton Hall before nightfall."

"Then you will be disappointed. You have at least six hours of riding ahead of you, and the sun will set in less than three."

"Six hours to the ranch?"

"About four hours to the northern boundary of Claybourne's property, and a good two-hour ride from there to his main house. Maybe twenty-five miles."

"Do you mind if I camp here by the creek then? It looks as good a place as any to spend the night."

"I do mind, in fact. You will come with me and stay the night in our cave."

Cave? thought Thomas. He didn't like being in close quarters and the idea of bedding down in the tight confines of a small mountain cave did not sit well with him.

Von Sievers noted his discomfort. "Are you familiar with the works of Jules Verne, Colonel, especially his book, *Mysterious Island*? You may recall that the castaways in the balloon were blown thousands of miles across the ocean, only to descend by chance on a remote island where they constructed remarkable accommodations inside a great natural cave."

He did know the work. "My own abode is not of that size or sumptuousness," said Von Sievers, "but I promise you it is far more comfortable than this mosquito-plagued creek bank. And, I have the finest wine cellar on the escarpment."

It was an invitation Thomas could not turn down. He helped the scientist gather his gear and load up the burro, and then he mounted Ulysses while Von Sievers walked the jenny across the creek, around a graveled bend, and a half mile farther along the creek. When they arrived at a spot where a rocky glacial moraine flowed down to the creek bank they turned towards the bluff and ascended a path that had been excavated out of the soft stone. It went up and across the face of the moraine at a forty-degree angle for about fifty yards before switching back the other direction and ascending higher. The switchback path changed direction three more times as it traversed higher and higher up the bluff until it leveled off at about two hundred feet above the creek and valley floor below.

When they reached the summit, Thomas saw that the gravel path terminated at the foot of a massive boulder twenty-five yards from where they stood. He was mystified until he turned his head up to the cliff and saw two cave openings, each about eight feet wide and six feet high. The one closest to him was partially covered by a movable gate made of sapling poles and evergreen branches, while the other was open to the elements. Von Sievers led them over to the open cave entrance where a milk cow, a handsome Morgan, another burro, and several laying hens were enjoying their evening meals. Natural light streamed into the cave from two fissures in the limestone ceiling and several dozen bales of hay were stacked across from a water trough. When he looked closer, he saw that the trough was being fed by a steady drip of water off the wall. Next to the trough was a forge and anvil and a lineup of various kinds of shovels, stakes, sledgehammers, and other digging and excavating tools. Several cases of dynamite were stacked on a ledge at the back of the cave.

"Quite something, isn't it?" said Von Sievers. "Let's get your horse settled."

Thomas unsaddled Ulysses, let him drink, and then backed him into a clean stall where he immediately shared a friendly nuzzle and some hay with Von Sievers's horse. The professor brought both horses a ration of oats and molasses in canvas buckets. Then he unloaded the burro and put him in a stall with his companion.

"This is amazing," he told the scientist. "All of this-inside a cave. I've never seen anything like it."

"Then you might just like the main house."

He went to the other cave opening, pulled aside the gate and led Thomas inside a well-lit rock chamber thirty feet wide by sixty feet deep. The vaulted ceiling was twenty feet high at the center point and there were four openings that let in light from outside. A fireplace had been carved into the soft stone, above which a wooden mantel was set. Directly across from the fireplace was a cast-iron cook stove with a pipe that went all the way to a break in the rock ceiling, and next to that was a wash basin below a large, spring-fed water cistern. Most remarkable of all was the whitewashing on the cave walls and ceiling. That, plus the natural light, made Thomas feel as if he was in the garden conservatory of a New York mansion, not in a limestone cave in the Colorado wilderness.

The overall effect of the decorated cave left him speechless. Large rugs and a suite of fine oak and walnut furnishings covered much of the hard-packed floor. Oil paintings, bookshelves, mirrors, and candle sconces decorated two of the walls. A cello and violin rested on a small-raised platform, and, as Von Sievers had promised, a tall wooden rack holding dozens of bottles of wine was fastened to a board that had been screwed into the rock. Beside the wine rack were two framed certificates featuring Von Sievers's name and certifications: one from the University École des Mines de Paris and the other from the Humboldt University of Berlin.

Thomas was drawn to the back wall where dozens of highly detailed pencil and charcoal drawings of living dinosaurs, specimens still in rock, reconstructed skeletons, ancient plants, birds, and sea creatures were attached to wires running the full width of the cave

Two long worktables sat below the sketches. They were covered with notebooks, microscopes, specimen jars, bone fragments, measuring instruments, reference volumes, and even several complete dinosaur skulls.

He turned to Von Sievers, but he couldn't find the words to express his sense of wonderment. The scientist solved the quandary for him. "Not bad for a field quarters, eh, Colonel?"

❖

There was a rustle in the embroidered tapestry hanging on one wall, and a woman emerged from behind it. Thomas could just make out the alcove that had been cut into the stone to form a bedroom as she stepped into the main room.

"This is my wife, Katarina," said Von Sievers. "Darling, please meet Colonel Thomas Scoundrel, who I have invited for the evening by way of apologizing for nearly blowing him up."

"Oh, dear," she said as she shook Thomas' hand, "I really must do something about my husband's social graces. Get to know them first before dynamiting them, I always say."

Thomas laughed. Katarina was small, with dark hair and quick, expressive eyes. He knew better than to assume that there was anything frail about her though. From prairie rattlesnakes to off-reservation Comanches and sporadic bursts of ferocious weather, life on the edge of the plains was not easy.

Von Sievers excused himself to clean up and Katarina invited Thomas to sit at the head of the walnut dining table, where she poured a glass of red wine for him.

"You work in the field with your husband?"

"Most days, yes. I map and mark out the areas where we will dig, and I catalogue the specimens we gather. I also clean and prepare the specimens that we sell to museums and private collectors."

"Like the small skull on the table over there?"

Katarina nodded and added, "That is from a juvenile Camarasaurus, a genus of quadrupedal, sauropod dinosaurs. But don't be misled by that two-foot skull. Had he grown to his full size he would have been sixty feet long and weighed over 40,000 pounds."

Thomas was impressed. "He must have had quite an appetite."

"Just plants, but you wouldn't know that from his teeth, which are razor sharp and over seven inches long."

"So how can you be sure he only ate vegetation? Seems like a waste of such big teeth."

Katarina reached over and lifted two large, smooth stones, each the size of a coconut, from the centerpiece on the table. She placed them in front of Thomas. "Those are gastroliths," she said. "Sauropods swallowed them to help grind the food in their stomachs. When the stones became too smooth, the beast would pass them. We have found piles and piles of them."

He picked another stone from the centerpiece. It was bigger than the gastrolith, veined in scarlet red and emerald-green, and had been polished to a high sheen.

"This one looks a bit different. It's quite beautiful."

He heard Von Sievers laugh. "That's because you are holding a piece of fossilized dinosaur dung," he said as he came back into the room in a fresh shirt and jacket. "It's called coprolite. Makes a lovely table decoration, doesn't it? Sadly, there is no market for them. There are veritable mountains of the stuff all around us."

"It reminds me of being in Washington, DC," Thomas said. "Mountains of the stuff."

Von Sievers chuckled as he poured more wine for everyone. "I hope you like venison, Colonel. My wife brought down a doe on the trail above us a couple of days ago. She cans much of the meat in a pressure cooker for us to have during the winter, but I carved several steaks for us to have this week. Your timing is perfect."

Von Sievers fetched the meat and then heated a cast iron skillet on the wood-fired cook stove. As his wife prepared a dish with potatoes, wild greens and onions, the paleontologist lathered olive oil, crushed rosemary, garlic, and salt and pepper on the steaks and then dropped them into the sizzling skillet. He seared them on both sides and then added a cup of dry red wine and some dried cherries. While the steaks simmered, he prepared a roux with flour and fat in which he whisked in some black-currant jelly, coriander seeds, and a bit more rosemary.

Katarina and Thomas sat at the table as Von Sievers finished the venison steaks and poured a little currant sauce on each one. He brought the platter to the table and then selected a bottle of Charles Krug California Syrah from the wine rack.

If he closed his eyes, Thomas thought, he could have been in the dining room at Delmonico's, or Pembray's at the Shore. But as he looked around the exquisitely furnished cave and out to the sun setting behind the Front Range, he belayed that idea. Professor and Mrs. Von Sievers's cave was, in fact, the finest dining room in which he had ever supped.

When they finished eating Von Sievers cleared the table while his wife prepared a simple crème anglaise and poured it over a rice pudding. "The reward of having a milk cow and laying hens," she said as she set a bowl before Thomas.

Over coffee, his hosts asked him to share his story. When he described his mission to confront Claybourne directly to determine if he knew anything about Rosalilia's disappearance, Von Sievers's sunny countenance turned grim.

"I know Claybourne well," said the scientist. "You cannot live or work anywhere within one hundred miles of his ranch and not either know him or know of him."

"And what is your assessment of the man," asked Thomas. "Is he capable of undertaking something as foul as the murder of a prominent Mexican citizen and the kidnap of his daughter?"

"Not only capable, but I think it fair to say, well within the scope of his experience. A few years ago, a group of settlers filed homestead claims for several thousand acres on the Mesa Verde, abutting Claybourne's property. Within a year mysterious fires destroyed their new crops, the saw mill they were building was 'accidentally' dynamited, and two homesteaders fell to their deaths in a deep ravine, not far from here, in fact. The rest of the homesteaders got the message and deeded their land over to Claybourne within weeks."

"Settling is a dangerous business," Thomas answered. "So, how is it that you and Katarina have been able to stay here?"

"We met with Claybourne when we first came to Colorado five years ago, to seek his patronage for our work. But my ambitions were far too small for his vision; he knew there were dinosaurs to be had out here, but he was only interested in giant, dramatic specimens, the kinds that could go on display like those you saw in New York. Most of the creatures who lived here millions of years ago were smaller than our modern dogs, and in my mind, all of them deserve to be excavated, studied, and catalogued. He chose instead to finance the work of Professors Marsh and Cope, who are battling it out right now to find the most gargantuan monsters of all, including the *Tyrannosaurus Rex*, the beastliest and most dangerous theropod of all. It's a perfect specimen to seek out if frightening children is your objective, but of limited interest to those of us looking at the bigger picture of flora and fauna in ancient Colorado."

Katarina brought a bottle of port to the table and poured three glasses. "We considered filing a homestead claim for this area, but, instead we made an appeal to the Department of the Interior to declare nearly 20,000 acres on and around the bluff to be of rare and important scientific value. Claybourne himself supported the petition, no doubt so he would not have to worry about having neighbors on his northern flank. In short order, the petition was granted, and we were given permission to stay and work for as long as we wished."

Von Sievers emptied his glass. "I will echo what your friend Marshal Masterson said about Claybourne. He is as powerful as he is dangerous, and you must understand that if you go up against him you are also challenging every sheriff, constable, and judge he owns."

"Which is every damn one of the sons-of-bitches," Katarina added with a laugh.

The sun had settled in behind the western hills by the time they finished dinner. Katarina lit the oil lamps and Von Sievers opened a new bottle of port. Then he and his wife took up their instruments and began to play. Thomas seldom envied any person or their circumstances. As he sat back in a comfortable chair and listened to the haunting strains of a Bach Prelude played by his new friends with exceptional passion and expertise, he fought the urge to wonder what life might have been like if Angela had not walked away from him that night in the hospital sixteen years ago.

He had no regrets about the life he had lived, including the women he had been distracted by along the way. He knew in his heart that he would always be a wanderer. It was his fate. And yet, as he watched Von Sievers and Katarina play their instruments with a shared intimacy he had experienced only once, on that single, shining evening with Angela, Thomas felt the familiar onset of the melancholy that dogged him anytime he settled in one place–or with one person–for too long.

He was about to confront a dangerous, unpredictable man. And even if he had nothing to do with Rosalilia's kidnapping that man would probably treat him as an enemy for merely asking the question.

As the last notes of the Prelude faded away in a perfect, harmonic conclusion, he took a final sip of port. Tomorrow the waiting would be over.

NINETEEN

Claybourne Ranch

The outriders galloped towards him when he was still a mile and a half out from Langton Hall on the Claybourne Ranch. He saw the dust kicked up by their horses before he could make out the three men. Thomas figured he'd let them do the hard riding in the afternoon heat, so he pulled Ulysses off the trail and waited for them in the cool shadow of a lodgepole pine.

A few minutes, later the riders swept up and formed a line across the trail to prevent him from moving forward. Their hands rested on their revolvers as the leader's horse took two steps in his direction. He looked Thomas up and down before he spoke. The man was smart enough to know the difference between an unemployed trail hand and a gentleman. He figured Thomas to be somewhere in the middle of that continuum; dangerous enough to watch warily and be ready to shoot on the spot, but just refined enough–and possibly influential as well– to be someone the boss might not want left dead on the side of the trail.

The leader cocked his hat back and asked, "You lost, friend?"

"I don't believe I am, not if this is Claybourne Ranch."

"It is, and you are trespassing, least wise you are if you weren't invited. Is that the case?"

Thomas shook his head. "No, I don't have an invitation. Is this how Mr. Claybourne greets all of his guests?"

"Actually, pard,' this is as warm as the welcome gets for folks who think they can just meander on up to the house when they feel like it."

Thomas smiled. If Claybourne kept this tight an eye on the approach to his house, he could only imagine how many guns were on watch inside the property.

"I'd like you to take something to your boss," he said. Then he reached back towards his saddlebag, only to hear three pistols cock as one. "Easy boys. Just getting a card." He kept an eye on the revolvers pointed at his head as he reached into the bag and pulled out a small leather wallet. He held it up for the men to see and then pulled out a single business card. The riders holstered their guns and Thomas leaned forward and handed the card to the leader. He considered asking the man if he could read but figured he had been extended all the hospitality he was going to get for the day.

The leader held the card close to his face. "Colonel Thomas E. Scoundrel, USA, Retired," he read aloud. "Fifth Avenue Hotel, New York City."

"My name is Moncton. You are a long way from home, Colonel. You have business with Mr. Claybourne?"

"I do. If you would be kind enough to take that card to him, I believe he will want to see me."

The rider nearest the leader spat a stream of tobacco juice onto the ground. "You expect jes' cause you got a fancy calling card that the boss will ask you to supper?" The other riders laughed.

"The question you should be asking is what your boss is going to do when he finds out I was here to see him, and you ran me off."

The riders exchanged glances. Then the leader said, "Elias, you run this back to the house. We'll follow along slow. If Mr. Claybourne invites the Colonel in, that'll be fine. If he don't, well, then me and the Colonel is going to have us a little chat about the importance of good manners." Elias took the card and rode off at a hard gallop. Moncton and the other rider flanked Ulysses and headed towards Langton Hall at a steady, flat walk.

A half mile on, the narrow road turned to follow the path of a clear, wide stream. They rounded a bend and heard a commotion in a stand of cottonwoods along the creek bank. Two cowhands emerged from the brush hauling an Indian boy of thirteen or fourteen by the scruff of his neck. The boy was shoeless and wore a loose shirt and baggy trousers. He was holding a sapling fishing pole.

Moncton reined to a halt, and the other rider pulled close to Thomas and took hold of Ulysses's bridle. The three men waited as the cowhands dragged the struggling boy over beside them.

"Damn Cheyenne whelp was fishing at the rocks again," said one of the men. "Second time this month we caught his sorry red ass down there."

"You didn't put the fear of God into him properly the first time?" asked Moncton.

One of the cowhands loosened his grip on the boy's shirt and delivered a hard open palmed blow to the side of the boy's head. Thomas saw tears form in the boy's eyes, but the child made no noise.

"He's a simple one," said the cowhand who had just belted the boy. "Doesn't know day from night, as far as I can tell. Can't talk, neither."

"Yes, apparently you didn't show him the error of his ways when you should have. You won't make that mistake again. When he goes back to Red Elk's village this time, we'll send a clear message along with him that even those ignorant prairie fleas will be able to understand."

"Yes, sir, Mr. Moncton, we sure won't make no mistake this time. We'll beat him real good."

"I think we can do better than a whipping," said Moncton. He pulled a skinning knife from his belt and handed it to one of the cowhands. "Is the boy right, or left-handed?"

"He had his pole in his right hand."

"Take him over to that rock and cut off his right thumb. And hack off his hair too. He won't be able to use a bow without a thumb, and he won't be able to sit with the men if he has no hair." Moncton smiled at his own ingenuity.

His men's faces remained impassive as they were given the brutal order; their expressions betrayed no surprise or reluctance. They simply nodded in unison and then dragged the boy towards a flat boulder at the side of the road. It was clear that Moncton and his men had meted out this kind of punishment before.

Thomas had seen enough. "You're going to cut off his thumb just for fishing in Mr. Claybourne's stream? Would he want that?"

Moncton laughed. "Mr. Claybourne would have us cut off more than his thumb, Colonel, but I figure since he is some kind of mental retard, there ain't much possibility of him mountin' one of them Cheyenne gals and making no offspring. A thumb will do."

Thomas yanked his bridle free and rode over to the boulder where the cowhands had splayed the boy across the rock and were trying to hold down his arm. The boy kept struggling, and one of the men balled up his fist and smashed it into his face. Blood spurted from his nose and lips, but he made no sound or complaint. He lay still and stared defiantly into the sky.

Thomas's right hand went to his holster. "That's enough. Let the boy up, now."

The men holding the boy down turned their heads in Moncton's direction. How far was he willing to go to make this punishment happen? "You thinkin' you'll take all four of us on over a little thing like this?" asked Moncton. "This ain't your business. We deal with trespassers as we see fit, and this little antelope turd has had his run of luck. It ends today. If we don't punish him proper, every son of a pus-sacked squaw in that village will feel free to come on our land and steal our fish. Now, back off, Colonel."

Thomas nudged Ulysses a step closer to the rock. "You've made your point, Moncton, and your men have demonstrated their bravery. Let's call it a day, shall we?" He tightened his grip on the Colt.

The four of them could take this crazy bastard out, thought Moncton, but he'd probably get at least one of them when the gunplay began. It was even odds as to which of them would be the winner of that .45 caliber prize. Not a bet he'd care to take at the Faro table.

Moncton was in a corner, but he wasn't backing down. He and the other mounted rider slowly drew their revolvers. Thomas pulled his, pointed it at the ground, and cocked the hammer back.

The boy's nose was still bleeding and in the hot afternoon sun the blood turned black against the light-colored rock. Thomas swung Ulysses around slowly so that he was not in a direct line of fire between the men holding the boy down and Moncton and his man. He knew this wasn't so much a stalemate as it was just a bucket of choices that ranged from bad to damn bad.

Moncton thought through his own list of options; if he shot the damn fool, it might turn out that the boss really did want to see him. Plus, he figured this Scoundrel fella probably knew how to use that hog-leg, and more than likely, one of his men was going to end up dead. Or he could let the Colonel have his way and release the boy, in which case he would lose face with his men, and have his ass handed to him by Claybourne if it turned out he didn't care less about meeting the Colonel.

Moncton and Thomas exchanged a hard stare. Then Moncton decided the standoff had gone on long enough. He reined his horse back, keeping his revolver pointed at Thomas. His partner did the same. Thomas kept his pistol pointed at the ground but got ready to raise it and begin firing. Moncton first, he decided, and then his man. Two shots each. The men holding the Indian boy on the rock would let him go when the firing started and reach for their own weapons, but Thomas should be a beat or two ahead of them. That would be plenty.

The sound of a galloping horse brought the slow-motion standoff to a momentary pause. A second later, Elias appeared from around the bend at a full gallop. He reined up beside Moncton, took in the scene, and said, "You fellars fixin' to shivaree without me?"

Moncton didn't take his eyes off Thomas as he replied, "The Colonel felt he had some cause to interfere with us for chastising that little red runt for trespassing. We were just about to wrap up the conversation."

Elias removed his hat and wiped his forehead with a bandana. "Maybe you'll want to hold off on that for the time being, boss. Mr. Claybourne says we should bring the Colonel up to Langton Hall. He asked the housekeeper to prepare a room and told the chef to make something special for dinner. Looks like the Colonel here is our guest."

Moncton reluctantly slipped his revolver back into its holster and the cowhand and Thomas did the same. Then Moncton rode over beside Thomas. "I don't understand why any white man would take things that far for a redskin-especially one he doesn't even know," he said.

"Maybe I just believe in fair fights. Now, as it appears I am Mr. Claybourne's guest for the evening, I would take it as a personal favor if you would let that boy go."

Moncton motioned to the men holding the boy down. They freed his arms and he sat up and wiped the blood from his face with his sleeve. Thomas rode over to the boulder and handed him a canteen. The boy drank deeply and splashed a little water on his nose and split lip.

"Don't take this as some kind of pardon, boy," said Moncton. "You come back on this land, there won't be any champions standing up for you. This was your one and only lucky day. Got that?"

The boy did not acknowledge Moncton's comment. He slid off the rock and handed back the canteen. Then he nodded to Thomas, turned, and trotted off over a low rise.

❖

When they rode under the timber gate at the entrance to Langton Hall a few minutes later the road transformed from red dirt to crushed rock that had been hauled from some distant quarry. Moncton pointed Thomas towards the hitching post beside the house that was reserved for guests. As his men headed to the stable, Moncton said, "A boy will look after your horse, Colonel. Just tie him there, and he will be along presently. He will bring your saddle bags to your room too. Go on up to the house along the walkway, seeins as they are expecting you."

Thomas couldn't help himself. He turned to Moncton and said, "Thank you. Perhaps we can have that talk about manners some other time."As he guided Ulysses towards the house, he heard Moncton spit on the ground behind him.

Claybourne had planted a grass lawn, a feature very few of even the grandest homes in the east could boast. It was bordered by manicured hedges and crisscrossed with pea-gravel walkways. In the center of the lawn was a ten-foot- high Italian stone fountain. Three life-size marble muses stood on a base in the center of the bottom tier with their heads supporting the elaborately carved tiers above them. Water poured out of each of the muses' pitchers into a pool by the aid of some mechanism Thomas could not see.

The main house was built in a style that reflected Noah's English heritage, with practical adaptations made necessary by both the Colorado climate and the availability of building materials. The steeply pitched, asymmetrical roof featured three front gables and two chimneys made of brown and red brick. The outer gables had double windows with elaborate fretwork around the peaks, and the middle gable sheltered a small balcony outside the second-floor bedroom. The walls were built with light-colored brick, and the bottom floor was considerably wider than the top. A shingled porch wrapped around the house, and the gable-shaped structure over the steps was centered perfectly in the middle of the structure. Three sets of double windows fronted the bottom floor on each side of the main entry doors, and Thomas counted eight wooden columns with fluted bases supporting the porch roof. A barn-red railing that ran the length of the porch was covered with dozens of flower-filled terracotta planters under which sat a row of neatly trimmed bushes. Thomas could only imagine the cost of constructing such a house out here on the edge of the plains.

He wrapped Ulysses's reins around a post at the side of the house and followed the Mexican tile walkway up to the porch. He removed his hat, brushed the dust from his vest, and went up the stairs.

There was movement behind the opaque leaded glass in the entry door. It swung open, and a smiling Noah Claybourne extended his hand.

❖

TWENTY

Langton Hall

"Wouldn't you agree, Colonel Scoundrel, that absent their stupendous accomplishments in winemaking there would be little reason for the country of France and its boorish people to even exist?"

Thomas raised his Baccarat wine glass to his host and gave the remarkable deep ruby red Michelot Nuits-Saint-Georges Pinot a swirl before taking another sip.

"I would certainly agree that this Pinot may be the finest wine I have ever tasted, Mr. Claybourne. My compliments on your selection."

Claybourne accepted the flattery with feigned indifference and a shrug of his shoulders. "Amassing my cellar has been a lifelong pursuit, one which I am grateful my daughter is now assisting me with."

Thomas raised his glass to Hyacinth, who nodded demurely in reply. He had struggled to keep his eyes from wandering from her doe-like, violet eyes to the ivory swell of her breasts, but the combined effect of her low-cut, iridescent green dress with an emerald pendent nestled happily in her bosom had doomed that attempt. He suspected that Hyacinth was aware that he had thrown in the towel, but she gave no hint of being offended. In fact, it seemed to him that the more he drank in her physical charms, the more engaged and animated her conversation became. As the evening progressed from drinks on the veranda to dinner in the formal dining room Thomas felt a special appreciation for the novitiate monks in medieval monasteries whose hands were tied to their bedsteads at night to prevent them from indulging in the forbidden joys of the onanistic *ménage à moi.*

"My wine purveyor said that drinking this pinot is like listening to the earth singing to the sky," Hyacinth was saying. "Of course, this vintage pre-dates the Phylloxera blight that has been devastating French vineyards for the past twenty years. Now it appears that the only way the French will be able to save their wine industry is by grafting their native vines onto root stock imported from California."

Claybourne chuckled. "*Quelle Horreur*. Can you imagine the shame and embarrassment of those arrogant vintners who have been reduced to pleading with the clods of the American West to rescue them from that tiny aphid?" He raised his glass: "To the sweet ironies of life, and the visitation of lady justice upon the smug Frenchies, eh, Colonel?"

Before he could reply the pocket doors leading from the kitchen slid open and two servers entered with covered silver platers which they placed on warming stands in the center of the table. Another server followed close on, and soon the table was covered with dishes.

At Claybourne's signal the kitchen staff uncovered the platters and began to prepare the plates. First up was a cold gazpacho soup loaded with fresh vegetables and topped with chiffonade of basil. It was followed by a simple, mildly sweet frozen fruit sorbet to cleanse their palates. Then, char-grilled tomatoes and onions with olive oil were presented alongside warm, crusty bread with butter and chives. The servers then set down gold-rimmed bone china plates on which they laid mesquite-grilled rosemary and garlic-crusted lamb chops over a bed of pine-nut rice pilaf. Two more bottles of the Saint-George Pinot made their way to the table, and, for a brief while at least, Thomas's senses were diverted from Miss Clayborne's bountiful allure to the extraordinary balance of flavors, smells, and textures coming from the kitchen of Langton Hall's chef.

Thomas felt a twinge of sadness when the table was cleared and the empty pinot bottles were whisked away. The evening had been bookended perfectly by Hyacinth's captivating presence and the superlative meal, and Claybourne had been every inch the perfect host. He inquired about Thomas's life after Pebble Creek Ridge, his friendship with the famous Wild West showman William F. Cody, and even asked for his observations about Von Sievers and the ongoing work at Dinosaur Bluff.

Hyacinth went into detail about the fishing tournament that would take over the ranch at the end of the summer. It was her responsibility to organize the contest, care for the guests, and manage the thousand details required to make such a major event a success.

"One of our guests this year will be the celebrated author, Mark Twain. Do you know his work, Colonel?" she asked.

"I have a copy of his book, *Roughing It,* in my saddle bag. I can't remember any time I have laughed so hard while reading."

"He is also something of an oenophile, whose personal cellar, I understand, is the finest in Connecticut," added Claybourne. "We will have a great deal to talk about at dinner."

"Didn't he say that the works of the great authors were like fine wine, while his were merely like water?" asked Hyacinth.

"To which he added, I believe, 'on the other hand, *everybody* drinks water,'" said Thomas. Hyacinth's soft laugh intertwined with his, and he watched her eyes widen and sparkle with a hint of what might lay ahead.

It had been a dinner for the ages, and he wished the evening could go on forever. But it was time to for Thomas to explain the purpose of his visit, to ask Claybourne about his man Matthew Cord, and to do all he could to discern if the most powerful man in Colorado had anything to do with the events surrounding Rosalilia's kidnapping.

For his part, Noah Claybourne was ready to learn why the Civil War hero turned adventurer had journeyed across the country and shown up unannounced on his doorstep. He did not like surprises.

❖

Noah lit a fresh cigar, blew out the match, and said, "Will you join me in my library, Colonel? I'm sure you have much to talk about."

Thomas rose, took Hyacinth's hand, and thanked her for the wonderful evening. She held his hand a moment longer than required by etiquette, and as she turned to walk away her breast brushed softly against his shoulder. She raised her head, and her violet eyes looked deep into his. Not quite an invitation,Thomas thought, but clearly a signal that the dance was well underway.

He turned and followed Claybourne across the living room and into a comfortable, oak paneled library. Bookshelves lined one wall from floor to ceiling and two leather club chairs faced one another in the center of the room, each with its own small side table. Noah went to the sideboard and retrieved a bottle of port and two glasses.

He held a glass out and said, "Unless you would prefer a single-malt scotch?"

"This is just right."

Noah poured for them both, set the bottle on Thomas' table, and settled into his chair.

"I appreciate that the skills of my chef are widely celebrated," Claybourne began in a slow, deliberate voice, "and I don't underestimate the appeal of my wine cellar to one with tastes as refined as yours, or the charms of my daughter as a hostess. But I don't expect that is why you have traveled all the way from New York City to see me."

Thomas regarded his host carefully before replying. Claybourne, thin and tall and angular, was sitting back in his chair like a coiled rattlesnake at rest. When it came to rattlers, Thomas knew that a strike could come in a split second, without sign or warning.

He chose his next words carefully. "I have come to ask for your help."

Claybourne seemed genuinely surprised. "My help?" He shook his head. "I am flattered. Of course, it seems strange that man as famous as you, someone who doubtless has friends at the highest levels, would need my assistance. Are you in trouble, Colonel? Or might you be seeking capital for some new business you are starting?"

"No, nothing like that. I am looking for news of a friend who has disappeared."

"Really? Have you gone to the authorities? I'm afraid I wouldn't know how to help with a manhunt. It *is* a manhunt?"

Thomas could tell that Claybourne had been thrown off by his blunt reply and that he genuinely had no idea why he had come to Langton Hall. "My friend Diego de San Martín was engaged several weeks ago to Rosalilia Verján, whose father was the Minster of the Interior for Mexico."

"Was?" inquired Claybourne in a voice devoid of feeling.

"Minister Verján was murdered on the night that my friend and Rosalilia were engaged. His home was ransacked and set on fire, his daughter was kidnapped, and my friend was grievously wounded."

Claybourne reached into his vest pocket for a match and relit his cigar. It was hard for Thomas to read his face in the lamp light.

"A distressing business, I am sure," said Claybourne. "And this happened in Mexico, you say?"

"Yes, in the city of Cuernavaca."

"Which is, what, more than fifteen hundred miles from here?"

Thomas nodded. He was good at poker and among the best at bluffing when he had a weak hand, but Claybourne's face did not betray even the slightest change in emotion. His eyes did not flicker or narrow, his lips did not draw back, his breathing did not change. If he knew anything at all about Rosalilia he was doing a masterful job of hiding it.

"Your friend is recovering?" asked Claybourne.

"All I know is that he was still alive in a hospital in Mexico City two weeks ago. I have no other news about him."

Claybourne nodded with an expression that was a mix of concern and empathy. Perhaps the man truly didn't have anything to do with all of this, Thomas found himself thinking. Noah stubbed out his cigar in a crystal ashtray and said, "These are terrible events, Colonel. I wish the best for your friend and his fiancée, of course. Still, I am uncertain where I fit in any of this, or why you felt that coming to me might help you to find the young lady. Surely, you don't believe that her kidnappers would not have brought her all the way here to Colorado?"

He decided it was time. "My friend was shot twice, but before he lost consciousness, he was able to make out the face of the man who was directing the assault and kidnapping."

Noah leaned forward. For the first time, Thomas saw something in his eyes other than mild curiosity or sympathy. A faint glimmer, a trace, a hint of shifting emotion.

"And?" Noah finally asked.

"Diego recognized the man as Matthew Cord, a mining engineer in your employ."

Noah blinked hard. He took a sip of port and said, "That is simply not possible. Mr. Cord is no kidnapper, nor would he have reason to harm anyone in Mexico. He is my employee, yes, and a very good one. But his job is identifying, extracting, and shipping minerals from Mexico to the United States, not murdering government officials and burning their homes. Your friend is mistaken. Preposterously mistaken."

Thomas went silent. Claybourne reached for the wine and said, "If I may ask, Colonel, with your friend in the hospital, how were you informed of these events?"

"I received a telegram in New York and was asked to come to Colorado as quickly as possible to meet with…" He hesitated for a moment, thinking how best to describe Itzcoatl. "To meet with a trusted friend who was with Diego during the attack. He told me everything I have shared with you."

"A trusted friend," repeated Claybourne.

"Someone I would trust with my life."

"And has this friend accompanied you in your search?"

"He has returned to Mexico," Thomas lied, "to be with Diego until he has recovered."

"Have you taken this story to anyone else? To the US Marshal, or the county magistrates, for example?"

Thomas lied again. "No, Mr. Claybourne. Only to you."

Claybourne went to the window, where he stood with his hands clasped behind his back. The light of the first quarter moon illuminated the splashing waters in the Italian fountain, and in the distance, lanterns burned low on the porch of the ranch-hand's bunkhouse.

"I hope that you can appreciate that news of this kind is most distressing. But I feel honor-bound to do everything in my power to assist you." He held his hand out. "Please, accept my help."

He rose and took Claybourne's hand. The man's grip was exceptionally strong and his expression was sincere and forthright. I am either losing my ability to read people or this man really doesn't know anything about Rosalilia and Diego, he thought.

"My field superintendent is here for the week, going over the account books," said Claybourne. "I am going to have a servant fetch him from the guest house and join us. He is privy to all my operations both here and abroad, including in Mexico. Let's find out if he has heard anything about this situation. I will only be a moment."

Claybourne stepped out of the library and Thomas went to the window and looked up into the star-swept sky. It appeared that Claybourne had not ordered Cord to attack Rosalilia's family, which meant that the mining engineer must have acted on his own. Even if that were true, however, he was still going to track the man down, with or without Claybourne's help.

A minute later he heard footsteps in the hall. There were voices, and he started to turn to greet Claybourne and the superintendent. But before he could move, something heavy struck him on the back of the head. Bursts of light exploded across his brain, and he crumpled down on one knee.

Then he was hit again, and the lights went out.

❖

TWENTY ONE

Claybourne Ranch

Moncton stood over Thomas's body, enjoying the sight of the famous hero unconscious and sprawled on the floor.

"What the hell did you hit him with?" asked Matthew Cord. "Boss doesn't want him dead."

Moncton held up a blacksmith's hammer. The two-pound head was wrapped in a heavy wool sock. "Didn't break the skin, but he is going to have the mother of all headaches when he comes to."

Elias joined the two men in the library and together they carried Thomas down the hall and out a side door, where a buckboard and team stood waiting in the cool night air. Claybourne was leaning casually against a porch column, quietly smoking his cigar.

"You want us to do him here or wait 'till we get him out in the brush?" asked Cord.

Claybourne flicked his cigar into a terracotta planter. "Is that as far ahead as you can think? Shoot him, bury him beneath some rocks, and expect that no one will come looking for him?"

Cord shrugged. Seemed to him that once a man was dead there wasn't much use fretting about what might happen next.

"Get him in the wagon, and cover him with a buffalo robe," said Claybourne. "Then saddle his horse and bring him around." Elias went off for the horse while Cord and Moncton loaded Thomas into the back of the wagon.

When Elias returned with Ulysses a few minutes later, Claybourne told him to make sure Thomas's Colt and holster were in the saddlebags.

"What are you fixing to do, Mr. Claybourne?" asked Moncton.

"Colonel Scoundrel is going to have a fatal accident at the Tamayo Ravine. That's a four-hour ride, and just off the ranch property. The trail along the ravine is pretty well-traveled, and that is an important detail for making this work."

Cord shot Moncton a quizzical look. When he killed somebody, it was a foregone conclusion that it would be in everyone's best interests to keep the body from being found.

"You can't simply shoot a man as well-known as the colonel and hope no one asks questions," said Claybourne. "For God's sake, there is a framed poster of him taking on the entire Confederate Army at Pebble Creek Ridge hanging in every damn saloon in America. That's why we are going to make sure that his death is an accident. Moncton and Elias will take him and his horse to the ravine, where he will have the unfortunate luck to fall a couple of hundred feet onto the rocks below."

Cord laughed. "And the horse?" he asked.

"Leave him at the top of the ravine. He looks well-trained; he will wait for a good day or more for the colonel to return. By that time, someone should come along the trail and find the horse, and with a little effort, see the colonel's body on the rocks. They'll go for help, and when they haul the body up and find no signs of foul play, the county magistrate will declare it an accident. The good colonel will merit a headline or two in the newspapers back East, and that will be it. He will be gone and forgotten."

Elias tied Ulysses to the back of the wagon and Moncton climbed up into the driver's seat. Elias checked to see that Thomas wasn't stirring and then swung up beside his partner.

"Make sure his revolver is loaded and in his holster when you send him over the edge," said Claybourne. "When they find him, there can be no sign that anything was amiss before he lost his footing and toppled into the abyss."

Moncton snapped the reins and the wagon set off towards the hills to the east.

⁂

Hyacinth watched the men load Thomas into the wagon from her upstairs bedroom window. She could not hear what her father was saying but she had no doubt that Colonel Scoundrel had paid his first and only visit to Langton Hall. She stepped over to the dressing table mirror and picked up a hairbrush. It was a shame that she wouldn't see him again. He was just the kind of man who could bring her some measure of amusement–for a short while at least. Not many of the right kind of men made their way out to the ranch these days; she was going to have to talk with her father and ask him not to be so quick on the draw next time.

Claybourne saw the curtain's rustle in his daughter's bedroom window. He sighed; he was going to catch hell from her–again. At least she understood what it took to grow and manage an empire like his. Someday she would be the mistress of Claybourne Ranch and its far-flung enterprises, a job in which there was no room for pity or regrets. In his heart he suspected she had already learned that lesson quite well.

The mining engineer stepped up onto the porch. "What about me?" he asked his boss.

"You are going back to Mexico, tonight. Take my private rail car from Denver, and no more than three men; I don't want you to arouse suspicions. Find the hospital where Diego de San Martín is recuperating, and see to it that he has, shall we say, a terminally serious setback."

Cord smiled. "It shouldn't be hard to find him. Everyone knows his family, and there are only one or two places a family as wealthy as his would take a family member for treatment."

Claybourne stepped to the edge of the porch and looked out across the prairie. The wagon was still faintly visible under the light from the summer stars. "One more small matter. The colonel said that San Martín had someone helping him in his search for his fiancée. That man came to Trinidad to meet with Scoundrel and has now returned to Mexico. Find him, and make sure he does not interfere with us again."

"I will do that. What about the Verján woman?"

"You have her at the line shack up in the Chambour Hills?"

"Yes, and two of my men are with her."

"They are clear that she is not to be touched, or harmed in any way?"

Cord nodded. "They understand that if they so much as pinch one of her titties I will cut their balls off and shove them down their throat."

Claybourne shook his head. The engineer was not exaggerating to please his boss. Matthew Cord did not possess a single redeeming quality. He was more feral than human and simply being in his presence made one feel unclean. And that, thought Claybourne, is precisely why he is invaluable to me. With Colonel Scoundrel, San Martín, and his accomplice gone, the only outside connections between the Mexican scheme and Noah Claybourne would be extinguished. Their plans would proceed without delay and in a matter of four or five months the maps of the United States and Mexico would be redrawn, Claybourne would amass vast new power, and he would become the undisputed kingmaker of American politics.

There was still the matter of Miss Rosalilia Verján, of course, waiting to learn her fate at Cord's mountain retreat. Until he saw her in person when Cord arrived from Mexico, he had intended to use her as a negotiating chip, should it come to that. But when he stepped into Cord's cabin and saw her tied to a wooden chair he was rocked to the core by her resemblance to his dead wife. He certainly had no romantic illusions that Miss Verján would consent to marry him. What she was going to do, however, was going to be every bit as satisfying. That thought brought a smile to Claybourne's face, and the resurgence of a familiar itch.

❈

Two hours out from Langton Hall, Elias heard a noise coming from the back of the buckboard. He climbed out of his seat to get closer and heard Thomas groaning under the heavy buffalo robe. Elias pulled the robe back and saw that the colonel was rolling his head slowly from side to side.

"The boy is coming around," he said to Moncton.

"You keep that sumbitch quiet," Moncton replied. "We got another couple of hours to go, and sunrise won't be far behind that. I want this bastard on his way to the bottom of that ravine before daylight."

Elias cut a plug of tobacco, drew his revolver, and sat against the sidewall of the wagon with the barrel pointed lazily in Thomas's direction. "If you can hear me, son, you best lie still. We'll get you out of this fix but only if you don't try to get yourself up."

Thomas could barely make out what Elias was saying. His vision was misted over, and the back of his head was throbbing so hard he thought it was going to explode. He tried to focus his eyes, but between the pain and the bouncing of the wagon as it rattled across one rut after another he just ended up becoming so nauseous that he had to turn his head and vomit.

"Oh, hell, boy, why'd you have to go and do that?" grimaced Elias. "He fetched up, Moncton, and now we got to smell that spew all day."

Moncton turned his head and said, "Find something to clean him up with. Boss wants him to take that tumble all nice and clean like."

Elias found a pile of oily rags in one corner of the wagon. He mopped up as much vomit as he could and gave a cursory wipe across Thomas' face. "Colonel, what in the hell did you eat for dinner? Smells like two dead skunks in a shit factory during a heat wave."

Dinner, Thomas thought through the veil of pain and queasiness pouring through his body. Yes, the lamb, the Saint-George pinot, Hyacinth's violet eyes. A million years ago. His eyes closed and he drifted away again.

❖

The wagon reached Tamayo Ravine just before daybreak. The five-mile-long slash in the skin of the earth was the product of centuries of erosion. It was fifty yards wide at its narrowest point and nearly one hundred yards across at its widest. There were no bridges across the ravine, so travelers had to ride completely around it before they could continue on their paths. In the winter a creek cut through the bottom of the V-shaped ravine, but in early July there were only jagged rocks, thorny bushes and a few struggling oak and pine trees clinging to the steep sides above the bone-dry creek bed.

Moncton drove along the edge of the precipice until he reached its deepest point. He pulled the wagon to a stop and he and Elias hopped out.

Elias checked to see that Ulysses was still tied securely to the back of the wagon. "Shame to leave this horse behind. He's a keeper."

"Everything has to look like an accident," Moncton replied. "It has to be perfect, and that includes having him found with his horse."

Elias looked down into the wagon, where Thomas was beginning to stir. "If it's all supposed to be so perfect, how are they going to explain why a perfectly healthy man riding a first-class horse managed to get himself into the bottom of that ravine? Don't seem natural."

"I've been thinking about that. What's just about the only reason a man would get down off his horse in the middle of the night?"

"Well, I expect it would be to get out his bedroll and make camp, lessen he strayed upon a loose woman or a full bottle, that is"

"Or to take a leak," Moncton added. He smiled at his own cleverness. "What we're going to do is unbuckle his gun belt and trouser buttons just before we push him over. Folks who find him will figure he went to relieve himself, stubbed his foot on a rock, and fell ass over applecart to the bottom of the gulch."

"I expect that's a pretty good idea, but why would a man meander over to the edge of a cliff in the dark just to walk his dog?"

Moncton laughed. "For the view, you dumb bastard, for the view. You know any man who doesn't appreciate a fine view while he's watering the plants?"

Elias couldn't argue with that proposition. He climbed into the wagon and sat Thomas up. The colonel's chin lolled on his chest for a moment, and then he began to raise his head. His eyes opened and he started to take in the sights around him.

Moncton pulled Thomas's revolver and gun belt from Ulysses's saddlebags and handed them to Elias, who wrapped them around Thomas's waist. Then Moncton dropped the tailgate of the wagon and jumped up beside Elias. He slipped his hands beneath Thomas's arms and Elias took his ankles. Together they pulled the semi-conscious colonel out of the wagon and half dragged him over to a scrub oak a few feet from the edge of the ravine. Elias leaned Thomas back against the tree and helped him to balance.

Moncton stepped in front of Thomas and said, "Don't take this personal or nothing Colonel. It don't mean we are engaged or anything." Then he loosened Thomas's gun belt and unbuttoned the fly on his trousers.

Thomas's vision was clearing, and he could begin to make out the words Elias and Moncton were saying. It was cold and the sun was just beginning to peak above the eastern ridges. He knew he was outside, but he couldn't get his mind to focus through the pounding and the dizziness. He had been whacked good; that's the only thing he was sure of. That and the fact that Claybourne was, in fact, every bit the rattlesnake he had originally thought him to be.

He tried to speak but could only mumble a faint, "Where am I?"

"Now, look who wants to be awake for this little send-off," chuckled Moncton. "Hold his arms tight, Elias. Don't want him doing any harm to himself before we do." He brought his face close to Thomas's. "That wouldn't be good manners, would it, Colonel? I know you wanted to instruct me proper in them. Sorry you won't get that chance."

Thomas felt two pair of hands grab him and hold tight at his elbows. Then he was pulled away from the tree he had been leaning against. He was aware that it was Elias holding his left arm and Moncton holding his right arm. He turned his head and saw Ulysses tied to the back of a wagon. He tried with all his might to clear the fog from his brain and to get his eyes to focus. That's when he realized he was standing on the edge of a cliff. He looked down into the deep, rocky, brush-strewn ravine and it all became clear to him. The wagon ride, Moncton and Elias's conversation, and now, the arms that gripped him tightly as they prepared to hurl him to his death.

He tried to get his arms and legs to obey his brain, to struggle, to fight, but his limbs were like jelly. He could not do much more than turn his head.

That's when Elias said, "Seein's as this is all supposed to look so natural and all, do you figure I ought to piss on his leg, so he'll stink a bit when they find him?"

Moncton let out a belly laugh. "You don't think he's going to piss his own pants the minute he starts flying through the air?"

Elias grinned in reply. "We ready, then?"

"We don't want to toss him off. It's got to be a natural fall. If we throw him, some bright marshal might figure the colonel had himself some help. We've got to get him to the edge and just let him go."

Elias nodded, and the two men began to push Thomas closer to the edge. He reached deep into his innermost reservoir of mental and physical strength, calling upon every fiber of his being to fight what was happening. He grunted, sucked in his breath, and gave it his best effort, but all he managed to do was to pull back a little from the hands that were holding him in an iron grip. It wasn't enough.

They had him right at the edge. He heard their boots dislodge a stream of rocks that rolled and bounced down the steep ravine wall to the dusty creek bed two hundred feet below.

He turned his head towards Moncton. "Why?" he asked in a hoarse whisper.

"Because it just ain't your lucky day, Colonel."

He nodded to Elias, and they released their hold on Thomas's arms. He pitched slowly forward and toppled down into the ravine.

"You have a smooth ride, now," Moncton called.

The sound of Thomas's body crashing into rocks and breaking branches echoed up to where he and Elias were standing. It was too dark to make out how far the colonel was falling, but there could be no doubt that every bone in his body was being snapped like a dried twig.

"Be light soon," said Moncton, "and folks will be coming along the trail. Untie his horse; let's git."

The wagon lurched over a rocky slope and was swallowed into the gray and purple landscape. As the sound of its iron-rimmed wheels faded to a whisper, the cry of an owl floated across the canyon. Ten minutes later, in complete silence, the July sun topped the eastern mountains and bathed the world in light.

Ulysses wandered to the edge of the ravine and looked down.

❖

TWENTY TWO

Tamayo Ravine

Later, the only thing Thomas would remember about the fall was the rush of the wind, the brightness of the sun peaking over distant hills, and the sensation of being stabbed in the side.

He was barely conscious when Claybourne's men dropped him into the ravine like a sack of old garbage, and the rocks he smashed his head against as he somersaulted down the steep bank slammed him into darkness again. What finally woke him up was the excruciating pain he felt in his chest when he gasped for air. Must breathe shallow, he thought. My ribs are broken, and the sharp end of at least one of them is cutting into my insides like a straight razor.

He tried to reach out with his right hand, but his arm didn't respond. Broken, he realized. He wiggled the fingers on his left hand and then raised that arm above his head. So, he had at least one good arm. When he tried to move his legs, it felt like they were made of lead. He could feel them, so he was pretty sure he hadn't broken his back. He ran his left hand over his face and felt congealed blood and dozens of tiny rocks that had embedded into his skin as he rolled down the scarped embankment. There was a gash on his forehead, his nose hurt, and his nostrils were clogged–broken, for sure. He felt a gob of something at the back of his throat, turned his head, and spat out a thick mass of dark blood. Thomas had seen plenty of black blood spit up by soldiers who had been wounded in combat, and he knew that if he coughed up much more, he would be a dead man.

He lifted his head a few inches out of the dirt and looked around. The sun wasn't overhead yet, so it was still morning. All he could see was brush, gravel, and small boulders. Then he raised his head as far as he could and squinted against the bright light. The narrow channel at the bottom was at least one hundred feet below where he lay. That was good news, if he had rolled much farther there wouldn't be an unbroken bone in his body.

He laid his head back on the rocks and weighed his options. He might be bleeding internally, and one arm and perhaps both legs were broken. There was no pain or throbbing deep in his groin, which he knew from the surgeon in the 109th was a sign that his pelvis was probably not broken. That, and the fact that he had only fallen a hundred feet or so when they dropped him over the side, was the only good news he could muster up. Then again, he had no idea how far it was to the top of the ravine, or if Moncton and Elias might be waiting up there to make sure he was dead. If they were gone, was it possible that he was anywhere near a trail or coach road where he might be discovered by someone passing by?

He coughed up more blood–this time bright red–and fought the urge to take another deep breath. Somehow, he had to move. He had to make it to the top of the ravine and then sort out the next step from there. If Claybourne's men were waiting he figured that a quick bullet to the head would be preferable to dying of thirst, bleeding, and exposure on this damn hill. With that thought in mind, he wondered why they hadn't just shot him in the first place and tossed his body into the ravine. Moncton must have wanted him to enjoy a long, slow, painful death.

There was no profit in such speculation right now, he figured. It was time to get moving. First, though, something had brought him to a stop, and it couldn't have been anything good, not given the steepness of the ravine walls. Better figure that out first. He was going to have to sit up to get a bearing on his location, and then he was either going to have to crawl up the hill on his side or his belly. No, that wasn't right. He would have to have to pull himself up the hill using only his left arm. If he couldn't get his legs moving to provide some push–or at least some traction by pressing his boots into the dirt–he was going to be in a hell of a fix.

He gritted his teeth and turned his upper torso slightly to the left. Then he pulled his left elbow back in line with his shoulder, planted his palm firmly in the dirt, and started to push his upper body into a half-sitting position.

That's when a new pain flared in his gut. He looked down and saw that a tree branch about an inch and a half in diameter had pierced his lower right side and was sticking up four or five inches above his abdomen. He dropped his head back onto the dirt. That's what had stopped his fall. He had fallen–or bounced– right on top of the bloody thing with the full weight of his body. He reached over with his left hand and gingerly rocked the branch a half inch in each direction. The movement set off a torch in his belly.

He closed his eyes and felt the urge to laugh. What else could he do? The branch had stopped his uncontrolled tumble and saved his life–for the moment, at least. If he had fallen two inches more to the right, the stick would have perforated his bowels or stomach, maybe both. He would have bled out and been dead by now. The branch must have only penetrated his flesh; not that such a fortuitous point of puncture made much of a difference. He was nailed to the side of this desolate ravine like a butterfly pinned to a cardboard science display, and the odds that he could pull himself off the jagged spear and crawl to the top of the hill were looking pretty damn bleak.

He let his left arm fall to his side and willed himself to go to sleep.

❖

When Thomas woke the sun was directly overhead, and it was hot. He rubbed his eyes with his good hand, turned his head, and cleared his throat. He didn't feel any new blood clots, but that was the only positive thing that was happening. He could tell that his face was badly swollen, and his lips were cracked and parched. What he would give for a canteen of cool spring water. His broken right arm throbbed mightily, and the area around the puncture wound in his abdomen was on fire. He still could not move his legs, and now even his shallowest breathing delivered quick, knife-like stabs to his lung. This was the junction of life and death, and while he knew he didn't stand a great chance of making it out of this mess, he sure as hell was going to be dead before nightfall if he didn't give it a try. The three turkey vultures gliding in wide, lazy circles a few hundred feet above him probably agreed with that assessment.

It had to be now. He pushed his upper body a few inches off the dirt with his left hand. The price he paid for that movement was a surge of intense pain where the stick had impaled his side. That little twinge was nothing compared to what was about to happen, he guessed. The way he saw it, he had to give himself one mighty shove to pull his body off the branch. When he did that, he had to immediately turn his torso to the left, so he didn't crash back down on the stick and get skewered a second time. What little strength he had was draining quickly. One chance, that's all he had.

From out of nowhere, Angela's presence gently infused his thoughts. He saw her face, felt her touch, and heard her soothing voice in the stillness of the sunbaked ravine. Then he was reminded of Walt Whitman's parting words in the hospital: *"Do anything, lad, but let it produce joy."* His 33rd birthday was three weeks ago. He wanted to stay alive to produce that joy, and to honor Angela's wish that he live a long, full, meaningful life. He wanted a 34th birthday.

Years ago his Jesuit mentor, Father Broussard, impressed upon him that Newton's first law of motion applied to the way we pursued our lives as much as it applied to the realm of physics. "An object at rest stays at rest, and an object in motion stays in motion–*and so do you*–with the same speed and in the same direction, unless acted upon by an unbalanced force," he often said.

I can remain at rest and die here on this flea-bitten hill, he thought. Or I can get myself in motion and keep pushing forward. As for any unbalanced force on the horizon that could doom his effort to failure, he figured if he could crawl, the vultures circling high above would have to find something a hell of a lot more dead than he was to have for their dinner.

❈

His upper torso was three inches off the ground now. To create enough momentum to pull himself off the branch and over to the left, he would have to push with his left arm and at the same time raise himself at the waist using only his abdominal muscles. Snapping his head forward might help a little, but with his legs immobilized, the strength to make the move had to come equally from his arm and abdomen.

Thomas took the deepest breath he could, sending a bolt of white-hot flame through his chest. He clenched his teeth, leaned his head back, counted to three, and then hurled himself up with every ounce of his remaining strength. There was a sucking noise as the branch pulled out of his belly and exited through his back, and when he twisted to the left, his broken right arm flopped uselessly over his chest. Then it was over, and he collapsed on his left side under the weight of the most agonizing pain he had ever experienced.

He lay motionless under the broiling sun. Blood seeped from the wound in his belly, dribbled across his body and dripped onto the bone-dry ground. The pain was paralyzing, and he could hear air bubbles and gurgling deep in his chest each time he exhaled. The only thing he could move were his eyelids. That's it, he thought. I will never move again. That certainty chilled him, even on this scorching July afternoon.

What a place to die, he thought. What a time to die. As badly as he felt about the dark cloud that was slowly enveloping him and would soon carry him away, he felt worse for Diego and Rosalilia. He would have to break the promise he made to Diego to find out what had become of her, and to bring her home if he possibly could.

He coughed and saw that the blood coming from deep inside was darkening again. Then there was movement a few feet from his head. He turned a few inches and saw one of the turkey vultures hopping towards him, its leathery red head dipping rapidly up and down, excited to begin feasting on the carrion it had been watching for hours from the sky.

"Not yet, you sorry son of a bitch," he whispered in a hoarse voice. He tried to spit at the giant bird, but his mouth was too dry to form any saliva. For his part, the bird was happy to back off a few feet, secure in the knowledge that his dinner would stop moving any minute now, and he could begin to tear away at the soft flesh to his heart's content. In return, Thomas was determined to keep his eyes open and make that damn bird wait a long, long time before it took the first bite.

❖

It occurred to him as he was dying that he had never given much thought to what was going to happen after he took his final breath. His mother read the Bible to him every night when he was a child, and his father had been a practicing Catholic at one point in his life, but the last time Thomas had been inside a church was almost ten years ago. That was in New Orleans, and he had crossed the holy threshold on that occasion only because he was hiding out from the authorities after taking part in an illegal duel with a wealthy businessman. If he had uttered any prayer at the alter that night, it would have been for the mounted posse to bypass the church so he could make his escape.

Whether his destination today was to be heaven or hell, he did not know. He didn't expect that any man really knew, and the more and the louder they blathered on about it–especially in church–the more he figured they had no idea either. He believed in God because he wanted to, not because anyone had ever told him he had to. Of course, his life hadn't exactly been a model of pious decorum. If there were angels keeping score of what he had done right and what he had failed at, he didn't think anybody would make betting odds on him being handed a set of wings and a harp when the vulture hopped over to begin nibbling on his appetizer.

To his surprise, his pain began to fade, and in a few minutes he didn't feel anything. He tried to move his head, but his neck muscles wouldn't obey his brain. He could work his mouth a little and blink, but the rest of his body had shut down.

The vulture was only a few feet away now. He slowly unfurled and then closed his six-foot wide wings, all the while keeping his black, lidless eyes focused on Thomas's face. Probably signaling his friends to get ready for supper, thought the main course.

Should he say a prayer? Is that what dying people did? Before an answer came to mind, however, the angels appeared. Just like that. Their faces came out of nowhere and hovered a few inches above his head. At that same instant, a giant shadow sailed over them, blotting out the sun as it passed. That would be the disappointed vulture flying away, he thought. Nice of the angels not to let the feast begin quite yet.

The angels' mouths were moving, but he could not make out what they were saying. He strained his ears and tried to see through the mist shrouding his vision. They made for a strange pair of heavenly beings, that was for sure. One had a massive, bear-like head with thick curly hair that fell to his shoulders, and an equally dark and unruly moustache and beard. His eyes were the brightest that he had ever seen. The other angel had the face of…an Indian? Three feathers stuck out of his shiny black hair, and his round, red face was marked with two diagonal stripes on each cheek, one yellow, one white. He was missing two front teeth, but his smile was as wide and cheerful as any Thomas could imagine on a human, or an angel.

Suddenly, the prickly rocks and dirt beneath his body vanished. He was floating, suspended in mid-air and drifting higher and higher into the clear, azure sky.

Strange for an angel to be missing his front teeth, Thomas thought as he slipped into the welcoming darkness.

❖

TWENTY THREE

Red Elk's Village, Colorado, July 1882

The old man liked to walk the hills outside the village at midday, where a great oak sat on a rise above the creek with outspread branches that shielded him from the burning sun. He could rest on a tangle of soft dry grass and contemplate the world and the spirits properly, as an elder should do.

This was his twentieth summer as *vehoe*, peace chief, of the nearly two hundred Cheyenne in his care. He had once been *notxevoe*, war chief, of many villages, but that was when he carried a young man's shield on his arm and a young man's pride in his heart. After sixty winters he was nearing the end of his journey. He knew that old men often fluctuated in misery between their fear of death and the torments of old age; they didn't really want to continue living, but they didn't know how to die. He was in no hurry to join his ancestors, but he did not fear the step into the divine light either. He often imagined how bright the heavens would be when he was joined together with the spirits of all those who came before him. There would be not a shadow to disturb the clear sky; the heavens would shine without pause. Day and night alternate only on the human plain below; when he saw the total light for the first time he would understand that until the moment of his death he had been living in darkness. Until then, he believed, his whole life was simply a journey towards a new birth.

When my time comes, he thought, I will leave this body where I found it and give myself back to the Great Spirit.

Red Elk rose from his resting place beneath the oak and looked back towards his village. Game and fish were plentiful this season and the winter had been mild. They had been here for four years, ever since he separated his people from the larger body of Cheyenne who were being moved by the US government to a new reservation in Montana. Colorado was his birthplace, and it was where he married his Arapaho wife and had his children. It was good to return, despite the pressure on him from the Indian Agents and the Claybourne people to give up his village and trek north to the reservation. Had they known how he had survived the cholera epidemic that killed half of all Cheyenne people in 1849 when white settlers rushing to the gold fields of California spread the disease, they would understand why he did not budge. If they were aware of the many battles he had fought, from the Washita River to Mud Springs, they would understand that a warrior, even one as old as he was, would not turn from doing what was right for his people. He had driven Crow and Pawnee raiding parties away from his villages, and he had forged alliances with the Arapahos and Lakotas to hold off attacks by Comanche and Shoshone in the prime buffalo hunting areas along the Platte River. He knew how to conduct war, and he knew how to keep peace.

At the same time, Red Elk had no illusions about his people ever becoming the masters of the plains as they had once been. Forty years ago, he stood on a high bluff and watched a mile-long caravan of Conestoga wagons carrying white settlers along the Emigrant Trail to settlements in Oregon, Utah, and California. His heart broke that day because he knew that his people's way of life was coming to an end. What would become of them now? He adjusted the bowler hat he had purchased at the trading post and unbuttoned his store-bought vest. Then he tightened the laces of the leather boots that were made in great iron factories far to the east.

What will become of us, he smiled to himself? We shall become them, and our souls will vanish in the wind.

Red Elk followed the dusty path back to the village. Two rows of fine tipis were scattered along the creek, where several boys were fishing. A group of young children raced past him, rolling a wooden hoop with a stick, and a girl of fifteen or sixteen paraded slowly past four young men as they brushed out their horses. The chief slowed his pace to see if any of the men would acknowledge the provocative action, and he was pleased to see that Hiamovi stopped brushing his horse long enough to share an open smile with the girl. There would be a wedding feast before winter, thought Red Elk, or sooner if the girl decided to sneak into her intended's tipi some night to close the deal a little more quickly. It would be wise to speak with her father, in any event.

When he reached the center of the village he saw a freight wagon with two men on the seat coming over the rise. The wagon was being pulled by two horses, not the usual four that would be needed to haul a heavy load. A Cheyenne pony and a black Morgan were tied to the back of the wagon, and as it pulled a little closer, Red Elk saw that the burly Scotsman, Hamish Mackenzie was driving, with Four Bears beside him. Several children raced out to greet the men and trotted alongside the wagon as it pulled into the center of the village and stopped.

Red Elk liked Hamish, who called himself a wilderness preacher and carried what he called "The Book" to towns, villages and settlements along the prairie. Red Elk and the rest of the villagers called him Christ-Man. The old chief wasn't so sure about the man's religion, but if the Great Spirit he worshiped permitted a man to hunt and fight and drink and wench as Hamish did, Red Elk was at least willing to share a pipe with him beside a fire under the stars and listen to his stories.

Hamish stepped down off the wagon and greeted Red Elk. The Cheyenne were a tall people, but the mountainous Scot towered over the tallest warrior in the village by at least four inches. His size was enhanced by his long hair and shaggy beard, but what Red Elk found most surprising about the giant was the gentleness of his voice; it was low and melodic and soothing. Hamish was a fine singer, a skill he learned in church in his native Scotland. The people of the village would crowd around the campfire after the evening meal to listen to Hamish sing everything from solemn hymns to rousing–and rowdy–sea shanties.

"Welcome, old friend," said Red Elk. "We did not expect to see you until the fishing games began at Claybourne Ranch some weeks from now."

"And I did not expect to be visiting you," replied Hamish. "I came across Four Bears this morning at the Tamayo Ravine. He found that black stallion wandering along the ledge looking for something on the slopes below. I climbed down the embankment and found this."

He went to the side of the wagon and pulled back a blanket. Thomas lay under it with his head on a bedroll. He was unconscious, and from the way his head was matted in dried blood and his right arm splayed out at an angle, Red Elk could see that he had suffered many injuries.

"This man fell into the ravine, but his horse did not?" asked Red Elk.

"Yes, I thought that strange," replied Four Bears. "But when we carried him up the ravine, I saw that his gun belt and trousers buttons were unfastened."

"What kind of man walks to the edge of a cliff to make water, unless he has enjoyed too much wine."

"Your village was the closest place we could think of bringing him," said Hamish. "Can your people look after him?"

"Do you know who he is?" asked the Chief.

"I looked through his saddle bags. There are calling cards inside that say he is a retired army Colonel. His name is Scoundrel. Thomas Scoundrel."

Red Elk leaned over the side of the wagon and looked down at Thomas. "An old enemy, perhaps? He looks too young to have shared in my fights. But he is a warrior and must be treated with respect."

He called two young men forward. "Lift the colonel with a blanket and carry him to my daughter's tipi. Then bring the healer and his women to the tipi and have them tell me if this man will live or die. If he is to live, he can remain, and we will help him. If he is beyond our medicine have him taken into the brush across the creek and let him die there with only the spirits beside him to prepare him for his journey."

Hamish started to object. If the medicine man pronounced the colonel beyond hope, there was always Claybourne's place, or even the town of Fletcher where he could take him for treatment. But when he looked at Thomas again and heard his short, gasping breaths, he knew that it would be a miracle if the colonel was alive when night came. Cheyenne medicine was his only hope.

He walked beside the men as they carried the colonel down to the creek. A small crowd of children followed them, and the commotion they stirred up brought Red Elk's daughter out of her tipi. She spoke with one of the men, laid her hand on Thomas' forehead and directed them to carry him inside. Then she nodded to Hamish, stepped into the tipi, and closed the flap.

A man could do worse than to see the face of Dawn Pillow above him when he took his last breath, thought Hamish.

TWENTY FOUR

Red Elk's Village

Thomas lay naked on his back on a doeskin blanket in the center of the tipi. Dawn Pillow had washed him gently with soft cloths as White Moon, the medicine man, crushed dried sage and herbs in a stone bowl. Then a woman entered the tipi carrying several jars of unguent pastes to spread on his wounds. She handed a burning stick to the healer, who laid it in the bowl. In a moment the tipi was filled with exotic scents. The medicine man began to lather the oily unguent paste onto his arm, face, legs and abdomen. The area around his belly wound was beginning to fester and swell, and when the healer applied paste to it, he instinctively recoiled and moaned. The medicine man shook his head, stood, and left the tipi. A few minutes later Red Elk stepped through the flap and motioned to his daughter to join him outside. They walked a few feet to the edge of the stream.

"White Moon says this man is already in the shadows and will soon step over to the other side," he said to Dawn Pillow. "He must be moved across the water now and left in the open so that his spirit can pass to the sky unhindered."

Dawn Pillow contemplated the water rushing over the smooth creek stones before she answered. "He could also live, Father. You yourself said that he is an esteemed warrior among his people and deserves our respect. Does he not also deserve the chance to live?"

"He deserves what every warrior does: a good death. That is enough. If it was me lying ill in your tipi, I would want you to let me go."

"And I would, Father, because I respect you, and I know that has always been your wish." She put a hand on Red Elk's shoulder. "But that is what you want for yourself. How do we know what this man wants? You have seen many summers come and go and you have witnessed generations of your seed grow into manhood. This man is young. Shall we deny him the greatest gift that a man can leave to the future?"

Her father turned his head and looked back into the village where children were playing, women were preparing food and doing quill work, and a group of young men were being instructed by an elder in the proper way to skin and butcher a deer.

"Is this the price I pay for sending you to the mission schools?" he asked with a gentle smile. "You will defy your father?"

She kissed him on the cheek and added, "The missionaries taught me to read and write and speak English. No one had to teach me not to defy you. From the day mother died I have respected you and cared for you. I always will."

"But you have not consented to marry any of the eligible men I have presented," Red Elk complained. "How is that showing me respect?"

She laughed. "I will marry the right man at the right time, and I will bear many strong sons and daughters who will make us both proud. What greater respect can I show?"

Red Elk could not argue the point. They had had this conversation many times since she came of age at fifteen. Now she was nearly twenty-five, and she was as stubborn and strong-willed as she was intelligent and beautiful.

"If you choose to care for this man, you must do it alone," he said. "I have spoken to our people and stated my desire. If you take responsibility for his life, no one, not White Moon or the Christ-Man, or any person, may help you. The path to his life or death shall be yours to walk, and yours alone. Consider that well."

Dawn Pillow nodded. Red Elk hugged her and started to walk away. "Father," she said in an urgent tone. He turned, and she said, "Your boot has come unlaced."

He started to look down and then remembered this was a game she had played with him when she was a child. He shook his head with a look of mock exasperation and walked away to join the group that was butchering the deer.

What father could deny anything to a daughter like her, he thought.

❖

Late that night Dawn Pillow changed Thomas's dressings for the third time. She mixed more of the unguent paste and covered his wounds. Then she took two narrow boards and made a splint with rags that she used to keep his broken arm still. Tomorrow she would attempt to set the bones. She had seen White Moon do it many times, and she knew if she waited too long the bones would not knit properly, and his arm would hang useless at his side for the rest of his life.

She pulled a cotton blanket over him and fed him a little soup. He moved his head and groaned occasionally, but for the most part he lay so still that she had to check from time to time to see that he was still breathing. She asked herself again if she was doing the right thing. Then she pulled her bedding close to him, stoked the fire against the night chill, and lay down beside him. If he was still alive in the morning, she was certain he would survive.

❖

Thomas did survive that first long night, only to fall into a pattern of alternating fever and chills that lasted for a week. Dawn Pillow never left his side. She mopped his sweating forehead with a cool cloth when he was feverish and piled buffalo robes on him when he began shivering uncontrollably. Once, despite the thick robes, his teeth were chattering so badly that she removed all her clothes and climbed in beside him, holding his body close to hers to keep him warm.

Despite her father's command that no one help her, a steady trickle of villagers came to the tent each day with soup, clean cloths, and wood for her fire. White Moon sent a boy to her each morning to inquire about Thomas's progress, after which he would send a new blend of herbs and unguents based on her reports. One of his medicines was a supply of dried peyote cactus, along with instructions on how to steep it in hot water to prepare a tea that would help reduce Thomas's pain and speed his healing. Hamish brought his saddlebags with clean clothing and shaving gear, and one of the older women spelled Dawn Pillow each day so she could bathe in the river. Red Elk was the only person who did not visit her. She was not troubled, though; she knew her father had already forgiven her for her defiance.

❖

He had no recollection of anything that happened during his first week in Dawn Pillow's tipi. Night and day, fever or chills, pain or sleep, nothing registered in his consciousness. That changed in his second week of recovery. As the fevers became less intense he became aware of people moving around him and of sounds coming from outside the tipi. He saw fleeting images of a tall, dark-haired woman leaning over him, spooning soup into his mouth, giving him tea, washing him, and once, he even dreamed he felt her warm, naked breasts and thighs rubbing against his freezing skin. He also had another visitation from the two angels who had hovered above him as he bled out on the brushy slopes of the ravine, and he began to experience dreams so realistic that he wasn't sure if he was awake or asleep. They usually coincided with the bitter tea that the young woman gave him in the afternoons. One dream, so real that he could feel the warmth of the sunshine, the chill of the wind, and the taste of food, was about an experience he had after leaving Mt. Pleasant Hospital at the end of the war.

He had retrieved his horse, Cornwall, from the army veterinary hospital on the Potomac River, and was beginning the long journey back to Ohio. The roads out of Washington, DC were clogged with men on horseback, in wagons, and on foot, who were also headed home after four years of brutal fighting. On his first night of travel he followed Walt Whitman's advice to find lodgings. He elbowed his way through a crowd at a roadside inn and introduced himself to the landlord. Although every room was taken, when the landlord learned that Col. T.E. Scoundrel of Pebble Creek Ridge fame was standing before him, he set up a cot in an alcove at the top of the stair landing. Nothing was too good for a bona fide Union hero.

The trip back to Wayne County took two weeks. There was really nothing there for him now, of course; his parents were dead, and the farm had been sold long ago to pay his father's gambling debts. But it was the only place he had any memory of, so he figured it was as good a place as any to think about what to do with his life now. His army pension might be enough to purchase a small farm, or perhaps he could start a business in Wooster. As he ambled west on his eighteenth birthday the only thing he knew for sure was that he had plenty of time to sort it out.

Nearly every farm he passed on the road had some kind of hand-painted sign hanging on a fence. Milk cows for sale, eggs by the dozen, and, especially, help wanted. Most able-bodied men had gone to war, and thousands died in battle. Others were coming back with wounds so severe they would never work again.

On the afternoon he neared his old home, he rounded a bend and saw a small, well-kept farmhouse with a newly painted red barn and a fresh-planted vegetable garden. A sign on a post said, "Help Wanted," and below that, "Apple Pie, 15¢." It was warm for late May, and he was hungry, so Thomas led Cornwall up the hard-packed dirt drive to the front of the house. He hitched the horse to a post, climbed the steps to the porch, and knocked on the door.

A couple of minutes passed, but no one answered his repeated knocking, so he prepared to mount up and ride on. That's when a voice cried out, "Hey there, wait up a minute," and a woman raced around the corner of the house just as he put one foot in the stirrup. What first struck Thomas about her were her flame-red, shoulder length pigtails. Her eyes were cornflower blue, the same color as the long sleeve gingham work shirt that she wore over men's trousers and boots. Everything about her was petite, except for her breasts, which looked as though were about to pop off every button on her shirt. Her freckled face was shining from the all-out run she had just made from the pasture.

"I am sorry it took so long to get up here," she said. "I'm mending the plow so I can get the late summer corn in." She put out one hand; "I'm Titia Freisch."

You certainly are, thought Thomas before clearing his mind and introducing himself.

"Come up to the house," Titia said, "I'll pour you some lemonade."

He re-tied Cornwall to the post and followed Miss Freisch up the stairs and through the screen door. Even from the back she had curves that would be impossible to hide no matter what she was wearing. She invited him to sit in the parlor while she fetched drinks and returned a minute later with two tall glasses of cold lemonade. "Are you on your way home, Colonel?" she asked as she sat down. "Do you have family in Wayne County?"

"I lived not far from here on a farm with my parents. Their name was Scanndréll."

Titia's eyes narrowed. "My daddy knew your daddy. Can't say they were on the best of terms, though."

"I'm afraid I have heard some version of that description of my father since I was a boy. All I can say is that in my case the apple fell a long, long way from the tree."

She laughed. "Is that why you changed your name to Scoundrel?"

"That's another story entirely, but it's probably as good a reason as any."

Titia cleared her throat. "No other family, no wife or children?"

He shook his head. You would think that anyone looking at him would see a young man of only seventeen or eighteen standing in front of them. But, when he was introduced as 'Colonel,' people tended to add a good ten years to his actual age. The power of advertising, he thought.

"And what will you be doing now that have returned home?"

"That is a good question. I have considered farming or opening a small business. Time will tell, I am in no hurry."

"Both of which, I would imagine, require some amount of capital?"

"Army pension, just enough to get a start at something."

The only sound for a minute was the ticking of the mantel clock and the rustling of the curtains on the open window. As he sipped his lemonade, Thomas couldn't help but think that Titia's mind was racing. Perhaps he had overstayed his welcome, and she needed to get back to her chores.

He finished his drink, and said, "I don't want to keep you from your work. The lemonade was fine. And, if you have an entire apple pie, I will happily buy it if you have some paper you can wrap it in."

It was almost as if he had startled her from a nap. She gave him a quizzical look and said, "Going? But there are no inns for miles. It will be dark in two hours. I insist that you stay the night as my guest."

"Miss Friesch, that is very kind of you, but I really couldn't impose. And after all, a single man staying the night in your home–what would your neighbors say?"

She laughed. "It's 1865, Colonel. Times have changed. The war is over, and the old ways will never return. I have a spare room, and I have every confidence that you are a perfect gentleman. It's settled; you are staying."

She stood up, and he could have sworn that she was pulling her shoulders back so that her more than generous bosom became even more pronounced in the form-fitting shirt.

"This is very hospitable of you," he said as he got up. "At the very least, please let me compensate you at the same rate as I would pay at an inn."

Titia nodded. "Let's get your horse settled in. Then I will make dinner."

❃

Thomas explored the barn, vegetable gardens, and the front pasture while Titia made dinner. She said she had twenty acres in corn and had just planted fall wheat. She was only able to get hired help once or twice a month, and so she labored alone seven days a week to keep the farm productive.

He was admiring her laying hens when she whistled out the back door. He washed his hands and face at the pump beside the door and entered the brightly lit kitchen. Her cook stove was a monster, with two separate ovens and a huge fire box. The walls were lined with shelves on which the Delft-blue and white dishes her grandparents carried over from Europe were displayed. The oak dining table in the center of the room could easily seat a family of eight, and Thomas had no doubt that someday, it would. He was equally sure that whoever was sitting at the head of the table when that time came, it would be Titia who was making the big decisions.

He sat at the table as she poured home-brewed beer into a crockery mug. Then she set a bowl of chicken and dumplings on the table, along with a plate of fresh biscuits and honey butter, and two baked apples stuffed with walnuts and brown sugar.

As they ate, she described how her mother had died in childbirth when Titia was ten, and how her father had dropped to the ground with a heart attack while plowing the field just the year before.

"You can appreciate how difficult it is for a woman to run a place like this by herself," she said. "The house and land are paid for, though, so I am not beholden to any bank. My needs are few, and I live simply. Still…." Her voice grew soft, and she looked down at the table with a sly smile, "I can't help but feel it's about time to find a man to park his shoes under my bed, if you'll pardon my being direct."

"No apology needed. No one is going to recover from the damage done by this war unless they are prepared to forgo some of the old customs and take chances."

Titia poured more beer and put a plate of fat strawberries on the table. "It is so refreshing to hear a man speak the facts so bluntly, Thomas. I'm sorry, may I call you Thomas?"

He nodded. The kitchen was very pleasant, the food was the best he had enjoyed in a long time, and truth be told, Titia didn't seem to mind the fact that he was spending a fair amount of time admiring her figure. He helped her clear the table and excused himself to go to the outhouse as she brewed coffee. Then they sat on the front porch, enjoying the mild evening and watching as the stars popped out and spread across the heavens. When a pair of shooting stars streaked across the horizon, Titia volunteered that this was the most enjoyable evening she could remember in ages. He was in complete agreement. If this was what married life was like, maybe he should give it a try someday.

When it grew cool, Titia blew out the lamps and led Thomas upstairs to the guest room. "I'll be taking my bath downstairs now," she said as she handed him an extra blanket. "You are welcome to use the tub in the morning if you'd like."

He thanked her for dinner and said goodnight, but before she turned to go, she bent her head a little to the side and raised her eyebrows at him, as if to say, "Why would you say that?" Then she smiled and headed down to her bath.

He took off his clothes and settled into the comfortable feather bed. He seldom wore a nightshirt, and it was comfortable enough that he even opened the window to let in fresh air. The stars were so bright that he could almost read by them. As he drifted off to sleep, he wondered about the questioning glance Titia had given him when he said goodnight. It would be years before he learned to read women's expressions; if he had possessed that ability tonight, he would have been out the door and on his horse before his hostess's bathwater got cold.

❖

He was on the edge of sleep when he heard the door creak. He sat up, startled, and took a moment to remember that he was still lying on top of the covers stark naked. A little lamp light spilled into the room from the hall, illuminating Titia's figure in the doorway. He was sure he could smell lilacs. As his eyes adjusted to the light, he saw that she was still wearing the gingham shirt, but it was completely unbuttoned, and she wasn't wearing any trousers or undergarments under it.

She walked over to the bed and dropped her shirt on the floor. "I hope you don't mind," she said in a sultry voice. "I wasn't ready for the evening to end."

Titia leaned over and kissed him on the lips and then stood and pulled her pigtails back behind her shoulders. Her breasts were every bit as magnificent as he thought they would be, proud and pouting, with half dollar-sized nipples that were as red as her hair. She rested her hand on his lower stomach, and let it trail down between his legs. When she felt his hardness, she said, "I guess you *don't* mind......." Then she lowered her lips on him, and he was lost.

❖

Thomas woke at dawn to the smell of coffee and lilac, and the feel of an ice-cold stick between his legs. He bolted upright to find Titia straddling his legs, just below his knees. She was nude and were it not for the icicle poking him in the groin, the sight of her amazing breasts and wide-spread legs would have had him rocketing back inside her in a heartbeat.

The last remnant of sleep cleared from his eyes, and he saw that it wasn't an icicle that she was holding between his legs. Instead, it was a fully loaded and cocked revolver. She had the barrel wedged firmly against his testicles, and in a voice that was octaves different than the sweet murmurings she blew in his ear when they were making love the night before, she said, "Good morning. We have business to attend to. If that goes well, there will be more of this..." With that she bent forward and placed a breast against his lips. The revolver stayed parked where it was.

His mind reeled. How could a person transform in a few hours from a passionate and sensitive lover to the coldly calculating monster sitting across his legs? And with a pistol on his balls? He didn't know much of the world, but he knew that he had better choose his next words damn carefully–and then get the hell out of there.

He ran one hand through his hair as he composed himself. "That's quite a good morning kiss, my love," he said in a surprisingly calm and endearing voice. Best to treat this as a lover's comedic gesture, he thought. He reached one hand up to caress her breasts. "But I had a different kind of good morning in mind."

He reached down and carefully guided the revolver away from his crotch. Then he placed her other hand between his legs and began to move it gently back and forth. A look of confusion crossed her face. He could tell she was weighing the circumstance, trying to decide if he was sincere, or if he was merely trying to save his manhood. Thomas knew what she was thinking. But if he was going to prove his sincerity, words alone would not do the trick. He had to do something to prove he wasn't lying, and that meant only one thing.

He kept stroking her breasts with one hand, while keeping pressure on her free hand to keep stroking him. She did not let go of the revolver, but he saw that her breathing was becoming a little more labored. Thomas closed his eyes and concentrated on putting on a physical display that Titia could not ignore. She would be certain that any man who thought that his balls were about to be shot off could not succeed at getting himself back in the saddle. But that's exactly what he had to do now.

He opened his eyes and smiled as warmly as he could. He pulled her down and kissed her full on the lips, all the while keeping her hand moving on him. Whether he was about to be crippled or not, he had to admit that it was starting to feel pretty good. He looked down at himself a moment later and saw that his concentration had paid off. She noticed too.

"Why don't you climb on board," he said quietly. "We'll talk business later."

"Really?" Do you mean that? You aren't lying?"

He reached down with his right hand and pulled the revolver away. He set it on the nightstand and then put both of his hands on her waist and pulled her up and onto him.

"Really," he said as he began to move inside her. She wrapped her arms around his neck and lowered herself onto his chest. When he felt her hips begin to gyrate, he knew he had bought himself a little time. But how was he going to get out of this mess–*and* keep the family jewels intact?

Afterwards, Titia became an animated chatterbox. She lay on her side and went on about how the two of them were going to work the farm, and perhaps raise milk cows and hogs to supplement what they made from corn and wheat. "We can buy more acreage," she said, "and we will be able to hire a full-time hired hand. When the children come–oh, we must get married right away–they will be able to help us, too."

He felt awful. His second romantic experience, and it had turned into a nightmare. He loathed liars and cheaters; he knew the pain from what his father's dishonesty had done to their family over the years. He wanted no part of that behavior. And yet, he knew that he was going to have to lie to Titia if he was going to be able to make it out to the barn, saddle Cornwall, and make a run for it. If she thought for an instant that he wasn't being sincere that pistol was going to find its way back between his thighs, and this time she was going to pull the trigger. He supposed he could tie her up and make his escape, but that meant possibly harming her, and he could not countenance that notion. No, he was going to have to talk his way out of this one and be ready to fly on a moment's notice.

The opportunity came sooner than he thought. Titia rolled out of bed and said she had to visit the outhouse. Thomas saw a questioning look in her eyes: would he be there when she came back? He turned on his side and raised himself on an elbow, resting his head in his palm. "Tell you what, you get your necessaries done and then get yourself back up here for one more ride. Then we'll figure out what to do with the rest of our day."

"You can do it again, already?" she cooed.

Thomas pulled the blanket down. To his own surprise, his steed was warming to the challenge. "Enough said?" he smiled.

Titia pulled on a pair of bloomers and a robe. Then she kissed him, gave his manhood a light caress, and said, "Five minutes." Thomas listened as she went down the stairs. When he heard the back door close, he flew out of bed, threw on his clothes and boots, and grabbed his hat. He stepped into the hall, then turned and went back into the bedroom, where he laid four $20 gold pieces on the nightstand. She could hire a farm hand for three months with that much money.

He raced down the stairs and out the front door. The sun was still drying the evening dew on the trees and grass, and the air was soft with the scent of apple blossoms and early roses. Beautiful place, he found himself thinking. Damned if I wouldn't like one like it for myself one day.

The barn sat at the left side of the house, fifty yards from the outhouse. He saw that the half-moon door was still closed, thank God. He raced inside the barn and grabbed Cornwall's blanket, bridle, and saddle, and threw them on and cinched up in record time. A few seconds later his feet were in the stirrups, and he was ready to bolt.

That's when the outhouse door slammed. He turned his head and looked out the back barn window. Titia was racing across the yard in his direction. Her robe was open, her bloomers were down around her ankles, and she was holding *his* S&W revolver in both hands. He froze; but, as frightening as it was to see her charging at him with a revolver that she was no doubt quite handy with, he was transfixed at the sight of her extraordinary breasts bouncing up and down with every stride she took. As for the sweet spot between her thighs shining in the morning light, heaven help me, he thought, I'm almost willing to let her shoot me just so I can nuzzle that magnificent canvas of nakedness one more time.

Fortunately, even at the tender age of eighteen, he had developed an acute appreciation for survival. He tapped Cornwall's flanks with both boots and leapt out of the barn. The first shot zipped past him a second later, smashing into the apple tree by the gate. The next shot passed so close that he felt a rush of air as it whizzed past his face. He desperately wanted to turn around in his saddle for one last look, but shots three and four convinced him to keep galloping with his head low and his knees tight against his horse. He ran Cornwall along the narrow road for at least a mile before he felt safe enough to slow to a walk.

He wiped the sweat from his face with the brim of his hat, and then, without thinking, he reached down between his legs and felt himself through his trousers. I can replace the revolver, he thought. You, I can't.

❋

Dawn Pillow noticed that as the colonel got through the worst of the fever episodes his dreams became much livelier. He talked to himself frequently, often in complete, coherent sentences. Tonight's dream, though, was unlike any she had watched him go through. He was hot enough that he had pulled off his blanket and was naked on the doe skin beneath him. That didn't bother her; she was raised with four brothers, and she had seen them without clothing from the time they were born until they became young men.

What amused her about this dream was the way he kept becoming physically aroused before trying to convince himself–or someone else, she could not tell–that everything was going to be fine. Then his aroused state would vanish, only to return a few minutes later with yet another round of assurances that all was well.

Just before she lay down to sleep Dawn Pillow watched as he reached down, took his manhood in hand, and said in a loud, clear voice, "…but I can't live without you!"

She covered Thomas with a light blanket and settled down to sleep beside him. What she would give to be inside that dream.

❋

TWENTY FIVE

Red Elk's Village

Thomas had been in Dawn Pillow's care for three weeks when the angels returned. He was able to walk a bit with the aid of a carved stick White Moon gave him, and this morning he was standing on the bank of the creek that flowed past the village. He was enjoying the dance of the light on the water and the orange and red flashes of cutthroat trout skimming the gravel creek bottom in search of caddisfly larvae when someone spoke to him. "Have ye decided not to die then, laddie?" the voice said in a distinct Scottish burr.

He turned to see an enormous fellow with a thick shock of black hair and an unruly beard standing behind him, hands on his hips, a wide grin on his face. Beside him was a short, round-faced Cheyenne man with a lop-sided smile, who, he immediately noticed, was missing two front teeth.

He shook his head. "I thought it was a dream. I thought you two were angels."

"Angels? *Us*?" laughed Hamish Mackenzie. "It's true I do my best to share the Word with heathens and civilized folks alike, but no one has ever accused me of being a divine messenger. As for my friend Four Bears, he may not look it today, but in his youth he was a mighty warrior, and many are the bones of his enemies that lie bleaching under the prairie sun. It's not likely he will be mistaken for an angel in the afterlife."

Four Bears acknowledged the compliment with a curt nod. Then he said, "You should be dead, you know."

"I'm sure that is true. I fully expected to take my last breath in that damn ravine and become vulture food, to boot. Thank you both."

He shifted the walking stick to his left hand and shook Hamish's hand with his right. He wasn't sure how to properly thank a Cheyenne warrior, so he simply nodded to Four Bears and touched two fingers to his forehead. "What I couldn't figure was how you tumbled into that mess," said Hamish. "My friend thought you fell over the edge while you were watering the flowers. Drunk, maybe. Your trousers were around your knees, after all."

Thomas thought back to the night in Claybourne's library, the ride in the buckboard under the stars, and the feeling of weightlessness when Elias and Moncton dropped him into the deep ravine. He tightened his grip on the walking stick. "I did not fall," he said in a quiet voice.

"Then the professor must be right," said Hamish. "He told me you were going to confront Noah Clalybourne about your missing friend, and when I told him we carried you here to the village from the ravine more dead than alive, he allowed as how he believed that snake had a hand in you being tossed down the cliff."

"Von Sievers? Does he think Claybourne knows I am alive?"

"That I cannot say with certainty," answered Hamish. "But the word among the local ranchers is that a white man got himself killed at Tamayo Ravine three weeks ago, and I would venture to guess that Claybourne thinks the same thing. You figure he'd like to finish the job?"

"I'm sure of it," he said with a slight smile. "Somehow, I've gotten myself mixed up with his plans, whatever they may be. He thought I might drop an anvil onto his little hourglass, and so he had a couple of his men drop me first."

Hamish laughed and slapped Thomas on the back. A spasm of pain shot through his body, and tears welled in his eyes, but the giant Scotsman took no note of his discomfort. "What now, then? Will you go to the law, or will you perhaps pay a visit to Langton Hall and stick a caber up Claybourne's arse and be done with it?"

"A caber?"

"Aye, a great wooden pole, tapered and de-limbed. A proper one is exactly nineteen feet six inches long, made with a larch tree and tapered at the top. Just long enough to shove through that bastard's innards."

Thomas scratched his head. "Are they for battle?

Hamish sounded exasperated. "No, laddie, they are for throwing. Have you no education? We toss them at the games. I learned from the great Donald Dinnie himself in Edinburgh. No man ever tossed a caber as straight and true as he."

Why am I not surprised that a mountain of a man like Hamish would toss trees for sport, thought Thomas. "Then perhaps you should teach me, and then I can pay a visit to Claybourne and corkscrew him with ten or twelve feet of it."

Now it was Four Bears turn to laugh and slap Thomas even harder on the back than Hamish had done. Thomas almost fell to the ground this time, but he held tight to his cane and remained upright.

"I think I'll head back to the tipi," he said. "Much more of this conversation and you two will finish what Claybourne's men got started."

His remark stung the Scotsman. Hamish clasped his hands together, his face tightened, and he stared hard at the ground. The man tosses trees for fun, thought Thomas, but he is as sensitive as a child. He raised his cane and tapped Hamish on the shoulder. The giant raised his head, and Thomas saw that his eyes had misted over. "Do I weigh more than one of your cabers, Hamish?"

"What's that now?"

"You carried me up the ravine. Couldn't have been easy, being dead weight and all. I was wondering how it compared to tossing a caber."

Hamish smiled. "Having not tossed you back down, of course I can't do a fair comparison. But if you'd like, we can ride out to Tamayo and give it a go. One toss should be enough."

Thomas laughed, reached up, and gave the best whack he could to the Scotsman's shoulder. It was like hitting a brick wall. Then he walked with the two angels back into the village to where Red Elk was reading a book on a camp stool in front of his tipi. He removed his spectacles and motioned for Thomas to join him. Hamish and Four Bears asked him to join them later and then made a beeline for the stew pot that was hanging above a cookfire near the stream. He pulled a stool next to Red Elk and eased himself down with the help of his cane.

"My daughter says you will live," the chief began. "From what I have been told of you in the days of your great war you are a famous warrior, and one who is hard to kill."

"It is true that I am in no hurry to travel across the water and join the Great Spirit," answered Thomas, in a veiled reference to Red Elk's order on the night he was carried into the village to leave him to die in the brush across the creek. He would not insult his host, but he wanted the old chief to know that he was aware that the only reason he hadn't become coyote food that night was because of Dawn Pillow's intervention.

Red Elk regarded Thomas like a curiosity in a display case. "A leader does not have the luxury of compassion when it comes to protecting his people, and no man who chooses how and when he will die can be called a coward."

He knew how important it was to the Cheyenne to meet death head on, with dignity and grace. "Then, what is a good and proper death?"

"My Sioux friend, Bad Soup, mounted his wife one night last winter and died during the act. She told me later that he knew his heart was about to burst, but he struggled on until he had helped her to reach the magic place, which is something all good husbands seek to do before satisfying themselves." He grinned. "That was a good death, my friend."

A skinny dog approached the men and lay down at Thomas's feet. He reached down and scratched its head. "I cannot argue with that. Of course, had your friend suggested to his wife that they hold off completing the ride until the morning, he might have lived to ride another day."

"Pride and vanity kill some men, Thomas, and stupidity kills even more. Then there are those who spend their lives thinking with the wrong head." Thomas looked uncertain. The wrong head? Red Elk laughed; he raised a finger and pointed at the top of his skull and then at his crotch. "The wrong head," he repeated and laughed again at his own joke. "When a man looks at the world only through the single eye on this head," he patted his crotch, "he will wander half-blind until he lays down his knife and fork for the last time."

"Like your friend."

"Oh, no, he was felled by his sense of duty to his wife, not by his lust. The story of Bad Soup's death is almost sacred to the Sioux these days, and to Cheyenne, as well."

Thomas couldn't help but chuckle. "Especially for the women, I'm guessing, given the sacrifice he made for his wife's pleasure."

Red Elk slapped his thigh and laughed. "Oh, yes, many are the wives who entreat their husbands to exert themselves in the fashion of Bad Soup when they are wrestling beneath the buffalo robes in their tipis."

"We all have our heroes," Thomas answered with a grin.

A group of children raced past them, and the dog got up to join the chase. Red Elk fetched two glasses and a clay jug from his tipi and poured two glasses of red wine. Thomas took a sip and said, "This tastes like a Bordeaux."

The chief nodded. "I developed a taste for two things when your government sent a delegation of Plains chiefs to Washington several years ago: good red wine and the music of Mozart. I am lucky enough be able to secure wine from the trader, Major Rhine. As for Mozart, sadly, I can only enjoy his music in my memory."

"And the book you are reading?"

Red Elk held up the thick volume on the table beside his stool. "*The Life of Genghis Khan.* A great general, all-powerful leader, master of his world six hundred years ago."

"You forgot to mention he was a monster, a man who slaughtered millions."

Red Elk nodded. "Few are the giants of history who did not sail to their greatness upon rivers of blood, Colonel. Your own people included."

"I won't argue that point. War has always been the common denominator of all civilizations and all cultures." He raised his wine glass towards the chief. "Here's to a day when warriors like us can only be found in history books."

Red Elk tapped his glass against Thomas's. "That day may come, but it is not a world you or I will ever see."

Red Elk refilled their glasses, and the two men sat quietly as the sun rose high above the village on the bank of the creek.

❖

He returned to Dawn Pillow's tipi late that afternoon. The combination of the red wine and warm weather overpowered him, and he quickly fell asleep on a bearskin in the corner. When he woke and looked up through the tipi vent, he could see a scattering of stars. Dawn Pillow had prepared a meal of smoked fish, squash soup, wild greens, and fresh summer berries. "Will you eat with me?" she asked when she saw he was awake. He joined her on a soft antelope rug in the center of the tipi.

As he had every day since he regained consciousness two weeks earlier, he marveled at her grace and beauty. Dawn Pillow was nearly as tall as he was. She wore her lustrous black hair straight, all the way to her waist. Her eyes were deep indigo, her lips were full and naturally red, and they always seemed to be formed in a half rosebud smile. She had a delicate nose, high cheekbones, and when she leaned close to him with washcloths or bandages, her almond skin smelled of ripe raspberry.

Dawn Pillow made her own long dresses and moccasins from supple doeskin, fringed with thin leather strings and bordered with multi-colored beadwork woven into intricate designs. In motion she flowed like a ballet dancer, and even when she was hurrying along her gait was smooth and liquid. He had vague memories of her singing to him when he was still teetering on the edge of death with fever and chills. Her voice was like a summer breeze rustling through Aspen leaves, and he caught a hint of cinnamon on her breath when she leaned into him to tend to his wounds.

During his long days of recuperation she spent hours reading aloud to him from books that Hamish and Von Sievers loaned to her. She had excelled as a student at the mission school; poetry was her favorite, and she read the works of William Wordsworth, Samuel Taylor Coleridge, William Blake, John Keats, Percy Bysshe Shelley, and Lord Byron with a level of passion and natural artistry that one would expect to find in an Oxford classroom, not in a buffalo-skin tipi on the edge of the vast American prairie. He was pleased to also hear her appreciation for the poetry of his friend, Walt Whitman.

Dawn Pillow told him the history of her people, who called themselves *Tsistsistas*, and she explained how the all Spirit Maheo grew weary of living alone in a dark void and decided to create a world from mud, which he placed upon Grandmother Turtle's back to carry. In time, her hair became flowers and plants, and because Maheo did not want her to be alone he pulled a rib from his right side and it formed into the first man, and then a rib from his left side, which he formed into the first woman. Finally, he gifted his creation with the buffalo so that all their needs from food to warmth to clothing could be filled.

He was enchanted by her storytelling; it was effortless and sincere and infused with love and appreciation for the world into which she had been born. "But," he asked her one night when she had finished another story, "you attended the white's schools, you speak and read English perfectly, you know music and poetry and the great literature of the West. So, who are you now? You aren't a Cheyenne in the way your grandmother was; you have as much of the ways of my people about you as your own, and your children and theirs will see even more of the old ways crumble into dust in their lifetimes."

She laughed softly and set down the beadwork she liked to do when telling him stories. "Life is not an either/or proposition, Thomas. Wisdom is recognizing the need to accept change and to discern what change is good. I have no fear of taking on the best things from your world, especially if they help me to grow and to experience life more fully. It does not mean that I must abandon the ways of my own people." She looked at him intently. "Can you say the same thing for yourself and your people?"

"Do you mean will we ever acknowledge the things the Cheyenne do better than us?"

"And make them a part of your way of life."

He felt a chill coming on and clasped his woven blanket tightly around him.

"I do not know the answer to that question, Dawn Pillow. Perhaps we will, someday. Ask your children's children when they are grown."

❖

When they completed their meal, Dawn Pillow heated water in a small kettle and handed Thomas a cloth and soap for his bath. She had bathed him daily for over three weeks; tonight, she said, he would do that by himself, and tomorrow, he would have to leave her tipi for good. White Moon had visited that morning and pronounced Thomas ready to take care of himself. His bones were knitting well, his wounds were nearly healed, and he showed no new signs of infection. It would be unseemly for him to remain in an unmarried woman's tipi for another day. Hamish had cared for Thomas's horse, and his saddle and gear would be ready for him in the morning.

As he finished washing himself Dawn Pillow came back into the tipi with his clothing in her arms. He had been wearing a loose nightshirt and deerskin leggings borrowed from White Moon, and he appreciated the care she had taken in washing and mending his clothing. He stood up with only a small blanket covering his waist and thighs and took the clothing from her. As he reached for his trousers his blanket fell to the floor, and he stood before her naked in the golden light of the oil lamp.

She was neither embarrassed nor offended; she had seen him without clothing several times a day for nearly a month. This time was different, though. He was no longer helpless, and she could no longer pretend to herself that he could not get by without her help.

There was a long silence in the tipi. Thomas did not move to get dressed and Dawn Pillow did not turn to leave while he put on his clothing. They simply looked into one another's eyes. He felt a mix of gratitude, respect, and, despite his best intentions, a growing sense of desire. He could not tell what she was feeling.

Finally, she said, "Put on your shirt and trousers and moccasins, and join me outside." Then she picked up the thick bearskin and ducked out the tipi flap. He dressed quickly and stepped out into a moonlit nightscape beneath a velvet black sky that was carpeted with endless ribbons of glimmering stars. There was a soft breeze off the creek and he could hear the water flowing over smooth stones, but the village itself was ghostly quiet. For the moment it was just him, the faint crackle of dying embers in the evening cooking fires, and a coyote calling mournfully from the distant hills.

It took a few seconds for his eyes to adjust to the dark, and a little longer to make out the form of Dawn Pillow waiting for him at the edge of the creek.

He went over beside her and took the bearskin from her outstretched arm. Then, without a word, she stepped into the creek. Thomas had no idea where she was going, but he plunged into the water after her. The cold water was only knee deep, but he still had to struggle against the strong current. Twenty yards on he stepped up onto the opposite creek bank and stood next to Dawn Pillow. He searched her eyes, but they offered no hint of where they were going. She said nothing, and he thought it best to remain quiet as she turned and walked swiftly through the soft, tall grass towards the tree line fifty yards from the creek. She wound through a stand of cottonwoods, into a small, circular clearing that was dappled with the light of the full moon. The ground was covered in a mass of lush, deep-green maidenhair fern, and dotted with clusters of evening primroses whose yellow blossoms fluoresced in the moonlight.

Dawn Pillow took the bearskin from his hands. She spread it out on the fern, and then, wordlessly, reached down to her ankles and lifted her dress over her shoulders, off her head, and laid it on the ground beside the bearskin. He felt his breathing stop. Her body seemed to glow in the bright moonlight. Her full, firm breasts dimpled in the cool night air, and he watched as if in a dream as she pulled her hair off her shoulders and slowly went to her knees in the center of the thick, soft bearskin.

Thomas removed his clothing and lowered himself on his knees directly in front of her. He started to speak, but she lay her hand gently across his mouth and shook her head. Then she raised her arm, pointed high into the sky and traced the arc of a line of stars from one horizon to the other. His eyes followed her movement, marveling at the spectacular cosmic display unfolding above them.

They remained face to face on their knees for several minutes, not speaking, not touching. Then Dawn Pillow leaned forward, kissed him full on the lips, and laid back on the bearskin. Before he lay down on her he watched a beam of moonlight bounce off a tree, linger a moment on a stand of flowers, and then spill across the glade to bathe her body in a pure, warm blanket of light.

He clasped his hands behind her head, lowered himself slowly onto her, and became a part of her body.

TWENTY SIX

Red Elk's Village

Thomas woke at first light. Dawn Pillow was not in the tipi, and it was cold. He washed his face with water from the pail in the corner and dressed quickly. It was good to wear his own clothes again. He wanted to see Dawn Pillow, thank Red Elk and White Moon for their hospitality, and then make his way to Major Rhine's to gather up his things and find out if there was any word about Itzcoatl or Diego.

He wasn't sure what to say to Dawn Pillow; their visit to the moonlit glade had been one of the most extraordinary experiences of his life, but a part of him wondered if his memory of the event was a product of the hallucinogenic tea that the medicine man had been using to help him sleep. The only thing he was completely sure about was that he wanted to see her again. He took his hat from a willow stand and looked around the tipi that had been his home for almost a month. Then he pulled the tent flap aside and stepped out into the chilly morning.

He expected to see the village stirring as usual; women going to the creek to fetch water, children helping to re-kindle the cook fires, and men tending to the horses. Instead, when he stepped out of the tipi, he found himself face-to-face with White Moon, who was dressed in the hawk mask and feathers he wore only for the most important rituals. White Moon's appearance startled him, and he fell back against the tipi. As he righted himself, he noticed that the medicine man had not come alone; standing behind him was an elderly woman, and behind her, another. One after another, a line of women and girls stretched from the front of Dawn Pillow's tipi all the way to Red Elk's tipi at the center of the village. Thomas could just make out the old man standing there stoically with his arms crossed across his chest.

Before he could ask White Moon what was happening, the medicine man raised his left hand to the sky and shook a wooden rattle. Then he leaned in close, opened his right palm, and blew a gritty, acidic powder in Thomas' face. His eyes watered, and he began gasping for air before his knees buckled and he went to the ground. Dozens of hands moved all over all his body; they removed his shirt and boots and trousers and then lifted him by the arms and dragged him to Red Elk's tent.

Two things happened before he lost consciousness; he felt himself being tied to a tree, and Red Elk appeared through his blurred vision and said, "You thought with the wrong head, Colonel." Then everything went black.

❖

He came to at dusk. His whole body hurt, and he was parched. As his eyesight cleared, he realized he had been tied in a standing position against a pole. His hands were lashed at the wrists behind him, and his shoulders felt like they were about to pop out of their sockets. Rope was also tied around his lower legs. He could only move his head. He looked down and saw that the only clothes he had on was the lower half of his long underwear. There was no rain, but his stomach and chest felt wet and sticky. As he pondered on that fact, an elderly woman walked up and spat on his abdomen. She noticed that he was conscious, so she held off the second spittle barrage and scurried away to tell the villagers that the shamed colonel was awake.

He struggled against the restraints, but it was no use; whoever had tied him to the pole had done it before, probably many times. He was going nowhere. Soon, people began to emerge from their tipis, get up from beside their campfires and leave their evening chores. The moon and stars illuminated the path they walked to the center the village where he was held captive. In a few minutes he was surrounded by over one hundred Cheyenne men, women and children. He felt a scrap of hope when he saw Professor Von Sievers in the crowd, but the look on the scientist's face said, "I am sorry, my friend, you are doomed and there is nothing I can do to help."

White Moon appeared out of the dark carrying two small pots. He dipped a brush into one and painted a green horizontal line across Thomas' stomach. Then he dipped into the other pot and painted a bright red circle on the underwear around Thomas' crotch. He tried to speak to the man, but his mouth was too dry to form words. He simply looked at the medicine man and shook his head back and forth in bewilderment. White Moon did not acknowledge his entreaty. He completed his painting and stepped back into the crowd.

Now, the old woman who spat on him approached. She was wearing a pair of doe-leather gloves to protect her from the poisonous oils on the leaves of the stinging nettles she had just picked. She grasped the ends of the nettles below the leaves and brushed them across Thomas's stomach. He flinched at the searing pain that felt like the sting of a dozen yellow jackets. Without looking down, he knew his stomach would already be blistering. The old woman wasn't done, however; now she pulled his underwear away from his body and stuffed the nettles deep into his crotch, all the while smiling at him the way a grandmother would look at a naughty child who had stolen a treat from the candy jar.

The agony inflicted by the nettles was unlike anything he had ever felt. His face broke out in a sweat, he gasped for breath, and his entire lower body felt as if it were on fire. He thrashed to the left and right against the restraints, but it only caused the nettles to shift deeper and the pain to escalate dramatically.

A moment later, two men planted flaming torches on either side of the pole to which he was tied. No one wants to miss a bit of the show just because it's dark, Thomas thought to himself. But what was the *rest* of the show going to consist of anyway? Most importantly, why the hell was he here? What was he being punished for? This entire village had just spent a month going out of it way to save his life. It just didn't make sense.

Then the crowd parted and Red Elk marched slowly up and stood in front of him. The chief of the Cheyenne said nothing. He didn't need to. Thomas finally understood that he was being punished for last night's woodland tryst with Dawn Pillow. It had not been a dream. He was guilty of thinking with the wrong head, and the nettles that were blistering and burning his body were only the warm-up. He could only imagine what the final punishment was to be. He lifted his head and returned Red Elk's hard stare with an expression that said, "Very well, then, do what you must."

The chief waved to a woman to bring a gourd of water. She lifted it to Thomas's mouth, and he drank deeply. When he felt he could get words past his swollen lips he said to Red Elk, "Will you leave it to your old women to kill me, then, and not do me the respect of giving me a warrior's death?"

"Respect?" growled the chief. "You dare speak to me of respect? You have defiled my daughter, disrespected my village, and brought shame upon us all. You do not deserve a good death. But let me put you at ease on that subject. I have no intention of having you killed. Come tomorrow, however, I promise you will find yourself wishing I had."

Thomas's eyes widened. He wasn't going to be killed? A wave of relief washed across him, almost enough to cool the blowtorch burning between his legs. But Red Elk had only delivered him from the most extreme punishment possible; when he saw the chief pull a skinning knife from his waistband and hold it high for the villagers to see, he knew he was not going to get off scot-free. Cheers and hoots filled the night sky as the chief turned back to him and said, "Believe me when I say that it gives me no pleasure to take away a man's ability to enjoy a woman. Still, a wrong has been done, and a price must be paid."

Son of a bitch, Thomas muttered to himself. That explained why White Moon had painted the red circle around his crotch. He looked into Red Elk's eyes and said, "Because in defense of his people, a leader cannot show compassion?"

The old warrior nodded. "You would have made a fine son, Colonel. We could have enjoyed many hunts and battled many enemies.

Have you any sons of your own?"

He shook his head. For him, having a family had always been something he would get around to in the future. Now, it was too late.

Red Elk turned to the crowd and raised a hand for silence. "I follow the old ways," he intoned. "When a crime is committed punishment must follow, but that punishment must reflect the harm done by the crime. A thief may have his fingers cut off; a murderer may be executed in the same way he took his victim's life. As for an outsider who lays with an unmarried woman in defiance of the law, there is only one punishment that is fitting. It is my family that has been shamed, and it is my duty to deliver punishment."

"My knife is sharp," he said to Thomas, "and my hand is steady. If you remain calm, I will cut away your testicles as quickly as you can snap your fingers. If you struggle my hand may slip, and I could cut off the trunk along with the branches."

Thomas looked out over the crowd, hoping to catch even a fleeting glimpse of Dawn Pillow. She was not there, but he was able to make eye contact with Von Sievers. The professor grimaced and shook his head at the gruesome carnival taking place around them. Had Dawn Pillow also been the recipient of Red Elk's primitive form of justice, Thomas wondered?

Torches were burning all around the darkened village, casting ghostly shadows on the tipi walls. The faces of the Cheyenne were ocher and blood red in the flickering light, a perfect complement to this evening's gory entertainment. Even before Red Elk made the slice, he found himself wishing the old chief would sever his carotid artery and let him die now, instead of turning him into a hapless eunuch.

Red Elk called forward the woman who had stuffed the stinging nettles between his legs. She yanked his underwear down and scooped the nettles away with a gloved hand. Then to add real insult to the forthcoming injury, she took a moment to fondle what Red Elk's knife was about to slice away. She beamed a toothless grin and then turned back to enjoy the laughter of the appreciative crowd who understood that Thomas's shame would only multiply over the years when he thought about the last time a woman had handled his manhood.

Red Elk now took a position slightly to Thomas's right side. He turned his body at an angle so that the villagers would have a clear view of the surgery. "Do it quickly, damn you," said Thomas through clenched teeth.

Red Elk sighed. Then he reached between Thomas's legs with his left hand and took hold of his scrotal sac. He stretched it out as far as he could, raised his knife into the air, and then slowly lowered it in front of Thomas' abdomen.

"Bite your tongue. It will help."

He leaned in with the knife to make the cut. Suddenly, shouts rang out, and an adolescent boy pushed through the crowd and came up to Red Elk so quickly that the startled chief released his hold on the colonel's jewel sack.Thomas was surprised to see that the intruder was the deaf-mute he had helped at Claybourne's ranch. The boy tipped his head to Thomas, and then placed his hand on Red Elk's wrist and guided the knife away from its intended target. Red Elk wrenched his hand back from the boy's grip and said, "What are you doing, boy? Get back to your parents."

"He is the deaf one," someone shouted from the crowd.

"He probably doesn't understand what is happening," said another person.

Thomas heard Von Sievers voice join in: "Please, let's find out what he wants."

Had the punishment been interrupted by anyone other than the handicapped boy Red Elk would have cuffed them on the head, or worse. But he was genuinely intrigued by the boy's action, and so he lowered his knife. The boy's eyes were wet with tears. He wiped a sleeve across his face and then turned and backed up against Thomas. As the people of the village watched in astonishment the boy dropped his buckskin leggings, pulled out his scrotum with one hand, and put his other hand on Red Elk's hand to direct the knife towards his body.

The chief pulled his knife hand back and turned to his people. "Does anyone know why this boy is offering to be punished in place of the colonel?"

White Moon separated from the crowd and came up beside the boy. He motioned for him to pull his pants up, and then he put an arm around the boy's shoulder.

"Somehow, this boy must be in the colonel's debt," the medicine man said to Red Elk.

"What kind of debt could possibly be so great that a boy would give up something so important?" asked the chief. Then in a loud voice he said to the villagers, "Does anyone know why this boy wants me to cut him in place of Colonel Thomas? Speak!"

A middle-aged woman stepped into the torchlight. "Salamander is my son," she said. "You know that he cannot hear or speak, but we sign, and he has told me about the colonel." Thomas strained to lean his head forward so he could hear them speak. The only sound in the village was the crackling of pine tree pitch burning in the torches.

"Why is your son doing this?" Red Elk asked.

The woman looked at her boy and nodded to him with an expression of love and pride. "Some weeks ago," she said, "Salamander was caught fishing on Mr. Claybourne's land. A group of men captured him and beat him for trespassing. Then their leader ordered two of them to cut off his right thumb so he could never enjoy fishing again." A slight smile crept across Red Elk's face. He was beginning to see where this story was going. "Go on."

"The colonel was on his way to visit Mr. Claybourne," she continued, "and he happened upon the men just as they pushed my son down on a rock and readied to cut him. Colonel Scoundrel asked them to stop, and when they did not, he drew his revolver and readied to fight them. None of Claybourne's men were prepared to die for a Cheyenne, however, and so my son was released. This is his debt to the colonel, and this is how he is willing to pay it in full."

Murmurs of approval swept through the crowd. These were the actions of a true Cheyenne warrior and a cause for celebration. Red Elk sensed the change in the crowd's mood and knew he had a very important decision to make. If cutting the boy instead of the colonel was the best course of action, the chief would do it without hesitation. He could also cut them both, but he doubted such an action would be pleasing to the Great Spirit. No, he decided, he would not cut them both, but if he moved to cut the colonel, he would have to get past the boy, and he knew he could not do that without causing the boy some harm. Such is the burden of leadership, he thought to himself.

Red Elk slipped his knife back into his waistband. When he did, Thomas realized he had been holding his breath for a long time. He exhaled and tried to figure out what was going to happen next.

The chief turned the boy around so that he was facing his people. Then he rested his hands on the boy's shoulders and asked, "How many among you would risk so much to pay a debt of honor? From this day on, Salamander is no longer a boy. He is a Cheyenne man. Give him your respect."

The villagers cheered, banged drums, and shook rattles as the boy's mother translated the chief's words to her son in sign language. He nodded his thanks to the chief and then walked over to where Thomas was still tied to the pole with his pants at half-mast. Without asking permission, the boy leaned down and pulled Thomas' trousers back up. This truly is a brave young man, thought Red Elk. Until that instant the chief was not sure if he was going to spare Thomas or not. Now, a boy had made the decision in his place. Even so, some price had to be paid for the colonel's transgression with Dawn Pillow.

"This boy has repaid his debt to you, Colonel," said Red Elk. "It is only for his bravery that you will remain attached to your manhood. I hope that in the future you will wield it with greater wisdom."

The chief turned to acknowledge the laughter and approving nods of his people. It was good to see that they agreed with that part of his decision. The next part would be more difficult. Red Elk was certain that last night's adventure was not the first time that his daughter had waded across the creek in the moonlight to meet a man, but there was no doubt that she had journeyed there with Thomas. By rights, the colonel must do penance for his transgression.

Red Elk drew his knife. The blade gleamed in the torchlight as he leaned forward and placed the end at the top of Thomas's left cheek, stuck the knife into the bone and then made a diagonal cut down to the top of Thomas' jaw. The knife was razor-sharp, and the cut was straight and clean. Thomas's eyes went wide as he felt the slash and the flow of hot blood down his face, but he didn't make a sound. He knew he could have been bleeding from a much worse place.

Red Elk wiped his knife on his vest. Then he stepped behind the pole and cut the restraints on Thomas's hands and feet. He toppled in a heap to the ground, but before he passed out, he saw White Moon lean over him with a familiar jar of ointment. The medicine man smiled, and Thomas closed his eyes.

TWENTY SEVEN

Streams and Meadows

He slept fitfully in the back of Hamish's wagon. Von Sievers had applied a plaster made with mud and herbs to the cut on his face but urged Thomas to get it stitched up as soon as possible. Hamish made coffee and bacon at first light and fed and saddled Ulysses. Thomas checked his gear, tested the action on his Colt, and loaded his rifle.

He swung up into the saddle as the sun crested the eastern hills and said, "I can't properly thank you both right now. But, if there is ever anything I can do to repay you, know that you can count on me."

The professor and the Scotsman nodded in reply. "Where now, Colonel?" asked Von Sievers.

"Denver, to see if I can get any word of Diego de San Mártin." And to find a great meal and then get stinking drunk for a day or two, he thought to himself. "I guess we will figure it out from there. Whatever Noah Claybourne has in the works, Diego's fiancée is somehow involved. I'm not done with that bastard, not by a long shot."

"Ye dinnae think it's time to get the federal marshal involved?" asked Hamish. "Seems to me there are crimes a plenty for him to be looking in to."

"I wish I could, my friend. I will telegraph Bat Masterson in Trinidad and ask if there is a marshal here in Colorado or the territories who can be trusted." He raised his hand up and felt the welting cut on his face. "But I just don't know." With that, he tapped his boot against

Ulysses' flank and rode away. As he left the path and joined the main trail a minute later, he heard the faint sound of Hamish's voice: "And don't forget where to stick that caber, laddie. Straight and true!" It hurt to smile, but it was worth it.

✽

He rode north and west all day, skirting stands of trees and random limestone outcroppings that dotted the valley floor. The trail was well-worn and mostly level and Ulysses eased through the prairie grass and scrub brush without effort.

He stopped along a quiet stream at midday and ate the cornbread and pemmican that Von Sievers had packed for him. He watched a swarm of trout glide past in the crystal-clear water and thought about the friends he had made in the past month; Bat Masterson, Major Rhine, Von Sievers, the Scotsman and especially, Dawn Pillow. Despite his love for the action and energy of the gambling table, Thomas was not a particularly sociable person. He was just fine keeping his own company. He had never been one to indulge in saloon banter with the fellas at the long bar, and on the trail, he was content to ride for hours without making conversation with anyone who might be with him. The open sky and the panorama of the natural world around him had always been sufficient. And yet, in the matter of a few weeks, he had made five new friends, each of whom he knew he could trust with his life.

He gave Ulysses a handful of grain and put his foot in the stirrup. He had no real idea where he was going, or what he was going to do when he got there. He had asked Rhine to send a note to Trinidad along with the revolver the Major had repaired, telling the marshal to be on the lookout for Itzcoatl and Diego. Beyond that, he just didn't know. He was worried about Dawn Pillow and certain that when Claybourne learned he had survived the ravine there would be even more men looking for him. They would make damn sure the job was done properly this time. He adjusted his hat, took up the reins, and let Ulysses choose his own pace when they returned to the trail.

❖

It was late afternoon when he smelled the coffee. He had been riding along a low ridge above a creek and was about ready to find a place to bed down for the night when the unmistakable aroma drifted up from a few hundred feet below. A moment later he saw two canvas tents set back about fifty yards from the stream. Between the tents was an open canvas pavilion stretched across four sapling poles. A table and four chairs sat under the protective covering, and in front of them he could just make out the campfire. That had to be where the coffee was brewing.

He picked his way down the ridge and slowly approached the tents. When he was within hailing distance, he shouted, "Hello the camp! Rider coming in!" He rode to within forty feet of the tents and reined Ulysses up. It wasn't just bad manners to ride uninvited into a stranger's camp: it was also an easy way to get a belly full of buckshot.

A moment later, a tall black man in his early thirties rounded the corner of one of the tents and walked easily in Thomas's direction. He wore a collarless riverman's shirt and suspenders over denim trousers and boots, and his left hand rested on a holstered revolver. Thomas kept his hands open and away from his sides as the man walked up to within a few feet of him.

"Afternoon," Thomas said. The man did not respond. He was looking Thomas over with the kind of experienced gaze that suggested he had been a lawman or soldier. The fact that he was completely bald somehow magnified the intensity of his thorough once-over.

"I smelled your coffee and wondered if you might feel inclined to share a cup."

"We might," replied the man in a deep voice, his eyes never leaving Thomas's hands. His natural command tone reinforced Thomas's belief that the man was used to being in authority. "Who are you, and where are you headed?" the man continued.

"I left the Cheyenne village south of here at daybreak. On my way to Denver."

"This ain't the fastest way there."

"I'm not in a hurry, and in any event, word on the prairie is that you folks make a fine cup of coffee."

The man did not smile. "And your name is…?"

"Scoundrel. Thomas E. From Ohio by way of New York."

The man showed the barest hint of a smile. "I know your name, Colonel. Never thought I'd make your acquaintance, though. No, I never did." He pulled his hand off his revolver and said, "Come on down. I'd be happy to share our coffee."

Thomas dismounted and followed the man around the tent to where his horses were tied next to two freight wagons. They left Ulysses and walked over to the campfire. The man grabbed a tin cup from a side table and pulled the blue and white-flecked enamelware pot off the iron grate in the fire. He filled the cup and handed it to Thomas, who took a quick sip of the fresh coffee.

"Man, that is good. I haven't had coffee in over a month."

"I'm guessing there is a story behind that," said the man. Then he touched his finger to his own cheek and said, "And maybe to that plaster on your face, too."

Thomas had almost forgotten the injury on his face. No wonder the man had given him an extra measure of scrutiny when he rode in. He smiled and nodded. "You didn't give me your name."

The man extended his hand. "Mose Triplett. Pleasure."

As Thomas shook his hand a woman came out of one of the tents and joined them. She had the look of the Creoles he had known in New Orleans.

"This is my wife, Calista," said Mose.

"And your business partner," she added in a distinct French-Creole accent. "He tries to forget that sometimes," she said, "but seein' as how I keep the books of the business, and I do the banking, I know how to keep his attention."

Thomas grinned. "I expect you do."

"Are you going to camp here with us for the night, Colonel?"

"I hadn't planned on that, but if it's fine by the both of you, I'd be much obliged."

"Let's ask Miss Mary," said Mose. "It'll be dusk in an hour, and she should be about done for the day."

"Miss Mary?"

"Our client," answered Mose.

"Our *first* client, and good Lord willing, not our last," added his wife.

Thomas took another sip of coffee. "Client? May I ask what business you are in?"

Mose pulled a business card from his pocket and handed it to Thomas. "M. & C. Adventures & Expeditions," he read aloud. "I get the M. and C. part. But what are adventures and expeditions?"

"You're in the middle of one right now," said Calista.

Thomas looked puzzled. His idea of adventure ran to the being-chased-by-angry-hostiles-with-guns sort of experience, not camping on the bank of a calm prairie stream on a warm summer night. "Drinking coffee?" he asked.

Calista giggled. "Adventure is in the mind of the beholder, Colonel."

"We were running a dry goods store west of Denver, and we did fine," said Mose, "but we both wanted something bigger, something better. For the past couple of years we have seen an increasing number of well-heeled folks from the east coming out to Colorado to fish and hunt for sport. When they get here they have to scrape around to find somebody who has time to lead them into the backcountry, and generally speaking, those ain't the finest sort of professionals."

"Our idea," chimed in Calista, "was to provide these folks with a professional experience. The best camp accommodations, the best guide service, and even connections with taxidermists to mount their trophies and ship them to their homes."

"Plus, we want them to have food and wine as good as anything they can get in the best big-city hotel," said Mose. "Calista sees to that, and friend, she knows her business."

Calista smiled at the compliment, and Thomas's eyebrows shot up at the mention of fine food and wine. This adventure & expedition business was sounding better by the minute.

Calista topped off his coffee, and Mose stirred the fire. "So, you are new to the business," said Thomas. "How did you find your first client?"

"She found us," replied Mose. "Came into our dry goods store looking for supplies. She was going to come out here and camp by herself, which we advised against. The Indian wars haven't been over for that long, and there's more than a few white men who are happy to do a little scalping, too. This ain't no place for a woman on her own."

"The short of it is that when we found out who she was and what she wanted to do, we made ourselves available," said Calista. "That was two weeks ago, and we have been camped here with her for nine days."

Thomas was genuinely intrigued. "And what was it that brought a lady from the east all the way to Colorado?"

"Fishing," said Mose. "In particular, what they call fly fishing. Damndest way to fish you ever saw. Miss Mary makes bugs–she calls them flies–from all kinds of materials, and then snaps them with a line across the water so the trout think they're catching dinner. When they hit the hook she plants in those flies, they learn that *they're* on the menu, not the bug."

"I know a little about the sport," said Thomas. "It's popular with some of the bankers I have worked with." He finished his coffee and handed the cup to Calista for a refill. "I've always been a hook, line and sinker fisherman myself, but the truth is I don't have the patience to sit for hours waiting for a nibble."

"Let's go down and meet her," said Mose. Thomas thanked Calsita for the coffee, and the two men walked down towards the creek.

"Were you in the army?" Thomas asked as they walked. "You carry yourself like a military man."

"I was with the 54th Regiment of Massachusetts volunteers. Joined when I was sixteen."

"I know them. Were you at Fort Wagner?"

"I was. And at Charleston and Grimball's Landing. Last fighting I saw was in Florida, at Olustee, under General Seymour. Seen my share of it, that's for sure. Like you, I suppose."

Thomas quietly nodded. He had been in conversations like this with veterans dozens of times since the end of the war. Without exception, they had all seen infinitely more carnage than he experienced in his one and only morning of actual battle at Pebble Creek Ridge. The fact that he was a national hero while the real warriors like Mose Triplett were mere footnotes to history would stick in his craw for as long as he lived.

"I saw a little," he said as they neared the creek bank. "I joined at seventeen, near the end of the war. Most of the fighting in my career was against the Sioux in '77."

Mose gave an understanding nod. Then they rounded a stand of tall bushes and were standing at the creek's edge, where Thomas was presented with one of the most incongruous sights he had ever witnessed. Standing on a large granite boulder in the middle of the creek with her back towards them was M. & C. Adventures & Expeditions' first and only client. She wore a long-sleeved blue chambray shirt, men's cotton duck trousers, and rubberized boots. A green wicker fish creel with a hinged top sat on the rock behind her, but what Thomas found most fascinating was the jaunty tam o'shanter on her head, and the long bamboo pole with side reel she held in her right hand.

As he watched, Miss Mary fed a length of line out from the reel, then snapped it quickly behind her head and cast it out onto the calm surface. She let it sit for a minute, then pulled the line back with her left hand and repeated the casting motion. This time he saw a trout poke its head out of the water, and a moment later, she was reeling in a fat cutthroat.

She turned to drop the fish into the creel and saw Mose and Thomas standing on the bank. She shot Mose a quizzical glance, and he replied with a reassuring nod. She gathered her fishing line, picked up the creel, and lightly hopped from the large boulder to a smaller rock near the creek bank. Mose stepped into the water and took the creel, which he handed to Thomas. Then he held out his hand to Miss Mary so she could make the final hop to the shore.

She walked up the bank, set down her pole and reel, and held out her hand to Thomas. "Mary Orvis, this is Colonel Thomas Scoundrel," said Mose. "He invited himself to coffee, and I wanted him to meet you."

Thomas shook her hand. She was in her late twenties, with short dark hair and quick, intelligent eyes set above an expressive mouth. "You look like you have been doing that for quite some time," he said.

"Since I was three, at least," she replied with an open smile. "My father, Charles Orvis, has been making rods and reels and pretty much anything else you need to fly fish since '56. I work with him."

"Miss Mary is writing a book," said Mose. "It's all about them flies they tie; she's got thousands of them up in the wagon."

She laughed. "More like hundreds, but my collection does look a bit like a museum. Are you staying for dinner, Colonel?"

"I can only contribute beans and cornbread to the table, but, yes, thank you, I would enjoy that very much."

❖

While Mary freshened up in her tent, Mose cleaned the fish she caught, and Calsita set the table beneath the canvas awning and began preparing dinner. When Thomas returned from unsaddling and feeding Ulysses, Calista asked him to check on the wine she was chilling in a submerged basket near the creek bank. He took his coffee and a camp chair to the water's edge, opened the basket, and felt four icy bottles. It was too early in the season to worry about mosquito swarms, so he unfolded the chair and sat on the mossy bank as dusk settled over the valley. The sound of water flowing over smooth stones and the orange and purpling of the Colorado sky were so relaxing that he nearly fell asleep.

"May I join you?" he heard Mary say.

Thomas stood and helped unfold the camp chair she had carried down to the stream. His host had changed into a simple cotton skirt and blouse, and when she sat down, she produced a bottle of sherry and two small glasses from her bag. She handed him a glass, uncorked the bottle, and filled both their glasses. He was about to toast her day on the creek when Calista appeared with a small table and a tray of cheeses and crackers. She set down the tray and handed them each a starched white napkin.

"You were serious when you told me that you were going to make this adventuring business of yours a gourmet experience, weren't you," said Thomas.

"Oh, yes, indeed. And with enough positive reports from folks like Miss Mary and yourself, we just might make a go of it." She bustled off to tend to dinner, and Mary and Thomas sat quietly, enjoying the sherry, the cheese, and the sound of the creek.

"You know, I believe she and Mose are going to make a fortune," Mary finally said. "I have friends in Boston and Newport and New York who would pay anything to experience all this."

Thomas looked across the creek to the grassland and trees that rolled in endless waves towards the eastern prairie, and then to the soft, darkening sky above their little camp. He leaned across and clicked his glass against Mary's. "Miss Orvis, you couldn't be more right."

Mose summoned them to dinner a few minutes later. Thomas was impressed to see crystal stemware and china plates on a linen tablecloth, and even a small candelabra hanging from a post in the center of the pavilion. An arrangement of fresh wildflowers graced the table, and each of the four place settings featured a calligraphy name card.

"We wouldn't normally join our clients at dinner," said Mose as he pulled out a chair for Mary Orvis. "But, seeing as how there is just the four of us, it fills out the table some and feels more like a full camp." Then he opened a bottle of stream-chilled Petit Chablis and filled their glasses.

A few minutes later dinner was spread out on the table, and Calista sat down with them to enjoy fresh grilled trout with almonds and garlic, smoked bacon hash, wild rice, sourdough biscuits, and dried fruit. Later, while they drank the second bottle of a delightful, semi-sweet Cru D'Alsace Riesling, Calista pulled a dutch oven from the fire and served up a fresh berry cobbler.

Stars blanketed the sky, and the chirp of crickets filled the air when they finished their coffee. Mose and Calista cleared the table, and Mary and Thomas lingered over a final glass of brandy.

"I don't wish to keep you from your work," said Thomas, "But if you have time tomorrow, I would love to hear more about what you do."

"That would be fine, Colonel. And if you want, I can take a look at that." She motioned towards the cut that Red Elk made on his face. "Your plaster is dried out, and I can see the edges of the wound. I have extra fine thread and needles, and I'm a pretty fair hand at sewing..."

He touched his hand to his face. The wound felt hot, and it had been throbbing more and more all day. It was time to close it up. "That sounds perfect. I seem to have gotten myself into many people's debt these past few weeks. I hope there is something I can do someday to repay your hospitality."

Mary chuckled. "Let's see how you feel about that after I've finished stitching you up."

❖

The sun was topping the eastern horizon, and it was getting warm when Thomas took his place on a camp chair behind Mary Orvis's "museum" wagon. Inside were custom built oak cabinets with glass fronted drawers packed with beads, feathers, tinsel, cork, balsa, as well as spools of wire and multi-colored thread. Above the cabinets were racks that held dozens of bamboo rods, and in one corner was a stack of handsome walnut boxes containing reels with ventilated spools made of nickel-plated brass.

"Are you ready?" she asked.

He nodded. She had cleaned his wound and applied some alcohol-based liniment before sterilizing a needle and attaching a short length of fine silk thread. Now she leaned forward and used the thumb and forefinger of her left hand to pull the wound together. Then she inserted the needle under the skin of his cheek and began deftly stitching the three-inch wound from top to bottom.

He clenched his teeth and gripped the sides of his chair as she sewed. She worked quickly, and less than a minute later she drew a pair of scissors from her trouser pocket, snipped off the end of the thread, and tied a small knot to keep it from unraveling. As she leaned back to admire her work, Calista appeared with two cups of coffee and a plate of fresh-baked biscuits with honey butter.

"That's a fine bit of stitching, Miss Mary," said Calista as she set the cups and plate on a side table. "I had to close up a cut on Mose's forehead last winter, and it was a pretty ragged result. A doctor couldn't have done no better job."

Mary took a sip of coffee and handed Thomas a small mirror. He held it up and examined her work. Calista was right; the stitches were thin and fine and bunched closely together. "If you ever give this up," he said, motioning into the wagon, "the medical profession would happily welcome you."

She smiled and then reached over and lightly touched the wound. "No sign of infection that I can see," she said, "and your skin doesn't feel hot. You'll have a visible scar, but then, people probably expect that sort of thing with a soldier. A sort of calling card, I suppose."

Thomas nodded. He appreciated her skill with a needle and thread as much as he was impressed by the fact that she had not insisted on hearing the story of how he got such a cut.

"How long will you be staying here?" he asked.

"Mose wants to move camp in a few days to a higher elevation. Different stream conditions mean different varieties of trout-and the opportunity to test different flies."

At dinner the previous evening, she had described how her company was producing hundreds of different fly patterns, along with reels, rods and other fishing gear. She explained that because of regional differences in the terms anglers used to describe flies, their customers were never sure if what they were ordering from Orvis was exactly what they expected to get. So, her father not only decided it was time to create a standard naming system for fly patterns, but also that his daughter would also be the one charged with the job of describing and cataloging each of thousands of fly pattern sent to them by fishermen from around the country. Her work included determining the history of each fly, information about the insect it was designed to mimic, and most importantly, how to tie it.

Thomas had flipped through some of her notebooks before bed last night; her research and drawing skills were exceptional. Now, as they finished their coffee and biscuits, he decided it was time to broach the subject of Noah Claybourne.

"I don't suppose it's a coincidence that you are here in Colorado about the time of the Claybourne fishing tournament?"

"No coincidence at all. In fact, I am here at the personal invitation of Mr. Claybourne. My company will be giving a dozen reels away as prizes, and I plan to enter the contest myself. Will you be joining us?"

He shook his head. "I don't expect that I will. I'm headed to Denver to meet a friend, and not sure where I may be headed after that. Anyway, I'm not in your league when it comes to angling. I'd catch more fish with a pistol than a hook."

"May I ask a favor then, Colonel?"

"If it helps in some small way to repay your hospitality, you sure can."

"Our company produces a catalog each year, and we sometimes include personal stories about the people who use our gear. It would mean a lot to our customers to know that someone as famous as you had fished with our products."

"Even though I don't know one end of a pole from the other?" he said with a wide smile. "That might not exactly be what you would call truthful advertising."

Mary thought a moment. "How about this: spend one more day here. I will teach you how to fly fish, and if you catch a dozen trout by sundown, I will outfit you with a complete kit to take when you leave. In return, you will allow my company to publish a statement from Colonel T.E. Scoundrel personally attesting to the quality of our products."

He pretended to weigh the pros and cons of the offer. He could use one more day of rest, and in any event, he was genuinely fascinated by her sport. Then Mary added, "Of course, it would mean having to eat more of Calista's cooking."

On the other side of the camp, Mose was exercising the horses, and Calista was setting the table under the pavilion. A soft breeze was picking up, and the sun sparkled on the surface of the creek. Mary sat quietly, waiting for his answer.

It wasn't a difficult decision. He reached out his hand and said, "Miss Orvis, meet your newest satisfied customer."

TWENTY EIGHT

Southern Arizona Territory

Geronimo Rivas used his boot to push away the charred stump that had once been the deputy sheriff of Monteverde. The corpse was still smoldering, and the stench of burning flesh filled the air. The buildings on the main street of the little town twenty miles north of the Mexican border were all ablaze, and as he lit a cigar, the front of the hotel collapsed into the street across from him. He took a deep breath and felt the familiar surge of physical excitement that he craved more than anything in life. Oh, he loved women–at least he loved to screw them–but nothing he experienced in bed could match the raw, primal sensations that coursed through his body during the act of destruction.

He watched his men race out of buildings holding under their arms the few valuables a desert shit-stain like this town had to offer, and he laughed at the sight of Armando–the newest and youngest member of his gang–trying to shove his little pencil into a woman from behind as she bent over the body of her dying husband.

Rivas had taken a woman himself when they swept into town an hour ago. She had just stepped out of the general merchandise store, and as his men began firing at people on the street and throwing burning torches into their businesses, he leapt off his horse and knocked her to the ground. She was young and strong, and she struggled, of course, but that only added to his enjoyment as he tore aside her skirt and underclothes and savagely penetrated her. He was done after a few violent thrusts. He stood, buttoned his trousers, and as she lay sobbing in the dirt, he put his revolver against her temple and pulled the trigger. Then he went into the store, where the shopkeeper and his wife were cowering behind the counter. The old man was struggling to load his shotgun, which made Rivas laugh as he shot the idiot in the face from a few feet away. When the wife turned to run, he casually placed two .45 caliber bullets in her back. Her body pitched forward and crashed through the door. Rivas grunted and then helped himself to a handful of stick candy from a jar on the counter. He put one in his mouth and slipped the rest into his vest pocket.

Outside, the chaos was total. Bodies littered the street, and several riderless horses raced past him towards the safety of the desert. At the end of the street, three of his men were tying the preacher and his wife together, face to face. They shoved the hapless couple into an empty horse trough and poured a five-gallon bucket of coal oil on them. One of the men struck a match, lit his cigarette, and then tossed the match on top of the tightly bound couple. The oil ignited immediately, flames enveloped the trough, and an almost inhuman chorus of shrieks and sobs rose into the air with the blue and orange flames. When the men tired of the noise, they emptied their rifles into the trough until the screams died away.

Rivas considered himself to be an expert on only one subject: annihilation. Humanity had been weakened across the centuries by the ideals of compassion, tolerance, and reverence for life, he believed, and those virtues were anathema to his credo of obliteration for its own sake. Over time, civilizing forces had squeezed out the more important human character traits necessary to thrive, like aggression, personal survival at all costs, domination, and control. Rivas had mastered those traits. He served his apprenticeship with his adoptive Mescalero Apache father in the 1860s and 70s in the war against the white settlers who were flooding into the territories like locusts. By the time he was sixteen, he discovered he not only had a knack for mayhem and murder, but a hunger as well.

Still, no matter what sophisticated people like his employer Noah Claybourne believed, taking a human life was not an easy thing to do.

Claybourne's kind killed from a distance by proxy, issuing death sentences from the comfort and warmth of the paneled studies in their mansions. They did not know the satisfying feel of a long, razor-sharp blade as it slipped between the ribs and pierced the heart, or the gurgling and sucking sounds a man makes as he fights for air when his throat has been slit. For Rivas, killing was as natural as breathing. Women, children, the elderly and infirm, it didn't matter; he had killed them all. Death was death, and he felt no need to apply moral distinctions to those he liberated from the toils of life. Finding reliable men who could pillage a town and rape, torture, and murder its inhabitants and then sleep peacefully at night was not so easy, of course. Fortunately, he was very good at recruiting men from among the ranks cowboys and drifters who were always hanging around main street saloons and whorehouses. He paid them well, and even more importantly, he let them indulge every depraved desire that their stone-cold, debauched hearts could conjure from the pits of their blackened souls.

He leaned against a post and re-lit his cigar. The screams of dying townspeople that permeated the air only minutes ago had softened to an occasional whimper. Even those would disappear soon; his men knew better than to leave so much as a puppy in this little town alive. Eleven men had just massacred a town of over one hundred, he thought. No one really fought back, and not a tinker's dam one of them had died bravely.

Mr. Claybourne's instructions had been clear; the devastation Rivas was to inflict on this town and the next was to be so brutal, so primitive, and so unthinkably hideous that the aftermath would bring tears to the eyes of the most hardened lawman and make headlines in every newspaper in the nation. Achieve that, and I will pay you even more than we agreed on, Claybourne told him three weeks earlier when they met at Langton Hall.

As he pondered on how much more to ask in payment for a job well done, one of his most experienced men rode towards him. A rope from the pommel of his saddle trailed behind him to the bound wrists of a fat, pink, and completely naked man he was dragging down the center of the rocky dirt street. The man was blubbering incoherently, and his face was a pulpy mass of blood and flayed skin. As transfixing as that picture was, it was the three-foot length of metal pipe protruding from the unfortunate fellow's rectum that really caught Rivas's attention.

The horse came to a halt. "Castillo," Rivas said with a nonchalant, approving nod.

"*Teniente*," Castillo replied, doing Rivas the respect of addressing him by his former military rank.

"Who have we here?"

"*Jefe*, I have the distinct honor of presenting to you *el alcalde*–the mayor–of this delightful little town. *Alcalde*, please meet *Teniente* Rivas, the new military commander of this district." The mayor turned his head in Rivas's direction. He coughed out a thick mass of dark blood, and then lay still, trying to catch his breath between deep sobs.

"So, Castillo, *mi amigote*, I know you are no friend of the political class, especially given their theft of your family hacienda when you were a boy. But, that pipe in his *culo*......is that any way to show respect for a man in his position?"

Castillo turned in his saddle and regarded the bleeding tub of lard behind his horse. "*Me parece* that this *cabron* has spent his entire life with his hand stuck up the ass of every tax-paying *campesino* in this flea-bitten territory. I am simply returning the favor on behalf of all of the poor, hard-working people he has robbed in the name of the government."

Rivas smiled. Then he untied his horse from the post and stepped up into the saddle. "You realize, of course, that your act of justice, as perfectly conceived and well-deserved as it may be, will not ever be known by those who would have most enjoyed it?"

Castillo looked puzzled. "Señor"?

"Next time, *pendejo*, kill the politician publicly *before* you kill his constituents. Let them revel in some small measure of payback before you cut their throats."

With that, Rivas rode off to inspect the carnage so that he could file his report with Noah Claybourne.

❖

TWENTY NINE

Southern New Mexico Territory

Demetria Carnál sat on her horse on a ridge above the town of San Rafael, three hundred miles east of the glowing embers of Monteverde. The midday heat was ferocious, and from her vantage point on the north slope of the Three Sisters volcanic cones not a bird or coyote or any living creature could be seen. The sky was as yellow as the endless landscape of dirt and sagebrush stretching miles in all directions, and why anyone thought that building a town here on the doorstep of hell was a good idea was beyond her comprehension.

Her trip from Claybourne's Colorado ranch had taken eight days; three days by train and five days on horseback, accompanied only by her trusted lieutenant, Ramiro. San Rafael was a day's ride north of the Mexican border, if you wished to pick your way through a maze of basalt canyons littered with razor-sharp cinder rocks that held the heat in like an oven. She could have already joined the two-dozen veteran *pistoleros* she had assembled for this job, but first, she wanted to see the town she was supposed to destroy.

Demetria had earned her title as the Bandit Queen of Northern Mexico honestly; she and her men had robbed banks, trains, stagecoaches, and trading posts from Hermosillo to Nogales, and Chihuahua to Ciudad Juarez. Her trademark lightning raids had garnered the attention of both Mexican and United States newspapers, and her penchant for sharing a portion of her personal earnings with the poorest of the poor made comparisons with the legendary English bandit Robin Hood inevitable. In truth, she spread a little money around in the towns she attacked as an investment to make sure they would not share her whereabouts with the authorities. It had nothing to do with needing to assuage her guilt for being a thief. She enjoyed her chosen profession and was comfortable in her role as the leader of a band of thieves. But, if the world wanted to think of her as a selfless benefactor of the needy, so much the better. As she saw it, if becoming a legend made her work easier and less risky, then she would accept the mantle.

She did suffer from one weakness, though, that should have disqualified her from rising to the top of the banditry business: Demertria did not like to kill people. That is not to say that she had not killed anyone; her bullets had snuffed out the lives of corrupt judges, sadistic *federale* soldiers, swindling politicians, and a score or more *bandoleros* who had tried to compete for business on her turf. In fact, she was only fourteen when she killed a man for the first time. He was the foreman at the *estancia* where her father was employed as head *jimadore* in charge of tending to the agave plants from which tequila and mezcal are produced. Early one morning while her father was working in the fields and she was alone in their shack, the foreman knocked on her door. When she did not answer, he kicked the door in. She had just bathed and was standing naked in front of her dresser. She spun around at the sound of the door splintering off its hinges and found herself face-to-face with the estate's greasy-haired, foul-smelling labor boss. The man's coal black eyes went right to the softness between her legs, and he growled with animal lust. He yanked down his trousers and smiled through yellowed teeth at the shock on her face at the sight of his erection. He took hold of his hardness in one hand and said, "Come *niñita*, and have a taste of this candy."

Demetria's mind raced; she knew with cold certainty that if she did not remain calm she would probably not live through what was about to happen. Somehow, she forced herself to smile at the monster. "Of course, *jefe*," she said in a tender voice, "but please, take me on the bed, not standing here like an animal. Let me do it to you properly."

The foreman grunted with pleasure and turned to walk to the bed in the corner of the one-room cabin. He couldn't believe his good fortune; this timid little *puta* was smart enough to know who was boss. If she performed well, he might let her live and pay her visits whenever he felt the urge.

The instant he turned, Demetria reached to the side and opened the top dresser drawer, where her father kept a loaded pistol beneath his nightshirt. She grabbed the gun and cocked back the hammer just as the foreman turned and sat on the edge of the bed. He still had one hand on his erection, readying himself for the treat he was about to enjoy. At the sight of the pistol leveled at his genitals, his expression changed from menacing lust to total confusion, and then, just as quickly, to blind anger. He roared and lunged off the bed towards her.

Had the foreman known that Demetria's father had trained her in the use of pistols, rifles, and even knives since she was six, he would not have been surprised that her expression was so serene and focused, or the instant that the barrel flashed, that her aim was so damn good. The first shot caught him on the side of his masculine pride, about halfway down the blood-engorged shaft. He started to scream in horror at the sight of half his penis being blown across the room, but, before his vocal cords could form the sound, Demetria calmly raised the barrel and blew his brain out the back of his head.

Late that night, after she and her father had buried the foreman in a thicket of cactus and thoroughly cleaned the room, they sat on the front porch for their evening game of chess. Her father poured two glasses of the estate's finest aged tequila and slid one across to the table to Demetria. It was the first time she had tasted the agave liquor and the first time her father had treated her like a grown woman.

He raised his glass to toast her and repeated the expression he had used every night since she was a baby when he put her to bed: *"La vida es sueño."* Life is a dream.

❋

Demetria shifted in her saddle and turned her face away from the scorching wind that was starting to blow across the desert floor. She did not like to dwell on her childhood and youth. She missed her father's kindness and wisdom every day, but what would he think of the adult that she had become? And, even if he shrugged off the bandit existence she had lived until now, how would he feel about her preparing to level the small town below, including any of the inhabitants who made the grave mistake of simply trying to protect their homes? Life, indeed, is a dream, a still voice of conscience whispered inside her. But the destruction she was preparing to inflict upon San Rafael could only be described as a nightmare.

Demetria motioned to Ramiro. Fort Cummings, where she was to meet her men in two days, was thirty miles to the north. She wheeled her horse and galloped towards the cool green hills in the distance.

THIRTY

Denver, Colorado

A few hours after receiving Itzcoatl's telegram in New York City two months earlier, Thomas was on a train headed West. During a layover in Indianapolis he penned a letter to the War Department requesting that his pension be made available to him at the Fort Lupton Trading Post, northeast of Denver. His personal mail would also be forwarded there, and he had given both Marshal Bat Masterson and Major Rhine the post's address should they hear any news about Diego.

The ride to the post from Mary Orvis's camp took a day and a half. Strapped to his bedroll was the fly-fishing reel and pole Mary presented him when he had mastered fly casting well enough to fill his creel with trout in a single afternoon. Much to his surprise, he had enjoyed learning how to prepare flies and how to seek out the best places in the stream to snap his line. Under different circumstances he might have enjoyed entering Claybourne's fishing tournament. He would also have enjoyed at least one more of Calista's gourmet camp dinners.

He reached Fort Lupton at midday. What was left of the once bustling army camp now sat in the shade of a scrub brush and rock-strewn hill. The barracks and walls had been torn down years before, and all that was left of former federal encampment were three long, low adobe and timber buildings and a horse stockade. He was surprised that the post was still a federally run operation, but in the lean years after the war Congress had cut army funding to the bone, and small outposts like Fort

Lupton were common from St. Louis to Sacramento.

He left Ulysses to get shoed at the farrier's, slung his saddle bags over his shoulder, and climbed the steps to the wide porch that fronted the trading post. Inside, the store was packed with dry goods and groceries of every kind, from bolts of dress-making cloth to hand tools, patent medicines, rifles, ammo, and bags of dried pinto beans. A hand-lettered sign offered "Meals All Day" and an elderly Chinese woman sat at a table sorting through a giant pile of colored glass buttons. The counter was covered with glass jars filled with candy, boxes of cigars, and an assortment of notions and toys designed to get people to let loose with the last of their pocket change. Behind the counter were several shelves of liquor, and next to the backbar mirror were rows of pigeon-hole mail receptacles, many of them packed to bursting.

He introduced himself to the proprietor and asked for a beer and a sandwich while the man found his mail. A few minutes later the store-keeper dropped a thick bundle tied with string on the table. Inside were two telegrams, along with letters from Annette, Bill Cody, and an old friend who managed the sugar plantation on the Hawaiian island of Lana'i where he had worked ten tears earlier. Most of the letters in the packet contained invitations for him to speak at veteran's conventions, association gatherings and business meetings from New York to San Francisco. Such requests had been a staple of his life since the romanticized versions of his exploits at Pebble Creek Ridge had been splashed across the front pages of newspapers around the country. He supposed he could make a good living doing lectures, but he turned every request down and always would.

The first telegram had arrived at the trading post ten days ago. It was from Diego, who had met up with Itzcoatl in El Paso Del Norte and was on his way to Denver. Did Thomas have any news of Rosalilia? The second telegram, posted three days ago from Trinidad, was also from Diego. He had spoken with Marshal Masterson, who told them that Thomas had been seriously injured but was on the mend and was headed to Denver. Thomas was pleased that Hamish and Von Sievers had gotten word to Major Rhine, who had, in turn, contacted

Bat Masterson. According to Diego's second message, he would arrive in Denver in two days and would be staying at the Windsor House Hotel.

He pressed his hand against his ribs, which were still painful from being dumped into the ravine by Claybourne's men over a month ago. Yes, he thought, I have news for Diego. He finished his beer, gathered up the rest of his mail to read later, and waved to the storekeeper. As he walked out of the trading post he caught sight of himself in a mirror behind the bar. He had lost weight, and his face was drawn and pale, except for the thin red wound that ran from his cheekbone to the corner of his mouth. It would be weeks before he regained his full strength.

"Remember, lad," Walt Whitman told him when he was discharged from the army hospital, "we go into every battle in life with what we have at that moment, not with what we would like to have."

This is what I have today, he thought as he stepped out onto the porch and scanned the cloudless horizon. It will have to be enough.

❋

The city of Denver was hot, dusty, and crowded when he arrived at noon the next day. He boarded Ulysses at a livery stable off Larimer Street and walked around the corner past the "Ladies Only Entrance" on 18th to the front of the Windsor House Hotel. Built two years earlier, the five-story sandstone and rhyolite façade was a proud city's symbol of its transition from a wide-open gold rush town to the main commercial center and railroad hub of the Rocky Mountain region. Major Rhine had told him that the hotel also boasted the best cuisine in the state and a wine cellar second to none.

He walked through the iron porte-cochère gate adorned with two Greco-Roman lampposts and waited for the top-hatted doorman in full Royal British livery to swing open the heavy brass door leading into the marble lobby. It was cool inside, and his first instinct was to turn to the left and head for the Cattleman's Room and its famous gaming tables. But he kept to the business at hand and went directly to the registration desk, where he selected a room with a private bath for $2.50 per day.

He hadn't soaked in a tub for months, and, other than the sponge baths Dawn Pillow gave him each night in the warmth of her tipi, his only baths for the past week had been in freezing cold streams.

He briefly considered registering under a false name; he had no doubt that Claybourne paid the better hotels to keep tabs on who was coming and going in town. But he was going to discover sooner or later that Thomas was still alive, and so he wrote out his full name and rank in clear, bold letters on the ledger page. The desk clerk's eyebrows rose, and a smile creased his face when he read the Scoundrel name, and Thomas knew it wasn't simply because a famous Civil War hero was gracing the Windsor with his presence. More than likely the clerk would get an extra $20 gold piece for getting the information to Claybourne's agents as quickly as he could. As Thomas took a complimentary newspaper from the desk and walked towards the ornate stairs leading to the guest rooms, he wasn't surprised to see the weaselly clerk scurry into a back office to share the news.

Before he went upstairs, he stopped at the concierge desk and asked for someone from the hotel laundry to come to his room in an hour. Then he went down an adjoining corridor lined with gift and clothing shops until he found the men's haberdashery. With the assistance of a very knowledgeable clerk, he selected three shirts, new underwear, a tie and jacket, and two pair of wool trousers, which he arranged to have hemmed that afternoon. Then he borrowed a menu and wine list from the hotel restaurant and went up to his room.

When the laundry maid knocked on his door few minutes later, he was naked. He wrapped a towel around his waist and handed the astonished young woman a cotton bag containing every piece of clothing he owned. He also gave her a dollar tip, with the promise of another dollar if she could get the clothing back to him by 7:00 p.m. The Irish girl was all grins; $2 equaled her pay for a full ten-hour day. She thanked the handsome colonel and rushed off to get his clothing to the head of the clean and press line.

He filled the tub with hot water, added some of the bath soap provided by the hotel, and pulled a small table into the bathroom on which he piled the rest of his unread mail. Then he settled into the tub to soak and read. Annette's letter was posted a few days after he bolted from her side at Delmonico's to go to Diego's assistance. In the weeks following the flying champagne cork mishap and the emergency telegram that waylaid his plans for a tumble in a rustic cabin's feather bed, he assumed their brief and unconsummated affair was over. Judging from the outpouring of affection and loneliness that marked her letter, however, that assumption was one-sided. *"I will get right to the heart of things, dearest Thomas,"* she wrote. *"I had hoped that our night together would have ended in a lover's embrace, not with you racing off to rescue a friend."* Thomas felt his heart deflate at those words. "*But this is who you are, and the man I love could do no less than sacrifice his own happiness to ensure the safety of another. I promise you this: on the night you return to me, every rapturous gate will open, and we will become as one."*

Thomas groaned. His moonlight encounter with Dawn Pillow notwithstanding, he had felt real affection for Annette. But, in the two months since their ill-fated dinner, he had grown increasingly convinced that he would never see her again. From the moment he strapped on his Colt and swung up into Ulysses's saddle at Major Rhine's, he knew that his life was meant to be lived wherever there were still frontiers. He craved the adventure that one can only experience by being in the thick of things, not on the edges of the action looking in. The year he had spent working as a New York City banker had been the most miserable period of his life. And now, not even the thought of Anette's extraordinary sensuality, or the promise that she would bounce him into bed the minute he came back to her, was enough to turn him from his course.

Despite that conviction, he felt a familiar wave of melancholy begin to envelope him. This happened only when his life slowed to a crawl, and at those moments the only things that kept him emotionally balanced was the surge of adrenaline he felt at the gaming table or the physical release he experienced in bed with the next beautiful woman. He was not foolish enough to think that he could live that way forever; but, at age thirty-three, he could not conceive of any circumstance in which a person, force, or outside event would be able to move him from his appointed path.

He carefully folded Annette's letter and placed it back in its envelope on the table beside the tub. The he turned on the tap for more hot water and reached for Bill Cody's letter. The man who the world knew as Buffalo Bill had been his good friend since they served together five years earlier in the Sioux Wars during the winter of 1877. Cody was already a famous showman who had been the subject of Ned Buntline's largely fictional dime-novels for over eight years when he returned to scouting for the army after the death of his young son, Kit Carson. He spent part of the year touring with performers and the rest of the year scouting for the army on the prairie. When Thomas was recalled to active duty and attached to the Army's 5th Cavalry Regiment by order of the Secretary of War, Bill was the regiment's Chief of Scouts.

Thomas had been amused when Bill showed up at the command post in Cheyenne, Wyoming, wearing the same costume he wore in performances; a bright red fireman's shirt over black velvet pants that were trimmed in red and appointed with silver bells and embroidery flourishes. Even more impressive to him than the outfit was the way that the veteran scout ignored the snide comments and ridicule from some of the troopers. In the end, Bill wore the gaudy outfit through the entire campaign.

In time, he grew to respect Cody for his seasoned trail wisdom, his sense of humor, his ability to speak plainly, and his fearlessness. The men might guffaw at his showman's sartorial splendor, but no one disputed his bravery or integrity. Cody and he were an odd duo in some ways; they were both national heroes, but where Cody craved the limelight and the adulation of crowds, Thomas kept to himself and did everything he could to downplay his hero status. Bill asked him to join his new Buffalo Bill Combination show so many times in the past three years that it had come to be a joke between them.

The letter he was holding from Cody was only a week old; it simply said, *"Colonel, I will be doing a little antelope hunting along McTimmonds Creek at the fork of the Nettles River, southeast of Denver. Expect to be there for five to six days from next Wednesday. I am told you are local, and if so, I invite you to share my campfire. We have much to catch up on. Sincerely, Bill C."*

This was Tuesday, so Cody would be arriving at his hunting camp tomorrow. As he added more hot water to the tub, he decided it would be a good idea for Diego and him to pay the scout a visit; he was convinced that Claybourne was the key to Rosalillia's whereabouts, but if he and Diego were going to move against the man, they would need every ally they could find. Theatrics aside, William F. Cody was a man you wanted in your corner when the big fight was on.

❖

At 6:30 there was a knock on his door. He was dressed in a new shirt, tie, and freshly hemmed trousers from the hotel haberdashery, much to the disappointment of the Irish laundry girl and the co-worker she had brought along to prove she had indeed met the famous Colonel T.E Scoundrel–and in the nude, no less. Her frown quickly vanished when he rewarded her with not one, but two shiny dollar coins.

He put away his laundered clothing, slipped on his jacket, and folded the unread Denver newspaper under his arm. Then he went downstairs to the restaurant and requested the quietest corner in the room. A few minutes later he was enjoying a half-bottle of G.H. Mumm champagne and an appetizer of oysters on the half shell. He opened the four-day old newspaper and was immediately stunned by the banner headline. After reading the opening paragraph, his stomach began to churn.

ARIZONA BORDER TOWN ATTACKED, 106 KILLED
WOMEN & CHILDREN AMONG THE SLAUGHTERED
ARMY GENERAL GREER VOWS SWIFT VENGANCE
By Tanner Fulbright, Special Correspondent
Monteverde, Arizona Territory, August 22,1882

In an attack of unparalleled savagery, a band of Mexican brigands under the command of a known Mexican regular army officer has attacked and demolished the western Arizona Territory border town of Monteverde, twenty miles north of Mexico.

Army Major General Winston Greer, the US Commander for

the Arizona and New Mexico Territories, told this correspondent that in all his years of service he had never seen such savage brutality. All 106 residents of the small mining town were butchered by the Mexican attackers. Their homes and businesses were burned to the ground, their livestock were killed, and many of the bodies showed signs of torture so heinous that we cannot describe them to the decent people who read this newspaper. Suffice it to say that this correspondent can only describe the indignities visited upon the poor residents of Monteverde before, during, and after the raid as a vision out of Dante's Inferno. I was personally sickened, and I will carry the images of slaughtered mothers with dead babies in their arms with me to my grave.

General Greer could not surmise a guess as to why the barbaric attack on helpless American citizens had taken place. "We often see small raiding parties from Mexico cross into the Territories to steal horses and cattle, and occasionally a life is lost," he said. "But this simply makes no sense unless we see it as an act of outright war."

Has Mexico declared war on us, this correspondent inquired of the General? "I am a military man, not a political figure or diplomat," he answered,"so I cannot provide your readers with an accurate answer to that question. However," he continued,"outside the battlefield, I can tell you I have never seen carnage on this scale. I have sent a report to the territorial governor and to the President of the United States. I am authorized on my own to seek out those who perpetrated this horrendous injustice, and even now, several companies of men under my command are in pursuit of the brigands."

A statement from the US State Department and the Secretary of War are said to be forthcoming.

-end-

The look on Thomas' face as he read the article drew his waiter's attention. He approached the table and said, "Sir, are you alright?"

He simply motioned to the front page of the paper and shook his head. "This is unbelievable," he said.

"Are you only now learning of the attack?" asked the waiter.

"Yes, I have been out on the prairie. I had no idea. Has there been further news?"

The waiter refilled his champagne glass. "Only a promise from our governor here in Colorado to offer our military department in support of General Greer's search for the bastards…" his voice trailed off, and he looked around the dining room to see if anyone else had heard his intemperate remark. "Sorry, sir."

"No need to apologize. You can't be human and not be sickened by this."

The waiter pointed a finger at the headline on the paper. "He is here with us at the hotel, you know. He arrived this morning."

"Who's that?"

"Tanner Fulbright, the reporter who filed this story. He was in Monteverde that day after the attack. I understand he is following the story."

Thomas thought a moment. Then he dug into his jacket pocket and fished out a calling card. "When you see Mr. Fulbright, would you please give him my card and ask if he will see me?"

"Of course, sir." The waiter pocketed the card and then pulled his order book from his apron. "And now, sir, may I ask if you are ready for dinner?"

Food was the last thing on Thomas' mind. He started to say no, then changed his mind. He was still healing from his wounds, and if what he had just heard meant what he thought it did, he was going to need every ounce of strength he could muster in the coming days.

"Just bring me whatever you would recommend. And a bottle of your best Bordeaux."

The waiter went to the kitchen to place the order and then returned with a basket of warm bread with chive butter and a bottle of Chateau Latour. "Our sommelier would normally decant this, but I thought you wouldn't mind if I took care of you this evening without too many other distractions."

Thomas nodded. He appreciated professionalism in all its aspects, no matter the trade or profession, and his waiter clearly understood his customers. He read and reread the front-page story over the next hour and a half as dishes were delivered to his table. The baked flounder a lá Chambord was excellent, as were the side salads and vegetables, but he ate tonight only for nourishment, not for pleasure. The Latour did garner his attention; it was one of the finest he had ever enjoyed. No doubt his bill would reflect that fact, so he took plenty of time to savor it.

It was late when the waiter brought him coffee and brandy. Thomas handed him a $5 tip, an almost unheard-of amount for a gratuity. "I will be meeting friends tomorrow," he told the delighted server, "and I want to make sure that you will be taking care of us."

As the waiter walked away, he read through the newspaper article one last time. Monteverde. It was the name of a town that Moncton and Elias mentioned while they were hauling him out to the ravine from Claybourne's house in the back of the wagon. He had weaved in and out of consciousness during the long ride, but he had near complete recall of what the hired guns talked about. Most of it focused on liquor and women's anatomy. Except for this part.

"You ever been out to that rat's ass of a town, that Monteverde?" Elias had asked Moncton as the wagon clattered along the rutted dirt road. "Copper mines and cactus, that's about all it's got to offer. The saloon only serves beer, and there ain't a whorehouse in fifty miles. Has two churches to make up for that deficiency, though."

"Don't know as I have been there," came the reply. "But if what the boss was saying about that little town is in the cards, I don't guess anybody will be paying a visit no more."

Somehow, he thought, Claybourne, Rosalillia, and the destruction of Monteverde were linked together. He finished his coffee and walked through the quiet lobby. He could hear laughter and piano music coming from the gaming room across the way. Tonight, though, the cards held no sway on him. He took his newspaper and walked up the stairs to his room. There was a lot to think through before he met Diego and Itzcoatl at the train station tomorrow afternoon.

❖

THIRTY ONE

Mexico City, July 1882

There was nothing Diego de San Martín could do to stop the dreams. They came to him every night in his bed at the Hospital de los Ángeles within minutes of being injected with another dose of morphine. He had a choice, of course; he could accept the excruciating pain where he had been shot in his abdomen and leg, and go without any sleep, or he could succumb to the seductive call of Morpheus and allow the doctor to administer another hypodermic.

He could not go in search of Rosalilia's kidnappers until he healed, and he would not heal unless he could sleep. The dreams were a small price to pay to earn his way out of the hospital then, but that fact did not make them any more tolerable. He craved the release the drug delivered, but he feared the price he had to pay for the brief respite from pain. Within minutes of the morphine being injected, a warm, numbing sensation coursed through his body. The ache in his broken femur receded, and the burning and tearing sensations in his gut calmed to a dull throb. Then he felt as if his body was being enveloped in a tight, warm cocoon, and the dream came.

He was standing outside his room in the open gallery of La Hacienda Verján on the night of his engagement party. The scent of night blooming jasmine filled the air, and the sounds of a Mozart string quartet floated up from the garden below. Then, the decorative candle sconces that lined the gallery walls began to flare, and one by one, they turned their twisted gargoyle faces in his direction, murmuring obscenities and condemnations at him. *"Coward, bastard, deserter, turncoat, apostate,"* they hissed in unison. *"You abandoned Rosalilia with a Judas kiss. You betrayed her. You let them take her. You could not protect the woman you said you loved. You were not man enough for her, but those who carried her away will have her legs open soon enough, and she will thank them for showing her what a real man is capable of doing."*

Then the doors along the corridor began to open slowly, and the engagement party guests filed out in slow motion. They lined up with their backs against the wall, and, one by one, they turned their heads to Diego and joined the grotesque sconces in their chorus of reproof.

The last guests to come out into the gallery were the Bishop and Rosalilia's aunt. She came out first, hunched over with her night dress pulled up to her neck. The corpulent Bishop was behind her, naked, his hands on the aunt's shoulders, and his fleshy, sweating ass pumping back and forth as he thrust himself into her again and again. The aunt turned her head to Diego, smiled sweetly and said, *"You will never have my niece like this,"* which caused the Bishop to begin to laugh wildly and slam home into her in an even greater frenzy.

Diego felt himself being pulled down the corridor, and as he passed the guests, they shook their fists and spit on him. When he reached the stairs, he saw the engineer Matthew Cord on the landing calmly smoking a cigar while stroking Rosalilia's long hair. Her eyes were closed, as if she were sleeping. Cord smiled up at Diego, lifted Rosalilia's chin, and gave her a long kiss on the lips. Diego struggled to move, but his feet were lead, and he had no choice but to watch as Cord began to move his hands all over his fiancée's body.

Then Cord slung Rosalilia over his shoulder, gave Diego a mocking half-salute, and walked through the open door and out into the courtyard. When Diego was finally able to move, he raced down the stairs and into the gardens. It was daytime, and the engagement party was in full swing. Guests danced, servers carried platters of food and drink to the tables, and the lake sparkled in the perfect June sunshine. He could not see Rosalilia or Cord. A ripple of laughter began to move through the crowd, and Diego went towards the elevated stage where the musicians were playing. There, struggling and kicking, he saw Rosalilia's father hanging by the neck from a wooden gibbet. Piles of fresh flowers were strewn around the base of the gallows, and, as Señor Verján's face began to turn purple, Diego watched helplessly as the old man pulled his sword from its scabbard and began to slash wildly in all directions. The orchestra played louder in time with the flying sword, and the assembled guests roared with laughter at Verján's futile gyrations. In the midst of the monstrous scene, Señora Verján sat on an upholstered chair in front of the gallows, sipping sherry and waving the crowd on.

Diego turned to leave the garden, and it was night again. Cord's men were streaming out of the house carrying paintings, silver, and furnishings. Two men were holding Itzcoatl's lifeless body above their heads. They carried the warrior over to the great fountain in the center of the courtyard and tossed him into the water. Diego raced over to help his mentor, only to watch as Itzcoatl's body sunk into the depths. The Aztec's facial expression was impassive, but his eyes burned into Diego with a look of complete and utter disappointment. A moment later, the dark green water swallowed him up.

"Diego, *mi amor*," he heard Rosalilia whisper. He turned and saw her standing in the back of Cord's freight wagon. Her arms were tied behind her, and her night gown was pulled down to her waist. Only her long hair covered her exposed breasts. Cord stood behind her, caressing and kissing her shoulders. Rosalilia looked into Diego's eyes, and in a plaintive voice, she recited a stanza from the book of Keats's poetry he had given her at their engagement breakfast that morning.

"O what can ail thee, knight-at-arms, Alone and palely loitering?
The sedge has withered from the lake, And no birds sing."

Diego tried to move, strained to reach out to her to pull her from the wagon, but his feet were rooted to the ground. Cord continued to lavish kisses on her neck and shoulders as the wagon pulled away from the burning hacienda. Her eyes never left Diego's. He had never seen an expression of such sorrow and pity. He collapsed to the ground, sobbing.

When a group of Cord's men surrounded him and began stabbing him with bayonets, he woke up.

❈

The dream never changed, night after night, for weeks, even when his parents moved him to a new hospital and later to a private, guarded clinic in Bosques de las Lomas for fear that Cord's men would return to kill him. Day and night, Itzcoatl's sons Xipil and Ácatl stood outside his door. No one would get past them.

Diego could only wait for word from Thomas as he sought answers in Colorado and from Itzcoatl, who was arranging for Diego to join him in EL Paso del Norte. The doctors told him that he would walk with a limp for the rest of his life, but that his gut would be as good as ever within a few weeks. His own timeline was slightly different; as soon as he could mount a horse and hold a gun, he would find and kill Matthew Cord and anyone else responsible for kidnapping Rosalilia and murdering her father. In his heart, he knew she was alive. He also knew that he could not have a better friend and ally than Thomas Scoundrel, who had walked away without hesitation from his career and his woman and traveled across the country to help his friend.

On the first morning of his seventh week of recovery, Diego got out of bed and walked to the clinic window. The gardens were in full bloom, and the sky was powder blue and cloudless. Several of the ambulatory patients were walking in the garden, and he saw his mother coming through the main gate for her daily visit. The parcel wrapped in brown paper she was carrying would be his revolver and a box of cartridges.

He was grateful for the presence of Itzcoatl's sons outside his door, but, until he had Rosalilia safe by his side, his pistol would be his constant companion.

❈

THIRTY TWO

Denver, Colorado, August 1882

The stable car attendant had never seen mounts as impressive as the two stallions the white-haired Indian was offloading at the Denver station. Their heavily muscled bodies, arched necks, and strong bone structure reminded him of the great *destrier* war horses that carried armored knights into battle in medieval times. The saddles and tack were equally splendid, as were the hand-tooled rifle scabbards he helped lash to the saddles when the train braked to its final stop in the terminal. No doubt these horses had come up from EL Paso del Norte for some special purpose or event.

Itzcoatl acknowledged the attendant with a wave and then instructed a porter to carry Diego's bags to the hansom cab stand and wait until the gentleman was ready to leave. He mounted his horse outside the station, took Diego's horse by the reins, and rode off to the livery stable where Thomas had boarded Ulysses. He would join Diego and the colonel at the Windsor later. Or rather, they would join him when they were done arguing on the arrival platform about which of them looked the worse for wear after their separate encounters with Claybourne's men.

"Twenty pounds, at least," Thomas was saying.

"I will take your twenty and see you by another five," replied Diego with a smile. "But, unlike you, I haven't gained any of my weight back."

"Ah, but I have had to buy new trousers because my old ones kept falling off," continued Thomas, "while yours look well worn. Hardly the look of a man who has wasted away to a twig."

"When *your* pants fall off, my friend," laughed Diego, "it has more to do with the fact that there is a beautiful woman in the room than it does with your not getting enough to eat."

Thomas grinned and shook his head. Then his voice grew serious. He noticed Diego's limp when he stepped down from the train. His friend had probably dropped closer to thirty or thirty-five pounds during his convalescence. "Are you ready for this?"

"Don't let my pallorous skin or the walking cane fool you, Tomás." He pulled his coat back and placed a hand on his revolver. "For an entire month in hospital, and during every minute of the journey from Mexico City, I have thought only of finding Rosalilia and punishing those who took her and killed her father. I am ready."

Thomas nodded. "I understand. But thinking is not the same as preparing. I have spent my fair share of time these past weeks trying to heal, just like you. What I know is that we are up against a small army of highly trained *soldados* who are very good at protecting the men I believe to be responsible for the crimes committed against the Verjáns and yourself. Not to mention the politicians and financiers who back these people up."

Another train puffed its way to a stop a few yards away from the wrought-iron bench on the platform where they were sitting. Diego stood, slung his valise over his shoulder, and took up his cane. "The Windsor is famous for its kitchen, and I am starving," he said. "Let's eat and make our plan."

❖

The waiter who took care of Thomas the previous evening seated the three men at a corner table that was partially obscured behind a semi-circle of tall potted ferns. Itzcoatl was uncomfortable with the starched tablecloth and linens, but it was the absence of tequila and mezcal from the bar menu that really put him off. He was about to leave and go elsewhere to eat when a busboy appeared at his side and pulled a tall blue bottle from under his coat. "From your waiter," said the boy as he handed the mezcal to Itzcoatl. "It's on the house." The Aztec grinned and handed the boy a tip. He uncorked the bottle and filled a small indigo glass that the boy also brought. "To civilization," he said to Thomas and Diego before downing the fiery liquor.

Over tomato salad, sautéed mushrooms, fresh-baked bread, and champagne, Thomas walked through everything that had happened since the day he got off the train at Trinidad. Diego's face clouded over when he described being hit in the head at Claybourne's and carried out to the ravine. He twice asked Thomas to repeat the conversation in the wagon between Moncton and Elias about Monteverde, and he agreed that Claybourne was up to his eyes in whatever was going on.

"Matthew Cord must be here in Colorado," Diego concluded. "And if he is here, so is Rosalilia. But, why? Why kill her father and *then* kidnap her? Even if Claybourne's intention was to use her to get permits and concessions for his mines in Northern Mexico, by killing her father, he lost his leverage over the Ministry of Mines. It makes no sense."

Thomas refilled their glasses. "Except, the kidnapping does send a clear message to whoever takes the job next. Their family is not safe either. Maybe that's enough for Claybourne." Then he added a hopeful note: "I also think this means that Rosalilia is alive, and Claybourne is going to have to prove that she is."

"I don't understand," said Itzcoatl before Diego could respond. "Why would that matter to Claybourne now?"

"Because he is going to have to demonstrate that if the next minister's family member is kidnapped, he will release them unharmed when they agree to his demands. If he can't produce Rosalilia before then, the new minister will assume that his family member will be killed no matter what, and so he will have no reason to negotiate."

They finished the champagne, and the sommelier made a splendid table side show of opening the bottle of Romanée-Conti ordered by Diego. "This is the finest wine in our cellar," explained the wine steward, "and probably the best wine in the world. We are allocated only five cases per year."

He poured three small tastes into crystal wine glasses and waited expectantly. Thomas and Diego swished their glass, examined the deep ruby colors, inhaled the extraordinary fragrances of violet and black cherry, and then tasted the wine. Itzcoatl raised his glass without ceremony and downed it in a single gulp. Then he pushed the bevel-cut Baccarat crystal glass aside and poured more mezcal into his glass.

The sommelier ignored the Aztec's barbarism and watched expectantly as Diego and Thomas savored their tastes. Diego's eyes closed, and a satisfied smile crossed his face. Thomas's eyebrows went up, and he shook his head from side to side. "I can't do justice to a description of the layers of smell and taste," he said. "The wine is that remarkable."

His remark earned a look of pride and satisfaction from the sommelier. "An Irish poet, Healy, I believe is his name, penned some words about Romanée-Conti a few years ago. May I recite them?

Diego shot Thomas an amused glance before saying, "Yes, of course, please, but only if you fill our glasses first."

The sommelier filled their glasses to the top. Then he took a step back, put one arm across his chest, and cleared his throat. "It was upon the occasion of his first experience with this wine that the poet was moved to write:

Within this opulent wine are the song of armies sweeping into battle, the roar of the waves upon a rocky shore, the glint of sunshine after rain on the leaves of a forest, the depths of the church organ, and the voices of children singing hymns. All these and a hundred other things are blended into one magnificence."

Thomas had expected to bust out laughing at whatever verse the wine steward was going to recite. He had dined in some of the finest establishments in the world, but this was the first time that he had heard of a restaurant employee reciting a poem about wine. However, as the last words of the poem faded away, he looked across the table at Diego and realized his friend had been as moved as he was.

As they enjoyed the wine, their waiter rolled a cart to the table and began uncovering dishes of grilled rib-eye steak, artichokes, and roasted onions. When he finished, a short, round little man in a tweed suit appeared from around the ferns. He was young and pale, and if the spectacles and moustache were intended to make him look more mature, the effect was unsuccessful. He looked lost, and he was clearly uncomfortable interrupting their meal.

"You would be Colonel T.E. Scoundrel?" he said to Thomas in a distinct British accent while looking down at the calling card he held in his hand.

Thomas reluctantly lowered his wine glass. Then he remembered: "Mr. Fulbright? The reporter?"

"The very same, sir. Your waiter asked me to introduce myself, but I can certainly meet you at a more convenient time."

"No, we need to speak to you now."

Thomas signaled to the waiter to bring another chair. Fulbright sat, and Thomas introduced Diego and Itzcoatl. The reporter ordered a whiskey, and Thomas asked the waiter to bring a full bottle. "You're going to need it," he told the reporter.

When the whiskey arrived, Thomas said, "We have read your coverage of the raid on Monteverde. A terrible event."

Fulbright looked into the distance. "More terrible than you can imagine, Colonel. The thought that civilized humans could inflict such savagery upon a helpless populace is really beyond comprehension."

"The three of us have seen more than our share of death in war, and so we have some idea of what you must have experienced. Still, I do not know these people," said Diego, "but I can dispel you of any notion that they are civilized."

Fulbright took a long, deep drink. "Are you agents of the government, or do you have some other special interest in this event?" he asked.

"Our interest is personal, but we do have information that may be of value to you. That is, if you are going to pursue the story further," said Thomas.

"My editors in New York have told me that I am to follow this story exclusively. The massacre is dominating the national conversation. Some in Congress are even calling for an invasion of Northern Mexico."

"There are parts of Mexico I would advise the American army to avoid," said Itzcoatl in a bemused tone. "For their health."

Diego looked into Fulbright's eyes. "Before we talk with you, Señor, please understand that for *our* health," he nodded in Thomas's direction "we need to know who you are and where your loyalties lie."

Fulbright looked thoughtfully at the three men sitting with him. He knew Colonel Scoundrel by reputation, and, judging from Diego's speech and clothing, he was clearly a member of the Mexican aristocracy. As for the wizened old man with the piercing blue eyes gripping the glass of mezcal like he was holding a revolver, who could know? His survival instinct told him to get up and leave, right now. He knew the Monteverde story was a dangerous pursuit; the closer he got to the truth about who was behind the slaughter and why, the more he would become a target. His journalistic instincts, on the other hand, shouted to him in an even louder voice: these were serious men. They knew something about Monteverde, and for the past few days he had run into one wall after another while seeking more information. It was time to take a new tack.

"As for who I am," Fulbright said, "my story begins at King's College in Cambridge, England, where I became mesmerized by the tales of your wild West. Savage Indians fighting settlers on the edge of the frontier, Buffalo Bill and the duel to the death with the warrior Yellow Hand, that sort of thing."

Thomas smiled at the mention of his friend's name. He leaned over and poured another whiskey for the young reporter and then waved the approaching waiter off.

"I have always loved writing; I have an eye–and an ear–for stories, and so my career in journalism was a foregone conclusion. I came to New York four years ago, and have worked my way west ever since, studying and writing about how the frontier experience distinguishes America from Europe. I am fascinated by the energy, practicality, and individualism of the American character. Especially the gunfighters. My title is "Special Correspondent," a moniker that does not, alas, translate to much in the way of a paycheck."

Diego nodded. "And your loyalties?"

Fulbright sipped at his whiskey. "Only one, sir: the truth."

"Have you done any business with Noah Claybourne?"asked Thomas.

"I know of him, of course, everyone in Colorado and the territories does. But I have never had occasion to interview him or write about him or his businesses."

Thomas looked at Diego and then at Itzcoatl. Both men nodded. Fulbright was telling the truth.

"I have a story to tell," said Thomas, "and when I am done you will appreciate why we are being cautious. It will take a while, so let's order something for your dinner. As our guest, of course." Fulbright beamed. He was hungry, and the storied Windsor restaurant was far out of his budget.

Diego called the waiter over and ordered a steak dinner for the reporter. Thomas was also able to persuade the sommelier to bring them a second bottle of the Romanée-Conti, and as they ate and drank, they got to know more about Fulbright. In return, the reporter peppered his hosts with questions about their backgrounds.

When the table was cleared, the waiter brought brandy and cigars. Fulbright pulled a small notebook and pencil from his jacket pocket and laid it in front of him on the table. That was the signal for the story to begin. It was late enough that the restaurant had quieted, and Thomas asked the waiter not to disturb them.

Diego began with the story of his engagement party and Matthew Cord's late-night raid on the Verján's home. He described the pitched battle in detail, including his discovery of Señor Verján's body, how Rosalilia was carried to the freight wagon, and when he was shot in the leg and abdomen. Itzcoatl picked up the story from there with detail about Diego's hospitalization and the lengths they went through to keep his whereabouts secret in case Cord was looking to finish the job.

Then, Thomas recounted his journey to Trinidad and his conversations with Marshal Bat Masterson and later, with Major Rhine. Fulbright perked up at the mention of the famous frontier marshal, and he was even happier when Thomas suggested he get in touch with the lawman. Finally, Thomas detailed his visit to Claybourne's home and described how he had been assaulted, tossed into a wagon, and hauled out to be dumped into a deep ravine after he brought up the subject of Matthew Cord and his role in Rosalilia's kidnapping.

"This is where the story becomes important for you," he said to the reporter. He recited the conversation between Moncton and Elias in which they referred to what they had heard from the "boss" about what was going to happen to Monteverde. "And here is where everything ties together; Cord, the mining engineer who led the raid on Rosalilia's home and kidnapped her, is an employee of Noah Claybourne."

Fulbright had been taking notes at a rapid-fire pace. Now he lowered his pencil and raised his head. "Cord works for Claybourne?" he asked in a disbelieving tone.

"He does," answered Diego.

"And you are sure that he was working for Claybourne in Mexico at the time?"

"There is no question about that," Diego replied.

"So, Cord kidnaps the daughter of the Minister of the Interior of Mexico, where Claybourne is trying to get permits to vastly increase his mining operations. Cord murders the Minister, and, you believe, spirits away his daughter here to Colorado as a warning to Mexican officials that they had better play ball, or their families may be attacked?"

Thomas nodded and refilled Fulbright's glass. "And you are convinced that Miss Verján is still alive only because Claybourne has to demonstrate to the next Minster that he will keep his word if they grant him the concessions he wants?" Fulbright asked. He looked exasperated. "This is all so remarkable. Claybourne, a respected businessman and philanthropist, dabbling in kidnapping and murder?"

"And perhaps far more than that," added Thomas. "If what I heard in the wagon that night was correct, Claybourne may also have something to do with the raid on Monteverde."

Fulbright shook his head. "This is just all too..."

Itzcoatl finished his sentence. "Too much. Yes, it is."

Fulbright ran his hand through his hair. "I cannot fathom why Claybourne would participate in the monstrous attack on Monteverde. He would lose everything, his family would be bankrupted, and he would surely hang. It makes no sense."

Diego set down his brandy glass. "Unless the prize is worth it, my friend. Even the wealthiest and most powerful men have hunger pangs, and the greater their hunger, the more risk they are willing to take to satisfy it."

"But what can he possibly hope to gain?" asked Fulbright. "Destroying a town in Arizona Territory and murdering a hundred innocent people will not get him any closer to obtaining mining permits to extract minerals on Mexican land. No, there is something more, much more, at play here."

Thomas was pleased to see that Fulbright's journalistic curiosity was now fully engaged. He raised his glass to the young reporter. "And you, Mr. Fulbright, are going to find out exactly what that is."

THIRTY THREE

Saltillo, Mexico, August 1882

Matthew Cord was entertaining two thoughts at the same time. First, the mouth on the whore who was kneeling between his legs should be declared one of Mexico's greatest national treasures. Second, he was going to be lucky if Noah Claybourne didn't have him shot for not finding and killing Diego de San Mártin in Mexico City as he had been ordered to do.

He looked across the private rail car at Billy, who was passed out drunk on the floor next to an equally inebriated, dark-skinned woman. At the front of the car Norton was still banging away like a piston-driven locomotive at the two women he had insisted on screwing at the same time. Cord decided to let the men be; the three of them would probably be repairing barbwire fences in the mountains next winter once Claybourne was done with them.

The trip had started on a positive note; their converted Pullman car was an oak paneled marvel with four pull down beds, a small kitchen, its own bathroom, and a full-time attendant who could rustle up a perfectly grilled New York steak or a young, spectacularly proportioned sporting gal–whatever best suited the occasion or the time of day. The trip from Denver to Mexico City took nearly four days, but Claybourne's private car was so well-provisioned that Cord and his men never had to set foot on a depot platform along the 1,400-mile trip. Outside their windows an endless panorama of Mexican desert scrub, distant mountain ranges, and scraggly pine forests baked in the summer heat. They arranged for the first women in Ciudad Juarez and then changed them out for fresh fillies in Zacatecas two days later. Now, on their return trip to Denver, they had traded the second batch for three more tarts in San Luis Potosi. Cord usually hated travel, but he had to admit that having Claybourne's wealth at his fingertips for this trip made the experience a hell of a lot more enjoyable.

They had arrived in Mexico City on a Sunday morning, and the streets of the capitol city of 300,000 residents were nearly deserted. According to the reports from Claybourne's private detectives that were telegraphed to them at each stop, San Mártin was being moved around the city to make it difficult for Rosalilia's kidnappers to find him. That was probably a smart move, Cord thought, not that it was going to do them any good in the long run. Claybourne simply worked through his Mexico City solicitors to build an overnight network of doctors, nurses, and sanitation workers who were happy to share information about the patients in their care in exchange for fresh United States currency.

A nun met the train at the private car platform in the central depot and handed Cord a note that said that he would find Diego on the top floor of the Hospital of the Sisters of Mercy in the San Ángel neighborhood. A man would be waiting for him in the hospital kitchen with more information. Cord briefly considered offering the attractive young novitiate a couple of twenty-dollar gold pieces to step into his car and spread her consecrated thighs for him, but he was already a day behind schedule. In any event, if he was going to have himself a religious ride, he preferred to take it by force. Nothing made his heart pound faster or his pecker grow harder than a woman who tried to fight him off. Add to that the fun of tearing off a nun's starched coif and veil and ripping open the front of her shapeless black habit to get to those untouched, honeyed breasts, and the image was almost enough to make him forget what Claybourne would do to him if he didn't find Diego and kill him today.

He cleared his mind and sent the nun on her way before snapping his fingers for a porter to call a hansom cab. It would be easier for one man to make it past the hospital guards than it would be for the three of them, so he left Billy and Norton at the station. He took only his knife; a revolver would draw too much attention, and frankly, he preferred a knife when he killed someone. He liked the personal connection it made, and the way his victim's horrified expression went from the initial shock of feeling the blade to the experience of agonizing pain, and finally, in the instant before they died, to a look of bewildered acceptance.

It was a twenty-minute ride to the hospital in San Ángel. Cord had traveled the streets before, but the European design of the wide, tree-lined boulevards and the Beaux-Arts blending of sculpture and design that characterized so many of the newer buildings in the city still impressed him. He told the driver to pull around to the rear kitchen entrance when they arrived at the three-story hospital. As the nun had promised, a man wearing a janitor's smock was perched on a stool inside waiting for him. Cord handed the man ten dollars, which got him a smock of his own, along with a pail and mop and directions to room 512.

"All of the rooms on the third floor are private," the janitor told him, "and some have guards hired by the families. As long as you get into and out of the room in less than two minutes, no one will interfere with you. Longer than that, and the guards will be on you. And I can tell you señor, they are very good at their jobs." Cord acknowledged the instructions without saying a word and then climbed the service stairs to the third floor. The door opened at the end of a long hallway that was well-lit by long banks of windows on both sides. He counted four rooms on each side of the corridor. Two had guards stationed directly outside the doors, but he could see from his vantage point that rooms 511 and 512 were unguarded.

He moved quickly down the hall with his pail and mop, smiled at one of the guards, and then stepped into room 511. He didn't want to go into Diego's room first in case his presence raised any suspicions.

Inside, an elderly woman with labored breathing was fast asleep in her bed. Cord saw a bottle of laudanum on a side tray. That and the woman's gray complexion told him that her time was very short. He stood quietly for a moment and then made sure his knife was loose in the sheath. He would enter room 512, slit Diego's throat–and the throats of any visitors he might encounter–and be back into the corridor in a matter of thirty seconds or less.

He opened the door and left the room. As he stepped across the corridor to 512, a guard down the hall motioned to him. Damn. He walked over to the man, who was fumbling with a cigarette he had just rolled. *"Tiene usted un fuego?"* asked the guard. Cord reached into his pocket and pulled out a pack of matches. He handed the box to the guard. "*Mantenerlas. Keep them.*" The guard smiled and accepted the gift.

Holding tightly to the pail and mop, he walked to room 512, stepped inside, and set down the cleaning tools. There were no visitors in the room. Cord pulled his knife from its sheath and walked towards the bed, which was encircled by a privacy curtain. He reached up and jerked back the curtain with his left hand as he raised the knife over his head with his right hand. The curtain flew open.

The bed was empty.

❃

Six hours later, in a dank iron and brick warehouse on the shore of Lake Xochimilco, Cord was studying the young man who was tied to the frame of a wooden chair. Claybourne's Mexican attorney maintained the nondescript building for business negotiations exactly like these. Billy had ripped the cane seat out of the chair and stripped the clothes off the man before binding his wrists and ankles. What was left of his testicles hung down below the seat frame, dripping blood onto the brick floor. The swollen skin around his eyes was turning yellow and deep purple from the ferocious beating Norton had just administered with a lead-weighted leather sap. His nostrils were slit open, and half of an ear lay on the ground beside his foot in a pool of sticky blood. His achilles tendons had been severed at the base of his heels, and the tendons behind both knees had been cut clean through.

Even if he were to be released right now–something the young man knew was not going to happen–he would never walk again, or hear well, or screw or bend his arms. In a moment of ironic clarity, he reminded himself that those disabilities were constraints that only hampered the living. Soon, he would journey to the other side where he would stand before *Huitzilopochtli*, the god of war and the sun, to deliver his account for how he had lived, and how he had died. His body would be whole again, and if his life was deemed worthy by the god, he would spend eternity among his ancestors. First, though, he had to die a noble death. As he listened to his lungs gasping for breath and felt the warm blood seeping from the cuts they had made along his legs and neck, he knew that time was not far off.

Cord took a drink of water and went over the day's events in his mind. When he discovered that Diego had been spirited out of the hospital shortly before he arrived, he paid another visit to the janitor in the kitchen. He impaled the man's palm on a wooden table with his knife and gave him ten seconds to explain exactly what had happened with Diego. It only took the terrified man five seconds to blurt out the story. Itzcoatl's sons Xipil and Ácatl had been guarding Diego day and night for weeks. Last night they had arranged for him to be taken away in a carriage. The janitor did not know where they had gone, but he begged Cord's forgiveness and told him that Xipil threatened him with death if he ever told anyone that Diego had been at the hospital.

The good news was that the janitor knew where Cord could find Xipil. The young man had a sweetheart, and, as it was Sunday, he would be walking with her in a park across town that evening. That news made Cord smile, which gave the janitor hope.

"Spare me?" he begged. He was shaking, and the front of his pants were soaked where he had wet himself in fear.

Cord pulled his knife out of the man's palm. "Thank you, señor," sobbed the janitor. As he stood, Cord rammed the knife up under the man's breastbone and felt it penetrate his heart. The janitor gasped and slid down to the floor. Cord withdrew his knife, wiped it clean on the man's shirt, and asked, "For what?"

❖

Later that afternoon, Cord, Billy, and Norton took a hansom to the public square in the wealthy residential neighborhood the janitor had described. Dozens of young couples were strolling arm in arm through the flowered plaza, while musicians played, vendors sold drinks and treats, and dour faced chaperones watched with hawk-eyes to make sure the young men accompanying their charges did not attempt to take any liberties. Cord called to a passing flower vendor. He gave the man five American dollars and a description of Xipil, with a promise of five more dollars when he pointed Xipil out.

It only took the vendor a few minutes. He led Cord and his men to a far corner of the plaza and pointed to where Xipil and his girlfriend were holding hands at a small table beneath the cascading blossoms of a blue jacaranda tree. Cord paid the vendor and sent him away. Then he and his men walked swiftly to the table, where Billy and Norton placed themselves directly behind the girl, and Cord planted his hands firmly on Xipil's shoulders. Cord leaned in and whispered, "Do exactly as I say, and she will not be harmed. If you fight or call out, my men will drag her away. They will screw her senseless, and then they will slice off her tits and mail them to her family. Do you understand?"

Xipil's eyes blazed, and Cord felt the young man's muscles tense. "Do you understand me?" he repeated. Xipil looked helplessly at his terrified girlfriend, and then over in the direction of her aunt, who was chattering animatedly with another chaperone and was oblivious to the scene unfolding at the table. Xipil bit into his lower lip, but he nodded. He was furious with himself for letting his guard down and for being captured so easily. These men were Americans, a thousand miles from home, which meant they could be here for only one reason. But, if they had known that Diego and Itzcoatl were about to board a train for Colorado to search for Rosalilia, they would have gone directly to the train depot to stop them. The fact that they had come for him instead meant they had no idea of Diego's whereabouts. Now, the only way Xipil could protect both Diego and his father was to remain quiet, no matter what. For once, he prayed, please see to it that the U.S. bound train pulls out of the Mexico City station on time. That would provide Diego with at least a small head start on the bastards.

Cord motioned for Xipil to get up and walk with him. Billy stayed with the young woman, and Norton came over and lightly pressed a small revolver against Xipil's back to make sure he complied. When they crossed the plaza, Cord waved to Billy to join them. A moment later the girl rushed over to her chaperone–who was still yammering like a magpie-and collapsed at the woman's feet. By then, Cord and his men had bundled Xipil into the hansom and were headed for the lakefront warehouse.

❖

Over the years, Cord had learned that the human body cold withstand an almost inexhaustible litany of injuries. He had seen men–and a few women–survive intentionally broken limbs, gouged eyes, severed fingers and toes, scalping, and repeated blows to the head and body from fists and other heavy objects. He was personally fond of the Chinese practice of *Ling chi*, also known as "slow slicing" or "death by a thousand cuts." This method of torturous execution had been practiced in China for more than two thousand years. With a razor-sharp knife, a skilled practitioner could flay nearly all the skin off the arms, shoulders, back, genitals, and torso of a person and then keep them alive for hours, even days.

The first thing he had done to Xipil after they stripped him and tied him to the chair was to carefully slice and peel off the top layer of skin from a large section of his abdomen. Cord nailed the oozing, book-sized patch to a post directly in front of Xipil before getting down to the business of interrogating him. He had only two questions: where was Diego, and who was with him?

Xipil did not scream or shout as the torture began. Instead, the minute they tied him up, he retreated as far into the inner recesses of his mind as he could travel. He recalled the ancient Aztec legends about the creation of the world that his father and grandfather told him when he was a child, and he imagined himself sailing high above the jungle canopy on the back of a winged jaguar. He heard his mother saying, "*Nimitztlazohtla, Nimitznequi,*" I love you, over and over in their native Nahuatl tongue. And each time Norton hit him again on his face or stomach with the lead weighted sap, each moment Cord sliced into another part of his flesh, Xipil retreated with the jaguar. He groaned, he twisted and thrashed in the chair, and he even shed tears for the life he knew he was never going to have. But he did not answer Cord, or even acknowledge his presence. The outcome of this event was foreordained the minute Cord walked over to his table at the plaza. Nothing he could say would change that.

When Billy stepped back from Xipil's broken, bloodied body a few minutes later, he was soaked in sweat, and Norton's arms were so tired from laying into the young man again and again that he could barely raise them above his head. Torture was a hard business.

Cord weighed his options. This man was a warrior. He was not going to break. He took another drink, wiped his sleeve across his brow and made his decision. He stepped behind Xipil's chair, yanked his head back by the hair, and ran his blade across the young man's throat. Xipil's head folded onto his chest. His journey with the jaguar was over.

The foolhardy Aztec might be dead, mused Cord, but it was he, not Xipil, who had failed the living. He felt no remorse for the savage torture and murder he had just committed, only fear of the price he would pay for not completing his mission.

❖

Two days after killing Xipil, Cord received a terse reply to the telegram he had sent to Claybourne about Diego's disappearance. "Come back" was all it said. Given his boss' volcanic temper, there was no telling what would be waiting for him when he set foot in Langton Hall. He briefly considered pulling the plug and relocating to New York or Chicago, but Claybourne's tentacles reached everywhere. He would not be able to remain hidden for long. His only choice was to return and take his lumps.

Cord poured a glass of bourbon from a crystal decanter and called for the attendant to close the blinds and prepare dinner. He was weary of the endless miles of shrub and rocks outside the train, and since Billy and Norton were sleeping off another drunken bout with their hookers, they wouldn't mind losing some daylight. As for what he was going to do to pass the time, fortune had supplied him with an amusement far more delicious than what his men were experiencing with their expensive companions.

He stepped to the back of the railroad car and opened the curtains that had been arranged to create a small, private bedroom. Tied and gagged on the bed was the young nun who met the train when they first arrived in Mexico City. After dispatching Xipil and throwing his body into the lake, Cord had taken a carriage to the convent at the edge of town. He bribed a groundskeeper to tell the beautiful novitiate that a family member needed to see her on urgent business. When she came out into the high-walled garden a few minutes later, he took her forcefully by the wrist and the back of the neck and marched her out of the garden to the waiting carriage. A wad of American dollars was all the driver needed to keep his mouth shut, and even to help carry the struggling nun into the private rail car when darkness fell.

Cord watched the naked woman struggle against the restraints. He threw back another shot of bourbon and felt the heat begin to rise in his loins. When he tore off her black woolen habit for the first time two nights ago, it played out exactly as he had fantasized. Her youthful skin was that creamy, her breasts were that full and firm, and the tightness between her legs was proof that no man had penetrated her before he did. She put up a good fight the first time he ravaged her, and she even began to pray when he ripped open her legs and forced his way into her. He slapped her so hard that her mouth was still bleeding an hour later when he pushed her lips down onto his crotch. The prayers stopped.

Now, he stood beside the bed, ignoring the pleading in her eyes as he thought about what he was going to do to her. Perhaps he would show her how a man pleasured a woman with his mouth, and then flip her over and give it to her in the *cula*. After that? Well, he wasn't completely heartless. When they reached Ciudad Juarez, he would arrange for her to be taken to the best, most exclusive bordello in the city. With the training she had received in his bed, the little nun might just become the most skilled *puta* the place had ever seen.

Three long blasts from the locomotive's whistle drifted back to the Pullman car, signaling that the train was about to begin the gradual ascent over the western spur of the Sierra Madre Oriental mountains. Cord finished his drink, pulled the curtains closed, and unbuckled his trousers.

THIRTY FOUR

Langton Hall

A small fire burned in a cast iron stove in Noah Claybourne's study every night of the year, even now, in the middle of a blazing hot August. He kept the windows open to capture the evening breezes because the purpose of the fire was not for heat. Winter or summer, Noah was nearly oblivious to changes in temperature, as he was to almost any outside physical stimulus. The fire burned because he was mesmerized by flame. The flickering, vaporous towers of blue and orange combustion had held him in their thrall since he was a child.

One snowy day before the family left England for America, his mother took him into the garden and showed him how to capture one, downy-soft snowflake at a time and examine it under a powerful hand-lens. "No two flakes are ever alike," she had told him. "Of all the billions of products of God's creation that manifest in nature each day, these are the proof of his infinite creativity. Every other physical being and substance, from people to trees and rocks and fish, have identical twins– many, in fact. But you could study the crystal structure of individual snowflakes every day for the rest of your life and never discover two that are exactly alike."

Noah was his mother's fifth and youngest child. That, and the fact that he had barely survived two childhood illnesses, made him her favorite. He cherished her, too, and did everything he could to please her. Then, in a single year between his seventh and eighth birthdays, he discovered that almost everything she had told him was a lie. His father wasn't the kind and generous man who put his family above all worldly pursuits, as she told him each night when she tucked him in bed after a story and prayers. Instead, Noah learned that he was prone to fits of black rage, often striking out violently at the tiniest provocation. He once saw his father beat a servant across the back with a fireplace poker for the crime of spilling a few drops of the cider she was bringing him. And one ice-cold evening when the new puppy he was given at Christmas would not stop whimpering, Noah watched in tears as his father tossed the tiny dog out into the snow and left it there all night to freeze to death.

On a bright Sunday morning the week before he turned eight, Noah raced out of the house to see if there were any new spring chicks in the coop's nesting boxes. As he went past the door of the outside cook shed, he heard muffled laughs and squeals. He climbed up on an empty barrel and looked through the grease-streaked window, where he saw his father standing behind one of the young kitchen maids, with his trousers around his ankles. She was bent over a chair, and her skirt and petticoat were billowing around her head. Noah watched with a combination of fear and fascination as his father thrust himself into the young woman again and again and again. By the time he finished and pushed her away, Noah was in tears. The girl righted herself and smoothed her clothing. His father pinched her cheek in what Noah assumed to be a sign of affection and then handed her a few coins from his pocket. The girl curtsied and scurried to the door, and Noah scrambled down from the barrel and raced out to the chicken coop, where he sat on a pile of hay and cried for an hour.

Until the day his father threw himself down the stairs of the Denver whorehouse and broke his neck when Noah was twenty-five, the two of them never engaged in anything other than the most cursory and superficial conversation. That circumstance suited Noah's father as much as it did him.

After the incident in the kitchen, Noah became increasingly reclusive. He spent hours in his rooms every day, reading books, playing cards, and assembling and disassembling an old flintlock pistol his father had given him over his mother's objections.

He also began lighting small fires all around the family property. He didn't want to burn anything down; he was careful to tend the flames and not let them get out of control. Instead, he had become fascinated with the unique properties of fire, especially with the way that the flames danced and flickered and melded one into another. He soon discovered that no two fires were ever alike; even if he arranged the same number of sticks made with the same wood in the exact same fashion and lit them under the same weather and wind conditions, each fire had its own personality and character.

Noah's mother had lied about snowflakes being the only perpetually unique manifestations of God's incalculable engineering skills. Fire, which was both a great friend and a deadly foe, was a creative force unto itself. It could twist and turn in endless, violent paroxysms, or it could wave in serene and tender dips and bows that almost seduced the observer into reaching out to caress it.

He did not completely disavow his mother's affections as time passed, but as the web of lies she told him about everything from her husband to the very character of the natural world itself continued to grow, he slipped further and further away from her. He never told her that what he had seen in the kitchen that day, or what he had discovered through his own observations of nature that disproved what she had told him. When she succumbed to typhus in America when he was thirteen, he did not weep or mourn. He simply moved on.

At age fifty, he trusted no one, believed in no one, and depended on no one. He married Hyacinth's mother so that he could have a legal heir, not because he loved her. When she died during childbirth, he simply engaged a wet-nurse and a nanny, handed over his child's care to them, and returned to work.

Noah was wise enough to understand that he was emotionally hollow and discerning enough to know exactly how the absence of love, trust, compassion, and empathy had impacted his development as an adult. But he did not care in the least that those closest to him considered him to be emotionally deficient. He regarded that character trait as his single greatest strength; it was the source of his ability to apply reason, logic, and cold, utilitarian thinking to any situation and then come to a decision about how best to protect and grow his interests. There was no place in his personal cosmology for even a shred of the anxiety that most other people experienced when making similarly important decisions. Regret and remorse were foreign attitudes to him; he had not become one of the richest and most powerful men in the country by agonizing over the consequences of the actions he had to take to further his business and political interests.

He stirred the coals back to life and thought about the philanthropic work he was doing that endeared him to the people of Colorado. More importantly, his high-profile donations also tied their elected leaders to his waistcoat strings. An opera house and hospital in Denver each bore the Claybourne name, and his recent endowment to the new State College meant that the largest new building on campus would also be emblazoned with his name–and graced by a ten-foot bronze statue of him, as well. The citizens of the state built their homes with lumber from his mills and bricks from his kilns. They baked their bread with flour from his granaries, grilled steak from his herds, and benefited from the daily deliveries of food and dry goods that came into the state on his railroad cars. Soon, the people of Colorado would raise glasses of beer branded with his label in their saloons and restaurants. He had made attempts to purchase the state's largest and most profitable brewery from that damn, obstinate German immigrant, Adolf Coors, but negotiations had gone nowhere. The old fool had dreams of building a family dynasty that would last for centuries. When the upcoming fishing tournament was over, Noah would turn his attention to squashing Coors and assimilating his business as he had done with dozens of other upstarts around the state. That thought brought a rare smile to his lips.

There was a tap on his study door, and his housekeeper brought in a tray with a light supper and a bottle of burgundy wine. Noah cleared a space on his desk and uncorked the bottle. He poured a glass and turned back to the pile of newspapers from all over the country that featured banner headlines about last week's raid on Moneteverde. By any measure one could apply, the raid had been an over-the-top spectacle of monstrous proportion. The breathless narratives of decapitated parents, slaughtered children, and especially, the description of the inhuman savagery inflicted upon the body of the mayor ("...*and a length of iron pipe protruded from the unfortunate man's nether regions...*") almost made Claybourne wince. Almost.

The quotes from politicians in the New York, Philadelphia, and Washington papers were exactly what Claybourne hoped to hear: *"Bestial,"* intoned one US Senator, *"Heinous and vile,"* said a congressman. Adding to Noah's satisfaction was the fact that at least a half dozen influential politicians called the attack upon the innocent border town, *"An outright act of war by Mexico against the United States."*

At a time when the nation was riven by an economic crisis and by the non-stop squabbling of the major political parties, the raid on Monteverde seemed to be the only event on which all the players were taking a unified stand. For its part, Mexico had issued both a flat-out condemnation of the raid and a forceful denial that any representatives of their government had anything whatsoever to do with the destruction of the little town.

Noah understood the rules of politics and the fickle nature of the electorate. The politicians he owned would soon begin applying pressure on the White House to bring American military might to bear against Mexico. The President and his cabinet would resist, of course, but when Demetria Carnál's upcoming raid on San Rafael in the New Mexico territory rivaled the brutality of Monteverde, the President would find himself boxed into a corner. At the very least, he would have to send army units into Northern Mexico to determine if the raids were being staged from there, and if they were taking place at the direction of the Mexican army. Leading that American military expedition would be General Winston Greer, whose loyalty first, foremost, and completely, was to Noah Claybourne.

He had directed Carnál to execute her raid as soon as possible, but in no case was it to happen later than the opening day of the Claybourne Ranch Fishing Tournament. More than five hundred contestants and distinguished guests would be gathered there, including Noah and his co-conspirators. With hundreds of eyewitnesses present to provide them an alibi, Claybourne knew that neither he nor any of his people could be connected to the events at San Rafael. So, when word of yet another massacre on the southern border reached Washington, no power on earth would be able to hold back Congress from declaring war on Mexico. Then, as Greer's brigade swept across northern Mexico in search of the attackers, it would simply be a matter of the general making an urgent recommendation to the President: to guarantee the safety of American border towns, the United States must take "temporary" control of a broad swath of the Northern Mexican states. At the same time, political pressure would be brought to bear on Congress and the President from people in every walk of life to take the next step and formally annex the land into three new American-controlled territories. They would be called South Arizona, Southern New Mexico, and South Texas.

Noah poured another glass of wine, opened a drawer and pulled out a map of Mexico that was marked with the names and locations of the new territories he intended to create. He ran his hand slowly across the document. In all, his audacious plan would add a land mass equivalent to the total square mileage of France and the United Kingdom to the United States. The region's vast supply of extractable minerals and the presence of an easily controlled *campesino* population to work in the mines was the sweetener.

He went over to the fire and gazed into the flames. Geronimo Rivas and Demetria Carnál would stoke the blaze he had started. When the fire was hot enough for long enough, he would hammer out a new destiny for America on an iron anvil entirely of his own making. He turned towards the window, and a fleeting thought crossed his mind: what would his father and mother have thought of their son's extraordinary accomplishments? He let the question pass; there was no need to formulate an answer. Instead, he raised his glass to the starry sky and toasted himself.

❋

THIRTY FIVE

On the prairie

Puffs of dust dotted the afternoon sky, signaling to Bill that the visitors heading his way were still an hour away. Looked to be three riders, maybe four. Whoever they were, he hoped they were bringing a jug with them. Louisa had searched the pack horse before he left home, and damned if she hadn't pulled out the four-bottle supply he had laid in for the trip.

He lit a cigar and walked down to the creek that snaked towards the green and yellow prairie stretching for miles in all directions. Then he sighed and got down to the business of preparing dinner. The skinned carcass of the pronghorn antelope he shot yesterday was suspended by a rope in a cottonwood on the creek bank. He slipped an apron around his neck and fetched the meat up to his camp. First, he removed its legs at the hocks and knees and laid it spread-eagled on its belly on a make-shift wooden table. If he were cooking for himself, he would simply have gone for the tenderloins that were located under the kidneys, up along the backbone. But it appeared that he would be having company, so he was going to need a more substantial cut to feed his guests.

Bill felt for the hipbone along each side, about three inches out from the center of the backbone and made a cut at right angles from the backbone to the flank of the carcass. Then he cut one side from the hip to the shoulder, loosening the long loin muscles from their center attachments with his fingers. He peeled out a piece of meat about twenty inches long and three inches in diameter, which he swiftly trimmed of sinew and fat before slicing into one-inch chops. That would be plenty to serve five or six people; if his guests wanted to carve out any roasts or chops to take with them when they left camp, they were welcome.

Then he checked on the pronghorn's hide, which he had determined was of good enough quality to have tanned. He rolled it up and hung it in the tree after treating the flesh side with a couple of pounds of salt. He was partial to the soft vests they could be made into, and Louisa–despite her attempt to leave him high and dry–would appreciate some new antelope hide gloves.

There were sweet onions and potatoes in the gunny sack outside his tent, and he rinsed them in creek water before chopping them into small pieces and putting them into a cast-iron kettle with a handful of wild greens he collected at the base of a rise a few yards from camp. If his visitors brought wine, he would pour a little into the kettle and let them simmer over the fire with salt and garlic. Beer would do fine too.

Next, he mixed some flour, baking powder, salt, and baking soda, and cut in some butter from a tin. He stirred in a cup of sourdough starter and turned out the dough onto a lightly floured board before kneading it until all the flour was mixed in. Then he patted and rolled the dough before cutting it into biscuits with a knife and laying them into a Dutch oven by the fire. He pulled his chair closer to the creek and sat down to await his dinner guests, whoever they might be.

The sky was beginning to soften and a cool breeze picked up across the creek when the riders got within a couple hundred yards of camp. Bill took up the field glasses that General Crook gave him after the Battle of Slim Buttes at the height of the Great Sioux War and focused them on the approaching men. He was pleased to see that one of them was his friend Thomas Scoundrel, who he had written some weeks back with an invitation to come out to the camp. He did not know the older man with the long white hair, or the dark-haired younger man beside him, but even from this distance, he appreciated the imposing silhouettes of their horses. There was a story worth hearing from these men, Bill was certain of that.

❋

Diego let Thomas take the lead as they wound along the creek and entered the camp. They had been riding for two days, and he was more tired than he expected he would be. Still, it was good to be back on his horse, and he found the grasslands, shrubs, and streams along the western boundary of the prairie to be a powerful tonic for the worry that had consumed him since the night Rosalilia was taken.

They passed a highline between two small cottonwoods where three horses were tied, and a man stepped from behind an oversized canvas tent and walked towards them. Diego figured him to be in his late thirties. He was about six feet tall, with dark features, quick searching eyes, an aquiline nose and rather delicate facial features. He wore his hair falling in long ringlets over his shoulders, and he was dressed in a blue flannel shirt and corduroy trousers tucked into high boots. He had on a broad-brimmed hat, and a white handkerchief was folded and loosely tied around his neck, no doubt to help keep the searing prairie heat off his back. What Diego found most interesting, though, was the apron around the man's neck that was splattered with drops of blood and what looked like baking flour. Thomas had only told him that they were meeting a trusted friend whose contacts in government rivaled Claybourne's. If Noah's hands were as deep in this mess as it appeared, Thomas argued, the long ride out into the prairie to seek this man's help would be well worth the journey.

Diego and Itzcoatl reined their horses up, and Thomas brought Ulysses to a halt. For a moment, he and the aproned man didn't say a word. They looked one another over to see what indignities the past year had visited upon the other. It only took Bill an instant to see that Thomas had most certainly had the worst of it.

Bill wiped his hands on his apron and tipped back his hat. "Thomas," he finally said with a smile.

"Hello, Bill." He turned in his saddle and said "Bill, these are my friends; Itzcoatl and Diego de San Mártin. Gents, this is William F. Cody, about whom, I apologize, I have told you nothing."

Itzcoatl touched his forelock with two fingers. Diego nodded. He wanted to say something, but he was too startled to speak. William F. Cody was *Buffalo Bill Cody*, the legendary army scout, hunter, Indian fighter, and showman. What was one of the most famous men in the United States–even the world–doing out here on the prairie by himself? Diego found his tongue at last. "We know your story well in my country, Mr. Cody. It is an honor."

"It's Bill," said Cody, "and if you are friends of Thomas's, the honor is all mine. Come on down. We'll tend to your horses, and I'll make dinner." He paused, and then added in a hopeful tone, "I don't suppose any of you fellas has brought along anything stronger than coffee to drink?

Itzcoatl pointed to a box attached to the side of the pack horse that was tied to his mount. As Thomas and Diego got down off their horses, Cody unlatched the box and peered inside. Then he turned to Itzcoatl with a wide grin and said, "Welcome, friend!"

❁

With the horses tethered and fed, Cody turned his attention to dinner. The temperature had dropped considerably as twilight settled in, and as he dropped the flour-drenched pronghorn chops into an oiled cast iron skillet and set it on the grate above the fire, Thomas uncorked a bottle of Bordeaux and poured three glasses.

"None for you, my friend?" said Cody to Itzcoatl, who shook his head when offered a glass. Instead, Itzcoatl reached into the box and pulled out a bottle of aged mezcal. Thomas saw the questioning look on Bill's face and said, "You might want to get a little wine in your stomach before you give that particular demon a try." Itzcoatl shrugged and poured a glass for himself.

The four men sat on camp chairs, and Bill let out a long, satisfied sigh after he tossed back his first glass. As Thomas gave him a refill, Bill turned to Itzcoatl. "Your pardon, sir, for my asking this," he said, "but, I fancy my knowledge of the various indigenous tribes of the America's to be second to no man's. I know the customs of the Athabascans in the far north, and I have studied a little of the language of the Mayan peoples of your Yucatan peninsula, and pretty much every tribe located in the thousands of miles in between. But, your countenance, your eyes, even your name, are entirely foreign to me."

Itzcoatl finished his drink and set down the glass. Then he drew his obsidian dagger and laid it across his lap. He looked into Cody's eyes and, in a voice that sounded like it had traveled through the centuries to make it to their twilight campfire, he said, "*Nehua notōcā Itzcoatl.* I am Itzcoatl, and my people are the Tenochca, who you call Aztec."

"I'll be dammed," said Cody in a half-whisper. "I did not mean to pry, and I meant no familiarity. But if you have the time, I probably have about a hundred questions I would like to ask."

Itzcoatl's eyes narrowed, and his voice grew deadly serious. "I have the time," he said slowly, "and I could tell you many stories about my people." Then he threw back his head and laughed. "But I do not know if I brought enough mezcal to finish them all!" Cody had been holding his breath for fear that he had offended the old man. Now, he laughed, and Thomas and Diego joined in.

Thomas poured more wine and then helped Bill get the biscuits and skillet potatoes and onions on the coals. When Bill dished up their plates a few minutes later, the first stars were appearing against the backdrop of the deep blue sky. They ate and drank in silence as the sky darkened to velvet black, and the light from the stars illuminated the tips of the prairie grasses rippling like waves in the soft breeze. A meteor streaked across the dome of the sky, and the rush of water over stones in the creek drifted harmoniously through the camp.

"I can see why you come out here, Bill," said Diego. "I don't believe there is any other place on earth quite like this. What a contrast it must be from your life on the stage."

Bill had helped himself to another bottle of wine and was drawing circles in the dirt in front of his chair with a willow branch. "Oh, yes, this place is sacred to me, in many ways. On the stage there is no sky, no stars, not even any dirt. Greasepaint and spotlights and applause take up the space, but they are no match for this." He waved his stick in an arc across the sky. "No match at all."

"Is it about the money, then?" asked Thomas.

"In some ways, I suppose it is. It may also be a way to play God, to stop from growing old by freezing time itself and re-living the best moments of your life again and again. That's really all I do in my shows." He looked embarrassed and set down the willow. "Perhaps I should stick with the wine and not philosophize," he said quietly. "You did not come out here to listen to a prairie sermon. They're not needed in a place like this."

The men stayed quiet as the great star-swept bowl of the heavens continued to turn above them, and a sliver of new moon appeared in the east. Diego fetched a bottle of brandy, and Cody gave him a cigar. Finally, Itzcoatl spoke. "My people say that God sleeps in minerals, He awakens in plants, He walks in animals, and He thinks in man."

Thomas chuckled. "Your people also slaughtered five thousand innocent captives in a single day on top of the Great Temple of Tenochtitlan. They tore out their beating hearts, cut off their heads, and rolled them down the sides of the temple to the cheers of the crowds."

Itzcoatl took a long pull of mezcal and then raised his dagger above his head. "And wouldn't that spectacle make a fine addition to your new show, Mr. Cody?"

❖

Itzcoatl rose at sunrise and shook off the lingering effects of the bottle of mezcal he had consumed the night before. He started a pot of coffee and dug out a dozen eggs that were packed for freshness in a bag of finely ground cornmeal. He also unsealed a small lard tub and fished out a pile of bacon. He stirred the coals, set the cast iron skillet on the grate, and dropped in the bacon. Then he warmed the leftover biscuits in the Dutch oven and set them on the table with a jar of honey. By the time the bacon was done, and the eggs were frying, the smell of brewing coffee had lured Thomas, Diego, and Cody from their bed rolls.

The clear sky promised a blazing day ahead as the men gathered around the log table and ate breakfast. Bill was excited to talk about the new extravaganza he was developing that would be called Buffalo Bill's Wild West.

"I have repeatedly invited Thomas to join my shows," Bill told Diego and Itzcoatl, "and he repeatedly turns me down." Thomas shrugged. "The legends that have arisen around the war time exploits of Colonel T.E. Scoundrel are not to be underestimated," Cody continued. "And in the Sioux Wars of '76 and '77, I myself witnessed him perform deeds of such heroic proportions that it would be a crime not to share them with a public eager to embrace the men–and women– who dare to cast their fates before the whims of destiny and chance."

"At a nickel per embrace," said Thomas.

"Make that a dime, dear boy, and I will make you rich" replied Cody with feigned indignation. He took a sip of coffee and changed the direction of the conversation. "But you did not come all the way out here to talk about my show. Diego and Itzcoatl have clearly traveled a great distance to join you, and, frankly, both you and Diego look as if you have been to the gates of hell."

Thomas appreciated his friend's discernment. "I need your help, Bill. *We* need your help."

Cody nodded, his face expressionless. "Go on."

For what seemed like the hundredth time in recent weeks, Thomas walked through everything that had happened since the night Rosalilia was kidnapped. Cody asked him to repeat the details of several of the events, and he asked several very direct and pointed questions of Diego and Itzcoatl, but he volunteered nothing until Thomas finished the story about meeting with the reporter Tanner Fulbright at the Windsor Hotel.

"I know Claybourne well," Bill said when he began to respond to Thomas' story. "In fact, it had been my intention until just a few minutes ago to seek his financial backing for my new show."

"I am very sorry to hear that," said Diego.

Cody waved his hand. "No, my friend, I am sorry. I will not take blood money. Investors abound. Decent ones are rare, but they do exist.

I will be fine." He looked at Thomas. "How can I help?"

"Can you go to Washington and share what I have told you with your friends in Congress? There are no doors closed to Buffalo Bill."

"I can," answered Cody. "And I can probably get an audience with anyone, including President Arthur. There is not much depth to the man, but the corruption and scandal that fester in the sewers of Washington have not attached themselves to him. At least not yet."

Diego was heartened by what he was hearing. The two-day ride out into the wilderness had not been a waste of precious time. But Cody's next words threw ice water on his hopes.

"The problem, Thomas, is that you have no proof of Claybourne's involvement at Monteverde. The scrambled conversation you heard in the back of the wagon right after you had been hit on the head and knocked unconscious is not going to be given any credence by those in power. Moreover, when someone as creative as me cannot fathom a reason for a man as powerful and influential as Claybourne to risk undertaking so nightmarish an action as the destruction of that little town, well, put yourself in the shoes of a typical Congressman. Why would he believe you over Claybourne?"

Thomas hated to admit it, but Cody was right. The evidence against Claybourne was scant, at best. And, truthfully, there was very little chance–especially since the massacre of one hundred innocent American civilians–that any politician in America would care about the fate of one Mexican woman who may have been kidnapped by an American.

Diego looked dejected. Itzcoatl gripped his coffee cup and stared hard at the table.

Cody took in the scene. "That is not to say that we can't get those audiences and make them listen to us, of course."

"Yes?" said Diego.

"Bring me something solid I can take to Congress, and even to the President if necessary. Find out who is conducting the raids, and who the hell is paying them. If you can connect them to Claybourne with a straight line, we have a chance. But only a chance. People like him play by different rules, and there are a lot of people in the club protecting one another's asses."

Thomas looked across the table at Diego. "We'll look up Fulbright and begin there. He is our best source of information."

"I know several officers in the Arizona Territorial Command," said Cody. "I will visit them and see if they know anything more than the Army is telling us. I might also pay Claybourne a purely social visit and see if I can sniff anything out."

Thomas rubbed the back of his head where Moncton had smashed him with the hammer. "You will want to be very cautious in that conversation," he suggested.

Cody smiled. "He has no idea what I know, and it's very possible he still thinks you are lying in the bottom of that ravine."

Thomas agreed. "I will telegraph Bat Masterson and Major Rhine and ask them to help coordinate our communication."

"Good men, the both of them," said Cody. "I wish we had more like them on our side. Now, I have a request: I could use a second set of hands in the next week. Can Iztcoatal come along with me?"

Diego looked at Itzcoatl, and the old man nodded solemnly.

The four men broke camp. Diego and Thomas rode off towards Denver to find Tanner Fulbright, while Cody and Itzcoatl turned south to question some of Cody's army contacts.

For the first time in two months, Diego allowed himself to feel hopeful.

❖

THIRTY SIX

Temptation Mountain

Rosalilia climbed out of the frigid creek, ignoring Reed and Spruce as they feasted their eyes on the curves of her body where the thin cotton nightshirt clung to her wet skin. She dropped the bar of soap on the grass, pulled her shawl from a tree branch and wrapped it around her shoulders before slipping into a pair of huarache sandals and following the well-worn path up to the cabin.

Six weeks had passed since the kidnappers brought her to the remote Colorado mountain. Her memory of the four-day journey from Cuernavaca to Denver was a blur. Cord's men accompanied her on the train, and one was beside her every minute except when she was allowed to go to the bathroom. They spoke only a few words to her during the long trip, and they would not answer any of her questions. She was terrified, exhausted, and overcome with fear for her family and Diego.

On the morning they left Mexico City, Cord had come onto the private car just long enough to give instructions to his men. "If any one of you so much as gives a squeeze to one of her titties, you are dead. Anybody not understand?"

Then he addressed Rosalilia. "You can see your family again, but only if you do exactly as you are told. You're going to be with us for a while, so settle in and make the best of it."

The one-room cabin in which she was held was perched at the edge of a grassy meadow ringed by stands of fir and aspen. Above the tree line, fields of rocky scrub and boulders swept up the steep grade. The ground was covered with huckleberry and wildflowers when she arrived in late June, and there were still several feet of snow on the mountain peak. Now, in August, the snow had melted off, and most of the flowers were gone, replaced by thickets of low-lying shrubs and seedling trees. Far to the west, rows of white-dusted granite peaks cut into the summer sky, and from the high plains to the east, warm breezes poured across the meadow in the afternoons. She could see for miles in all directions from the crest of the hill behind the cabin, which was as far as she was allowed to walk. But no matter where she looked, there were no other signs of human habitation. Cord had picked the location well. Escape would be nearly impossible.

She did not venture out of the cabin for the first week, except to visit the privy. Then, a little at a time, she began to take several walks each day around the meadow, with Reed or Spruce always in tow. Her keepers had been picked as carefully as the location; they did not speak much to her, or to each other, for that matter. Reed was middle-aged, tall, and fair. Spruce was young, short, and swarthy, with a perpetual frown on his face. Whatever Cord was paying them, it was clear that they did not fancy themselves as babysitters.

There was a shelf of books in the cabin, and she devoted herself to improving her English by reading aloud from them for several hours each day. After a week of eating nothing but beans, salt pork, and jerky, she asked the men if they could hunt for some meat and gather a few wild greens. That afternoon Reed brought in a brace of rabbits, which she butchered, browned in bear fat, and made into a savory stew with potatoes and local greens. It hadn't been her intention to become the cook, but from that day forward, the men brought her something every day to prepare. When she went outside each morning at first light there would be a wicker basket on the porch containing venison or partridges, brook trout, or rabbits, always with an assortment of wild berries and vegetables. They also rustled up sacks of corn meal and flour to make biscuits and breakfast mush, and a bottle of brandy to simmer away some of the gamy flavor in the meats. She settled quickly into the new routine, and the men were delighted to be eating well-prepared food, but she drew the line at sitting with them to dine. Diego was coming for her, and when he did, he would kill the men who took her, including Reed and Spruce. She wanted nothing to do with dead men. So, each evening when the food was ready, she took a plate outside and sat on a log bench until the sun began to set and they called her back to the cabin.

Every ten or eleven days a rider leading a pack horse came through the trees a hundred yards below the cabin. His routine never changed; he offloaded supplies, visited with the men for an hour or so, and then disappeared back into the forest. Since the rider never stayed the night, she assumed that wherever he came from was no more than a half day ride from the cabin.

One afternoon during her fourth week in captivity, Reed slipped on a rock and fell onto a pile of broken pieces of razor-sharp slate. Spruce hauled him up to the porch, and Rosalilia cleaned and sewed up his lacerated calf. Then, every day for a week, she changed his bandages and applied fresh poultices to stave off infection. When he was able to walk, Reed brought her a small bag of striped peppermint candy. She accepted the gift without saying a word.

Her watchers had been given explicit orders not to lay a hand on her, but they were men, and their orders did not prevent them from undressing her with their eyes, or from finding excuses to accidentally brush up against her breasts or her rear end when they walked past her in the confines of the small cabin. They slept on cots out on the porch, but she knew they sometimes watched through the windows while she undressed for bed. She could deal with that. If either one tried to come into her bed, however, she would pull the dagger Diego gave her from under her chemise and run the bastard through the heart.

When the sun streamed through the window on the morning of her forty-third day on the mountain, Rosalilia decided that her only hope of making it through this ordeal would be to escape and somehow find Diego. She was certain he would be searching for her, and she was equally certain that he would not be coming alone. Itzcoatl would accompany him, and, since she had been taken to the United States, she knew that Thomas Scoundrel would play some part in delivering justice to Cord and his men as well. The American colonel and her fiancé were like brothers.

She wasted no time making a plan. When she prepared breakfast that morning she secreted a little corn meal in a flour sack under her bed, and later that day she sliced some of the venison haunch she was preparing for dinner into thin strips to dry into jerky. Over the coming days she rendered some of the venison fat into tallow and mixed it with dried berries and jerky to produce a dozen pemmican bars, which had been a staple food of the native peoples of the Americas for centuries.

It wasn't much, but Rosalilia estimated that she could live for four or five days on the pemmican. There were streams everywhere on the mountain, so she was not concerned about going without water. With a little luck, she would find a way to distract her captors and then head down the mountain in the general direction the rider came from with their supplies. She would try to pick up his trail and take it wherever it led. The problem, of course, was to get away from the cabin with enough of a head start so that she could find a rancher or hunter to help her before Reed and Spruce discovered she was gone and lit out after her.

The solution that eventually presented itself was far from ideal, but she knew that it had the best chance of giving her precious time to get ahead of the men and make her way down the mountain. Adding to the difficulty of the whole idea was the fact that she wouldn't be able to make her escape until just before daylight. There was no possibility that she could hike down the mountain slope in darkness; there were too many arroyos, boulders, rock piles, and thorn-filled brush thickets to navigate safely. An early morning escape was her only chance.

❖

Three days later she felt ready. After dinner that evening, she surprised Spruce by coming back into the cabin early and asking him if she could have a drink. The rider who supplied them brought several bottles each time he visited, and the men had routinely asked her if she would drink with them, but she had always turned them down. Spruce was surprised, but his ear-to-ear grin made it clear that he figured she was looking for a little male companionship.

"Reed, get your ass in here," Spruce shouted out the door. "The little lady fancies having a drink with us."

Reed bounded up the steps and grabbed a fresh bottle from the shelf above the fireplace. "Good on you," he said to Rosalilia. "We really ain't half bad when you get to know us." He poured three glasses, and Rosalilia raised hers high and then downed the fiery liquid in one gulp.

"Now, hold on there, missy," said Spruce "don't you go getting yourself ahead of the game here. Hell, the dancing hasn't even begun!"

She forced herself to laugh, and Reed smacked his palm on his thigh and let out a loud, "Yee-haw!"

The bolt of whiskey hit her system like a hurricane, and she had to struggle to compose herself so that her next words sounded sincere. "You boys have yourselves a couple more drinks, and then we can talk about just what kind of party you have in mind."

The men shared a look of total disbelief, but they weren't about to let the opportunity slip away. Reed re-filled their glasses, and they toasted their amazing turn of fortune. Their captive was beautiful, and from what they had seen through the windows when she was getting ready for bed, she also had a magnificent body. As for Cord's admonition not to touch her; hell, if it was her idea to take a bounce or two with them, who would be hurt, and how would he ever know?

Rosalilia reached up and loosened her hair ribbon. She shook her head from side to side and then pulled her tresses off her shoulders so they would have an unobstructed view of her bosom. Then she gazed directly into their eyes, smiled softly, and slowly undid the top button of her blouse.

Reed let out a whoop, but she put her forefinger across her lips and in a hushed voice said, "Now, boys, we can have ourselves the best party of your lives, but it has to be my way and my timing. We do it my way, and Mr. Cord never hears about it. Do you agree?" With that she loosened another button, and the men could see a hint of her cleavage.

"Oh, I'm all in," smiled Reed.

Spruce smacked his lips and said, "I'm with you, partner. All the way." He would have preferred to take on this little spitfire by himself, but if she intended to offer up that sweet little quim in equal measure to them both, why the hell not share?

"Good," said Rosalilia. She undid the third button, and the men had a clear view of the tops of her breasts through her silk chemise. "Here is what we are going to do. I like you both, but I am not the kind of woman who will take on two men at the same time, so one of you is going to have to go first, while the other one waits outside."

On cue, the men's eyes widened in anticipation for what was ahead. "And how do we settle on who slides in there first? Toss a coin?"

Rosalilia had thought this part through carefully. "Now, where's the sport in that?" she answered coyly. "I'd like to see this party go all night, if you two are men enough to handle it."

Reed grabbed himself by the crotch. "Damned straight we are!"

Rosalilia smiled demurely and wet her lips. "Oh, I'm sure you are," she said, while opening the last button on her blouse. Now the men could see the outline of her breasts clearly, and the smooth, tight skin of her abdomen. "Here's how we're going to decide which of you will join me here…" she patted the bed, "and which of you will have to cool his heels–and other things– out on the porch."

She went across the room and took two full bottles of whiskey from the shelf. As she handed each man his bottle, she intentionally grazed his chest with her nearly exposed breasts. Reed was practically drooling.

She stepped back, unfastened the stays on her skirt, and let it drop to the floor. All she had on now was her short chemise and a pair of half-bloomers. She sat on the edge of the bed, giggled sweetly, and slowly crossed her legs. The men followed her every movement like they had puppet strings attached to their heads.

"In my experience," she began in a sultry voice, "the best men in bed are also the best men at the bar. Is that true?"

Reed and Spruce shook their heads vigorously up and down. "Each of you has a full bottle. The man who finishes his bottle first, and then can show me that he is actually ready to get the deed done, will be the first in my bed." She looked pointedly in the direction of their crotches so that her meaning would be crystal clear.

"Now wait here just a minute," said Reed. "You want us to each drink a full bottle and then show you how upstanding we are, and, based on that, you'll pick one of us, lay back, and go for a ride? That some kind of joke?"

Spruce wiped his hand across his mouth. Hell, he'd been as hard as a crowbar since she undid the first button on her shirt. What more did he have to prove? Something smelled wrong with this little party idea. He looked over at Reed and saw that his partner was thinking the same thing.

"And what the hell are you planning on doing while we're sitting here drinking?" Reed growled.

Rosalilia knew she had to do something quickly. Cord's threat to kill them if they touched her notwithstanding, if she didn't get them to agree to go along with her idea right now, they might upend everything and just take her right on the spot. She remembered back to the night in Cuernavaca some years ago when her great-aunt was telling her about men in general, and sex in particular. "Don't ever tease a man and think you are in control," the old lady had advised. Then she shocked her niece by saying, "A stiff dick has no conscience, and it cannot reason. Don't ever forget that."

If she was going to have any chance of escape, Rosalilia was going to have to violate her great-aunt's sage advice. The men were looking increasingly unsettled, as if they were about ready to scrap her game and just toss her on the bed and be done with it. They could figure out how to deal with the boss' fury later. So, what she did in the next few seconds would determine whether her plan had any chance at all, and whether she was going to get out of this mess with her knickers intact.

She closed her eyes for a moment and envisioned Diego coming for her. Then she took a deep breath and pulled one corner of her chemise down, fully exposing her breast. She wet two fingers in her mouth and began to caress her nipple. "What am I going to be doing while you are drinking?" she cooed. "A little more of this, I expect. A girl needs to get ready in her own way, you know." Then she covered her breast back up. "Of course, if you aren't up to the contest..."

Reed shot his partner a questioning glance. "You going to do more of that rubbin' business while we drink?"

"Count on it," replied Rosalilia softly. "Lots more."

Reed uncorked the fresh bottle and took a long swig. Then he pulled a chair over by the bed and sat down. "You get to rubbin,' we'll get to drinking." Spruce took his bottle and pulled a chair to the other side of the bed. "And don't be pulling no tricks," he warned.

Rosalilia laid a hand lightly on his thigh. She trailed her fingers up close to the bulge in his trousers and said, "Oh, I hope to have something much better to pull than tricks."

Spruce gave a little shout and slapped himself upside the head before taking a long pull on his bottle. "Let's commence on to it then, gal."

❖

It took less than an hour for the men to finish their bottles. Rosalila spent the time perched in the middle of the bed. She took her time lowering her top before beginning to lightly rub her breasts with one hand and her thighs with the other.

She knew the risk she was taking. They had to drink until they passed out, or she would be forced to keep her end of the bargain. She watched as Reed's eyes became increasingly watery, and his voiced slowed to a thick slur. But even when his bottle was almost empty, he showed no signs of giving up. On the other side of the bed, Spruce massaged his own crotch between sips of whiskey, never letting his eyes stray from her full, naked breasts.

Outside the cabin, slivers of gray were beginning to pierce the black curtain of darkness. Sunrise was less than an hour away, and she knew that if something didn't give soon, the men were going to finish their whiskey and take their prize. She couldn't fend off the two of them with just a dagger.

Suddenly, Reed lurched up from his chair and swung his empty bottle above his head. "I'm done, you little bitch. Now, get them pants down." He moved towards her and started fishing himself out of his button-fly trousers. Then, a disgusted look crossed his face. "Hell's fire, of all the times a guy has got to take a leak." He turned and wove his way to the door, threw it open, and stumbled out onto the porch. A minute later Rosalilia heard a grunt and then a crash as Reed toppled down the stairs.

Spruce chuckled at his good fortune. He lifted his bottle and drained the last of the whiskey with a satisfied grin. He would be the first to push this big-tittied, stuck–up aristocrat onto her back and ride her good and hard, the cowboy way. Rosalilia sat dead still, terrified of what was about to happen, wondering if she could reach her dagger. Then, a silly smile crossed Spruce's face, and he exploded in his pants from all the rubbing he had been doing while watching Rosalilia play with her breasts. He grimaced at the realization that his rodeo would have to wait, and then the bottle slipped from his fingers and fell to the floor. A minute later his head lolled forward onto his chest, and he began to snore.

Rosalilia did not hesitate. She leapt off the bed, threw on her clothing, and took Reed's jacket from a peg on the wall. She pulled the bag of food she had been adding to each day from under the bed, tossed in a tin cup and the one kitchen knife they had, and headed for the door. Then she stopped; both men wore revolvers. She could not leave them behind for them to chase her with. She went over to Spruce, who was passed out in his chair, pulled his revolver from its holster, and dropped it into her bag. Then she went out to the porch. In the breaking light, she could just make out Reed lying on his side on the ground at the bottom of the stairs. She knelt next to him and saw that a pool of blood was forming in the dirt beside his head. She pushed him over, retrieved his revolver, and checked to see that it was loaded before slipping it through her belt.

Her breath was visible in the gray dawn air, and the emerging shapes of rocks and trees on the steep slope below reinforced the wisdom of her decision to wait until light to make her escape. Since they had been brought up the mountain in a wagon and dropped off without additional horses, Spruce and Reed would have to follow her on foot. They knew the terrain better, but she had a head start. That and the .45 caliber revolver at her side were her only advantages.

Rosalilia slung the bag over one shoulder and started down the slope. She would look for the trail, but, if she couldn't find it, she would follow the course of the stream to the valley below. Someone down there would help her. They had to.

THIRTY SEVEN

Denver

The note from Tanner Fulbright asked Thomas and Diego to meet him at 8:00 p.m. at Pell's Oyster House on Arapaho Street, between 13th and 14th Streets. It was ten days since they dined with the British reporter and three days since they returned from their prairie meeting with Bill Cody.

They descended the steps from street level to Pell's basement location, which was at least twenty degrees cooler than at ground level. Oysters were kept in ice water and fed with oatmeal and flour during their journey from the east coast, but restaurants had only a couple of days to serve them up before they went bad and so, when possible, restaurants located below ground to better keep the oysters chilled.

"I've never much cared for oysters," said Fulbright as he slipped into a dark walnut and leather trimmed booth beside Thomas. "Too damn slippery for my taste."

"Then you haven't had them properly prepared," replied Diego. "They can be extraordinary."

"You mean they're not just served raw, with lemon?"

Thomas laughed and slid a menu across to the reporter. "Fifty-one styles," he said, "and only three of them are raw."

A waiter stopped at their table, and Diego ordered two bottles of *Schloss Gobelsburg* Riesling and a plate of crackers. "Would you like some time to examine the menu?" asked the waiter.

"My friends, trust me on this," Diego said before turning to the waiter and saying, "let's start with two dozen, roasted with butter, créme fraîche, Pernod, shallots, and tomatoes. Can you do that?"

The waiter looked thoughtful. He had never heard of that recipe. He scribbled it down and said, "I will talk to chef and be right back."

"Ah, but I am not quite done," said Diego. The waiter raised his eyebrows. "Please also ask your chef to prepare a sauce with equal parts hollandaise, Velouté, and unsweetened whipped cream, to be served on the side."

The waiter jotted his notes and left for the kitchen. "I know hollandaise," said Fulbright, "but what is Velouté?"

Another waiter brought the Riesling and crackers and poured three glasses of the cold, semi-sweet wine. "It is one of the five mother sauces of French cuisine," said Diego. "Basically, it is a light chicken or fish stock sauce that is thickened with a blond roux."

As Diego talked, Thomas saw a tall man in a chef's jacket and hat step out of the kitchen alongside their waiter. The waiter pointed to their table, and the chef read the recipe notes dictated by Diego before giving Thomas a cursory wave and returning to his kitchen. No telling what that meant, Thomas thought.

"And, so, Mr. Fulbright, have you had any luck with your inquiries?" asked Diego.

The reporter pulled his notebook from his pocket and flipped it open. "In fact, I believe I have," he said, "and it has come from a most unusual place." He waited a beat for a question from Diego or Thomas, but they simply stared at him with open expressions. "Yes, well," continued Fulbright. "I have been operating on the assumption that if Claybourne is in fact behind the attack in Monteverde, the men in his employ who carried it out are either from Denver or would have to come here to report directly to him. Ergo, I believed I would find the connection right here in the city."

Fulbright was pleased with himself. He took another drink of wine, and downed two crackers before Thomas said, "Tanner, Denver is a town of thirty thousand people, hundreds of whom are coming and going on any given day. How the hell do you think you can find anybody who might have direct knowledge about what happened in Monteverde?"

Fulbright looked like he had been slapped in the face. He set down his glass and sat back in the booth. "How?" he said. "But I already have." He looked exasperated. "Look, Thomas, finding people and getting them to talk is what I do, and I am damned good at it."

Diego interrupted. "You found someone who was at Monteverde? And they talked? Do they know anything about the whereabouts of Matthew Cord?"

"And is there a connection to Claybourne?" added Thomas in a rush.

Fulbright beamed. He lived for moments like this when people who had judged him to be something of an inconsequential mouse learned that, in his hands at least, the pen truly was mightier than the sword and that this was one mouse who walked where lions feared to tread. He took another sip of wine and said, "Yes, gentlemen, to both of your questions. But, let me tell you the complete story so you will have all the information that I have gathered. There are still pieces to fill in, but I am more convinced than ever that the scheme Claybourne has set in motion is nothing short of breathtaking."

The diminutive journalist turned towards Diego and laid a hand on his wrist. "I also have reason to believe that your Rosalilia is not only alive, but that she is being held somewhere not far from here."

Diego's eyes went misty, and he pursed his lips. "You are certain?"

"The man who told me was drunk," Fulbright replied, "but he had first-hand knowledge of the attack on her home in Cuernavaca, details about her kidnapping and transport here to Colorado, and he personally overheard Cord giving instructions to the men who were charged with taking her to a cabin in the mountains."

Diego bolted up from the table. "Where? Where is this cabin? We go now!"

Fulbright shook his head and motioned for Diego to sit down. "I don't know the location. The man I talked to didn't either; I'm sure of that."

"How many cabins can Claybourne own?" asked Thomas as Diego reluctantly took his seat. "There must be a way to find out. We'll visit them one by one."

Tanner fiddled with his empty wine glass and said, "Noah Claybourne owns more than 800,000 acres of land across some 1,200 square miles. That's bigger than the state of Rhode Island. And scattered across the prairies and mountains and canyons on his ranch are dozens of cabins, line shacks, bunk houses, and hunting lodges. It would take until next spring to visit them all. Rather a needle in a haystack situation, I'm afraid."

"Two months," Diego said bitterly. "Two months to get out of the hospital, to travel to Colorado, only to be told I am no closer to Rosalilia now than I was the night she was taken?"

"On the contrary," said Fulbright, "we are very, very close. You to finding your fiancée, and me to sorting out the reasons that one of the richest men in America has been funding his own little war on the Mexican border. They really are the same story, you know. Solve one mystery, and we will solve them both."

The waiter appeared with a cart and began setting plates and glasses on the table. "I have no appetite," said Diego, "I'm going back to the Windsor. You can find me in the bar."

"Hold on, then," said Fulbright. "You need to hear the full story, Diego. I have good leads, and it will take the three of us to follow up on them."

"Leads that will take me to Rosalilia?"

"Leads that will explain what Claybourne is up to, which will take us to Cord, who will take us to your fiancée. The road is not straight, my friend, but it does lead to her."

Thomas smiled at Diego. "When all you want to do is break down Claybourne's door and beat her location out of him?"

Diego shook his head. "Sometimes simple plans are the best."

"You wouldn't get within a mile of Claybourne," said Fulbright. "Since the raid on Monteverde, he has doubled the number of men patrolling around Langton Hall. He says it's in preparation for the big fishing tournament that begins in three weeks, but according to what I have heard, he is beefing up his personal security for an entirely different reason."

"And that is?" asked Thomas.

"He knows that Diego is on his way to Colorado. He doesn't know he is here yet, but that won't take long for him to discover."

"How does he know?" asked Diego.

"Because he sent Matthew Cord to Mexico City to find you and kill you. Cord returned a few days ago and had to tell his boss that he had failed. All he knew for sure was that you were not in the city. Claybourne assumed that you would turn heaven and earth to find her, Diego. He knows you will not rest until you free her and kill him. He's not taking that chance."

Diego's eyes took on a faraway look. "On that, he and I are in perfect agreement," he said quietly.

"We're going to eat those special oysters of yours," Thomas said. "And while we do, Tanner is going to tell us everything he knows. Then, we'll map out a plan."

Diego nodded in agreement, even though every fiber in his body wanted to ride to Claybourne's and take his chances with the guards. But, when Itzcoatl taught him to hunt all those years ago, he often told the boy that learning how to wait was more important than knowing when to pull the trigger. Bitter medicine, he thought. He had already waited two months. But, in his heart he knew it still wasn't time to pull the trigger.

❖

"Is this your recipe?" the chef asked Thomas as the waiter put two covered silver platters and a small sauce tureen on the table.

"It's his," he answered, nodding in Diego's direction.

"Sir," said the chef, "I have never used hollandaise, Velouté, and unsweetened whipped cream in the preparation of roasted oysters before tonight. I tasted them in the kitchen–it is a superb combination."

He doffed his tall, starched cap and added, "My compliments."

"My pleasure," replied Diego.

"May I ask your permission to make this dish available to our customers on a regular basis?" said the chef. "It is that good."

"Are oyster houses a competitive business?" asked Thomas before Diego could reply.

The chef looked around to make sure no one was listening. "Like you wouldn't believe. There are six here in Denver alone, so the addition of a recipe this extraordinary, well, it would really help us to stand out."

Diego chuckled. "Please, use the recipe as you wish. I promise I won't share it with the competition."

The chef smiled and snapped his fingers for the waiter, who appeared with a silver ice bucket containing two bottles of cellar-aged Bollinger Rosé Champagne.

"By way of thanking you," the chef said. He turned to go and then asked Diego, "Do you have a name for this recipe? For our menu."

Diego shook his head. "No special name," he replied.

"Actually, there is," Thomas said. He looked at the chef and said, "Call them *Oysters Rosalilia*."

"I like the name," said the chef with a wide grin. *"Bon appétit."*

❖

As they ate, Fulbright explained that he had begun his search for information about Claybourne in the county assessor's office. The tax records indicated that among the properties Noah owned in Denver was the very building that housed the bar and bordello where his father had committed suicide fifteen years ago. What better place to find his men, especially if they had just spent weeks in the desert pining for the delights of the town's famous fleshpots and gambling dens.

The sporting house still existed, but Fulbright quickly discovered that Claybourne's ownership was not common knowledge among the employees. So, every night for a week, the reporter plopped himself down at a table in a dark corner of the well-appointed bar and made friends with an assortment of whores, bartenders, waiters, and their customers. The combination of his clipped British accent and spectacles, plus his cover story of writing a novel about the bawdy houses of the Wild West designed to titillate the European upper crust, was sufficient to generate a steady stream of people who wanted to sit down and tell their stories in hopes of being a part of the book.

After six nights of gathering nothing more interesting than detailed descriptions of the sexual peccadillos of the American cowboy, he was about to give up. Then, on the seventh night of waiting patiently at his table, a friendly bartender pointed out a tall, thin cowboy seated at the bar. "That fella just came back from Mexico City," said the bartender. "He's been braggin' on how great their whores are as compared to ours. Don't know if you were interested in any south of the border pussy tales for that book of yours, but that gent seems to have loads of 'em."

Fulbright invited the cowhand to his table and bought him dinner and a steady stream of the bar's best whiskey. It wasn't long before the man was sufficiently lubricated enough to begin telling stories about his employer, Noah Claybourne, and his immediate boss, Matthew Cord. Fulbright moved gingerly towards his ultimate objective of finding out what the man might know about Monteverde. As it turned out, though, the cowboy was more than eager to spout everything he knew, and it was more than the reporter could have hoped for.

"He worked directly under Cord in Mexico," Tanner told Diego. "In fact, he was one of the men who invaded your fiancée's home after your engagement party."

"*Dios mío*," said Diego. "This *maricón* is a dead man."

"Cool your trigger finger," said Thomas. "I'm pretty sure Tanner is going to be adding a lot more names to the list."

The waiter brought coffee and a dessert tray to their table, and the reporter continued his story. "We already knew that Cord was negotiating with Rosalilia's father for exclusive mining rights for Claybourne's enterprise along the Arizona and New Mexico Territory borders. What I was told was that when Señor Verjan turned his proposal down for the last time, Cord was ordered by Claybourne to sack the house, kill the old man and take Rosalilia."

"And how would a low-level cowhand like your guy know information like that?" asked Thomas.

"Matthew Cord is a prideful, strutting character who likes to look important. He has a trusted team of about a dozen Americans he uses for jobs like this, and when he explains the job, he tells them why they are doing it and for whom. He portrays his own role in these affairs as much more important than they really are, of course. In his telling, Claybourne is a minor character behind the scenes, while he is the one who scripts all of the action."

Thomas nodded. That made sense. If your life is on the line you want to know the big picture, no matter how much your boss is paying you to do his dirty work.

"But why bring Rosalilia to Colorado?" asked Diego. "Right to Claybourne Ranch? Seems like that would be showing his hand."

"And how the hell does this tie into the attack on Monteverde?" added Thomas.

"I have some of the pieces to that puzzle, but not all of them," answered Fulbright. "The cowhand told me that the scuttlebutt around the ranch was that Claybourne held an all-day meeting with some very powerful national politicians and military officers, coincidentally not long before the raid on Monteverde."

"Was that an unusual sort of thing for him to do?" asked Thomas.

"In some ways, no. Claybourne has political and business interests all over the country, and he routinely meets with important people."

"So, what made this meeting so noteworthy?" said Diego.

"It was the presence of three people that piqued this cowboy's interest. One was General Winston Greer, who happens to be the army commander responsible for protecting both the Arizona and New Mexico Territories."

"And the other two?" asked Thomas.

"Ah, that's where it gets very interesting. One was a half breed Mescalero named Geronimo Rivas. He is a Mexican national, who was once an officer in the Mexican army. Today he is a notorious bandit, albeit one who has plundered almost exclusively in his native country. He is a cattle rustler, bank robber, kidnapper…you name it. Frankly, those are just the kind of credentials Claybourne would be looking for if he wanted to wipe out some unfortunate little town like Monteverde."

"So, who was the other interesting guest at the meeting?" asked Thomas.

"This one I am excited to learn more about," answered Fulbright. "She sounds perfect for a newspaper series. My readers in the United Kingdom would eat the stories up."

"*She*?" said Diego.

"Yes, Demetria Carnál. Sometimes she is referred to as the bandit queen of northern Mexico. A bit of a folk hero, it seems."

"And her resume is similar to that of Rivas?" said Thomas.

"Quite. She is credited with robbing more than a dozen banks, stealing payroll from stagecoach lines, and torching any number of freight warehouses. Rumor has it that she is also something of a Robin Hood character."

"She steals from the rich and gives to the poor?" asked Diego. "I thought that kind of thing only happened in your English legends."

"Who knows," he said. "At the very least it makes her a leading candidate for a profile by yours truly." Fulbright finished his glass of champagne and poured a cup of coffee. "Now then," he went on, "I have saved some of the most intriguing things I learned for the last. Just before the cowboy slumped over drunk, he shared what I am sure will prove to be the most important part of the puzzle for you gentlemen. According to him, Claybourne has made Matthew Cord responsible for coordinating all communication with Rivas and Carnál. The cowboy himself has carried several messages back and forth between Rivas and Claybourne at Cord's direction. But what exactly are they communicating about? That is what we need to find out and quickly if my hunch is correct and Claybourne is planning another attack along the border. What I am certain of is that if we find Carnál and Rivas, we also find Cord. And when we find him…" He didn't need to finish the thought. Finding Cord was the key to rescuing Rosalilia and bringing a hammer down on both Cord and his boss.

The three men finished their coffee and brandy, and the conversation turned to what they should do now. Thomas had listened carefully to Fulbright's report, and his mind was racing. The more he thought it over, the more convinced he became that Fulbright had it right: the best way to find Cord would be to track down Rivas and Carnál.

"Do you have any idea where either of the bandits might be right now?" he asked Fulbright.

The reporter adjusted his spectacles and smiled. "I thought you'd never ask."

❖

THIRTY EIGHT

Denver

It was after midnight when Thomas left the Windsor Hotel. He walked for several blocks along streets that were dimly illuminated by flickering gas lamps until he reached the Daniels and Fisher Department store on 16th street. He could see the building from several blocks away because it was one of the few structures in the city that had installed the new electric lighting provided by Colorado Electric's thirty-five horsepower, direct current Brush-Swan dynamos. The store had also installed electric arc streetlights on the sidewalk to replace the old gas lamps.

He was fascinated by the way that electric light was transforming life in the cities. For as long as he could remember, in every city he had visited around the world, pedestrian and carriage traffic would evaporate shortly after dusk. They picked up a little when the smoky kerosene streetlamps were replaced with gas lamps, but, with the introduction of electric lighting, nightlife in cities was transformed. He figured that the pickpockets, muggers, and prostitutes who relied on darkness to ply their trades were probably not happy with the change, but for most people, electric light meant they didn't have to be trapped inside their homes each night when darkness fell.

After lingering in front of the store for a few minutes he turned the corner and walked six blocks to the area along Market Street simply known as The Row. The sidewalk became busier the closer he got to the stretch of gambling halls and brothels that had earned Denver the reputation of being the most sinful city west of the

Mississippi. He passed Belle Binard's establishment, where a signboard promised fourteen rooms, five parlors, twelve 'boarders,' choice wine, liquors and cigars. *"Strictly first-class in all respects,"* the sign proclaimed. He poked his head inside the next business, Jennie Roger's House of Mirrors, because tales of its floor to ceiling mirrors in oval frames carved with the figures of nude women were legendary among wealthy men who sought out only the most exotic sporting houses when they traveled.

The mirrors were impressive, but the row of sad-faced women in white brothel gowns sitting on plain wooden chairs could only have been attractive to cow punchers who'd spent too much time swatting horse flies and swallowing trail dust. He ignored the barker who offered him a two-for-one deal and stepped out of Jennie's in the direction of his real destination, directly across the street. The Pearl was a handsome, well-maintained, three-story building. A liveried doorman was on duty at the main entrance, and as he walked across the street, Thomas watched two older gentlemen in formal evening attire alight from a hansom cab and enter the business.

"Bar or sport?" asked the doorman as he approached.

"Bar for now."

The doorman swung open the massive leaded glass and oak door and directed him to go through the first door on the right. He went down the paneled hall and walked into one of the most beautiful bars he had ever visited. It was filled with potted palms, gas chandeliers, and carved oak tables and chairs. The mirrored back bar rose two stories to a vaulted ceiling decorated with plaster frescoes. A tall ladder on wheels was affixed to a rail so that the barman could climb up to retrieve the rarest liquor and wines from the Olympian heights.

He settled into a small booth in the corner and ordered a bottle of California Syrah from the waiter. As he waited for the wine, he gazed around the room. A dozen men were eating and drinking, and a middle-aged woman–the madam, he assumed–was making her way from table to table to inquire whether the gentlemen were looking to engage any of her girls. The woman was carrying a list under her arm; no doubt it contained descriptions of the girls and detailed notes about their special talents.

The waiter uncorked the wine just as she reached Thomas's table. "Good evening, *chéri*," she began in a distinct French accent. "Welcome to the Pearl." She looked him over and added, "I am sure I would have remembered a gentleman as handsome as you, so I will guess this is your first visit to our club?"

He nodded. "It is, but the unique qualities of your establishment are famous everywhere, even in New York where I am from."

"I am flattered. And would you care to hear about our ladies? We have a new girl just in this morning from Jamaica. She is dusky and full-bosomed, and she has the sweetest Caribbean accent."

He slid a five-dollar bill across the table. The woman snatched it up with a quizzical look. "I will want to visit with you later this evening, I am sure."

"And this?" she asked, holding out the bill. "Do you wish to pay for your girl in advance?"

"That is for you. When I am ready, I do not want you to offer me anyone but the best, freshest, and most talented girl in your house. Can you do that?"

The woman leaned over and pecked him on the cheek. "It will be my pleasure…and then yours."

He watched her walk away and wondered again if he was being foolhardy. The Pearl was the business Tanner Fulbright had described. It was owned by Noah Claybourne, and he was here because he wanted to make his own inquiries. Fulbright was a fine reporter, but he knew that he was not very experienced with the people who lived and worked in places like this. He had been around them his entire adult life. He knew how to talk to them, how to question them, and he understood intuitively when it was a better course of action to push harder for information or back off before somebody stuck a dagger between his ribs.

He sipped his wine and nibbled at the chocolates the madam sent over with her compliments and watched with amusement as the two older gentlemen who had entered the club before him were introduced to a couple of scantily clad, prospective dates. The young women slowly twirled to show off their wares, they flirted and cooed and teased, and then, when the deals were made and the madam paid, each girl dropped into the lap of her intended. Despite what Thomas had asked of the madam when he gave her the five dollars, he had no intention of engaging one of her girls. He had never paid for sex; it wasn't so much that he had any kind of moral compunctions or religious scruples that prevented him from visiting prostitutes. Instead, it was the fact that–for whatever reason, whether fate or charm or providential timing–willing partners had always been available when he was in the mood. The idea of paying someone to pretend to enjoy his company was a thought he could not countenance.

Across the room, the gentlemen stood up with their girls and headed upstairs. Thomas caught one of the men's eyes and raised his glass to the old gentleman. The man grinned and waved enthusiastically in return. "Good luck to you–and to your heart," he thought to himself.

❖

For the next hour, he drank the syrah and watched a steady stream of men and sporting girls perform their parts in the two-act play that was the sex for hire business. Act One: Negotiate. Act Two: Fornicate. End of performance. That is, except in those instances where an Act Three might have to be performed if a "soiled dove" happened to pass along any one of several debilitating social diseases to her customer. In those cases, the sequence of acts became, Negotiate, Fornicate, and *Medicate*. Thomas had seen the effects of an array of sporting house maladies among his fellow soldiers. Some were funny, but all too many had gruesome aftermaths. Chief Red Elk was right: a man needed to think with the head on his shoulders, not the one between his legs.

He was smiling at his own private joke when a familiar looking man entered the bar and took a chair at the opposite side of the room. He snapped his fingers for the waiter, leaned forward, and rested his elbows on the table.

Thomas blinked and stared hard. There was no mistaking him: it was Claybourne's hired gun Elias, who, together with Moncton, had hauled him out to Tamayo Ravine, tossed him in, and left him to die. He squeezed his wine glass so hard that the glass stem broke. A busboy appeared quickly to clean up the spill, and the waiter brought another bottle of wine. Thomas scooted his chair back into the darkness of the corner and watched the waiter bring a mug of beer and a plate of sausages and cheese to Elias. When the madam appeared to make her sales pitch, he leaned forward and strained to hear the conversation.

The Frenchwoman did not greet Elias as her *chéri*. That told him that Elias was not a favored customer, even though he was employed by the brothel's owner. He could only hear snatches of their sentences; "Younger this time," Elias was saying, "and, by God, send me one who doesn't use the word 'no'." He watched the madam shake her head before saying something along the lines of, "that's not something most of the girls will do…you'll need to pay more money for that." Elias growled at her, but he dipped into his wallet and pulled out a wad of bills.

Elias tore into his beer and sausages, and a few minutes later the madam returned with one of her girls. She wore a simple green dress, and Thomas estimated that she could not have been older than sixteen or seventeen. She was thin and blonde, with a pale complexion. Looking at her in profile, he also noticed that she had a bit of a tummy. Pregnant, no doubt. That meant she wouldn't be able to work much longer, which could explain why she was willing to take on whatever special requests Elias had made to make a few extra dollars.

Elias nodded to the madam and grunted at the girl to sit down while he finished his beer and food. He didn't say a word to her until he was done. Then he pushed back his chair, stood up, and simply said, "Let's go." Romantic devil thought Thomas. He watched Elias and the girl go up the stairs and disappear down the hall. Then he asked the waiter for a sandwich and settled in to wait for Elias to finish his ride.

Cord's hired man came down the stairs an hour later. He stood at the bar and tossed down another beer and then made his way to the door. Thomas put three silver dollars on the table, waited a few beats, and followed Elias out onto the street. It was just past 3:00 a.m., pitch dark except for the faint light from a scattering of gas streetlamps. Only a handful of people were about. He matched Elias' stride, staying back about twenty-five feet. They passed the last of the brothels after four blocks and were about to enter the city's more respectable business district when Elias stepped off a curb and turned into an alley. He went over beside a waste can, unbuttoned his trousers and began to relieve himself against a brick wall.

Thomas went quietly up behind Elias as he was buttoning his pants, and when the trail hand wheeled around, he found himself face to face with the man he was sure he had killed at the ravine eight weeks ago. Two things happened in rapid-fire succession: Elias' eyes went wide in shocked recognition, and Thomas grabbed him by the shirt with his left hand, made a chisel fist with his right hand and struck Elias hard in the throat just above the thyroid cartilage of his larynx.

There was a crunching sound as Elias's neck cartilage collapsed. Then he wrapped his hands around his throat and crumpled to his knees. His head snapped back, and he made a series of deep, raspy, sucking sounds as he fought for breath. Thomas watched impassively as Elias's arms dropped to his side, still trying to draw a breath as blood began to fill his lungs. When Elias looked up at him his expression didn't communicate hate or fear. Just surprise. A moment later blood gushed from his mouth, and his head dropped to his chest.

Thomas pulled Elias's wallet from his jacket pocket and removed the cash. When he turned to walk away, Elias slid dead onto the dirty pavement.

❖

The bartender at the Pearl was surprised to see the tall, young American return. Perhaps he had changed his mind about engaging one of the girls.

"Are you ready for your party?" he asked.

Thomas shook his head. "The girl who was with the cowhand at that table," he said, pointing to where Elias had been seated. "Blonde, looks like she might be pregnant. I want to talk to her."

"Can't do that, mister. Seems she took ill after her romp with that son of a bitch. Not seeing anybody for the rest of the night."

Thomas pulled out the money he had taken from Elias' wallet and peeled off a ten-dollar bill. The barman's eyes widened. "That's yours when you bring her here to me. Tell her I just want to talk. Just talk."

Five minutes later the madam appeared with the young girl in tow. Her blonde hair was unkempt, her lips were bruised and bleeding, and one of her eyes was swollen shut. She walked with a limp, and she held one arm across her abdomen as if she had a terrible stomach-ache.

The young girl looked wordlessly at the floor, but the madam's eyes were blazing with fury.

"He did this to her?" Thomas asked quietly.

"He did," replied the madam coldly. "Friend of yours?"

"Not hardly. What's your name, child?" he asked the girl.

"Lisette," answered the girl in a tiny voice.

"Your real name. The name your family gave you."

The girl raised her head. "Margaret. That's my real name."

"And where are you from?"

"St. Louis."

"Do you have family there? Can you go home?"

"I wish I could," whispered the girl.

The madam shot a questioning look at Thomas but said nothing.

"Give me your hand, Margaret," he said gently. The girl extended her hand timidly and he put Elias's money in her palm. A look of disbelief crossed the madam's face.

"There's almost three hundred dollars there. Plenty enough to get a good doctor, buy some new clothing, and take the train home." He turned to the madam. "Does she need to buy her way out of here?" It was common for prostitutes to build up big debts at the houses where they worked. Until their debts were paid, they couldn't go anywhere but the bedroom.

Madam shook her head. "She has not been here long enough to owe anything."

Margaret clenched the money in her hand, and tears began to flow down her cheeks. "Will you give me your word that you will help her get fixed up and make sure she gets on that train?" he asked the madam. "I can pay you more for your help."

"I will do that," said the madam in a motherly voice. "And you do not need to pay me a cent." With that she waved over another girl, who wrapped an arm around Margaret's shoulder and lead her to the stairs. The girl wiped her nose on her sleeve, smiled at Thomas, and walked up the stairs.

"How did you convince that rattlesnake to give the girl so much money? He has done this before to other girls without so much as a simple apology, but if you know his employer, you know why we can't do anything about it."

"I know his employer, and he knows me. As for how I convinced him to do the right thing, let's just say I didn't give him a choice."

"But when he comes back, what will I do then?"

Then she saw a cloud cross his face, and she understood. "But he won't be back, will he."

Thomas rested his hand on her forearm and smiled. Then he turned and walked to the door.

"Dieu vous protége." Go with God, she whispered as he stepped back out into the night.

❖

It was blistering hot the following afternoon when Thomas, Diego, and Itzcoatl rode through the gates of Major Rhine's ranch northeast of Denver. Thomas said nothing to his friends about killing Elias. The death of that one man, deserved as it was, brought them no closer to finding Rosalilia. It settled part of a score and he knew it would please Diego to learn that one of the men who threw his friend into the rocky canyon had been served a full measure of justice, but he chose to keep the event private for the time being.

Rhine greeted them warmly and called for his ranch hand to see to their horses. Then he led them up onto the covered porch, where Anaya brought them clay jars of cold Coors beer and a plate of bread and cheese.

"Your hospitality is most appreciated, Señor Rhine," said Diego, "as is your kindness in agreeing to be the conduit point for our communication with Mexico and with Marshal Masterson. I am in your debt."

Rhine nodded and then listened intently as Thomas and Diego brought him up to date on everything that had happened since Thomas left his ranch more than a month earlier.

"It appears that the two of you are just plain damn hard to kill, or maybe you're just the two luckiest fellas on the continent," said Rhine.

"Little of both, I expect," answered Thomas with a grin.

Anaya returned to the table with more food, and when she set the plates down, she put her hand gently on Thomas's jaw and turned his head towards her. "Your woman give you that?" she asked, looking at the long scar that ran down his cheek to the top of his jaw.

"Actually, it was her father," he replied. "He was aiming somewhat farther south, but that's where his blade ended up."

Anaya nodded in understanding. "You are a fortunate man, Colonel. My father would not have missed."

The men laughed, and Anaya refilled their jars. Then Rhine asked what their plan was.

"The reporter, Fulbright, believes that the bandits Claybourne hired are preparing more attacks on border towns," said Thomas. "He has a good idea where they are holed up right now. Diego and Itzcoatl will go to the Arizona Territory to track down Geronimo Rivas, and I will go to Las Cruces in New Mexico Territory to find Demetria Carnál. Matthew Cord is sure to be near to one of them. When we find him, we find Rosalilia."

"You make it sound simple," said Rhine.

Diego chuckled. "I am under no such illusion, nor is Tomás or Itzcoatl. But we cannot sit and wait for fate to deal us a kind hand. One of these *ladróns* will deliver Cord to us, whether they wish to or not."

"*Ladrón*?" asked Rhine.

"Thief," answered Diego. "And for our respective journeys, we will require supplies. Tomás tells me that is your business."

Rhine held his hands up, palms outwards. "My armory is yours to explore," he said with a smile. "After dinner we can evaluate your needs and line you out with any gear you may need."

"Do you have any news since your last letter?" asked Thomas.

"None about the raid on Monteverde. The national newspapers are flogging the story daily, and they seem to be succeeding at whipping up the public's desire to extract a pound of flesh from the Mexican government for the murders of all those innocent civilians."

"Many innocents have died in Arizona, and so now many more innocents must die in Mexico?" asked Diego.

"That seems increasingly to be the national mood," said Rhine somberly. "And, speaking of the death of innocents, I have something to give you."

He went into the house and returned a moment later with a letter in hand. "This came by special courier a few days ago," he said. "The envelope was addressed to me, and I opened and read it, but the message was not for me. It comes from your father."

Diego reached for the envelope. "The letter is actually for Itzcoatl," said Rhine in a soft voice. Diego looked surprised but he made no comment when Major Rhine handed the letter to the old Aztec. They waited in silence as Itzcoatl fished a pair of spectacles out of his vest pocket, unfolded, and read the letter. His expression never changed. A minute later he re-folded the letter, slipped it into his vest, stood up, and walked away under the orange twilight sky in the direction of the creek.

Diego and Thomas looked at Major Rhine. "Itzcoatl's son, Xipil, is dead," he explained. "Tortured and murdered. He was taken at gunpoint from a park in Mexico City where he was sitting at a table with his fiancée. They found his body in a lake two days later. According to Diego's father, the boy's body had been so badly mutilated that they would not let his mother see it."

"Xipil," murmured Diego. "So young, so brave. He and his brother never left my side while I was recuperating. They guarded over me, just as their father has done for me my entire life."

Anaya set bottles of whiskey and mezcal on the table and handed glasses to the men.

"According to Diego's father, the last people to be seen with Xipil at the park before he was taken were known employees of Matthew Cord."

"Cord!" spat Diego. "Again. Will we ever..?"

Thomas looked towards the creek, where Itzcoatl stood rock still on the bank, his shadowy form a silhouette against the dying light.

"We will," he said in a determined voice. "I promise you, we will."

⁂

THIRTY NINE

Organ Mountains, Southern New Mexico Territory

Ulysses picked his way up the rocky trail in the shadow of the granite spires of the Organ Mountains. At the lower elevations, the trail was marked by golden Mexican poppies, mesquite tress, and creosote bushes, and as they rode higher up the slope, they passed through scattered stands of junipers. Now, at about four thousand feet, the landscape was dominated by ponderosa pines, mountain mahogany, and gnarled oaks. Several mule deer skittered across the trail as they wound their way up, and when Thomas stopped for water at a spring that flowed from a rhyolite outcropping, he gave a wide berth to a tuff of volcanic ash where a pile of diamondback rattlers was coiled under the edge of a rock.

The needle-tipped mountains were the first things Thomas saw when the train from Denver pulled into the siding at Ft. Selden, twelve miles north of Las Cruces. Their rocky crevices and folds rose like an island from the floor of the Chihuahuan Desert and dominated the horizon for as far north and south as he could see.

Stopping at the fort was a purely military courtesy. It was protocol for high-ranking officers to introduce themselves to the local army commander when they were traveling, and in this instance, it was also a way for him to learn if the army knew anything about Demetria Carnál and her band of brigands.

The fort was laid out in the shape of a cross, with a line of well-maintained structures and corrals radiating out from the central headquarters building. Thomas dismounted in front of the HQ and watched as a group of black soldiers from the 125th US Colored Infantry Regiment were put through their paces on the parade ground. He had served beside them in the Sioux Wars, and he learned to respect their grit and professionalism, and to appreciate the nickname given to them by Plains Indians: Buffalo Soldiers.

The commanding officer was in Las Cruces on business, and so the duty sergeant sent a runner to fetch 1st Lieutenant P.M. Price.

"Colonel Scoundrel, it is an honor," said the fresh-faced lieutenant when he bounded into the office. "We had no idea you were in the territory."

"I'm assisting a friend in the search for a group of Mexican nationals who are reported to be in the area. But I am not on active duty at present and simply hoped you might have some helpful information."

"Of course. Please, sit down." The lieutenant motioned to a desk in the corner of the room and then asked the sergeant to bring coffee.

"Anything stronger?" he asked Thomas.

"A shade too early in the day, thanks all the same. What is your duty assignment here, Lieutenant?"

"I am a Field Astronomer with the Corps of Engineers. Four years ago I lead a mapping expedition in this area, and I have returned to complete our survey of the *Sierra de Los Organos* Mountains, what we now call the Organs."

Thomas took a drink of coffee."Then you are just the man I want to talk to. Do you know the location of the old Jacinto Trading Post? I understand it is located in a remote foothill region."

"Is that where you think you will find the Mexican nationals you are seeking?"

"Could be. I was told on good authority that they were at the post a week ago."

"Is there a name I might recognize?"

Thomas hesitated. He did not want to invite the army to join in his search, but he really did need some help. "Demetria Carnál," he answered calmly.

"The bandit woman? Here in Doña Ana county? What on earth…?"

"That is my question, as well."

"Is it possible, Colonel, that Carnál could have any connection with the events at Monteverde? Our standing orders are to increase border patrols and report incursions by anyone who could have hostile intent."

Thomas chose his words carefully. Whatever else happened, he had to find and talk to Carnál before anyone else—especially the army–had a chance to interrogate her.

"I believe she may have information about a friend of mine who was kidnapped in Mexico. That is my only interest in her at present."

"I understand," replied the lieutenant. "Any idea why she would be up in the mountains, just thirty miles north of the Mexican border?"

"No idea at all. What exactly is up there?"

Lieutenant Price went over to a large wall map and motioned for Thomas to join him. "This is from our '77 expedition," he said. "The old trading post is halfway up the mountains, about here." He pointed to a spot twenty miles southeast of the fort. "Legend has it that the original log post was built by the Spanish explorer Juan de Oñate when he came north from the Valley of Mexico with five hundred Spanish settlers and soldiers in 1595. In the last two hundred fifty years the place has been abandoned more than it has been occupied. It was a line shack for a local rancher for some years, and I heard a few years ago that one of the wealthiest families in Las Cruces had expanded it into something of a summer retreat to get away from the heat. It's high enough that the average temperature is probably twenty or thirty degrees below what it is down in the valley."

"And they still own it?

"As far as I know, yes. It's actually a perfect spot for something like that; there is a natural spring, stands of pine and oak, lots of grass, and plenty of game meat."

"The family who owns the place, do you know them?"

Price nodded. "It belongs to the brother of Antonio Resposo, who was the vice-president of Mexico under Porfirio Díaz. He owns ranches, a mine, and a couple hundred thousand acres of raw land and timber around here."

Thomas took a chance. "Would you happen to know if the Resposo family does any business with a man named Noah Claybourne?"

"The Colorado land baron?"

"The same."

"I seem to remember something," said Price. He went over to a tall wooden cabinet with multiple drawers, opened one and rifled through it. "Here it is. This is a copy of the grant giving Claybourne and Resposo permission from the territorial governor to exploit any and all mineral rights up and down the length of the Organs, including the right to build any structures they need to make that happen. That's about forty miles of potentially valuable dirt. Quite a coup, and it didn't cost them a dime."

He gave the document to Thomas, who scanned them quickly and handed it back. He did not believe in coincidence. Demetria Carnál was staying at an isolated place in the mountains that was owned by Claybourne and Resposo. And, she also had some connection to Geronimo Rivas, who Thomas believed had led the attack on Monteverde.

"This is exactly what I was looking for," said Thomas. "If you wouldn't mind having one of your men sketch a map of the best route to that post, I would be much obliged."

"I will do that myself, Colonel. I am the post cartographer, after all. Will tomorrow morning work for you? The major will be back from Las Cruces this afternoon, and he'd have my hide if he found out you were here but didn't stay for dinner. We have plenty of room in the officer's quarters too. You can stay the night and be off in the morning."

"That sounds just right. If you don't mind, I'll look after my horse and then throw my things in my room before I clean up for dinner."

He saluted the duty sergeant and stepped out onto the porch alongside the lieutenant. "By the way," he asked Price, "Is a black sergeant named McReady still posted here with the 125th?"

"Old Obidiah? He sure is. Must be five years past mandatory retirement, but we'd be hard pressed to run this place without him. Would you like me to let him know you are here?"

"I really would, and thanks for everything."

A private materialized out of thin air and picked up his saddlebags. "This way, sir," he said, and they walked across the parade ground to the officer's quarters.

❖

Thomas left the fort at dawn. Lieutenant Price had sketched an excellent map of the trails he should follow along the base of the Organs. He marked the arroyos, washes, and moraine fields to avoid and included a dotted line showing the best path to follow until he reached the switchback trail that would lead him up to the isolated lodge where Tanner Fulbright believed he would find Demetria Carnál.

His dinner with Fort Selden's commander had not provided any new information about the raid on Monteverde. The army had scoured hundreds of miles of territory around the town and come up empty handed. General Greer ordered more patrols around other towns in the area in the event the raiders returned, but officially, the army was taking the position that the attack had been a one off.

After dinner, he met Sergeant McReady at the bar in the sutler's store. Obidiah was coming on sixty, and he wouldn't be able to hold off retirement for much longer. The wiry, ever smiling, consummate professional soldier was a favorite friend. As a former cook with the 109th Ohio during the war, he was also one of a small handful of people who knew the real story of how cook's assistant Private T.E. Scanaddrél was elevated to the rank of full colonel at the Battle of Pebble Creek Ridge. Thomas noted that the sergeant was limping when he came through the door.

"What will you do when you pull the plug?" Thomas asked when they sat down at a table with a bottle of whiskey.

"No plans, least wise none I have thought through," said McReady. "I still have family in Ohio, and they have a little farm, but, God's truth, I can't see myself steering a plow in the shadow of a mule's hindquarters for the rest of my days. Just can't see that."

Thomas poured a whiskey and slid it across the table. "Maybe you don't have to. You've been recruiting, training, and supervising men and managing supplies for the past fifteen years. Why not keep doing that?"

"You mean they've gone and started a new regiment for old colored sergeants who are headed out to pasture? Who we gonna fight–pensioners from the War of 1812?"

Thomas grinned and handed an envelope to McReady. "I had something a little more modern in mind. I wrote that last night; it's a letter of introduction to my friend, Bill Cody."

"The showman?"

"Yes. He is organizing a new wild west extravaganza, and it's going to be a big affair. Trick-riders, pitched battles between Indians and cavalry, the world's best pistol and rifle shots, the works. He plans to take it to every major city in the country and even over to Europe. Says he plans on performing for the Queen of England herself."

"Imagine that," said Obidiah as he turned the envelope over in his hands. "But what's this old man got that folk would pay to see at a show like that? They got so few old black cripples in their own towns that they'll be happy to cough up a dime to see a live one hobble across the stage?"

Thomas didn't take the bait. "Somebody's got to organize things. Somebody has to bail the wranglers out of jail when they get drunk, manage railroad schedules, deal with provisioners, keep the rolling stock rolling, things like that."

"Things I've been doing for over thirty years."

"And you can do it sitting on your ass if that makes you happy."

Obidiah turned serious. "I ain't never done a day's work on my backside, Private, and I never will."

"That you won't, not if you are working for Cody. He needs somebody like you that he can depend on to keep things humming along smoothly in the background so he can focus on running the entertainment up front with the crowds."

Obidiah nodded. "And I thank you for the opportunity, Thomas. Couldn't see myself ending my days in a rocker at the old soldier's home."

"Hell, as if they'd have you."

The two men laughed and finished their whiskey. They sat quietly for a few minutes and then Obidiah said, "You know, if there is ever anything I can do for you, find me. I'll be there."

"That might be sooner than you think," answered Thomas. He poured two more whiskeys and told his friend about Diego, Rosalilia, their suspicions about Noah Claybourne, and their search for Cord, Geronimo Rivas, and Demetria Carnál. He also told the sergeant about being dropped into Tamayo ravine, his recovery at Red Elk's village, and the recent news of Xipil's murder at the hands of Matthew Cord.

"Son, that's a powerful mountain of trouble you're walking into," said Obidiah. "And you are certain the law can't help you out?"

"Claybourne *is* the law in Colorado and probably here in New Mexico Territory, as well. No, we are on our own in this mess."

Obidiah stared hard at Thomas. Then he raised his glass and smiled. "Like I said, you call for me, and I'll be there."

※

It was late afternoon when Thomas swung around a boulder at the top of the switchback trail and stopped to get his bearings. That's when it occurred to him that he hadn't mopped the sweat off the back of his neck in some time. Lieutenant Price was correct; the temperature had gone down from over one hundred degrees on the valley floor below to a comfortable seventy-five or so at this elevation. He could see for miles through the shimmering waves of heat that flowed across the landscape below. The location for the mountain retreat had been picked well; whether you wanted to get out of the summer furnace or hide out, it was an ideal spot. And anyone making their way up the zig-zag trail would be visible for hours before they could get close enough to be a threat.

Then the silence was broken by the sound of a Winchester rifle lever being worked. "Son of a …" he began. Why the hell hadn't he been paying attention to his own advice?

The voice from atop the boulder to his right was slow, calm, and confident. "*Buenas tardes, señor.* Have you had a pleasant ride up our mountain?"

Thomas looked up at the sentry who was holding the rifle on him. He wore a dark hat and clothing, capped off by a garish yellow bandana. His relaxed posture was a ruse. The intense focus in his eyes belied his casual stance. This man was a seasoned professional who would not hesitate to shoot if he thought it necessary.

He slowly removed his hat and beat some of the trail dust off his shirt before answering. "Pleasant enough," he said. "Especially when the temperature began to drop, and the diamondbacks went to sleep. Been watching me for long?"

"All day my friend, though I did take time for a nice lunch and even a short siesta. But now that you have arrived, I am afraid I must do my duty and either allow you to pass or throw you down into the canyon. Such is the way of the world in which we live. *Entiendes*?"

"Yes, I understand. But I've been thrown down enough canyons this year. I would much prefer to be allowed to pass."

"As would we all, *amigote*, but *la jefa* is very strict about such things, and so I must follow the rules or face the possibility of being pitched into the canyon myself."

"Your leader is a woman," he replied in matter-of-fact voice.

"Somehow, my friend, I think you already knew that." He turned the rifle away from Thomas and rested it in the crook of his arm. Not a reprieve, Thomas knew, but at least a sign that the sentry was still not sure what to do. "And where have you come from today?" asked the sentry.

"I left Fort Selden at dawn."

"Fort Selden? Are you a military man?"

"I was. Now I am simply trying to find a friend."

"Up here? At the top of a desert mountain in the middle of nowhere?"

The sentry pulled a hand-rolled cigarette from his shirt pocket with his right hand as he balanced the rifle in his left. He struck a match, took a couple of puffs, and said, "Why do you think your friend is here?"

"She is not here. But I think Miss Carnál may be able to help me find her."

The sentry was not surprised that he knew *la jefa's* name. "You risk your life for a woman? *Ojalá*, my friend, hopefully she is worthy of such courage, foolish though it may be."

It was time to appeal to the man's sense of honor. "She is the fiancée of my best friend. She was kidnapped near Mexico City and carried here to the United States. I gave my friend my word I would help to find her."

"And you believe Señorita Carnál may know of this woman's whereabouts?"

"I am sure of it."

The sentry went quiet. Then he said, "Ride ahead around that bend, and tie your horse in front of the cantina. They will know I have given you permission to pass but understand that does not mean you will be allowed to speak to *la jefa.*" He grinned and added, "They could decide to throw you into that canyon themselves."

Thomas touched the brim of his hat in thanks. "Such is the way of the world in which we live." His put his heel to Ulysses's flank and continued up the trail.

He was not sure what to expect when he passed between two tall boulder stacks and saw the layout for the first time. In the past few days he had heard it described as a trading post, a hunting lodge, and a cantina. In fact, none of those descriptions were accurate. The two story, U-shaped structure directly in front of him was every bit as fine as any of the best haciendas he had visited with Diego in Mexico. A multi-colored tile roof covered pale pink stucco walls that were covered with roses and climbing bougainvilleas and studded with rows of balconied French windows. A fountain large enough to swim in sat in front of the steps leading up to two massive oak entry doors, its pentagonal walls emblazoned with hundreds of hand painted tiles depicting flowers, frogs, and vibrantly colored exotic birds.

To the left and just behind the building was a corral with more than a dozen horses in it, and to the right was a smithy, a well-kept barn, and a smokehouse. He could just see inside the central courtyard where classic Corinthian columns supported Arabic style arches on both floors around the rectangular space. Pots of flowers and towering ferns were interspersed with wrought iron tables, and a smaller version of the great fountain in front of the building made soothing, splashing sounds that echoed around the courtyard.

He rode up to a hitch rail in front of the main entry doors and dismounted. This place hadn't been built on a whim; the cost of transporting all the building materials and furnishings up miles of rocky switchback trails must have been staggering. As for the architectural, construction, and landscaping costs, it was clear that this was the summer retreat of someone of real substance. Still, as incongruous as the existence of this magnificent estate on top of a mountain in the Chihuahuan desert might have been, the fact that it could also be the hiding place of the notorious bandit queen was an even greater mystery. It was time to find out.

The late afternoon sky was softening into evening as Thomas tied Ulysses to the post, unholstered his revolver, and slipped it into his saddlebag. It wouldn't be much use against the number of hardened *pistoleros* that Carnál was reputed to ride with. He patted Ulysses on the muzzle, went up the stairs, and swung open one of the huge doors.

The room was at least forty by sixty feet. Oversized tiles covered the floor, and oak tables lined two of the walls. There was an ornate oval-shaped bar in the center of the room, with shelves packed with whiskey, tequila, mezcal, brandy, cognac, and imported liqueurs. An oversized ceiling fan pushed cool air around, and afternoon light streamed in from a bank of high, narrow windows. Behind the bar was a wide staircase leading up to a gallery lined with rooms overlooking the courtyard. Terracotta pots filled with flowering plants were everywhere.

He took all of this in in a few seconds. He would have taken more time to appreciate the design and decor had it not been for the two other notable features present in the high-ceilinged room: the eighteen or twenty hard-looking men who raised their heads from their drinks and stopped their conversations when he stepped through the door, and the stunning, dark-haired woman in a white silk blouse and tight riding breeches who was standing with her back to the bar. She was staring at him, too. Unlike her men, though, Demetria Carnál was smiling.

FORTY

St. Petersburg, Russia, March 1881

Sergey Petrovich Baklanov relived the ten minutes on the banks of St. Petersburg's Catherine Canal in every daydream and nightmare.

Sunday, March 13, 1881, was cold and snowy, and the wet fog that blanketed the city was a reminder that the Russian spring was still weeks away. Sergey was one of six Cossack bodyguards accompanying Tsar Alexander II on a routine visit to the riding academy at Mikhailovsky Manège for the military roll call ceremony that morning. The Tsar was riding in a closed bulletproof carriage that was a gift from Emperor Napoleon III. Behind the carriage were two sleighs carrying city dignitaries, and behind them, Sergey and four of his fellow Cossack guards rode on horseback.

There were scattered crowds milling along the newly built pedestrian sidewalk, and as he rode, Sergey's eyes swept the area for any signs of trouble. Suddenly, a young man stepped out of the crowd holding something under a white handkerchief. He raced up to the Tsar's carriage and tossed the bundle under the horse's hooves. An explosion rang out, and Sergey saw the young man fly though the air and crash into a fence. He raced his horse forward, ignoring several badly wounded people, and pulled up alongside the carriage. His friend Nickolai, who had drawn the duty to ride up beside the driver, was dead, blown almost in half. Sergey leapt off his horse, drew his saber, and together with the other Cossacks guards, formed a tight circle around the carriage. He pulled open the carriage door and saw that the Tsar and the Polish nobleman traveling with him appeared to be shaken but were otherwise unhurt.

"What has happened?" demanded the Tsar.

"We will find out, Majesty," replied Sergey. "It appears to have been a bomb. Please stay in the carriage until we secure this area."

As he spoke, the chief of police, who had been riding in the sleigh behind the Tsar's carriage, opened the other door.

"Your Majesty," said the hefty official in an almost breathless tone, "we have captured the villain who threw the bomb. All is well; it is safe now."

"Then I will view the scene," said the Tsar. "I will not be thought a coward by my people."

"Majesty, I ask that you do not leave the safety of your carriage until we reach the riding academy," said Sergey. "There may be other assassins in the crowd."

The Tsar nodded. He liked Sergey and knew that he and his family would never have reason to fear when the tall Don Cossack was with them. Even so, with all the civil unrest that was bubbling in Russia, he could not be seen running from danger.

He leaned forward and said, "No, Sergey Petrovich, I will walk among my people and let them see that their Tsar has no fear of these barbarians."

Sergey extended his hand and helped the Tsar alight from the carriage. The other Cossack guards stepped forward to form a tight circle around him as he walked over and began greeting some of the astonished passersby. The Tsar of all the Russias did not often mingle with his subjects. This was an extraordinary moment, and Alexander knew his bravery in the face of such danger would go a long way towards quelling some of the resentment that so many felt for him.

A young girl and her mother stepped forward to greet him, and Alexander leaned down to take the child's hand. Just then, a massive explosion tore through the crowd, and Sergey was thrown to the ground in a blast of superheated fire and wind.

He lay still for a moment, unable to see or hear. Then he willed himself to sit up and peered through the smoke, snow, and fog at the carnage in the street around him.

Dozens of people lay in the street and on the sidewalk. Bits of flesh, pieces of clothing, and chunks of one of the sleighs were scattered like children's toys in a messy nursery. The cries of the wounded mixed with shouts from the police for everyone to stay where they were. No worries on that front, thought Sergey as he roused himself to his feet. One of the sleighs was on fire, and two of his comrades were sprawled dead on the ground. Then he saw the Tsar. Alexander lay on his side, bleeding profusely from his abdomen and legs. The child he had been about to greet lay at his feet alongside her mother. They were both dead.

Sergey made his way to the Tsar, leaned down and helped him into a sitting position. Half of Alexander's face had been torn off by the blast, and there was a gaping wound in his abdomen. Several policemen appeared out of the fog, along with the doctor who accompanied the Tsar any time he left the Winter Palace. They lifted the mortally wounded monarch and placed him in one of the sleighs. Sergey watched the sleigh race across the canal bridge and disappear in a veil of snow and fog.

That is when he realized he had been badly burnt on his left arm. His wound was nothing, though, compared to what would happen next. He and the other Cossack guards had failed in their duty to protect the Tsar. No matter the reasons, there would be no mercy shown to them. No investigation, no trial. The Cossack guards–those who survived the blast–would be publicly hung on the banks of the river before the sun went down this night.

Sergey mounted his horse and rode swiftly away from the devastation along the river. He galloped to the Cossack barracks and arrived before word of the assassination was received. He packed one small bag, retrieved what money he had in his footlocker, and was back on his horse in less than five minutes. As he rode under the barracks gate and into the city, he ripped off his epaulets and officer's insignia and tossed them into a snowbank.

That was the beginning of a month-long journey that took him by rail and coach through Germany, Belgium, France, and finally, to Barcelona, Spain, where he bought passage on a Dutch trading vessel bound for Veracruz, Mexico. Sergey knew that the reach of the Tsars knew no boundaries, and he intended to travel deep into the interior of Mexico and live out his life in anonymity in some small village.

When he debarked in Veracruz he had no money. He practiced Spanish and English with the ship's crew for hours every day on the voyage across the Atlantic, but on the morning he slung his bag over his shoulder and walked down the gangplank he was far from fluent in either language. He made his way to Mexico City, where there was a community of Cossack expatriates. He was sure they would offer him some help, but they could not endanger their own safety by openly protecting an enemy of the state. He was an unwelcome stranger in a very strange land.

❖

As the American stepped through the doors of the Hacienda de Jacinto, Sergey was one of the hostile faces that confronted him. He had been in the employ of Demetria Carnál for nearly six months, since being introduced to her by a German arms merchant who hired Sergey to arrange for security for his shipments of rifles, cannon, and ammunition to both sides in the ongoing turmoil that passed for politics in Mexico. Sergey rose quickly in Demetria's band; his organizational abilities, command presence, and his skills with revolver and sword made him a stand-out. Unfortunately, his talents also made him a rival of Ramiro Ortiz, her trusted chief lieutenant.

Last night, Ortiz and Sergey had almost come to blows as they argued about tactics for the raid they were going to conduct inside New Mexico Territory. Demetria stepped in before blood began to flow, but she knew that the conflict between the two men would have to be resolved quickly–and permanently. They could not serve together, and neither man was going to walk away quietly. In her mind, that left only one solution: personal combat to determine which man would lead, and which would leave–or die. Sergey watched the American approach the bar and introduce himself to Demetria. She poured him a drink, and they talked for a few minutes. Then she led the American over to where Ramiro was seated and asked him to come to Sergey's table. She told Ramiro to sit opposite Sergey and then she addressed them both.

"Sergey Petrovich Baklanov and Ramiro Ortiz,"she said, "let me introduce Colonel Thomas Scoundrel, a retired United States army officer of some renown. It seems the colonel has been searching for us for some time."

Thomas nodded at the two men, uncertain about why their leader had brought him to their table. From the expressions on their faces, one thing was clear: these men were not friends.

The room grew silent as Demetria talked. In a voice intended for everyone to hear, she said, "Most of you have been with me for several years. We are more than bandits, we are *familia*. We fight together, we bleed together, and we share in the profits of our labors. Together. *Siempre*."

Thomas was taken aback by her quiet, unquestioned authority and sincerity. He was also enraptured by her beauty. But his eyes only lingered on her figure long enough for her next words to slap him back to the dangerous reality of his present circumstance.

"We all know that an organization such as ours must have clear and absolute lines of command and respect, in equal measure," she began. Looking at Sergey and Ramiro she added, "in recent weeks, those lines have been blurred, and the harmony I demand within our ranks has been turned upside down. It cannot continue. It will not continue." She looked at Ramiro, and then at Sergey.

"I have spoken with each of our warring comrades here. Neither wishes to leave. Each wants to serve as my most trusted *teniente*. But only one can do so. The solution from the old days was for such rivalries to be settled by personal combat. In many things, the old ways are still best. Therefore, I have decided that Ortiz and Baklanov will solve their differences once and for all. Right now."

At those words there were loud shouts from around the room, and tequila glasses were slammed down on tabletops. Demetria knew her men were as tired of the dispute as she was, and she also knew that after two weeks of being confined to this mountain top–luxurious as it was– they needed to blow off some steam. There was nothing they loved more than an old-fashioned *mano a mano* resolution to an argument, and the bloodier, the better. As their leader, it was her job to maintain order and harmony within the ranks. She had provided Sergey and Ramiro with a graceful way out, but neither man would accept it. So be it, she thought. One of them might die, but it would be by his choice, not hers.

When the room calmed, Demetria said, "*Mi mejor amigos*, my only hesitation at settling this dispute in the arena before today was that I did not feel qualified to act as judge in such a matter. Nor could any of you. These two men are our friends, and that means that none of us can act as a referee must, fairly and honestly. Now, however, *Dios* himself has provided a solution in the form of a respected military officer and hero. Colonel Scoundrel will referee the fight. He will administer justice fairly, and any decision he makes will be final."

There were shouts of agreement across the room, and Demetria's men raised their glasses in salute. Thomas looked at her, and whispered, "Me?"

She replied with a smile that was almost feline. "Oh, yes," she said in a soft voice. "And you will perform your task to the complete satisfaction of my men and me. If you do not, you will join the unfortunate loser of this combat at the bottom of the canyon."

Thomas shook his head. That damned canyon again.

Demetria raised her hand for silence. Looking at her in profile, her dark hair glistening in the late afternoon light, her olive skin aglow, her breasts taut against her cloud-white blouse, Thomas felt like he was in a dream.

All eyes were on Demetria. "*Soldados*," she said in a ringing voice, "prepare these men for combat."

❖

FORTY ONE

Organ Mountains

Twilight slipped into darkness as Demetria's men pounded stakes into the ground to form a twenty-foot circle in front of the hacienda. They strung a sisal rope at waist height around the perimeter and then planted a dozen torches topped with pitch and burlap inside the arena.

They'd done this before, Thomas thought to himself as a woman wove through the crowd with a wicker basket filled with clear bottles of tequila and blue bottles of mezcal, handing out the fiery liquor like a grandmother sharing candy at a birthday party. It felt like a summer fiesta, with seasoned meat grilling on outdoor grates, a guitarist playing a passionate tune, and shadows from the torches dancing on the walls of the hacienda and licking up the sides of the fountain.

He was reaching into the basket for a bottle of tequila when someone pulled his arm back. "Perhaps you should stay with something you know," said Demetria, who had come up beside him quietly. "My father was a *jimadore* who spent his life tending the agave plants and distilling the finest tequila. But even he would not drink it when important decisions had to be made."

Then he noticed that she was holding a bottle of red wine and two glasses. "From California. Perhaps not as refined as the French varietals I understand you prefer, but I think it will do for this occasion."

He had no idea how a bandit leader isolated in the wilds of New Mexico Territory could have learned about the wine preferences of an

American army colonel, but it was a stark reminder that she was not to be underestimated.

Demetria filled their glasses, and made a toast: "To a swift, decisive and successful bout."

"And how do you define success?" he asked as he sipped the excellent wine. "By what you will gain, or by what either Sergey or Ramiro will lose?"

She laughed, and he was struck by how long and smooth her neck was. "I win no matter what," she answered. "Either man would make a fine *teniente*, and with you here to choose a victor if there is a draw, I will be held blameless if your decision is not shared by my men."

He looked out over the noisy crowd that was forming around the arena. Blood was running high, and the anticipation of the battle to come flowed like an electrical arc through the courtyard.

"But *I* will not be held blameless. No matter the outcome of this fight, I could still end up being the only one who gets tossed down into the canyon."

Demetria looked into his eyes. "Or you could win a prize beyond your wildest imagination," she said in a soft, low voice. "Better for you to think on that prospect, wouldn't you agree?"

With that she re-filled his glass, but before he could respond with an equally provocative reply, she turned and melted into the crowd. Then, a shout went up, and Ramiro emerged from the hacienda and descended the steps to the makeshift arena. He was about thirty, medium height, long black hair, built like a side of beef, Thomas noted. He was shirtless, and the scars of past battles crisscrossed his thickly muscled abdomen and back. Ramiro leapt easily over the rope and planted himself in the middle of the circle to the cheers of his *compadres*.

The next shouts announced Sergey's arrival. The Cossack walked deliberately; his eyes fixed straight ahead. Like his opponent, he was shirtless, but where Ramiro was solid and stocky, Sergey was tall and thin. His pale skin was untouched by the sun, and he had the longest arms Thomas had ever seen on a man. His blond hair was cut unfashionably short, and his blue-gray eyes reflected the flames of the burning torches. He also seemed exceedingly calm, almost as if he was walking to his morning bath instead of a fight to the death. Thomas figured that all bets were on the more muscular, rugged-looking Ramiro to win, but something about the Russian's demeanor told him that the betting crowd was wrong. Sergey stepped over the rope and stood at ease across from Ramiro with his arms casually crossed. Thomas set his empty glass on the fountain ledge and watched Demetria enter the rope circle and raise her hand for quiet.

"*Amigos*," she began, "each of these men has claimed the privilege of being my most trusted *teniente*, my right arm and counselor. Neither man will withdraw his claim, and therefore we have come to this moment in the arena, a moment of decision."

With that, she raised a three-foot, razor-sharp machete high above her head. The crowd roared its approval, and Demetria played to their energy by holding the blade at an angle that reflected the orange light from the torches onto their faces. Then she walked to the far side of the arena and mounted the machete on two nails that were affixed to a post.

She returned to the center of the circle and said, "At Colonel Scoundrel's command, the combat will commence. Both men will attempt to take the machete from its resting place and use it to dispatch his opponent. There are no rules. And should it come to that, no mercy shall be asked for, and none shall be granted." She paused a moment and then, in a solemn voice, added, "One of our band will die tonight. It is not a cause for celebration, but it is our way, and it is our law."

The crowd applauded and shouted at her pronouncement, but Thomas was left wondering what role he was expected to play. If there were no rules, why was he here? They didn't need a referee–they needed an undertaker. Demetria looked at him from across the arena. She smiled warmly, and then she dropped the boom.

"One last thing; it would not do for our new friend Tomás Scoundrel to be relegated only to the simple act of signaling the start of this combat. A warrior of his status and reputation would be dishonored if that is all we asked of him tonight. Don't you agree?"

A fresh round of cheers and catcalls greeted her words, and for the first time, Thomas felt the mesmerizing power that Demetria exercised over her men. Like all great leaders, she knew when to cajole, when to command, and when to surprise. Was he about to be given the "prize beyond imagination" that Demetria dangled in front of him just a few minutes ago?

"And, so," Demetria continued, "to make this night's contest even more satisfying, we will give the good colonel a second, small responsibility: he will stand in front of the post on which I hung the machete, and the combat will commence at his command. And then, *mis amigos*, the colonel will remain there during the fight, where his job will be to prevent either combatant from taking down the machete and using it on the other."

The crowd exploded with boos and curses. What was the point of hanging up the machete if it wasn't going to be used to hack one of these bastards to death? Was their leader going soft?

Demetria raised her hand again for quiet. "Have you so little faith in me," she said in her loudest voice yet, "that you would think I would deprive you of the spectacle you so richly deserve? *Ojalá que no!* I promise you will not be disappointed."

He looked around to see if there was any possible way he could escape, only to notice the two men with drawn revolvers who had come up beside him while Demetria was talking. One of the men shrugged and poked him in the ribs with the barrel of his Colt.

"If either man succeeds in getting past the colonel and liberating the machete," Demetria was saying, "then the colonel must pay a price for not doing his duty. Once the holder of the machete has put away his opponent, he will give the weapon to me, and his job will then be to prevent the colonel from leaving the arena. No weapons; just bare knuckles."

Laughter rippled across the crowd. This was more like what they had been hoping for.

"As to what price the combatant will have to pay if he cannot keep the colonel inside the ropes, well, I will leave that up to a vote from all of you."

The crowd began to cheer, and one of his guards slapped him across the back. "A bad night for you, *amigo*, no matter what happens, eh? Or perhaps you thought your reward would be a moonlight dinner with *la jefa*?" His companion laughed, and the two of them motioned for Thomas to cross over the rope and enter the arena. They marched him over to the post with the machete and ordered him to turn around and face the crowd.

Demetria's extraordinary face and figure faded from his mind. Right now, a simple dinner–even without a romantic ending–sounded pretty good.

❖

He leaned back against the wooden post and considered his situation. Sergey and Ramiro were standing as still as statues at the center of the ring, ignoring the shouts of onlookers who were pressing up against the rope. Everyone was waiting for his signal for the fight to begin. What were his strategic options when the battle commenced, he wondered. Would the combatants go right at it until one of them was unable to move? And if that happened, would the victor have enough strength left to fight past him for the machete and then to kill him? Or might the two men join forces and come at him together, figuring it would be best to take him out of the picture first and then fight it out for the machete? If he tried to take down the machete now, the guards would shoot him dead. But if they came at him together, he would not be able to hold them off. No, his only chance was to take out the winner of the combat after one of the two was killed. There was no other possible way out of the arena. Even then there was no assurance that Demetria would allow him safe passage off the mountain. He wiped droplets of sweat from his forehead with his sleeve and steeled himself for what was about to come.

It was dark, and the light from the full moon bathed the hacienda courtyard under a soft, white blanket. The air smelled of liquor and tobacco, and the burning pitch in the torches crackled in harmony with the chirps of thousands of late summer crickets.

Demetria looked across the arena at Thomas and called out: "In your own good time, Colonel."

Sergey and Ramiro turned their heads in his direction and at the prize hanging on the post above his head. He felt the intensity of their gazes as they gauged what kind of fight he might put up when they came after the machete. In that moment he realized that they were going to fight one another before they came for him. Even though he was certain he would only have to face one of them, he felt no sense of relief. The only things he knew for certain about these men was that they knew how to fight, and they would have no qualms about killing each other–or him.

He took a deep breath and slowly raised both arms above his head. The crowd quieted to a whisper, and, in the loudest and calmest voice he could muster he said, "May God have mercy on every worthless *hijo de puta* here. And on your leader, too."

Demetria shot him a startled glance. He had expected her to react to his words with fury, but instead, he saw hurt in her eyes. No time to wonder about that right now, he thought.

He planted his left leg forward, drew back his shoulders, and raised his fists as if he were about to enter a boxing match. Left hand high and forward, right hand back and low, cocked and ready. Then, in his best command voice, he shouted, "Gentlemen, you may commence the fight."

Squeals and whoops and roars poured out of the crowd, and for added dramatic effect, someone blew a few notes from the Mexican army cavalry charge on a brass bugle.

Ramiro bowed his head, bent his arms at his elbows, clenched his fists, and raced headlong at Sergey's middle. He's a wrestler, thought Thomas. Not surprising, since the Sioux, Comanche, Mescalero, and other tribes in the region were famous for their grappling skills. Ramiro was going to try to get the Cossack on the ground and pound him into submission. He had seen that technique used many times against US army troopers during the Sioux Wars of '77. It was a crude but brutally effective tactic.

Sergey, however, was more than ready for the charge. In a flash, he turned his body perpendicular to the low-flying bandit and pushed down and forward on Ramiro's neck. Then, using Ramiro's own momentum, Sergey swung behind him and planted a powerful, booted kick between Ramiro's legs. Like most of the men watching, Thomas winced inwardly at the pain the Cossack had just visited upon Ramiro's balls.

Ramiro fell flat to the ground but quickly shook it off and leapt back to a standing position. If the man was in pain, his face didn't show it. He began to circle Sergey, shuffling in long, wide strides, his head bobbing up and down, looking for an opening. Sergey kept his arms at his side and turned his body so that he was always facing his opponent. Suddenly, Ramiro dropped to the ground, placed one hand back beside his hip, and used it as a lever to pivot around and behind Sergey. He grabbed Sergey's right ankle with his right hand, wrapped his left arm around the Cossack's upper thigh and flung himself back up to his feet. It happened so fast that Thomas could hardly believe what he had just seen.

Now, Ramiro was holding Sergey's leg up at a 45-degree angle from the Cossack's body. Sergey tried to keep his balance on one leg, but Ramiro didn't give him time to fight to free his leg. The bandit stepped back, twisted his left hip outward and pushed Sergey's ankle up high while pulling down on his thigh. The combination of forces threw the Cossack hard on the ground, with Ramiro right on top of him, pummeling Sergey's abdomen with both fists.

Forgetting his own peril for the moment, Thomas had to admire Ramiro's technique. So did the crowd, who were yelling and stamping their feet louder than ever before. Any man who had been in a real fist fight knew that throwing blows at their opponent's face was almost always a waste of time. Odds are your fist would simply glance off a cheekbone or forehead, and, even if you were lucky enough to connect with a nose or jaw, your first punch probably wouldn't do that much damage. The best way to fight was to go for the soft tissue areas of the abdomen, kidneys, groin, and thighs. Kick a kneecap or gouge an eyeball if you could, but if a gut punch knocks the air out of your opponent's lungs, he will be incapacitated, if only for a moment. That could be long enough to choke him out, get behind him, and break his neck or to grab a rock from the dirt and open up his skull.

Sergey went into defensive mode. He threw his right arm across his chest, put his right leg over his left, and turned to the right and on to his stomach. Ramiro followed behind, wrapping one arm around the Cossack's torso to hold him down while continuing to hammer his fist at Sergey's kidney, over and over. Sergey lifted his body enough that he was able to shove his left hand under his neck. Then he reached up and back and took hold of Ramiro's right arm just above the elbow. As Ramiro struggled to free the hand he had been using to beat the Cossack, Sergey pulled his legs up under his knees, tightened his grip on Ramiro's arm, and, in a lightning fast move, yanked Ramiro's body off of him and into the dirt.

The move startled Ramiro, and he tried to quickly roll away so that he could stand up and take the fight back to Sergey. But the Cossack was too fast for him. Sergey dug his right hand into the rocky arena soil and threw a handful into Ramiro's eyes before the bandit could stand up. Then, Sergey fell on top of Ramiro, pushing his left hand against Ramiro's throat while grasping the unfortunate man's already bruised crotch in an ironclad grip with his right hand.

The crowd in the hacienda courtyard had never seen anything like this battle. They were used to a more traditionally brutal, old-fashioned *mano a mano* contest in which the combatants traded punches back and forth until one of them collapsed to the ground in defeat. In a few breathtaking moments, their new Cossack compadre had turned all the old ways upside down. Ramiro, one of the toughest and most hardened members of their band, had been blinded, strangled, and emasculated as quickly as a man could down a glass of tequila.

All eyes turned towards Demetria as Sergey continued to squeeze the air and the manhood out of her former *teniente*, Ramiro, but she remained impassive. When she said no rules, she meant exactly that. She would not interfere.

Thomas knew that Ramiro was close to death. Sergey did not let up, and a moment later, Ramiro's face turned blue and purple, his gasps for air ended, and finally, his feet stopped kicking. Even then, the Cossack did not loosen his grip on Ramiro's throat or his crotch. A stillness fell over the crowd. They had been prepared for mayhem–they dearly wanted mayhem–and they fully expected that one of the men would die tonight. But not like this. None of them expected to see death meted out in such a cold and clinical fashion. Where was the fun in that?

A minute later, Sergey let go of Ramiro's lifeless body. He stood, brushed some of the dirt off his trousers, and then looked across the ring in Demetria's direction. She approached the rope and asked for silence. Then, she simply said, "Sergey Petrovich Baklanov, you have finished only half of your task." She pointed at the post behind Thomas. "The machete awaits."

Her words brought the crowd back to life. The machete! Of course, the spectacle was not yet over. Their leader had anticipated a less than ideal conclusion might be possible in the first combat, so she had set it up so that there would be a second battle. They shouted their approval, stamped their feet, waved their fists in the air, and called for the second round to get underway immediately. The woman who had been handing out liquor from the wicker basket sighed and went back into the hacienda to refill her supply as the guitarist struck up a new, livelier tune.

That's when Thomas realized he had not relaxed since the combat had begun. He was still in his fighting stance, with fists tightly clenched. He willed himself to relax and looked across the ring at Demetria, but she turned her gaze from his and walked away. This was it. He would have to fight the Cossack. At least he knew better than to take the fight to the ground. It would be fists and elbows flying, teeth tearing, and heads butting. But, no matter what happened, he had to stay upright. He would be no match for Sergey if they fell to the ground.

The moon was directly overhead now, and its light mingled with the flames from the torches, making it bright enough to read a book. The cry of a coyote drifted from the boulders below, and an owl swooped low over the crowd. The bird was probably curious at the commotion, thought Thomas. That might be a useful characteristic for an owl, but curiosity sure as hell hadn't gotten him anywhere these past several months. Except maybe dead.

As the crowd chanted and whistled, Sergey walked slowly across the arena, until he was just a foot in front of him. My God, Thomas thought, the Cossack wasn't even breathing hard after his fight with Ramiro. He looked over at the two guards who had been watching him since the fight began and saw that they were still ready to shoot if he tried to escape. Then, an idea crossed his mind: if he was able to survive being thrown down into a canyon once, maybe he could survive it again. A slim prospect, but maybe his only chance. Then he looked into Sergey's calm, almost bemused face and concluded that it would take a miracle for him to defeat Demetria's new *teniente*.

Sergey kept his hands at his sides, but that was no consolation. The Cossack had begun his fight with Ramiro the same way. Thomas tensed and readied himself for the first blow. But, instead of taking the first swing, Sergey cracked a slight smile and, in a heavily accented voice asked, "What are you doing here, Colonel?"

He was almost too surprised to answer. Why wasn't Sergey going for the machete? That was Demetria's price for allowing him out of the arena alive, and the Cossack did not impress Thomas as someone who would choose to engage in light banter before he choked the life out of you.

"I might ask you the same question," he finally said.

"I came here from Russia because I failed in my duty. Had I stayed, I would have been killed."

"You could have been killed tonight. You might still be killed."

Sergey chuckled. "With all respect, Colonel, I do not think the outcome of a battle between the two of us would end with my death."

Damn the man to hell, thought Thomas, but he is probably right.

Sergey looked around at the crowd. "They expect a show."

"They had one. What the hell else do they want?"

"What all peasants want, I suppose; good beer, a soft bed, a warm woman, and now and then, a little excitement."

Why am I not surprised that the man is also a philosopher, thought Thomas. He didn't know how to reply.

He sighed. It was time. "Shall we get to business, then?"

"Business?" asked Sergey.

Thomas turned and looked up at the machete hanging on the post. "The machete. The next death. The show."

Sergey shook his head. "But there isn't going to be a show," he replied. "At least not between you and me. Not today."

"But Demetria, her orders, what the crowd expects…."

"*Blyad* to her orders. That means screw them, Colonel. If there is going to be another fight, it will be you and me against every last one of these *cabrones*. I have no quarrel with you."

Thomas was almost relieved. Still, it was hard to feel confident about his immediate prospects while the mob was howling for blood.

"Excuse me," said Sergey. He reached above Thomas's head and took down the machete. Then he smiled. "You didn't think it could turn out this way, did you?"

"I never expect things to turn out for the better. Because, in my life, they usually don't."

"Shall we see what future the fates have in store for us?" asked the Cossack.

"Might as well."

They stood shoulder to shoulder and stared out into the crowd, where the revelers were slowly beginning to realize that they were going to be cheated out of the second act in tonight's entertainment. They would not take such a betrayal in good humor.

The guards raised their pistols and pointed in Thomas' direction. He could not hear the hammers cock over the angry cries of the crowd, but he had no doubt they were preparing to fire.

"Hold your ground for as long as you can," Sergey whispered. "I can take out at least a couple of them with the machete; then perhaps we can get a weapon for you off one of their bodies." He turned his head. "I regret I did not get a chance to know you better, Colonel

Thomas Scoundrel."

"Likewise, Captain Baklanov."

Then, with the swiftness of an exploding pressure cooker, a half dozen men boiled forward, tore down the arena ropes, and charged towards Thomas and Sergey.

Sergey raised himself up to his full height, lifted the machete above his head, and began to swing his arm in a wide, circular motion. Whatever else happened now, the first man to walk into his path was going to be cut in half.

Thomas drew his breath and went into his fighting stance. Then, a flying tequila bottle glanced off the side of his head, and the fight was on.

FORTY TWO

Organ Mountains

Two of Demetria's men careened past Sergey and flung themselves on Thomas. As he was going down, he saw Sergey's machete flash, and the severed arm of one of the men who were attacking him fell in the dirt beside his head. Boots kicked him in the ribs, and he felt hands gripping his ankles as someone tried to pull him out of range of the Cossack's flying blade so they could kill him without fear of being sliced to pieces.

He rolled onto his side just in time to avoid a boot in the face, but the respite was brief. A bearded man holding a skinning knife dropped to the ground beside him and raised his blade in the air. Thomas's legs were still being held tightly, and someone else was kicking him relentlessly in the back. There was simply no way to escape the knife that was about to be plunged into his gut.

Then, a shot rang out, followed by a second. Were the guards trying to steal the knifeman's thunder and claim the privilege of killing the *gringo* for themselves? Then, almost in slow motion, the bearded man with the knife toppled over backwards onto the ground. At the same instant, the hands pulling on his legs let go. He pulled himself up to his knees as everything in the arena came to a halt. The man whose arm Sergey had cut off was leaning against a post, clutching the bleeding stump of his arm and moaning wildly. A second unfortunate, who had also stepped into the path of the Cossack's swinging machete, lay at Sergey's feet with a long, deep gash across his back. Like everyone else who had joined in the melee, Sergey was now standing motionless. Thomas shook his head to clear his vision and watched as blood dripped from Sergey's machete to form a puddle in the dirt.

Three more shots were fired in rapid succession, followed immediately by the sound of Demetria's voice.

"Enough," she cried. "All of you will lower your weapons and cease this fight, or I will personally cut out your entrails and feed them to the dogs."

Thomas could see her under the light of a torch on the hacienda steps, about fifty feet from where he knelt. There were seven men in the arena with he and Sergey, and dozens more were forming a protective semi-circle around their leader. He had never seen a vision as beautifully terrifying or thoroughly exciting as the sight of Demetria Carnál at that moment. Lit by flame and moonlight, her skin aglow, her eyes flashing, she was a tall and commanding presence who looked for all the world like a Greek goddess on the steps of an Acropolis temple. Where gray-eyed Athena wielded a spear in battle, Demetria brandished a pearl-handled revolver, and the body in the dirt next to him was all the testament to her shooting skill that he needed. He got up off his knees and nodded to Sergey. The Cossack smiled back and dropped his gore-stained machete to the ground.

"By whose permission did you men rush into the arena and attack my guest *and* my new *teniente*," Demetria demanded to know.

Sergey blushed when his *comandante* made her first public pronouncement of his elevated status.

"We are *bandidos*, yes," she continued, "but are we not also people of honor? Do we not live by rules, and have those rules not brought each of you more money and tequila…," she paused a moment and added, "and more beautiful women to your beds than you could ever have dreamed of?"

The men around her cheered, but those who had come into the arena to attack Thomas and Sergey–those who were still alive–stood quietly, their expressions downcast. They knew that taking matters into their hands would come at a great price.

"And what am I to do with those of you who have defied my orders?" she asked. "Two are dead, and Sergey Petrovich has seen to it that our friend Estéban will never again be able scratch his balls and his head at the same time."

Her men exploded in laughter, while the sobbing, one-armed Esteban cursed his bad fortune.

"We have had enough bloodshed tonight. It is time to celebrate the ascension of Sergey as my most trusted *soldado*. Therefore, I order that you who defied me must leave this camp. Tonight. Gather your things and be off this mountain before the first light of dawn catches your miserable *culos* in our presence. *Teniente* Sergey, your first duty in your new position is to see that my orders are carried out."

Sergey saluted *la jefa* and motioned for the attackers to follow him out of the arena. As he passed Thomas, the Cossack said, "It's like I told you, Thomas; you could never have imagined any of this happening, could you?"

Couldn't he? Had Demetria intended all along that Thomas and Sergey were never going to fight? Had this been a test for Sergey, and even for him? Before he could give that idea more thought, he saw Demetria turn to the guards who had kept him at gunpoint all night. She gave them instructions, and then, without looking in his direction, she wheeled and trotted up the steps and through the great doors of the hacienda. The guards walked swiftly towards him, but this time, he was glad to see that their pistols were holstered.

He was about to discover what it meant to be Demetria Carnal's "guest."

❈

The guards walked him up the stairs and into the hacienda. They went around the bar and through a side door that led down a long, candle-lit corridor. At the end of the hallway was a single door. One of the guards rapped his knuckles against the wood, and a sturdy middle-aged woman swung it open.

"*Bunea suerte con eso*-good luck," said one of the guards. The two men began to laugh and turned to go back to the bar.

The woman placed her hands on her hips and gave him a thorough once-over. It was apparent that she was not pleased with what she saw. "You smell like a pig," she said. "Follow me."

She led him across the small room and through another door into a large, wood paneled space with tile floors and a window that looked out into the fields behind the hacienda. There was a low fire burning in a corner stove, where two copper kettles were steaming away.

An oval-shaped wooden bathtub sat on a platform in the middle of the room, which Thomas could see had already been filled with hot water.

"Well?" said the woman. "*Vamanos*. Get in. Now."

He was perplexed. Five minutes ago, he was fighting for his life. Now he was being ordered to take a bath. He was exhausted, and his side throbbed from being repeatedly kicked. But there didn't seem to be much point in arguing. He raised his eyebrows to the mistress of the bath to signal he was ready to undress, and she could leave the room. She replied with a droll smile and turned her back, but she did not leave.

He sat on the bench, pulled off his boots and clothing, and piled them on a side table. Then he went up the platform steps and swung one leg over the side of the tub. The water was hot, but it felt good. He settled in and looked around for soap and a washcloth, but his keeper had something else in mind. She came up on the platform with a long-handled scrub brush that she soaped up and began to work up and down his back. He hated to admit it, but it felt good. Then, she poured a pitcher of warm water over his head and began to wash his hair. Only when that was done did she hand him soap and a cloth so that he could finish washing himself.

A few minutes later he was clean, toweled off, and ready to get dressed. That's when he noticed that his clothing and boots had been taken away. In their place was a neatly folded pair of loose linen trousers, and a soft, long-sleeved, pull-over cotton shirt. A pair of leather sandals sat on the floor beneath the clothing. He was slipping them on when the door opened, and his guards appeared. Now that he was clean himself, he could smell how badly they reeked of sweat and tequila. Small wonder the bath woman said he smelled like a pig.

"Let's go Colonel," said one of the men. They led him back into the main hall, where Demetria's men were drinking and celebrating the appointment of their new *teniente*. The guest of honor himself was at the bar with his arm around a young woman. He turned as Thomas walked past, raised his glass in salute, and then gave a whistle of approval at Thomas's appearance.

The guards marched him up the stairs to an open gallery that looked down on the main courtyard. There were two bedrooms on each side of the gallery, and, at the far end, a set of double oak doors marked the entry to the hacienda's master suite. The guards swung the doors open and motioned for Thomas to enter. It was an impressive space, with a high, vaulted ceiling, a crystal candle chandelier, vases of fresh flowers, fresco wall paintings, and an enormous four-poster bed perched on a tiled platform. A set of French doors opened out to a small balcony above a private, moonlit courtyard with its own fountain and gardens, and the scent of plumeria rising from a mass of flowering shrubs outside the windows filled the room. The most intriguing decoration in the room was the brightly burnished copper bathtub that sat directly in front of the open doors, with the front of the tub pointed to the outside so that the bather could enjoy the spectacular view. He noticed steam rising from the tub. It had been prepared exactly as his had been, no more than an hour earlier.

He shot the guards a questioning glance, but they said nothing. One took him by the arm and directed him to stand with his back against one of the bed posts. Before he could object, the other guard wound a rope around his waist and secured it tightly to the post. He began to struggle, and the other guard reluctantly drew his revolver and pressed it into his stomach.

"*Oye, amigo*, listen to me," said the guard with the pistol. "Whatever else happens here tonight, you have my word–and *la jefa's*–that you are going to live. Your clothing is being laundered, and your horse is being fed and cared for. Our orders are to see you down the mountain at first light. *Relajarse*-relax, Colonel."

For the second time tonight, he was rendered speechless. He offered no resistance as the guard with the rope pulled his arms behind his back and lashed his hands together just above his wrists. Then the guard knelt and bound his lower legs tightly at his ankles.

"Do not struggle, *amigo*," said the guard when he finished his work. "Your bindings will only tighten, and the rope could cut through your skin."

"And, now what?"

One guard walked to the door and stepped out into the corridor. "Now what?" said the other guard. "My friend, the ways of *la jefa* are known only to her. I do not know what is next, for you, but I do not believe it will be very pleasant." He grinned and patted Thomas's shoulder. "Be brave. Tomorrow you will be on your way home." Then he left the room and shut the doors behind him.

❖

Thomas had been in many strange situations in his life. He was once chased down the middle of Park Avenue in New York City by a band of club-wielding Tahitian warriors, which, as bad as it seemed at the time, was not as terrifying as the morning in Ohio when Titia Friesch exploded from the outhouse with her bloomers around her ankles, her extraordinary breasts bouncing in the wind, and her revolver blasting away at him as he rode for his life to the woods at the edge of her farm. And, when he was twenty-three, a winning hand in a poker game in Hawaii made him half-owner of a pineapple plantation on the island of Lana'i and paved his way to a swim in a cobalt-blue lagoon with Hawaii's last royal princess.

Five years ago, during the winter campaign against the Sioux in Montana, he got separated from his troop and found himself alone and surrounded by a band of thirty Sioux fighters who were intent on relieving him of his scalp. He had cursed, dropped his empty revolver into the snow and prepared himself to meet his fate when a huge, coal-black wolf appeared from behind a snow drift and calmly walked in a straight line between him and the Sioux. The wolf stopped and swung his head slowly in Thomas's direction and then towards the Sioux. They took it as a sign from the Great Spirit that the American solider was to be left unharmed. One of the warriors rode forward and tapped his shoulder with his lance. Then, the Indians turned their horses and disappeared into an afternoon flurry.

His life, he thought, had been a montage of moments like those. He was just thirty-three, but he sometimes felt like he had lived for a hundred years. The chafing at his wrists and ankles from the rope amplified his melancholy. He hoped that Diego and Itzcoatl were faring better in their search for Geronimo Rivas in Arizona Territory. Were they getting any closer to discovering where Rosalilia was being held? Thomas lowered his head to his chest and closed his eyes, overwhelmed by the feeling that he had failed his friend, and maybe even signed Rosalilia's death warrant by sharing his story with so many people. And now, instead of continuing the search, he was tied to a damn bed post in a hacienda on top of a remote mountain. God only knew how far away he still was from where Rosalilia was being held, or what was in store for him now.

"You can sleep at a time like this?"

His head snapped up, and his eyes opened at the sound of Demetria Carnál's voice. This was the second time tonight that she had snuck up on him.

"Not sleeping. Thinking."

"*Claro que sí*, of course. Given your reputation, however, you will have to forgive me if I don't take that remark too seriously."

Demetria was standing less than a foot in front of him. She was wearing the same form-fitting silk blouse and tight riding breeches from earlier tonight, and for the first time, he noticed that her eyes were a deep, sea green.

He shook his head. "Your information is correct about at least one thing," he said.

"Only one?"

"I prefer red wine over white."

She laughed softly and then reached out a hand and brushed his cheek with the backs of her fingers.

"And so, I may have paid for intelligence on you that is not accurate? You are not a soldier and adventurer?"

"I am."

"And you are not also a famous romantic and despoiler of innocent young women?"

"I have never taken anything that was not willingly offered."

"Ah, you believe that a woman can be the equal of a man?"

"In a war of wits–or on the battlefield of love," he turned his head towards the bed, "I have known women who could outmatch any man."

"Then you see us as creatures to be out maneuvered, or perhaps even tamed?"

"I see women as worthy adversaries in the only contest that really matters."

"Sex?"

"No," he replied softly. "Love."

Demetria pulled her dark hair back off her shoulders and placed her hands on her hips. "You surprise me, Colonel Tomás Scoundrel. It may be that I have not been given the complete picture about you."

"Perhaps I could talk better with my hands untied?"

She smiled and shook her head. "Oh, I think it is a little early for that, *querida*. I like you just where you are."

The moon was peaking outside the window, and its light spilled over the fountain and flooded the room. "Just what else is it that you think you know about me?" he asked.

Demetria turned serious. "I know that you are a famous hero of your American Civil War. That you arrived in Colorado two months ago in search of something or someone and that you have made some powerful people very angry since you arrived."

"Like your boss, for instance?"

Her eyes flashed. "I have no boss, Colonel."

"Your employer then," he countered. "Noah Claybourne. You met with him at his ranch outside Denver."

She did not seem surprised that he knew Claybourne's name or that she had been seen at his ranch. She was quiet for a moment and then she reached down and slowly pulled her blouse loose from her trousers.

"I did. And he has offered me work. But to be honest with you, I have not yet decided whether I will take it."

"I don't see Claybourne as the kind of man who would take kindly to being turned down." He was struggling not to let his imagination flare at the sight of Demetria loosening her blouse, but he could tell he was very close to losing that battle. He decided to take a chance.

"Geronimo Rivas doesn't seem to have had any qualms about butchering an entire town for Claybourne."

That remark did surprise Demetria. "How much, exactly, do you know about Claybourne's plans?"

"Truthfully? Not all that much. But what I do know should be enough to alert the authorities to begin an investigation."

Demetria chuckled. "Of Claybourne? Oh, Tomás, you are new to the ways of the world, aren't you?"

She was about to say something else when the door opened, and the woman who had bathed Thomas earlier came into the room with two pitchers of hot water. She was followed by another woman carrying more water and a wicker basket filled with rose petals. They poured the water into the tub, sprinkled in the rose petals, and then left without saying a word or making eye contact with Demetria or Thomas.

Demetria walked to the door and dropped the heavy latch into place. Then she went around the room and blew out all the candles except for the one on the table next to the tub. Its light danced across the copper and mixed with moonlight bathing the room in soft light and shadows. Smoke from the extinguished candles blended with the scent of plumeria blossoms, and for a moment, he almost forgot that he was tied tightly to the bed post.

Demetria came close and ran a hand through his hair. "We have so much to talk about. However, you do have an advantage over me."

"Really?"

"Yes, you have bathed. You are clean, head to toe, while the dust of a long day fills every pore of my body. You said earlier that a man and woman can be evenly matched, but in this instance, I have to say that I feel a bit less than your equal." She reached out and stroked his face again. "At least as it relates to being equally clean."

She took three steps back, leaned over, and undid her boot buckles. She slipped them off and then began to unbutton her white silk blouse. First, she undid the buttons at her wrists, and then she worked her way slowly from the bottom button to the top. When they were all undone, she tugged at one sleeve, then the other, and then she pulled her arms out of her blouse and tossed it onto the bed.

She stood still for a moment, permitting his eyes to pour over the rise of her breasts under the thin silk chemise and down to the curve of her hips and thighs. Without speaking, Demetria unfastened the stays at the side of her riding breeches, and pulled them down over her waist, below her knees, and into a heap on the floor. She stepped lightly out of them and used her foot to slide them over by her boots. He had to remind himself to breathe.

Her panties, like her chemise, were made of white silk trimmed with a narrow band of lace. They hugged her hips tightly, and he could clearly see the outline of her Venus mound. Demetria put her hands back on her hips and lowered her gaze so that he could just make out the top of her face. "You don't mind, do you?"

His throat had gone dry, and he coughed. "Mind?"

"If I take my bath before we…talk."

He could only shake his head, as much in wonder as it was to signal her that he had no objection to her bathing.

She stepped forward, placed her hands behind his neck, and kissed him full on the lips. Then she pulled back and whispered "I won't be long. Don't go anywhere."

Demetria turned and walked over to the copper tub. With her back to him, she pulled her chemise over her head, and then slipped her panties down around her ankles. She took much longer than she needed when she bent over to pull them off. His eyes went wide, his mouth tried to form words, and his heart raced as he watched her spread her legs ever so slightly before she bent over at the waist and leaned in to test the temperature of the water. Moonlight dappled her inner thighs and illuminated the contours of her pubis, and the glow of the flickering candle caressed her derrière like a pair of lover's lips.

Satisfied that the water was just right, Demetria stepped into the tub and slipped into the scented water. He could only see the back of her head, the curve of her long neck, and the top of her back. He watched in a trance as she reached over to the side table for soap and a cotton wash cloth and began to lather her body. For a moment, the splashing of the fountain in the courtyard below was the only sound in the room.

Then Demetria extended one arm out from her body and ran the washcloth slowly up and down its length. As she washed, she began to speak. "Do you know the plumeria flower, Tomás?"

"Is that what we are smelling right now?"

"Yes, their fragrance peaks at night, especially during a full moon. The aroma is overpowering to male sphinx moths, who desperately try to harvest nectar from the flowers." She transferred the washcloth to her other arm and continued. "But the plumeria is a fraud because it does not produce any nectar. It releases its scent as a way of tricking the moth into dashing from one flower to another to find the nectar it needs to survive. That is how the plumeria assures pollination and the survival of its species."

Demetria turned her head to the side. "Have you ever considered that the human female employs much the same technique in the mating dance with men?"

"A more apt comparison in that situation would be to the behavior of the black widow spider, I think. She entices a mate, teases and seduces him, and then devours him so that she will have plenty of food energy stored for her children."

Demetria laughed and dropped her washcloth to the floor. He started to move to pick it up, only to be reminded that he wasn't going anywhere until Demetria decided he could.

In reply, Demetria slowly stood up in the tub. He watched as tiny rivulets of water trickled down her back and around several rose petals that were clinging to her olive skin. The water drifted to the cleft between her buttocks and followed the shape of her upper legs before dripping back into the water. Then, with her head high and her shoulders back, Demetria turned slowly around to face him. Thomas unconsciously sucked in his breath as sparkling beads of crystalline water formed on her taut, upright breasts, slid down across her stomach and rolled into the dark patch between her legs.

"But I do not tease," she said in a faraway voice. "And I certainly do not devour, though, if I did, I think you might enjoy the experience."

A light breeze blew through the open French doors, ruffling the curtains and setting the candle to dance. Demetria stepped out of the tub, and without saying a word, came up to him. She knelt and untied the rope around his ankles, and then she got behind him and undid the rope at his waist and around his wrists.

He began to rub his lower arms to get the blood flowing, and then Demetria was standing directly in front of him. Her eyes were wide and shimmering, her nipples had ripened into tiny pink berries, and the dampness in her hair was intoxicating.

"Now, my dear colonel, we are very close to being equal." With that she reached down, took hold of the hem of his shirt, and pulled it over his head. Then she pressed forward and moved her breasts back and forth against his chest. She began to kiss him, and she slipped one hand down into the front of his linen trousers. She grasped his hardness and began to caress it softly. She placed her other hand on his and guided it down between her legs.

Thomas had been on the edge of delirium from the moment she had loosened her blouse. He could not remember ever wanting a woman as much as he wanted Demetria. He continued kissing her, gently stroking her thighs and feeling her become wet. Her emerald eyes went misty, and she was breathing hard and fast. It was time to take her to the bed.

And then, suddenly, it wasn't. For the first time in his adult life, thoughts and images began to filter up from the depths of his conscience that had no connection to the explosive desire that was taking hold of his mind as much as it had already taken control of his body. Demetria's lips were melting his heart, and her hand was working magic on his hardness, but in his mind's eye, a vision of Rosalila struggling against her kidnappers arose. And even as he marveled at the soft, creamy heat between Demetria's legs, he suddenly recalled what it felt like to be thrown down into Tamayo Ravine by Claybourne's men. As waves of desire competed for total control of his being, he could not help but remember how it was his promise to Diego to bring his fiancée back to him that had energized him to pull his broken, bloody body out of danger so that he could honor his oath.

The room swirled around him; moonlight and plumeria, the taste of strawberry on Demetria's lips, the magnetic pull of her thighs, the tickle of her firm nipples against his, and more than anything, the deep, almost primal need he had for her to keep stroking him, to pull him deep inside her, and to experience the rush of release when he reached the peaks of ecstasy with her.

Demetria began to kiss his neck and chest. She went to her knees and lavished warm kisses onto his stomach as she pulled his trousers down to the floor. She moved her head lower, and then, in an action that surprised him more than anything he could ever recall, he cupped her face in his hands and gently said, "We need to talk, my darling."

He stepped back and let her stand up. Her expression was a mix of bewilderment and concern. Had she insulted him? Was he perhaps married, or did he simply not find her attractive? She didn't know what to say. She took two steps back and wrapped her arms defensively around her chest.

He reached forward and placed his hands on her shoulders.

"I'm sorry," she said. "I should not have assumed you wanted the same thing that I did."

He wrapped his arms around her and held her tightly. "And there you would be wrong again, Demetria. From my heart, I tell you that I have never desired a woman in my life more than I want you right at this moment. But if I don't tell you right now why I have come here and what I have committed to do for my friend, I will never forgive myself. And you wouldn't forgive me either."

He pulled his head back to look in her eyes. She was crying, and her body was beginning to shake.

"I don't take this kind of thing lightly, Tomás. I am no whore. I–"

He put a finger on her lips. "I know. I know who you are. I would not have allowed myself to be tied up or waited while you bathed if I didn't know what kind of person you were."

Demetria sniffled and then laughed. "As if you had a choice in any of those things, Colonel."

"Demetria, if you felt enough for me that you were prepared to share your complete being with me tonight, would you hold onto that feeling long enough for me to explain why the journey I am on is so important to so many people? After that, you can love me, or you can have me tossed into the canyon, whichever you choose. I will abide by your decision."

She smiled. "Very well, *querida.* But I think we should get dressed first."

A few minutes later they were seated on wrought iron chairs on the balcony. Demetria opened a bottle of imported Bordeaux and filled two glasses. Thomas took a sip and marveled again at her grace and beauty. And, for a moment, he felt a pang of regret for having passed on what might well have been the most extraordinary romp of his life. At least I lived up to Red Elk's admonition to think with the right head for once, he thought. A small consolation if Demetria decides to throw me to the wolves tomorrow, but, right now, in this moment in the hacienda at the top of the mountain, he felt content with the decision he had made.

Demetria looked over at him. "Are you ready?"

He nodded, took another sip of wine, and began his tale.

❖

The sun was peaking over the eastern ridges when he finished talking. Demetria went back into the bedroom twice as he told his story; once to get more wine and again for a blanket to cover her against the night chill.

He described the last three months in more detail than he had ever shared, from the telegram he received at Delmonico's in New York that began his quest, to his journey West. He told her about his encounters with Bat Masterson and Major Rhine, and about the night that Claybourne's men beat him and threw him into the canyon. He described his convalescence in Red Elk's village, and, to his own surprise, he was even comfortable telling her about Dawn Pillow and the scourging he had received when her father discovered what had happened across the river on that starry night. He talked about his meeting with Professor Von Sievers, reuniting with Diego and Itzcoatl, and how they had gained at least some information about Demetria and Geronimo Rivas from the reporter Tanner Fulbright.

Demetria asked him to go into greater detail on several issues, and to speculate about what he expected might happen next. Her questions were pointed, incisive, and clear. Exactly what he would expect from a leader.

His story ended after the trip to New Mexico Territory and his climb up her mountain. Before she could ask more questions there was a knock at the door, and the laundry woman brought in a tray with coffee, a bowl of eggs scrambled with cilantro, fresh biscuits, and local honey. They ate quietly out on the balcony, and when they were finished, Demetria reached over and took his hand.

"I have never known a man like you. It's not just what you did–or more correctly, what you didn't do-last night. For that, I respect you, but it is what you are doing for your friends that really sets you apart."

"Don't spread the word. It could be bad for my reputation. Especially the part about last night."

Demetria laughed. "Your secret is safe with me, Colonel." She filled their cups with fresh coffee and said, "But now we must make a plan. You say you need to get back to Denver without Claybourne knowing you have returned, and I must figure a way to deal with the unfinished business I have with him. My men won't like the fact that I am passing on a lucrative job, but I have made unpopular decisions before and lived another day."

The sun was beginning to warm the high desert around them, and people were coming out of the hacienda to begin the day's work.

"Let's go for a ride," said Demetria. "I need to tell you everything I know about Claybourne's scheme in Mexico, but such a conversation would not be safe to have between these walls."

"You don't even trust the laundry woman who scrubbed my back?"

"She is the only person here that I do trust. In her youth, she snapped the neck of a federal police official who tried to rape her in the woodshed behind the hotel where she worked. She was the original *jefa* of this band. I trust her with my life."

Thomas shook his head. What a world. Then Demetria turned in her chair, placed her hand on his forearm, and graced him with a smile that was brighter than the rising sun.

❖

FORTY THREE

Manzanita Flats, Arizona Territory

Geronimo Rivas was as mad as hell. There was nothing new about that, he was almost always furious at somebody or something, usually for the thinnest of reasons. The fifteen men waiting behind him on the rise overlooking the small town knew better than to approach their boss when his mood was cloudy. Since that was pretty much all the time–except when Rivas was killing somebody–he rode alone, camped away from the group at night, and seldom talked with any of his men about anything except the job at hand.

It was the job at hand today that was the root of his anger. Matthew Cord arrived at his camp a week ago to tell him that he was going to have to pick a town to target, and fast. The success of Claybourne's plans hinged on there being frequent, brutal attacks along the Mexican border, but that *hija de puta* Demetria Carnal had yet to launch a single raid in New Mexico Territory. Cord had no idea why she had faltered. He would visit her soon enough, but in the meantime, Rivas was going to have to pick up the slack. The attacks had to continue so that the national news would become overwhelmed with heart-rending stories about the slaughter of innocent civilians along the border, which would force the politicians to take action against Mexico.

Rivas had spent weeks planning the next raid to follow up his success at Monteverde. He scouted several towns, appraised their defense abilities, and even tasted a few of their best whores before settling on Oro Blanco, a community of about two hundred ranchers and farmers located in a pleasant river valley twenty miles east of Tombstone.

He had given serious consideration to conducting a late night, lightning raid on Tombstone itself. That wide-open town had become legendary both for the vast silver deposits it was extracting from local mountains, as well as for the pitched gun battle that had taken place last October in an empty lot next to C.S. Fly's Photographic Studio, a few doors down from the O.K. Corral. Rivas knew all the players in the fight; lawman Wyatt Earp and his brothers Virgil and Morgan had once rousted him after a night of drinking and faro at the Bird Cage Theatre, and he had ridden with the men they killed, Billy Clanton and the McLaury brothers. For Rivas's money, the wrong bastards were gunned down in the fight. The thought that peckerwoods like the Earps and Doc Holiday, the tubercular former dentist who rode with them, had killed his friends and lived to walk away was more than he could stomach.

His hatred for the Earps placed Tombstone high on the list of towns to hit when Claybourne gave him carte blanche to pick his targets. Unlike Monteverde or Oro Blanco, however, Tombstone had a population of almost seven thousand, most of them silver miners who would know how to shoot back when the fireworks began. Plus, Tombstone had installed telephone lines the year before, which meant he would lose the element of surprise almost as soon as the shooting began. Hell, before the smell of gunpowder had drifted away from the O.K. Corral shootout, telephones all over town were ringing to spread the news. Rivas knew that damn contraption, more than any other single invention of the past quarter century, spelled doom for his way of life.

He figured the happiest man in Tombstone the day the Earps murdered his friends was the undertaker who had installed one of the new gadgets in his office. Five minutes after he got the call and learned there were three bullet-riddled corpses gathering flies in the dust, he was racing down main street to claim the prizes ahead of his competitors. By the next afternoon he had the bodies of Tom and Frank McLaury and nineteen-year-old Billy Clanton laid out in open coffins in the display window of his shop for all the world to see. Rivas figured the undertaker probably also got a piece of the fee that C.S. Fly charged any curious onlookers who wanted their pictures taken with the corpses of the noted desperados.

❖

Tombstone got a pass from Rivas. But when Cord informed him that he needed to get something done within a week, he knew he would also have to give up on the fat prize at Oro Blanco and find someplace that he could reduce to ruins without having to do much advance planning. His search led him to a rocky landscape of juniper, manzanita brush, lowland oaks, and pines along the border with New Mexico Territory on the leeward slope of the Mule Mountains. After three days of hard riding, he found a collection of canvas tents, ramshackle cabins, and false-fronted main street businesses that snaked along the path of an ancient dry wash, where a hand painted sign nailed to a scrub oak welcomed him to the town Manzanita Flats. It was the perfect location for the next burnt offering in Claybourne's Mexican scheme.

The residents of the little pueblo were mostly disgruntled Swedish miners and their families who left Tombstone when the mine owners chopped their daily wages from $4.00 to $3.25. Six months after the first tent stakes were driven into the old creek bank, new mining claims were producing enough marketable ore that the camp evolved into a small town with a general merchandise, a church, and a school. No saloon, Rivas noted sourly when he rode down the muddy main street to get the lay of the land. His men had always enjoyed watching saloons go up in flames after they had rescued every bottle of whiskey from their shelves. They'd have to bring their own red eye to this party.

The men he encountered around town were big, strapping Swedes who looked like they could handle themselves in a fight, but he was pleased to see that none of them were wearing sidearms. Most of the horses he saw were not much more than farm plugs, which meant he didn't have to worry about being chased out into the desert in the event the townspeople put up a successful defense. What sealed his choice of Manzanita Flats for the next raid, though, were its women. Rivas had always been partial to blonde hair, and whenever he walked through the door of a new whorehouse, he always requested the lightest haired filly in the stable. The dozen or so women he observed around Manzanita Flats were blonde, tall, and as ripe as summer strawberries. Probably that juicy too. The thought of getting a look under their billowing skirts took some of the sting away from the pain of losing out on the opportunity to demolish Oro Blanco. This was going to be some fine pickings.

Rivas swung around in his saddle. His men were lined up behind him on the rise above the wash, checking their pistols, loosening the long knives in their leather sheaths, and making sure their saddles were securely cinched. He was pleased to see that the only emotion visible on their faces was a mix of bloodlust and impatience. No signs of fear for what could be waiting when they galloped down the rise to smash the town, or so much as a hint of compassion for the dozens of men, women, and children who were going about their last few minutes on earth. He had picked the men carefully; not a one of them would hesitate to trample a child under his horse's hooves, or to slit the throat of somebody's bed-ridden grandmother. As for the Nordic women his *soldados* were about to violate on the streets in broad daylight, well, that would be as close to heaven as these miserable sons of bitches would ever get. That thought made *Teniente* Geronimo Rivas smile.

The sun was about to top Mule Pass Mountain, and ribbons of heated air were starting to rise from the parched, brush covered ground. Hot business was best done on a hot day, thought Rivas. He raised his hand to get his men's attention. It was time.

❖

Diego and Itzcoatl had been tracking Rivas and his men for two days, taking care to stay at least two miles behind them. Diego's left leg had gone numb from the throbbing pain where the bullet had crushed his thigh bone the night Rosalilia was kidnapped, but Itzcoatl knew better than to suggest they rest. Geronomo Rivas was their best possible link to Matthew Cord, and only Cord knew where Rosalilia was being held up in Colorado. Diego would not stop until he had Rivas under his gun, telling everything he knew.

The two men waited quietly on the bluff across the dry wash while Rivas assembled his band on a rise several hundred yards away. Diego could just make them out with his field glasses. Sixteen riders, including Rivas. He watched as the men checked their weapons and dropped their bedrolls and saddlebags onto a pile on the ground. They were going to charge light and fast. Then he turned the binoculars towards the town and watched a handful of locals going into businesses, loading wagons, and taking the opportunity to visit before the sun rose higher and the blast-furnace heat drove them indoors. He had no doubts about what was going to happen.

"And so, *tecolote*," said Itzcoatl, "what shall we do? Wait for the butchery to stop and then follow Rivas to a place where we can safely separate him from his men?"

Diego considered their options. They could ride down into the town and alert the residents to what was coming, though it was uncertain they would arrive before Rivas's men. They could also simply wait out the inevitable and continue tracking Rivas when the carnage was complete. Or, he mused, he and Itzcoatl could head off the marauders before they crossed the dry wash and try to inflict as much damage as they could. Two against sixteen. Thomas would call those sucker's odds.

Itzcoatl regarded him closely. "It has the feel of your engagement night, does it not?"

Diego nodded. When he charged against Cord's men as they forced Rosalilia into the wagon outside her burning home, it wasn't the smartest move he had ever made. He looked over at Itzcoatl before tapping his heel against his horse's flank. No, not the smartest. But it was the best.

Itzcoatl pulled back his silver hair and tied it with a piece of string so it wouldn't fall across his eyes during the fight. Then he drew his horse up alongside Diego, unsnapped his knife sheath, and drew his rifle from its scabbard. "We are still men, Diego, and we must live with honor. Rosalilia would understand."

Diego smiled. She would. The people in the small pueblo below were about to be attacked by brigands as fierce and bloodthirsty as any he had ever known. Without warning or help, the town would be laid to waste just as Monteverde had been. He followed Itzcoatl's lead and pulled out his own rifle.

Itzcoatl pointed to a stand of brush and boulders a hundred feet away where they could take up a firing position. With luck, they could stop at least a few of Rivas' men from making it across the wash. As for the others, Diego figured that once they were spotted, they would have to leave the safety behind the boulder and take the fight directly to them. Whatever they did to slow down the attackers would give the townspeople precious time to grab their weapons and fight back. It would have to be enough.

They rode down to the boulders, dismounted, and looped their reins on the branches of a creosote bush. Then they checked their ammunition and took up positions behind a sandstone rock. A moment later, Rivas and his men started slowly down the rise in single file. In a minute they would be within range of Diego and Itzcoatl's rifles.

Suddenly, Itzcoatl tapped Diego's shoulder. "Off to the west, about a quarter mile, on top of that mound. Look."

Diego raised his field glasses and focused where Itzcoatl was pointing. Four men on horseback were holding their own binoculars and appeared to be focusing on the town, not on Rivas and his men. That was strange. What was even stranger was that the men were wearing the uniform of the United States Army Cavalry.

Diego handed the glasses to Itzcoatl. "The one in the middle, the big fellow, is wearing the insignia of a Major General."

Itzcoatl surveyed the scene. "Are they going to stop Rivas?"

"I hope to God they do, and I hope they have at least a full company of men somewhere close by to help."

Rivas and his men were about to reach the base of the rise.

In a minute they would cross the dry wash and ride up the five-foot embankment to the southern end of main street. Then, they would form a skirmish line and unleash hell on Manzanita Flats. Diego turned his binoculars back in the direction of the US Army soldiers. They were not moving, and none was holding a weapon.

"*Por el amor de dios*. "They're not going to intervene." He shook his head. "It looks as if Claybourne also owns the American military."

Itzcoatl raised his rifle and sighted in. "And so, we shoot?"

"Once again I have placed you in the middle of an impossible fight," Diego said softly, "*Lo lamento*. I am sorry, my friend."

The Aztec smiled. "At this distance it will be difficult for them to hear our rifles, so we will take out the ones at the back of the line first. That will give us a few seconds before the riders in the front figure out what is happening."

Diego couldn't help but chuckle. That was how the old man taught him to shoot game birds when he was a boy. He pulled his rifle up against his shoulder and peered down the barrel through the iron sights. "And so, we shoot," he said calmly.

Itzcoatl's rifle barked first, followed in an instant by Diego's. Three heartbeats later the last rider in the line heading down into the wash was knocked out of his saddle by a pair of 405 grain, .45-70 Winchester bullets. Itzcoatl and Diego immediately re-cocked their lever actions, ejecting the first spent shell and pushing another one into the chamber. Their next shots cracked in the still morning air as one, and a second rider near the back of the group fell forward, toppled under his horse's neck, and landed on a pile of loose shale.

❖

Major General Winston Greer saw the puffs of smoke above the brushy thicket before he heard the retort of the shots. He and his adjutant turned their binoculars in the direction of the smoke and saw two horses tied to a creosote bush. Greer could just make out the silhouettes of two men behind a boulder.

In the space of five seconds, two of the attackers were lying dead on the ground. A moment later, the general watched Rivas' men begin to scatter around the wash so they wouldn't be such easy targets. Then, he saw Rivas turn his horse in the direction of the shots and point towards the boulder. He waved his arm in the air, and the thirteen men remaining in his command drew their rifles and fired a volley. Pieces of brush flew into the air, and shrapnel from the boulder exploded all around, but the fusillade did not deter the men who were shooting at them. Greer saw one of Rivas' men clutch his abdomen, lean low in his saddle, and then whirl his horse and gallop back towards the safety of the rise.

His attempt at retreat was useless; Rivas calmly raised his rifle and shot his own man in the back. The man pitched forward, slid off his horse, and collapsed into a thorn bush thicket. Exactly what a commander had to be prepared to do, and a lesson to the others, thought Greer. But, what now? Would Rivas assume he was under attack by a sizeable force and order his men to retreat, or would he soldier on and complete his mission?

The general's aide solved part of the problem. "Sir," said Colonel Alphonse, "whatever happens here, we cannot be identified. We must leave, right now."

General Greer agreed. He hadn't wanted to be present for this attack; not because he was squeamish about the sight of dead civilians, but because he feared he might be seen by someone who could tell the newspapers or Congress that a general officer of the United States military had sat idly by as another town was razed to the ground and its citizens butchered.

Unfortunately, Noah Claybourne felt differently. He was furious that Demetria Carnal had yet to attack San Rafael over in New Mexico Territory, and so he sent Matthew Cord to order Greer to personally oversee Rivas's next attack. Whatever Rivas was about to do now, Greer could not wait to see. He turned his horse, motioned to his men, and galloped away from the chaos.

❁

Rivas was startled when the first shots rang out from behind the boulder a hundred yards up the wash. His men had scouted the area the night before and reported that no one was in the vicinity except the residents of Manzanita Flats. He had only selected the flea-ridden pueblo as his target a few days ago, and no one outside his own men and General Greer knew his plans. The shooters could not be the law, and he did not believe for an instant that any of the Swedes in town could have seen them coming, assumed what was going to happen, and then positioned themselves to begin firing at his men, all in the matter of a few minutes. But he had a decision to make, and it had to be done immediately.

❖

Diego and Itzcoatl continued their steady pattern of fire, but now the attackers were racing their horses in circles around the wash so they would be much harder to hit. As Diego sighted in on his next target, he saw Rivas raise his arm and point directly at him. Diego fired and missed, and the last shell ejected from his Winchester. Itzcoatl fired twice more, and then his rifle, too, was empty. Both men reached into the canvas cartridge pouches at their waists and began to swiftly reload; one cartridge in the chamber, fifteen in the magazine. In the twenty seconds it took to reload, Rivas's men formed a semicircle and began to charge towards the boulders. When they were about seventy-five yards away, four of the riders broke off from the group and began to sweep around to the right, and a moment later another four broke to the left. They're going to flank us, thought Diego. Four will hit us on each side from the rear, while the other six charge straight at us. A smart military tactic.

A salvo of bullets slammed into the boulder, peppering Diego and Itzcoatl with tiny shards of sandstone. Diego fired as fast as he could into the center of the charging group, and another rider dropped onto the ground. Out of the corner of his eye he saw Itzcoatl leave the safety of the boulder and position himself next to the creosote bush opposite the side where the horses were tied. The old man was going to take on the two sets of riders who had flanked them.

Diego's next shot took down the rider next to Rivas, causing the leader to swing his horse around and lead the four men remaining with him to a stand of boulders twenty-five yards away. The moment they turned their horses around to ride for cover, Diego pivoted to the rear and fired at the clutch of riders coming up from behind. Dust from the charging horses mingled with rifle smoke and shouts, and he heard Rivas order his men to take positions behind the rocks. As he started to fire at the riders who had just flanked them, he suddenly saw a bright red bloom appear on the back of Itzcoatl's right shoulder.

They fired volley after volley at the attackers. Two men fell from their horses, and the remaining four wheeled and galloped to the relative safety of a copse of twisted oaks.

"Re-load," shouted Itzcoatl. Diego went to one knee and dug into his cartridge pouch. A few seconds later he nodded to Itzcoatl, who kneeled and did the same. Then Diego swung around behind Itzcoatl, went back to his knee, and faced towards Rivas and his men as they began to fire from their positions in the rocks. Itzcoatl backed up against him and fired at the men who had come up behind them and were now taking cover in the scrubby trees.

"Is it bad?" shouted Diego between shots. He could feel the blood seeping from Itzcoatl's shoulder and onto his own back.

Itzcoatl fired twice in rapid succession before saying, "Ask me tomorrow, after I sleep off the mezcal I am going to drink tonight."

Diego almost smiled as he squeezed off his next shot. Then, he heard a dull, thumping sound, and felt Itzcoatl's back push against his. The old man had been hit a second time. As painful as it was not to turn from the fight to check on Itzcoatl, Diego continued to fire methodically towards the rocks where Rivas and his men were sheltering.

Then, three horses flew out from behind the oaks in front of Itzcoatl. They swung in a wide arc, charged over to where Rivas was crouched behind a pile of rocks. The riders leapt from their mounts to the ground behind the rocks, and the horses came to a standstill, unsure of what to do. That was a mistake. Itzcoatl quickly dropped two of the horses, and Diego dispatched the third. Whatever else happened, at least three of Rivas' men would have to continue the fight on foot.

By Diego's count, they now faced only ten attackers. Still one mother of a lopsided battle, he thought, but one he still had hopes they could walk away from. He turned and took stock of Itzcoatl's wounds. At least one bullet had passed through the Aztec's shoulder, and another had creased his side. The old man's face was ashen, and his left arm was trembling. That's when Diego saw that he had also been shot through the elbow.

"Can you make it to your horse? I will lay down all the fire I can to keep them down for a few seconds. Get to your horse, ride south on top of the embankment until you are out of range of their fire, then double-back on the road and get some help from the men in town. They must have heard the shooting by now."

Itzcoatl coughed, and drew a deep, wheezing breath. He was clutching his rifle in his right hand, and Diego saw that he had somehow managed to pull out his obsidian dagger with his left hand, even though he could barely bend his elbow.

"I think I'll stay, *tecolote*," whispered Itzcoatl in a gravelly voice. "The weather is better here, and I don't want you to get lonely."

Diego placed the palm of his hand gently on Itzcoatl's face. "I can make you go, you know."

Itzcoatl frowned. "Have I taught you nothing all these years? The gods decide who shall come and who shall go when the battle is on. Remember, Diego, that they loan us to each other only for a short while. I have fight in me still. Honor my wish."

Before Diego could reply, a stream of shots rang out from the rocks. They smashed harmlessly into the huge boulder above them, but until they stopped, Diego could not peer around the rock to return fire. He was about to pull Itzcoatl over against the rock and see to his wounds when two men crashed out from the creosote bush and jumped onto them.

One of the men knocked Iztcoatal off his knees and began to pummel him ferociously with his fists. The other man wrapped his arm around Diego's neck and flung him down into to the dirt. Diego's rifle went flying, and the man began slashing at him with a knife. Diego rolled to his side, got back to his knees, and parried the next knife blows with his right forearm. He pulled his knife out with his left hand, and when the man raised his arm to deliver a killing strike, Diego thrust his knife up into the man's lower abdomen. The man lurched back and struggled to recover his balance, but before he could right himself, Diego withdrew his knife from the man's gut and plunged it straight into his neck. Hot blood sprayed onto the ground from the man's severed artery, and he fell in a heap into the dust.

Diego jumped to his feet and raced over to where Itzcoatl and the other attacker were thrashing around on the ground. Diego saw a glint of steel and heard Itzcoatl's breath expel in a rush. He reached for the man's knife arm just as Itzcoatl stuck his dagger into the attacker's side. The man went to his back, and Itzcoatl finished him off with a deep slice across the neck.

The firing from the rocks started up again, and Diego knew the next wave of attackers would be on them in a heartbeat. He reached for his rifle with one hand, and with the other, pulled the old man closer to him. He kneeled, cocked his rifle, and pointed it at the bushes, before looking over to assess Itzcoatl's condition. The Aztec had wounds in his side, shoulder, and arm. His lower belly was bloody, and his right leg had a deep gash from the thigh to the knee. He was conscious, but Diego did not think he could sit up on his own.

Before he could speak, the branches of the creosote bush parted again, and three men rushed towards him. He fired once, and the lead man dropped. Then, to his amazement, Itzcoatl pushed himself up to his knees, leaned forward, and tackled the second man as he raced towards Diego. As they began to struggle, the third man smashed Diego's face with the butt of his rifle. Diego countered with a blow to the man's groin, only to feel the bite of a knife as it sunk into his shoulder and knocked him on his back.

The man pulled out his revolver, straddled Diego's body, and smiled. Then he raised his gun into the air and fired twice. A signal that it is safe to come over, thought Diego. He turned his head and saw Itzcoatl and his opponent on their knees, just inches apart. The haft of Itzcoatl's stone dagger was protruding from his attacker's stomach. The man was gasping for air, his eyes were panicked and wild, and a gush of urine was soaking the front of his trousers. Itzcoatl's countenance, in contrast, was serene, almost contemplative. He could just have well been sitting at a lakeside picnic table, telling favorite stories to his sons and Diego, instead of dying under a broiling sun in the New Mexico desert. Itzcoatl looked his way. He smiled and whispered something in the Aztec tongue, and then his eyes closed, his arms went limp at his side, and he lowered his head to his chest.

❖

The man with the revolver motioned for Diego to stand up and walk in front of him around the boulder to where Geronimo Rivas and four men stood waiting. Another man was rounding up the horses that had been loosed when the fight began.

Rivas looked Diego over and then gave a curt nod to the man holding the gun. The man raised his revolver and struck Diego on the side of the head with the barrel. He went down to one knee with blood trickling out of his ear.

"Who are you, *pendejo*?" growled Rivas. "And why have you and your ancient amigo attacked and killed my men?"

Diego straightened up, only to have the man with the revolver cuff him upside the head again. He put his hand against his ear, and said, "I would guess that you are Geronimo Rivas, the butcher of Monteverde."

Rivas smiled. "Is that what they are calling me? I am flattered."

He grunted, and Diego was pistol whipped a third time.

"Judging from your horses and your gear, you are a wealthy man. Tell me, why does an aristocrat search the desert for me? The US Army is not doing a good enough job of that without your help?"

Several of Rivas's men laughed.

"My name is of no importance to you," said Diego. "And to be precise, I am not searching for you. I have business with your boss."

Rivas crossed his arms over his chest and spat a cheek full of tobacco juice on the ground. "My boss? A man of my stature has no boss. Look around you. Do I look like someone who needs a boss?"

"No, but you do look like someone who needs seven or eight new men."

At that, the man with the revolver smashed Diego straight in the face. Blood gushed from his nose, and he had to struggle not to fall again.

"Amigo," said Rivas, "it is hot, and I have work to do, even with the few men you have spared me. We will talk again later, and I will see how smartly you speak after I cut out your tongue and throw it to the dogs."

He signaled for Diego to be taken away and turned to go.

"Work to do for Matthew Cord and Noah Claybourne?" said Deigo. "Work you had better get done if you don't want to lose *your* tongue?"

Rivas whirled and drew his revolver. "You have surprised me twice today, *maricón*." He thumbed back the hammer. "And twice is the limit." He pointed the barrel at Diego's stomach. "Too bad about the old man. He was a warrior."

Then, a shotgun blast rang out, followed by another and then another. Diego looked up at the embankment a hundred feet away and saw a dozen or more men standing along it in a long row. All had rifles or shotguns, and in the instant it took to realize they were up there, four more men appeared, also holding weapons. Several women also arrived on the ridge, and then more men, until at least twenty-five armed residents of Manzanita Flats were looking down on Rivas and his men.

None of the Swedes said a word. Rivas took a step back and waved for the man who had been gathering their horses to hurry over. A few seconds later they were mounted. They started to gallop away, but before he reined his horse to join them, Rivas rode over to Diego and smashed the side of his head with his rifle butt.

"Hasta luego," he said. Then *Teniente* Rivas spurred his horse and raced away into the desert.

Diego weaved unsteadily on his feet for a moment and then

collapsed onto the hot, stony ground.

❖

He awoke several hours later in an unfamiliar room. A man with a shotgun across his lap was seated in a rocking chair in the corner. Diego bolted upright, only to fall back onto the bed with a searing pain in his head.

"Not your best day," said the man with the shotgun, in a heavily accented voice.

"Not by far," answered Diego.

The man called to the other room, and a minute later, a small crowd of men and women were standing around his bed. An older man stepped forward and introduced himself as Alrik Karlsson, the leader of the town. "There are nine bodies scattered around the wash," he began. "Eight look like hired guns. The ninth is a silver-haired old man who looks out of place with the others."

Diego nodded. "Yes," he said, "he was with me. For my whole life, in fact…" His voice trailed off and his eyes misted over.

One of the women came forward with a mug of tea and honey. He drank deeply.

"Are you up to telling us what is going on?" asked Karlsson. "Why were you and that old man fighting those men. Why here? Who are they?"

Diego sat up against the headboard. "Do you know what happened in Monteverde a few weeks ago?"

"Of course," said Karlsson. "We have been keeping watch in the event those monsters came our way. That's how we came upon you. What does your fight have to do with Monteverde?"

"The man who knocked me down? His name is Geronimo Rivas. He is the outlaw who led the attack on Monteverde. And, for reasons I really don't understand, they were planning on doing the same thing to your town this morning."

The room fell deathly quiet. Then one of the men said, "But, how can that be? Why us? We have no money; we haven't offended anyone."

Diego finished the tea and then said, "Who you are and what you have is of no consequence to these people."

"But what were you doing here?" asked Karlsson.

"We were tracking Rivas."

"Just the two of you? Not the army? That makes no sense."

Diego ran his hand through his hair and asked for another pillow to be wedged behind his back. "Here is my story," he began.

❖

The next evening a cooling wind blew down from the neighboring mountains and across Manzanita Flats. Diego had been patched up, fed, and bathed. The town carpenter built a simple pine coffin for Itzcoatl, and the entire population of a very grateful town gathered at the cemetery to listen to the preacher say a few words over the grave. Diego would keep Itzcoatl's rifle and dagger, but he asked Karlsson to sell the horse and saddle and use the money to purchase materials for the new school the town was building.

After dinner, Diego limped up to the cemetery. He carried a folding chair, a bottle of mezcal, and a blue glass. When the sun dipped below the western mountains and the stars carpeted the ink-black heavens, he poured a glass of mezcal and settled onto the chair beside Itzcoatl's grave.

First Xipil, and now his father, Diego thought. Both killed in the effort to find Rosalilia. He knew better than to question whether his friends' deaths were worth it. Since he was a boy, Itzcoatl had hammered home the importance of living with honor. It is better to die for *something*, he would say, than to live for *nothing*. Itzcoatl died, as he had lived, by that credo.

Diego finished his drink and then poured the rest of the bottle out onto the rocky grave. He stood with his hands on the wooden chair for support, looked up into the glittering night sky, and recited the prayer that Itzcoatl had spoken every night since he was a child:

Only for so short a while you have loaned us to each other because we take form in your act of drawing us, and we take life in your painting us, and we breathe in your singing us. But only for so short a while have you loaned us to each other. Because even a drawing cut in obsidian will fade, and the green crown feathers of the Quetzal bird will lose their color, and the sounds of the waterfall will die out in the dry season. So, we too, shall die because only for a short while have you loaned us to each other.

He leaned the empty bottle against a rough wooden cross the Swedes had pounded into the hard dirt. Then he turned and walked back to the little town by the light of a million stars.

❃

FORTY FOUR

Leadville, Colorado, September 1882

As Thomas struggled to breathe, he reflected that Demetria Carnál's plan to get him back into Denver without alerting Noah Claybourne had sounded a lot better in the garden of her New Mexico hacienda than it did here on the station platform at Leadville. The journey from Las Cruces had taken three days, and as the train wound higher and higher up into the Rocky Mountains from the sweltering desert floor, he was struck by how spectacular the scenery became, and how much more pleasant it was with daytime temperatures at least thirty degrees cooler than in New Mexico. When he stepped down from the passenger car in the early afternoon light, though, he was also reminded that something as simple as breathing was a whole different proposition at 10,000 feet elevation than it was at sea level. A liquor drummer who sat beside him for much of the journey had warned him about what the locals called "thin air" sickness, but until he had experienced having to breathe faster and deeper to get enough oxygen into his lungs to function normally, he didn't appreciate how right the salesman had been.

"Leadville was a fly-speck in the dirt fives year ago," said his traveling companion, "and this year they'll pull $20 million in silver out of the mines. Thirty thousand people live up here. Can you believe that?" Then he laughed. "Of course, it takes a man a week or so to adjust to the altitude, which means he won't be able to partake in the amusements for a spell. You know, God engineered the pecker to perform some amazing feats, but to get the job done right, a man's John Thomas requires a strong supply of blood, and that blood needs lots and lots of oxygen, which you will find in short supply in Leadville. Get my drift?"

He completed his joke–which Thomas was certain the man told to anyone would listen–by pointing his index finger up straight and then letting it droop down slowly beside his thumb.

"But business is good despite the thin air," Thomas replied.

"Brother is it," said the salesman. "I sell my product in eighty saloons, three dozen sporting houses, and twenty-one gambling rooms. The miners hereabouts are well-paid, but I'm blessed by the fact that they spend the biggest slice of their payday cake at establishments who do business with me. You'll see that when you get your high-altitude legs under you and make your first turn around the town."

As the porter handed him his bag and hailed a hansom for the ride to the Clarendon Hotel, he was determined to take that turn sooner rather than later. He would stay for one night, and then board the narrow-gauge train for the six-hour journey northeast to Denver, where Sergey Baklanov would be waiting with Ulysses. They would telegraph Bat Masterson about their plans, and then ride out to Major Rhine's ranch, where Diego and Itzcoatl were already waiting. With a little luck, Demetria would arrive soon after them. The fishing tournament was just two weeks away and Thomas was hopeful that Claybourne would be so occupied with entertaining notable guests from around the world that he would back off the search for he and Diego for a few days.

The cab deposited him at the Clarendon, which was adjacent to the Tabor Opera House. A six-foot high playbill in the display window advertised a presentation on "The Decorative Arts," to be presented that evening by the Irish lecturer and self-promotion genius, Oscar Wilde. Tickets were $1.25 Thomas noted as the doorman took his bag and led him into the lobby. Any other time he would have enjoyed such a spectacle, but he only had the energy for dinner and a bath. The train for Denver left at 6:00 a.m.

His third-floor room looked out across a wide dirt street to a row of false-fronted saloons, restaurants, and smaller hotels.

The Clarendon was the finest place in town, and the desk clerk bragged that its restaurant was the best in the world, at least in the category of dining establishments located two miles above sea level.

He took a bath, dressed for dinner, and dropped off his laundry to be cleaned overnight. Then he went down into the opulent dining room, which he was surprised to see was nearly deserted.

"Everyone in town has gone to the Tabor to see Oscar Wilde," his waiter explained. "You wouldn't think a bunch of silver miners would be interested in a lecture on the arts."

"He has a reputation as a witty and funny fellow," Thomas replied, "though I have no idea what he has actually done other than crisscross America opining on the meaning of color and form. Good luck to him, though. If he can line them up at five bits a seat and hold their attention for an hour, he probably deserves to be famous."

He was famished for a good meal after three days of the dry eggs and stale sandwiches served on the train and followed his waiter's recommendation for pan-seared venison with garlic mashed potatoes, steamed summer squash and wild rice soup. He also asked for a bottle of Charles Krug California zinfandel, which he drank while flipping through the newspaper he picked up at the desk. When the waiter poured a second glass of wine, he told Thomas, "You'll want to make sure and read the crime blotter at the back. It's the only reason most folks read the rag."

He followed the waiter's advice. The best way to get to know a town–after visiting its best gambling spots–was to read the local crime reports. He wasn't disappointed when he scanned Leadville's crime reports for the past several days.

POLICE BLOTTER

On the 26th of August, Mrs. Joe Ward attempts the death of her husband by use of her little pistol. No damage done.

The 27th was the also the date upon which Billy Nuttall chewed an ear off Chris Wagner.

On the night of the 28th, a crazy woman escaped from the poor

house and wandered to the city. On the same day, a Mr. Jacobs was knocked down and kicked in the head by one of the fire horses, which became unmanageable on the corner of State Street and Harrison Avenue.

Also on that day, Joseph Hennessy, the sawyer at the Morning Star Mine, had his head badly lacerated by falling against a buzz saw. Whiskey and stitches were applied at the scene.

On the 29th was recorded an accident to Superintendent Charles of the Matchless Mine, who fell down a shaft 180 feet deep but was saved from instant death by his clothes catching on a nail.

And, on the 30th, the South Park train ran into a charcoal team belonging to A.C. Drake and killed both horses, the driver escaping with his life and vowing to find another occupation.

❖

When the perfectly cooked venison was set before him, he folded the paper and slid it across the table. As he did, a headline on the bottom of the front page that he hadn't noticed before caught his eye:

Nine Mexican Nationals Killed
in Arizona Territory
Reputed to be members of notorious outlaw gang

Tombstone, August 29, 1882
by Tanner Fulbright, Special Correspondent

The United States Federal Marshal for the southern district of Arizona Territory reported today that the bodies of nine men, all of whom are reputed to have been members of the Geronimo Rivas outlaw gang, were discovered in a dry wash on the eastern edge of the small mining town of Manzanita Flats, thirty miles east of Tombstone.

Residents of the town contacted the marshal after hearing a ferocious gun battle raging just after dawn on the morning of the 26th. According to town leader Alrik Karlsson, with whom this correspondent spoke personally, several men from the town went down into the wash when it was clear that the fight was over. "Bodies were scattered around the wash," said Karlsson, "and it appeared that all of them had been shot, some of them multiple

times.

As for who did the shooting, and why such a battle had taken place in this isolated corner of the territory, neither Karlsson nor any other residents of Manzanita Flats could volunteer any information. They did not see any of the combatants alive, nor were there any survivors of the fierce encounter.

"We are concerned, of course, especially after the massacre at Monteverde a few weeks ago," said Karlsson. "But, unless the marshal can tell us anything more, I'm not sure we will ever know what to make of all this."

Thomas poured another glass of wine. There was no doubt in his mind that Mr. Karlsson knew far more than he was telling. He read on:

Information relayed to this correspondent by a scout for the US Army (who wishes to remain anonymous) says that officials believe that the Mexican outlaw and cattle thief Geronimo Rivas was operating in the area at the time of the gun battle. General Winston Greer, the American commander in the territory, has not issued a statement on the event. All we can be certain of at this time is that the carnage that took place at Monteverde has not run its course. We shall continue to investigate.

-end-

He read through the article one more time. Then, deep in thought, he set the paper aside and finished his meal.

❖

Hours later, in the orange glow of light from the streetlamps that spilled into his room, he looked at his pocket watch. It was nearly 3:00 a.m. and he had tossed and turned since he went to bed four hours earlier. Now he got up and went to a chair beside the window. Despite the hour, there were lots of people moving along the street, and the sounds of pianos and fiddles drifted out the open doors of a half dozen saloons.

He kept going over and over the content of Fulbright's article in his mind; he knew what the reporter hadn't shared with his readers, of course: Rivas was in Noah Claybourne's employ and quite probably was responsible for the massacre at Monteverde. The fact that nine members of his gang had been killed in the dry wash at Manzanita Flats was beyond coincidence. He was certain that Rivas had also been present and that, for reasons unknown, someone had stopped him and his men from reducing the little mining town to rubble the way they had crushed Monteverde.

But, who? It could not have been the army–not with Greer in command at least. And in any event, if the army had stopped the attack, they would not have left the bodies lying in the dust before disappearing into the desert without filing a report.

No, someone else had killed Rivas's men and sent the bandit leader scurrying into the brush. Thomas could almost not allow himself to consider the obvious possibility. Could Diego and Itzcoatl have come upon Rivas's gang as they prepared to descend on Manzanita Flats? Had they been able to thwart the bandits, just the two of them? And if they had, why didn't Alrik Karlsson or anyone else in the small town share that information with the US marshal? And then the biggest question of all: were Diego and Itzcoatl among the nine who were killed in the wash that morning?

He was not a worrier by nature. He faced things head on; if he couldn't go through them, around them, or over them, his habit was to move along and not let the issue hang around his neck like a lead weight. But tonight was different. He didn't have much information, but what he did have pointed to the very real possibility that Diego and Itzcoatl were dead.

When he found himself pacing back and forth across the room, he knew he had to do something. The train left in three hours, and he wasn't going back to sleep. He got dressed, went downstairs and headed across the street to a brightly lit saloon called "Wyman's." That would be as good a place as any.

❖

The saloon was ablaze with light, cigar smoke, and laughter. Tiers of box seats lined both walls, and an empty stage graced the center of the huge room. Two signs on the wall caught Thomas' attention; one read, *Please Do Not Swear*, while the other admonished guests, *Please Do Not Shoot the Piano Player. He Is Doing His Best.*

In normal times, he would have headed directly for the gaming tables. But as he began to elbow his way through the crowded room he was drawn to an unusual sight: seven large tables had been pulled into a circle around a smaller table and were crowded with men in work clothing. At the head of one of the tables sat one of the most striking individuals he had ever seen. He was well over six feet tall, thin and angular, and dressed like a theatrical dandy. He wore a tight black velvet coat framed with lavender satin piping and frills of lace at the wrists. He had on black satin knee breeches with silk bows above black silk stockings, and the silver buckles on his black patent leather shoes gleamed in the garish lamp light. Completing the remarkable ensemble was a white silk waistcoat from which hung a gold watch fob, a floppy bowtie, a pair of white kid gloves, and a black velvet cape that was slung rakishly over one shoulder. His unruly hair hung to his shoulders, and as he passed the table, Thomas was certain the young man's milky face had been dusted with powder and rouge.

The man was speaking in an animated, Irish-accented voice to the dozens surrounding him, and as Thomas passed the table, he caught the middle of the conversation. "And what a sign!" the man was exclaiming. "Please don't shoot the piano player? How wonderful that someone other than me recognizes that bad art merits the penalty of death." Then he sighed melodramatically and added, "And thus, the aesthetic implications of your Colt revolvers, no?"

Thomas smiled to himself and pushed on past the laughs and hoots of the man's rapt audience. As he waved for the barman's attention, he had no doubt that he had just encountered the Irish wit, Oscar Wilde.

❧

He took a seat at the far end of the bar and sipped at his brandy. He willed himself not to jump to conclusions about Diego and Itzcoatl and tried to focus on formulating a plan that would allow him to get close to Noah Claybourne and discover what had become of Rosalilia. On that count, it would not matter if Diego had perished in the dry wash. Thomas would find her, free her, and take her back to her family in Mexico. Or, he mused, he would die in the attempt.

He was roused from his thoughts by the scent of cologne and turned to find Oscar Wilde seated on the barstool next to him. The Irishman hailed the bartender, asked for a champagne cocktail, and then turned towards Thomas.

"You look damned near out of place here as I do," said the poet.

"Really?"

"Oh, not your dress, dear fellow, but rather, your demeanor. Are things in your world so appallingly bleak?"

Thomas managed a half smile. He was struck by Wilde's wide, doe-like eyes, and the way he looked as if he had been poured, long and limp, out of a glass onto his stool.

"Perhaps I should have attended your performance this evening, Mr. Wilde. Word has it that no one leaves the theatre after seeing you without a new spring in their step and a smile on their face."

Wilde took his champagne from the bartender and raised his glass to Thomas. "*Merci*, Colonel Scoundrel, for your kind observation."

"*Merci à vous*. But, how do you happen to know my name? I don't believe I have been introduced to anyone in this establishment."

"A man as famous as you cannot enter a tavern anywhere in America without someone recognizing you. As it happens, one of the miners with whom I descended into the Matchless Mine for a tour a few hours ago served under your command in the Sioux Wars. He was quite excited to see you walk through the door. Chattered on and on about you, and, of course, pointed to that…" Wilde turned his head towards the eight-foot-wide painting hanging dead center on the wall behind the bar. "My dear Colonel, is it true that this very representation of your fabled heroic deeds in the final hours of your nation's civil war hangs in a place of honor in every watering hole in America?"

Thomas looked up at the painting, which had become a fixture of saloon décor since the early 70s. He had trained himself over the years to ignore it, something that was impossible to do once a bar manager learned that the hero of Pebble Creek Ridge was drinking in his establishment. The perspective was from high in the air and showed the valiant young colonel on his war steed waving the American flag in the face of hordes of Confederate attackers. The sky was blue and cloudless, and the Rebel soldiers were boiling with blood lust, but Scoundrel's countenance was serene, almost beatific. He held the flag high in one hand and was firing his service revolver at the Rebel leader with the other. Most magnificent of all was the fact that his horse, Cornwall, was reared back on his heavily muscled hind legs. The effect of the placement of horse and rider and sun-drenched flag suggested they might sail off into the air at any moment. Thomas had always found the painting to be garish as well as inaccurate, but its mix of vibrant colors, swirling action, and especially, the selfless, demi-god like aspect of the vastly overmatched colonel had immediately become a favorite of the more than two million veterans who had fought for the Union.

He sighed. "A liquor magnate in Chicago commissioned the original. Then he sent it on tour of some of the most prominent establishments that sold his product. It was such a hit that a trio of investors got the rights to manufacture and sell reproductions. And, boom, just like that, it appeared on the back bar wall of every tavern, saloon, whorehouse and cantina from New York to San Francisco."

Wilde motioned to the barman to fill his glass and pour Thomas another brandy.

"And you aren't pleased by that tour de force of free advertising?" he asked in an incredulous tone. "Your speaking fees alone must have trebled the moment the first painting was hung in a public place."

"I don't do lectures."

"Well, then, a biography? Surely you have authorized a publisher to at least do that? It would sell millions of copies and make you a very wealthy man."

"No book, either, though many publishers have approached me."

Wilde looked genuinely perplexed. "No lecture tours, no book...

honestly, my friend, those in the public eye like myself would crawl naked over broken glass to get such attention. Please, and I mean no offense or disrespect, please tell me: why?"

He looked up into the Irishman's face. "Because it wouldn't be true," he said quietly. "None of it. I'm not really a hero. Heroes were buried where they fell."

Wilde scanned the American's face to discern if he was being sincere. Then he threw his head back and let out such a great laugh that half the patrons in the noisy bar looked his way.

"True?" he said through his laughter. "Dear heaven, Thomas, I'm starting to think that whoever it was that told me you were a fellow Irishman was sorely misinformed. This," he brushed his hands down in front of his absurdly dandified outfit, "this is theatre. It is make-believe; it is a fantasy piled upon a nightmare ladled over a mountain of bovine excrement."

He turned on his stool and gestured towards the gaggle of miners on the other side of the bar. They roared back and slammed their glasses on the tables in anticipation of the great man's return to tell more stories.

"Célébrités like us prosper only because our audiences are willing to suspend their disbelief for a few brief hours while they are in our presence," Wilde continued amidst the clamor. "And even then, we who educate and entertain are able to succeed only because the people leaning forward in their seats so as not to miss a single word want so desperately to be lifted out of the muck and mire of their everyday existence, if only for an evening. That is as true for the wealthy as it is for the downtrodden, by the way. The rich try to conceal their sorrows beneath exquisitely tailored clothing, but to no avail. Fine silk or rough woolens; it doesn't matter. Everyone you meet is fighting a great battle of some kind. I offer a brief respite from the struggle." He reached out a hand and laid it on Thomas' shoulder. "They don't want to hear truths, *mon amie.* They have had it up to their ears with truth. They know that truth is a wretched, bitter, and barren companion who mocks their every step through life, right up until the glorious day that their suffering is brought to an ignominious conclusion in the icy embrace of death."

Thomas shook his head. "And in place of truth, you give them what?"

Wilde's face broke out in a wide grin. He stood up and threw his velvet cape back over one shoulder. Then he raised his head high, looked out upon his admirers, and raised his arms above his head to get their attention. A great shout came from the crowd, and a chant of "Wilde, Wilde, Wilde," rang across the saloon.

"I give them this," said the Irishman, making a half bow to his admirers.

He turned back and reached out his hand for Thomas to shake. "Being Irish," he said, "I have always had an abiding sense of tragedy, which, I am glad to say, has sustained me through temporary periods of joy. I suspect, dear colonel, that you have your own ways of dealing with melancholy, just as you have of hiding from the burdens of the fame that the world wants to thrust upon you. God bless your journey."

With that, Wilde stepped forward and melted into the cheering throng. Thomas finished his brandy, left a tip for the barman, and went out into the darkness.

❋

FORTY FIVE

Near Temptation Mountain

Rosalilia reached the base of the mountain at midday. She left Reed unconscious in the dirt outside the cabin seven hours earlier and then scrambled through the low brush and thick stands of conifers that spilled down to the valley floor several miles below. The pre-dawn air had been laced with frost when she began her escape; now, the sun lazed high in the clear Colorado sky, and the temperature was soaring.

She didn't care about the weather. The race down the slopes towards freedom felt exhilarating after six weeks of confinement with only Cord's hired guns for company. As for the performance she put on to distract the men so she could make her escape, that was something she was going to put out of her mind forever. She could only imagine the sacrifices that Diego and Thomas were making in their effort to find her; what she had done to lull Spruce and Reed into a sense of false complacency last night was nothing compared to what she knew her fiancé and his best friend were probably enduring on her behalf.

The trail from the cabin to the valley floor was well marked, courtesy of the rider who delivered supplies to the cabin. Once she passed through the last stand of sub-alpine trees and shrubs, a clear panorama of grassy meadows and low, rolling hills stretched for miles before her. Even though she could finally see to the horizon, there were no signs of farms or ranches. No chimney smoke, no structures, no roads. Someone had thought carefully about where she was to be held prisoner, and they had gone to great expense to see to it that she stayed there until they were ready to exchange her for ransom–if that was the purpose for her kidnapping, of course.

But, why? What was so important about her that a Colorado land baron would reach thousands of miles into Mexico, attack her home on her engagement day, ransack the villa, and spirit her away on a private rail car? Was it a simple kidnapping for ransom? If that were the case, she had no doubt her father would have paid the ransom by now. He loved her dearly, and he was a wealthy man. Kidnapping was a fact of life among the Mexican aristocracy and the reason their homes had fortress-like outer walls and private guards. No, there was more to this story than an ordinary kidnapping. She knew the kidnapper's leader, Matthew Cord. He had come to her home on several occasions to talk with her father. The last time she saw him he was slamming the door of Señor Verján's study. The mining engineer stormed past her in the courtyard, his eyes black with anger, his face a twisted ball of rage.

The events of the past weeks had to be tied to the business her father had been negotiating with Cord, whom, she learned from her captors, was in the employ of Noah Claybourne. As for the fate of her parents and family, she could only pray. No matter how many of Claybourne's men had attacked her home, however, she knew in her heart that Diego and Itzccoatl would have fought them off, and they would have survived. She would not allow herself to believe otherwise.

When she emerged from a stand of scrub oak and whipsaw brush and realized she had finally reached the base of the mountain, Rosalilia experienced a fleeting moment of pride. Young women of her station were discouraged from engaging in strenuous physical activity in public. In fact, a mere bead of perspiration on the brow of a proper lady was considered a sign of lower-class status, and there was no chance that any of her society friends would have attempted the dash she had just made down the mountain. Those same friends had been mortified when

Rosalilia took fencing lessons, along with instruction in shooting, knife throwing, and horseback riding. She had worked hard to excel at each of those sports, a fact that endeared her to Diego far more than her social graces, finely tuned as they were.

She drank her fill from a nearby stream, pulled some pemmican from her bag, and took a moment to rest on a fallen log to ponder the next move. The only thing she was certain of was that Reed and Spruce were on her trail, probably only a few hours behind. If they caught up with her, all bets were off. She gathered up her bag, checked the action on the Colt revolver, and then strode purposefully out into the prairie.

After an hour of pushing through thick grass and navigating around randomly scattered mounds of crushed shale, she came to a long, low hill that rose several hundred feet above the surrounding landscape. She was dead tired, but it would be faster to go over the hill than around it. She made her way up the slope, stepping carefully around dozens of deep, brush-lined fissures that crisscrossed the ground. Looking down into one of the seams she saw that it was lined with razor sharp rocks that protruded from its ragged sides. Probably the remains on an old volcano. If she slipped into one, her escape would come to a very quick and violent end.

The view from the top was dominated by a flat, sparsely vegetated landscape painted in muted browns and greens that unfolded in waves in all directions. It only took a moment for her eyes to find a narrow road cut through with wagon ruts running north to south about a half mile distant. As she picked up the pace and walked swiftly in the direction of the wagon trail, she caught sight of something even more exciting: a few wisps of dust were rising in the warm air currents just a few hundred yards up the road. Someone-or something- was moving in her direction. She ran as fast as she could through the grass and brush, hoping against hope that she could make it to the road before the traveler passed by and was swallowed up by the prairie.

The closer she got to the trail, the more certain she was that she was about to be rescued. A moment later saw that the dust was being kicked up by an old-style prairie schooner of the type that had dominated the trails to Oregon and California thirty years earlier. The wagon was about twelve feet long, narrow and low, and its arched canvas top was tattered and grimy from years in the open.

Rosalilia hid behind a cottonwood and waited as the wagon approached. She knew she would be taking a huge risk by announcing her presence; these could be Cord's men, which meant her rescue could turn into a hellish nightmare far worse than the one she had escaped from that morning. But she really had no choice; she had no idea how far she was from a farm or town, and she would be taking an even greater risk if she allowed Spruce and Reed to catch up to her. She had to take the chance, she decided, and she stepped out from behind the tree and planted herself in the middle of the road.

Her heart leapt when she saw there was a man and woman seated on the wagon bench. The man was holding the reins loosely as his four horses plodded along the red dirt trail, while the woman in the calico dress and bonnet beside him was bouncing a small child on her lap. A family! Tears welled in Rosalilia's eyes. A family. Surely, they would take her in and help her get to the nearest town, where she could find a sheriff and tell her story. And if they had a telegraph, she could also communicate with her family in Cuernavaca.

❖

The driver and his wife were astonished when they rounded a pile of dun-colored boulders and saw a young, attractive woman standing in the middle of the trail. Her dress was torn and muddied, there were fresh scratches on her arms, and her hair was pulled back in a ponytail. A cotton rucksack was slung over one shoulder, and she was smiling.

The woman didn't need to wave them down. The man reined the horses to a halt and clambered down from the wagon, followed by his wife and child.

"Well, now, sister," he said as he approached Rosalilia, "how on earth have you gotten yourself way out here on the far side of nowhere?"

"Are you alright, honey?" his wife added. "Is anyone with you?"

Rosalilia shook her head, almost beside herself with relief. "I'm alone, and I'm fine. But there are men after me who mean to do me harm, and I must get to the sheriff. Can you help me, please?"

The man and his wife exchanged a worried glance. No one invited themselves to trouble out here on the prairie. The woman looked and sounded like she was educated, and she sure as hell shouldn't be alone in the Colorado wilderness, but no matter what they did, they knew they might be bringing a load of trouble down on themselves for simply extending a helping hand to a stranger in need. In the man's experience, good deeds seldom went unpunished.

Finally, the wife spoke. "Of course we will help you, darlin. Don't you concern about a thing." She stared hard at her husband before turning back to Rosalilia and saying, "Let's get you in the back of the wagon. We're only a half day's ride from town. We can take you right to the sheriff's front door."

The man pulled the canvas covering on the back of the wagon aside and helped Rosalilia climb over the gate and into a space filled with boxes of canned goods and farm supplies.

"We're headed back to our homestead from a trip south," said the woman. "There's a blanket and a pillow we use for our daughter there in the center. You lay yourself down and get some rest. Looks like you could use it. Help yourself to the canteen on that peg and the biscuits in yonder little bag. Made 'em this morning. We'll make a necessaries stop in a couple of hours, and you can attend to your business then if you have a call to."

Rosalilia reached over the back of the wagon and took the woman's hand. "I can't thank you enough for your kindness. My family will be coming for me, and they will see to it that you are rewarded."

The man closed the back up, and a minute later the wagon lurched forward and settled into a steady, swinging gait. Rosalilia lay down with the pillow and blanket. Until this moment she had no idea how exhausted she was. It only took a minute for the gentle rocking of the wagon to put her to sleep.

She had no idea how much time had passed when she was

awakened by the sound of people arguing at the front of the wagon. She crawled back to the canvas curtain and peeked out one side. It was late afternoon, and they had stopped in front of a small ranch house. The voices next to the wagon grew louder, and suddenly there was movement, and the curtain yanked open.

Standing just inches from her face was a man with a badly bruised and swollen face, his head swathed in bandages. Rosalilia drew back in horror at the sight of her captor, but there was no where she could escape to this time.

"Time to finish our dance," growled Reed. He leaned forward and slapped her hard across the face. Then he put one hand behind her neck and jerked her upper body against the wagon gate. The motion knocked the wind out of Rosalilia, but before she could take a breath, Reed raised his hand from her neck up to her ponytail, yanked her head back, and slammed his fist into the center of her face. Hot blood gushed from her nose, and the world went wobbly.

Then, a calloused hand reached under her shirt and squeezed her breast so hard it made her gasp. The last thing she heard before she blacked out was Reed saying, "What do you say we go along home now, sweetheart."

❖

FORTY SIX

Claybourne Ranch

Adolf Coors seldom smiled. It wasn't in his German nature, and it didn't fit with his philosophy of work, which was his only philosophy of life. He believed that a man should be measured not by the hours he put in or the money he piled up, but by the quality of his work product. By that measure, the thirty-five-year-old German immigrant was already a success. He had tramped the hills and valleys around Denver for months in '73 looking for the perfect combination of location and water. When he found the right spot on Clear Creek, about fifteen miles upslope from Denver, he brought in a partner and started his dream brewery.

The beer business was ferociously competitive. Coors decided early on that the only route to success would be to use only the best water along with the finest, perfectly roasted malt, and, true to his character, he personally oversaw every aspect of the business at all levels of production, marketing, and distribution. In the previous year he had sold four thousand barrels of beer. Make that four thousand forty-four, he thought with a hint of a smile as he wheeled the heavy freight wagon beneath the arched gate leading up to Langton Hall. He nodded down at a boy of about twelve who was directing delivery traffic. The boy's eyes widened at the sight of the three massive, black and gray Percheron work horses as they pulled the gleaming, freshly painted beer wagon onto the property. Twenty barrels of beer were stacked like cannons in two rows on each side of the glossy blue wagon, pointed at forty-five degree angles towards the sky. Two more barrels were lashed with rope to each side, and a brightly painted gold and blue signboard was fastened to the center of the wagon on top of the barrels proclaiming Coors to be the best beer in America. The boy pointed to a staging area to the left of an enormous provisions tent, and Adolph swung the wagon in that direction.

A delivery like this would normally have been done by a pair of his employees, but the Claybourne fishing tournament was far more than just another wealthy man's party. It was Colorado's social, political, and business event of the year, an opportunity for Coors to mingle with significant potential customers from around the country, as well as a chance to rebuff Noah Claybourne's latest offer to buy him out, this time face-to-face.

The amount of activity on the grounds of Langton Hall was impressive. At least a dozen freight wagons were parked around the huge central tent, offloading crates of vegetables, fruits, eggs, baking supplies, meats, and hard liquor. Adolf counted six A-frame cooking spits, several of which were already manned by crews slowly turning sides of beef, whole pigs and chicken over hot coals. Three brick ovens had been assembled to produce bread and rolls, and the aroma of fresh baked bread drifted over the entire area. A trio of Mexican women were slapping homemade tortillas on flat iron grills next to steaming pots filled with tamales, while four more tended to the contents of giant iron kettles hung by chains over wood fires. Several children shucked piles of sweet corn, and an assortment of cooks, carpenters, gardeners, decorators and kitchen workers swarmed the property making last minute preparations for the fishing tournament that would begin in just two days. Coors noted that there were at least ten rather handsome outdoor privies lined up just outside the compound, too. That boded well for consumption of his product.

The Denver newspapers had been covering the fishing tournament in increasingly breathless tones for weeks. As Coors waited in line for his wagon to be unloaded, he picked up yesterday's edition of the *Rocky Mountain News* on the seat beside him. Details of Claybourne's tournament and the famous guests who would be in attendance were splashed in bold headlines across the front page. Adolph harumphed through the litany of archdukes, viscounts, and assorted other minor European and Russian royalty who would be at Langton Hall. None of them could do any good for his business, and he figured they had made the journey west mostly to enjoy a free holiday with gourmet food in a spectacular setting. He similarly dismissed the need to seek out some of the other famous figures who would be guests at the tournament, including the author Samuel L. Clemens and the Italian opera composer Giuseppe Verdi. Where was the prospect for profit with the likes of them? The actress Lily Langtry was another story. She had traveled from her home in London, and wherever she went, the public followed her every move in the papers. She would be worth striking up an acquaintance with, as would the pugilist John L. Sullivan, whose legendary bare knuckles fight a few months earlier against Paddy Ryan in Mississippi had earned the champ a new nickname: His Fistic Holiness. Adolf could envision a color broadside poster showing Sullivan in a boxing stance alongside a display of Coors beer in every saloon that served his product. That made solid business sense.

A moment later a boy whistled to Coors and motioned for him to pull his Percheron team and wagon up to the provisioning tent. Adolf set the paper down and snapped the reins. When his beer was unloaded, he would present the bill for payment, and then make his way through the organized chaos around Langton Hall in search of new business.

❖

In contrast to the noise and bustle around Langton Hall, it was deathly quiet in the mansion's dark-paneled dining room, where a dozen men sipped their coffees and waited for Noah Claybourne to respond to the report that had just been delivered to the group by Geronimo Rivas. The success of their plan to force Congress and the President to send troops to northern Mexico had depended on a series of swift, brutal attacks against American citizens in the border regions of the Arizona and New Mexico Territories. Rivas's merciless assault on Monteverde several weeks earlier had gone as planned, and the entire nation had been predictably horrified and outraged at the massacre of over one hundred innocents.

And then, nothing. Demetria Carnál did not follow up with a fresh attack in New Mexico, and Rivas and his men had been unsuccessful in their attempt to cover for Carnál's failure with their unscripted attack on Manzanita Flats. The political momentum that Claybourne counted on to quickly forge a national consensus for imposing American military control across a huge swath of Mexico had faltered, and if that momentum was not regained immediately, the entire scheme could collapse.

Claybourne had been staring at the tabletop for several minutes. Finally, he raised his head and spoke in a quiet but deliberate voice.

"The failure of the one will not become the failure of the many," he began. "I will not permit that. We will adapt, we will reposition, and we will strike even more forcefully than originally planned. Great accomplishments come at great cost and usually only after unforeseen obstacles are overcome."

Heads nodded around the table.

Claybourne fixed his gaze upon Geronimo Rivas, who was standing next to the map at the head of the table. "Where is she?" he said slowly.

"Last we knew for sure she was up in the mountains outside Las Cruces."

"That would be at my villa," said Antonio Resposo, the former vice president of Mexico. "She and her men gathered there to plan their attack. The caretaker of the property reported that they departed almost two weeks ago, but he did not know where they were going."

"They certainly did not pay a visit to San Rafael, which was their intended target. Do we know why Miss Carnál chose to defy her orders?"

Resposo and Rivas shook their heads.

"A twinge of conscience, perhaps?"chimed in Senator Mack. "Maybe in the end she just did not have the heart for it."

"Conscience," said Claybourne in a flat, far away voice. "In her chosen profession? I think not, Senator."

General Winston Greer cleared his throat. "There is more to the story, Mr. Claybourne."

Noah raised his eyebrows. "Do tell, General."

"One of my scouts was with her and her men. He reported to me that she had a visitor, an American. The day after he arrived, she ordered her men to pack up, and by midday, they were headed down the mountain."

"Your man did not go with them?"

"His orders were to return to my headquarters as soon as she departed the villa."

Noah nodded. "And this visitor, this American. Who was he?"

"Interesting fellow," replied Greer, "a hero of the War Between the States, and someone whose name you may know."

Claybourne's long fingers pressed into the tabletop. "Yes?"

"Retired army colonel. Name of Scoundrel. Thomas Scoundrel."

Claybourne shot a withering glance down the table at Matthew Cord. He took a deep breath. "Strange, my understanding was that the colonel was killed in a tragic accident out at Tamayo Ravine a couple of months ago."

Greer shrugged. "Seems to have been healthy enough to disappear into Carnál's private room for the entire night."

There were muted chuckles around the table until Claybourne balled his fist and smashed it down on a pile of papers. He and Cord were the only ones in the room who knew the details of Scoundrel being beaten and tossed two hundred feet down into the ravine. And yet, the man was alive. There had been rumors that he had somehow escaped death at Tamayo, but, until this morning, that's all they were: rumors. Cord looked across the room at Claybourne and knew they were both thinking the same thing; the murder of their hired hand Elias in a Denver alley near the whorehouse Noah owned had been no random criminal act. Elias had helped to throw Thomas into the canyon, and now, the colonel was exacting his revenge.

"General," said Noah in a thoughtful tone, "what is the greatest enemy of the solider who is preparing for battle."

"That would be fear, sir. Fear has vanquished more armies than cannon fire."

"And what," continued Claybourne, "would you say contributes more to failure on the battlefield than any other cause."

Greer looked down at his coffee cup before speaking. "Chaos. Disorganization. Uncertainty."

Claybourne shook his head in agreement. "Exactly. And where are we today with our plan, gentlemen?" He stood and walked around to the map. Without warning, he smashed an open palm against the map and sent it crashing to the ground.

"We are standing on the precipice of fear," he continued, "and we are reaping the consequences of chaos and disorganization. The exact enemies of victory that the good general has just identified."

He leaned forward and placed his hands on the table. "But we have time to change our course, and by God, that is what we are going to do, starting this instant."

Heads nodded around the table, and Claybourne saw renewed confidence and energy in his co-conspirators' eyes.

"Mr. Rivas, you will assemble your men immediately. Take my train to southern New Mexico, find wherever it is that Miss Carnál is hiding, and kill her."

Rivas could not suppress a grin. Killing that insufferable bitch would be the high point of a long and bloody career.

"And you will not just kill her like some lamb at slaughter," continued Claybourne. "You will see to it that her death is worthy of a Homeric poem, very, very public, and terrifyingly memorable. One for the ages, so to speak. I want people to talk about the brutality of her death for years. Am I clear?"

Rivas nodded with delight and turned to go. "One more thing, Lieutenant," added Claybourne. "After you dispatch Carnál, I want you and your men to return to Colorado and pay a visit to Tipton."

That order startled every man in the room. Tipton was a small religious settlement of several hundred people, only fifty miles southeast of Langton Hall. It was inside Colorado, and hundreds of miles north of the targets they had agreed would be the most likely to motivate the United States government to act against Mexico.

Assistant secretary of State Wharton Geve spoke. "Sir," he began, "mindful as I am that we need to proceed as quickly as possible with the most direct action we can that will further our cause, I cannot see how an…," he paused, "how this activity you propose at Tipton fits within our strategy. Will the government believe that the attackers here in Colorado are the same bunch who have been operating hundreds of miles closer to the Mexican border?"

"They will believe what they are told to believe," replied Claybourne. "In this case, they will be convinced that the Mexican raiders have accomplices here in Colorado."

Even Rivas look surprised at that remark. He had no accomplices.

"The Cheyenne village south of the ranch has long been a thorn in my side," said Claybourne. "Red Elk has spoken publicly of his desire to rekindle his tribe's warrior past and to reclaim land and prestige he believes were taken from his people. I'm afraid, gentlemen, that the old fool is about to do just that."

"He only has a couple dozen men who are young and healthy enough to even be considered warrior material," said General Greer dismissively.

"And yet Mr. Rivas had even fewer men when he so brilliantly and completely razed Monteverde," replied Claybourne. Rivas accepted the compliment with a smile.

Before Claybourne could continue, the door opened, and two kitchen workers came in with more coffee and trays of pastries. Noah waited for them to finish and leave the room.

"After Tipton has experienced Mr. Rivas's inimitable flair, General Greer will grant an interview to that young English reporter whose vivid dispatches about Monteverde have been instrumental in rallying so many to our cause. What is his name?"

"Fulbright," answered Greer. "I know him."

"Good," Claybourne answered. "He will naturally seek you out after the raid on Tipton. You will regale him with all the sordid, stomach-turning details, of course, and then with something else of equal value to our plans. You will provide the reporter with unequivocal proof that the savage Chief Red Elk and his blood-thirsty Cheyenne warriors were in league with the border raiders and played a significant role in the torture and murder of innocent civilians. Manufacture evidence, plant it, invent it, whatever may be required to convince Fulbright that the Cheyenne were at Tipton. His pen will be every bit as mighty as Mr. Rivas's sword in putting steel into the backbones of the Washington politicians who will be asked to bring justice to Mexico and to the last of the red warriors."

Greer nodded. This plan just might work.

"Then," Claybourne said, "under the authority the President has given you to deal with the raiders, you will destroy the Cheyenne village and every last one of the god damn gnats in it. At the same time, you will report to the President that, unfortunately, the Mexican raiders who joined with Red Elk to flatten Tipton escaped to the south just before you arrived on the scene. You will proceed to the border in pursuit, and, as you do, Mr. Rivas and his men will visit the town of San Rafael and finish the job that Demetria Carnál left unfinished. The combination of the raids on the two towns will inflame the politicians to a point where they cannot choose any course of action but to declare war against Mexico. And, you, General, will just happen to be poised at the border when the order to invade comes from the President."

The men around the table nodded and murmured in agreement, and Senator Mack raised his coffee cup in salute to Claybourne. Like the other conspirators, he had been worried that Carnál's failure at San Rafael might spell doom for their project, and with it, an end to his career–or even his life–once they were found out and he was tried in federal court.

"Any questions, Mr. Rivas?"

Rivas grinned and shook his head. He understood exactly what he was to do. He was a craftsman, happiest when he was able to do the work for which he was so uniquely suited. First, he would personally violate Carnál in every way a man can ravage a woman, and then he would order his men to do the same. When they were done, he would tie her up and ever so slowly flay the skin from her twisted, broken body and feed it to the dogs. Finally, he would open her abdomen with his knife and watch her terrified eyes as her intestines spilled out on the ground in front of her and her life dribbled to a close. Of course, he would see to it that a few of her men were allowed to live so that they could share the story for years in every saloon and gambling hall in the West.

Rivas walked down the hall towards the front door, unsurprised in the least that he had become rock hard while thinking about how he was going to deal with that bitch of a bandit queen.

Claybourne returned to his seat at the head of the table. "The fishing tournament begins in two days. You all are about to be my guests at one of the most public and visible events in the West. Each of you was formally invited, and no one will ever suspect you came here for any reason other than to enjoy the sport and the company. Rivas and the estimable General Greer will do their parts, and we all will be immune from suspicion as events unfold." A smile creased his face. "Victory and treasure is within our reach, gentlemen. Congratulations to us all."

❖

A half hour later everyone but Claybourne and Cord had left the room. Noah lit a cigar and contemplated the events of the morning. He was content that he had put everything in motion necessary to achieve his ambition. In a matter of weeks, he would effectively control every aspect of mining, ranching, railroad construction, and irrigation development on a land mass larger than Texas.

He went to the window and looked out over the small tent city that had been erected in front of Langton Hall for the three-day fishing tournament. He saw Hyacinth talking to Nickolas Buckwright, who was responsible for assigning spots along the rivers, ponds, and streams on the ranch to over one hundred contestants each morning. He also spotted the Coors brewery owner, who was engaged in conversation with the owner of one of Denver's largest restaurants. This would be as good a time as any to make a final offer for the German's business. Noah had long wanted to own a beer company, and the German's was the best in the state. Coors had twice turned his offers down. It was time to up the ante; but, if the German turned him down today, there were other ways to persuade him.

Claybourne turned to Matthew Cord. "Find Colonel Scoundrel. Spend any amount of money you may need to locate him. When you find him, though, do the job yourself. I want to be sure this time."

Cord smiled and left the room.

FORTY SEVEN

Cheyenne Village

Diego joined Thomas at Red Elk's village late in the day, and the two friends walked to the crest of a nearby hill. Autumn light filtered through golden aspens and orange oaks, painting shapes in soft purple and moss green across the landscape, while cook fires dotted the rows of tipis lined up along the creek below. Thomas could smell the aromas of stew in the iron pots and trout smoking on sticks that had been jammed upright into the coals. Hunting had been good that season, and the rains plentiful. The village would have plenty of stores of dried meat and fruit to last through the Colorado winter.

His reunion with Red Elk had been brief and cold, and he had caught only a glimpse of Dawn Pillow as she walked past her father's tipi. Professor Von Sievers and Hamish Mackenzie had visited the old chief earlier in the day at Thomas's request and shared what they were learning about Claybourne's plans to settle old scores with the Cheyenne once and for all. Based on that information, Red Elk allowed Thomas into the camp and invited him to join the council fire after the evening meal.

Major Rhine and Marshal Bat Masterson had worked diligently to coordinate all the telegraphed communication between Thomas, Diego and their growing band of allies in the search for Rosalilia. That included Demetria Carnál, who would arrive at the village in the morning with Sergey Baklanov. She had her own business to conclude with Claybourne. His power and influence reached deep into Mexico, and until she either reached an accommodation with him–or saw him shot, imprisoned, or hung–there wasn't any location, no matter how remote, that would be safe for she and her men. The fact that her objectives mirrored Thomas' in so many ways only bolstered her belief that their small company could at least delay Claybourne until the United States authorities could conduct an honest investigation into the raid at Monteverde.

Diego had barely spoken a word since he rode into camp. He handed his horse over to a boy, shook hands with Red Elk, the professor and Hamish, and immediately asked his host's pardon for a few minutes while he spoke with Thomas in private. Red Elk pointed to the hill where he took his daily constitutional, and Diego and Thomas walked up to the summit in silence and settled on a log overlooking the village.

Diego sat wordlessly for several minutes. Then, as the faint outlines of stars began to appear in the evening sky, he raised his head towards the heavens.

"Itzcoatl," he sighed, and then his words trailed off. He took a deep breath and tried to fight off tears.

"I figured," Thomas said softly. "Manzanita Flats?"

"You know about that?"

"Only what I read in Fulbright's article. It said nine men had been killed in a dry wash, and since Geronimo Rivas was mentioned, it stood to reason that you and Itzcoatl were mixed up in it somehow."

"There were sixteen of them, Tomás. Sixteen. Itzcoatl fought like the jaguar king. I have never seen such bravery. We both were sure we were going to die there, but he did not relent, not for an instant. He saved my life."

Thomas looked out to the horizon. "That was his purpose in this world, Diego, from the day you were born. He died fulfilling that purpose. He would call it a good death, my friend. Dying in bed at a ripe old age would not have been his choice."

Diego forced himself to smile. "He *was* a ripe old age."

"You buried him there?"

Diego nodded. "On a hill, facing the land of his ancestors."

"When this is over, I will help you to take him home. We will place him next to his son, Xipil."

"I would like that."

They sat quietly as the sun dipped below the western mountains and a crescent moon appeared against a sea of glimmering stars. Then they walked down the hill to join the group that was gathering around the council fire in the center of the village.

❖

A dozen of Red Elk's warriors sat on logs around the fire with Diego, Thomas, Von Sievers, the medicine man White Moon, and Dawn Pillow. She had been cordial but distant with Thomas. He could not blame her. Her father had nearly banished her from the village after her moonlight tryst with Thomas in the glade across the creek. He wasn't going to complicate things further for her.

Red Elk poured some wine into a tin cup and passed the jug along to Hamish Mackenize, who filled his pewter mug to the brim before handing the wine to Four Bears. Then Thomas stood and began to speak. Over the next hour he detailed everything that led up to their meeting tonight. The crackling of the council fire, water pouring over smooth rocks in the stream, and the sound of wine jugs clanking against tin cups were the only other sounds in the village while he talked. He took note of Dawn Pillow's face when he described the circumstances around his meeting with Demetria Carnál at the mountain top hideout. He did not share the details of his adventure in Demetria's bath and bedroom, of course. He didn't have to. She filled in the blanks for herself.

"Your tale has the weight of my people's greatest legends," Red Elk said when Thomas finished speaking. "Even so, it is hard to believe in this modern age that Claybourne would think he has the power to change the destiny of nations."

"And yet, that is exactly what he believes," said Diego. He liked the old chief and appreciated the wisdom and clarity with which he spoke.

"He understands what is at stake if his scheme succeeds–and also if he fails."

"His power is truly this great?" asked White Moon.

"It is," answered Thomas. "He controls politicians and judges, and sheriffs and banks. One of the army's most senior commanders is in league with him, which means every solider in the Southwest is at his beck and call."

Thomas was surprised when Dawn Pillow weighed in. "Your government is fine with this? The murder of innocent civilians, the theft of hundreds of thousands of acres of land, not to mention having my people used as scapegoats for the destruction of Tipton?"

"They do not know," replied Diego. "Nor does my government in Mexico. Claybourne's plan is to move fast, put unbearable pressure on the politicians by enraging the public with tales of the massacres, and then to strike into Mexico swiftly and decisively."

"Can it really work?" asked Red Elk.

Professor Von Sievers set down his cup. "Oh yes," he said. "In fact, if the information we gained yesterday from our source inside Langton Hall is correct, Geronimo Rivas is looking for Miss Carnál right now. After killing her and her men, he will descend upon Tipton and murder every man, woman, and child there and then burn the town to the ground."

"And they truly think they can make the world believe that my people would do such a thing?" asked Red Elk. "How will they prove it?"

"They don't have to prove anything," said Hamish. "General Greer will be in charge of sorting out who did what, and when he tells the world that you and your warriors did the deed in the employ of Mexican raiders, the die will be cast, and you will be visited at dawn by a full regiment of US Cavalry bent on revenge. They will show your people no quarter."

A young brave leapt to his feet. "We will fight them then, and we will take many blue coats to the other world with us!"

His outburst was met with cheers and whistles from the other young men. They had lived in fear long enough. It was time to gather clubs and lances and bows and meet the American soldiers as their ancestors had done.

Red Elk raised his hand for silence, and the shouts and war cries died away. "If what the colonel and his friends have told us tonight is true, that is exactly what Claybourne and the others will want us to do. Our deaths would only prove to the world that we were trying to hide our guilt for the massacre at Tipton."

"But we would at least have our pride and die standing up like men," said the warrior who ignited the outburst. The other young men nodded their heads and murmured in agreement.

"Your pride will be small comfort to your impoverished widows and starving children," said Red Elk.

"I am afraid that Claybourne could not allow them to survive," said Diego. "No one could be allowed to live who might know the truth. Not even the children."

Thomas was surprised when Dawn Pillow walked over to the fire and spit into the flames. Her eyes flashed, and she held her head defiantly. "Are you saying we have no recourse, then?" she said, staring hard at Thomas. "That we should sit back like sheep to be led to slaughter? Can you not hear the absurdity and cowardice of your own words? Would you not fight for your people, no matter the odds against you, no matter what those who will write history might say about you in years to come?"

Thomas shook his head. Dawn Pillow's words stung. He waited for the people around the council fire to quiet before he spoke. "No, that is not what I am saying. In fact, we have a plan that we think can beat Claybourne at his own game and protect your people for years."

"So, we pack up camp in the middle of the night and flee to a reservation?" said Red Elk dismissively.

"That would do you no good," answered Von Sievers. "It would only make you look more guilty of the raid on Tipton, and the army would still pursue you."

Red Elk crossed his arms and glared into the fire. "Then, what is your plan?"

Thomas and Diego shared a glance. "You cannot beat the army in a fight, fair or otherwise," Diego said, "and you can't escape their reach by running away. There is only one thing you and your people–especially your warriors–can do that will guarantee your safety."

Every head around the fire arched forward. Dawn Pillow relaxed her clenched fists, and Red Elk took a long drink of wine and waited. Hamish clasped his hands behind his head and smiled in anticipation of what Thomas was about to pronounce.

"The Claybourne fishing tournament begins the day after tomorrow," Thomas continued. "Hundreds of important people from all over the world will be at Langton Hall for the sport and festivities and so will reporters from some of the leading newspapers in American and Europe. The finest anglers in the world will be there to test their skills. They will pay their entry fees and register for the contest at first light on the morning of the first day. Whoever catches the greatest weight in fish over the next three days will win a silver cup and $5,000 in cash."

Red Elk turned to White Moon and raised his hands, palms up. What madness was Colonel Scoundrel spouting? The Cheyenne people were at the junction of life or death, and this fool was talking about fishing? He was about to turn to leave when Thomas resumed speaking.

"You and your people cannot fight. You also cannot hide. There is only one thing you can do, something Claybourne would never expect you to do: you must attend the tournament. The press will see you there, which means the whole world will see you there. Hundreds of prominent and influential people who have nothing to do with Claybourne's schemes will also be witnesses to your presence. No one will be able to claim that you were involved with a raid on Tipton or anywhere else. You will be covered."

Red Elk was perplexed. He gestured at the warriors and elders gathered around the council fire "Us? At the largest and most exclusive gathering of wealthy white men in the West? And what do you expect us to do there, Colonel? Serve food? Clean the kitchens, or perhaps empty the latrines?" The crowd around the fire cheered the chief's words. The idea that they would be allowed to attend such an august gathering of

American and European elites who believed that the Cheyenne were barely human was laughable.

But, not to Hamish. He had been waiting for this exchange. He stood up and walked over in front of the fire. His imposing physical presence was magnified by a shock of unruly hair above a thick, tangled beard. He scanned the crowd and waited for them to fall silent. Then, in the booming voice that he used when preaching to large crowds outdoors, he called out, "Don't be barmy, man. Ye'll not be attending as servants. You and your lads are going to enter the tournament."

As dozens of astonished expressions fixed on Hamish, a burning log collapsed at the center of the fire, and the Scotsman raised his head to follow a shower of orange sparks as they trailed up into the sky. Then he let out a great laugh, and shouted, "Ye'll be fishing!"

※

Thomas and Diego left Red Elk's village at dawn. They rode southeast towards Arapahoe County to meet Demetria and Sergey at the Kansas Pacific Railroad coaling stop in Byers. At the same time, Professor Von Sievers and Hamish headed northwest to meet with Major Rhine along Box Elder Creek. Rhine would have information from Bat Masterson about the marshal's efforts to connect Claybourne to Geronimo Rivas and about Bill Cody's trip to Washington to garner support from the congressmen they would need when Senator Mack and his fellow conspirators began to clamor for war against Mexico.

"Did you arrange our schedule so that your woman would not meet your woman?" joked Diego as they picked their way across a stream that had breached a section of the coach road.

"Hadn't thought about it in those terms, but I have to confess I did wonder what might happen if a barrel of rattlesnakes and a box of dynamite were tossed together into a small closet. Dawn Pillow and Demetria are alike in a lot of ways, but each tends to be a little headstrong in the romance department."

"You know, *amigote*, your life would become far less complicated if you found one woman who could put up with you for the rest of your life."

"I thought about it once. It didn't take."

Diego grew serious. "She died, Tomás. Years ago. And she would be the first one to agree with me. Really, how many more bedroom windows do you plan on climbing through in your life?"

Thomas put his heels to Ulysses flanks and galloped ahead. "I don't know," he laughed... "how many are there?"

⁂

They arrived in Byers an hour before the train and settled into chairs at a table outside the cantina. A woman brought them beer and a plate of soft, thin pancake shaped bread filled with venison seasoned with wild onions and herbs. When the train swung around a stand of pines and steamed to a halt under the coal chute, Diego and Thomas paid their bill and walked across the dirt road to the small depot.

Sergey and Demetria were the only departing passengers. The train would reach Denver in two hours, and unless you wanted to hunt jack-rabbits there wasn't much to see or do out on this arid plain. The porter swung their bags down, Thomas made introductions, and Diego and Sergey went back to the livestock car to offload the horses.

Thomas and Demetria were silent for a moment. Then he took her hands in his. "Thank you for coming."

She leaned in and kissed him lightly on the lips. "*De nada*, my Tomás. Your journey is also mine. We each have our reasons to find these bas-tards and rid the world of their stinking existence."

He picked up her bags and Sergey's and lead her back across to the cantina. They took the same table he had shared with Diego, and Thomas ordered drinks for everyone.

Even after two days of hot, uncomfortable train travel, Demetria looked wonderful. She wore a simple dark blue cotton shirt over men's black denim trousers and boots and a hand-tooled leather vest that did little to hide her exquisite form. Thomas could have stayed there for hours, just drinking her in. Perhaps Diego was right about settling down, he mused as the server set their drinks on the table.

Then Diego and Sergey walked up with the horses, and the spell was broken. Demetria filled them in on what had transpired since she and Sergey left the mountain, and Thomas detailed the plans they made the previous evening at Red Elk's village.

"And your Cheyenne friend, she is well?" asked Demetria coolly.

Diego could not hold back a wide grin. He loved to watch Tomás squirm.

"Well enough, I suppose. I actually did not see that much of her."

"Que triste," replied Demetria. "How very sad. And after all the two of you went through together."

"Why do I feel like I am missing something important here," said Sergey. "Should I know this Dan person?"

"Her name is Dawn, *teniente*, and yes, I have no doubt you will meet her," Demetria replied.

Thomas sighed. He did not blame Demetria for unsheathing her verbal rapier, but he had never been one to indulge in chatter whose purpose was simply to slash and destroy. It was time to move on.

"There is something you both need to know right now," he said. His tone softened the sharpness in Demetria's expression. "Claybourne and his fellow conspirators met several days ago at Langton Hall to move forward with their plans." He looked into Demetria's eyes. "Those plans include your death."

Demetria did not look surprised. "Many have put me on their lists. None have succeeded."

"These people are different," Diego said. "Geronimo Rivas himself has been tasked with tracking you down and killing you. You know him as well as anyone; you know what he is capable of."

"And where is this man looking?" asked Sergey.

"That's the good news," replied Thomas. "He left for Las Cruces two days ago on Claybourne's private train. Their information indicated you were still in the area."

"Then we have time," said Demetria."It's almost a two-day rail journey there from Denver."

"I wouldn't count on us having much time,"said Thomas. "Claybourne's ears are everywhere; I expect that they discovered you weren't in Las Cruces by the time Rivas pulled out of Denver station. They probably also know you were headed this way. I'd guess Rivas got a telegram at a watering station midway to Las Cruces and that he turned around and is headed back to Denver right now."

Sergey's fist slammed on the table. *"Dermo!"* he said.

"Sorry?" said Thomas.

"A Russian curse, I believe" replied Demetria, "and apparently a good one, because he uses it often."

The server brought more drinks and asked if they wanted rooms for the night. She had two. Thomas cast a glance across to Demetria. This would be interesting.

"Yes," Demetria told the woman. "My three companions will take one room; I will take the other."

Thomas lowered his head and smiled inwardly. Apparently being within fifty miles of Dawn Pillow was enough to put Demetria off any notion of romance.

"What shall we do now?" asked Sergey.

"Tomás and I have talked about that all day," said Diego. "We're going to have to split up for a while. Rivas will not slow in his pursuit of you, Demetria. The man is really nothing more than a killing machine, and he is very, very good at his work."

Demetria watched Diego's gaze drift off into space when he said those words. Thomas gave her a look that said, 'I will explain later,' and then he picked up on Diego's thought. "Either Rivas finds you in his time and on his terms, or you and Sergey find him on yours."

The Cossack nodded. The colonel's observation made strategic sense. It was always better to be the hunter than the prey.

"He won't be hard to find," Thomas continued. "He leaves a wake of destruction and chaos wherever he goes, even if it is just breaking up a saloon or goading a poor cowhand into a gun fight. It will be like tracking a whirlwind in a Sunday service. He will stand out."

Demetria reached over and placed her hand on Thomas' wrist. "We can do this," she said quietly. "And you and Diego?"

"I will seek out Matthew Cord and invite him to tell me where he took Rosalilia," he replied through tight lips.

Demetria knew about Cord and his sadistic penchant for torture and murder. She could only imagine what kind of invitation Diego would extend to a beast like that.

"Where will you go, Tomás?"

"By now Claybourne knows I'm alive, and he can't allow that, because I know too damn much about his Mexican scheme. He will be surrounded by his own small army, and more than a few US Army troops too. Plus, hundreds of people from all over the world are descending on Langton Hall right now for his three-day fishing tournament. I can't sneak through all of that. If I want to get to Claybourne, I am going to have to walk right up to the front gate and announce myself."

Demetria raised her eyebrows. "Just like that? And what will you do then?"

He grinned. "Then… I will grab a fishing pole."

FORTY EIGHT

Langton Hall

Nickolas Buckwright stepped up to the podium on the speaker's platform at first light. Below him, hundreds of people milling around the grounds in front of Langton Hall began to loosen their coats and scarves as warm air flowed out of the flatlands and gullies that crisscrossed the prairie expanse. This was Buckwright's fifth year officiating at the Claybourne fishing tournament and the first year that the contest had been extended from two days to three. He loved everything about the event, from the smell of the fresh-sawn lumber used to build the platform to the potpourri of languages spoken by the international contestants.

Lined up behind him on folding chairs was a who's-who of politicians, wealthy businessmen, military officers, and celebrated individuals from the worlds of art and sport. Hyacinth Claybourne had spent the better part of the previous year seeking out and inviting well-known people who could help to give the event a level of social prestige that would rival any event held back east in Newport or Saratoga Springs.

The actress Lily Langtry was seated next to the governor, holding an open parasol against the early morning mist, while boxer John L. Sullivan sat with his arms-crossed and head down next to a thoroughly bored Senator Mack. Buckwright had marveled at the quantity of beer and rye whiskey the pugilist had downed the night before. Seated at the end of the second row nearest him was the author Samuel Clemens, who was holding a cup of coffee, browsing a Denver newspaper and pointedly ignoring Giuseppe Verdi, the Italian composer of *Rigoletto* and *La Traviata*, with whom Clemens had argued about American culture the previous evening.

After downing a bottle and a half of Claybourne's best port, Verdi had loudly opined to his fellow dinner guests that as long as books like Clemens' *Tom Sawyer* were among the most popular works in the nation's literature, America could not be regarded as anything more than a culturally primitive wasteland. Clemens pushed his dessert plate aside, stubbed out his cigar, and leaned forward to respond to Verdi's insult, only to be interrupted by Oscar Wilde, who had just finished three standing room only performances in Denver. The flamboyant Irishman had been in top form all evening, both delighting and mortifying the glittering assembly with his quick and witty retorts and mildly scandalous asides.

"No culture in America, maestro?" Wilde said. "Perhaps you should broaden your definition. Why, only last night, while traversing the heart of Denver in search of entertainment, I heard a Bach prelude played on a banjo in front of a saloon, and I later witnessed a comedic ballet performed by three…," he looked around the table with a wide-eyed, smiling expression that signaled that he was about to push the boundaries of propriety, and continued with, "….three of the loveliest fallen angels one could imagine. Arms akimbo, legs kicking high, bosoms jouncing in time to the tinny piano. When the ladies took their bows, hundreds of men leapt to their feet, cheering wildly. That, sir, is culture!"

Wilde's colorful description of his visit to a well-known sporting house elicited chuckles from the men and more than a few disapproving glances from the ladies. Even Noah Claybourne allowed a smile to briefly crease his face.

Verdi shook his head and tossed back another glass of port. "You make my point for me, my dear Mr. Wilde. Plunking a few notes of Bach on a riverboat guitar is a bastardization of high culture, not an example of it. And as for your dancing trollops, I hope you are not suggesting that the spectacle of a crowd of ill-mannered cowboys gawking at the legs and undergarments of a trio of frontier harlots compares in any way with opera, which is, as all educated persons know, the pinnacle of humanity's cultural accomplishment."

There was a smattering of applause around the table following the composer's reply. Wilde, however, was not prepared to concede. "The pinnacle, Signore? But isn't an opera an entertainment in which a man who gets stabbed in the back belts out an insufferably tedious aria, instead of bleeding out on the floor like any normal person would do? And where a tenor and a soprano who want to make love are prevented from doing so by a baritone? Is that the pinnacle to which you refer? Give me an organ grinder and a monkey, please. At least that audience gets honest value for their penny and peanuts."

Verdi slammed his hand on the table, knocking over his glass. But the laughter around the table confirmed that Wilde had the better of the argument.

Veridi pushed back his chair and stood up; his face was florid from the wine and his anger.

"Sir," he said to Wilde, "I understand that dining rooms are where you perform for *your* peanuts, but all witticisms aside, I have no doubt that when you die, it shall either be at the end of a hangman's noose, or in the agonizing throes of some vile social disease."

The room went silent, and a servant carrying a tray of coffees froze in place. This verbal duel had gone far beyond the kind of lighthearted dinner banter they were accustomed to.

Wilde, however, felt no sense of embarrassment or shame. He had honed his conversational skills to a sharp edge in the salons of Europe. It was impossible to insult him, and no conversation was complete until he had the last word. As for what others might think of him, that was the least of his concerns in life. "Popularity," he often said, "is the one insult I have never suffered."

Out of respect for his opponent, Wilde also stood. He placed his hands on the back of his chair, nodded in the direction of his host, and returned fire.

"Whether I die on the gallows, or in the venereal ward of some public hospital, Signore Verdi, depends on which I embrace more tightly: your bloated cultural ideals or…" he paused for effect, "your mistress."

With that, Wilde sat down, satisfied that his final salvo had vanquished the famous composer. Verdi's face darkened. He flung his napkin on the table, glared at Claybourne, and stormed out of the room. Everyone seated around the banquet table knew they had just witnessed an epic battle of wits; one they would be talking about for years. After several moments of silence Samuel Clemens raised his whiskey glass and saluted the Irishman. "By God, sir, that was a corker. A corker."

Clemens's remark had the effect of a relief valve on a pressure cooker; the emotional intensity of the past few minutes dissipated, and people began quietly chatting about what had just transpired.

"Pity about that," Claybourne said to the group, "and I am sure that Mr. Wilde meant no genuine disrespect to Signore Verdi. I am sorry he left, but I will speak to him in the morning and smooth things over."

Wilde raised his glass to his host. "Thank you, sir, and yes, you are correct, I meant no disrespect. On the other hand," he continued in a sly tone, "has it not been your observation, as it has been mine, that some cause happiness wherever they go; and others, *whenever* they go?"

At that, the room erupted in raucous laughter. Hyacinth clapped her hand across her mouth in to hold back her laughter, and the famously dignified Lily Langtry pulled a handkerchief and dabbed away the tears in her eyes. Mary Orvis rocked so hard with laughter that she spilled her tea onto the starched linen tablecloth, and John L. Sullivan used the cover of the moment to pour himself a large glass of whiskey to accompany his eleventh stein of beer. It had been a dinner party for the ages.

❖

Now, just minutes after sunrise, most of last night's dinner guests were assembled on the platform with Noah Claybourne to witness the opening of the tournament, except for Oscar Wilde, who seldom appeared in public until late afternoon. The hundreds of guests packing the compound in front of the platform had breakfasted on biscuits, cinnamon rolls, bacon and coffee, and the aroma of beef and pork roasting on giant spits drifted across the yard. At a long table flanked by the flags of Colorado and the United States a dozen men and women were busy signing up the contestants. After they paid the $100 fee, each fisherman was handed two sheets of paper and a cotton bag tied with a red ribbon. One piece of paper listed the tournament rules, the other was a map showing where on Claybourne Ranch they would be fishing that day. The bag contained their lunch; two roasted beef sandwiches, slabs of cheddar cheese, apples, and a stoneware bottle filled with Coors beer.

Each morning at daybreak the contestants would return to the registration table to receive a map to that day's location. Moving a couple hundred people to pre-determined spots around an area as large as a good size city was a logistical challenge, but it was the only way Buckwright felt he could ensure that each fisherman got an equal shot at the most productive locations. The nearest stream was an hour's ride from Langton Hall, the most distant was a two-hours away. When the contestants arrived at their designated spots, volunteers would assign them a one-hundred-yard stretch of waterway that was flagged at each end with a bright orange pennant for their exclusive use. The angler could be accompanied by no more than one assistant and one pack horse to help with gear and meals, but that person was not allowed to get within ten feet of the water. Volunteer wardens would be riding from location to location to enforce the rule, and anyone caught in violation would be tossed from the tournament.

Two contestants wore tartan kilts and woven caps, dozens were dressed in short woolen trousers tucked into rubber boots, and others had on cotton duck pants and plaid jackets. Their assistants had already loaded poles, reels, canvas or wicker creels, tackle, bait and flies, picnic lunches and canvas-wrapped water canteens onto their pack horses.

A murmur rippled through the crowd as Mary Orvis approached

the registration table. Claybourne had been pleased when she accepted the invitation to come to Colorado and become the first woman to compete in this internationally recognized event. Her appearance would generate a lot of positive press. When Orvis signed her name and turned to join Mose Tripplet alongside their horses, the dignitaries on the raised platform applauded politely. She waved to them and disappeared into the crowd.

With the final registration complete, Claybourne prepared to give Nicholas Buckwright the go-ahead to announce that the tournament was officially underway, and fishermen could leave for their assigned spots. But, before he could raise his hand, Moncton tapped his shoulder and whispered, "Boss, look, over there at the end of the registration table. It's that son of a bitch, Colonel Scoundrel."

Claybourne swung his head towards the table. Sure enough, it was the colonel. He was dressed in denim jeans, a blue chambray shirt and leather vest, and he was bareheaded. A canvas bag was slung over one shoulder, and he was holding the fly fishing rod and reel he was given by Mary Orvis. The fool hadn't even tried to sneak in, thought Claybourne. Damn his hide to hell!

"How…" said Claybourne through tight lips. "Dozens of riders have been covering every approach to Langton Hall for days, with express instructions to deal with Scoundrel if he had the temerity to show his face on the ranch."

"Looks like the colonel was a might smarter than our men," offered Moncton.

"Do you think so?" asked Claybourne. He was about to say more when he realized that Buckwright and most of his guests were looking expectantly in his direction, waiting for him to signal the opening of the first day of fishing. He would have to deal with the failure of his riders later.

Claybourne rose and joined Buckwright at the podium. He raised his arms in the air for attention and shouted, "Friends, I welcome you here for the opening morning of our fifth annual, world-class fishing competition!"

Shouts and cheers greeted his words. "Each angler has been given his–or her, in the case of Miss Orvis–map and instructions for the day. At 5 p.m. the judges will open the scales to begin weighing and recording each fisherman's catch for the day. The scales will close at 7 p.m. sharp, and no fish will be accepted after that. The winner of the competition will be announced at 8 p.m. on the third day after the weights have been tallied. The man or woman who has delivered the greatest total weight of fish will be declared the winner and will receive a silver cup and $5,000 in cash." He lifted the engraved cup from a nearby stand and held it up to the applause of the crowd.

"The festivities here at Langton Hall will commence at sundown each day," Claybourne continued. "There will be food and music, fireworks, and no doubt, a little beer." Even more cheers and shouts followed those words.

"And, I have a special announcement to make, courtesy of our good friend, the dinosaur collector, Professor Von Sievers. It seems that even the heavens are celebrating what is happening here this week. According to the professor, a great comet will appear in the skies above us tonight, one so huge and bright that it will even be visible to the naked eye during the day tomorrow. It will deliver a spectacle not seen on our planet for over a thousand years. That display will be a–"

His words were cut off in mid-sentence by the sound of gunshots, and a great commotion coming from the timber gate at the entrance to the compound. Hundreds of heads turned in the direction of the hullabaloo, and many of the guests on the platform rushed over to the railing to see what was happening. General Greer tapped his aide, and they hurried down the steps to take charge of the company of infantry bivouacked near the barn.

A thunder of horses' hooves reverberated in the compound, mixed with the battle cries of a dozen Cheyenne warriors in full war paint and dress. At their head rode Chief Red Elk in a flowing feather bonnet, bright red vest and beaded leggings. He held his reins in one hand and an eight-foot battle lance in the other. The Cheyenne swept in at such speed that nothing could have stopped them.

Moncton pulled a pistol from his jacket and went up alongside Claybourne. John L. Sullivan leapt protectively to Lily Langtry's side, and Samuel Clemons dropped his newspaper off the edge of the platform. Signore Verdi clung to the arms of his chair, frozen with fear. Why had he consented to travel to this barbaric land?

Everyone was thinking the same thing: were they under attack? Had the Indian wars flared back up after six years of peace? And where was the army?

Claybourne was furious, not fearful. Perhaps the Cheyenne had discovered his plan to blame them for the slaughter that Rivas was scheduled to carry out against Tipton. Red Elk could have come to pre-empt that plan, and perhaps even to mete out his idea of justice before that attack could take place. He watched the warriors stampede past the platform, and as they passed, he saw that none of them were armed except for Red Elk. No rifles, no hatchets, no spears. If they weren't here to attack him, what was their game?

Red Elk and his warriors whirled their horses to a racing stop in front of the registration table, where the frightened officials were glued to their seats. The old chief thrust his lance into the dirt and swung down off his horse. The other warriors waited on their horses as he pulled a leather bag from a shoulder strap and strode up to the table. The crowd held its collective breath as Red Elk opened the bag and poured a pile of cash onto the table in front of the wide-eyed registrars.

The bloodthirsty savages who had just scared the crowd within an inch of their lives hadn't swooped in to scalp the men and ravish the women.

They were here to fish.

❖

As the adrenaline levels in the compound began to settle back to normal, Claybourne huddled on the platform with Buckwright, Senator Mack, and General Greer. There was no way they were going to allow the Indians to participate in the tournament. Things like that just didn't happen. The contestants and guests who filled the compound represented the crème of American and European society, entertainment and business. It would be undignified–and possibly life-threatening–for them to have to compete against this band of primitives.

"Maybe so," Senator Mack said, "but they do have the registration fees, and I don't believe the rules for the contest included a prohibition on any particular group of people."

Claybourne looked at Buckwright to deliver a more acceptable answer. "That's correct," said the rancher. "Hell, we have two Russians, a couple of limeys, a Mexican *caballero,* and at least three Scotsmen waiting to head out to their fishing holes."

"No pygmies?" Claybourne asked with disdain.

"Look around, Mr. Claybourne," said Mack. "That Fulbright fellow is over there talking to Red Elk, and the female *Times of London* correspondent is about to swoon over them young Cheyenne bucks."

In fact, as Claybourne watched, several of his guests left the platform to mingle with the warriors. Social novelty, he concluded, an adventure they would brag about at society dinners for the rest of their lives. He also saw Mary Orvis, who was explaining the workings of a flyrod to Red Elk, and the Scots preacher, Hamish somebody or other, engaged in conversation with Colonel Scoundrel.

"Which suggests, what, exactly?" Claybourne followed up to Senator Mack.

"I think I can answer that," said an unfamiliar voice. Claybourne turned to see that Samuel Clemens had joined them.

"What are your thoughts, Mr. Clemens, or do you prefer to be called Twain?" asked General Greer.

"Oh, I am perfectly satisfied to be hailed by either moniker, though if writing a check is part of the proceedings, I prefer that it be issued in the name my parents gave to me."

Claybourne almost smiled. "Your reputation for wit would seem to be no lie, sir. I suspect you would also have carried the day against Signore Verdi last night."

Clemens took a draw on a fresh cigar. "We'll need more than wit to sort this problem out, gentlemen. I am a fair talent at reading crowds, and I'd say this one is more than fairly disposed to send our Cheyenne friends packing, even if it requires a bit of physical persuasion to get them herded in the right direction."

"And, why, precisely, do you see that as a problem?"

"Well, sir," replied the author, "in part it's because this isn't a military campaign approved by Congress, like it was against the Sioux in '76"

"We don't need to kill them," said an exasperated General Greer. "Just get their stinking carcasses off the ranch."

Clemens raised his eyebrows. Ignoring Greer's comments, he turned to Claybourne. "As I see it, sir, you aren't facing a military use of force problem here."

"No?"

"Look out there," continued Clemens, pointing to the crowd. "I'd bet that most of the folks from hereabouts would love to follow the general's lead and run those boys out of here on cactus limbs."

Greer nodded.

"On the other hand," said Clemens, "most of your honored guests would probably enjoy nothing more than to see the Cheyenne go head-to-head with the white fishermen. As for the reporters…" He gestured to where a half dozen reporters representing major American and European newspapers were in rapt conversations with the young Cheyenne men.

"In the next week or two, there will be dozens of stories about this little hurricane on front pages from Chicago to Paris. I promise you that most of the sophisticates who read those stories will be pre-disposed to take the side of the Cheyenne. No, Mr. Claybourne, you don't have a military problem. What you have on your hands is what the advertising boys would call a public relations problem. I believe Senator Mack understands that kind of situation."

Mack nodded in agreement. He hated to have to accept Clemens's premise, but the writer was correct; Americans in the East considered the frontier closed and its red inhabitants defeated and subjugated. Kicking the Indians when they were already down wasn't the American way. And besides, he was up for re-election next year, and stories that made him look like a bully would dampen his prospects for victory. No, he did not need this kind of disaster.

As for Claybourne, the events of the last few minutes probably meant that his plan to blame the attack on Tipton on Red Elk was doomed. He would have to figure out another path, and quickly.

Buckwright, too, felt a sense of urgency to get the Cheyenne problem resolved. "One way or another, we need to get this tournament going," he said. "Daylight is burning, and we need to get these folks out on the water, or we're going to miss the best fishing of the day."

"And so, my options are what," asked Claybourne. "Let the Cheyenne register? The locals might take matters into their own hands, and we could end up with a pile of dead Indians. But if we deny them entry and toss them off the ranch to keep our neighbors happy, we'll catch hell in the press. Not a very attractive pair of choices."

Samuel Clemens considered both arguments. He smoothed his mustache with a thumb and forefinger. "There might be a third way, Mr. Claybourne. I believe we can find common ground and bring both sides together."

Claybourne was interested. "What is your suggestion?"

"Allow me to address these folks. I have some experience in the persuasive arts, and all humility aside, people do tend to listen when I speak."

Claybourne considered the request. Clemens was one of the most famous men in America, and his dinner speeches had made him one of the most sought-after banquet guests in the world. Still, he could not afford to have this situation collapse; he wanted to kick the Cheyenne off his land and lay the blame for the raid on Tipton on them. In fact, if he did kick them out, it would make it that much easier for people in the east to believe that Red Elk and his men had been so humiliated that they took their vengeance out on the little town. He scanned the anglers, guests, reporters, and locals who were busy coming to their own conclusions about how to deal with Red Elk and his warriors. That pot shouldn't be allowed to boil for too long.

Noah made his decision. He would let Clemens speak, hope for the best, and then get with Moncton and Cord to deal with Colonel Scoundrel once and for all.

"Mr. Buckwright," said Claybourne. "Would you please get the crowd's attention? Mr. Clemens has a few words to say."

❖

The registrar who took Thomas's money and gave him his first day fishing assignment barely batted an eyelash when he read the famous colonel's name on the sign-up sheet. He had been registering a steady stream of dukes, viscounts, railroad tycoons, eastern publishers and even a Hungarian prince since an hour before daybreak. A lowly America colonel didn't merit much attention compared to those luminaries.

He and Hamish had edged towards the middle of the crowd just as Red Elk and his warriors hurtled into the compound. Thomas had no doubt that Claybourne had spotted him by then, which meant he had also ordered his men to make damn sure that he didn't walk away from the next visit to Tamayo Ravine. The middle of a crowd was the best place to be for the moment.

"They're parleying about something up there," said Hamish, indicating the small knot of men gathered at the front of the platform.

"They've got to decide whether to allow Red Elk and his men to enter the tournament. I know Claybourne's preference."

"Aye, he wants them dead, but them soldier boys weren't fast enough on the trigger when the Cheyenne flew through the gate, and his balls would be in a wringer if he brought harm to 'em now." The enormous Scotsman grinned. "Still, wasn't their entry the loveliest sight ye've beheld in a long time?"

Thomas was about to agree when he caught sight of Hyacinth Claybourne standing at the end of the platform closest to him. The sun was rising behind her, painting a soft golden glow around her head. She was dressed in a tight riding coat and breeches, with boots that went up to her lower thighs. He knew he was staring, but the combined effect of the early morning light, her natural radiance, and the rush of events in the past few minutes caught him off guard. She made eye contact with him, smiled, and then turned to talk with Signore Verdi.

"Lovely?" he finally said to Hamish. "Oh, yes."

The sound of a single gunshot cracking in the cool September air brought conversation in the compound to a halt. Heads turned towards the platform, where Nicholas Buckwright was laying his revolver on a wood podium. The guests behind him took their seats, and the crowd settled down to hear the announcement. Red Elk and his men stood by their horses, ready to make a run for it if Claybourne had decided they should be thrown out, or worse.

"Ladies and gentlemen, may I have your attention," Buckwright began. "I know we all want to get on with the main event, and I assure you that we will get you out to your locations as quickly as possible. Don't worry; this time of year the cutthroat don't wake up for breakfast any earlier than we do. They'll be getting hungry just about the time you are setting your first hook."

Buckwright's remarks were met with a bit of laughter and a great deal of relief. Anticipation for the start of the competition had been building to a head for days, and the surprise appearance by the Cheyenne warriors was just about enough to make the pressure cooker explode.

"Now, friends, we thought we had everything wrapped up and ready to go when our…" he paused for a moment. "Our Cheyenne neighbors decided to pay a call."

"Send the bastards home," came a shout from the crowd. "Ride 'em out on a rail," yelled someone else. A chorus of cries and curses peppered the compound, and a cheer broke out when a cowhand climbed up on a beer barrel and twirled a lasso above his head. "I got a welcome necktie right here," he cried. "Line them up, I'll decorate 'em one neck at a time."

Approving hoots and catcalls met the cowboy's suggestion. Red Elk's warriors circled around their chief, prepared to fight with their bare hands if it came to that.

Buckwright rapped the podium for order, and the crowd quieted. Behind him, General Greer whispered an order to his aide, who scrambled off the platform and trotted over to where two dozen soldiers had assembled on the steps of Langton Hall, rifles at the ready. Hamish shot Thomas a questioning glance. "In case this goes sideways," Thomas said in a dour tone. Red Elk saw the aide leave the platform, too, and looked over at Thomas with an expression that said, "This was your solution for my people? To be shot down like dogs?"

"I hear you," Buckwright said in a loud voice. "And I understand your feelings. We all have our opinions about this situation, and I assure you that Mr. Claybourne cares about what you think and is committed to doing the right thing.

"Then let's get to the hangins," shouted the cowboy on the barrel. A round of laughter and applause greeted his suggestion, and he took a mock bow.

"We actually had something a little different in mind," answered Buckwright. He looked out over the crowd, uncertain if he, too, was about to become an object of their growing frustration.

"As you all know, we have been fortunate to be able to host a number of well-known people at this year's event." He turned to the guests seated behind him. "From the world of opera, the distinguished composer, Signore Verdi." A smattering of applause rippled through the crowd.

"Of course, you all know the truly remarkable stage actress, Miss Lily Langtry, who has traveled from London to be with us." The applause continued and grew louder.

"And, John, could I ask you to stand? Ladies and gentlemen, John L. Sullivan, the finest bare-knuckle fighter on earth." Sullivan stood and waved one hand in the air to the thunderous applause of the crowd. "Thank you, John," said Buckwright as the fighter sat back down. "To tell you the truth I was getting a little worried that we might have to call on your special talents to quiet some of these folks down."

"It'd be an honor to be knocked on my arse by you, Mr. Sullivan," shouted the cowboy with the noose. The crowd roared, and the cowboy took his second bow of the day, this time a bit too low. He tumbled off the barrel and was picked up by a couple of his friends.

At least they are laughing, thought Buckwright. Maybe they'd get through this mess in one piece after all.

"There is someone else we have been privileged to welcome this week," continued Buckwright. "The author Samuel Clemens, who most of you know by *his nom de plume*, Mark Twain. I have a personal affection for his books *Innocents Abroad* and *Roughing It*, and I have read *The Adventures of Tom Sawyer* to my boys again and again. Fine work, damn fine work. Mr. Clemens has been observing our little convocation this morning, and he has asked if he might say a few words to us."

The crowd applauded, and Buckwright motioned to Clemens, who stood and walked slowly to the podium. The author was a few weeks shy of forty-seven, and his thick, wavy brown hair and walrus mustache were flecked with gray. His suit looked like he had slept in it, and when he stepped up to the podium, he halted a moment to put a match to his ever-present cigar.

"War is about to break out, and Claybourne sends an author to calm the crowd?" Hamish asked. "A little mad, that."

"Or a little genius," replied Thomas. "Claybourne can't afford for this event to go south. It means too much to him and to his scheme. If Clemens can lower the temperature a bit, so much the better for everybody." As he said that, he noticed that the soldiers had stepped down from the porch and were now only a dozen yards from the circle of Cheyenne warriors surrounding their chief. He could not conceive of anything the author might conjure up that would dissuade this crowd from dealing with the Cheyenne in their own way. For the first time that morning, he wished he hadn't left his revolver in Ulysses's saddlebag.

❖

FORTY NINE

Langton Hall

The prairie landscape, cold and gray and purple only minutes earlier, was warming to a palette of cornflower blue and browns by the time Clemens and Buckwright shook hands. The author stepped to the podium and briefly raised one hand to shade his eyes against the rising sun. There was chattering in the crowd as people tried to sort out what to expect from the famous man of letters. In truth, Clemens was wondering the same thing himself. He took a long draw on his cigar and set it on the edge of the podium. Then he turned to acknowledge his host, faced the crowd, and began to speak.

"My friends," he began, "forgive me if my remarks seem a bit unprepared. The fact of the matter is, they are completely unprepared. Not only that, but I will confess to you all that in my many years of delivering well-seasoned speeches to diners whose bellies are overflowing with good food and even better drink, this is the first time I have risen from a seat on the dais at the conclusion of a rodeo spectacle the likes of that we just witnessed."

A bit of polite laughter greeted his opening remarks. He touched his hand to his forehead. "My respects to you and your warriors, Red Elk. You ride like the wind."

Red Elk acknowledged the compliment with a nod, and Clemens continued. "Some among you may be wondering why I of all people on this stage would be asked to speak at such a time. That would be especially true of the journalists among us this morning who assume that what the characters in my books said about Indians was what I believed in my heart about them. I submit to you that any conclusion along those lines is simply a function of the journalist's inability to discern truth from fiction. By way of proof of that statement, I encourage you to read the stories about our Cheyenne friends' ride into this compound a few minutes ago when they appear in the paper in the next week or so. You were here. You saw exactly what transpired. But I promise that when you read the story on the front page of the *Times* next week, you will wonder how you managed to miss the extravaganza these reporters will describe. How did you not see the ferocious and bloodthirsty warriors attacking innocent, unarmed civilians? Where were you when a handful of brave soldiers and cowhands risked their lives to stop the attackers in their tracks and bring them to their knees?"

Fulbright and his fellow reporters were bunched together in front of the platform, notebooks in hand, pens at the ready to capture Clemens' remarks. He was always good copy. But his frontal attack on their integrity had them glaring with indignity instead of scribbling notes about his comments. The author could not help but notice their discomfort.

"Now, I see I have captured the attention of the scribes among you who will be telegraphing their fantastic version of events to their editors this afternoon. I assure you that their feigned outrage concerns me not in the slightest. I have been the recipient of their so-called even-handed journalism too many times to fall for their fainting spell.

Let me share an example: a few years ago, I was accused by a major eastern newspaper of loading an Indian up with beans that had been lubricated with nitroglycerin, and then sending him in an ox wagon over a stumpy road along the shores of Lake Tahoe."

The crowd roared with delight at the imagery.

"That bit of slander was bad enough on its own, but the fabulist pretending to be a journalist was not satisfied with one stab in my back. No, he had to go on to fabricate an even more outrageous punchline to the story. '*In reply to my query as to whether the story about the nitro-soaked beans and the Indian was true*', wrote the reporter, '*Mr. Clemens, in a voice more suited to an aggrieved schoolmaster than a noted author, replied, "Such a thing, on its face would be impossible, of course. After all, no one would risk oxen in that way."'"*

Nicholas Buckwright had to hold his breathe to stop laughing, but most of the people on the platform and in the crowd had no such reservation, and Clemens had to stop his speech until the gales of laughter subsided enough for people to hear him again.

"You would think that the reporter would have wrapped up the story at that point and moved on to some other fresh assassination against my character," he went on. "Sadly, when one of these budding Shakespeares become enamored of even the briefest of his own ruminations, stopping him from digging the hole deeper is almost as hard as taking aim at a single fly in the dead center of a swarm buzzing around a pile of buffalo droppings." The author paused for effect. "In plain terms, friends, once they get a taste for manure, reporters can't give it up."

Hamish slapped Thomas on the back and joined the crowd in another round of uproarious laughter. Only the reporters standing sullenly at the edge of the crowd were silent.

Clemens took another puff on his cigar. "No, this dedicated reporter had not milked the last drop of sensationalism from the story of the unfortunate Indian and the nitro-lubed pinto beans. In the breathless conclusion to his story, he added, '*Never once during our interview did Mr. Clemens express the slightest regret or remorse for what must have been a particularly gruesome death for the poor Indian when the explosive beans ignited in his intestines. Only the oxen were the beneficiaries of his compassion. What a sad commentary on a man who some regard as a giant of American literature.*'"

Clemens looked out across his audience. When their laughter died to a whisper, he said, "In all fairness to the truth, which is something to which I aspire in my work, I must add this: it is actually true that I have been a party to and a witness of the volatile explosions that can result when a sufficient quantity of beans are packed into the intestines. Frequently, in fact. I say this as someone who has dined with Her Royal Highness at Windsor Castle, and with presidents, potentates, and politicians around the world. Especially politicians. No person living is immune from the causes or safe from the consequences of this most fundamental of chemical reactions. It is as natural as the air we breathe." He waited a moment, and then added, "and especially of the air we do our best *not* to breathe."

He winked in the direction of his audience and concluded with, "and if the little runt of a reporter who created this fairytale had been honest, he would have acknowledged that while nitroglycerin might enhance the pyrotechnics of the event, it is not a necessary ingredient for this particular stew to make its presence known, no matter how much perfume and cigar smoke might be circling the room when an eruption occurs."

Clemens paused and took a moment to relight his cigar. Senator Mack leaned over to Noah Claybourne. "What the hell is this fool up to? How is this getting us anywhere?"

Claybourne didn't acknowledge the comment. His patience was ending as fast as his temper was rising. If Clemens didn't wind things up quickly, Noah was going to have to take matters into his own hands. As he went over the possible actions open to him, he made eye contact with Colonel Scoundrel, who was standing alongside the Scots preacher in the center of the crowd. Thomas stared straight back at him with a calm, relaxed expression, not at all what Claybourne would expect from a man who only had a few hours to live. Claybourne turned his gaze back to Clemens, who had lit his cigar and resumed speaking.

"...which brings us to this auspicious moment in the history of the relations between the white man and the red," Clemens was saying. "I don't pretend for an instant that the gulf between the races isn't vast; too much blood has been spilled on both sides over these past fifty or more years to just let things go and hold hands at a picnic."

"You damn right," came a shout from the back of the crowd. "As long as there is a single Indian left breathing in the territory none of us can sleep easy," yelled another voice.

"Well, now," answered Clemens with a wry smile, "I can't speak to your sleeping habits, but I will remind you that Colorado isn't a territory anymore; it's a state. Statehood means that some modicum of civilization has been established here and that folks have decided that it's better to settle down and seek a little prosperity and peace than it is to seek more fights with the tribes."

"And you think these vermin are civilized?" came another voice from the crowd. "They don't understand the meaning of the word!"

Clemens smiled and squinted against the sun as it peaked over the hills. "That wouldn't surprise me, friend, seeing as how so few people of the so-called educated class understand it either. I'm a simple man, and my take on it is this: it seems to me that what we call civilization is really nothing more than the limitless multiplication of unnecessary necessities."

Faces in the crowd looked perplexed at that remark, so Clemens took another tack. "That just means that I think we confuse our ability to provide a lot of goods and services that none of us actually needs to survive with what it means to be civilized. Take Congress, for example, or that new telephone device that is popping up everywhere. The former is a pit of barbarism and graft, and the latter will spell the end of human intimacy. Trust me on that."

His remarks brought smiles and understanding nods from the crowd–and a bit of throat-clearing displeasure from the politicians seated behind him.

"No, friend," Clemens went on, "you are wrong when you say the red man is not civilized. They labor to produce only what they need to survive, and they aren't burdened with so many unnecessary necessities the way we are. They've got the whole civilization thing down to a neat little package. No fat, no corruption. Sounds pretty admirable to me.

"Which brings us to this bright and glorious morning at the home of our most generous host, Mr. Noah Claybourne." The crowd applauded Claybourne, and he stood to acknowledge their appreciation.

"And so, good people," said Clemens, "here we are, on the cusp of beginning three days of fine sport and good company. The invitation to the tournament did not specify to what degree or other of civilization you must have attained to pay your $100 and join in the contest. It simply said, 'all anglers are welcome.' I look out into the crowd and see men from Scotland and Ireland, England, Germany, Russia and Wales. I see ranchers and tradesmen and even a banker or two with their fishing poles at the ready. No authors, I am ashamed to note, but perhaps we can rectify that oversight next year. The fairer sex is represented, too, in the person of Miss Mary Orvis, and I am even told that one of the most famous heroes of the war between the states will be trying his luck on the water. Is that true?" He looked out over the crowd.

"Colonel Thomas Scoundrel, are you among us?"

Thomas stepped forward and raised his hand. He would normally have hated being recognized this way, but it provided him one more layer of protection against any sudden attack from Claybourne's men-at least while he was with this crowd. There was wide applause at the mention of his name, and he nodded in thanks for the recognition before stepping back alongside Hamish.

"A finer assembly of representatives from so many nations and cultures would be hard to imagine," Clemens said. "As to the question of allowing Chief Red Elk and his associates to join the contest, how can we deny them that privilege when we have opened the doors to people of different beliefs from so many lands? Of course," he added with a smile, "that is unless those who have already registered for the contest think the Cheyenne are just naturally better at catching fish than they are. Is that the case, ladies and gentlemen? Are you afraid these boys will whip you good and hard if they are allowed to compete?"

A rowdy chorus of "no!" and boos met Clemens's challenge. "Not bloody likely, mate," shouted the lone Australian competitor. "Bring 'em on, I'll show the red buggers what a real fisherman can do."

Clemens seized on the opening provided by the Australian. "Good on you, friend," he exclaimed. "There's nothing like beating somebody fair and square at something to show the world who really has earned the right to be called the best." He puffed his cigar, glanced back at the guests behind him, and then into the crowd waiting expectantly on his next words. It was time.

"We don't need to nitro up the beans or ride anybody out on a rail. What we need to do is get out there and show the world that real champions don't duck the difficult situations. They run right at them!"

His words earned a solid round of cheers and applause. Clemens turned around towards Claybourne and his guests, then back to the crowd. He gripped the sides of the podium, stood up tall, and in his loudest voice called out, "What do you say we sign these fellas up and get to fishing?"

Amidst the cheers and shouting, Red Elk led his warriors over to the registration table to make their 'Xs' and receive their maps.

Thomas and Hamish took advantage of the pandemonium to slip through the crowd, mount their horses, and ride out in the direction of their assigned stream.

❖

FIFTY

Streams and lakes on Claybourne Ranch

The osprey soared in great, lazy circles hundreds of feet above the prairie. Fall was approaching, and a million years of instinct was awakening in the bird, encouraging it to prepare for the long migration to its South American breeding grounds. Preparation meant building extra stores of energy, and that required flying over dozens of creeks, rivers, and lakes in its daily search for fish.

This morning, though, the osprey's world looked dramatically different than usual. Dozens of men on horseback were traversing the low hills and grassy flatlands in all directions and planting themselves on the banks of the bird's favorite hunting grounds. Their tiny camps were mushrooming across the prairie, marked by colorful flags and small canvas huts. Wherever the bird flew, from lake to creek to brook-fed pond, men were standing on the banks or wading into the water with poles and nets. Others sat on camp chairs set back from the water's edge or busied themselves tending to campfires.

The osprey was not used to this kind of competition. Still, the instinct to hunt, and to begin the journey south to find a mate who would return with him in the spring was more powerful than any concern he felt for his safety. Today, the humans were going to have to share the water with him.

❋

Thomas snapped his line into a pool at a bend in the creek where the water flowed around a partially submerged rock, just as Mary Orvis taught him. He was about to whip it back and repeat his cast when a flash of brown and white swooped down towards the middle of the creek directly in front of him. He watched as a giant osprey hovered a moment, stretched its talons out in front of its head, and then plunged into the water. A second later, the bird emerged with an eight-inch trout clasped in its leathery claws. The osprey flapped its wings a few times, rose into the air, and carried its breakfast across the creek to a limb on a dead tree.

"I'm doing this all wrong," he called back to Hamish, who was pouring a cup of coffee at the fire he had built the requisite ten feet from the bank of the creek.

"Did ye mean the fishing, or this damn hide-and-seek ye're playing with Claybourne?"

"A little of both, I suppose. Diego is on Matthew Cord's trail, and Demetria and Sergey are on their way to Tipton to alert the town to Claybourne's plans. Major Rhine says that Bat Masterson is headed this way with a couple of federal marshals, and I have no idea where Bill Cody is. I just feel like I could be doing more."

"Aye, you could, but as long as you are in this tournament you are visible to the public, and Claybourne can't lay a hand on ye. We'll pack up early, and be among the first back to Langton Hall, unless you had some notion of trying to win this damn contest. You can mix with the crowd and do a little look-see then. Folks'll be drinking and dancing soon enough, which means they'll be talking. We'll learn plenty, ye can count on that."

Thomas nodded and checked his line before casting again. "No plans to win, but as long as I'm here I might as well not embarrass myself."

"How do you suppose Red Elk and his lads are doing?"

"I heard one of the judges say that Buckwright was sending them to a lake where there isn't so much as a single live polliwog to be found. Apparently, letting the Cheyenne in the tournament was humiliating enough for him and Claybourne; the idea that they might actually win was more than they could stomach."

Hamish warmed his coffee with a pour of whiskey from his saddlebag. "In my experience, Indians have a way with nature that we cannot begin to fathom. Nay," said the Scotsman with a shake of his head, "it's way too early in the day to be counting those boys out."

❖

It might have been too early to dismiss the Cheyenne's chances in the contest, but when Thomas counted only eleven small to mid-size trout in his creel that afternoon, he knew his first day in the tournament had been a bust. He hadn't forgotten that the reason he was in the contest was to get information that would bring them closer to finding Rosalilia, but at the same time, he was a gambler, a highly competitive personality who didn't like to fail at anything.

The contest warden who came by their stream at 3 p.m. was surprised to see he and Hamish already packing up, but he signed off on their map as required by contest rules and wished Thomas better luck on his second day.

As they neared Langton Hall, a few of the other contestants swung onto the road beside them with their catches hanging off the sides of their packhorses. Spirits were high, and when Mary Orvis rode over a hill with Mose Triplett, the smile on her face told Thomas that at least one contestant had enjoyed a very good day on the water.

They rode through the gate just after 5 p.m. amid the sounds and smells of a summer fiesta. A trio of banjos was performing on the speaker's platform, and servers were carrying platters of beef, pork, barbequed chicken, and tamales to set on tables around the compound. Baskets of fresh bread and tortillas were being kept warm on grates above low fires alongside kettles of baked beans and piles of roasted, late-summer corn in the husk. Children scampered around with bags of popcorn and caramel apples on sticks, and, at the very center of the compound, an open tent covered a dozen kegs of beer that were chilling on slabs of ice provided by the Coors brewery.

Eight brass and iron scales from the Howe Company of Vermont had been hauled over by the registration table, and judges were starting to weigh and record the days catch. Thomas was mollified to see that several other anglers had done about as poorly as he had, so he felt a little better about getting in line to have his paltry nine pounds of trout officially recorded. As the judge handed him a receipt, Mary Orvis and Mose set three large fabric creels on a scale. She was already being trailed by a reporter, and a small crowd gathered around when the judge announced that she had brought in forty-two fish, at a total weight of twenty-seven pounds. The crowd applauded, and Mary looked past the reporter to smile at Thomas. He returned her smile and then joined Hamish at the tent where the kegs of iced beer were being tapped.

The scales would be open for another two hours, which is when the real party would begin. He planned to use that time to gather all the information he could about the whereabouts of Matthew Cord and possibly even find some leads to Rosalilia's location. Then, he and Hamish would meet at the campsite being set up by Professor Von Sievers in the small tent city that was popping up outside the gates of Langton Hall.

"Keep a sharp eye, out, Thomas," counseled Hamish as the Scotsman left to meet with a local rancher who was reported to have seen Cord only a week ago. "Claybourne is watching your every step, and if you wander off alone, one or another of the bastards who work for him will try to slip a knife between your ribs."

Thomas managed a grim smile and then accepted a ceramic jar filled with cold beer from an elderly Mexican woman who was filling and handing out jars as quickly as she could move.

He was about to take his first drink when a familiar voice said, "And I thought you only drank wine."

He turned to see Hyacinth Claybourne. She was wearing a brown cotton skirt with a blue bolero vest over a starched, high collared white blouse. Her hair was done simply, parted in the middle and falling to her shoulders. He was struck again by the fact that even standing still, Hyacinth radiated the refined energy and charisma of a prima ballerina–or, given who her father was, perhaps a more apt comparison would be to a leopard who is poised to leap.

He raised his beer to her and took a sip. "Any port in a storm, you know. May I get one for you?"

She nodded, and he shouldered his way through the pack of men around the beer tent, returning a minute later with her drink.

"Shall we walk?" she asked.

They took a turn through the crowd, stopping for a moment to watch a juggler toss balls into the air and set them whirling around and around to the delight of group of children who clapped and cheered each time he added another ball to the mix. They swung around the weigh-in scales, where a long line of fisherman stood waiting to have their catches tallied, and wandered to the edge of the graveled compound, where one of Claybourne's prize stud bulls was on display in a special corral.

"It doesn't seem quite right, does it?" said Hyacinth when they paused to look the gigantic bull over.

"What is that?"

"Such a magnificent creature, bred from a long line of other prize studs, wasting away in this silly pen instead of doing what of God and nature intended him to be doing every day."

"Well, in his defense, I would say that even the most adept practitioner of his rather unique talent has to take a break every now and then."

"Really," said Hyacinth in a soft, low voice. She touched his forearm. "How very sad for him… and for the willing partners who lose out because the poor boy needs a nap."

Thomas knew that he was being drawn into the dance, and, for a moment, an image of Demetria sitting beside him on the balcony of the hacienda in the Las Cruces mountains stirred in his mind. He had been completely taken with her, but after the night that she bathed in front of him while he was tied to the bed, there had been no further signals from her that suggested a romantic encounter was in the offing. Their relationship had become all business, and if there was one thing that Thomas E. Scoundrel was not accomplished at, it was business.

"We all need a nap from time to time," he finally said.

"And do you, Thomas? Is it time for your nap?" Hyacinth leaned in close and brushed her lips lightly across his.

"I had one earlier," he said with a smile. "I couldn't fall asleep right now if I tried."

"Von Sievers comet makes its appearance tonight," she said. "With the fireworks and bonfires going on down here, I suspect it will be better viewed from a hilltop. Why don't I have the kitchen prepare a meal for us, and I'll ask the stables to hitch a matched pair to a carriage. We can ride up the hill and watch the comet without all these distractions. With champagne, of course."

"Of course."

"Meet me at the stables in an hour," Hyacinth said. "I'll bring a blanket for the chill."

She squeezed his arm and took pains to let her breast brush against him when she turned to walk away.

❖

Darkness was folding around them as Thomas drove the team to the crest of a grassy hill a half-mile from Langton Hall. Hyacinth pointed to an oak tree whose outstretched branches would provide cover from the evening dew, and he parked the carriage and staked the horses out to graze. When he leaned into the wagon to fetch their picnic, he noticed that there was a pile of blankets and pillows laid out in the back. Either she got chilled easily, or she had made this trip before and knew how to prepare.

He hauled two wicker baskets and an ice-filled bucket over to the blanket Hyacinth was spreading beneath the tree. Below them, lights from torches and lanterns were beginning to twinkle all around Langton Hall, and the faint sound of guitars and concertinas drifted up their way with the breeze. The ice-bucket contained two bottles of Pommery & Greno Brut champagne and two crystal flutes. As he uncorked one of the bottles, Hyacinth laid out a spread that included thin-sliced roast beef with mild horseradish crème on toast, along with fresh-sliced peaches and an assortment of cheeses. They were famished, and, in short order, the food was gone and the second bottle of champagne was open.

It was dark now, and the sounds of revelry from below mixed with the chirps of crickets and a few late-season tree frogs. Thomas scanned the cloudless sky to the northwest, just below the crescent moon where Von Sievers said the comet would make its appearance. It only took him a minute to see a smear of curved white light moving at a swift pace towards the southeast.

"Look," he said to Hyacinth, "there, halfway between the horizon line and that point directly above us."

She scooted over against him on the blanket and pressed back against his chest as she turned her head skyward. Her hair smelled of violets, and her perfume reminded him of the exotic floral aromas that permeated the air in the coastal village he had lived in on Tahiti. He brushed her hair from the back of her neck and began to softly kiss it from below her ear to the top of her shoulder. Hyacinth purred and raised one hand to loosen the buttons on the front of her blouse so he could continue his kisses around her neck and across her upper back. Then she turned her head and he leaned forward to kiss her on the lips.

Suddenly, a stream of fireworks began to rise from behind Langton Hall, exploding in whirls of red and silver pinwheels that continued to arch higher and higher in the air with each new volley. He wrapped his arms around Hyacinth and pulled her back tight against his chest. As the fireworks spread across the sky in a shower of blues and greens and shimmering reds, he caressed her full breasts through her silk chemise and continued to lavish her neck and creamy shoulders with kisses.

"Just a minute, my darling," Hyacinth said. She stood and walked over to the carriage, returning a moment later with two pillows and several thick blankets. She spread out the blankets and propped the pillows against the base of the oak tree. As a splash of iridescent fireworks popped across the sky above them, she patted the pillows. "Lay here," she said in a soft, throaty voice. Thomas did as he was told, laying back with his head on the pillows. Hyacinth stepped away, and all he could see above him were cascading fireworks, the crescent moon, and the great comet as it traveled unerringly on its ceaseless journey across the galaxy.

Then a shadow, all curves and soft angles, appeared in the darkness in front of him and knelt down. Hands pulled at his boots, unfastened his trouser buttons, and pulled them down and off his ankles. Fingers worked his shirt buttons and stroked his chest. Finally, wordlessly, the form straddled his legs, and lowered itself onto him.

He wrapped his arms around her lower back and helped her begin to move rhythmically up and down and back and forth. Then he reached up to feel the heat of her breasts and then pulled her face down to his for a long, deep kiss. She sat back up and planted her palms on the blanket on either side of his legs so that she could lean back and ride faster and faster. Her breath came in short, labored bursts, and he felt every muscle in her body begin to tense as she neared her climax.

Far below the hilltop oak under which they lay, a final crescendo of fireworks rose majestically into the starry night from behind Langton Hall. The riot of colors soared upwards in a wild frenzy of glittering light and explosions. Almost on cue, Hyacinth thrust down hard on Thomas one last time. She sighed and then wilted onto his chest.

They lay quiet for several minutes. Thomas would have preferred to keep the match going, but something inside told him that she had no intention of helping to deliver the grand finale to his own fireworks show.

❖

The pyrotechnics were over, and the party around Langton Hall was ebbing to a close when Thomas reined in the carriage in front of the stables. Hyacinth hadn't said a word during the journey down the hill. Now, she leaned over and gave him a perfunctory peck on the cheek before climbing down from the carriage and walking briskly away towards the main house. He handed the horses over to a stable groom and walked past the bonfires towards the tent encampment outside the gates where Hamish and Von Sievers were probably already bedded down for the night.

As he neared the pen in which the prize bull was held, he felt compelled to stop. The bull was standing in the dead center of the corral, his coal black hide rendering him almost invisible in the weak light coming from Langton Hall. Thomas rested his hands on a wooden cross post and stared hard into the massive beast's eyes. The bull raised its great head and contemplated the man in front of him with what seemed like a sense of curiosity. Or, was it more a sense of familiarity, a recognition of a kindred spirit, wondered Thomas. One tired, empty stud bull to another.

Regret was a foreign emotion to him. And yet, as he nodded to the bull and turned to walk towards the timber gates and the darkness beyond, he felt a hollowness in his soul that he had never experienced before.

❖

Noah Claybourne watched from the window of his study as his daughter stepped out of the carriage and hurried towards the main house. Her sexual habits had never been of any real interest to him; he turned his head the other way each time she used up another one of his cow hands before sending them packing, hat and hard-on in hand. This time, though, was different. Riding up into the hills with Colonel Scoundrel in full view of a crowd of people was her way of punishing her father for not letting her toy with the colonel the first time he had come to their home. She knew about the incident at Tamayo Ravine, and she was intelligent enough to know that the colonel's fate was sealed the minute he walked through the gate and registered for the tournament. None of that mattered to her, though. The fact that she had been able to scratch her itch *and* slap her father in the face at the same time by simply lifting her skirts was undoubtedly a personal triumph for her.

Hyacinth had miles to go before she would be ready to manage the ranch, he reminded himself for the hundredth time. He sighed and poured another glass of port. Then he pulled the curtains wider and watched Scoundrel stop in front of the prize bull, pause a moment, and then disappear into the ink black night.

Perhaps it was best that the colonel had enjoyed a romp on his last night on earth, Claybourne decided. And even better that it had been with a woman as cold and unpitying as his daughter.

There was a tap at his door, and he turned and motioned for Moncton to enter. Claybourne watched as his employee nervously turned his hat over and over in his hands. He had every right to be worried, thought Noah.

"There will be no mistakes tomorrow," Claybourne said.

Moncton nodded slowly. "None," he answered.

FIFTY ONE

Carbon Creek on Claybourne Ranch

Two hours after daybreak on the second day of the tournament, Thomas was casting his line in waist deep water on a gravel-bottomed stretch of Carbon Creek. The chest pockets on his rubber waders were filled with flies and hooks given to him by Mary Orvis, and three fat cutthroat trout were already cooling in the wicker creel on the mossy creek bank across from him.

Hamish had picked up the map to today's location from the judges so that Thomas would not have to tempt fate again by showing up in Claybourne's front yard. Protective crowds or not, Thomas knew that Claybourne wanted him dead and would be looking to make that happen as soon as possible. He waved to Hamish as the Scotsman mounted his horse for the ride to Von Siever's cave, just an hour from where he would be fishing. Major Rhine would arrive tomorrow, and Hamish would catch up on any information he had gathered from Bat Masterson and Demetria. With luck, Diego would also join them. The preacher had been reluctant to leave Thomas alone on the creek, but both men knew that the time for getting information about Rosalilia was growing short.

❖

A half hour after Hamish and his horse were swallowed up in the pine forest that swept down from the neighboring hills, Thomas changed out his rig to a setup that Mary told him was her sure-fire bet for catching morning trout. He was snapping the pole behind his head to make his first cast with the new fly when he heard the screech of a red-tail hawk from the other side of the creek. The glare from the rising sun and the shine off the creek surface made it impossible to see the bird, so he turned back to complete his cast, but in the instant before his fly hit the surface, he heard the unmistakable sound of horses galloping through water.

Two riders were bearing down on him from about seventy-five yards away, straight out of the rising sun. That was an attack strategy he had seen used by the Comanche, who were probably the best horsemen in the world. He held up one hand to shade against the bright sunlight and watched as both men raised their lever-action rifles and pointed them in his direction. He dropped his pole and started to push through the fast-flowing water towards the creek bank, where his holstered Colt was slung on the end of a fallen tree branch. The current made the going slow, but he knew that the riders were about to go from knee-deep water to a waist-deep stretch, so their forward momentum would be slowed down too.

When he was ten yards from shore the crack of the first rifle shot echoed across the creek, followed by two loud splashes as the riders and their horses hit deep water and began to flounder. Thomas felt a brief instant of relief and took a moment to turn his head upstream. Sure enough, the horses were struggling against the deeper water, but that did not stop one of the riders from getting off another shot that hit the water just a few inches from him. He was only six feet from the bank and a few seconds from retrieving his revolver and evening out this fight.

Then he heard horses galloping on dry land, and his heart sank to see two more riders racing right at him along the near-side creek bank. Four attackers, not two, were about to box him in. The riders on land pulled their pistols when they were about fifty yards away from his campfire and began peppering the creek with .45 caliber bullets.

He knew he wouldn't make it to his revolver. He thought about diving into the water and letting the current take him downstream, but his rubber overalls would quickly fill up with water and hold him in place like a sea anchor. He couldn't stay in the creek, and he couldn't leave it. It looked like Claybourne was about to finish the job his men had botched at Tamayo Ravine.

❖

More gunshots rang out, and a bullet whizzed through the side of his waders, just below his chest. Anchor or not, he was going to have to take his chances swimming downstream. He took a deep breath and dove to the bottom of the creek, pulling himself across the smooth gravel in what he hoped was the right direction. He could see through the crystal-clear water as bullets streaked all around him and smashed into rocks and submerged branches. But, as he had feared, the waders ballooned with water and made it almost impossible for him to move.

Horse legs and hooves began pounding the stream bottom all around him, and his lungs screamed for air. One of the hooves connected with his left side at the same instant his lower right leg was grazed by a bullet. If I only have a minute to live, Thomas decided, I'm not going to spend it on the bottom of this damn creek.

He yanked at the shoulder straps of the waders with every bit of strength he had left, fighting the burning in his lungs and the pain in his side and leg. Somehow, in the chaos of gunshots and stomping hooves, he pulled the waders down and off his boots. Staying under water would be ideal, but his head was pounding, and he felt weak from lack of oxygen. Whatever fight was left in him was going to have to happen on the surface.

He pulled close to the underbelly of the horse closest to him, reached up, and yanked with all his might on the boot in the stirrup a foot below the surface. Then he bent his knees and flung himself straight up. He gasped for air when his head breached the surface, but he kept his hold on the attacker's boot. As his eyes came into focus he saw that the man had a revolver in one hand. He pushed against the side of the horse and raised his hands up to the man's waist. He heard the revolver's hammer being pulled back, and immediately tightened his grip on the man's belt and pulled down as hard as he could. The man tumbled into the creek, which made the animal thrash and kick even harder than it had been.

Thomas was on the side of the horse opposite the two riders on the creek bank. They were holding their fire for fear they might hit their companion. He took advantage of the brief respite to yank the man's head out the water by his hair and to begin pounding him repeatedly in the face. The revolver had fallen into the creek and was lost, but he was able to pull the man's knife from his belt as he continued to pummel him.

Bright red blood from the man's mouth and nose mixed with the clear stream water around them, but before he could maneuver the knife up to a place where he could stab his attacker's throat, the other rider in the water swung his horse around and charged. Like the men on the creek bank, this man could not risk firing his gun for fear of hitting his comrade. So, he rode his horse right at Thomas, hoping to knock him away. But, the horse resisted, and instead of charging it held its position and swung its head wildly from side to side. The horses became entangled, and as the man struggled to hang onto his rifle with one hand and the reins with his other, Thomas delivered a final blow to the head of the man he was fighting in the water. A moment later the man stopped moving, and Thomas let his limp body float away with the current.

Then he pushed his way between the horses and plunged his knife into the rider's thigh. The man pulled the knife out and tossed it into the water before leaning forward and kicking the riderless horse, which backed away from the brawl and began making its way to the safety of dry land. With the other horse no longer providing him with cover, he was exposed to the riders on the bank. He had no other weapons, and he knew it would only be a moment until they would be able to take a clear shot at him. He grabbed at the attacker's shirt, trying to shake him off his horse, but the man was strong and simply pressed his legs harder into his horse's flanks.

He continued to pull at the man with all his remaining strength, but the bastard wasn't letting go. The only good news was that it took two hands to cock a lever action, and since he had to use his left hand to hold his reins and fight to hold his horse steady, he was no better off than Thomas, at least for an instant. He didn't hesitate long; the man swung his rifle around in his right hand, grasped it by the barrel, and smashed the stock against the side of Thomas's head. He splashed back into the water but quickly pulled himself up and pressed against the flank of the horse again. The minute he pulled away from the horse he would be an easy target for the riders on the bank.

The man raised the rifle butt again and struck Thomas hard on the shoulder. He clung tightly to the saddle and tried again to reach up to the man's waist and pull him down. Suddenly, the sound of multiple rifle and pistol shots exploded all around them. Had the riders on the bank decided to take their chances and shoot at him, even if it meant hitting their friend?

The rifle butt slammed into his head again, and his vision blurred. He didn't know how much longer he would be able to hold onto the saddle and fight to pull the man into the water. Then he heard more splashing in the water, close to where he was fighting. He looked over the top of the horse as the rifle butt swung his way again. As the walnut stock glanced off his jaw, he saw two amazing sights; first, a brown and white pinto was charging across the creek right at him, and he saw the muzzle flash from a rifle firing in his direction. It looked like another one of Claybourne's men had weighed in to end this battle once and for all. But there was something about the horse that didn't seem right. Then the pinto was only a few feet away, and his sight cleared enough to make out the rider. It was Demetria Carnál. She was controlling her horse with her legs and firing a repeating rifle at the riders on the bank.

The noise and intensity of the gunfire increased and seemed to be coming from all directions now. Thomas wondered just how many people had joined in the battle. Before he could make out the action on the creekbank, though, the rider above him swung his rifle one more time and cracked it against the side of his skull. His grip on the saddle loosened, and he started to fall back into the water. As he did, the rider released his left hand from the reins and used both hands to cock his lever action. He wouldn't miss this time.

In that same instant, Demetria swung her pinto in front of his attacker and lowered her barrel at his gut. But, before she could pull the trigger, one of the attackers on the creek bank took aim and fired at her. The bullet slammed into her shoulder, and she pitched sideways off her horse and into the creek, face down.

Thomas felt like he was falling backwards into the creek in slow motion. As he fought to remain conscious, a dark shadow arced high in the bright blue sky above him. It sailed gracefully through space and crashed onto the head of the rider he had been battling. The man dropped the rifle and fell off his horse, a look of disbelief in his eyes. His expression was understandable: he had just been taken out by the flying skull of a juvenile Tyrannosaurus rex.

Thomas tried to shake off the searing pain and dizziness caused by the last blow to his head. He couldn't make sense of the dinosaur skull, but that confusion would have to wait to be sorted out. He couldn't hold himself up any longer. He fell on his side in the waist deep water and tried to prepare himself for what he knew was his inevitable death.

At least the shooting has stopped, he thought. The last thing he saw before he faded into darkness was the body of Demetria Carnál floating serenely past him in the cold, clear water.

Thomas came to with a start and bolted upright in his bed. A lightning bolt of pain surged through his head, and he fell back.

"The lad is awake," he heard Hamish say.

A moment later he was encircled by friends: Von Sievers, Sergey, and Mose Tripplet stood around Hamish, who was seated comfortably in a rocker with a double barrel Greener shotgun on his lap.

He reached up and felt the bandages that were wound tightly around his head. "How?" he asked, "Where?" and, "Demetria. Tell me about Demetria."

"One answer at a time," said Von Sievers. "Demetria is over there." He pointed across the room to a cot on which Demetria lay, covered in blankets and being ministered to by Von Siever's wife.

"The bullet passed through her shoulder. It's a clean wound, Thomas. She needs to rest, but she should be fine if it doesn't get infected."

Sergey grinned. "It will take a lot more than that to take her out of the game, Colonel."

The pounding in his head was receding, and he was able to look around just enough to realize that he was in Von Siever's mountain side cave.

"What time?" he asked.

"It's after 9," Von Sievers answered. You've been here since before noon."

He looked at Mose. "How did you get here? Why?"

"That's easy, Colonel. Miss Mary saw that you weren't at the weigh-in. She sent me snooping, and a deaf-mute Indian boy got my attention and guided me out here."

That was the second time the Cheyenne boy had come to his rescue. "What happened at the creek?"

"I met the professor a few minutes after I left camp," answered Hamish. "He was hauling a load of specimens to a museum buyer and wanted to get them delivered before everybody showed up here later in the day. Demetria was riding along with him. We were just about to turn east when we heard shooting coming from Carbon Creek. I figured you'd gone and got yourself all bungled up in something, so we thought we'd better pay you a visit. Miss Carnál lit out ahead of us, and we followed in the wagon as fast as we could. Sergey was a good mile back, but he caught up quick and struck at them two men on the creek bank faster than a mongoose springs on a cobra. First time I ever saw a Cossack at war. It's not a sight I will ever forget."

The huge Scotsman touched his forelock in respect, and Sergey smiled in return.

"I saw her in the water," Thomas said. "But I also saw something so strange I'm almost afraid to mention it."

Mose propped a pillow behind his back, and Sergey handed him a glass of brandy.

"And what would that strange thing of yours be?" asked Hamish, with a wink to Professor Von Sievers.

"I know I was about done for out there in the water, but it looked for all the world to me like a dinosaur skull fell out of the sky and knocked Claybourne's son of a bitch off his horse."

His friends laughed. "Did more than knock him off his horse," said Hamish with a grin. He reached down beside his rocking chair and lifted the T-Rex skull. "My friend here was the last thing that bastard ever saw in his pitiful life."

Even in his pain, Thomas couldn't help but smile. "You didn't have a gun?"

"Nah, and you should have seen the expression on the professor's face when I reached into the wagon and grabbed the prize of his collection."

"The most expensive prize," added Von Sievers.

"Aye, all that is true enough. But that arsehole had cocked his rifle and was going to pull the trigger, so I tossed the closest thing at hand. Wish it had been a caber, mind you, but a fifty-pound dinosaur skull was the best I could do."

"Fifty pounds?" said Thomas.

"And at fifty feet," laughed Von Sievers. "Has to be a world record of some kind."

As the men laughed, Katarina came over with a bowl of soup and scooted everyone away. She spooned the soup into Thomas's mouth slowly, and when he was done, she brought a bedpan to him and started to slip it beneath the blankets. He put a hand gently on her wrist and said, "I'll take care of my business when the time comes. In the outhouse, if you don't mind."

"We'll see about that, big talker. But if you mess in my bed, you won't like where that T-Rex skull ends up."

The men burst into laughter once again. Thomas turned his head to look over at Demetria, who was sleeping soundly. Then he closed his eyes and drifted off.

⁂

FIFTY TWO

Langton Hall & Claybourne Ranch

Noah watched from the front porch of Langton Hall as the contestants lined up to receive the maps to their fishing locations for the third and final day of the competition. He was pleased to see that Colonel Scoundrel was nowhere to be seen. There had been no word from the men he sent to Carbon Creek yesterday to deal with Scoundrel, but that was as expected. After their job was complete, they were to join Geronimo Rivas for the attack on Tipton.

The Mescalero half-breed was one of the few people he knew would always get the job done, especially if it involved wanton slaughter. Rivas would strike the small town late tonight while the final celebration of the fishing tournament was in full swing in front of Langton Hall. Claybourne, Senator Mack, General Greer, and the other Mexican scheme conspirators would be highly visible among the revelers. Not a shred of responsibility for the horrors that would soon be visited on the men, women, and children of Tipton could be assigned to them.

He accepted a cup of tea from a passing servant and turned to go back into the house where he was about to meet with the others to confirm their next moves. The senator, Congressman Renton, and assistant Secretary of State Geve would return to Washington as soon as the news of the massacre at Tipton broke, where they would lobby hard for an immediate intervention by US troops against the raiders in the northern Mexican states. General Greer would also leave at once to assume personal command of US forces in the Arizona Territory and await permission from President Arthur to take the battle directly into Mexico. Claybourne's plans had not gone perfectly, thanks mostly to Demetria Carnál's failure to flatten the town of San Rafael, but he approached war the same way he did business; adapt to changing circumstances quickly and make as few mistakes as possible. Do that, he believed, and victory will always be yours.

Despite Carnál's treachery, he was confident that he had acted quickly enough to keep the public and political momentum building in support of military action against Mexico. Rivas would deal with the bandit bitch soon enough, but for now, the only thing that mattered was the big plan and the big prize. In a matter of months the United States would control an enormous swath of Mexican territory from Baja California to the Gulf of Mexico. While General Greer enforced American control with an iron fist, Claybourne's political army would press hard for permanent annexation of the Mexican lands. That might take several years, but in the meantime, he would hold absolute sway over all mining, timber and ranching in the region. American troops would enforce his contracts, and the American taxpayer would foot the bill.

As he passed by the portrait of his father in the hall, a half-smile crossed his face. The elder Claybourne could never have amassed the human or financial resources to pull off anything even remotely as spectacular as what his son was about to do. Noah closed the study door, set his tea on a table, and prepared to issue the final orders for the crowning achievement of his life.

❖

"You're becoming my best customer, you know," Major Rhine said to Thomas. They were standing beside Rhine's wagon outside the entrance to Von Siever's cave complex, where the Major had arrived with news and supplies shortly after dawn.

Thomas adjusted the bandages that were wrapped around the top of his head. His left eye was swollen almost shut, and his jaw ached mightily. But he was alive, thanks to the friends who came to his rescue on Carbon Creek yesterday.

"I'm glad to help keep your business afloat," he said, "but I really am going to do my best not to have to shop with you quite so frequently."

Rhine grinned and handed him a new Colt revolver and three boxes of bullets. "You've still got your Winchester"

"Yes, Hamish gathered up Ulysses after the fracas, and most of my gear was still intact."

Rhine leaned back against the wagon and lifted his coffee cup from the open tailgate. His voice became serious. "You're up against at least three dozen of Claybourne's men at Langton Hall and a full company of army infantry, to boot. Make it one hundred forty of them. There are a half dozen of us, that is, if Diego makes it back from his search for Matthew Cord. You're a gambler, Thomas, you can read those odds."

"Any word about Bat Masterson or Bill Cody?"

"Masterson telegraphed from Trinidad two days ago. He is on his way with two federal marshals he says we can trust, but I don't know when they will arrive. As for Cody, he sent a telegram from St. Louis four days ago. I could tell he didn't want to take a chance the message might be intercepted. It pretty much just said he was on his way."

Thomas shook his head. "So, what you're saying is that we might end up with a total of ten men to take Claybourne on?"

"If that. The bastard owns every judge and politician in the state and half of the lawmen too." He set his cup down and raised one hand to shield his eyes against the rising sun. "We can't take them head on, Thomas. We have to find another way."

"And what about Tipton?"

"Sergey and Demetria got word to them about Rivas's plan to attack. That piss ant is going to find out that Mormon farmers know how to fight. Most of them were in the war, so it's not going to go anything like the massacre at Monteverde. They'll be ready, and any man that didn't have a weapon yesterday will have one today because that's where I'm headed now." He pointed to three cases of rifles and boxes of ammunition in his wagon. "My contribution to the effort. Three-hour ride there, three back. I'll be at Claybourne's by early evening."

Thomas stepped forward and shook his friend's hand. "I don't know how to thank you."

Rhine climbed up into the seat and took up the reins. "How about you just stay alive long enough to pay your bill?" Then he flicked the reins and the wagon began to move. "I'll be there, Thomas."

❖

Thomas watched the wagon head down the narrow gravel road and disappear around a bend. Then he went back into the cave, where Von Sievers was cleaning his shotgun and Katarina was making more coffee. Sergey had left an hour earlier to meet Dawn Pillow at Red Elk's village to get ready for what might happen when the tournament ended and the Cheyenne lost the protection that being in the contest had provided.

He went across the cave and pulled a chair close to Demetria's cot. She had been feverish and in and out of consciousness through the night. Katarina was concerned about how much blood Demetria had lost, but all she could do was change the bandages each time they soaked through and give her a tablespoon of opium-tinted laudanum every few hours when her pain ramped up. He lay his hand gently on Demetria's wrist. She turned her head and gave him a soft smile.

"I am so very sorry," he said.

"For what?" she replied in a hoarse voice. "For not taking advantage of the opportunity I gave you up at the hacienda when I finished my bath?" She tried to laugh but could only cough.

"Perhaps," he said, giving her arm a squeeze. "Just don't expect me to be such a self-disciplined gentleman the next time."

"Will there be a next time, Tomás?"

He leaned forward and softly kissed her forehead. "I promise."

Demetria's eyes closed and she went back to sleep.

He went over to the table where Von Sievers was cleaning his weapon.

"This isn't your fight, my friend. Katarina is here and so is your work.

Things with Claybourne will come to a head soon enough. Take care of yourselves, and I will come and see you when the dust settles."

Von Sievers did not reply. Instead, he pushed his chair back and motioned for Thomas to follow him outside. He walked over to the adjacent cave and went to the back where several cases of dynamite were stacked against the limestone wall.

"Help me with these, would you?" asked the professor.

He lifted one case, and Thomas took another. They carried them to a wagon parked outside and set them gingerly on a pile of loose hay. Von Sievers packed more hay around the boxes and then covered them with a heavy tarp.

"You fixing to free up some new specimens?" asked Thomas.

"Something like that. What about you?"

"Hamish went to Langton Hall to get the map for today's location. I'm meeting him at the junction. Diego might be with him, so I expect we'll go to our spot and figure out how to get to Claybourne. That might be possible with hundreds of people celebrating the end of the tournament."

"And if you can't get to him?"

"This is our best chance to find out where Rosalilia is being held. If we don't do that soon, I'm afraid…" His voice trailed off, but he didn't have to finish his sentence. Von Sievers had come to the same conclusion himself.

The professor put his hand on Thomas's shoulder. "Take it from someone who has spent his entire life looking for unlikely things in unexpected places. Sometimes, your gut is the only thing you should listen to."

❁

Two hours later, Thomas sat waiting on Ulysses at the Denver junction. It was almost noon and hot for mid-September. He was unfastening his canteen when two familiar figures rode out from a stand of pines to the west and headed in his direction. He took a long drink and patted Ulysses on the neck. "It's time, boy."

Diego looked him up and down when he and Hamish pulled close. "I didn't think it possible that you could have looked worse than when I saw you after your visit to the bottom of the ravine. But, once again, Tomás, you have proven me wrong."

Thomas smiled despite himself and wheeled Ulysses alongside Diego. "What news?"

"Matthew Cord is nearby. No doubt he is on his way to report to his boss."

"Where did you learn that?"

"I ran into one of his men at a small cantina on the outskirts of Denver. He was happy to share the information with me."

Hamish laughed. "Oh, aye, as happy as a man can be at the point of a gun."

"It was actually a knife," said Diego, "and where I had it pressed made it easier for him to sing, which he did in a lovely falsetto voice."

"And where is this man now?" asked Thomas. "Should we talk with him some more?"

Diego shook his head and tapped his horse's flank with his boot. Hamish and Thomas matched him, and the three men began moving along the trail.

"The answer to your question, Tómas, is, no, we can't speak to him now. When I left him in the stable behind the cantina, he was no longer in possession of his tongue. Or his balls. He told me what he knew. That was enough."

They rode along the trail for half an hour, then turned east and climbed a grassy hill. Below them was the small lake that was indicated on the map Hamish was given by a tournament judge. They rode down to a flat area near the water and tied their horses to a pile of fallen limbs. Hamish unpacked a bag filled with venison and vegetable-stuffed pancakes that he had grabbed from the kitchen tent at Langton Hall, and the three men sat on rocks and ate in silence.

"You know, Thomas," Hamish finally volunteered, "if one of them tournament wardens happens along while the three of us are this close to the lake, ye'll be in violation of the rules, and they'll disqualify you from the contest."

Thomas grinned. "Was I in danger of winning?"

※

Hamish started a fire and prepared coffee while Diego and Thomas shared everything they knew, from the status of the trail hands and troops protecting Claybourne, to what Diego had learned about Cord's movements during the past week.

"He has made two trips to the west," Diego said. "He leaves just after daybreak and returns not long after dark. He wasn't going into Denver, and I'm pretty sure he doesn't have a woman stashed away somewhere near, so the only reasonable guess I can make is that he was checking on Rosalilia."

"Why would he feel he needed to do that," wondered Thomas. "Doesn't he trust the men who must be watching her?"

"Or maybe he is simply looking after his employer's ace in the hole,"said Hamish as he walked over with two cups of coffee. "Claybourne's men have cocked up one job after another. They couldn't kill Thomas, though God knows they have tried enough times. Demetria is still alive, and Red Elk and his warriors have the run of Claybourne Ranch, at least for another day. He's got to tighten control, or risk losing everything."

"That makes sense," said Thomas. "When the time comes for him to apply pressure to government officials in Mexico City, he will have to prove that Rosalilia is not only alive, but unharmed. Otherwise, they will know that if any of their family members are kidnapped, there is no point in negotiating. Cord's job is to make sure she is safe."

"I will thank him for that just before I cut his heart out," said Diego. "What is our next move?"

"We will ride into the compound with the other contestants tonight. It will be chaos, the biggest night of partying yet, and we'll use that cover to our advantage. You get to Cord; I will find a way to get to

Claybourne. Hamish will watch my back; Rhine will watch yours."

The Scotsman nodded. He was glad they were done with the planning and waiting. It was time to knock some heads together. "Aye, get to them, that's all well and good. But once ye have them by the scruff of their necks, what then?"

Thomas and Diego exchanged a glance. What then? What if neither Cord or Claybourne would tell them where Rosalilia was being held, despite their most persuasive questioning? These were men of enormous personal discipline and great physical strength to boot. They weren't going to fold like cheap $2 suits.

"Itzcoatl often said that people bend, or they break, or they hold their ground depending on how important the fight is to them," Diego finally said. "If Rosalilia means more to them than their grand scheme to take control of northern Mexico, I don't expect they will break. If she isn't, by the time they see a few of their fingers lying in the dirt in front of them, they will talk to save their hides."

Hamish looked at Diego. "But it won't save them, will it?"

Diego shook his head and sipped his coffee.

❖

It was late afternoon when Hamish and Diego broke camp and began the ride to Langton Hall. Thomas would follow a half hour later and make his approach from the east. Although his heart wasn't in it, they decided that the best way for Thomas to stay alive for the ride across the crowded compound would be if he came in with fish for the final day's weigh in. He was recovering at Von Siever's cave yesterday and so hadn't gone to the weigh-in. Now he would take his chances that Claybourne wouldn't have him shot on the spot in front of hundreds of onlookers. When Sergey arrived, he would figure out a way to move against Claybourne.

By the time Hamish and Diego rode out he had a dozen fish in his creel. He was sure to come in dead last among the tournament's hundred competitors, but at least he would have a cover for riding past the gate guards and into the compound. The further in he made it, the better his chance of getting to Claybourne.

He packed up Ulysses and swung into the saddle. His eye was getting better, but his vision was still a little blurry. There was no fresh blood around the bandages covering his head, so he unwound them and tossed them into the campfire coals. It was a two-hour ride to Langton Hall, and there wasn't a cloud in the sky. A pair of buzzards were circling high off to the east, but this time it wasn't him they were keeping a hungry eye out for. A light breeze floated off the prairie, just enough to set the big bluestem and indian grasses waving like an ocean current. This was a beautiful place, and for just a moment he allowed himself to wonder what it would be like to settle down here with Demetria. But, only for a moment.

❖

An hour later, the trail veered to the west and followed along the base of a brush-capped ridge. He saw movement at the top of the hill to his right, about one hundred yards off. A four-horse team topped the crest from the eastern slope, and he could make out two men sitting on the bench seat of an open freight wagon. He reined up as they continued down in his direction, and a minute later, he saw that it was Von Sievers driving the wagon, with Red Elk on the seat beside him. Trotting alongside the wagon was Salamander, the deaf-mute boy who had come to his aid the night Red Elk punished him for his moonlight tryst with Dawn Pillow,and tied to the back were two saddled horses.

The professor and Red Elk waved at Thomas, and as the wagon pulled closer, he was struck by the wide grins on their faces.

"You're done fishing?" he asked Red Elk when the freight wagon braked to a stop next to him.

"Four Bears has taken our catch to the weigh-in," replied the chief, "not that there were many fish in the pond that was assigned to us." He struck a match on the side of the wagon and lit a pipe. "But we were here, and we have done our part."

"Not quite all of it," said Von Sievers with an ever-widening smile. "There is one last thing we need to do before you take your catch in to be judged."

Red Elk laughed, and Salamander climbed up on the back of the wagon. The boy looked anxiously at his chief, but the old man raised his hand and motioned for Salamander to stay put.

"What are you doing in the wagon?" Thomas asked.

Von Sievers and Red Elk exchanged smiles, and the chief waved his hand at Salamander, who began to pull back a corner of the heavy canvas tarp covering the four foot by eight foot freight bin.

"Colonel Scoundrel," said the professor in an official tone of voice, "we think you had a pretty good day on the water."

Thomas looked at the corner of the tarp that Salamander had just pulled back and sucked in his breath. "What in the holy hell…"

Von Sievers, Red Elk and Salamander burst out in laughter at the sight of Thomas's wide eyes and open mouth. His reaction was understandable: beneath the tarp was a glistening mass of fresh trout, stacked in a heap at least three feet high. As Thomas shook his head in disbelief, Salamander peeled the tarp back several more feet. The entire wagon was filled, stem to stern, with what must have been more than a thousand fish.

Thomas took off his hat and ran his hand through his hair. "How? Where? Who did this?" was all he could think to say.

"Red Elk knows a small lake that was not far from the pond he and his men were assigned to fish," said Von Sievers.

"My people have pulled fish from that deep lake for hundreds of years," added the chief. "It is fed by underground streams that flow from springs high in the mountains. In bad times it has been a source of fish to salt and dry for the winter, and in good times we let the fish multiply so that it will be there when we are in need."

Thomas shook his head. "And Claybourne's people knew nothing about this place?"

Red Elk set down his pipe and spat on the ground next to the wagon. "What do his kind know of the land and the spirits and the animals who dwell upon it?"

"But, how? How were you able to catch so many fish in one day?"

Von Sievers reached behind his seat and pulled out a short length of primer cord and a stick of dynamite. "Science," he said with a grin.

"You blew those fish out of the lake?"

"You helped," replied the professor. "We loaded those two cases at my place this morning, remember? Red Elk and his men spent three hours tossing lit sticks into the lake from a canoe, starting at the center and working their way to the shore. Each time another stick blew, we waited a few minutes for the shocked fish to float to the surface. Then it was simply a matter of scooping them up with nets and piling them in the wagon under a wet canvas tarp."

"But the contest wardens," said Thomas. "How could they allow you to do this? It has to be a violation of the rules."

Now it was Red Elk's turn to laugh. "One warden came by the morning of the first day of fishing to check on us," he said. "I made sure that several of my warriors were sharpening their knives as he approached, while others were throwing spears and tomahawks at targets attached to trees."

"Targets that just happened to look like white men?" said Thomas.

Red Elk nodded. "The warden rode within fifty yards of the pond, waved to me, and then put his heels to his horse and raced back to Langton Hall. That was the last time we saw any tournament officials."

"And I have actually studied the tournament rules carefully," added Von Sievers. "No mention of dynamite anywhere in them."

Thomas patted Ulysses on the neck, shook his head, and chuckled. "But why give them to me? Why doesn't Red Elk take them in, and score a win for the Cheyenne? That would turn polite society on its head."

"You mean on its ass," said Von Sievers. "Yes, it would be quite a victory. But we were thinking in more practical terms."

"When you take the wagon to the judging table," continued Red Elk, "and are declared the winner, Claybourne won't be able to touch you. The newspaper people will swarm around you for hours.

And while that is happening, my men and I can put a lot of distance between Langton Hall and ourselves. You win, we win."

Thomas had to admit to himself that it made sense. "What are the judges going to think? They'll have to assume I cheated somehow."

"They can assume all they like," said the professor. "But in the absence of a report from a warden or some other eyewitness, they'll have to take your word for it. You are an officer, and by definition, a gentleman. Just tell them the bait you used is an old family secret, one you are honor-bound not to disclose. That way you won't have to lie."

Red Elk knocked his pipe against the side of the wagon and filled it with tobacco from a pouch at his side. "The assumption, Colonel, will be that you are the best god damn trout angler in the world."

❖

Thomas helped Salamander to cover the fish up while Red Elk and Von Sievers untied their horses from the back of the wagon. Salamander secured Ulysses and hopped up on the seat beside Thomas. The chief and the professor would get to Langton Hall first, where the weigh-in for the final day of the tournament would end in three hours. Thomas waved goodbye to his friends and shook the reins. The heavily laden wagon lurched forward in the soft afternoon air and then settled into a steady gait along the narrow dirt road.

❖

FIFTY THREE

Langton Hall & Claybourne Ranch

Three days of world class food and wine, stimulating dinner conversation, and a parade of characters worthy of a new book were not enough to keep Samuel Clemens from growing restless. As he smoked a cigar and sipped a noble port on the guest platform in front of Langton Hall, he was thankful that the fish being weighed near the judge's table were the last of the tournament.

He had enjoyed his time with Lily Langtry and the boxer John L. Sullivan, whom Clemens found to be a very well-read chap for one who made his living beating the hell out of people. The composer Giuseppe Verdi, in true fashion, had continued his tedious libretto on the superiority of European culture to the point that Claybourne's guests would turn and walk the other way if the Italian happened to head in their direction. As for that Irish dandy Oscar Wilde, if Clemens had to endure one more evening of the playwright's sophomoric *bon mots*, he might take the pistol down from above the dining room fireplace and shoot the jackeen dead.

The only real excitement since the tournament began had been when the Cheyenne warriors swept into the compound with their feathered headdresses, scarlet-ocher face paint and ribboned battle lances. The experience was electrifying, though the number of small puddles that bloomed on the platform and in the gravel around the compound as the raid was unfolding confirmed to the writer that for some, the prospect of being scalped or ravished had an immediate and deleterious effect on bladder control. That episode, at least, had provided him with fodder for a tale or two and might even have made the trip west worthwhile.

He settled back into his chair and accepted another pour of wine from a server. The golds and reds of late afternoon had softened into twilight purples, and dozens of torches were being lit on the grounds around Langton Hall. A great yellow harvest moon was rising, and the crowd milling around the bonfires and food tents was in a fine mood. A fiddle was playing somewhere, and he could smell the glorious scents of a roast pig being raised out of a trench and unwrapped.

Directly across the stage, Noah Claybourne was holding court for several reporters. Clemens could only imagine what the event cost the man to put on. The tournament entry fees would barely cover the cost of prizes and expenses for the judges and wardens. Add to that enough fresh food to feed hundreds of people for three days, plus the rivers of beer, wine, and whiskey that flowed non-stop–and all the help necessary to serve it up– and the price tag would be serious, even for a land baron as rich as Claybourne.

He continued to observe the activity around the food and beer tents, where he noticed two other people with whom he had enjoyed interesting conversations over the past few days. The German brewery owner Adolph Coors was supervising the off-loading of another dozen barrels of beer. Coors had a fascinating personal story and impressed Clemens as probably the hardest working individual he had ever met. Mary Orvis was also a charming dinner companion. She had taken the time to show him her wagon filled with flies, reels, poles and fly-making materials. It was the kind of complex, artistic pursuit that Clemens had always been attracted to. He waved at Mary as she stepped away from the scales after weighing in her final day's catch. Word around Langton Hall was that she was the angler to beat.

He was reaching for a match to re-light his cigar when a runner pushed his way through the crowd and leapt up onto the stage. The man rushed over to Claybourne and motioned for him to end his interview with the reporters. Noah broke away from the little group and walked swiftly over to the platform railing. Clemens looked in the direction the runner was pointing, just inside the tall timber gates that marked the entry to the compound.

Claybourne stiffened, and his countenance darkened at the sight of a tarped freight wagon making its way slowly across the compound. As the wagon got closer, Clemens saw that Colonel Thomas Scoundrel was driving the four-horse team. Sitting next to him was a Cheyenne youth with a smile as wide open as the Colorado prairie.

A dozen heavily armed men surrounded the wagon, matching its pace as it rumbled forward. Clemens recognized several of them as Claybourne's ranch hands, though why they were encircling the colonel's wagon like it was carrying a prisoner to the gallows was a mystery. He took another glance at Claybourne and saw that the man was clenching the top of the wooden railing so hard that his knuckles were turning white. His face was skewed in anger, and his lips were trembling. The author had hoped that a few more story ideas might pop up before this event was over; as he shifted his gaze from Claybourne to Colonel Scoundrel, he determined that he had just been dropped into the middle of a corker.

Like everyone else in the crowd, the author was trying to make sense of what the colonel and the Cheyenne boy were up to. He checked his pocket watch; it was six minutes till eight, at which time the scales would close, and the tournament would officially be over.

The crowd parted for the wagon and fell into line behind it as it inched towards the judging table. Most of the people in attendance knew who Colonel Scoundrel was, and there had been a lot of speculation about him missing yesterday's weigh-in. Whatever was in the wagon would tell the tale.

❃

Thomas pulled the team and wagon parallel to the weighing table, set the brake, and acknowledged Nicholas Buckwright and the other judges with a salute. As the wagon came to a stop, Hamish stepped forward out of the crowd alongside Adolph Coors and one of Coors' burliest employees. The huge Scotsman reached under the springs on one side of the wagon and pulled out the heavy L-shaped wooden crank that was stored there, while Coors pulled another crank out from under his side. They inserted their respective cranks into the receivers at the front of each side of the wagon and waited for the signal.

Thomas looked down from his seat and caught Mary Orvis' eye. She was standing next to Mose Triplett by the scales with her arms crossed and a quizzical look on her face. He smiled at her, nodded to the judges, and then signaled for the lift to begin. Salamander scrambled over the tarp to the back of the wagon and loosed the ties at either side and then returned to his place on the seat beside Thomas. Hamish took a deep breath and began to turn his crank, and Coors and his man leaned together into their crank on the other side.

A silence fell across the compound as people strained to see what was going to slide out from under the canvas tarp when the back of the wagon was cranked up to a sufficient angle. John L. Sullivan stepped over beside Clemens and nudged his arm. "I have no idea," said Clemens, "but judging from the number of Claybourne's guards circling around the rig, I wouldn't be surprised if it was full of gold bullion."

Noah ignored Lily Langtry, Oscar Wilde, and Verdi as they came chattering up to the rail alongside him to watch the drama play out. Instead, he glared at Moncton with an expression that told him to get down into the crowd and close to Scoundrel. The hired gun didn't have to be told that if the colonel wasn't dead soon, Claybourne would do the job himself, and probably cut Moncton's throat in the process. As he climbed down off the platform, Moncton heard General Greer instruct his aide to have a squad of soldiers assemble behind the judge's table in case the arrival of the wagon meant trouble.

❖

Hamish put his back into turning the wooden crank, and Coors and his man bent into their work with every ounce of strength they could muster. Adolf and his employee routinely lifted one-hundred and thirty-pound barrels of beer, and their arms were as thick as heavy tree branches. Hamish planted himself like a mighty oak, pulled with everything he had, and a moment later the back of the freight wagon creaked and began to rise. After a minute of slow, steady cranking, the three men's exertions raised the back of the wagon to a 30-degree angle.

The crowd pressed in close to the wagon, forcing Claybourne's men against the wooden sides until there was nowhere for them to go. Up on the platform, there was complete silence. Noah was standing as rigid as a marble statue, but of all the hundreds of people waiting to see whatever came tumbling out the wagon, he alone did not care. No matter what Colonel Scoundrel was up to, he would be dead before the sun came up. Rivas and his men would have flattened Tipton by now, and his conquest of northern Mexico would proceed as planned.

Clemens watched Claybourne's face. He studied people for a living, and he was damn good at it, but this was one façade he could not penetrate. The man was a sphinx.

The author turned back to the freight wagon, which was lifting into the darkening sky one mechanical click at a time. He was impressed by the brute strength of the three men turning the cranks, especially the bearded giant who was raising one side all by himself. He made momentary eye contact with Colonel Scoundrel, who was standing up on the seat with the Cheyenne boy watching the freight box make its ascent. Clemens touched his hand to his forehead, and Thomas returned the salute before turning back to watch the back of the wagon inch higher and higher.

Light from torches, bonfires and the full moon illuminated the compound and sent shadows dancing across the gravel and up the sides of Langton Hall. The sound of a server dropping a tray of dishes startled the crowd, and then a smattering of shouts and laughter rose from the people who were closest to the wagon. Hamish stepped back from his crank and motioned for Coors and his man to stop their work.

The Scotsman yelled, "Now, Thomas!"

Thomas and Salamander dropped onto the wagon seat. Thomas snapped the reins, called to the four-horse team, and lunged the wagon a few feet forward. As he did, the deluge was unleashed.

Clemens started to laugh as hundreds, maybe thousands, of fish began to slide out of the wagon and splash onto the gravel in front of the judge's table. The crowd surged back to avoid being crushed under the weight of the trout, but two of Claybourne's men didn't leap quickly enough and were swallowed up beneath a pile of wet, slippery fish. Their companions set down their rifles and waded through the mounds of trout to rescue their friends, to the delighted roar of the crowd.

Buckwright and the other judges climbed on top of their table and watched in astonishment as the fish tsunami continued to flow out of the back of the wagon. On the guest platform, everyone but Clayborne was laughing and slapping one another on the back. John L. Sullivan forgot himself for a moment and lifted the famously proper Lily Langtry up by the waist so she could get a better view of the spectacle. But before he could put her down and sputter out an embarrassed apology, Langtry kissed him on the cheek and raised her arm to wave to Thomas.

Chaos engulfed the area around the wagon. People scooped fish up and threw them in the direction of the scales, and they cheered Thomas and Salamander when they stood on the wagon seat and waved. Somehow, Mary Orvis made her way over, and Thomas leaned down and gave her a hand up. When she was standing beside him, he yelled out, "I'm so sorry. You should have won this contest."

She could barely hear him above the din of the crowd, but in reply she simply leaned forward and planted a kiss on his lips. "Oh, Thomas," she shouted in reply, "this has been the most exciting part of this whole damn tournament. It's wonderful!" She hugged him and then turned towards Mose Triplett, who had come up alongside the wagon with her. Mose helped her down, and then the former soldier turned outdoor-adventure-leader grinned at Thomas and led Mary away from the crush.

The crack of a gunshot thundered in the evening air, followed by another, and heads turned towards Nicholas Buckwright, who was standing atop the judge's table. He holstered his revolver and raised his hands for quiet.

"Ladies and gentlemen. It's eight o' clock sharp. The fifth annual Claybourne fishing tournament is officially over. Before we announce the winner and get to celebrating, I have three things to say. First, let's offer our thanks to Mr. Noah Claybourne for his generosity and hospitality this past week." The crowd applauded and shouted their approval at the stage, which forced Claybourne to acknowledge them with a curt smile and a wave.

"Second," Buckwright continued, "you're going to have to forgive us judges, but there is no way in hell that we are going to take the next three days to weigh the fish that Colonel Scoundrel has just delivered." He turned to the other judges and said, "And third, given the size of that pile of fish, and with my fellow judge's concurrence, I vote that we proclaim Colonel Thomas Scoundrel the winner of the tournament."

All four judges raised their hands. Against the background of deafening shouts and applause, Buckwright carried the winner's silver cup over to the wagon and handed it up to Thomas, who lifted it high in the air for the crowd to see.

"I'll get your cash prize from Mr. Claybourne later this evening," Buckwright told him. "As I am sure you can imagine, folks are going to have a lot of questions about how you were able to catch so many fish. What would you like me to tell them?"

Thomas smiled. "The bait I use is an old family secret. When I snag one, he blows up to the surface so fast he never knew what hit him."

❖

A trio of fiddles and guitars struck up a jig over by the beer tent, and, at the invitation of Buckwright, folks began scooping up trout to take back to their homes and camps. Thomas handed the silver cup to Hamish for safe-keeping and immediately found himself surrounded by

Tanner Fulbright and three other reporters. He waved to Salamander and watched as the boy began filling a large basket with fish to take back to the village.

As Fulbright was asking his first question on behalf of the readers of the *Times of London*, Moncton squeezed through a line of onlookers and headed for the little group encircling Thomas. When he was ten feet away, Claybourne's hired assassin unsnapped his holster and began to withdraw his gun. No one in the crowd noticed. Moncton locked eyes on Thomas, his intent clear. He was going to kill Scoundrel right here, in front of hundreds of people, consequences be damned. Two thoughts flashed through Thomas's mind: first, his own revolver was in a saddlebag with Ulysses, wherever Hamish had taken him. Second, in the midst of this raucous crowd, Moncton might be able to pull off his murder without getting caught. The sound of a single shot would be swallowed up in an instant with all the noise that was echoing around the compound.

Then Moncton was only six feet away and his revolver was pointed straight at Thomas's gut. Someone bumped against Moncton, and he was briefly pushed off his path, but he quickly righted himself. Fulbright kept talking, the other reporters bent their heads and scribbled at their notes, and Thomas realized that the stream of people elbowing their way over to Coors's beer tent were preventing him from moving in any direction. Now only three feet separated him from his murderer.

Moncton's expression was impassive. No smile, no sneer. He was focused on taking aim, and in the blink of an eye, he would be so close that it would be impossible for him to miss. Thomas steeled himself for the bullet that was about to tear into his body.

Suddenly, a look of complete surprise crossed Moncton's face. He blinked, shook his head, and then stumbled to the ground onto a pile of fish, two feet from where Thomas was standing. Folks had been slipping and falling in the slimy mess all over the compound, but they got back up quickly, wiped the glop off of their clothing, and went about their business–usually to the laughter of their friends. Moncton lay still where he fell. The haft of the hunting knife protruding from his side explained why.

Thomas looked up from Moncton's corpse and saw his executioner standing a few feet behind the body. As people continued to rush past without paying attention to the dead man, Salamander looked calmly into his eyes. He nodded slowly, turned, and melted into the crowd.

Fulbright hadn't missed a beat with his questions since Moncton stepped out of the throng and came at Thomas. Neither he nor the other reporters were aware that anything was amiss with the man who had slipped onto a pile of fish right in front of them. Most importantly, Thomas thought, none of them had seen the face of the Cheyenne warrior who came to his rescue.

FIFTY FOUR

Langton Hall

Hamish materialized out of the stream of people flowing back and forth across the compound. He looked down at Moncton's body and then made eye contact with Thomas, who was about to respond to a question from Fulbright about the tournament.

"I'm sorry, Tanner," Thomas said, "but we're going to have to finish this interview later." The journalists from New York, Chicago, and St. Louis shrugged off the dismissal by the contest champion; there were plenty of famous people to interview at Langton Hall tonight. They flipped their notebooks closed and went off in search of Claybourne's other notable guests to get their comments about the tournament's rousing conclusion.

Fulbright stayed with Thomas. "We have more things to talk about than fish, Colonel."

Thomas nodded and signaled for Fulbright to follow him over to where Hamish was standing over Moncton.

"Isn't that one of Clayborne's men?" Fulbright asked. "Is he drunk?"

Hamish leaned down and wrenched Salamander's hunting knife out of Moncton's side. "Dead drunk, laddie," he said. He wiped the knife clean on Moncton's trousers and slipped it into his belt. Then he lifted the body as easily as he would pick up a pile of rags and slung it over his shoulder.

"Where to?" he asked.

Thomas pointed to an outbuilding in a darkened corner of the compound, and the giant preacher strode off like he was carrying a five-pound sack of potatoes. Thomas followed him, with a very nervous Fulbright in tow. No one paid attention as they walked around behind the building, where Hamish quietly dropped Moncton behind a pile of empty food crates.

"Weren't he one of the dobbers who tossed you down into that ravine?" asked the Scotsman.

"He was," answered Thomas in a faraway voice. "His name was Moncton."

"Well, Mr. Moncton," Hamish said as he threw two more boxes on top of the corpse so it would not easily be found, "it seems your ticket has been well and truly punched. And did you get the pleasure of doing the deed yourself, Thomas?"

"No. It was the boy."

"By the saints," whispered Hamish.

"Boy?" asked Fulbright, his voice cracking. "A boy did this?" He looked around nervously and then repeated his question in a whisper. "You say a boy killed this man? Colonel, what is happening here? How can you watch a man be murdered and then allow his body to be tossed onto a trash heap like so much garbage?"

Hamish lay a massive hand on the reporter's shoulder. "This was justice, not revenge, lad. That feller had a gun on Thomas and was about to pull the trigger. The colonel was unarmed. The boy…or rather, the young man, stopped the scabby walloper. That's all."

Fulbright turned to Thomas. "I have to know what is going on, Colonel. A man is dead."

Thomas looked hard at Fulbright under the shadowy orange light of a nearby torch. The reporter was shuffling side to side and rubbing his hands as if it was freezing outside. "More people are going to die tonight, Tanner. If they don't, everything we talked about at dinner that night in Denver with Diego is going to happen."

"Claybourne's Mexican scheme?"

"And another Monteverde, maybe several of them."

Hamish looked around the torch and moonlit compound, where

the music and dancing were in full swing. "We need to leave, Thomas. Now."

Thomas followed Hamish's gaze to the steps of Langton Hall, where six of Claybourne's men were huddling with several soldiers.

"They'll begin a search for Moncton any minute," said Hamish. "Best we get out to the camp."

"Come with us, Tanner," Thomas said to the reporter. "We could use your help to pull everything together."

Fulbright looked uncertain. "I'm not going to kill anyone," he finally said.

Thomas laughed. "And no one wants you to. We need to share information, and especially, we need you to do what you do best."

The reporter looked perplexed.

"To tell the story, lad," Hamish interjected. "To the whole damn world."

Fulbright nodded somberly, and the three men made their way around the fence to the gate, where they slipped out into the night.

❖

It was after 9 p.m. when Diego and Major Rhine rode into the tent city outside the gates of Langton Hall. Light from dozens of campfires cast a reddish glow that drifted out to the edge of the prairie, and the smell of savory roast pork and spilled beer floated on the soft night breeze. Hamish and Fulbright were deep in conversation, and Von Sievers and Thomas were putting up another tent to accommodate the new arrivals as Rhine and Diego rode into camp. The men sat on logs that had been placed on either side of the campfire, and Hamish filled their coffee cups and passed around a bottle of brandy. Thomas immediately asked Von Sievers about Demetria.

The professor chose his words carefully. "She seems to be holding her own," he said. "Her fever comes and goes, and there is still a lot of pain. But she is awake most of the time now, and that is a good sign."

"When this is over..." Thomas started to say.

"She will stay with us until she is well enough to travel," Von Sievers said.

Diego looked at his friend through an unfamiliar lens; he had never known Tomás to express this level of concern for a woman. Perhaps the wanderer was finally ready to plant some roots.

Major Rhine poured a slug of brandy into his coffee and shared his news about Tipton. "I got there not long after Demetria and Sergey left. They alerted folks to Rivas's plan, and riders had gone out to the neighboring farms to call everyone into town. By the time I rode up there was a barricade across main street and a dozen rifles took beads on me. I had done some business with one of the men, and he had the others stand down."

"Did you give them the rifles?" asked Thomas.

Rhine nodded. "Three cases and fifteen hundred rounds of ammo. By the time I pulled out an hour later there were at least fifty men patrolling the perimeter of the town. According to what I learned, Rivas should be arriving there any time now with his men. I'm afraid he's not going to like the welcoming committee that's waiting for him."

"What will he do when he finds out that Tipton is heavily fortified and won't be going down like Monteverde?" asked Diego.

"He'll come back here," said Hamish, "that's the only thing he can do. And when he does, Claybourne will turn him around and point him at some other small town, one we won't be able to warn in time. Claybourne must have another Monteverde, or a couple of 'em, or his plans will sputter out."

"Which is why people have to die tonight," said Fulbright in a grave tone.

"Aye," said Hamish, "a few bastards will die here and now, or many innocents will have to die later."

Diego stirred the fire with a stick. "When I telegraphed Tomás in New York the day after Rosalilia was kidnapped, I had no idea how big all of this would become. I knew we would be up against a powerful enemy, but I did not imagine we would also have to battle the army and most of the lawmen in Colorado, or that the very fate of my country would be at stake. It is almost too much to comprehend."

"This is still about finding Rosalilia," said Thomas. "It has always been about finding her."

Diego leaned over and patted his friend on the knee. Then he stood up and limped out to the edge of the darkness.

"The numbers are against us," said Major Rhine.

"And that's only going to get worse by midday," added Von Sievers. The other men looked at him with questions in their eyes. "I overheard one of Clayborne's people tell the kitchen manager to prepare for another fifty men to be here tomorrow afternoon."

"But the tournament is over," said Hamish. "After breakfast, most of the folks here in the camp will pack up and head home."

"These aren't more guests," answered Von Sievers. "It's a detachment of fifty regular infantry from Ft. Cottonwood. They're coming to reinforce the attack that General Greer is going to level on Red Elk's village."

"Counting the soldiers he already has in place around Langton Hall, that means we could be facing two dozen of Claybourne's men and a hundred and fifty troops," said Thomas. "It's a safe bet that Greer asked Cottonwood to dispatch their most seasoned fighters."

It was quiet around the campfire. Then, Fulbright cleared his throat. "The men arriving tomorrow might be professionals," he said, "but many of the men with Greer right now are anything but seasoned," he said. "They're the opposite, in fact."

Diego stepped back in from the shadows. "What do you mean?"

"The ones who travel closest to Greer aren't really soldiers; they are his personal bullies, rather like his own version of the old Roman Praetorian guards whose job was to protect the emperor above all else."

"And they were some of the best fighting men on earth," said Diego.

"These men are a far cry from that," said Fulbright. "I have been talking with them at mess and in the beer tent for over a week. Most are former deserters, paroled criminals, or just guns for hire who like wearing the uniform."

"Why would Greer trust men like that to protect him?"

asked Hamish.

"Simple," replied Major Rhine. "The jobs he asks them to do don't fall under the rules of the Uniform Code of Military Conduct. Remember, they probably helped to butcher the civilians at Monteverde, and putting the Cheyenne village to the torch is just the kind of thing they live for."

"But won't they follow Greer's orders, no matter what?" asked Hamish.

Thomas had been listening carefully. He set down his coffee cup. "They might," he said. "Depends on how much opposition we can muster up in front of them. They're probably not used to having anybody shoot back at them."

"That's a lot of maybe's and what if's," said Von Sievers.

Tanner Fulbright looked into the fire and in a quiet voice said, "It's doesn't necessarily have to come down to us facing them one on one," he said.

"How is that my friend?" asked Diego.

"What if we can manufacture some reason that would compel Greer to send most of his soldiers far into the prairie at daybreak to put down some kind of emergency? Not sure what kind, but if we could…"

Major Rhine picked up Fulbright's thought. "Maybe if Greer got a report that a few dozen mad-as-hornets Tipton farmers with rifles and shotguns were headed towards Langton Hall to pay Rivas and his boss a personal visit?"

"Claybourne would be furious," Diego added. "But he would still have to send Greer's men out to stop them."

"He won't be angry after he thinks it through," Thomas said in a thoughtful tone. "What's going to make Claybourne see red at first is when Rivas tells him he couldn't wipe Tipton out because someone got advance notice to them, and they had fortified the town. Claybourne absolutely had to have those people slaughtered. But it will only take him a minute to re-organize and take another stab at it. His new plan will be simple: Greer's men ride out to kill the farmers in the morning, and Rivas heads back to Tipton to finish the job he had to leave undone tonight. When it's over, Claybourne can still make it look like both massacres were done by the Cheyenne."

"And by the time the detachment from Ft. Cottonwood arrives tomorrow afternoon," continued Rhine, "Greer's men should already be back at Langton Hall. Then they'll join the new arrivals and take out Red Elk's village as originally planned. The regular army soldiers will believe whatever they are told about how the farmers died and Tipton was flattened. Claybourne still achieves everything he wanted to, only by a slightly different route."

The sound of music and laughter drifted across from the compound, and sparks from the huge closing night bonfire floated high into the clear night sky. Whatever else was going to happen in the next few hours, the party was not slowing down.

"We can do this," said Diego. "But even if we can get Greer to send most of his men on a wild goose chase into the prairie in the morning, we will still need help to deal with the men who will remain around him, not to mention Claybourne's hired guns."

"I have an idea," said Thomas. "First, we need to round up everyone we can and have them come out here for a meeting. Let's say three hours from now. Tanner, can you get to Langton Hall and talk quietly to Sam Clemens and John L. Sullivan? Make that Adolph Coors too. He has a beef with Claybourne, and I think he'll want to help. And, do you know Mose Triplett, the guide who has been accompanying Mary Orvis? Get word to him, would you?"

Fulbright nodded. "I can do that." As he stood to go, Von Sievers added, "Don't you think we should also ask the reporters for the other newspapers to come, as well? The more places this story appears, the stronger our case will be against Claybourne."

"Oh, aye," said Hamish. He slapped the diminutive reporter hard on the back, and said, "it will make for a grand story, me boy, and I wouldn't be surprised if some publisher asked you to write a book about it when the dust settles, and that's the truth."

Fulbright straightened his glasses and stood as tall as he could. Then he did a military about face and marched purposefully in the direction of Langton Hall and his destiny.

"There is one more group we need to invite," said Thomas as they watched the young reporter fade into the darkness. "Professor, can you get to the Cheyenne village and ask Red Elk, his daughter and Sergey Baklanov to join us? We'll need all of them."

"I can, but there is someone who can do it a lot faster than me," said Von Sievers.

"Really?" asked Diego.

Von Sievers raised one arm into the air and waved it back and forth. An instant later they heard a horse galloping, and Salamander appeared out of the darkness on his pony as if by magic.

"He's been out there the whole time?" asked Thomas.

"Somebody had to be ready to warn us if Claybourne's people were headed this way," answered Von Sievers. He went over beside the horse and made a series of hand signs. The boy nodded, whirled his horse around, and shot off over the hill.

"You can sign?" asked Diego.

"We've been teaching each other for months," said the professor. "The boy is actually very bright."

The men returned to their seats around the fire, and Hamish added brandy to their coffees. The full yellow moon was at its peak, and a light breeze pushed through the tall grass outside the camp.

There was a lot of planning to do before the sun came up, Thomas thought to himself, and a lot of killing to do after. He looked through the flames and into Diego's eyes and knew his friend was thinking the same thing.

❖

FIFTY FIVE

Claybourne Ranch

Two hundred yards east of the sprawling tent camp, Von Sievers found a natural amphitheater dotted with grass and small boulders that was perfect for the midnight meeting. A stand of trees that had been knocked down by lightning would shield them from winds blowing off the prairie and provide them with places to sit, and when Major Rhine and Hamish followed the professor back, they started a fire in a hollow of a dead tree. An orange glow from the bonfires at Langton Hall off in the distance signaled that the party there was still underway.

"Whiskey or coffee, or both for everybody?" asked Hamish as he added wood to the fire.

"We'll need clear heads tonight," said Rhine.

"Aye, so I'll make sure we have plenty of both."

The moon was softening to a dull yellow-white and a scattering of clouds were drifting off the mountains when Thomas and Diego arrived and tied their horses to the back of Rhine's wagon. "Salamander will guide folks in," Von Sievers told them. "And then he will ride the perimeter and alert us if any of Claybourne's men show up."

Diego lit a cigar and leaned against a tree trunk. It had been almost three months since Rosalilia's kidnapping. It felt like a lifetime, but he could only imagine what it had been like for her. He had survived gunshot wounds that left him crippled, journeyed thousands of miles across Mexico and the southwestern US, and suffered the personal agony of watching Itzcoatl, his best friend and mentor, killed in the battle against Geronimo Rivas. The search for Rosalilia had also resulted in the murder of Itzcoatl's son, Xipil, by Matthew Cord, the deaths of Claybourne's men at Carbon Creek, and Moncton's final exit from this world only hours earlier. And what about Moncton's partner, Elias, who had helped beat Thomas nearly to death before tossing him down into Tamayo Ravine? Thomas had not said anything, but Diego felt certain his friend had evened that score back in Denver. The trail was growing bloodier by the day, and in the morning, even more men were going to die, some by his own hand.

He walked over to the fire, where Thomas was cleaning his revolver and Von Sievers and Rhine were listening to Hamish's bawdy tale about a voluptuous, dark-tressed ghost who legend said would appear on the eve of battle and tease Scottish soldiers to the brink of madness by slowly undressing in front of them before fading away in a wisp of perfumed smoke. For men who might only have a few hours to live, my friends are putting on a good face, Diego thought. He tightened his leg brace and said a blessing for his good fortune.

❖

The men around the fire heard footsteps and made out figures walking down the darkened slope towards their camp. Behind them, a horse and rider were silhouetted against the waning moon. Salamander waved and rode back towards the tent encampment.

A moment later people began to file into the amphitheater. Tanner Fulbright was accompanied by the reporters from New York and Chicago. Samuel Clemens and Adolph Coors came next, followed by John L. Sullivan and Mose Triplett. Thomas welcomed the men and motioned for them to find seats on rocks or logs around the fire.

"Well, this is damned irregular," Clemens said to Thomas.

"And yet, you agreed to come."

"Hell, yes, I'll go anywhere I think a story is brewing, and unless my compass has gone haywire, I'm guessing you and your friends are sitting on an epic tale."

"You can be the judge, Mr. Clemens, but I promise all of you that this meeting will not be a waste of your time. We have invited each of you for very specific reasons, and when the rest of our group gets here, we'll tell you exactly what is going on."

Coors took a step closer to the fire and spread his hands out over the flames. "That sounds fair enough." Then, ever the business promoter, he turned and began a conversation with the reporters.

Diego introduced himself to Clemens and offered him a cigar. The author passed it under his nose and clipped the end off with a pen knife. "If this smokes as good as it smells, the hike out here will have been worth the effort," he said.

Hamish approached the knot of people, handed one bottle of whiskey to Sullivan, and set two more bottles on a flat rock for the others to share. Even the world's greatest bare-knuckle boxer felt a little intimidated in the presence of the towering Scotsman, but after Sullivan uncorked the bottle and took his first drink, they fell into conversation like old friends who hadn't seen one another in years.

Clemens lit his cigar, inhaled, and smiled at Diego. "As good as it smells, my friend." Then he turned to Thomas. "I have looked forward to meeting you for some years," the writer said, "although I must say that no amount of imagination I could have conjured for the circumstance could have done sufficient honor to the way it has actually come to pass." He looked around the small camp and added, "When those fish poured out of the back of that freight wagon tonight, I liked to wet myself, I was laughing so hard. Has your entire life been like this? Adventure, I mean. The unexpected. Danger and intrigue, that sort of thing?"

"If you are asking if I get up each morning thinking I am going to find myself in the middle of a mess like this one, the answer is no. Somehow, though…"

"Somehow, trouble just naturally bypasses others and drops into Tomás's lap, no invitation required," finished Diego with a smile.

"Which I would conjecture makes you slightly less than warmly welcome at most social gatherings," said Clemens.

Before Thomas could reply, a voice called out from the top of the ridge. "Hello, the camp!"

He turned in the direction of the shout. So did Major Rhine, who had just handed new Winchester rifles and ammunition to Mose Triplett and Von Sievers. The men took several steps forward into the darkness and raised their rifles towards the ridge until they were able to make out Salamander, who was leading three others down to the camp on horseback.

Red Elk, Dawn Pillow, and Sergey tied their horses to the branches of a downed tree and came over by the fire. Thomas was struck once again by the way Dawn Pillow walked, as if she was made of liquid: effortless and flowing in a way he had never seen with another woman. She kissed Hamish on the cheek, acknowledged Von Sievers, and then came over to him.

"Sergey told me about your friend. I am so very sorry. How is she?"

Thomas was surprised to be greeted so warmly, but then, nothing he had experienced with the Cheyenne healer had been ordinary. "She is fighting. That's the best I can tell you. Von Siever's wife is caring for her. We just don't know."

Dawn Pillow lay her hand gently on Thomas's forearm. "I will ask the professor if there is anything I can do." Then she walked over and joined her father, who was accepting a light for his cigar from Clemens.

Thomas knew that the people assembled around him were about to hear a story so fantastic that it might leave some to question his sanity. It also struck him that he was about to ask some of them to risk their lives to help rescue a woman they had never met. The funny thing was, he figured each of them had a good reason to say yes.

Then Diego made eye contact with him; it was time to begin.

❖

Thomas climbed onto a stump in the center of the grassy circle a few feet from the fire. Fifty yards up the slope, Salamander rode guard around the amphitheater. Thomas didn't have to call for everyone's attention. Some were sitting, some standing, but all eyes were on him as he began to speak.

"It's difficult for me to find the right words to tell you how much Diego and I are thankful that each of you are here," he began, "so we will just get right to it. We have a story to tell. It begins in Mexico, and at first, Diego thought it was his story alone. But over the last several months the story has grown much bigger. It involves all of you, and, in fact, it concerns our entire nation and the country of Mexico as well. I'm going to ask Diego to start the tale. I will pick up at the point that I became a part of the story, and then I will ask the *London Times* reporter, Tanner Fulbright, to give you his perspective. He has looked under more rocks in pursuit of the truth than any of us, and he has put his life in danger every bit as much as Diego and I have." He looked over at the reporter. "That OK with you, Tanner?"

Fulbright nodded, and Thomas noted that his colleagues were looking at their bantam-size associate with a newfound respect.

"One other thing," added Thomas. "Some of you were dragged out of bed to come here, and others might conclude that they have no dog in the fight when our story is complete. I understand. Please feel comfortable leaving anytime you wish. We only ask that if you choose to leave that you keep this meeting secret until daybreak. By then," he said with a half-smile, "all hell will have broken loose, and you'll most likely be ducking for cover. Our time is short, so, if anyone would rather not hear us out, this is the time to leave."

Heads nodded around the fire, but no one spoke up, no one objected, and no one stood up to leave. That's a good sign, Thomas thought, at least for now, but it was probably curiosity more than resolve that was keeping some of them here. Wait until they found out what they had waded in to.

"Good enough," he said. "I'll ask Diego de San Martín to speak first."

Diego set down his coffee and went over beside Thomas. For the first time in months, he felt nearly overcome with emotion. So much anguish, so much death, and so many lives destroyed since his quest to find Rosalilia had begun. He scanned the faces of the people gathered around him, and then he turned his gaze down and looked deep into the fire.

"Three months ago," he said as he raised his head, "I became engaged to Rosalilia Verján. On that same day, I held her dead father in my arms, I watched her taken by men in the employ of someone you know well, and I was wounded so severely that I spent a month in hospital before I could come to Colorado from Mexico City to find her. This is my story."

Diego began with the engagement party and the attack on Rosalilia's family. Several people in the group gasped audibly when he described the moment he recognized Matthew Cord, an employee of Noah Claybourne, as the leader of the assault and kidnapping.

"Someone very close to me sent a telegram to my friend Tomás Scoundrel, who was living in New York City. It simply said I needed his help and asked him to come to Colorado at once. He was dining with a beautiful young woman when he received the message, and before sun-up, he resigned from his job, said goodbye to his lover, and took the first train west to come to my aide."

Diego looked at his friend. "I will never be able to repay him for what he has done. But now, the story is his to tell."

Thomas took his place on the stump and began with his arrival in Trinidad and his meetings with Bat Masterson and Itzcoatl. He detailed his first encounter with Claybourne, and how Moncton and Elias had beaten him and left him for dead in Tamayo Ravine. From his convalescence at Red Elk's village under Dawn Pillow's care, to befriending Hamish, Von Sievers, and Major Rhine, he went over his search for clues about where Rosalilia had been taken–and why. He also described his meeting with William Cody and Cody's offer of help.

He shared his reunion with Diego and Itzcoatl in Denver and the pattern of growing information about Claybourne that led them to believe that something much bigger than a simple kidnapping was taking place. And he explained how Diego and Itzcoatl had thwarted

Rivas's attack on Manzanita Flats and the terrible price that small victory had cost. With that done, Thomas asked Fulbright to tell the group everything he knew.

The spectacled British reporter hopped onto the stump and in precise, clipped tones told the group what he had learned, starting with the connections he drew between Claybourne, Geronimo Rivas, and the massacre at Monteverde. He told them about Demetria Carnál and how she had turned against Claybourne, and then he shared all she knew about his plans with Thomas and Diego.

"This is the part you are going to find very difficult to believe. It was stunning for me to accept, but nonetheless I assure you that everything I am about to say is true."

Fulbright went into every bit of information he had gathered about Clayborne's scheme to use Monteverde and other massacres to pressure the US Congress and the President to order General Greer to occupy northern Mexico, which would become new US territories under Claybourne's control.

Thomas watched the expressions on the faces of the people around him turn from curiosity and concern to outright shock and disbelief. The idea that one of the nation's wealthiest, most respected and powerful businessmen could have organized a cabal of politicians, military, men and even foreign leaders to carry out a conspiracy of such grand proportions was astonishing.

The reporters from New York and Chicago had their heads down and were scribbling furiously. Samuel Clemens had stubbed out his cigar and replaced it with a tin cup of whiskey, and Adolph Coors was pacing back and forth with his arms crossed tightly over his chest. The brewer had plenty of his own reasons to battle Claybourne before tonight; he understood now why Thomas had asked him to be here. John L. Sullivan had slowly migrated close to Diego and looked ready to take on anyone foolish enough to try and do harm to Rosalilia's fiancée.

"That is everything I know at present," Fulbright concluded. He got down off the stump and returned to stand beside the other reporters. Thomas smiled when he saw the reporter from Chicago slip her arm through Fulbright's.

"Where does that leave this enterprise, then, Colonel?" asked Clemens. "You have clearly asked us here tonight because there is more to the story, and by more, I mean more that is happening right now."

Thomas looked over at Red Elk, who had been standing silently near Rhine's wagon for the past half hour while the story was being told. What he was about to ask of the Cheyenne, Thomas thought. What he was about to ask of everyone.

"We believe that everything is coming to a head tonight," Thomas said. "Claybourne's scheme has always been time-sensitive, and time is something he is nearly out of. He needed a quick follow-up to the attack on Monteverde to keep political pressure on Congress and the President to agree to the occupation of northern Mexico. Demetra Carnál foiled that plan when she refused to attack San Rafael in New Mexico territory. Claybourne's back up plan was then to wipe out the town of Manzanita Flats, but Diego and Itzcoatl intervened, and Claybourne was pushed back for a second time."

"Claybourne made his third attempt earlier today. He sent Geronimo Rivas and nine men to attack the Mormon farming community of Tipton, which is only a couple of hours from here."

"Ten men against an entire town?" asked Coors. "How can that be possible?"

"That's all it took for him to murder one hundred ten men, women, and children at Monteverde," answered Fulbright. "They had the element of surprise, and the townspeople weren't armed."

Coors nodded. "But what about Tipton? I know some of those people. Are we too late to help them?"

Sergey came close to the fire. "Miss Carnál and I rode to Tipton on the first day of the fishing tournament," he said. "We told them what was happening, and they began building barricades on the spot. And yesterday Major Rhine took them a load of rifles and ammunition. Whatever else happened there today, I am sure that Tipton did not become another Monteverde."

"And where might this Miss Carnál be now?" asked Clemens.

"Some reason she couldn't be here?"

Sergey looked at Thomas, but neither of them could find the words.

Diego answered for them. "Two days ago, Tomás was fishing on Carbon Creek. We felt it best for him to be in the tournament so that he could come and go around Langton Hall without Claybourne's men being able to touch him. They have been trying to get that job done for over a month. While he was fishing, five of Claybourne's riders attacked him, three from the water, and two from land. Tomás took one out, and while Hamish and Sergey were dealing with the others, Demetria rode into the creek to help Tomás. She stopped one of the riders in the water, but another one on the creek bank shot her before he himself was killed. She is with Von Siever's wife, but I do not know her condition."

"And those five men," asked Clemens, "have they been arrested?"

Major Rhine chuckled. "Let's say they have been brought to justice."

"Aye," added Hamish, "they won't be needing any lawyers."

The expression on Clemens' s face explained that he finally understood the full magnitude of the story that was unfolding around him. "Very well, Thomas," he said. "Here we are, assembled under a starry sky in the middle of the night. What now?"

Thomas looked at Diego, then to Hamish, Von Sievers, Major Rhine, and Sergey. Each man nodded to him.

"Now we take the fight to Claybourne," he said. "By now he will have been informed–probably by Geronimo Rivas himself–that the attack on Tipton failed. Claybourne will have no choice but to turn Rivas around and send him after some other unsuspecting town. He has to have another Monteverde, or his scheme loses momentum and political support."

"The trouble is," interjected Rhine, "we have no way of knowing what that town might be."

"Which is one of the reasons we need to act now," said Thomas.

"You can't notify the authorities?" asked the reporter from Chicago.

"Claybourne owns them," answered Von Sievers. "And by the time even half of this story makes it to your newspapers another town will lie in ruin, Red Elk's village will be laid to waste, and General Greer will be occupying northern Mexico at the request of the President of the United States. Nothing will be able to stop that train once it is in motion."

"You say it's time to take the fight to Claybourne," said Sara Joliette, the New York reporter. "But there are a lot of soldiers around Langton Hall, and only a handful of you. How do you think you can get past them?"

"You're right; Greer has a full company of one hundred troops," answered Thomas in a matter-of-fact voice. "Claybourne has another two dozen or so hired hands around the place, and Rivas can bring nine seasoned killers with him to the fight. We also know that a detachment of fifty army regulars are on their way from Ft. Cottonwood and will arrive tomorrow afternoon to reinforce Greer when he carries out the original plan to punish the Cheyenne for attacking Tipton."

"I think I understand what George Custer must have felt like when he looked down on the Indian villages lined up for miles along the Little Big Horn," said John L. Sullivan.

Red Elk spoke for the first time. "He felt what all fools do before they die. Nothing."

Thomas shook his head and smiled. "I knew the general. His arrogance was his undoing, but we have no such illusions about our little band." He looked up to the ridge where Salamander was passing once again. The air was cooling, and he waited as Hamish added more logs to the fire before he continued.

"Our first task is to reduce the number of men we are up against. Major Rhine came up with a plan that should help us to get everything done before the reinforcements arrive from Cottonwood. Major?"

Rhine took a place by the fire. "Demetria Carnál has someone inside Langton Hall who has provided us with information about Claybourne's activities. She is a maid who recently found herself pregnant by one of Claybourne's men–one of his favorites, as it happens. It seems the young man's affections turned sour when he learned about her condition. He paid her off with $50 and then told the household manager about the girl. The manager said she would have to leave her job as soon as her belly started to swell."

"Bastards," muttered Dawn Pillow, to the sympathetic laughter of the men around the fire.

"Maybe so," continued Rhine, "but her boyfriend was also one of the poor sons of bitches out on Carbon Creek the other day. He and Sergey's blade had a bit of a run in, and the lad was last seen floating down the river."

"Claybourne trusts this maid, and so we brought her to the camp this morning and made her an offer: if she could convince Claybourne that the story we were about to feed her was true, we would rent a house for her and her mother and pay all of her expenses for the first year after the baby is born."

"And what story was that?" asked Clemens.

"She will go to Claybourne two hours before daybreak," continued Rhine, "and tell him that her lover came upon a couple of dozen heavily armed farmers boiling out of Tipton in the direction of Langton Hall, no doubt to find Rivas. He turned his horse to run, but one of the farmers winged him with a rifle shot. The young man was able to ride to the maid's house and is being cared for by her mother."

Mose Triplett spoke up. "Based on that information, we expect that General Greer will order a detail of his men to ride out at once and head off the farmers before they get to Langton Hall."

"Which peels at least some of Claybourne's protectors away," said Clemens.

"More than a few," answered Triplett. "I'd bet he will send at least eighty. They have no reason to believe that Claybourne is in any danger, and since reinforcements are on the way from Cottonwood, there is no reason for him not to send most of them."

"Which leaves that Rivas fellow and his men, plus Claybourne's two dozen?" asked Coors. "That is still a sizeable opposition."

"I don't think so," said Thomas. "When Claybourne learns that Tipton was not destroyed, he will have no choice but to pick another town. He absolutely must have another massacre for his plan to stand a chance. But it will only take a minute for him to realize that with most of Tipton's men riding his way, there is no one left to protect the town."

"So, he'll send Rivas back to finish the job in town while Greer's men squash the farmers out on the prairie?" asked Clemens. "That's a hell of a plan, Colonel." The author took a draw on his cigar. "It also makes perfect god damn sense. Perfect."

"Greer will blame the massacre of the farmers and the destruction of the town on Red Elk," continued Diego. "When the fifty soldiers from Cottonwood arrive, they will help Greer's men to destroy the Cheyenne village, and then they will head south to the Mexican border to await the orders to invade."

"Once Greer's soldiers and Rivas and his men have departed Langton Hall, we will make our move," Thomas added. "There will still be anywhere from thirty to forty men around, though most of them will be sleeping in the bunkhouse. I will get to Claybourne and bring him back here. Diego will search for Matthew Cord and do the same if he finds him. When we have Cord, we will find Rosalilia."

"What about the rest of the conspirators?" asked Fulbright "They can't be allowed to get away."

"When we have Claybourne, the entire plan falls apart," answered Diego. "We will contact the federal authorities here and in Mexico and let justice take its course."

"Greer won't go down easy," said Von Sievers. "Neither will Rivas. And as soon as Greer's men figure out that there never were any farmers coming to attack Langton Hall, they will ride back at a full gallop and join the fight. Rivas will do the same when he sees that Tipton is still being guarded."

"We don't expect them to give up easily," said Hamish. "That's why the other lads and I will back up Thomas and Diego at the house. Sergeant Triplett, Captain Baklanov, and Professor Von Sievers will hold the main gate, while Red Elk, Dawn Pillow, and their warriors wait on the ridge outside the compound for the rats to flee the sinking ship. And that, I promise you, they will do. The important thing is that we snatch Claybourne and Cord and get the hell out before the soldiers and Rivas return."

Mose and Sergey shared a smile when Hamish referred to them by their military ranks.

"They will not pass," Red Elk said simply.

Thomas turned to Tanner and the other reporters. "None of you should risk your life by coming into the compound with us. If you want to report on what happens, I suggest you go back to Langton Hall now, and then meet on the speaker's platform a half hour before daybreak. You can take cover up there if you have to, but it's the only place where you will be able to see what is going on."

"What about all of the other guests inside Langton Hall?" asked Clemens. "When the shooting starts they are going to be in a bad way. I'm not sure the world would be the worse for wear if Mr. Wilde and Signori Verdi shuffled off their mortal coils, but I do have a real affection for Miss Langtry, and would be sorely upset to see her harmed."

"You are right," said Diego, "Which is why we asked you and Mr. Coors and Mr. Sullivan to come tonight. Your job will be to go back into Langton before the rest of us arrive and gather up the guests. Take them out to the stable and keep watch until it's over."

"Babysitters?" asked Sullivan with a look of disgust on his face.

"Bodyguards," replied Thomas. "It's not just possible but highly probable that one or more of Claybourne's men will want to grab a famous guest or two to use to negotiate their way out when the battle turns against them. You'll have to stop them in their tracks."

His words brought a grin to Sullivan's face. Stopping people in their tracks was language he understood.

"Mr. Coors, Mr. Clemens," Thomas continued, "you didn't sign on for this fight. We won't think less of you if you choose to remain here in camp until the dust settles."

Coors looked defiant. "This country has been good to me and my family," he said. "I was ready to battle Claybourne to stop his takeover of my brewery in any event. But there is much more than my business at stake now. I will fight."

Samuel Clemens laughed softly and took a sip of whiskey. "It is rumored that I served in the army for a period of two weeks during the

War Between the States, and on the losing side, no less," he said. "Seems to me that I now have an opportunity to rectify that lapse in judgment. Count me in, Colonel."

❖

The moon had shrunk to the size of a nickel and drifted low in the heavens since they started talking. Stars filled the expanse of sky from horizon to horizon, and the rustle of bluestem grass merged with the crackling of logs on the fire and the yip of a coyote celebrating a successful hunt.

Thomas went over to Diego and handed him a tin cup that Hamish had filled with equal parts coffee and whiskey. He noticed how close Sergey was standing beside Dawn Pillow and wondered for a moment if the two of them had made the trip to the moon-dappled forest glade across the creek.

He tapped his cup against Diego's, and the two men raised their drinks in salute to their friends around the fire.

❖

FIFTY SIX

Langton Hall

US Senator Terrance Mack came down from his room after being awakened by a servant at 4 a.m. In the foyer at the bottom of the stairs, Assistant US Secretary of State Wharton Geve was pouring coffee from a silver pitcher for himself and Congressman Renton, and on a chair beneath an ornate gilt mirror, former vice-president of Mexico Antonio Resposo looked as if he were about to fall back asleep.

"Are we meeting out here?" Mack asked Resposo.

"Mr. Claybourne is finishing some minor business, and said he will be with us shortly," answered Resposo. He seemed as irritated as Mack to be kept waiting, even by someone as important as Claybourne.

The door to Claybourne's library opened, and a house maid scurried out, went down the hall to the front door and stepped out into the darkness.

Claybourne came to the doorway and signaled for the men to join him. Inside, a fire was burning in an open fireplace, and the long conference table was set with muffins, toast, fresh fruit and pastries. General Greer and his senior aide, Colonel Alphonse were seated on one side of the table, and on the other side sat Geronimo Rivas.

Senator Mack got right to it. "Trouble, Noah? We weren't supposed to meet until 8 a.m. It's still a good two hours before sunrise."

Claybourne ignored the impertinent question. "Please, gentlemen, sit down. Help yourself to something to eat."

He waited for everyone to settle in and then went to the head of the table, where he stood with his hands clasped behind his back. "No plan goes from start to finish without a few twists and turns along the way," he began. "We have had our share of unexpected incidents, but, considering the magnitude of our undertaking, I am confident that we are poised to realize our every aim."

"And yet, you have called us from bed in the middle of the night," said Secretary Geve. "How does that comport with your assertion that everything is on track?"

Noah Claybourne was the only human being Mack had ever known whose smile could send chills down your back. He turned that kind of smile towards Geve, and the diplomat shrank visibly back in his chair.

"A misstep here and there does not constitute failure, my dear Mr. Secretary," said Claybourne in an emotionless voice, "particularly when one considers the number of initiatives we have in motion across thousands of miles of this continent at this very moment.

"In fact, I called you here at this early hour because I am making a few last-minute course changes to our plan. They will not hinder or slow down our progress, I assure you. But circumstances have arisen that must be dealt with, and events are unfolding rapidly."

He walked to the window and looked outside, where the great bonfire that had shone across the landscape for miles last night had burned down to embers. Several lanterns were still burning on their posts, and kitchen staff were bringing in trays of food and coffee for the last of the celebrants to enjoy before they left for their homes. Adolf Coors's crew was striking the beer tent and preparing to haul off dozens of empty wooden kegs. Claybourne made a mental note to confront the German one last time about purchasing his brewery. There would be no further negotiations. Noah had a hundred ways at his disposal by which he could crush a business. If it came to that, Coors would feel the weight of his boot before the end of the day.

He turned back to the group. "I received two pieces of news in the past twelve hours that demanded a great deal of my attention, including information I was given only moments ago."

That might explain the young housekeeper who had just rushed out of Claybourne's office, thought Mack.

"In each instance, the substance of the news caused me to re-think some of the most important final steps we are taking before General Greer leaves for the border and the occupation of Mexico-or, rather, I should say, the occupation of our new territory."

Claybourne sat down, filled his teacup, and squeezed in a little lemon.

"I was quite concerned about the information that Mr. Rivas delivered to me last night, but then, out of the blue, a solution has presented itself that will leave us in a stronger position to persuade Congress and the President to our way of thinking." He sipped his tea and continued. "Fortune favors those who do not become slaves to their plans," he said. "And this morning, gentlemen, fortune favors us."

Mack felt some of the tension go out of the room at those words. Like his fellow conspirators, he would not rest easy until the President authorized the invasion of Mexico. The moment the first American soldier set foot across the border, the attention of Congress and the press would be focused only on punishing Mexico and protecting American lives. No one would be interested in Claybourne and his group.

"As you all know," Claybourne said, "Mr. Rivas was scheduled to pay a surprise visit to the little burg of Tipton yesterday. That performance was to have been the final act in our graduated plan to garner support from politicians and prominent businessmen alike to squash the Mexican invasion, protect our people, and, of course, to be compensated for the costs associated with having to mount such an operation."

"Only a handful of people knew about Tipton, including those of you in this room. Absolute surprise was the minimal requirement for Mr. Rivas to prevail. And yet…"

"I was betrayed," spat Rivas. "Someone got to Tipton and warned them what was coming." He slammed one palm on the table.

Claybourne was not used to being interrupted, but in this case he knew that Rivas's passion would help soothe the concerns of anyone at the table who might be upset that he hadn't consulted them about what steps to take next. So, he said nothing and simply raised one hand in

Rivas's direction to signal him to continue.

"Some *hijo de puta* right here in this house told them when I was coming and why," Rivas said. "The farmers barricaded the street and mounted dozens of heavily armed men on boulders, in trees, and on rooftops. There were rifles and shotguns everywhere. We rode to within fifty yards and turned around. I was not going to lead my men to slaughter."

Senator Mack couldn't help but smile at the irony of a butcher like Rivas being offended at the idea of a slaughter.

Rivas's dark, cold eyes drilled into the face of each man at the table. "I will find the *cabrón* who did this to me," he said slowly. "And when I do, I will gut him like a fish and hang him by his own entrails."

Claybourne let that statement sink in before he talked. "I was concerned for many reasons when I got this news. First, the attacks on Manzanita Flats and San Rafael were also deflected by treachery. We needed Tipton to keep the fire under our cause red-hot. Second, Mr. Rivas is correct: there is a traitor somewhere in Langton Hall. They will be discovered, of course, and when they are, Mr. Rivas will deal with them exactly as he pleases."

Vice-President Resposo spoke up. "Tipton was, as you say, a very important piece of our strategy. How will we recover the momentum we have lost? Will you pick another target?"

"It would have to be done right now, as in *today*," said Congressman Renton. "Greer has to leave for the border when the detachment arrives from Ft. Cottonwood, although I don't know how he will be able to deal with the Cheyenne as originally planned. We cannot stretch this out indefinitely. Too many cracks are appearing in this plan."

Heads nodded around the table. There would have to a fresh target, and it would have to be dealt with before the sun went down tonight.

"I agree," said Claybourne. "When Mr. Rivas returned and informed me of the failure at Tipton, my mind went exactly where yours are now. No Tipton also meant no retribution against the Cheyenne because we wouldn't be able to blame them for the event. And so, I called Mr. Rivas here this morning to plan for the application of his, ahem, rather unique specialty in a new place. My intention as you waited in the foyer was to outline when and how that would happen." He smiled. "Not where it would happen, of course. After all, it is possible that the traitor is here with us right now."

That remark got an immediate response. Senator Mack stood up "No, sir, I cannot countenance such an accusation against any one of our members. We have all risked too much and become invested too deeply with our fortunes and our lives to commit such an act. The traitor, sir, is not here."

"Sit down, Senator," said Claybourne, "this is not Congress. No speeches are necessary. Other matters take priority right now, but in due time, we will root out the bastard, and we will deal with him."

"Or her," added Resposo.

"Or her, yes," said Claybourne. "But concerning where we go from here; my mind went immediately to the selection of a new target for Mr. Rivas to visit. I was prepared to make that announcement to you when I received the second piece of news from an unlikely source. An hour ago, a housemaid who has been in my employ for several years knocked on my bedroom door."

Eyes widened and eyebrows raised around the table. "No, gentlemen, that is not one of her assigned duties, though I understand that one of my foremen has been putting it to her for some time. This girl has earned my trust over time, and I assure you that there is not a political or spiteful bone in her body. So, she knocked, and I sat on a chair by the window and listened to her story.

"It seems her young man had been sent out two days ago to track down a mountain lion that has been ravaging our stock. A few hours ago, as he came around a stand of cottonwoods just outside Tipton, he ran headlong into thirty or forty farmers galloping hellbent out of town and in this direction. He was surprised, of course, but he knew nothing of Mr. Rivas's intentions, and so he had no reason to fear the farmers until they recognized him as my employee and began shooting at him. He turned to escape, but one of the farmers was a good enough aim that he shot the boy in the back. They left him on the ground and rode past him, but he was able to mount his horse and ride to the house where the maid lives with her mother. He is being cared for there as we speak."

"And how long ago did this happen?" asked Mack.

"No more than three and a half hours," replied Claybourne.

"Jesus," said Congressman Renton. "And you think they are headed here?"

"I am sure of it," replied Claybourne in a calm voice. "No doubt they believe Mr. Rivas is here, and they wish to do him the courtesy of a return visit. I expect they have paused for a bit somewhere not far from here to send a scout ahead and then to make their plans."

"This is no laughing matter," said Senator Mack.

"I couldn't agree more," replied Claybourne. "I must confess the news set me back on my heels a bit."

"A bit?" interjected Geve. "A town we needed flattened is still there, and an army is headed this way to kill us all? A bit?"

General Greer spoke. "There are armies, Mr. Secretary, and there are armies. Thirty minutes ago, I ordered seventy-five troops from the detachment stationed here to ride out and intercept the farmers. They are commanded by a highly competent officer, and their orders are clear: there will be no survivors."

Claybourne poured more tea. Daylight was an hour and a half away, and by noon the last of the tournament revelers would be out of the compound.

"And so a bunch of farmers are killed in battle," said Mack. "How does that advance our cause?"

"How, indeed," replied Claybourne. He stood and walked over to the fireplace. "Here is how the intersection of fate and fortune have smiled upon us today. A few minutes ago, I thought we were about to send Mr. Rivas to a new target, and I believed we would need a new strategy for attaching the responsibility for the attack on the Cheyenne. And then, serendipity: a simple, neat solution has been dropped in our lap."

The men around the table looked at him with questioning glances.

A neat solution?

"The farmers who are gallantly racing towards us to protect their honor have made something of a strategic mistake, haven't they."

A light went on in Senator Mack's head. He looked around the table and knew that every man there was coming to the same realization.

"With all of their fighting age men out on the prairie, Tipton is completely unprotected," Mack said. "So, Greer's soldiers will take care of the farmers…"

"And Mr. Rivas and his men will leave here in five minutes to finish the job in the town," said Claybourne with a satisfied smile.

"When my men have dealt with the threat on the prairie, they will leave behind evidence that proves the farmers were ambushed by the Cheyenne," said Greer. "And they will also place letters on Red Elk's body from senior Mexican authorities that promise him a great deal of money in exchange for dealing with Tipton. Vice President Resposo has seen to it that those letters are perfect and will hold up under any investigation." He nodded to Resposo, who accepted the compliment with a diplomatic smile.

"Rivas will also leave behind evidence proving that the Cheyenne attacked Tipton," Greer went on. "Then, later today, we will gather up the reporters who have been covering the tournament and take them out to the ambush site on the prairie, and then into Tipton to view the atrocities committed by the Cheyenne on behalf of the Mexican government. In two days, their stories will be splashed across the front page of every newspaper in the nation. Any political opposition to the occupation of northern Mexico will vanish overnight."

"And the Cheyenne?" asked Resposo.

"When the detachment from Ft. Cottonwood arrives this afternoon, they will be tasked with helping with the clean up on the prairie and in Tipton," said the general. "When they see the carnage Rivas leaves behind, those boys will beg to be in the first wave when we hit the village."

"You see, gentlemen," Claybourne said in a soft voice. "Fortune and fate truly have joined forces to give us victory when we most needed it."

The room cleared a few minutes later. General Greer went to

prepare for the campaign against the Cheyenne and the journey to the Mexican border, and Rivas left to assemble his men for their return to Tipton.

As he stepped out into the pre-dawn darkness, Rivas felt a sweet, primal throbbing spread through his groin. He had learned long ago that the only way to satiate the raw lust that took hold of him at times like this was to wade headlong into rivers of blood and mayhem. Somewhere in Tipton, perhaps still asleep and warm in her bed, one of the little town's juiciest pieces of quim was about to meet him–and his knife. That would calm the fires… for a while.

❖

Claybourne was standing alone at the window when a pocket door slid open and Hyacinth stepped into his office from the adjoining library. Matthew Cord was drinking coffee in a wingback leather chair behind her. "At first light, you will ride up to the cabin and see that Miss Rosalilia Verján is secure," said Claybourne. Then he turned to his daughter.

"You heard?"

"Everything," Hyacinth leaned forward and kissed him softly on the cheek, something she seldom did. "You are brilliant, you know."

Noah brushed his lips against her forehead and smiled.

❖

FIFTY SEVEN

Langton Hall

A half hour before sunrise the wind spilling off the prairie was tinged with a hint of frost. Thomas pulled his coat tight and looked around the compound to make sure everyone was in place. He was kneeling behind a fence post next to Hamish, looking across the gravel yard to Langton Hall where every window in the three-story building was ablaze with light from lamps and candles. No surprise there, he thought. Claybourne had set events in motion that would spell success or failure for his enterprise, and he knew that the next several hours would determine exactly how his scheme was going to play out. He was waiting, just as Thomas was.

By now, Von Sievers, Sergey, and Mose Triplett would be in position at the main gate, ready to defend against any of Claybourne's riders who would have to come into the compound that way from the bunkhouse once the fireworks started. Over behind the stockade where the prize bull was penned, Diego and Major Rhine were hunkered down, waiting for Thomas's signal. The plan called for them to circle around to the right, go down the covered porch, and break down the door leading into the kitchen. There was a small bedroom off the kitchen where the maid told them that Matthew Cord slept when he was at Langton. When Thomas and Hamish heard them go in, they would breach the front door and seek out Claybourne.

Red Elk and his warriors were in place in a hollow at the base of a tree-lined ridge five hundred yards to the east, ready to intercept

Claybourne's co-conspirators if they tried to flee. Salamander would be the only one of their group in motion. He would carry messages from the compound out to Red Elk and circle around Langton Hall looking for the first soldiers or hired guns to come piling into the fight once it got started.

Clemens, John L. Sullivan, and Coors had returned to Langton an hour ago. When they heard the kitchen door crashing in, they would roust the other guests from their beds and lead them down the back stairs and out to the stables.

The sky was softening in the east, and the light from the stars and moon was fading. Thomas heard the screech of a red tail hawk, which was Salamander's signal that said he had made another pass around the buildings and seen nothing. A few kitchen staff were going back and forth across the compound, readying the last meal for the tournament goers who were still outside in the tent encampment. Breakfast was scheduled to begin in an hour, but there were going to be a lot of hungry stomachs today; when the bullets started to fly, folks were going to get as far away from Langton Hall as they could. Those who stayed behind would either be shooting, or, Thomas reminded himself as he watched the four reporters quietly ascending the steps to the speaker's platform, they'd be taking notes.

There was a rustling sound, and Hamish tapped him on the shoulder. "Someone's coming." A second later they made out the form of a man scooting towards them on his hands and knees from behind a water trough. When he got closer, Thomas recognized Four Bears. The gap-toothed Cheyenne pulled himself over between them and took a moment to get his breath.

"Well, man?" Hamish finally asked. "What is it?"

"Red Elk sent a scout to an escarpment four miles to the east to watch for the soldiers," wheezed Four Bears. "He just flew into the hollow with news; the Mescalero and two of his men are riding this way fast. They will be here in a few minutes."

"Thomas?" asked Hamish.

"He got to Tipton faster than we expected and figured out fast that he got snookered again. The minute he saw that the farmers were still manning the barricades and not riding this way across the prairie like he expected, he high-tailed it back as fast as he could to tell Claybourne."

"And the rest of his men?" asked Hamish.

"He probably sent a couple of them to find Greer's detachment and tell them that there aren't any farmers out there for them to attack. Rivas's men and the soldiers will be along presently."

"Which means we have less time than we hoped for," said Hamish. "A few minutes before Rivas gets here and probably no more than an hour for the soldiers to return–maybe less if they really put their spurs to it."

Thomas nodded. Their plan depended on having enough time to get into the house, secure Claybourne and Cord, and extract information about Rosalilia by whatever means it took.

"We'll tell Diego," Thomas said. "Four Bears, go back to Red Elk and tell him we are going into the house right now. Be ready for anybody trying to escape."

"And if the soldier boys get here before we're done?" asked Hamish. "Do you want Red Elk to hold 'em off?"

Thomas looked at Four Bears. "Tell Red Elk that the soldiers are not his problem. If he goes after them, there will be hell to pay, and Greer and the whole US army will figure they have permission to kill every living thing in the village. Tell him to stick to the plan. Watch for the men who helped Claybourne put this damn thing in motion and leave the army to us."

Four Bears grinned and high-tailed it back to his horse.

"Leave the army to us?" asked Hamish as he watched his friend speed away. "Ye don't think that might be a wee bit much for us to handle?"

Thomas loosened the holster strap on his revolver and adjusted his hunting knife in its leather sheath. "Hell, I don't know. If we make it through the next ten minutes, ask me again."

Hamish laid a hand on Thomas's shoulder. "That we will do, laddie, and when the time comes, I'll be dancing at your wedding." He pulled a hatchet from his belt and checked its edge. "If ever you get wise enough to settle down, that is."

"Someday, my friend,"Thomas said with a smile. He looked across the compound. No kitchen workers were present, and no figures were visible in the well-lit windows. "Rivas expects trouble, so he won't come through the main gate. He'll swing around to the west and come over the ridge behind the smokehouse. Let's go," he said, and they sprinted across the open space towards the stockade where Diego and Rhine were waiting.

They raced past the bull, who pawed the ground and gave a muted snort at the disturbance in his routine, and around to the back of the enclosure, where Diego and Rhine were waiting with their revolvers drawn.

"I didn't expect to see you again until after," Diego said.

"Things have changed," said Thomas. "Rivas and two of his men will be here any minute."

"Didn't take him long to figure things out," said Rhine. "Now what?"

"We stick to our plan. You and Diego work your way down the porch. When I hear you knock the door down, Hamish and I will go in the front. Claybourne will be downstairs, either in his office or the library. He'll hear the kitchen door too and head down the hall to see what's going on. We'll be in his living room before he gets there."

"That's a damn heavy door," said Rhine. "Way thicker than the one on the kitchen."

"Which is why the fellow who tosses cabers for sport will be the one to kick it in," said Thomas. Hamish acknowledged the compliment with a somber nod of his head.

Diego put his hand on Thomas' forearm. "Whatever happens," he said, "I want..."

Thomas interrupted: "I've already got one volunteer to dance at my wedding. Make it two, and we'll call it even."

Diego smiled and tightened the brace Von Sievers had given him to help support his bad leg. Major Rhine checked the pair of tomahawks that crisscrossed his back and then tightened his gun belt. "Might as well make that three, Colonel," he said.

A dog barked near the smokehouse, and they heard a match strike as someone fired up a lantern by the woodshed. The breeze had died down, and a smear of light was spreading on the eastern horizon. The world was coming to life. Thomas looked at his friends. Diego bowed his head a moment and then said, *"Vamanos."* Without another word, he and Rhine trotted around the right side of Langton Hall and disappeared into the dark gray morning. A few seconds later, Thomas and Hamish heard a crash and the splintering of wood. The battle was on.

Mose Triplett was standing under the great timber arch that led into the Langton Hall compound when he heard the kitchen door cave in. Von Sievers and Sergey Baklanov left their positions at the sides of the gate and came up alongside him. Mose pulled out the unlit cigar stub he had been absentmindedly chewing on and tossed it away. "Gentlemen," he said, "I believe it's time to go to war." With that, three lever action rifles cocked as one in the soft morning air, and then there was another, even louder crash.

❖

The speaker's platform stood six feet above the gravel compound, and there was a small shed at the west end to protect guests from inclement weather. It sported a shingled roof, several benches, and a small wood stove around which the reporters were now huddled, waiting for whatever was about to be unleashed around them. Tanner Fulbright had been in battle before, but his colleagues from Chicago and New York had never seen real conflict up close. As they walked back to Langton Hall from the meeting with Thomas and Diego two hours earlier, the reporter from the *Times* asked him what it was like to find yourself in the thick of battle. His first reaction was to reassure her, but on reflection, he decided it was best to tell the truth, niceties be damned.

"Three years ago, I was attached to the field command of Major General Sir Frederick Roberts when he led the Kabul Field Force into central Afghanistan, and fought the Afghan Army at Charasiab," he told the correspondent. "We met them on a hot, dusty plain at mid-day, our 3,000 men against their 5,000. The noise of cannons and rifles and shouting and screaming was almost more than my mind could bear. In fact," he said with no hint of shame, "when a half dozen Afghan soldiers popped up out of a trench and began swinging their swords a few feet in front of me, I actually soiled myself."

As they hurried along in the moonlight, the *Times* reporter looked at him with an expression that was a mix of empathy and horror. "Oh, but I could never," she said, "I would never, I simply can't conceive of allowing such a thing to happen."

Fulbright saw movement across the compound and was just able to make out Thomas and Hamish walking swiftly towards the stairs in front of Langton Hall.

"It will happen," he said quietly. "But I promise none of us will think the worse of you for it when this is over."

Then he motioned for his fellow reporters to stand up and retreat into the shadows as far as they could, out of the line of fire.

❖

Rhine took the lead and raced down the porch to the side kitchen entry. Diego stood to one side as the Major kicked hard, just below the knob. He kicked a second time, and the window shattered. A third kick, and the door flew open in a hail of splinters and glass shards. They stepped into the huge kitchen, where two startled cooks were stirring pots of oatmeal.

"Get out," shouted Diego, waving his revolver in their direction. The men dropped their ladles and retreated to the porch.

"This way," said Rhine. He went across the kitchen to where a pocket door was set into the wall next to a shelf packed with spices. It was exactly as the maid told them it would be. Now Diego took the lead; if Matthew Cord was here, he wanted to be the one who confronted the bastard- just before he killed him. Rhine pointed his revolver at the door as Diego grabbed the handle and slid it rapidly open. Both men rushed into the small bedroom, pistols at the ready.

A lamp was burning on a side table, and the covers on the bed were pulled back. An open suitcase on a chair was filled with men's clothing, and an empty rifle scabbard hung from a peg on the wall. Diego could smell burnt tobacco from the cigarette Cord had been smoking only moments earlier. Rhine went across the room to the open window, where the curtains were flapping softly in the morning breeze.

"The son of a bitch got out."

Diego holstered his revolver. "But we know he is here. We'll find him."

They heard shouts from somewhere in the house and the sounds of furniture toppling over.

"Tomás!" said Diego.

The two men started towards the double doors that lead into the dining room when they heard horses come to a stop outside the kitchen, followed by a man's voice ordering his companions to wait there for him. Diego knew the voice; the last time he heard it was in the heat of battle in a dry wash at Manzanita Flats.

Major Rhine grabbed Diego by the arm. "I'll go. You help Thomas and Hamish."

Diego knew that Rhine feared that his crippled leg would hold him back. That was true, but it didn't matter. Geronimo Rivas killed Itzcoatl, and Diego was going to deliver justice to the bastard.

He pulled his arm free and smiled at the Major. "Not this time, *amigote*. This one is mine."

There was no time to argue. Rhine nodded and stepped aside. Diego pulled Itzcoatl's obsidian dagger from his belt and went out through the broken kitchen door.

❖

Thomas and Hamish leapt up the stairs in front of the main entrance to Langton Hall only seconds after Diego and Major Rhine broke through the kitchen door. The enormous Scotsman drew back his shoulders, turned his body at an angle, and then rammed into the heavy double doors with the force of a locomotive snowplow. The massive doors shook, but they did not budge. Hamish took three steps back and smashed into the doors again and then again. Thomas was about to fire his revolver into the locks when Hamish stepped back to the edge of the porch for one final try. Sweat was pouring down his face, and his tangled hair covered his eyes. He shook his head, roared, and then lowered his shoulders and rammed into the door so hard that the porch boards shuddered beneath Thomas's feet.

The thick etched glass on both doors cracked, and the right-side door flew off its hinges. The door crashed into the foyer, with Hamish on top of it. Thomas started to kneel to help his friend up, but something stopped him in his tracks.

Noah Claybourne was standing in the hall outside his office, just twenty feet from where the doors to his home had just been battered down. Thomas was surprised to see that Claybourne was dressed formally, in a black suit, white shirt and bow tie. What wasn't surprising was that Claybourne had a Colt revolver pointed right at him. His eyes were focused on Thomas, but his facial expression did not show a hint of concern.

Thomas reached for his own revolver, but before it cleared his holster, the sound of a .45 caliber explosion thundered in the confined space of the hallway.

❖

Diego stepped out of the kitchen just as Rivas was swinging down from his horse. The top edge of the sun was cresting the hills to the east, and a cool wind was picking up off the prairie. Diego saw the cooks scurrying off in the direction of the bunkhouse, but there were no other people in the compound. Then he heard another crash inside the house, followed by the crack of a single shot.

It took Rivas a second to recognize Diego in the pale morning light. The Mescalero's eyes went right to the obsidian dagger Diego was clutching in his right hand, and he knew in an instant what Diego was thinking. Revenge was one of the handful of emotions that Geronimo Rivas was capable of feeling. He gauged his opponent in a heartbeat; the man already looked exhausted, and the brace on his leg told Rivas that he was a cripple as well. That, plus the way the Rivas knew that hate could blind a man and cause him to make mistakes, lead the killer to keep his pistol in its holster and instead reach for his own knife. He preferred to kill with a blade, to feel flesh and muscle and organs give way to the razor-sharp steel, and he even reveled in the sensation of being covered with the hot, sticky blood of his victims.

Rivas calmly raised his knife in salute to the man he was about to eviscerate. "Are you here to atone for the sin of allowing that old man to die by my hand in the desert?" he asked. "If so, I am happy to help you cleanse your guilt. With blood, of course." He stepped away from his horse to give them ample room to fight.

"His name was Itzcoatl," said Diego.

"An Aztec? Ah, that would explain the stone dagger. Leave it to an aristocrat to bring a medieval weapon to a modern battle."

Diego turned his body at an angle, bent his left arm at the elbow and raised it up protect his ribs, head, and neck. Then he drew his right hand back and gripped the dagger with the tip pointed at Rivas's abdomen. Itzcoatl had taught him to never stay head-on with an enemy in a knife fight; instead, he should move in at forty-five-degree angles from either side to increase his chance of landing his slashes and to make it harder for his opponent to slice him.

Out of the corner of his eye, he saw Major Rhine unsling his tomahawks from the belt that crisscrossed his back and pass behind him, but he never let his gaze leave Rivas's face. The butcher of Monteverde looked very confident, and that was a point in Diego's favor. Overconfident fighters were prone to make mistakes in the first few seconds of a bout; in a knife fight that could be a deadly mistake. On the other hand,

Diego mused, if I was a healthy warrior in the prime of his life facing a worn-out fellow sporting a leg brace, maybe I'd be cocky, too.

Rivas held his knife out and began to circle Diego with short, shuffling side steps. A half-smile creased his face, but his dark eyes did not blink, not even when he suddenly lunged forward and slashed at Diego's defensive arm.

❖

When the front door of Langton Hall crashed in, the four reporters rushed out of the lean-to and over to the railing at the edge of the platform. The *Times* reporter winced when she heard the gunshot that followed a moment later. Fulbright already had his notebook opened when she reached over and placed her hand on his. When no other sounds came from the house in the next few seconds, she asked, "Is it over?"

He liked the feel of her hand. "No," he replied quietly. "It hasn't even begun."

❖

Thomas flinched when Claybourne fired his revolver, but, to his amazement, he did not feel a bullet slam into his body. He looked to his right, where Hamish had been about to get up, but the Scotsman was still kneeling, and he was clutching at his side where a puddle of dark liquid was seeping between his fingers.

He turned his eyes back to Claybourne. A second shot was on its way, and this one would be for him.

Claybourne took three steps forward, keeping the barrel of his gun pointed at Thomas's midsection. Doors slammed upstairs, and Thomas could hear people running. That would be Coors, Clemens, and John L. Sullivan taking the guests to the back stairs and safety, he thought.

Claybourne paid no attention to the activity above him. He took two more steps towards Thomas and said, "You just might be the most difficult man to kill I have ever known."

"I'm sorry to have caused you so much trouble," replied Thomas, "but I'm afraid I can't say the same thing about your employees. They die rather easily, but then, I suppose it is hard to find good help."

A streak of anger flashed in Claybourne's eyes, and Thomas took the instant of that distraction to let his right hand go towards his revolver.

Claybourne responded by thumbing back his revolver hammer. "I think not, Colonel Scoundrel." Then he smiled, and said, "By the way, how does any self-respecting man go through life with an embarrassment of a name like that? Have you no pride?"

"One might ask the same about your mental condition." He heard a half laugh and saw that Hamish had struggled to his knees beside the fallen door. Hamish looked Thomas in the eyes and grinned.

Claybourne began to move his barrel back and forth in front of the two men. At this distance he couldn't help but hit vital organs, but his vanity demanded that he respond to Scoundrel's insult before he killed the man. "Our definitions of sanity bear no resemblance to one another, Colonel. Look back through the ages and ask yourself how many great men made their marks on history by virtue of the application of your pathetically weak definition of mental competence."

Thomas took a step to the left, trying to create as much distance between himself and Hamish as possible. "You think you will be remembered by history as a great man, Noah? I think you will be a tiny footnote, if even that. On the other hand, I suppose it's possible that some mental illness might be named after you. That would be a fitting legacy for the Claybourne name. Your father did commit suicide by throwing himself down a flight of stairs at that Denver whorehouse, didn't he? And your daughter? A bag of rocks possesses more humanity than she does."

A few rays of sunshine began to stream into the room, and Thomas wondered how Mose, Sergey, and Von Sievers were doing out at the gate. He glanced down at Hamish and figured that he was wondering the same thing.

Claybourne was not shaken by Thomas's insults. "History, my dear

Colonel is written by the victors. In a matter of weeks, my associates and I will take control of northern Mexico, and with it a vast reserve of mineral wealth. You won't be alive to see it, of course, nor will your oversized friend. I will live out my days as the undisputed titan of the west, and someday, my daughter will follow in my footsteps."

Thomas took a chance. "Yes, you and she do share a great deal in common; generations of in-breeding have a way of producing congenital idiots." He took another step and then stopped when Noah said, "That will be enough moving, Colonel. Stay where you are."

"Those are the exact words your daughter used when she was done screwing me in the back of your wagon. Is that what she says when she finishes with you?"

Claybourne's eyes flickered. His cheeks flushed, his lower lip trembled, and his shoulders tensed. Hamish saw Noah lose his concentration and took the opportunity to grasp both sides of the oak door, pull back, and push himself up to his feet. Thomas and Claybourne were momentarily startled at the sight of the giant Scotsman deadlifting the three-hundred-pound door and holding it out in front of him like a shield. Then Thomas leapt behind Hamish and the protection of the door, and Claybourne began firing. The first bullet lodged in the wood, the second smashed through the door's leaded glass window and streaked out into the compound, and the next two shots also hit the solid wood without penetrating.

Thomas pushed hard against Hamish's back, and the two of them propelled the door forward. Their combined weight and the mass of the door knocked Claybourne down onto the floor on his back, leaving only his right arm visible. He still had a grip on his pistol, and two thoughts flashed through Thomas's mind: was Noah alert enough to pull the trigger after being crushed, and, how damn many shots had he already fired? He pulled himself off Hamish while the Scotsman kept his weight on the door and reached for his revolver.

His holster was empty. His Colt had fallen on the floor, and he could just see the butt sticking out from under the back corner of the door. As he bent to grab it, the sound of a revolver hammer being pulled back echoed in the hallway.

❖

As Rivas struck with his knife, Diego raised his left arm high and twisted his torso to the right, but he didn't move fast enough; Rivas's blade cut into the back of his defensive arm, just below the elbow. Had he been a half second slower or had Rivas delivered an undercut at that same location, the tendons under his elbow would have been severed, leaving him with no ability to block Rivas' attack.

Now, Diego did the unexpected. When Rivas attacked frontally, he anticipated that Diego would block with his arm and then step back, away from the second slash that would come within a second or two. But rather than move backwards, Diego quickly transferred his knife to his left hand, pulled his right arm close to his chest, and planted his right foot a few inches forward. Then he whipped his right leg behind him and to the left in a half circle motion, at the same time swinging his left arm in a wide arc with the blade of his knife pointed outward from his upraised palm.

Rivas was not prepared for such a swift move, especially from an opponent he had already determined was an exhausted cripple. He tried to pull back, but the swiftness and power with which Diego kicked his leg and swung his knife arm gave him a momentum that was unstoppable. Before Rivas could blink, Diego was behind him, and his knife was already biting into Rivas' right shoulder. The blade went deep, then withdrew, and before he could react, Rivas felt the blade press hard against the side of his neck. His right arm was frozen because of the shoulder cut, and he dropped his knife to the ground. His only option was to drop to his knees and try to pick the knife up with his other hand. What he didn't understand is why the *pendejo* behind him hadn't already plunged his knife into his neck and severed his carotid artery. That's sure as hell what he would have done if their roles were reversed. Instead, Rivas felt a boot on his back, and he was pushed face down into the dirt.

❖

Major Rhine saw the knife fight begin as he passed Diego and Rivas, but his focus was on the two men waiting on their horses at the other end of the porch. It was light enough now to make them out, and he was glad to see that they were looking away from the house in the direction of the gate. They had no reason to believe trouble would be coming from inside the compound, but there was no way they could miss the gunshots that suddenly rang out from inside the house as Rhine approached them.

The two dozen men camped behind the smokehouse probably heard the gunshots too. Rhine knew they were mostly ex-soldiers who had been cashiered out of the regular army and were now acting as General Greer's personal hired hands, but professionals or not, they were armed, and their job was to protect Claybourne and Greer and he expected they'd come pouring into the compound pretty quickly. He wasn't worried about the ranch hands sleeping in the bunkhouse a hundred yards outside the gate; Sergey, Von Sievers, and Mose Triplett would hold them off. For how long? That part he didn't know. At best they had an hour before the seventy-five men Greer sent after the farmers returned, along with the rest of Rivas's men. Time just wasn't on their side.

When he was within ten feet of the men, the one nearest swung around in his saddle. He reined his horse, drew his revolver, and aimed at Rhine. In the heartbeat between the time he thumbed back the lever and started to squeeze the trigger, Rhine let his first tomahawk fly through the still morning air. It spun around twice in its two-second flight, and cut into the base of the man's neck, just above his sternum. Rhine reached back and withdrew his second tomahawk as the man dropped his revolver, clutched his throat with both hands, and slid off his saddle onto the ground.

His friend heard the tomahawk strike and whirled his horse around, his revolver blazing. One shot struck a pole on the porch next to Rhine's head, another shattered a hanging flowerpot just above him. Before the man could shoot again, Rhine's tomahawk punched into his chest at dead center. The heavy blade cut through his breastbone, severed a main artery and sliced his heart in half. A look of surprise crossed the man's face, but he was dead before the reins slid out of his hands. He slumped forward with blood spraying from his chest and fell into a flower box that ran along the porch.

Rhine left the men-and his tomahawks-where they lay and trotted back towards Diego just in time to see Rivas fall to the ground, and Diego push his boot onto his neck. The Major climbed up the porch steps and surveyed the compound. No soldiers yet, and all was quiet in the bunkhouse across from the gate. He waved to Mose Triplett, who was standing on a boulder next to one of the gate's supporting timbers. Triplett waved his rifle from side to side, the signal that all was well.

Diego kept his boot on Rivas as he bent at the waist and made a swift cut across the tendons behind the Mescalero's right knee. When Rivas reached back reflexively to protect his leg, Diego ran his blade across his bicep, slicing deep through sinew and muscle.

Rhine looked up and down the porch. It had been less than two minutes since they crashed through the kitchen door and the fight began, but he knew their luck wouldn't hold much longer. Claybourne's men would be on them quickly. If they didn't find Cord, the plan called for them to back up Thomas and Hamish, and then to help get Claybourne away from Langton Hall to a place where they could extract information about Rosalilia from him.

"Diego," he said. "Finish it. We have to move."

Diego turned his head and nodded, and Rhine saw there was not so much as a whisper of either fury or triumph in his eyes. His expression was calm and resolute.

"Yes, *puto*," said Rivas. "Show the world your *cojones* and finish it. But then, you are a civilized man, so perhaps you should call for the sheriff and not take the law into your own hands. The law must be upheld, eh *compadre*?"

Diego slid his boot from Rivas's shoulder to the center of his back, allowing the bandit to lift his head out of the dirt. Then he raised Itzcoatl's *tecpatl* dagger high above his head. "For only a little while do you share us with each other," Diego said to the sky. "This is the eternal law." He pulled Rivas's hair back with his left hand, and with his other, he ran the razor-edged knife across the killer's throat.

As a pool of blood flowed onto the dirt around Rivas's head, Diego sheathed his knife and followed Major Rhine back into the house.

FIFTY EIGHT

Langton Hall

Thomas leapt up and Hamish rolled off the door onto the carpet, holding his hand tight against the wound in his side. He pulled himself into a sitting position against the wall and fought to catch his breath. If that bullet had struck his abdomen two more inches to the left, it would have pierced his gut and delivered a certain and painful death. Then he heard the hammer on Claybourne's gun pull back, followed by a hollow click as the hammer struck an empty chamber.

Thomas heard it too. Claybourne was out of ammo and trapped to boot. He turned from scanning the floor for his revolver and leaned down to check on Hamish.

"I'm fine, boyo," wheezed the Scotsman. "Grab the bastard and get him away from here. I'll be right behind ye."

Claybourne wasn't waiting. He slid his empty gun away and began struggling to get out from under the heavy door. First, he turned to his stomach and pushed to his hands and knees. Then he lifted with his legs and back, shimmied out, and bolted up to his feet.

It looked like he was going to make a run to his office, but a door opened at the end of the long hall and Diego stepped out of the kitchen, followed by Major Rhine. Noah stopped, turned to the left, and flew up eight carpeted stairs to the landing. Thomas left his revolver where it lay and raced after him. He put his right hand behind the newel post and used it as an anchor to generate enough momentum to hit the landing in two strides. He was moving so fast that he banged into the grandfather clock that was positioned in a corner. He pulled back, swung to the right, and threw himself up the stairs just as Noah was about to reach the second-floor hallway. He grasped the hem of Claybourne's coat with both hands, wedged his knees against the front of a step, and yanked back with all his strength. Then, he simply let himself fall backwards. His head hit a stair tread at the same instant that Claybourne's body somersaulted over and behind him and crashed into the clock.

Claybourne lay in a heap on his side, and blood was matting the hair on the back of his head where he had collided with the corner of grandfather clock. Thomas fought to focus through blurred vision and realized that his head had careened off the stair and come to rest on Claybourne's knee. He shook off the pain rocketing up his back and scrambled to his feet.

A few feet below him, Major Rhine was attending to Hamish, and Diego was starting up the stairs to help him drag Claybourne away from Langton Hall. Then, shots rang out in the compound. "I've got him," said Thomas. "They'll need your help out at the gate."

Diego tapped his forehead in a quick salute and went out through the opening where the entry doors used to be.

Thomas wiped his face with his sleeve and looked down at the unconscious body at his feet. Rapid-fire shooting continued outside as he leaned down and put his hands on Claybourne's shoulders, pulled him to a sitting position, and swung him around. Claybourne's head lolled on his chest, and his breath came in short, labored bursts, but Thomas did not see any obvious signs of broken bones. He started to drag Claybourne down the stairs when a hail of bullets shattered a first-floor window directly below him.

In the second it took to turn towards the sound, Claybourne roared back to life. From his seated position, he hit Thomas full force in the abdomen with his open right hand, followed immediately by a punishing upward blow into Thomas's crotch with his left. Thomas felt the air leave his body and a searing pain between his legs drove him down on one knee.

Claybourne shot up to his feet and delivered a powerful kick to the center of Thomas' chest. Then he pulled a glass-framed landscape painting off the wall and smashed it against Thomas's head. Exhausted, Noah leaned back against the wall to catch his breath. His next blow would be to Scoundrel's neck. If there was any life remaining in the whoreson at that point, he would use his bare hands to choke the last breath out of the fool.

Thomas fought to hold back the pain that was paralyzing his body. His lungs were screaming for air, one eye was swelling closed, and he felt blood dripping from his scalp and ear. Out of the corner of his good eye, he saw Rhine at the foot of the stairs with his revolver cocked, looking for an opening to shoot past him and take Claybourne out. Claybourne saw the Major too. He bent low, dropped onto the stairs and skittered up to the hallway like a venomous spider. Rhine fired twice, but both bullets hit stair posts, showering Thomas with wooden splinters. Before Rhine could fire a third time, Thomas was on his feet and running up the stairs.

Noah wheeled around and threw a punch just as Thomas reached the top step. The blow glanced off Thomas' jaw but carried enough force to send him flying back down the stairs. He reached out his hand and was able to stop his fall by grabbing onto an oak baluster. Then he righted himself, leaned forward, and charged back up. Noah could have used that moment to run down the hall to his bedroom and retrieve a pistol, but he chose to make his stand here and now. He planted his feet squarely and began to deliver a flurry of punches to take Thomas down before he could get off the stairs. Thomas had no choice but to take the first several hits head on; but, when Noah swung and missed on his fourth or fifth blow, he was able to drop his defensive posture. He lowered his head, clenched his fists, and surged forward as Claybourne was winding up to deliver a final haymaker.

Rhine raced up to the landing, trying to get a clear shot at Claybourne, but he and Thomas were banging back and forth against each other, and their arms were almost intertwined as they alternately threw and defended against one another's strikes. The Major had no choice but to aim and wait.

As they struggled, Thomas thrust his arms forward and wrapped them around Claybourne's waist. He pulled him close in a tight bear hug, raised up on the balls of his feet, and then slammed Claybourne to the floor. Thomas's punches were connecting. He struck Claybourne above the right eye and opened a cut along his eyebrow, then pummeled him in the solar plexus with both fists while pounding his knee into Noah's groin. But, when he raised his hand to deliver a killing blow to the soft tissue of Claybourne's neck, Noah thrust his hands up and stopped Thomas' fist in mid-air. Thomas fought to pull his hand back, but Claybourne was too strong. He held on for a few heartbeats and then briefly loosened his hold. Now he grabbed Thomas's wrist with both hands, yanked downwards, and at the same time, pushed over onto his side. The leverage he generated threw Thomas to the floor, and in a heartbeat, Claybourne was on top, battering Thomas's stomach and kidneys with his fists.

Rhine took two more stairs and leveled his revolver at Clayborne's back. But before he could fire, Claybourne swung off Thomas, grabbed him by his shirt, and in a sweeping move, pulled him to his feet and pushed him over against the stair railing. One good shove, and Colonel Scoundrel would plunge to his death on the foyer floor below.

Thomas felt vomit rising in his throat from the repeated punches, and his vision began to blur again. When he felt himself being pushed against the railing, he brought his arms close to his side and then thrust his hands up to Claybourne's face. He put his fingers under each side of Noah' s jaw and began to shove his thumbs into Claybourne's eyes. In response, Noah spread his arms out wide, and then slapped his open palms hard onto both sides of Thomas's face. Thomas reeled back, and his upper torso bent backwards over the top of the stair railing.

Rhine finally had his opening. He fired once, hitting Claybourne in the left shoulder. The bullet knocked him back into a mirrored hall tree, shattering glass and sending him to his knees. Thomas turned from the railing and advanced on Claybourne with his fists raised, but Noah wasn't out of the game yet. He grabbed an eight-inch shard of broken glass off the carpet and staggered to his feet, taking care to keep Thomas between himself and Major Rhine's Colt.

He clasped the glass dagger so tightly that it cut into his palm, and blood began dripping to the floor. "It's past time, Colonel," he hissed. He moved towards Thomas just as Rhine leveled his revolver again. The Major squeezed off the shot, but as he did, more bullets tore in from the outside, smashing into the foyer and stairs. One struck Rhine in his left calf. His hand dropped just as the gun went off, sending the bullet that was meant to finish Claybourne spiraling harmlessly into a stair tread. The impact of the bullet that hit his leg spun Rhine around. He lost his balance, tumbled backwards down the stairs, and fell onto a side table topped by a tall vase filled with wildflowers. The table collapsed under his weight, and he slumped to the floor, motionless.

Hamish had been propped against the wall as the fight raged around and above him. Now he willed himself to ignore the fire raging in his side and went over to where Rhine lay. The Major's breathing was shallow, but he was alive. Hamish needed to find the damn revolver that Rhine had dropped and finish the job he had started.

Fifteen feet above Hamish, Thomas and Claybourne continued to struggle. Hamish searched for the gun and watched out of one eye as Claybourne slashed back and forth at Thomas with the glass shard. Thomas stayed out of range by sliding back and forth along the railing until Claybourne stopped the wild swinging and raised the glass knife above his head to make a final, downward stab at Thomas's neck. As soon as Noah's arm went up though, Thomas grabbed his elbow with his left hand, and grasped his wrist with his right. Then he pushed Claybourne's elbow back against his chest while twisting his wrist down and to the left. The move helped him pivot around behind Claybourne and take control of his knife hand. With one hand holding the knife flat against Claybourne's abdomen, Thomas punched him so hard in the kidney that he heard a muffled groan, and the sound of air expelling from Noah's lungs.

It had to end now, Thomas thought. He banged his forehead hard against the bloody bullet hole on Claybourne's shoulder, and as Noah shuddered with pain and stumbled forward towards the stair railing, Thomas released the grip on his arm and took two steps back.

He didn't have enough strength for another round. He took a deep breath, cocked his right leg back, and then kicked with every ounce of strength remaining in his body. His boot caught Claybourne squarely in the middle of the back. A look of surprise crossed Noah's face, but it was too late to stop what was about to happen.

Hamish watched from below as Claybourne crashed through the carved wooden railing. He was looking down when he sailed out into nothingness, so his skull and neck were the first parts of his body to smash into the ground. His head fractured when it hit the corner of the fallen oak door, and the sound of his neck snapping like a dry chicken bone made Hamish flinch.

❈

There was still plenty of shooting going on out by the timber gate, but for the moment, no one was shooting into Langton Hall. Hamish saw that Rhine was coming around, and he brushed several flowers off the Major's head and helped him sit up. Thomas wobbled his way gingerly down the stairs, wincing with each step he took.

"That, my friend," said Hamish, "was the finest donnybrook I have ever attended, and God willing, when the sun goes down tonight I will be able to say it was my last."

"Are you alright?" asked Thomas when he got to the foot of the stairs.

Hamish looked down where the bullet had gone into his side. "Through and through," he said. "The bleedin' is slowing, so I'll sacrifice a little whiskey to clean it up, and we'll have another go at these fellas. Ye don't look so good yourself, you know. Not sure about the Major."

Rhine answered for himself. "I've got a bullet in my leg that we'll have to dig out later. I'll bandage it with a cloth; but there is a lot of business to be settled outside."

Thomas nodded and walked over to where Claybourne's broken body lay alongside the door that Hamish had knocked down. The sneer frozen onto his face showed that even in death, he remained true to his character.

"A hell of a thing," Thomas said, almost to himself.

"More than you know," added Rhine, who had gotten off the floor and limped across the foyer. He, Thomas and Hamish formed a semicircle around Noah's body.

"How's that?" asked the Scotsman.

Rhine pointed to the oil portrait of Noah's father on the wall directly above his son's head. The elder Claybourne's face was tight and drawn, and his eyes stared vacantly to a point far off on the horizon.

Hamish let out a soft whistle, and Thomas allowed himself a smile. He looked at the portrait and then down at Claybourne. He knew what Major Rhine meant.

"Like father, like son," he said.

The three men gathered up their weapons and walked out into the bright morning light.

As Fulbright said, the battle was just beginning.

❖

FIFTY NINE

Langton Hall

Thomas surveyed the battleground from behind a pillar on the covered porch. It was not a reassuring sight. Sergey, Diego, Von Sievers and Mose Triplett were taking fire from outside and inside the compound. Eighteen of Claybourne's hired guns had taken positions seventy-five yards to the east of the gate behind a row of temporary outhouses that had been set up for the tournament. At the same time, twenty-four of Greer's private soldiers were taking shots at them from behind the thick adobe walls of the smokehouse behind Langton Hall.

"If those army boys knew how to shoot, we'd be in trouble," said Rhine when he came up beside Thomas.

"They're not regular army," replied Thomas. "Mercenaries and penny-ante drifters, and Greer isn't paying them enough to risk their hides."

Then a volley of bullets slammed into the front of the house a few feet from them, and the men at the gate laid their fire on the smokehouse to force the soldiers back behind the building.

"Regular or not, they're shooting our way, and we best find a new place to visit," said Hamish.

Thomas looked at Rhine's bandaged leg. "Can you run?"

Rhine laughed. "I wasn't much of a runner before this, but I expect I can get up to speed for a bit."

"How about you?" Thomas asked Hamish.

"You just point, lad, and I'll show ye how fast a Highlander can waltz."

"We'll go out to the west, past the judging tables, and around the bull pen," said Thomas. "From there, the fence will provide us cover to the gate. I'll go to the boulder with Mose and Diego. Hamish, you're with Von Sievers; Major, you park beside Sergey."

"Aye, and then what?" asked Hamish.

Thomas pulled his revolver from its holster and checked the cylinder. "Then we figure out how to beat these boys back so we can go after Matthew Cord. He's our last connection to Rosalilia."

The men nodded at Thomas and drew their own guns. "Fire in the direction of the smokehouse as you run," said Thomas. "Anything we can do to keep them behind that wall."

With that, he fired a shot, and the three men ran into the compound.

❖

Sara Joliette hadn't wet herself yet, but she figured it could happen at any second. The *Times* reporter was huddled in the corner of the hut on the speaker's platform beside Tanner Fulbright and the reporters from Chicago and St. Louis. They watched as Thomas and the others made their way across the compound and disappeared behind the bull pen.

"Let's get to the house," said Fulbright. "More places to hide, and maybe we can get a better idea of what is going on."

The reporters were scared, but they followed Fulbright's lead down the steps and across the compound to the bullet spattered front entrance of Langton Hall. They stepped over broken glass and splintered pieces of the entry door and walked over by the stairs.

Sara felt bile rise in her throat when she looked down at Claybourne's contorted body. Then a voice called from down the hall. "Come through the kitchen," said the St. Louis reporter. Sara followed Fulbright into the kitchen and out onto the porch, where the Chicago reporter was standing next to Rivas's body. "Two more down there," he said, pointing to where Major Rhine had tomahawked the bandit leader's men.

Sara fell back against a porch pillar and held one hand over her mouth. "I can't do this," she said in a soft voice.

Fulbright took her arm.

"We're going upstairs to one of the bedroom terraces," he said. "We can see everything going on for miles from up there. Get your notebook ready-it's time to do your job."

"Is this what you expected?" asked Sara.

"Knowing Colonel Scoundrel and Diego de San Mártin, yes, it is exactly what I was expecting." He looked down at Claybourne's corpse and, in a near whisper, added, "Retribution." Then he motioned for the other journalists to follow and went back into Langton Hall.

❖

General Greer cursed himself for ever letting his best men go off on the rabbit hunt against the Tipton farmers. He paced anxiously inside the roomy, high-windowed smokehouse, while his fellow conspirators sat on the floor against the adobe walls.

"General, this is entirely unacceptable," said Senator Mack as more rounds struck the building. "This was not part of the plan. And, where the hell is Noah?"

That was the question, thought Greer. He figured Claybourne might have bolted when the shooting began. No matter, they would meet up later at their usual meeting place outside Denver.

"How many men are shooting at us?" wondered Antonio Resposo. "Who are they, and why haven't your men stopped them?"

"It doesn't matter," Greer replied to the former Vice-President of Mexico. "Some piss-ant lawmen, probably. My men are riding this way right now and will be here any minute. They'll mop up these sons of bitches faster than you can tie up your bootlaces."

"Let's hope so," said Congressman Renton. "We've got to keep our plan moving or we'll all end up swinging from a tree."

The back door opened, and a soldier's form was silhouetted against the blue morning sky.

"Yes, Corporal?" said Greer.

"You said to keep an eye on the back stairs of the house," said the soldier. "Looks like Mr. Claybourne's guests are fixin' to head home. They piled down the stairs a few minutes ago and went into the barn."

"Are they still there?"

"Yes, sir. Nobody's pulled out yet."

"Have Sergeant Wills assign you three men and get over there. Make sure none of those folks leaves the barn. None of them. Do you understand?"

The corporal nodded and closed the door. Claybourne's famous guests were at Langton Hall to serve three purposes: to elevate the importance of the fishing tournament to people around the world, to provide cover for the conspirators if there was ever an investigation of Monetverde, and, as a last resort, to serve as hostages if things went to hell and Greer and company had to negotiate their way out of the country. The notable guests were fine with the first purpose, of course, but they had no clue about the second or third. They were one step closer to figuring it out, though, thought Greer. And if they did, he would have no choice but to order the deaths of some of the most famous people in the world.

❖

Thomas raced from the edge of the bull pen to the timber gate and flew around the boulder to where Mose and Diego were calmly and steadily firing their rifles at the men hiding behind the outhouses. Hamish and Rhine took up their positions with Von Sievers and Sergey behind the massive timber uprights that framed the gate and joined in firing in the opposite direction, to where Greer's men were dug in behind the smokehouse.

Diego glanced at Thomas and let out a low whistle. "I think you need a doctor, my friend."

"I'm in better shape than Hamish and the Major. They both took bullets. I just took some fists and a painting to the head."

Mose fired a shot through the center of one of the outhouses. "We're not getting anywhere with this, Colonel. Every so often a rifle pokes around a corner and fires, and we return fire, but we're mostly wasting ammunition."

"They're not going to risk anything until Greer's men get here," said Thomas.

"How many are coming?" asked Diego.

Thomas saw movement at the side of the center outhouse and fired a shot.

"Seventy-five is the number I heard."

"The shooters behind the smokehouse are biding their time too," said Diego. "We can hold them off for a while, but we need to figure something out before the rest arrive. They will simply swarm around us and wait for us to run out of bullets."

"Ideas?" asked Thomas.

"That depends," said Diego. "Since you didn't bring Claybourne with you, I have to assume he was in no shape to travel."

Thomas squeezed off two more shots and re-loaded his revolver. With Claybourne dead, Matthew Cord was their only hope for finding Rosalilia.

"I'm sorry, Diego. I did my best."

A sudden flurry of gunshots exploded from behind the outhouses, but this time the shooters were aiming away from them towards the other side of the inner compound. They turned to see Salamander leap his horse over the compound fence from the west, pull behind the judges table, and swiftly dismount. He sprinted over to them as Thomas, Diego, and Mose laid down heavy covering fire. The deaf-mute Cheyenne ran over beside Von Sievers and began hand-signing. A minute later, the professor dashed over behind the boulder.

He gave Thomas the same once over as Diego had and then said, "Bad to worse, gentlemen. Red Elk's scouts say that the seventy soldiers Greer sent to intercept the farmers from Tipton are only twenty minutes away."

"Damn," said Thomas.

"So, we get the hell out of here and regroup with the Cheyenne?" asked Mose.

"That might be our only choice," said Diego.

Von Sievers raised his rifle and fired two more shots at the smokehouse. "I don't know about that," he said. "What if Red Elk sends a dozen warriors out to meet the soldiers, but instead of engaging them, the Cheyenne fire off a few shots and then race out towards one of the eastern canyons. The Captain in command will have to send a bunch of them after the war party. In fact, he'll probably send all the regular army troops. Greer's mercenaries wouldn't be up to the job."

"Which means only a few soldiers would be coming back here," added Mose. "I like those odds."

Diego and Thomas exchanged glances."Could work," said Thomas, "but the Cheyenne would have to understand they couldn't harm a single hair on any soldier's head. Do that, and the entire US Army will descend on them and their village."

"Yes, but how long can the Cheyenne keep the blue legs busy?" Sergey called from the other side of the gate.

Thomas saw an arm poke out from the side of an outhouse. He fired and saw the bullet strike the man in his shoulder. He dropped to the ground and was quickly dragged back behind the privy by his comrades.

"Long enough for us to figure out where to go from here," Thomas said.

Mose and Diego nodded in unison. "Tell Salamander what to do, Professor," said Diego.

Von Sievers made a series of hand signs to Salamander, who signaled that he understood. He raised his hand in goodbye and ran back to his horse.

Thomas and the others fired a volley against the shooters behind the toilets and the smokehouse as Salamander swung up on his horse, galloped to the fence, and flew over the rails towards Red Elk's camp.

"That's a fine boy, professor," said Mose.

"For a quiet type, yes, he is," answered Von Sievers.

❋

The stables at Langton Hall were new. The two-story barn-board structure with twenty horse stalls and an enormous hay loft sat fifty yards behind the main house, and, for the moment at least, it was not in the line of fire.

Samuel Clemens, Coors, and John L. Sullivan had shepherded the other guests away from the main house according to the plan, though none of them were happy to be roused at 4 a.m. and given only a moment to dress. Once they heard gunshots and crashes coming from downstairs, though, they raced down the back stairs in the chill dawn air without further complaint.

Once inside the barn, Clemens ascended the steps to the hay loft with Lily Langtry, Verdi, and Oscar Wilde in tow. They made themselves as comfortable as was possible on bales of summer alfalfa hay and spoke in hushed tones in the light of a kerosene lantern.

Sullivan and Adolph Coors kept watch through the front windows on the bottom floor, while Mary Orvis peered out the back window. They saw Rhine and Diego disappear down the long porch on the far side of the house and watched a minute later as Hamish beat down the main entry door and flew inside with Thomas right behind him. Then they held their breath as the sounds of breaking glass, splintering wood, and gunshots echoed around the compound. As the sky continued to lighten, they were able to make out the soldiers gathering behind the smokehouse, and Thomas's comrades standing guard at the gate to hold off Claybourne's riders, who were pouring out of the bunkhouse and taking up positions behind the line of outhouses.

"This is intolerable," complained Giuseppe Verdi when Clemens instructed him to find a place to sit and stay put.

"Loathe though I am to concur with the *maestro* on any issue," chimed in Wilde, "being roused from a comfortable bed in the middle of the night and marched out to a barn under threat of duress is hardly what I would call a hospitable act. And the smell, my God; this place reeks of horse apple."

At that moment a bullet tore through the upper window at the front of the stable and lodged in a beam just a foot above Wilde's head. The lanky Irishman jumped headfirst into a hay pile and stayed there until Clemens tapped his boot with his cane.

"Are they shooting at *us*?" cried Wilde as he emerged from the hay and pulled straw from his hair and dressing gown. "But that is absolutely savage. My agents assured me that your wild west had been tamed. Don't they know who I am?" He looked around. "Who *we* are?"

Lily Langtry had been sitting calmly on a hay bale. Now she pulled out a bottle of port from her bag that she had snagged from a hall table when they rushed out of the building. She took a sip and handed it to Clemens. The author took a pull and passed it on to Verdi.

"This would be a good time to tell us why we are here, Mr. Clemens," said Miss Langtry, "and what exactly all of the shooting is about."

Clemens was impressed by her spunk. He hung the lantern from a peg, lit his cigar, and exhaled a billow of fragrant smoke.

"That is a fair request, ma'am, one I will honor momentarily, if Mr. Wilde would be so kind as to hand me the jug."

He took a deep swig from the bottle and launched into the complete story, from Rosalilia's kidnapping and Thomas's near-death experience in Tamayo Ravine, to the grand story of Claybourne's Mexican scheme, including the massacre at Monteverde and the role played by Greer, Senator Mack, and the other conspirators. Sunlight was beginning to filter in through the stable windows when he reached the part about last night's meeting on the prairie.

"As for the rest," Clemens finished, tilting his head towards the staccato sound of gunfire erupting around the compound, "I suspect the tale is not yet complete."

Wilde shook his head. "But this is positively Shakespearean," he said, "Homeric, really. The fate of nations, titans at battle. It is beyond extraordinary."

"It is all that," answered Clemens, "and I'd give the royalties on my next book to know the ending."

"But this could be your next book," said Langtry, raising her hands and looking around the barn and out towards the battlefield. Clemens was about to answer when there was a stirring on the ground floor, and the sound of a side door opening. Clemens motioned for the others to remain quiet and went over to the edge of the loft to see what was going on below.

Two soldiers had come through the door and were standing in front of Clemens and Coors, while Mary Orvis remained in the shadows at the back of the stable.

"General Greer wasn't told you folks were coming out here," said one of the soldiers.

"Really?" said Coors. "Is there some reason we should have to ask permission of the military before we take a stroll outdoors?"

"When there's a revolution on his doorstep, yes, he has every right to know where you are and where you are going," replied the soldier with two stripes on his sleeve.

"You're a bit misguided, lad," Sullivan said as he took two steps towards the soldier who was doing the talking.

The soldier put his hand on his holster. "It's Corporal, sir, and I have my orders. You and the rest of the guests will remain in here under our watch."

"Watch?" laughed Sullivan. "Watch this!" With that he threw a lightning fast undercut punch that lifted the Corporal two inches in the air. The soldier's knees crumpled, and he fell unconscious to the ground.

The other soldier froze in amazement at the sight of the world's most famous boxer in action, but Adolph Coors did not freeze. He grabbed a pair of heavy blacksmith tongs from a peg on the wall and swung it against the side of the soldier's head. In a moment, he was lying on the ground beside his friend.

Clemens was about to call down congratulations when he heard a lever action rifle being cocked. He looked down to see two more soldiers coming out of the darkness at the back of the barn. Their rifles were pointed at Coors and Sullivan, and they were marching Mary Orvis in front of them.

"Step over there," said one of the soldiers, waving the barrel of his gun towards an empty stall. "Don't think I won't shoot. Now get."

The soldiers were almost directly below the loft, with their backs to Clemens.

"Help me," Clemens whispered to Oscar Wilde. The poet raised his hands as if to say, 'with what?' when he saw Clemens walk over to a double wide hay bale. Clemens began to walk one end of the bale towards the edge of the loft, and Wilde bent to help with the other end. The Irishman was surprisingly strong, and in a few seconds the heavy bale was perched lengthwise at the edge of the loft.

Below them, Coors, Sullivan, and Mary Orvis were starting to walk to the stall their captors wanted them to enter. The soldier's backs were still to the loft, and Clemens waved to Sullivan to get his attention. The boxer raised his eyebrows in acknowledgment and winked at Coors. Adolph raised his eyes to the loft and put the picture together for himself.

Clemens now used his hands to make a 'back-up' motion so Sullivan and Coors could get the soldiers to step back a few feet.

"Do you want us to move your friends?" Sullivan asked the soldiers.

"Big of you to care," came the reply. He looked over at his friend, who simply nodded. The unconscious soldiers were splayed out on the ground a foot or two in front of the soldiers holding the rifles. The guards took a couple of steps back so that Sullivan and Coors could drag their friends out of the middle of the stable.

As soon as the soldiers moved back, Clemens nodded to Wilde, and the two of them put their feet against the hay bale and kicked it over the side.

Verdi and Lily Langtry had tiptoed up to the edge, and now they watched as the bale flew through the air and landed squarely on the heads of the soldiers below.

The men were slammed to the ground, but before they could gather their wits, Coors and Sullivan relieved them of their rifles and had them pointed at their midsections.

Clemens and his cohorts, in what the author would refer to as the "Great Hay Bale Battle" in after-dinner speeches for years to come, hurried down the stairs and joined their friends.

Lily Langtry's eyes were shining with excitement, and even the reliably dour *Signori* Verdi was beaming with delight. Oscar Wilde couldn't help but put a foot on the back of one of the unconscious soldiers and pose with one hand in his vest like a big game hunter with his trophy. "Oh, but for a camera I would be the most famous man on earth within the week," he sighed.

Clemens went over beside Sullivan and Coors. "As I see it, gents, we still have two problems: what to do with these boys and what to do about our own situation." Given the steady gunfire pinging around the compound, Clemens summation of their present circumstance rang true with the others.

"As for them," said Coors looking down at the four soldiers, "we tie them up."

He went over by the wall to a wooden box filled with three-foot lengths of twisted sisal rope. He slid the box over by the soldiers and then turned to Mary Orvis. "Do you happen to know how to tie a knot?" he asked.

Mary put her hands on her hips and began to laugh, and in a minute everyone joined her, except for Adolph. He had been working day and night in the beer tent during the tournament and was the only one among them who had not witnessed Miss Orvis demonstrate her remarkable knot-tying skills for the other contestants.

Mary dipped her hand into the box, pulled out two lengths of rope, and in a heartbeat joined them together with a double fisherman's knot.

"How tight do you want them?" she asked Coors.

Then, to the accompaniment of the symphony of gunshots playing around Langton Hall, Mary Orvis bound the four soldiers' tightly at their wrists and ankles.

❖

SIXTY

The prairie and Langton Hall

After twenty-four years in the Army, Major Lucious Crane was preparing for the death-knell of mandatory retirement that loomed just six months away. The cavalry was all he knew: from Hampton Roads to Shiloh, Antietam to Sherman's March to the Sea, and a dozen battles in-between, he lived his entire adult life in the saddle. He had been stationed in Colorado since the Sioux Wars ended five years ago, where his reputation as a tough but fair commander made him General Greer's choice to manage the training of all new Army recruits in the region.

Crane had no love for war, but he had to admit that his finest hours had been spent leading men into battle against well-matched enemies. He had engaged the Rebs in sweeping cavalry attacks across artillery-splashed fields, and in ferocious hand-to-hand combat in trenches, on mountain slopes and in tall green forests of ripening corn. The Confederates had been a determined enemy, but they could not rival the horsemanship of the Comanche, or the bravery and discipline of the Sioux. Plains warriors had been his greatest foes, but until a few minutes ago, he thought his Indian-fighting days were long past.

His orders that morning were to double-time it from Langton Hall and intercept a force of forty to fifty insurrectionists who were marching from the town of Tipton to Claybourne Ranch. General Greer's orders were specific: Crane and his seventy-five regular army troops were to chase down the combatants from Tipton and squash their attempted rebellion. "Obliterate" was the word the General had used.

"They have massacred women and children," Greer told him as his men assembled in the pre-dawn darkness. "They mean to kill Mr. Claybourne and his guests and occupy his ranch to draw more people to their cause. We must make an example of them that is not lost on anyone contemplating such a foolhardy association. Not one of the seditionists is to walk away from the battlefield. Not one. Do you understand your orders, Major?"

Crane heard them clearly, but as he led his column of men to the east out of Langton Hall, he was also deeply troubled. He had heard nothing of an insurrection or of an armed militia operating in this part of Colorado. As for the claim that these were the men who had laid Monteverde to waste, why didn't Greer come out and say it directly? Crane knew the savagery that had been inflicted on that poor little town. If the men riding from Tipton were responsible, he would have no problem meting out the justice they deserved. But only if they put up a fight. If they chose to surrender in the face of his superior force, he would take them to the stockade at Denver and let the federal authorities deal with them, according to the law. That might not satisfy General Greer's command to "obliterate" the men, but Crane was a soldier, not an executioner. He would undertake this assignment to the best of his ability, using all his command experience and skill, but only in accordance with the established rules of warfare and the dictates of his conscience. Better to face a court-martial for disobeying an order than experience the personal moral consequences of presiding over a slaughter, he thought, even if it cost him his pension.

Two hours out of Langton Hall, a soldier rode up behind the column at a hard gallop and fired his rifle in the air to get their attention. The troops slowed their horses to a walk and allowed the rider to catch up.

"General Greer's compliments," said the messenger to Major

Crane. "You are to turn about and double-time it back to Claybourne's."

"And why is that?"

"The General says there are no rebels coming from Tipton. The story was a ruse to get you and your men to leave Langton Hall unprotected. Word is that a band of brigands led by Colonel Scoundrel are actually the ones who are planning an attack."

Major Crane shook his head. He knew Thomas Scoundrel well and had served beside him in the winter of '77-'78. Scoundrel was many things, he thought, but a brigand was not one of them.

"You sure about that, son? Did General Greer identify Colonel Scoundrel by name?"

The corporal looked at the ground. "No sir, not by name, but there is a lot of talk going around. Somebody mentioned Indians, too."

Soldiers and gossip, Crane thought to himself. Glued at the hip.

"Did the General say anything else?"

"No sir, just that you were to haul ass-sorry, sir, it's what he said."

Crane knew that nothing would be sorted out until he returned to Langton Hall. He gave the order, and the column swung about at a trot and rode back through their own dust.

❋

They had been following the stage road for an hour when Crane saw movement on a grassy ridge a hundred yards to the south. He blinked a couple of times to make sure he wasn't seeing cottonwood shadows thrown by the rising sun. Then he saw the movement again, like a long line of curtains flapping gently in the breeze.

"Captain Benjamin, would you please halt the column."

Benjamin raised one hand in the air, and a sergeant called out for the soldiers to come to a stop.

"Ben," said the Major, "What the hell is that on the rise over there?"

The captain pulled his field glasses from a pouch on his saddle and focused where the Major was pointing. Then, he let out a low whistle.

"I'll be damned, sir. Looks to be a war party. Cheyenne. And they're sure enough dressed for the ball."

He handed the binoculars to Crane, who sighted in on a line of Cheyenne in full war dress sitting stock-still on their horses at the crest of the ridge. "I count twelve. Rifles, lances, and they're mostly young bucks, too."

"No law against going out for a ride, I suppose," said Benjamin. "I mean, there hasn't been a lick of trouble with the Cheyenne for what, four years?"

"No law, that's true, but I'm guessing this bunch is from Red Elk's village. They have been on notice for years to pack up and move north to the reservation in Montana."

Sergeant Albion rode up beside them. "Should I send a trooper over for a parley and see what those lads are up to?"

Crane thought for a moment. "They're not making any moves, and I don't know of any reason to interfere with them. Could be on their way to a wedding for all we know."

"Shotgun wedding?" laughed Benjamin.

"Our orders are to double-time it back to Claybourne's," said Crane. "Sergeant, give the–"

Before Major Crane could finish his sentence, the sharp cracks of rifle fire rippled through the morning stillness. He raised the binoculars and saw puffs of smoke appear as the Cheyenne warriors fired a second volley.

"At us?" asked Benjamin. "From that distance? They're wasting bullets."

"Swing our boys around, Mister," came Crane's reply. "Looks to me like we have found the real insurrectionists. I'll take B Company and see what Red Elk is getting at. You get the rest of the men back to Claybourne's, full out. Tell the general we have been engaged by the Cheyenne. We will come to Langton Hall presently."

Captain Benjamin saluted and started to ride away when he was stopped by Major Crane.

"Ben," said the Major. "What the corporal said about Colonel Scoundrel being mixed up in this…whatever you ride into when you get to Langton Hall, believe me when I tell you that Scoundrel is no part of any kind of insurrection. I trust him. You can too."

"Understood, sir."

Then, Captain Benjamin and twenty-five soldiers peeled off the column and galloped towards Langton Hall, while the fifty men of B Company formed up behind Crane. "You gentlemen know the drill," he barked. "Hard charge over open ground. If the Cheyenne keep firing, you are to return fire. If they high-tail it, we will pursue. If they do not surrender, you are free to engage. Check your weapons now and spread out wide."

He checked his own revolver and then shouted, "Sergeant Albion, you are with me." More shots rang out from the rise, and Major Crane signaled for his men to charge.

❖

Four Bears sat on his horse in the center of the line of warriors waiting on the rise. He knew that Hiamovi and the other young fighters were disappointed at Red Elk's order that they not harm any of the soldiers. Firing over the soldiers' heads to simply get their attention was a cowardly act, they thought. Each of them wanted to fight, to plunge his lance into the heart of a worthy opponent and live to tell the tale to his grandchildren around the council fires years from now. Even so, Four Bears knew he could depend on each of them to follow his orders. He signaled for one more harmless volley to be fired, and, when the soldiers began to ride their way, he swung his pony around and raced off. His warriors followed, their headdresses and lances shimmering in the morning light. At the entrance to a box canyon two miles away, Salamander, Dawn Pillow, and several dozen women and elders waited to put Red Elk's plan into motion.

❖

From his position at the boulder near the gate, Thomas saw a stable door swing open. Samuel Clemens stepped outside and waved his arm from side to side. That was the signal that everything was well. Diego and Mose Triplett continued to fire whenever they saw movement around the outhouses, while at the other side of the gate, Hamish, Von Sievers, Rhine, and Sergey Baklanov shot back into the compound each time a soldier poked his head out from behind the smokehouse.

We are seven against at least thirty, Thomas thought. We can't get across the compound and back into the house, or out to the tent encampment where our horses are tied. The stalemate was bad enough on its own, but he knew things were going to go downhill fast when the regular army soldiers returned from their wild goose chase. Rivas's men are still out there, too, he reminded himself. They should return at about the same time as the soldiers. He and his friends were already pinned down by Claybourne's cowhands firing from the front and by Greer's private soldiers shooting from behind. How long could they hold out once another seventy-five soldiers–every one of them a battled hardened veteran–joined the fray?

He saw Sergey flinch when a bullet struck the timber post next to him and showered him with splinters, and he noticed that Major Rhine was using a downed tree branch to support his wounded leg. Just then, Mose shot a ranch hand dead center in the chest when the man stepped out from behind an outhouse to get a clear shot. The cowboy went down hard, but his friends did not attempt to pull him back.

Diego lowered his rifle. "Cord can't be far from here, Tomás. I must go after him before he gets away again. We may not have another chance."

Thomas knew how hard it would be for Diego to leave his friends at the gate, outnumbered and outgunned. He also knew that there was no other choice if there were to have any hope of finding Rosalilia. He dug into his saddlebag and tossed a pouch of cartridges to Diego and then whistled for the attention of the men at the other side of the gate. When Hamish looked over, he made a hand-signal and pointed into the compound to where Salamander had tied his horse a few minutes ago. Hamish understood and turned to speak to the other men.

Diego put his hand on Thomas's shoulder. "I am sorry to leave you like this."

Thomas smiled. "It's why we came here in the first place, Diego. Go, find Cord, and get to Rosalilia. We'll hold things together here."

Diego clutched his rifle and raced to the other side of the gate. Each of the four men there shook his hand, and then they joined with Thomas and Mose to lay down cover fire as Diego ran into the compound, circled the judges' table, and disappeared behind an outbuilding.

"All good things to you and Rosalilia, my friend, *y vaya con dios*," whispered Thomas. Then he sighted in on the barrel of a rifle as it peaked out from behind an outhouse and squeezed the trigger.

❖

SIXTY ONE

On the prairie

The little box canyon had been gouged out of millions of years of accumulated limestone and shale deposits by a river that completed its work a millennium ago and then dried into the very earth it had sculpted. The entrance to the canyon appeared out of nowhere, a slash in the ground seventy-five yards wide and a quarter mile long that gradually sloped down over one hundred feet below the surrounding landscape until it abruptly terminated into a sheer rock wall that rose straight up to the sky.

The landscape around the canyon was a flat sea of brush, gravel, and boulders, with a few scrub pines and creosote bushes holding in what little topsoil remained. Salamander leapt off his horse at the canyon entrance, where thirty women, children, and elders from his village were at work under Dawn Pillow's direction.

The villagers were piling limbs, dried grass, branches, and sticks along the sides of the entrance to the canyon, leaving a path wide enough for four horses to ride abreast. Exactly the way the cavalry was trained to charge, thought Salamander.

He signed to Dawn Pillow that Four Bears and the warriors had intercepted the soldiers, and the chase was on. She smiled and signed for him to take his position. Then she called out to her people and told them it was time to go. They used brushy limbs to sweep away their tracks and hurried to safety among a jumble of enormous boulders that were scattered around like a child's forgotten toys. They would wait there until Dawn Pillow gave the signal.

Salamander surveyed the scene to make sure that everything looked natural, with no traces of the dozens of people who had been working there all night. Then he wheeled his horse and galloped back in the direction that Four Bears and the warriors should be coming from. He stopped a half mile later beside a flat rock under a pine tree to retrieve the bag he had hidden last night. Inside were two small pots of paint, a beaded vest, and a war bonnet made with eagle feathers tipped with gray and accented with black horsehair. The feathers' bottoms were wrapped with vivid red yarn and were sewn onto a felt skull cap. Strips of white rabbit fur dropped from each side, and a multi-color brow band and beaded temple rosettes signaled that the warrior wearing the head dress was a man of great physical and spiritual strength.

He painted stripes on his face, adjusted his vest, and then carefully pulled the headdress on. It fit snugly-a good thing since his task called for him to ride flat out for a mile or more. For a brief instant, he wished that he had a trading post looking glass so he could admire his reflection before he rode into battle. He immediately dismissed that thought as childish, swung up onto his pony and grabbed his battle lance from its resting place against a pine. Today was his fifteenth birthday. It was a good day to become a warrior.

❖

Red Elk sat on his horse in a thicket of brushy pine fifty yards from where Salamander stopped to put on his paint and bonnet. The old man watched as the boy prepared for battle, and a memory of his own first ride onto a field where the enemy was waiting to take his life rekindled feelings he had not known for decades.

Red Elk believed that every young man should know the bittersweet experience of battle, even if only once, and even if no blood was shed. Hard times created strong men, the chief understood, and strong men created easy times. But easy times, in turn, created weak men, and weak men always went on to create more hard times. Red Elk knew that many did not understand the truth of that never-ending cycle, but no matter the state of the world, every family's responsibility should be to raise warriors, especially during the easy times.

He turned his horse and rode deeper into the stand of pine without making a sound. He would not interrupt the boy on the day he fully became a man.

❖

Four Bears loved the feel of the wind on his face and the sound of horses sprinting beside him under the cloudless sky. It had been years since he rode into battle, and he had forgotten how powerfully the blood surged through the body when you were riding full speed towards the enemy. He looked at the smiles on the faces of the eleven young men racing beside him and knew they were feeling the same emotions.

He led his men at a full gallop towards the soldiers, who were strung out from east to west in a long line, with their commander at the center. The officer held a sword above his head, but the others had not yet drawn rifles or revolvers. A wise man thought Four Bears. He is waiting for us to make the first move.

The Cheyenne did not disappoint. Four Bears thrust his lance into the air, which was a signal for the Cheyenne to fire once more and then turn and race towards the box canyon a mile distant.

❖

The sun was topping the eastern horizon as Crane and his men began the chase. Red Elk's warriors pounded along the dirt coach road, throwing up clouds of pewter-colored dust that choked the soldiers and limited their vision. Crane estimated they started the pursuit two hundred yards behind the Cheyenne, who continued to fire randomly as they swept deeper out into the prairie.

It had to be a trap, of course. Crane knew Cheyenne tactics from hard personal experience; there had to be a bigger purpose to their attack than he could figure, at least now. The outcome of a pitched battle between fifty seasoned soldiers against a dozen or so young warriors was not in question. Were the Cheyenne simply trying to keep him from riding to assist Claybourne and General Greer against the insurgents at Langton Hall, whoever the hell they might be?

Crane pressed his horse forward and decided that he would give chase for another half mile. He needed to determine if there was a larger war party hiding somewhere, and if so, to figure out their intentions. An attack on a single Army patrol would gain nothing for the Indians except misery and death. Ten years ago it might have been a different story; the Cheyenne and their allies could field a formidable fighting force that could hold its own against an entire regiment. But in the years since, the tribes had been dispersed to reservations around the West and had shown no signs of trying to regroup for further fighting.

The soldiers sailed up a rise on the road, and for the first time they had a clear view of the landscape ahead. The Cheyenne were approaching a field of boulders, where they would be lost to sight for a few moments. That could be the ambush site, thought Crane. He signaled to Sergeant Albion, who nodded his understanding. The sergeant raised his hand in the air, and the soldiers of B Company slowed their horses to a trot.

"You think those boys have friends around the rocks?" asked Albion.

"That would make sense if I could figure out why they're pulling this stunt," replied Crane. "There's just no reason for them to be trying to start a war."

"When did an Indian need–" Albion's words were cut off by a barrage of gunfire from the rocks.

"Left and right," shouted Crane. The fifty men in his column immediately split into two separate groups, one swinging to the west, the other to the east. Then, just as quickly as it started, the sound of gunfire evaporated in the morning air. Albion shot a questioning look at the Major. "Damned if I know," said Crane. He raised his hand and motioned for the columns to halt and then regroup behind him.

A moment later, his men were assembled, carbines at the ready.

But there was no sound and no movement around the boulders. Suddenly, a solitary warrior rode out from behind a rock and stopped, followed by the other Cheyenne. The first warrior remained at his station as his comrades swung into a single file and headed away at a slow, steady gait.

"They sheathed their rifles," noted Albion. "Maybe they finally figured we have them outnumbered four to one."

"I don't think so. One of those boys is staying put. Let's see what he has to say. Hold the column and come with me."

Crane and the sergeant rode towards the warrior. When they were a hundred feet apart, the Cheyenne calmly raised his rifle and fired a shot that sent a puff of dust into the air in front of Crane's horse and then lowered his rifle.

The major shook his head in disbelief but raised his hand to stop his men from returning fire. "Do you know this area?" he asked his sergeant.

"No, sir, never had a reason to come out this way. Seems pretty flat other than that rock field. Not much in the way of trees or brush, neither."

"I'd like to send a scout out there, but we don't have time. I want to catch that buck, and then get to Claybourne's fast."

Crane turned to his men. "Ride him down," he ordered, "but don't shoot him unless you have to. I want to talk to him."

Fifty soldiers shot forward and raced towards the bravest-or craziest-Cheyenne warrior they had ever encountered.

❖

Salamander laid his rifle across his saddle, wheeled his horse, and galloped towards the canyon. So far, Red Elk's plan had gone just as they hoped. For it to work completely, the soldiers had to pay enough attention to him that they weren't aware they were riding into a box canyon. That would take some doing.

It was only a hundred yards to the canyon now, and he turned in his saddle and fired off a final round above his pursuer's heads.

Even though he had been there a dozen times, Salamander was still surprised when he realized he was headed down the rocky slope that led deep into the canyon. He hoped it would also be a surprise to the soldiers.

❋

Major Crane flew after Salamander, with his men close behind him. When he passed between a pair of boulders that were encircled with piles of brush, the sight barely registered in his mind. A few seconds later, he noticed that the rocky trail was dropping down at a steep angle, but by then it was too late. He swung his head around and tried to look back through the dust. There was movement behind the column, but it wasn't horses, which meant the other Cheyenne were not behind them. They were only fifty yards behind the warrior. It was time to end this.

Sergeant Albion felt his heart sink when he figured out that they were riding down into a canyon, but the major pressed on. Then, looming straight ahead, he saw the rock wall that marked the box end of the canyon. He looked up to the rim of the canyon, but there were no Cheyenne warriors lined up there waiting to shoot down on them like fish in a barrel. When he looked back towards the canyon entrance, he thought he saw smoke rising. Must be dust, he thought.

Salamander galloped at a dead heat up to the rock wall and yanked back on the reins at the last second. He slung his rifle over one shoulder, leapt off his horse, and dug one hand into a crack in the limestone. Then he began climbing upwards, hand over hand. He was about twenty feet up the sheer face when Crane and his men came to a racing stop at the wall beside his horse.

"Sergeant," commanded Crane, "send two men to the rear and see what the hell is going on back there." He looked up again to make sure no Cheyenne had approached the rim of the canyon above them. "Company, form two lines and spread out tight against each side of this damn box. If they come at us from above, let's be hard to hit."

The column split in two, and a minute later the soldiers and their horses were pressed tight against the canyon walls. Whichever side the attack came from, the soldiers on the opposite side who would be in the line of fire would immediately make their way to the other side. And if the Cheyenne placed themselves on both sides of the canyon rim? Crane didn't want to consider that possibility.

He sat on his horse and watched Salamander continue to scramble up the rock face of the canyon. What was he doing?

The sound of galloping horses announced the return of the troopers who had been sent to scout the canyon entrance.

"Big fire," shouted one of the scouts as he rode up to Major Crane. "Flames are too high and deep to ride through."

"Any sign of their warriors?"

"Can't see anything through that fire. No way to tell what's on the other side, but it keeps getting bigger, like somebody is throwing more fuel onto it."

Crane could see the smoke and flames licking high into the sky at the canyon entrance. The fact that no one was shooting at them from the rim above was puzzling. It seemed like somebody wanted to bottle them up for a while.

"I want to talk to that damn spider," he said, pointing to Salamander, who was now halfway up the wall.

In response, Sergeant Albion raised his rifle and fired a shot. It hit rock just a few inches from Salamander's face, kicking up shards of limestone that splattered his forehead and neck. Albion cocked his rifle again. He wouldn't miss this time. Before he could squeeze the trigger, Major Crane reached over and stayed his hand.

"I want to talk to him. I don't want him dead."

Albion lowered his rifle. "Beg your pardon, sir, but how do you propose we get him back down here?"

Crane shrugged his shoulders. He didn't have a clue, and the fire raging at the canyon entrance limited his options. He was about to speak when he saw movement on the canyon rim directly above him. He looked up and made out the figure of a tall woman in a doeskin dress. Her hair was swept back so that it would not get in the way of the bow that was slung over one shoulder. Without asking, Crane was sure she knew how to use it.

The warrior who had led them into the canyon had made it to the top. He pulled himself up over the ledge and walked over beside the woman.

"Who are you?" shouted Crane. "What do you want?"

"I am Dawn Pillow, daughter of Red Elk, Chief of the Cheyenne. And you are?"

"Major Lucious Crane, United States Army," he shouted back. "And apparently, I am your guest."

Crane was certain he saw her smile.

"Only for one hour, Major. My people will feed the fire only for that long, and then you and your men will be free to leave."

"Why? So your warriors can attack civilians someplace else?"

"We are not at war with civilians, or anyone else, except for those who attacked Monteverde and wish to make it look as though we were responsible."

"Holding fifty US soldiers hostage like this doesn't help your cause."

"When the fires die down, make your way to Langton Hall," said Dawn Pillow. "Find Colonel Thomas Scoundrel. He will explain everything." With that, she and Salamander turned and disappeared from the canyon rim.

Scoundrel again, thought Crane. But why hadn't she told him to talk to General Greer, the commander of all army forces in the southwest? He was at Langton Hall, as well. As for Captain Benjamin and the twenty-five troops he had sent to Claybourne's, God only knew what they were riding into.

He gave the order for his men to dismount and rest and reached for his canteen.

One hour.

❖

SIXTY TWO

Langton Hall

A half hour had passed since Thomas, Hamish and Major Rhine sprinted out of Langton Hall, across the gravel compound and over to the cover provided by the boulders on either side of the great timber gate. Thomas and Rhine joined Mose Triplett on one side, while Hamish took up a position behind the boulder on the other side with Sergey and Professor Von Sievers. Diego had made his way out of the compound several minutes earlier to search for Matthew Cord.

Claybourne's ranch hands poured out of the bunkhouse when the firing began and were now taking pot shots at them from behind the row of privies that had been set up for the tournament fifty yards outside the gate. Inside the compound, Greer's private soldiers were waiting in reserve behind Langton Hall for the order to pile on. Despite being outnumbered six to one, however, Thomas and his friends felt confident about their chances–for the short-term, at least. Unless the ranch hands or soldiers found the courage to mount a frontal assault on their position, the battle was going to rage on until one side ran out of ammunition. They had to make every shot count, Thomas thought to himself, and find a way to either hang on until help arrived or get the hell out of there and link up with Diego or Red Elk on the prairie.

Mose began to press his last ten .44-40 cartridges into his Winchester. "Is it true you Cossacks can stay in the saddle for two or three days without rest?" he called across to Sergey as he loaded the rifle.

Sergey popped off a shot towards the smokehouse and said, "My friend, if my horse was in front of me right now, I am sure I could stay in the saddle for a month, or however long it took to get back to mother Russia."

Von Sievers laughed. "Make that the Müller-Thurgau vineyards along Lake Konstanz in Germany for me."

"I'll take the Isle of Skye in the Hebrides in the spring," chimed in Hamish as he lobbed two shots in quick order in the direction of the outhouses. "A stone cottage on a cliff above the sea"

"What about you, Mose?" asked Thomas.

"The Gulf Coast. In early summer," Triplett answered. "Calista and me on the boat, hauling in a full load of shrimp." He finished loading his Winchester and fired a shot that knocked the handle off an outhouse door.

"I'll take my ranch, any season of the year," volunteered Rhine. "Anaya and my dog. That's all I need." He looked across at Thomas but knew that of all the men facing death at the gate this morning, Thomas was the only one who would not be able to answer the question. Scoundrel had no roots and no home or loved ones to return to.

The Major squeezed his ammo pouch and estimated that he only had about a dozen rounds remaining. One of the men was going to have to make a supply run to the tent camp where his wagon was parked. Before he could alert Thomas, a bullet creased the boulder next to him, and he felt flakes of razor-sharp stone cut through the back of his shirt.

Then Von Sievers called out and pointed towards Langton Hall. Rhine and Thomas looked across the compound and saw Fulbright and the *Times* reporter waving at them from a second story bedroom terrace. When Thomas made eye contact, Fulbright pointed to the north.

"Holy shit," muttered Rhine.

Thomas could only nod in agreement. On the slope seventy yards behind the outhouses, a line of mounted soldiers had appeared and taken up position.

"I count twenty-five," said Hamish, "Including an officer."

"They look to be regular army," added Mose, "not saddle bums like

Greer's men at the smokehouse."

Thomas shook his head. The good news was that there were only twenty-five soldiers. That meant at least fifty had fallen for Red Elk's plan and were somewhere out on the prairie instead of joining the fight. He turned to Rhine. "What do you think their play will be?"

"They're professionals," said the Major. "First thing they'll do is size things up. It won't take but a minute for them to see we are pinned down, and they can just wait for us to run out of ammo. They don't have to do anything heroic."

"I'm guessing they'll send somebody in to talk to the general," said Mose. "All they know right now is that there weren't any farmers marching here to burn down Claybourne's place."

"And what do you suppose the general will say to them?" asked Hamish. Thomas noticed his voice was labored. The effects of the wound he received earlier was growing more pronounced. The Scotsman needed a doctor.

"No mystery there," answered Rhine. "He's going to order them to finish the job."

As they watched, a man appeared from behind a line of brush and approached the soldiers. Thomas recognized him as one of Greer's personal troops. The man spoke briefly to the officer, who immediately turned his horse and galloped along the same path that Greer's messenger had taken. His men stayed put on the rise, biding their time.

"He's going to get the order," said Von Sievers. He and his comrades stopped firing. It was silent as each of the men at the gate contemplated what was surely going to happen in the next few minutes.

❖

Captain Benjamin could make no sense of the scene outside the grounds of Langton Hall. When he and his men passed through the tent encampment a hundred yards from the gate, folks shouted to him about a big fight going on, but they were staying put and had no idea who was shooting at who. He rode on to a rise outside the compound where a dozen or more cowboys armed with rifles and revolvers were kneeling behind a row of privies. Every few seconds one of them would lean around the corner of an outhouse and take a shot towards the large boulders at either side of the massive timber gate. Was one of the men behind those rocks Colonel Scoundrel? And if it was, who was firing towards the gate from the cover of the adobe up by the main house?

As he tried to sort out the situation, a runner approached from a thicket of brush. The man wore a shabby uniform and hadn't shaved in days. One of Greer's private mercenaries, thought Benjamin.

"General Greer is holed up in that adobe smokehouse," said the runner, "and they's a passel of big shots in there with him."

"Why?" asked Benjamin. "And who the hell is shooting at everybody from there at the gate?"

"Couldn't say," came the reply, "but when I told the general that you fellas had come back and were waiting on the rise, he told me to fetch you to him, pronto. You can ride around there to the west and come in from behind. You'll be out of range of them rustlers."

Benjamin ordered his men to stand fast and galloped off to report to General Greer. He swung his horse around a stand of cottonwood, rode over a grassy knoll, and found himself behind the irregulars who were shooting from their knees and bellies in the direction of the gate. He shook his head in disgust at their lack of military discipline. The fools hadn't even posted a sentry to make sure no one could sneak up behind them. He approached to within a few feet of the smokehouse and then whistled to get their attention. The men recognized him and made way so he could tie his horse to a post. He knocked on the back door and was surprised when Greer himself pulled it open. Six or seven men were sitting on the plank floor of the thick-walled room. He recognized Senator Mack and Congressman Renton and an official from the State Department. The aristocratic looking Mexican gentleman smoking a cigar was the only unfamiliar face.

"Where is Major Crane and where are your men?" barked the general.

"On the rise just beyond the gate, sir. Twenty-four are with me, the rest of the company are with the major in pursuit of hostiles."

"Hostiles?" said Senator Mack before the general could ask the same question.

"We were attacked by a band of Cheyenne. Major Crane is riding them down a few miles to the east. He will be along as soon he can."

"Makes sense," said General Greer," although you and your men are going to have to do double duty until they arrive. Two things: first, I want you personally to go around to the stables and make sure that Mr. Claybourne's guests are there and that they stay put. I sent four men to check on them a while ago, but they have not reported back. Those guests are important, and there will be hell to pay if any of them are harmed. Understood?"

Benjamin didn't understand Greer's order any more than he could figure out what was happening at the gate; he simply nodded in reply.

"Then," said Greer, "I want you and your men to take out those damn insurrectionists. Every mother's son of them. You are to consider them to have been tried and found guilty. And that being the case, by God, you will do your duty. Are my orders clear?"

Captain Benjamin blinked. The commanding officer of all US forces in the western United States had just ordered him to murder five men. "Sir," he asked, "do I understand correctly that one of the men firing from the gate is Colonel Thomas Scoundrel?"

The general's face became florid. "Captain," he said through grit teeth, "it wouldn't matter if Jesus Christ almighty himself was out there shooting at us. I am a goddamn Major General in the United States army and the men in here with me are important members of our government. We will not be insulted and threatened this way. You have your orders. Now follow them, or I will have you tied to a wagon wheel and lashed for insubordination, and then I will cashier your sorry ass out of my army. Am I clear?"

Benjamin looked around the room. From the expressions on the faces of Greer's associates, it was evident that he had no allies in the group. Major Crane's last words to him were that he should trust Colonel Scoundrel. He was going to have to figure things out, and quickly.

He saluted the general, opened the door, and stepped out into the bright morning light. The shooting had slowed down considerably. Saving ammunition, he surmised. He mounted his horse and rode around behind Langton Hall to the barn. As he passed the house, he saw two bodies lying in the dirt near the kitchen entrance. Above them, several civilians were standing outside on a second-floor balcony. One of them even appeared to be taking notes. Benjamin shook his head. This was the damndest situation he had encountered in his dozen years in the army.

He tied his horse behind the barn, pulled off the saddlebags, and slung them over his shoulder, and tried the door. It was locked. He pounded several times and heard footsteps inside. "Friend or foe?" asked someone in a high-pitched, Irish lilt.

"Captain Benjamin, US Army, Sixth Cavalry. Please open the door."

As strange as the circumstances leading up to this moment had been, he was not prepared for the sight that awaited when the door was unbolted and opened. Standing directly in front of him, a hammer in one hand, was the poet and playwright Oscar Wilde, resplendent in an ermine trimmed, mauve-colored dressing gown. On Wilde's right was the famous pugilist John L. Sullivan, who had his fists up and at the ready. Next to the fighter was the author Samuel L. Clemens, whose only weapon, Benjamin was relieved to notice, was a freshly lit cigar.

His mouth was already agape when he recognized the woman standing behind Clemens. It was Lily Langtry, surely the most beautiful and revered actress in the world. He stammered a moment and lowered his pistol.

"Son, from the look on your face I believe it fair to say that you have no clue about what has been going on around here," said Clemens.

Benjamin could only nod. That's when he saw four soldiers laying on the ground with their wrists and ankles tied. He stepped back and raised his revolver.

"Oh, do put your gun away," said Miss Langtry. "We've had quite enough of fisticuffs and derring-do this morning."

Benjamin was not ready to do that. "Who are they?" he said, pointing to the bound men. "Who did that to them?"

"Actually, we all played our part," answered Wilde. "I myself was really quite brave, if you must know."

"Miss Orvis here tied them up," said Signore Verdi. "She really is very good with knots." Mary accepted the compliment with a smile.

Clemens sighed. "We don't have much time, captain. I've got a story to tell you, and only a minute or two to get it done before even more hell breaks loose around here. Do you want to know what's going on, or not?"

Benjamin knew that the decision he made in the next few seconds would determine whether his future lay in the army, or in a cell at a federal stockade. Greer was a pompous fool, but he was also his senior commanding officer. On the other hand, Crane had made no mention of Greer. He only said that he should trust Scoundrel.

Benjamin holstered his revolver, and the group gathered around as Clemens sketched out what they knew about Claybourne, Greer, Rosalilia's kidnapping, and the whole Mexican scheme.

"That is the big picture, captain," Clemens said when he was done. "Now you pretty much know what we do."

"I need to talk to Colonel Scoundrel," Benjamin finally said. "Is there some way I can get to him at the gate?"

"There is," said Adolph Coors as he stepped out of the shadows with a cocked revolver in his hand.

"Have you been there the entire time?" asked Benjamin.

"Of course," said Coors, "and with this pointed at your heart." He shrugged off the captain's astonished expression. "Trust is in short supply around here today."

Benjamin smiled. "So, how do I get to him without getting shot?"

"I will take you," Coors answered. "You might want to take off your hat and jacket, though, if you don't want Greer's men reporting that you have been talking to the enemy."

Benjamin removed his jacket and hung his hat on a peg. He thanked Clemens and the others, and then he and Coors went out the side door, around the judges table, and along the fence just as Salamander had done an hour earlier. A few shots were fired at them from behind the outhouses, but the bullets harmlessly struck fenceposts and rocks. Seconds later they were standing beside a very startled Hamish and Von Sievers.

"This man needs to speak to Scoundrel," said Coors. Then the stocky German turned and hurried back to the safety of the barn.

Hamish, Sergey, and Von Sievers used up much of their precious remaining ammunition to cover Benjamin as he dashed across to the boulder at the other side of the gate.

"Colonel Scoundrel?" he said. Thomas nodded and fired another shot towards the smokehouse.

"Benjamin, sir, Captain, attached to Major Crane, whom I believe you may know."

"You picked a strange time to pay a call," said Thomas, "but I'm glad to see you. If you have a message, you had better talk fast, because the boys and I probably only have a dozen rounds left between us."

Benjamin pulled his saddle bags off his shoulder. If coming over to talk to the colonel instead of shooting him didn't end his career, what he was about to do certainly would. "You have more than that, sir," he said. He unstrapped the saddlebags and poured their contents onto the ground. The pile included six boxes of cartridges, three hundred rounds in all.

Hamish grinned when Thomas tossed three boxes over to him. Rhine loaded his revolver with the fresh ammo and began raking the area around the outhouses as Sergey and Von Sievers reloaded and opened up on the smokehouse.

"Why did you come alone?" asked Thomas. "Didn't Greer have a task in mind that would require quite a few of your men?"

"He did, sir. You and your men have been deemed guilty of insurrection."

"And you were ordered to deliver justice?"

Benjamin could only nod. He felt ashamed for not standing up to Greer when the general ordered him to act as an executioner.

Thomas knew the risk the young soldier had taken by refusing the general's order. "The good news, Captain, is that there is life after the army.

A bullet whizzed past Benjamin's head, and he pulled back against the boulder.

"What now, Colonel?"

"Major Crane should be released from the box canyon by the Cheyenne any minute, and he'll hot foot it this way. When he gets here, just make sure he is careful about which side he picks."

"How did you know he went after the Cheyenne?" asked Benjamin.

"It may not look like it right this minute, son," volunteered Major Rhine, "but at least some of the things happening here today are part of a plan." Benjamin could only shake his head. Another volley of shots came their way from behind the smokehouse before he asked, "What about Mr. Claybourne? Where is he in all of this?"

Thomas fired a shot and then turned. "Where he is, Ben, is dead."

Benjamin slumped back against the rock. Claybourne dead. One of the most powerful and influential men in the country. Everything Clemens had told him in the barn appeared to be the truth.

"What are your orders, Colonel Scoundrel?"

The captain's question took him back five years to the Sioux Wars and his service in Montana. That was the last time he had been in a position of command authority, but as he formulated his answer, he realized that he felt right at home. "Rejoin your men on the rise," Thomas replied. "Send a rider to intercept Crane and tell him not to fire on us when he arrives. Then, take your men around to that little hill behind the smokehouse and wait. You'll be on an elevation above and behind Greer's men, but do not engage them until and unless your major orders you to. You are all still subject to the chain of command, but as of this moment, none of them have violated military law."

"Except for me," said Benjamin.

"That's one of the burdens of command, captain. Sooner or later we each must face circumstances that put us out there by ourselves. But your men haven't been dragged into this mess yet. Maybe you can get them out of here with no harm done to themselves or their careers."

"Yes, sir."

"We'll cover your return to the barn now. Let the folk inside know we will come for them when we can."

Benjamin's gun belt held an army issue revolver and fifty rounds of ammunition. He took it off and handed it to Thomas. "I can get another," he said. Then, as Thomas and the others laid down cover fire, he raced to the other side of the gate and into the compound.

They watched a minute later as Benjamin rode out on the ridge behind the smokehouse, looped around the perimeter of the compound, and joined his men on the eastern rise. The column followed him back to the slope behind the smokehouse, where they would wait for Major Crane. The cowhands hidden behind the outhouses and Greer's men at the smokehouse figured the soldiers were getting into position to attack the gate. With luck, they all thought, this mess would be over soon. None of them had signed on for this kind of duty.

Captain Benjamin watched the ongoing firefight from his position on the hill and hoped against hope that Major Crane would also refuse to follow Greer's order to kill Colonel Scoundrel and his friends. But the only thing he was sure of this minute was that his life wasn't the only one that was about to be turned upside down.

"If that young man doesn't get himself hung today, he has a fine future in the army," said Rhine.

Thomas was about to reply when Hamish shouted, "Ye'll not like this, boys." He pointed out beyond the tent encampment, where fifteen dark-clad riders had materialized out of the powder blue sky and were thundering towards them with pistols and rifles drawn.

"Rivas's men," said Thomas softly. He buckled on Benjamin's revolver, spun the cylinder, and took aim.

❋

SIXTY THREE

Langton Hall

Hernán Castillo did not know that his boss, Geronimo Rivas, had bled out and died a half hour ago in the soft brown dirt next to Langton Hall's kitchen. That knowledge would not have changed his trajectory this morning, however. He and *el teniente* had shared a common destiny since they were young men first taking up a life of crime and mayhem. That each would die a violent death and leave no one behind to mourn them was never in question. It was only a matter of time and place and circumstance. Who knows, perhaps Castillo would eventually have grown weary of Rivas's iron-fisted command and slit *el jefe's* throat one night while he slept. No one led a band like theirs forever.

When the rider from Claybourne intercepted Castillo and his fourteen men on the way to destroy the town of Tipton, the bandit had been furious for two reasons; first, like Rivas, he lived for the days when he was unleashed to perform wanton slaughter upon helpless innocents. Only during the act of murder did the stone-cold shell that should have been his soul feel alive and purposeful. The second thing that enraged him was that he and Rivas had been deceived. When he found out who was responsible he would rip the *maricón* from his balls to his throat with his dullest, rustiest blade. That *cabrón* would know pain at its deepest level.

As he and his men galloped over a rise and swept through the encampment near Langton Hall, he was pleased to see fear on the faces of the people who poured out of their canvas tents as they rode past. They flew through the camp and rode up to the crest of a low, brush covered hill, where Castillo motioned for his men to halt.

A gunfight was taking place around the enormous timber uprights that formed the gate leading into the Langton compound. Castillo could make out six defenders, three behind a boulder on one side, and three more crouching behind another boulder directly opposite. They were being fired upon from outside the compound by a dozen or more ranch hands who were squatting behind a row of outhouses just below Castillo's position and from inside the compound by a group of soldiers around the smokehouse.

Castillo pulled his binoculars from a saddlebag and surveyed the area. He did not recognize any of the shooters behind the privies, but there was one man firing from the gate who he did know: the American officer, Colonel Scoundrel. Despite Claybourne's best efforts, the *pendejo* was still alive.

"Well, Colonel," Castillo thought to himself, "at least you have done me a service by telling me who it is I am to be fighting on this lovely morning." The *teniente* was probably in the house with Claybourne and General Greer, waiting for him to arrive so they could squash Scoundrel and his *compadres* together. Castillo wasn't surprised that neither the ranch hands or Greer's private *soldados* had taken the initiative and simply charged into the open against Scoundrel. Direct action of that kind takes a special kind of courage, and no matter what kind of lies the roughest-looking men spew when they are drinking tequila in the safety of the cantina, Castillo knew that very few of them had the *cojones* to ride headlong across open ground to engage an enemy who was firing real bullets at them.

He looked up and down the line of men assembled around him. None of them had any such qualms. They were paid well to fight, no matter the odds against them, and the fact that they had been denied the pleasure of ravaging Tipton and its female inhabitants that morning only increased their desire to get down to the business of killing some-one–anyone–right now.

He could not see how many soldiers were firing at Scoundrel from behind the smokehouse, but between his men, the ranch hands, and Greer's private guard, there were probably fifty guns about to be leveled against the six unfortunate men at the gate. As he did the calculations in his head, he saw a line of mounted cavalry appear on the rise behind the smokehouse.

"More of the general's men?" asked the rider next to him.

Castillo nodded, raised his binoculars, and counted the new arrivals. "Twenty-five. They appear to be regular army. Let's get to business before the bastards try to take our prize."

He tightened the black bandana around his forehead and pulled his rifle from its scabbard. His men did the same. Then he turned his horse around and faced them. Their horses were pawing at the ground, and his men's eyes were shining in anticipation of the battle to come.

"Those brave fools at the gate are waiting to be properly introduced to us."

"Con un abrazo?" shouted one of his men.

"Yes, Luis, with a hug," answered Castillo. "A bullet up the *culo* or a knife in the heart will do just fine too."

His men laughed and then followed him when he put his heels to his horse and charged down the rise.

❖

Thomas watched and waited as Rivas's men formed a flying-V behind their leader and followed him down the slope. He knew these men would not hesitate or look for hiding places like the ranch hands and Greer's bodyguards had done; they were seasoned professional killers who knew the tactical and psychological benefits of a full-speed, merciless attack. He looked over at Hamish, who was leaning back against a boulder as Von Sievers and Sergey took up firing positions. The Scotsman's wounds were draining his strength, but he still made eye contact with Thomas and smiled before raising his rifle and firing towards the riders.

Sergey and Von Sievers followed suit, and then Thomas, Mose Triplett, and Major Rhine opened fire. When Rivas's men were seventy yards from the gate, one pitched forward off his horse and was trampled by two of the riders behind him. It did not slow the attackers. They rode up to within twenty yards of the gate and then swung their horses around and began racing back and forth in a wide circle in the fashion of the Comanche, firing furiously at the defenders. The ranch hands who had been taking occasional shots at Thomas and his friends were astounded at the ferocity of the attack, and they sat back in relief to watch the spectacle unfold around them. Greer's guards behind the smokehouse were also elated to see Rivas's men join the fight. They held their fire and waited for what they expected would be a swift and brutal end to the standoff.

Thomas and the others fired in unison again and again, popping behind the boulders for cover for a second or two and then leaping back out to get clear shots. He saw two more of the riders go down, and then in the corner of his eye, he saw Sergey knocked down to one knee, followed by Von Sievers, who was spun around by the force of the bullet that hit his shoulder. When the professor went down, Hamish roared to life, pulled away from the boulder, and waved his arms in the air. Then he pulled himself up to his full height and strode directly towards the line of riders, steadily firing his rifle until it emptied. He tossed it aside, and drew both his revolvers, firing ceaselessly as he kept walking towards the riders.

Thomas, Rhine, and Mose poured everything they had at the attackers directly in front of Hamish. It was an amazing sight; the giant Scot looked as big as the horses charging towards him, and the sheer wildness of his relentless counterattack caused the riders to swing around and gallop back towards the rise. Fourteen men had raced down against them; only eleven would regroup for the next attack.

Hamish returned to the gate, where Von Sievers was helping Sergey to his feet. The professor packed a wad of cotton under his shirt on top of his shoulder wound and then tore a strip of cloth from the bottom of the Cossack's shirt and wrapped it tightly around his leg above the knee.

Sergey reloaded his rifle as Von Sievers tended to him and then waved over at Thomas.

"They won't wait long," said Mose. "A minute to reload, and they'll be on us."

Thomas nodded in agreement. The ammo Captain Benjamin gave them would be gone after a second attack, and he knew that Rivas's men would not be favorably disposed to accepting their surrender. He looked around at his friends and knew they were fully aware of what was about to happen.

"Diego," he thought, "I hope you have made good use of the time we have given you and that Matthew Cord is under your knife right now telling you where to find Rosalilia."

❖

SIXTY FOUR

Langton Hall

Captain Benjamin could only sit and watch when Rivas' men swept down to the gate. He had already defied General Greer's orders by not remaining with Claybourne's guests in the barn. If he intervened now in what looked to be the likely slaughter of Colonel Scoundrel and his companions, he would be guilty of enough violations of military law that life imprisonment in a federal stockade would be the best sentence he could hope for.

He grimaced when he saw two of the men defending the gate go down and was astonished at the sight of the enormous, shaggy headed man who yelled into the sky and then walked towards the line of attackers, firing steadily as he went. When the riders pulled back and rode to the rise to regroup, Benjamin found himself fighting the urge to ride down and join Colonel Scoundrel before the next wave hit.

"I don't like this," came a voice at his side. Trooper Thorne, the best sharpshooter in the company, had pulled his horse up beside the captain.

"It ain't right, sir, and you know it."

"We have our orders, Trooper," Benjamin replied. "The most senior commanding general in the west is in that smokehouse down below. He makes the call, not us. We can't help them."

"Sir, you know my enlistment was up last week, right? That means I am a civilian now."

"I do, and I'm hoping you re-up."

"I'm thinking what I'm going to do is take a little time for myself and think things over."

Benjamin turned in his saddle. The riders would attack the gate any second now. He didn't have time for this conversation.

"What the hell are you talking about, Thorne? Get back in line; we'll talk later."

"Can't do that, sir. I'm no longer in the military. But I do wish you luck with this mess." With that, Thorne swung his horse around and rode away from Benjamin and his men.

Under any other circumstances, the lieutenant would have arrested Thorne on the spot and let the brass figure out what to do with him. Claiming civilian status was a legality that might or might not protect the trooper in a court-martial. But this was not the time to speculate. Benjamin lifted his binoculars and looked down to the gate. All six men were re-loading and readying themselves for the next assault. Three of them looked to be in bad shape. Then he looked up to the rise where the attackers were lined up waiting for the order to swoop down and finish off Colonel Scoundrel and his men.

He watched the leader of the attackers raise his hand, and he steeled himself for what was about to happen. Then, the crack of a rifle shot rang out from somewhere behind him, followed immediately by two more. Benjamin watched as one of the attackers toppled from his horse, followed a second later by another, and then a third man was thrown back in his saddle by a bullet to the chest that knocked him to the ground. The lieutenant whipped his head around and saw Trooper Thorne lying in a prone position about twenty-five yards behind and above him. His rifle was resting on a rock, and he was peering through his Malcom scope to sight in another shot.

The riders he had just taken out were at least one hundred yards away. Quite a feat for an army sharpshooter, or rather, Benjamin corrected himself, for a civilian who had just picked sides in the fight raging below.

Thorne stood up and saluted, and Benjamin's men started to cheer until the lieutenant raised his hand to tamp down their approval.

Bad enough that he would have to explain why he allowed a civilian to engage in the fight; he didn't need to see every one of his men face punishment for insubordination at the same time.

"That's all we can do for you, colonel," Benjamin whispered to himself. "But now you'll have just eight bastards barreling down against you instead of eleven."

❖

Thomas and the others heard the shots. They saw the three attackers fall from their saddles and then they watched as Rivas's men pulled back a dozen yards into a thicket that would obscure the sharpshooter's vision. A moment later one of the attackers emerged from the brush and rode down to the ranch hands who were huddled behind the outhouses.

"Parlay?" shouted Von Sievers from the other side of the gate.

"They're coordinating the next attack," replied Rhine. "They will charge straight at us, and the cowboys will be behind them on foot."

"That will probably inspire Greer's boys up at the smokehouse to join in too," added Thomas.

"Well, somebody back there is helping us," said Mose. "Maybe they'll weigh in again."

"That's unlikely," said Rhine. "I don't know how one of them was able to defy orders and shoot those three, but the minute that shavetail captain commits his men to help us, they're all going to hang."

Thomas considered their situation. It was time to get away from the gate and into the safety of the compound.

"Sergey," he shouted. "We need to get to a better defensive position. You three get over behind the speaker platform. We'll cover you. Then cover us when we make a run for it."

Sergey waved and passed the word to Hamish and Von Sievers. Each of the men had been wounded, so when they lit out for the compound, they did it more at the speed of a hobble than a run. Mose, Thomas, and Major Rhine laid down a line of fire in all directions and then raced into the compound themselves and joined their friends behind the wooden platform.

"These pine boards won't protect us for long," said Von Sievers. "Rivas's men are still fresh, and they'll figure out a new line of attack pretty quickly."

"Count your ammo, fellas," answered Thomas. "We'll spread out behind the footings and get ready. If there's any good news at all it's that things can't get much worse."

"I don't know about that, Colonel," said Mose, pointing out to the east. A column of soldiers appeared out of the rising sun, headed directly towards them.

"The rest of Greer's men," said Rhine. "Fifty, if we heard the numbers right."

Thomas and the others watched as the column approached Rivas's men on the rise. An officer split off from the group and rode over to talk with the bandit leader.

Hamish took a deep breath, and Thomas could hear a wheezing sound coming from deep in his lungs. The giant's face had turned pale, and one arm hung limp at his side. The Scotsman saw the concern on Thomas's face and smiled.

"If ye've invited any other guests to this party, Thomas, my boy, this would be a good time to let us in on the list."

He held his hand out and opened his palm. Thomas counted five bullets.

"You see," Hamish said, "I only have five party favors left."

SIXTY FIVE

Langton Hall

The private would have given anything to be in the fight at the gate instead of taking this message to General Greer. So, he stood outside the smokehouse door for ten long seconds before squaring his shoulders, standing straight, and banging on the door until Colonel Alphonse appeared and waved him in. The private looked around the room and felt more confused than ever; the gun fight was one thing, but why the hell were so many important men hiding out in here?

General Greer got off his folding chair. "What do you have to report, boy?"

"I've just, just…" he began to stammer.

"Get it out, private," barked the general. "What is going on inside Langton Hall? Where is Mr. Claybourne and Lieutenant Rivas?"

The private had to get it over with. "Dead, sir," he answered with his eyes downcast.

Heads popped up all over the room. "What did you say?" roared Greer.

"They are both dead, General. Mr. Claybourne is at the foot of the stairs in the foyer. It looks like his neck is broken."

"And Rivas?"

"Outside the kitchen, on the ground. The knife is still in his gut."

"You are certain they are both dead?"

"Yes, sir. No doubt about it."

"Have you been out to the barn, Private? Are Claybourne's guests still there?"

"Yes, they are sir. No one has left. And Colonel Scoundrel and his men have left the gate and taken up positions inside the compound."

Greer wheeled to Colonel Alphonse. "Organize the carriages and horses. We will all leave together and then split up a mile east at the Denver junction. Half of us will go into town from the east, the others will come in from the north. Natural like."

Alphonse left to arrange for their escape. The men in the smokehouse stood up and formed a circle around General Greer. This was not part of the plan.

"What now, General?" asked the Assistant Secretary of State.

"Now we return to Denver. My troops will deal with Colonel Scoundrel and any Cheyenne still alive, we will plant the letters from Mexican officials to prove the Cheyenne were in this all the way, and the result will be that the Indians and Scoundrel's co-conspirators will take the blame for Monteverde and Claybourne's death. No one will ask about Rivas."

"What about the reporters?" asked Senator Mack. "They're still here. We need them on our side."

"They'll see our men kill the people responsible for Monteverde," said Greer, "and then they will come to Denver to interview the heroes who delivered justice to the murderers. I will give them all the evidence they need to prove our case. In the unlikely event they don't accept our evidence, or if they question anything we tell them, well, there is always plenty of space on the prairie for a few more graves."

"In other words, no matter what happens, we are covered," said former Mexican Vice-President Resposo. "No one will be able to connect us in any way to all of this."

The door opened, and Colonel Alphonse entered. Major Crane and his fifty men had arrived, Alphonse told him and were waiting alongside Rivas' men for their orders.

"Good. Send a messenger to Crane and tell him to ride around the compound and wait on the hill behind us," said Greer. "And, have the messenger tell Rivas' men and the shooters behind the outhouses that I want them to wait until they see our horses and carriages ride out the gate, and then pour into the compound and rain down hell on Scoundrel and his men. Major Crane is to wait for the attack to commence before he rides down and finishes the job. Make sure he understands that we are responsible for the safety of several dignitaries and that we will be moving them to safety. He needs to be ready to protect them."

"I don't think Rivas's men will have any problem with that order, sir," Alphonse replied, "but those hired guns of Claybourne's are a different story. If they knew he was dead, they would high-tail it out of here immediately. With him gone, they won't be seeing another payday."

"They are paid $20 per month?" asked Greer. "Tell them they will each collect $200 when the job is done. In gold. But, by God, I want them to bring this to an end the minute we are gone. Between Company B, Rivas' men and Claybourne's little army, there will be at least one hundred men on top of Scoundrel and his boys. Shouldn't take but a couple of minutes to finish the job."

Alphonse saluted and stepped outside. It was only 6:30, but shimmering waves of warming air were already flowing off the prairie, and with no clouds on the horizon, it promised to be another sweltering day. Greer's private soldiers were scattered around behind the smokehouse, grabbing smokes and water, glad for the temporary respite from the shooting. Not one of the former troopers was worth a damn, Alphonse thought, and he expected that Colonel Scoundrel and his men would take many of them down in the first few minutes of the upcoming fight.

He looked up the hill to where Captain Benjamin and his twenty-five troops were waiting. When Crane joined them and they rode into the compound with Rivas's men, the slaughter would begin. Alphonse was glad he would be riding towards Denver with Greer and the politicians when the final shots were fired. He had no qualms about taking lives in battle, and the massacre at Monteverde was a political necessity that had not troubled his conscience. But he was still a military officer, and certain traditions and behaviors should be upheld when fighting another officer. Colonel Scoundrel would meet his end in a hail of hundreds of bullets. Not the most noble of deaths, but at least it would be quick.

He motioned to his messenger to join him and looked down to where Thomas and his men were hidden among the timber posts that supported the speaker platform.

"It's just not your day, Colonel," he said under his breath.

❖

Tanner Fulbright and the other reporters watched from their vantage point on the second-floor terrace as Thomas and his friends made their dash back into the compound.

"The fight is coming to us," said Fulbright to the little group. "The men behind the smokehouse and Claybourne's hired guns are going to swarm the platform any minute. Looks like the army troops who just arrived may be in on the final attack too. We need to leave, right now."

"To where?" asked Sara.

"We'll take the back stairs and make our way to the barn. Clemens and the rest are there, and perhaps we can all figure out the best way to get back to Denver."

The reporters from Chicago and St. Louis wasted no time tucking their notebooks in their pockets and heading for the door.

"What's going to happen to them?" wondered Sara, looking down at the men who had just taken cover beneath the speaker platform.

"Colonel Scoundrel would be the first to say that we should look out for ourselves."

She shook her head. "Can't we do anything to help them?"

Fulbright took her arm and steered her back into the house. "We can tell the whole damn story to world. That's the important thing now."

They crossed through the bedroom and went out into the hall. There had been no gunfire for several minutes, but the quiet was almost as distressing as the sounds of battle had been. Tanner started for the door at the back of the hall when he heard a low, guttural moaning coming from below, like the sound a wild animal makes when its mate has been killed. He and Sara went to the broken railing and looked down into the foyer where Claybourne had met his end an hour earlier.

Hyacinth Claybourne was on her knees next to her father's body. Furniture and paintings lay smashed all around the room, and one of Claybourne's arms was splayed across the splintered door that Hamish had knocked down when he and Thomas forced their way in. Her hair was tied back, and she was dressed all in black, from her riding trousers to her shirt and boots. Fulbright saw that she was also wearing a gun belt with two holstered Colts.

Hyacinth heard them come to the railing. She put one hand on her father's forehead and held the other across her breast. Then she slowly raised her head and looked straight into the reporter's eyes. The mix of pain and rage in her expression was so intense that Sara could almost feel Hyacinth reaching up and slapping her across the face. Sara stumbled back from the broken railing and would have fallen if Fulbright had not grabbed her by the arm.

Hyacinth's gaze did not change as her hand slid from her father's forehead down to one of the Colts at her waist. Fulbright grasped Sara's hand tightly and yanked her towards the back door. When they got to the bottom of the stairs, scattered gunshots began to ring out in the compound. Fulbright was certain that this would be the fight's final round.

As they hurried behind an outbuilding and headed for the barn, Sara took Fulbright's arm. "Did you see her eyes," she asked. "I have never seen anything like them. Violet and black, and..."

Fulbright completed the sentence. "Lifeless."

They reached the barn door and knocked.

❈

While Fulbright and the reporters made their way to the barn, General Greer addressed his fellow conspirators. "With Colonel Scoundrel dead, the Cheyenne village flattened, and Rivas's men disbanded and back in Mexico, no one will be around to dispute our version of this morning's events."

There was no response to his comment. The men in the room were getting their own versions of the story straight in their minds. Being politicians, that was the kind of exercise they were proficient at. Each of them was also acutely aware of one of life's greatest truths: it is the victor, not the vanquished, who gets the privilege of writing history in a way that reflects best upon them.

Senator Mack broke the silence. "What about Noah?" he asked.

"Claybourne?" replied Greer. "I barely knew the son of a bitch. Like each of you, I was simply a guest at his big event. I had no idea things would turn out this way."

The influential men who had pinned their fortunes on the success of Claybourne's Mexican scheme up until that moment were silent. None of them was going to volunteer a word to the contrary. Tomorrow, it would be back to business as usual. Today, the order of business was personal survival.

The sounds of a carriage wheeling up to the back door of the smokehouse got Greer's attention. "Get your things together," he said. "The fishing tournament is over."

❖

SIXTY SIX

Langton Hall

Five minutes after they raced into the compound and took up positions beneath the wooden speaker's platform, Thomas and his friends were trying to make sense of the lull in the fighting. If Rhine was right and Rivas's men and the hired guns behind the outhouses were coordinating an attack, their situation was about to go from dire to hopeless. Perhaps their attackers were also planning on having Greer's private soldiers rush the platform at the same time. That would put between forty and fifty guns against their six. Bad odds made worse by the fact that they only had about two dozen rounds of ammo between them.

Mose Triplett and Sergey had taken positions at the forward posts under the edge of the platform. They would signal when the charge began. Rhine and Hamish were sitting with their backs against a post, nursing their wounds and contemplating what lay ahead, and Von Sievers was on his knees a few feet from Thomas, pressing his bandage against his shoulder to staunch the flow of blood. It didn't look to be working.

Thomas's mouth was so dry from the heat and gunfire smoke that he couldn't form words when Katarina Von Sievers suddenly ducked under the west side of the platform and rushed over to her husband. She was dressed in canvas trousers and a long flannel shirt, and she had a revolver on her hip. Before she knelt beside the professor to tend to his wounds, she unslung a large satchel and a canteen and tossed them over to Thomas.

"From your army friend up on the hill," she said. He undid the flap, and he and Hamish lit up in grins at the sight of boxes of fresh ammunition. Hamish tossed boxes to the others and began to reload his revolvers. Thomas took a sip from the canteen and passed it around.

"How did you get here?" he asked Katarina, "and where is Demetria? Is she alright?"

Von Siever's wife continued bandaging her husband's shoulder as she spoke. "When he didn't come home this morning, I knew something was wrong. Major Rhine's wife is with Demetria. I sent for a doctor, too. On my way here, I came across Salamander, who was gathering up more Cheyenne to join Red Elk. He told me what was happening and showed me how to get into the compound undetected."

Katarina looked into Thomas's eyes. "She is in bad shape. I just don't know what else to tell you."

He reloaded his rifle and revolver and choked back his emotions. Demetria dying, his new friends facing almost certain death in the next few minutes, all because he had chosen to help Diego save Rosalilia. Each man there had stepped up without even being asked. None of them owed him anything, and yet each of them had willingly placed himself in harm's way for the sake of friendship and doing what they felt was right. They all knew the likely outcome of the next attack against them; still, no one complained, and no one tried to sneak out of the compound to safety. They chose to stay and fight for reasons they did not feel compelled to explain. Thomas had never experienced such a complete sense of gratitude.

Major Rhine made eye contact with him, shook his head, and grinned. "It's Todd," he said.

"What?" said Thomas. He didn't realize he had asked Rhine a question.

"You asked what my name was," said Rhine as he tore off a length of fresh bandage to wrap around his leg. "But no one has called me by that name since I was a boy."

Now it was Thomas's turn to smile; he noticed that Rhine had looked pleased when Katarina referred to Anaya as his wife.

Rhine turned back to Von Siever's wife. "What else did you see out there?"

"Men are swarming everywhere. Eight or nine just rode out of the brush on the eastern slope and joined a couple dozen others behind the outhouses. Looks like they are all gearing up."

Mose turned around from his position at the front of the platform. "That's good to know, Miss, thank you. Too many boulders and fences are blocking our view of things."

"The major was right," added Sergey. "They're going to come at us in a group."

"That's how I would play it," said Thomas. He turned to Katarina. "Did you see anyone at the barn?"

Before she answered, Katarina reached into a bag and pulled out a bottle of laudanum and a spoon and ladled some into her husband's mouth. Then she handed the bottle to Hamish. The Scotsman shook his head, but she said, "You will take some, you great clod, or I will hog-tie you and force it down." Hamish smiled and took his medicine and then passed the bottle to Rhine, who took a shot and then threw it forward to Sergey, who did the same before handing the medicine off to Mose.

"Good lord," said Katarina, "is everybody here shot up?"

Thomas smiled for the second time that morning. "Pretty much. So, the barn?"

"It's a busy place," she answered. "A minute after they opened the door for me those reporters arrived, and everybody began to compare notes. The only thing they agreed on was that they had to get some help to you boys. Clemens is filling canteens to bring to you, and that boxer is headed this way too. Oh, and Oscar Wilde and that Italian composer are heading to the encampment outside the gates to gather up anyone who is willing to help."

Her husband burst out laughing at that statement, and as Thomas and his friends imagined the sight of the spindly, gaudily dressed Irish poet and the diminutive and imperious opera composer trying to motivate a bunch of dumbfounded tournament goers to set aside their fishing poles and pick up their revolvers, they all began to laugh.

Katarina waited impatiently for the chortling to subside and then said, "Claybourne's death should have stopped all this."

"It can't," said Thomas. "Too many powerful people were part of Claybourne's scheme; as long as any of us are alive, they are at risk."

"You mean they want to kill all of you? And the reporters? My God how is this possible?"

Her husband got to his feet and began to reload his revolver. "Not only is it possible, it is also their only conceivable course of action. Eliminate us and then blame the Cheyenne and us for the massacre at Monteverde. Greer and his men will be heroes. We will go down in history as mass murderers."

Katarina's eyes brimmed with tears. "Give me some bullets," she said to Thomas.

The professor looked over at Thomas and shook his head. "My dear," Von Sievers said to his wife, "I have made it a habit not to contradict you, and because of that, our marriage has flourished. But right now, you must listen to me. Greer and his men cannot take the chance of allowing harm to come to the people in the barn. They are too famous, and too many questions would be asked. So, I want you to go there, right now. Stay until the shooting stops, or I come to get you. Now, go."

Katarina cast her eyes around the space under the platform where the six men were preparing for the final battle. She looked into each man's eyes and smiled. Then she wrapped her arms around her husband, kissed him on the lips, and walked swiftly back into the compound in the direction of the barn. Von Sievers watched as she hurried off, wiped the moisture from his eyes, and turned to check his revolvers.

"We're outnumbered and pinned down," said Hamish. "What are they waiting for?"

"I wish I knew," Thomas replied.

❖

Lucious Crane led his men in a wide arc around Langton Hall and rode up the hill to join Captain Benjamin. He could see activity behind the line of outhouses to the east, where Rivas's men and Claybourne's hired guns had joined forces. Inside the compound, he saw Greer's private guard waiting behind the smokehouse, and he could just make out movement around and beneath the speaker's platform.

He swung his horse over beside the lieutenant, removed his hat, and wiped the sweat from his forehead with his sleeve. "Ben, just what in the hell have we stepped in? A messenger brought orders from General Greer for me to wait up here with you until he and his group have left the compound."

"And then?"

"And then we are ordered to ride down and engage Colonel Scoundrel and his criminal co-conspirators. That is, if they are still alive when the general's flunkies are done with them."

"Sir, Colonel Scoundrel is not the criminal," said Benjamin. "That's the only thing I am sure of today."

Crane brushed his hand through his hair and put his hat back on. As he did, a carriage pulled up to the back door of the smokehouse, followed by a second wagon and two troopers leading four horses by the reins. "Then please enlighten me, Captain, but do it fast. Looks like the general is about to skedaddle."

Captain Benjamin recounted his brief conversation with Scoundrel at the gate a few minutes earlier. Crane shook his head.

"A scheme to take over Northern Mexico. Led by Claybourne and Greer? Who in the bloody hell is going to believe that?"

"You said I should trust Colonel Scoundrel, sir."

"That I did. And I meant it. But good God almighty, you are talking about a full-scale revolution, and probably a war with Mexico."

"We only had a minute to talk, sir. I had to get back here per the general's orders. I left Scoundrel and his men a pouch of ammo and I…"

"You did what?" asked Crane.

"They are outgunned by almost ten to one sir. And they were running dry. I wanted to give them a fighting chance."

"You quite probably just ended your military career, Ben. The general will throw every charge in the manual at you, and they'll stick."

A warm breeze picked up, and Crane and Benjamin watched as the smokehouse door opened and three soldiers began hauling out suitcases and bags. Outside the compound, Claybourne's hired guns were forming a skirmish line around Castillo and his fighters, while directly below them, Greer's mercenaries were checking their gear.

"Who is in there with the general?" Crane asked.

"His aide Colonel Alphonse, a US Senator, the assistant secretary of state, a congressman, the former vice-president of Mexico, and a couple of other swells."

Crane made a low whistling sound. "That's quite a line-up. Guests for the fishing tournament, though. No proof of criminal conspiracy there."

"Yes, sir, but Greer ordered the other civilian guests to be placed under guard in the barn."

"Mark Twain? And Miss Langtry?"

Benjamin nodded. "And the fighter John L. Sullivan and a few others."

"Why would Greer want to separate them from the politicians?" wondered Crane aloud.

"Ace in the hole. Bargaining chips if things go bad. Greer could trade those folks for just about anything, including safe passage to Mexico."

"Let's say you are right, Ben, and that what Colonel Scoundrel told you is true. Claybourne and Greer were responsible for the massacre at Monteverde. Can we prove it?"

"There are four reporters from major newspapers here who have solid evidence, sir. And Scoundrel believes that the Verján woman is alive and being held captive by Claybourne's mining superintendent, Matthew Cord. She can make an eyewitness connection to Claybourne."

"I'm pretty sure than General Greer and his friends have proof of their own that exonerates their asses," said Crane. "It might come down to Scoundrel's word against theirs."

Benjamin shifted in his saddle. "Which is why they want him dead, sir."

Crane looked hard at the captain. Both their careers were on the line, and he had already been hoodwinked once this morning when the Cheyenne led him on the wild-goose chase into the box canyon. But he had been serious when he told his second in command to trust Colonel Scoundrel. Now he would have to trust him too.

"You took him ammo?" asked Crane.

"Twice. Once at the gate, and a few minutes ago I gave one hundred rounds to Professor Von Siever's wife to take to them."

This was it. Crane had to pick a side. No matter who turned out to be right, Greer or Scoundrel, there would be a court of inquiry, and if he had any intention of staying in the army, whatever he did now would be coldly and dispassionately autopsied by a panel of high-ranking officers. There was the right way to do things, the wrong way to do them, and then there was the army way. The situation before him now would require that he do a little bit of each, in perfect balance.

"One hundred rounds won't do it," Crane finally said. "You said Thorne hasn't signed his reenlistment papers?"

Benjamin nodded.

"Good, we need a civilian for this job. Tell Thorne that he is going to steal five hundred rounds from the supply wagon and take them to Colonel Scoundrel and his men. Take a couple of rifles, too. Then, send eight men to the barn to watch over the folks in there."

"Anything else, sir?"

The major reined his horse to the side and prepared to talk to his men. "Yep. You can pray that those boys down at the platform know how to fight. We'll find out as soon as Greer and his men are out of here. For now, we sit tight."

❖

SIXTY SEVEN

Langton Hall

Mary Orvis hung four water canteens over Sam Clemens's shoulders, and Lily Langtry went to the hay bale where John L. Sullivan was seated and helped him sling six more across his back. "Are you boys sure you want to do this?" asked the actress. "If that young captain was right, the men on the hill will be fighting their way into the compound any minute now, and once you go out there, you may not be able to get back here safely."

Sullivan stood up and adjusted the canteen straps. "I figure if we're in for a penny, we're in for the pound," he said. "Besides, there's a war going on out there, and I can't abide the thought of being outside the ring while fists are flying inside."

Clemens stubbed out his cigar for the first time since they had been hauled out to the barn an hour before dawn. "Well spoken, my friend, but I will remind you that it isn't flying fists you should be worried about. A .45 packs a lot more wallop than even your considerable knuckles do."

Sullivan grinned and walked to the front door of the barn where the Cheyenne youth, Salamander, had just left with the Oscar Wilde and Giuseppe Verdi.

The young warrior was guiding the duo out to the tent encampment so they could plead for help for Colonel Scoundrel and his men. Sullivan didn't think it likely that any of the tournament contestants would be up to joining in, especially if it meant taking sides against the man who had just fed and entertained them for the past week. Still, the effort had to be made.

There was a knock at the back door, and Adolph Coors lifted the bar and swung the door open for the men Major Crane sent to guard the notable guests. "We best go," said Clemens. He held tight to the canteens and slipped out the front door with Sullivan. There were armed men on horses stationed around the privies outside the gate, but for the moment, no one was shooting into the compound or out of it. They made their way along the fence, keeping behind outbuildings as much as possible. When they were directly across from the speaker's platform they ran across the gravel and ducked under the front of the six-foot high structure, right into the raised barrels of Mose Triplett and Major Rhine's Colts. A few feet behind them, Sergey had his rifle pointed at Sullivan's head.

"Whoa, now boys," said Triplett. "Who are you, and what the hell are you doing out here?"

Sullivan and Clemens came to a halt as an astonished Rhine sized up the situation. He recognized both men and lowered his revolver. Mose and Sergey followed suit.

"Don't you know what's going on out here?" asked Rhine. "This is no time to pay a social call."

Sullivan pulled two canteens off his shoulder and handed one to Rhine and the other to Mose. "This ain't social," said the boxer. "I've never heard the referee count past nine myself, but I can count higher than ten, and the numbers I'm seeing aren't exactly on your side."

"You're here to fight?" asked Mose.

"That we are," replied Clemens. "Now, where is the colonel?"

Rhine pointed to the back of the platform, where Thomas was huddled with Von Sievers and Hamish. Rhine whistled to Thomas to indicate that Clemens was a friendly and then slapped the author on the back to send him on his way. Sullivan stayed at the front of the platform and accepted a revolver and a box of cartridges from Mose. "You know how to use that?" he asked the prizefighter. Sullivan checked the cylinder and slipped the gun into his waistband. "Fists aren't the only answer to life's problems," he replied.

Sergey shouldered his rifle, pulled his saber from its scabbard, and thrust it into the post next to Sullivan, where it would stay lodged until he needed it.

"No, they aren't," he said to the boxer with a wide smile. He stuck out his hand. "Welcome to the last round, my new friend. We are very happy you have joined us."

❋

Thomas was taken aback at the sight of the most famous author in America shuffling towards him underneath the platform with a load of canteens. When Clemens ducked under the ledge and stood up straight, he shook Thomas's hand.

"Forgive my manners," said Clemens as he set the canteens on the ground. "I know I was not invited to this little féte, but curiosity and a Yankee sense of fairness tend to compel a man to act rashly at times like this. And so, here I am, at your service."

Thomas and Von Sievers were speechless, but Hamish rose to the occasion by pulling a flask from his vest pocket and handing it to Clemens.

"Don't mind if I do," said the author as he took a swig. "Shame I don't have a cigar to go with that. Now, what's the situation, and what can I do?"

Thomas quickly described the events of the past two hours, including Claybourne's death, his conversation with Captain Benjamin, and the likelihood that any minute now they were going to be attacked from outside and inside the compound.

"We don't know what they are waiting for," he told Clemens. "They outnumber us by nine to one, and that's not including the seventy-five regular army troops under Major Crane."

"You think Benjamin was able to convince the major to hold off?" asked Clemens.

"Perhaps," answered Von Sievers. "But General Greer has no such reservations. He needs us dead, and fast."

"Looks like his plans may have changed," said Clemens. "The captain told us that Greer is planning on high-tailing it out of here this morning. And when John L. and I came across the compound just now, we saw a carriage and a couple of wagons parked behind the smokehouse. Soldiers were loading bags into them."

"That makes sense," said Hamish. "With Claybourne dead, the whole Mexican plot falls apart. Greer and those politicians with him are only concerned with saving their own stinking arses."

"And to do that, you boys have to die," Clemens said quietly. "That would sew things up pretty sweetly for the general, that is, if he could pin the massacre at Monteverde on you."

"We're convinced that is his plan," said Thomas. Then he looked into Clemens' eyes. "But things have gotten more complicated for him now. I'm sure he wanted you and the other guests to be kept safe, no matter what happens this morning. That makes sense, since he could also use you as bargaining chips if things went south for them and they had to negotiate their way out. But with you here, Mr. Clemens, and with the other guests in the barn having full knowledge of Claybourne's scheme…"

Clemens took another pull on the flask. "He has to kill us too. And the reporters. And now that damn Irish playwright and *Signore* Verdi have gone out to the tent camp to ask for their help. That's a powerful lot of killing the general will have to do."

Thomas nodded. That was Greer's only play. Eliminate anyone with knowledge of the Mexican scheme and then figure out who to blame for the murders of so many prominent people.

Clemens handed the flask back to Hamish and said, "First, gents, my name is Sam. I'd be obliged if you dropped the 'Mr.' Second, I have known the date and circumstance of my death since I was a boy. I came into this world with Halley's Comet, and I intend to go out with it when it returns. That's in twenty-eight years, by the way. I have to say I was a little concerned when that comet showed up here a couple of nights ago, but the good professor here positively assured me it was not Halley who was paying us a visit."

Von Sievers smiled, but Thomas winced at the memory of Hyacinth Claybourne riding him like a stallion-for-hire beneath the oak tree as the comet streaked across the sky. It seemed a lifetime ago.

"Now, then," continued Clemens, "this isn't the time to invite a storyteller like me to go on with one tale after another. The battle is upon us, boys. Give me a gun and tell me what to do."

"We're not going to have a clear view from back here when the riders come through the gate," said Thomas. "So, directly above us is a small structure, about twice the size of a privy. It was used to store supplies but should be empty now. It has a solid door with a small window, and you can see the compound gate clearly from inside."

"You want me to be the lookout," said Clemens. "Not exactly the most dangerous job around here."

"It will be when you fire a couple of shots to let us know they are coming," said Hamish. "That will alert them that someone is up there, and, friend, they'll be on top of you like butter on toast."

"After you signal, climb over the back railing, and get back down here with us," added Von Sievers.

While they talked, Major Rhine and the other men who had been standing guard at the front of the platform came back and joined them.

"Something's stirring out there," said Rhine. "It won't be long now."

Then, the sound of a single shot from behind the smokehouse echoed around the compound. It was followed immediately by a shot from outside the gate.

"We're not the only one with signals," said Thomas. "They're getting ready." He turned to Clemens. "You sure about this, Sam?"

Clemens accepted a Colt and a box of cartridges from Rhine and slipped the revolver into his belt. Then he climbed onto a wooden crate that was leaning against the platform, reached up to a crossmember with both hands, and without missing a beat, pulled himself up and over the railing. He was on the platform and heading for the storage shed in a matter of seconds.

"Now, who would have thought a writer could pull that off?" asked Hamish.

Before Thomas could answer, two shots rang out on the platform directly above them.

❋

Major Crane surveyed the scene from the rise fifty yards behind the smokehouse. He saw Clemens climb up onto the platform just as Castillo and seven dark-clad riders swept down the rise towards the gate, firing their rifles as they galloped.

"Thought they were going to wait for the general to clear out," said Benjamin as he rode up beside the major.

Crane looked around. The men waiting behind the smokehouse below him weren't making any moves towards the platform and neither were the hired guns behind the privies. Only Castillo's men were in motion.

"It's a feint," said Crane. "They want to rattle the colonel and his men and get them to draw back so the general can make his escape. When they're gone, every man jack down there will be on Scoundrel."

It took just ten seconds for the riders to charge down to the main gate. Crane had to admire the skill with which they kept up a steady stream of fire as they rode. No doubt they'd had plenty of experience.

Castillo's men spread out when they got inside the compound, forming a skirmish line that stretched from the bull pen across to the judge's table. Then they began to advance steadily at a fast walk, pouring hundreds of rounds into the wooden platform. Smoke billowed around them under the hot sun, and shreds of splintered wood flew like knives around the area. If a bullet didn't take you out, a razor-sharp three-inch length of wood could do the job almost as well.

As Castillo's men continued the barrage, the door to the smokehouse flew open and General Greer, Colonel Alphonse, and the other men who had been waiting inside ran out and climbed into the wagons. Four soldiers on horseback took up positions around them, and as soon as they pulled around the smokehouse Castillo's men formed a protective wall around the wagons and escorted them at a gallop outside the compound. In a minute the riders and wagons were at the top of the eastern hill. Castillo's men lined up and waited as the wagons continued along the trail to the Denver post road.

"Cowards," muttered Benjamin.

"The general sees it as a strategic retreat, Ben, and that's what his after-action report will say. Keep that in mind. There's a powerful lot of power in those wagons, and if it comes down to their word against ours, you and I will be sharing a cell in a federal stockade."

"So, we can't help Scoundrel," said the lieutenant.

"No, we can't help him *yet*," answered Crane. "He's going to have to help himself, first."

❖

Thomas and his friends fired steadily at Castillo's men when they came through the gate, but none of the attackers went down. He was surprised when they slowed their horses to a walk, but it all made sense when the wagons appeared from behind the smokehouse and hurtled out of the compound under the protection of the riders.

A minute after Greer and his escorts passed through the gate, Sam Clemens materialized at the rear railing. "You want me to stay on lookout, Colonel?" he called down. Thomas gave him a thumbs up, and Clemens retreated into the shed.

Sergey was reaching for another box of cartridges when an unfamiliar voice called out from behind an outbuilding between the platform and the smokehouse. "You behind the platform...friend coming in!"

"Keep your hands in plain view," cautioned Rhine.

The voice laughed. "If I do that, I'll have to drop the case of ammo I'm bringing you. Which will it be?"

Rhine looked over at Thomas, who nodded. "Come ahead," said Rhine, "but slowly."

A second later, recently retired army Trooper Thorne came around the corner of the outbuilding. A rifle was strapped to his shoulder, and he was lugging a heavy wooden box. Rhine and the others kept their guns trained on him until he came up beside them and set down his load.

"That's quite a scope you have on that rifle, trooper," said Rhine as he holstered his revolver. "Had cause to use it lately?"

"I might have fired it a few times about twenty minutes ago."

"Three times, by my count," said Thomas, thinking on the three riders the sharpshooter had downed. "Thank you, and welcome."

Thorne introduced himself and shook hands all around. "I'll be staying with you, sir, with your permission, of course," he said to Thomas.

"I didn't think the army could take sides in this one," said Von Sievers.

"They aren't," replied Thorne. "My enlistment is up, and I decided to spend my retirement with you fellas."

"And that box of ammo? A gift from your major?" grinned Hamish.

"Something like that, or leastwise that's the story we'll tell when they haul us in front of the court martial."

"What are the major's intentions?" Thomas asked.

"Looks like no matter what he does, his ass and his career are both in a sling," said Thorne. "All I know for sure is that when it comes down to it, Major Crane will do the right thing."

Thomas nodded. The mess they were wrapped up in had more tentacles than a barrel full of octopuses.

"Thorne, how about going topside and setting up by the shed. You'll have a clear field of fire but not a hell of a lot of cover."

Thorne saluted and started to climb up to the railing.

"Something you should know, Thorne," said Thomas. "There's a fella up there you will recognize. Just want to prepare you for the shock."

Hamish pried the top off the ammo crate and passed the boxes around as someone on the ridge outside the gate began to bark commands in Spanish. Castillo wouldn't come alone this time. Along with his riders would be at least eighteen hired guns from behind the privies, and another two dozen from the smokehouse. They would be surrounded.

Counting volunteers Clemens, John L. Sullivan and Trooper Thorne, the odds had narrowed considerably. In fact, thought Thomas, if he was sitting at his favorite gaming table in Trinidad, he'd be fine with six to one odds.

A warm breeze blew into the compound, and two dogs began to bark. Then, Clemens's revolver roared again, and the fight was on.

SIXTY EIGHT

Langton Hall

Castillo's plan for the assault on Colonel Scoundrel was not complicated; his men and Claybourne's hired guns would attack the platform from the front, while Greer's soldiers would move down from the smokehouse and swarm the defenders from the rear. In the unlikely event they encountered more resistance than they expected, Greer had authorized him to make use of Major Crane's seventy-five cavalry troopers to deliver the final death blow.

The irony of joining forces with the US Army to kill Scoundrel and level the Cheyenne village in an act of government sanctioned retribution for the massacre at Monteverde was not lost on Castillo. Of course, like any true artist, his ego would have preferred that his role at Monteverde be known to the world. His work had been spectacular, after all. But the idea that Thomas Scoundrel was about to be demoted in the eyes of history from a celebrated war hero to the monstrous architect of the slaughter of over one hundred innocent civilians was so delicious that it brought a rare smile to the bandit leader's face.

General Greer's aide had told him about the deaths of Rivas and Claybourne when he rode out to make arrangements to cover Greer's escape. Castillo had shown no emotion at the news; death was the currency of his profession, and he had no special bond with either of the dead men. He would finish the job, and then collect his pay from Claybourne's daughter. If she balked at the increased price he was going to demand, he would help himself to her body first and then take her money. In fact, he would probably take her by force even if she did agree to the new terms. Who was going to stop him? He enjoyed the sensation of power and control when he forced a woman to spread her legs, but there was something even more satisfying about putting it to an aristocrat, especially when he flipped her over and rammed his steed up the hapless lady's *cula*. And of course, when he was done with the mistress of Langton Hall, he would let his men line up to take their turns. Then, after collecting what he was owed, he would ransack and burn the place.

❖

The sun was hot on Castillo's back when he motioned for his riders to line up outside the gate. That was the signal for the men who had been taking potshots at Scoundrel and his men from behind the privies to form up behind them, but he knew that the only benefit those cowboys would bring to the fight would be as targets to drain the defender's ammo. As for the former soldiers waiting to charge down the path from the smokehouse, the bandit leader could only shrug. If any of those spineless drifters were lucky enough to kill some of Scoundrel's men, so much the better, but his expectations of them were very low. The truth was that this fight, like almost all fights, would end in a bloody flurry of bayonet and knife slashes, flying fists, and murderous choke holds. His men knew what to expect in the next few minutes, but Claybourne and Greer's people had no inkling of the hell into which they were about to descend. Experience told him that many of them would be bleeding out in the gravel around the platform before they reloaded their revolvers for the first time.

Castillo looked down the line and studied the faces of his men. Delivering mayhem was their purpose in life, and now, with rifles cocked, knives loosened, and fresh plugs of tobacco in their cheeks, they awaited the order to unleash death. Castillo did not give speeches before a battle. He didn't need to. He simply smiled at his men, thumbed back the hammer on his revolver, and raised it above his head. For the next few minutes, he would ride and shoot and stab and even bite like a wild animal if it came to that. The devil who rode with him lusted for the buckets of gore he was about to spill, and Hernán Castillo was not one to disappoint *el diablo de muerte*.

❋

Major Crane broke his cavalry company into three formations. He stayed in the middle on the rise directly behind the smokehouse nearest to the platform where Scoundrel and his men were preparing for the onslaught. Benjamin took twenty-five men to the east, where they could intercept anyone coming into or out of the compound through the gate. The final twenty-five troopers, under the command of the First Sergeant, rode over next to the barn. They would help protect the guests and wait in reserve to assist if Crane had to enter the scrap.

Crane's orders to his men were clear; do not fire unless fired upon, and do not, under any circumstances, take the first shot. As for the orders given to him by General Greer to stand in reserve and be prepared to engage Colonel Scoundrel if circumstances warranted, Crane could only pray it would not come to that. He dearly wished he could talk to Scoundrel and learn more about the Claybourne business, but the clock was ticking, and the battle was afoot. Events were about to be shaped by action. Conversation would have to wait.

Crane's men had just wheeled into position when Castillo and his riders started down the hill at a steady clip, followed by the hired guns. When they reached the gate, the sergeant in command of Greer's mercenaries gave the command for his men to fix bayonets, form three lines of eight men each, and double-time it down the slope to the rear of the platform.

Castillo's men rode through the gate, separated into two groups and took up positions at opposite ends of the compound, outside the range of fire from the platform. Per Castillo's orders, the hired guns spread out and advanced at a fast walk towards the front of the platform, and when Castillo fired his revolver into the air, they began sweeping the structure with pistol, rifle and shotgun fire. At the same moment, Greer's men leveled their bayonets to chest height and rushed the back side of the platform.

✱

Thomas held his pistol in an iron grip. He, Rhine and Hamish were at the front of the platform watching Castillo's advance from behind the cover of the tall logs on which the structure rested. Sergey, Von Sievers, and Mose Triplett were at the back of the platform readying for the assault that would come from the smokehouse, and John L. Sullivan was pacing back and forth in the shadows underneath the platform. His job was to deal with anyone who got past his friends and tried to make it through to the other side.

Above them, leaning on a rail at the back of the platform, Thorne was sighting in to take his first shot. Samuel Clemens cracked the shed door a few inches and waved to the sharpshooter. His revolver was cocked, and whatever the others thought about his willingness and ability to fight, he was ready. His heart might be pounding a bit loudly, but his hands were steady, and he was fully prepared to take the head off the first son of a bitch who came up onto the platform. The author ran his hand through his hair and reached absentmindedly for the cigar that should have been in his pocket. Then he held his breath when the line of gunmen boiled towards the platform.

Their orders were to advance without stopping, firing ceaselessly at anything that moved under, on top of, or around the platform. What these men did not know was that the second part of the plan that Castillo described to them was a lie. "My men will be right behind you on horseback," he had told them a few minutes earlier. "Between us, we will storm them with a solid wall of lead they cannot escape. In fact," he laughed, "those *cabrones* won't even have time to take aim." That assurance, plus the promise of $200 in gold for each man, fortified them with enough Dutch courage to charge the platform with total confidence that they were going to achieve an effortless victory.

Castillo felt no loyalty or obligation to the men he was urging forward to slaughter, and he felt no remorse as he signaled for his own men to hold fast until the first attack was over. Who knew, maybe those cowpunchers would get lucky and connect with one or two of Scoundrel's men. If not, Scoundrel's ammo supply would still dwindle, his men would tire, and Castillo and his men would come to the fight fresh and ready.

When Castillo's riders pulled back at the same moment the men on foot began to advance towards the platform, Thomas and Major Rhine understood the plan. Thomas stepped out from behind a timber, fired twice, and ducked back under cover as two of the hired guns fell to the ground. Hamish dropped one man, fired again, and struck another. Rhine's first shot caught one of the attackers in the shoulder. The man spun around and was immediately struck in the head by a misplaced shot from one of his own men.

It only took a few more seconds for the thirteen or fourteen men still advancing on the platform to figure out that Castillo was not behind them as promised. Their line broke, and they scattered all over the compound, diving behind water troughs, scrunching down behind the judge's tables, and taking refuge behind outbuildings. They weren't out of harm's way, though; Trooper Thorne sighted in from the top of the platform and dispatched two of the gunmen who made the fatal decision to poke their heads up to see what was happening.

"Now, *teniente*?" said Castillo's new second in command. Castillo was pleased to be properly addressed as *jefe* of this band, but it was not yet time to expose his men to the fight. Let the cow punchers and the soldiers from the smokehouse thrash around a few more minutes. By then, Scoundrel's energy and ammo reserves would have been seriously depleted. Then he would surge in and wipe out whoever was unlucky enough to still be alive.

❖

The only good news for Mose, Von Sievers, and Sergey was that the approach from the smokehouse to the rear of the platform was so narrow. Three men with rifles standing side by side could barely squeeze down the path. Once all three columns of soldiers were in motion, however, there was no way for the men in front to come to a halt without getting trampled by the men rushing up behind them. They had no choice but to advance.

Mose took time with his first shot. It hit one of the soldiers in the first line, and an instant later Sergey took down the man next to him. As the press of soldiers surging down the path intensified, the scientist in Von Sievers understood that no power on earth could stop or even slow their forward momentum. He carefully took his first shot, only to have his pistol strike an empty chamber. Before he could fire again, three soldiers threw themselves on top of him, slashing and punching and kicking as they pushed him down on the ground. As he went down, the professor saw Sergey and Mose disappear under a pile of blue coats and swinging rifle stocks.

Von Sievers thudded to the ground on his back with one of the soldier's knees in his gut and hands around his throat. He reached down, unsheathed his boot knife and thrust it straight up into the man's neck, severing the carotid artery. Blood sprayed into the faces of the two who were pounding him with their boots and fists, and when they jerked back to wipe the blood from their eyes, Von Sievers pushed up on his knees and shot them with his last two bullets. But that did not provide him a respite; two more soldiers ducked under the platform, and they were on him before he could pull his other revolver. He was shoved back into a timber so hard that his vision went blurry, and the air was forced out of his lungs.

He willed himself to move, and when one of the soldiers drew back his rifle to run him through with a bayonet, he braced himself for the searing impact of the cold steel that was about to rip into his abdomen. At that instant, though, his attention was drawn to the gold-flecks of light streaming through cracks in the floorboards above him, especially the way they illuminated the blade of Sergey's cavalry saber as it arced through space. He heard winter wind rushing through trees, and then the severed head of his attacker tumbled through the air and slammed into the soldier standing next to him.

The man drew back in horror, but before Von Sievers could pull back the hammer on his Colt, John L. Sullivan pushed past him. The boxer's arms were pressed tight against his side, and then, as fast as a rattlesnake strike, he punched the soldier so hard with his left fist that Von Sievers heard the bones in the man's jaw shatter. Before the soldier hit the ground, Sullivan followed up with a rocketing right-hook to the side of his comrade's face. That unfortunate fellow's mistake was recognizing the world-famous pugilist and allowing himself to be momentarily awe struck in the presence of the celebrity. Sullivan's blow knocked the soldier back against a post, where he was impaled through the heart an instant later by Sergey's blade.

❖

A few feet away, three soldiers from the smokehouse brigade had surrounded Mose Triplett. They were too close to fire their weapons, so they slashed and stabbed at him with their bayonets. Mose parried the first thrust and pushed the soldier backwards with his rifle stock. A second soldier swung to the right, and his blade sliced across Mose's thigh. When the soldier pulled back to deliver a killing blow, Mose spun his rifle around by the barrel and smashed the man in the jaw. He immediately swung the rifle back and got off a shot just inches from the first soldier's gut. The man was knocked off his feet and tumbled into the path of the two other soldiers coming at him.

With Sergey and Von Sievers doing battle behind him, Mose was on his own. That's when he saw that there were a dozen more soldiers pushing their way down the narrow path. He dropped his rifle, pulled his revolver, and fired at point blank range at the two closest to him. The other soldiers halted in their tracks, but only until their sergeant stepped to the head of the column and exhorted them to finish the job. "There's only one of them, damn you all," shouted the sergeant. "Hitch up your balls and get the son of a whore." The soldiers regrouped, brandished their bayonets, and prepared to rush him again.

As they started for him, Mose heard a rifle bolt slam home somewhere above his position, followed by four shots in quick succession that tore into the middle of the line of attackers. Greer's men panicked and ran back towards the safety of the thick-walled smokehouse, leaving four of their comrades in the dirt. Mose stepped away from the timber pillar and looked up to see Trooper Thorne leaning over the platform railing a few feet above him.

Mose touched his hand to his forehead. "Much obliged," he said.

Thorne smiled and lowered his rifle, and then turned back towards the shed as Sergey and Von Sievers came up beside Mose.

"They won't be long," said the Cossack. "They're going to figure out how to get past our sharpshooter pretty quickly. Might even leave the smokehouse and go around and join the rest of the bastards coming at us from the front."

"If they do, can't we get out of here?" asked Von Sievers. "Go around the barn, head to Denver, and get help?"

"We wouldn't make it far," said Mose. "There are too many of them, and they have horses. No, we have to make our stand here."

Sergey turned and shouted, "Colonel, what's your situation?"

Thomas emerged from the shadows under the platform. "Kind of like you fellas. The hired guns are scattered around the compound behind anything that will protect them, and the riders have split into two groups and are waiting just far enough back that we can't hit them."

Von Sievers pulled a roll of bandage from a bag and handed it to Mose, who wrapped the bayonet cut on his leg. "We have plenty of ammo, thanks to Crane, but we can't hold out here forever. They're going to come at us like hornets, and next time those damn *bandidos* will come with them."

"Options?" Thomas asked the group.

"How about a vacation?" yelled Rhine.

Thomas and his friends laughed. Then he said, "Looks to me like we have only one course of action available to us: we hold this platform, and we kill as many of them as we can until they realize the cost of taking all of us out is higher than they are willing to pay."

Heads nodded all around, and Thomas added, "I can't ever thank you all enough for what you have done today. But I also want you to know that you have done enough. You can make your way over to the barn and stay there until this is over or slip out into the prairie and disappear. I won't hold it against you, and there would be no shame in doing that."

Hamish had come back as Thomas was speaking. The Scotsman put a hand on his shoulder and said, "Ye're daft if you think that any of us is leaving this little party, laddie. Hell, we haven't even gotten to the caber tossing."

Thomas felt his eyes moisten, but before he could answer, Thorne shouted from his vantage point above them. "Colonel, off to the west, men coming in fast."

They looked out past the barn to the thick grass and low hills that spread in waves towards Denver and the distant mountains. Thomas could just make out a solitary figure a hundred yards out, galloping hard in their direction under the cloudless sky. He was slapping the reins against his horse's neck with one hand and holding onto his hat with the other. A moment later the man's urgency became clear; a dozen or more riders were galloping all out a few hundred feet behind him, and they were closing fast. Three heartbeats later, Thomas recognized the rider. It was Diego.

"I hope to God he figures out what's happening here before he rides into the wrong camp," he said.

"We need to lay down cover fire," said Mose. "Keep them cow hands down and discourage the *bandidos* and the soldiers behind us from going anywhere until your friend gets here."

Thomas nodded, and they took up positions and began firing steadily all around the compound, anywhere an attacker could be waiting. They were going to burn a lot of ammo, Thomas thought, but it was Diego's only chance to get into the compound alive.

Diego's horse flew over a rise, swept along a line of scrub pines, and hurtled towards the five-foot fence that encircled the compound. Thomas could see lather on the horse's jowls and the straining and heaving of its chest muscles from the exertion of the race. He expected Diego to bring his horse to a halt at the fence and climb over, but the stallion kept coming at top speed.

Then the horse was at the fence, and Thomas watched as Diego pulled lightly on the reins. The horse sailed into the air, floated over the fence, and landed in the graveled compound without losing a beat. The men kept up their fire as the horse charged past them, swung around to the back of the platform, and came to a dead stop.

Diego slid off the saddle and collapsed into Hamish's arms.

SIXTY NINE

Langton Hall

The riders chasing Diego swept on past the compound and up to the same spot on the rise where Castillo's men had been gathered only a few minutes earlier.

Castillo watched them through his binoculars and recognized them as Matthew Cord's hand-picked gunmen. Fortune had favored him again and delivered fifteen more experienced fighters to help take out Colonel Scoundrel. Even counting for those who had been killed in the first attack, Castillo would be in command of at least fifty men. The next charge would be the last, he vowed. Then he instructed his men to hold their position and galloped out the gate to meet with the new arrivals.

Major Crane watched Diego's race to the compound too. When the pursuers settled on the rise outside the gate and were joined by the leader of the dark-clad riders, Crane knew that the tide had turned dramatically against Scoundrel. But before he decided how to deal with the new development, he picked up his field glasses and looked out into the prairie for signs of any other activity. A company of infantry from Ft. Cottonwood was scheduled to arrive later in the day, which Crane saw as another complicating factor in this increasingly knotty situation. With Greer and Colonel Alphonse gone, Crane would be the senior officer on site, and it would be up to him to order those soldiers to either help squash Scoundrel or come to his aid. He needed to figure that one out fast.

When he turned his binoculars to the northeast, he saw something that added yet another layer of manure to the mountain of buffalo chips he was struggling under this morning; General Greer's party had bolted out of the compound fifteen minutes ago and should have been well on their way to the post road to Denver. Instead, they had come to a stop less than a half mile away. He counted one carriage, three wagons and four escort soldiers parked beneath a stand of cottonwoods. The passengers were milling around in the shade, and Crane quickly saw the cause for their delay: one of the wagons had lost a wheel, and two men were pounding away on its rim with hammers. Given the small size of the escort party, it made sense that general had kept everyone together for safety. The proper thing for Crane to do now would be to send a squad of soldiers out to help the general and his associates. Instead, he slipped his binoculars back into the saddle bag and did nothing. That was his first overt court-martial offense of the day.

It was quiet in the compound, but Crane could see that the cow punchers who had led the first attack from outside the gate were doing everything they could to stay hidden. Behind the smokehouse, the soldiers who had made it back after their failed assault were licking their wounds, and many were taking cover inside the building. Even if the cowhands and Greer's soldiers sat the second act out, at least two dozen veteran fighters could still take part in the next charge against Colonel Scoundrel and his men. Crane figured that the most likely scenario would be for Castillo's men and Cord's riders to combine forces for one final, ferocious, head-on charge. When the shooting started, the rest of the men would remember that if they wanted to collect their $200 bounties, they would have to take part in the final act. So, no matter how the coming battle played out, Scoundrel was going to be massively outnumbered.

He pulled a writing pad and pencil from his saddle bag and scribbled two copies of a terse, three-line order, and had them delivered to Captain Benjamin and the First Sergeant. Win or lose–whatever the hell that looked like–Crane knew the words he had just written would be the final instructions he would ever give as a US Army officer.

❖

Sergey and Mose slipped back to the front of the platform and joined John L. Sullivan on watch. The quiet was unnerving. They could see occasional movement around the tables and outbuildings, but no one was attempting to shoot at them. They had no illusion that it would stay that way, of course.

Thomas and Hamish tended to Diego while Von Sievers and Rhine kept an eye on the path from the smokehouse. Then two legs dangled over the platform above them, and Samuel Clemens's head appeared through the railings.

"Any chance we've seen the worst of it, Colonel?" the author asked.

"I'm afraid not, Sam. They've got fresh reinforcements, and they're planning their next move. It won't be long."

"Very well, I will return to my post."

"Mr. Clemens, a moment," said Diego. He fished into his vest pocket, pulled out a cigar, and handed it to Thomas, who reached up and gave it to the very happy author.

"God bless you, son," Clemens said, "and remind me to make you the provisioner at our next soirée." The men at the base of the platform heard the rasp of a match and a satisfied sigh, and then Clemens was back at his post.

Thomas wiped Diego's face with piece of cloth. His friend's left eye was swollen shut, and there were scratches across his face and neck. A small patch of hair was missing from behind his ear, and blood was oozing from the wound.

Hamish poured some water from the canteen on Diego's head and then gave him some to drink. "Ye've had a bit of a rough day, my friend," he said.

"All worth it," replied Diego.

"You clearly found Cord," said Thomas, "or from the looks of things, he found you."

"A little of both, I'd say. I happened on his man, Hayes while the fool was taking a dump behind a rock about five miles from here. I'd like to say that the knife I poked in his ribs before he got his trousers back on scared *la mierda* out of him, but he'd already taken care of that little matter. So, I pushed his face down in it while I asked him a question or two."

"Did he know where Cord was?"

"Better; he knows where Rosalilia is being held. He saw her two days ago, and said she is fine."

"What about Claybourne's death?"

"He does not know, and Cord probably doesn't either, at least not as of this morning. But when he does find out, there will be no reason for him to keep her alive, Tomás. I have to get to her, now." He struggled to stand up, but his knee buckled, and he collapsed back on the ground.

"Ye'll not be going anywhere for a bit, yet, lad," said Hamish. "But I promise you we will get out of this set-to as quickly as we can, and we'll all go and fetch her together."

"Do you have directions to her location?" asked Thomas. "Can we find it?"

"Not without Cord's man," answered Diego. "I pulled him back between a pile of boulders, and I tied and gagged him and covered him with some loose brush. He'll be there when we are ready."

"The men chasing you," Thomas said. "Who are they?"

"Cord's best guns. Hayes was with them when they stopped to water their horses. Apparently, they thought it odd when one man slipped behind a rock to empty his bowels, and a different man returned in his place. I was able to put two of them down, but, as you saw, the rest insisted on accompanying me back here. I apologize to all of you for bringing them with me."

"We will get to her in time," said Thomas. "I promise."

❖

Matthew Cord's lieutenant agreed with Castillo's plan to surge into the compound with everything they had and simply overwhelm the defenders.

"First, though," said Castillo, "there is something we have to take care of." He handed Cord's man the field glasses and had him train them on the back of the platform.

"They have a sharpshooter back there," said Castillo. "He is good. He can't take us all out, but if he figures out who the leaders are, he can concentrate on us, and that could spoil both our days."

Cord's man turned in his saddle. "Byrnes," he called. "Front and center."

A tall, thin man rode forward and halted. "Byrnes is a good as they come," said Cord's lieutenant. He handed the binoculars to Byrnes and waited as he scanned the platform.

"See him?" he asked.

"Yes, sir, I do. About one hundred ten yards out. He's mostly staying behind that little outbuilding, but he sticks his head out now and then."

"Can you take him?"

In reply, Byrnes slid his rifle out of its scabbard and pulled the waterproof oilskin cover from the scope. He pulled a bullet from the belt around his waist, loaded the rifle, and held it up to his eye.

"Permission to fire, sir?" he asked.

"Send the son of a bitch to hell," came the reply.

❖

Sam Clemens had just taken a draw on the excellent cigar Diego gave him when he heard the crack of a single rifle shot, followed by a crashing noise outside the shed. He tried to push the door open, but something was blocking it. He set down his cigar and put his shoulder into it, pushing as hard as he could. The door began to move, and a second later it was open wide enough for him to step through.

"Get out here," he heard Thomas say. "Stay down."

Colonel Scoundrel was on his knees beside Trooper Thorne's lifeless body. Clemens saw the red bloom of the entry wound on his chest, and the fist-sized hole in his back where the bullet had exited. He scooted over on his knees and cradled Thorne's head in his hands. "Oh, my boy, my dear, dear boy," said the author, rocking slowly back and forth.

"They have a sharpshooter of their own," said Thomas in a quiet voice. "You'd best get back down with us."

Clemens stared him in the eyes. "I don't believe I will do that, Colonel. My job is up here, and it isn't done."

Thomas nodded and placed a hand on Clemens' shoulder. "It doesn't happen like in your books, Sam. War is more awful than mere words can describe."

Clemens looked at him with steely resolve. "Oh, I know that all too well, Thomas. Take the boy down with you, will you? I've got to get back to work."

With that, Clemens stood up and went back into the shed. He left the door open and checked his revolver. Then he reached for his cigar and began scanning the horizon for the attack they knew was coming any minute.

❖

SEVENTY

Langton Hall

It was 7 a.m. when Captain Benjamin slipped his pocket watch into his jacket and loosened his shirt collar where a line of sweat was beginning to form. The sun was small and pale above the waves of prairie switchgrass, but the breeze had died away and the scattered morning clouds that had promised a sliver of relief from the heat were nowhere to be seen.

He instructed the sergeant to give permission to the men to loosen the top brass button on their wool shirts, not that it would help much. Soldiers weren't a patient lot, and all they knew this morning as they waited beside their horses and felt the temperature ratchet up was that they were being held in reserve in the event they were needed to help quell an insurrection. What that meant was anybody's guess.

On the rise behind Langton Hall Major Crane was sitting stock still on his horse, waiting for the shot that would signal the final act. He knew there were men hiding all around the compound, but no one was moving down there, or around the speaker's platform where Colonel Scoundrel's men had taken up positions. He also had a clear view of the trees and brush beyond the gate where twenty or more riders were holding position, but it was quiet with them as well.

The hardest thing for the captain to stomach about their present circumstance was that the orders from General Greer left no room for speculation; Crane's company was to sit tight when Claybourne and Greer's men attacked Scoundrel and engage if and only if Scoundrel was somehow able to get the upper hand and hold the attackers off. If that should happen, Crane had been ordered to finish the job and kill Scoundrel and every one of his men. A fair and just payback, the General insisted, for Scoundrel's involvement at Monteverde.

Benjamin reached for his canteen, only to flinch as a fusillade of bullets announced that Castillo's men were about to charge. He signaled for his men to mount up, and when the riders in black flew down to the gate, he fought the urge to disobey his orders and unsheathe his rifle.

❋

Thomas felt the ground shake as Castillo and Cord's men thundered through the gate. The pounding of hooves, men's shouts, and rifle and revolver shots reverberated around the compound. There was no time to wish his friends good luck. He cocked his rifle and raised it to his cheek. Then he pointed into the center of the swarm of horses and men flying towards him and opened fire. He knew without looking that his friends were doing the same thing.

When the shooting began, Fulbright and the other reporters in the barn climbed the stairs into the hayloft and went to a window that provided a birds-eye view of the compound and the surrounding area. Lily Langtry, Mary Orvis, and three of the soldiers Crane had sent to look after them followed a minute later, while Adolph Coors remained below, pacing back and forth with his hands behind his back. A moment later, he checked his revolver, opened the front door, and strode out into the compound.

❋

Castillo was smiling as he galloped through the gate. Smiling because he was in his element, smiling because he could taste and smell the blood he was about to spill, and smiling because *el diablo de muerte* was about to be unleashed once again to visit unspeakable pain and misery upon the flesh of his enemies. What a glorious morning!

As Castillo's men swooped into the compound, Claybourne's hired guns emerged from their hiding places and moved as a group towards the platform, blasting away with pistols and shotguns. Greer's men followed suit, surging down the path from the smokehouse. There are at least sixty of us now, Castillo crowed to himself. They would make fast work of the men defending the platform. He wheeled his horse around and waved his men on, sending half to one side of the platform and half to the other. He stayed to the middle and began firing around and below the wooden structure. When all thirteen of the bullets in his rifle were gone, he pulled out one of his revolvers and continued shooting.

❖

Thomas, Hamish, Diego, and Rhine took positions behind the heavy support pillars along the north side of the platform. Along the south side, Sergey, Mose, and Von Sievers readied themselves to fire on the men coming down from the smokehouse. John L. Sullivan climbed over the railing and dropped down on the pine board surface of the platform where he took cover next to the shed door. Clemens was waiting to send the first attacker who came his way straight to hell, and he smiled at the boxer when Sullivan drew his pistol and began firing into the sea of riders streaming into the compound.

Thomas had been under heavy fire before, especially during the Sioux Wars, but those battles did not compare to the avalanche of lead being thrown at him from all directions right now. On top of that, the men shooting at him weren't bothering to take aim or conserve ammo. Hundreds of their rounds slammed into the pillars and boards on the platform, showering the area with dirt, splinters and rocks.

As he reached for another cartridge box, he was surprised to see Adolph Coors appear at the corner of the platform nearest the barn. The German brewer didn't say a word; he simply nodded at Thomas, leveled his revolver, and joined in the shooting.

Then, Sergey called out. Thomas turned his head just in time to see

Diego's horse collapse on the ground. Mose and Von Sievers crouched down behind the dead animal and used him for cover as they continued to fire up the path at Greer's personal bodyguard. Their aim was deadly; Thomas counted six soldiers on the ground, a fact that was not lost on the attackers. They slowed their advance and took up firing positions behind two small outbuildings.

When a dark-clad man wielding a bayonet dipped under the platform and ran full-out towards Thomas, Hamish appeared out of nowhere. The giant Scotsman decked the man with one punch and then lifted his unconscious body and threw it onto the three men who were racing up right behind him. They were knocked down into the dirt, only to come face-to-face with Adolph Coors and his revolver when they tried to get back up. Thomas almost smiled as the brewery owner ordered them to drop their pistols and then marched his prisoners over to the barn.

❖

As the battle raged in the compound, Major Crane decided to ride down for a closer look. It meant losing his view of the gate and the prairie beyond, but he figured all the combatants were in the arena by now. As soon as his horse had picked its way down to the smokehouse, though, he was jolted by the distinctive blare of a cavalry bugle ringing out above the gunfire. He could not see where the noise was coming from or who was blowing the horn, but it was clear that more guests were arriving for the party.

Thomas heard the bugle, too, but like Crane, his field of view was severely limited. All he could see when he leaned out from behind the pillar to take another shot was a pack of armed men on horseback and on foot pushing forward towards the platform. When he turned his head to look back towards Sergey, two trail hands appeared from around a pillar and knocked him to the ground. They rained punches and kicks down on him as he struggled to his knees, but before either man could take a kill shot, a hail of bullets from Sergey and Von Sievers took the attackers down. There was no time to thank them; a half dozen more attackers were rolling up behind their fallen comrades.

Next to Thomas, Rhine was backed up against a timber by a soldier who was trying to impale him against the post with a bayonet. And directly in front of him, two men had jumped onto Hamish's back in an effort to bring the giant down. Thomas watched as Hamish threw himself back against a pillar to smash the men, but they hung on and the struggle continued. Hamish spun around, and he and the men on his back careened into Mose Triplett, who had been holding off a trio of attackers with only his knife. The entire group fell to the ground in a tangle of flying fists and feet. Thomas stepped over towards the mayhem, only to see more men coming at him from the compound. Where was Diego and Von Sievers. Had they fallen?

Behind the men coming at him with pistols and knives was a line of at least a dozen more waiting to finish the job if the others failed. He was nearly out of ammo, but that didn't matter; he had no time to reload. Thomas picked up a fallen rifle, lowered the bayonet, and backed up against a timber.

Then the bugle sounded again, this time closer, louder, and longer. There was also a roaring sound, like waves crashing on rocks in a storm. And then, above the din of the dozens of guns that had been firing ceaselessly, even more guns began firing, and these sounded like they were coming from outside the compound. The men coming at him hesitated, and when their fellows in the compound began shouting at them, they turned and raced back into the compound.

Hamish and Mose reappeared from under the clutch of attackers they had been wrestling, and Rhine kicked away the cow hand he had been fighting. That's when they saw that the soldiers attacking the rear of the platform were also pulling back.

"What has happened?" asked Diego, who had come up behind them so stealthily that no one had noticed. Thomas smiled to see his friend was alive. Then he took his first breath in what seemed like an eternity.

❖

The people at the hayloft window had a perfect view of the events taking place around the compound. Adolph Coors handed off his prisoners to Crane's soldiers and then joined the group to watch as the battle below them ebbed back and forth.

Fulbright called for their attention when two of the attackers climbed up through the railing and raced across the platform to fire down on Thomas and his friends, who were about to be trapped like fish in a barrel. But the moment they set foot on the stage, the shed door flew open, and Samuel Clemens stepped out. The people at the window held their collective breaths as the author calmly raised his Colt and fired, knocking one of the attackers to the ground. Before they got over that shock, John L. Sullivan leapt out from behind the shed and put a bullet in the center of second attacker's chest. Then he picked up the bodies and tossed them one at a time over the railing onto the heads of the surging attackers.

"I never imagined…" said Lily Langtry. "Mark Twain, of all people. And he can write such gentle stories. I just never could have believed it."

Sara was the first to spot the battle flag flapping in the breeze on the hill outside the gate and the first to hear the bugle call.

"Who are they?" Coors asked, pointing at the five men riding in a circle around the flag. "The man carrying the flag. What is he wearing…some kind of circus costume?"

"And who are all of those people behind them?" asked the Chicago reporter.

"As to your first question," said Tanner Fulbright in a hushed, disbelieving tone, "the man with the flag would appear to be the great western showman, Buffalo Bill Cody himself."

"And the men with him?" asked one of Crane's soldiers.

"I believe the man in the bowler hat is Marshal Bat Masterson," answered Fulbright. "I do not know the others."

"All those people running behind them," said Mary Orvis, "is that Mr. Wilde and *Signore* Verdi leading them?"

The men and women at the window shook their heads and shared glances that said, are we really seeing this? Behind Cody and

Masterson, dozens of men were pouring through the gate. Leading the column was Wilde and Verdi, side by side, with grins as wide as the prairie they were marching across. They had made it to the tent encampment a few minutes earlier, but they weren't having any luck convincing tournament goers to come to Scoundrel's assistance. That changed when the most famous celebrity in America galloped into the camp and urged them on. Cody's short, impassioned plea had every man buckling on weapons and forming up in a battle column in short order. Five minutes later the Cody Crusaders–as Buffalo Bill would call them in his next dime novel–were double-timing it to save the men at the platform.

❖

When Crane heard the bugle, he rode back up to the hill to rejoin his men. He was pleased to see that Captain Benjamin was waiting for him.

"Ben?" said Crane.

The captain handed field glasses to Crane. "You won't believe this."

Crane raised the binoculars and looked out upon the most amazing sight he had ever witnessed. One hundred yards out and closing fast under the tourmaline sky, William F. Cody was galloping towards Langton Hall. He had on a red fireman's shirt and black velvet trousers, and his long hair cascaded down from under his creme-colored, broad-brimmed hat. His reins were in one hand, and in the other he held the bright red and blue flag used at the dramatic conclusion of his Wild West extravaganza when the heroic cavalry charged into the arena to save the homesteaders from certain death at the hands of the pitiless Indian warriors. Four men rode alongside Cody: an older black man in a cavalry sergeant's uniform, the lawman Bat Masterson, and two other men wearing federal marshal badges.

The black sergeant raised his bugle and blew three long notes, which is when Crane saw a throng of civilians come over the rise behind Cody's group. At the head of the troupe were two distinctive figures, a short, stocky fellow dressed in formal evening clothing, and a lanky, impossibly tall man with flowing locks who was wearing a violet and green dressing gown that Crane was sure was trimmed in fur. Whatever sideshow the leaders had escaped from, there was no doubt as to the intent of the dozens of men with them. They were armed, and they looked determined.

Cody swept into the compound and planted his flag in a patch of dirt by the fountain. As he and his men came to a halt, Castillo sized up Cody's little band, and ordered his men to swat the flies away. It was time to pulverize Scoundrel and his pathetic supporters with one final, brutal charge. As he turned to wave his men back into action, however, Wilde and Verdi's army appeared and began to pour through the gate. For the first time since the battle started that morning, Castillo found himself looking around for a way to bolt if it came to that.

He fired at the golden-haired rider in the garish red shirt, but his shot went wide and hit one of the marshals riding next to a man in a bowler hat. Cody saw the marshal go down and pressed his horse forward. Sergeant Obidiah McReady was right behind him; he drew his saber amid the chaotic scrum of horses and fighters on foot and plowed into a group of Claybourne's hired guns, slashing away with deadly effectiveness.

Castillo drew back, but Cody advanced on him without pause. The bandit leader fired again and missed, but Cody's return shot struck Castillo's horse in the leg. As the animal went down, Castillo swung off the saddle and landed on his feet, where he was immediately encircled by several of his men. They backed up to the fountain as a group, firing in all directions.

❖

It was time for Crane to act. "Ben," he said, "take your men down, and hold the shooters behind the smokehouse right where they are. They're out of this fight."

Benjamin smiled and galloped over to gather up his men.

They quickly surrounded Greer's private soldiers, disarmed them, and sat them on the rocky ground behind the adobe building. The captain was not surprised that the expressions on the faces of the men who had been thrown back three times by Scoundrel were ones of relief, not humiliation or fear. None of them was up to a fight anything like this one had been. Benjamin left five men to guard the prisoners and returned to his place at Major Crane's side.

❋

A minute after the newcomers rode into the compound with bugle blowing and flag flying, Diego called for Thomas and Mose to come to the front of the platform. At first all they could see was a clutch of unfamiliar men on foot going at it tooth and nail with Claybourne's hired guns. Then Thomas saw a flash of red streak through the crowd, topped with a hat he would recognize anywhere. A moment later, a horse moved out of his line of sight, just in time for him to see Bill Cody take down one of the dark-clad riders with his saber. Coming up behind Cody was old Obidiah himself, and a few feet from him, Thomas was heartened to watch Bat Masterson drop one of Castillo's men with a single pistol shot.

"Time to finish this,"called Sergey as he raced past with Major Rhine and Von Sievers in tow. Mose swung up onto the platform to join Sullivan and Clemens, and Thomas reloaded his revolver and trotted out into the chaos a second later. He was aiming at a dark shirted rider when he saw Wilde and Verdi jog into the compound at the head of their little army. Their appearance made him do a double-take, almost as if he had been transported into one of Cody's big-tent performances. He waved as they flowed into the compound and began pounding on what remained of Claybourne's company of hired guns, and when Wilde caught sight of him, Thomas saluted the Irish poet. Wilde waved back, and then made the same half bow he had given to the miners at the saloon in Leadville. Then one of Claybourne's men slammed into Thomas, and he turned back to the fight.

❋

Sara Joliette watched the changing tide of battle from the barn window and marveled at how anybody in the throng below could tell friend from foe. She saw fists and sabers swinging, heard pistols crack, and even saw some of the newcomers from the tent camp swinging wooden clubs as they pushed their way across the battlefield. Screams and shouts mixed with the sounds of glass breaking, horses whinnying, and pistols and shotguns firing without pause.

"When will it end?" she asked of no one in particular.

Fulbright pointed to Major Crane, who was sitting on his horse on the hill behind the smokehouse.

"When he is ready for it to," he said.

⁂

Thomas smashed the flat side of his rifle butt into the face of the cowboy who had launched at him, and then tried to make his way over by Cody and Masterson. They were swinging their horses in short, tight circles, firing and slashing relentlessly at Castillo's riders. Thomas raised his hand to fire at the dark shirt nearest him when he felt a swarm of wasps stinging his wrist and forearm. His revolver flew out of his hand, and the man who shot him rode closer and pointed his pistol at Thomas' head. Before he could fire, a horse with a US Army saddle blanket on its back pushed out of the crush of men and animals thrashing away in the compound. The cavalry rider rammed his horse into Castillo's man, and Thomas watched as Obidiah's saber sliced diagonally from the man's face down to his stomach, pitching the bandit to ground.

"Horse for you, Colonel," shouted Obidiah.

Thomas smiled and swung up into the saddle. It felt good to be back in the cavalry. He rode over beside Obidiah and saluted. The old sergeant snapped a quick salute in reply and then galloped back into the heart of the fight.

Then Thomas started towards Hamish, who was swinging a club at a pair of cowhands. He touched his heel to his horse's flank, only to pull back when he spotted the bandit leader struggling with someone next to the pen in which the prize bull was kept. Thomas started towards him just as the dark shirted killer pulled his knife out of the back of his opponent and pushed the body aside.

He raced across the compound and leapt off his horse. The man seemed to recognize him; he pulled his revolver, fired, and missed. He thumbed back the hammer for a second shot, only to strike an empty chamber. With no time to reload, the bandit tossed his revolver aside and drew his knife.

"So nice to finally meet you, Colonel Scoundrel," said the man as he advanced. "I became acquainted with two of your friends at Manzanita Flats some weeks back, but I am afraid I had to leave the old white-hair in the dirt with only my bullet in his gut to keep him company."

Thomas stopped in his tracks. "Rivas is dead," he said.

"That is true, *amigo*. My name is Castillo, *teniente* to former *Comandante* Rivas, and had you been favored by God to live past this morning you would have come to know my name by my deeds."

"You think highly of yourself, Castillo."

The bandit nodded and smiled in acknowledgment. Then he stepped forward with a slashing blow. Thomas parried the thrust with his forearm and punched Castillo hard on the jaw. The bandit fell back against the railing of the bull pen, but quickly righted himself and raced forward. Thomas was able to grab his knife hand at the wrist, and the men struggled for possession of the blade, pushing and kicking and punching. When the knife flew out of Castillo's hand and landed inside the pen, he slipped between the rails to recover it. Thomas followed him, acutely aware that once inside the enclosure, he would be facing not one, but two formidable enemies: Castillo and the twelve-hundred-pound prize bull.

Castillo had no such concern. He retrieved his knife and began circling Thomas, looking for an opening into which he could step and deliver a killing strike. He favored a path that took the blade up under the armpit where he could puncture a lung and sever arteries with a single stab. Other knife fighters tried for the heart, but Castillo knew that the soft tissues under the arm were far easier to penetrate than the breastbone.

Thomas stepped from side to side as Castillo circled him. For his part, the bull was already weary of his guests. The eyes of the thickly muscled beast widened, and he snorted and glared at the men who had intruded upon his domain. Then he began to toss his coal-black head forcefully about. When the massive bull widened his stance, lowered his head, and began pawing at the dirt, Thomas knew there would be no further warning; there were about to be three contenders in this fight to the death.

He took several steps away from Castillo and then turned sideways as if he was about to launch a kick. Castillo kept the knife high and matched his retreat. When Thomas turned, so did Castillo, and that move put him between Thomas and the increasingly angry bull. Thomas knew that he had to do everything he could not to engage Castillo again. If they got tangled up wrestling or throwing punches, they would simply become an easier target for the bull to attack. On the other hand, he thought, I can't dance away from that knife forever. Something has to give.

The problem was solved a heartbeat later. Castillo took a step to the side, pulled his knife hand back in line with his rib cage, and prepared to plunge his knife straight into Scoundrel's stomach. At that same instant, the bull lunged forward and swung his powerful neck, thrusting one of his horns into Castillo's back. Then he raised his head and lifted Castillo a foot off the ground. When the bull shook his head again, Castillo was dislodged from the horn. He fell to the ground and collapsed onto a fresh pile of manure.

Thomas didn't wait. He turned to the fence, put his hands on the top rail, and swung over, hitting the ground outside the pen just as the bull impaled the bandit a second time, this time in the side. After the second strike, Hernán Castillo made the last and poorest decision of his life: his best defense, he was certain, would be to play possum. The bull would tire of the game and leave him alone. He turned on his side, pulled his knees up to his chest in the fetal position, and lay as still as he could. In response, the bull raised one hoof and smashed it down on Castillo's head. Then he did it again and again and again.

Thomas forced himself to watch the bandit's head being rendered into a bloody pulp. When the bull finally stopped and backed serenely away to the other side of the pen, Thomas looked him in the eye and said, "You're not like a grizzly, are you, boy. Possums just make you mad."

Turning his gaze to the dead bandit, he added, "It's a shame you weren't raised on a farm with bulls, *Señor* Castillo." Then he picked up his revolver and waded back into the fight.

❖

SEVENTY ONE

Langton Hall on Claybourne Ranch

Major Crane scanned the horizon with his field glasses, hoping that General Greer's wagon had been repaired and was on the way to Denver. But the men and wagons who parked beneath the cottonwoods a half hour ago were still there. The only good news was that two men were in the process of slipping the iron and wood wheel back on the wagon, and it should only be a minute or two before the group was on its way. He put the binoculars back in his saddle bag and contemplated the list of charges he would face if Greer returned to Langton Hall right now and found that his orders had not been carried out. On the other hand, with the fight still blazing all around the compound, who knew what could happen?

It was time to make the big decision: did he let the fight in the compound rage on and reach its natural conclusion, or did he ride down with his men and end it now. He knew how Captain Benjamin would vote; in fact, he knew what every one of his men were feeling. Thomas Scoundrel was a puzzle, to be sure, but he was also a celebrated war hero, someone every man in his command respected. Most importantly, he was one of them.

Crane removed his hat and mopped his brow with his sleeve. Then he unlaced the stay holding his rifle in its scabbard and called over to Captain Benjamin.

"Ben, what do you say we wrap this up?"

Benjamin grinned and unholstered his revolver. "How do you want to do this, Major?"

"We go down in force and surround the folks in the compound. At my command each man will fire three shots into the air, and when we have their attention, I will order them to lay down their arms. Anybody who doesn't, well, we'll deal with that if that happens."

Five minutes later, Major Crane and seventy mounted soldiers rode down the hill and entered the compound. Colonel Cody and the volunteers from the tent camp were still mixing it up with Claybourne's remaining fighters, and Crane could see at least four of the dark shirt riders slashing away with bayonets and knives. The scene was more like a riot than any battle he had been in.

The troopers formed a solid line along the compound fence, and at Crane's command, began walking their horses slowly towards the speaker platform. In front of them, the arena was packed with men kicking, gouging, stabbing, and punching, and Castillo's riders were firing at anyone they didn't recognize. When they got halfway across the compound, Crane saw the bearded giant raise a struggling cowboy over his head and toss him into the crowd as easily as a child throws a rag doll across the playroom. Samuel Clemens and Sullivan the boxer were on top of the platform taking shots at dark-shirted riders, and as he was trying to make sense of everything that was swirling around him, Buffalo Bill went flying past in pursuit of a pair of ranch hands who were racing for the safety of the outhouses.

Crane raised his rifle towards the sky and fired three times. His men followed suit, never losing a step as they continued to press the crowd against the platform. The combined effect of several hundred rounds being fired off at once, along with the steady advance of the cavalry troops had the desired effect; combatants began to untangle, gunshots died out, and the shouting faded.

"You will all drop your weapons and cease fighting now!" shouted Crane. Then he said, "Company, take aim." At those words his men leveled their rifles at the people in the crowd.

❖

Up at the barn window, Sara Joilette turned to Fulbright and said, "Is he going to execute them?"

"No, he's going to get their attention," Fulbright replied. Then he turned to the other reporters. "It's time for us to go out there and do our job."

Two hours earlier, none of the reporters would have dared to venture into anything that remotely looked like a gun fight. After what they had witnessed in the past hour, however, nothing could hold them back from getting their stories. They climbed down from the loft, and their guards stepped aside and allowed them to leave.

❋

Thomas stood beside Diego and Von Sievers and set his revolver on the ground. Within a minute, the hundred men crowding the compound had all tossed down their weapons. Crane's troopers kept their rifles leveled at the fighters until every single gun lay on the gravel.

As Crane's men saw to the weapons, Mose, Sergey, and Hamish made their way over beside Thomas. They were joined a moment later by Clemens and John L. Sullivan, and then two of the horses standing in front of them moved apart, and Major Rhine stepped between them and limped across the compound.

"Captain," ordered Major Crane, "sort out who is who. Put Claybourne's hired guns and Castillo's men under arrest and have them taken into the barn. Then hand them over to the federal marshals."

Benjamin rode away to begin the task of sorting out the attackers from defenders, and Crane rode over to where Thomas and his group were standing.

"Colonel Scoundrel," said Crane with a smile. "I am glad you seem well, sir, but you have given me pretty much the damndest morning of my life."

Thomas returned the salute. "It's good to see you, as well, Lucious."

Bill Cody and Bat Masterson rode up beside Major Crane and got down from their horses. Cody embraced Thomas, and Masterson patted him on the shoulder before walking over to talk with Rhine.

"We have a lot to talk about, Colonel," said Crane. "I need to know everything that brought you all to this point, and I need to know quickly."

Thomas nodded, and as Crane's soldiers worked their way through the compound sorting out who to arrest and who to allow to leave, the little group took seats on the benches behind the judge's table. They were joined by the four reporters from the barn, and over the next few minutes, they walked through the events of the past two months, right up to the battle this morning.

"It's almost all too fantastic," said Crane when Thomas finished the story.

"Real enough to me," said Clemens, "and every one of these boys here, and especially those who won't ever join us again."

Thomas looked around the compound, where the bodies of at least a dozen men lay where they had fallen. There were more behind the platform, including the body of sharpshooter Trooper Thorne. Claybourne, Rivas, and Castillo were dead, too. It had been a bloody morning. He glanced over at Diego. They knew that as bad as the morning had been, the killing wasn't over; they were going to retrieve Matthew Cord's man where Diego left him and make their way up the mountain to find Rosalilia. Anyone who got in their way would die. But Major Crane did not need to hear that part of the plan.

"What happens now, Major?" asked Diego.

"If everything you have said about Greer and the other conspirators checks out, Marshal Masterson and I will arrest them and take them in front of a federal magistrate. Despite everything I have heard today, though, I want to make it clear that it won't be easy to get a court martial to find Greer guilty of anything."

Bat Masterson shook his head in agreement and added, "The same is true of the civilians; the rules aren't the same for congressmen and high government officials as they are for ordinary folks."

"Do you mean they could just walk?" asked Von Sievers.

Neither Masterson nor Crane replied. Sometimes, even when something as monstrous as the massacre at Monteverde happens, temporal justice is powerless against the power, corruption, and money that people like Greer and Senator Mack can bring to bear.

"We've got a lot to sort out," Crane said to Bat Masterson. The marshal nodded, and they headed over to Langton Hall to begin the grim business of assessing the results of the fight that had raged over the past two hours.

Katarina Von Sievers made her way through the people milling around the compound and sat down to clean and dress her husband's wounds. Mary Orvis came to check on Mose, and Major Rhine and Diego went to collect the saddle and tack from Diego's fallen horse and find him a new mount.

Hamish was checked out by the army surgeon, who wanted the Scotsman to find a cot and stay on it for a week, but there was nothing that was going to stop him from accompanying Thomas and Diego on their journey to bring Rosalilia home.

Thomas went over to Clemens and shook the author's hand. "You're a warrior, Sam," he said. "I was proud to have you stand with us."

Clemens had scrounged a cigar from someone, and other than the dirt and bloodstains on his linen suit, he looked none the worse for his first real wartime experience.

"You know, Colonel," Clemens said, "I make my living telling stories about the trials and tribulations that have marked my passage through life, and truth be told, I have tended on rare occasion to gild the lily just a bit."

Thomas smiled.

"But," Clemens continued, "I don't expect that I will ever share this day's events or my role in them with anyone, and I will ask everyone to honor my request to remain an anonymous participant. That includes the official reports that will be filed by Major Crane and Marshal Masterson, and any stories filed by those damn reporters. I will not speak of what I did up on that platform this morning in my writing, or in my speeches. No sir, I will not."

Clemens stubbed out his cigar on the judging table and stared off into space. "Do you find that a strange request from a man who lives as public a life as I do, Colonel?"

He put his hand on Clemens's shoulder. "It's pretty much the only thing I have heard today that does make sense, Sam."

Clemens shook Thomas's hand again and then headed over towards the platform, where Bill Cody, Oscar Wilde, and Giuseppe Verdi were already regaling a crowd with their versions of the morning's spectacle. The author walked up the steps and went to the rear of the platform to gather up the few personal items that Trooper Thorne had left behind. When he passed the story-telling trio, he ignored Buffalo Bill's invitation to join them at the dais and bask in a little public adulation

Before Thomas left with Hamish to go out to the tent encampment and collect their horses and gear, he borrowed a pencil and some paper from Katarina and jotted a quick note to Demetria.

"Tell her I will come as soon as I am able," he said to Katarina. "Tell her…" His words trailed off.

Katarina took his hand. "I know what to say, Thomas. Stay safe."

❖

A half hour later, Thomas and Hamish rode back through the compound gate.

The perspective from horseback was quite different than it had been when they were on their feet in the thick of the fight. The bodies had been cleared from the gravel, but everywhere they looked, windows and doors were smashed and broken, fountains were knocked over, and fence rails pushed down. When Thomas rode past the platform and counted the hundreds of bullet holes in the support timbers and railings, he marveled that any of them had made it out alive.

"Amazing, no?" said Sergey as he appeared out from under the platform with his saber.

"It is. How's the shoulder?"

"My shoulder will heal, and my leg as well. That was some fight, Colonel Scoundrel. Now that I have seen you in action, I am glad that we did not have to face one another in the arena that night on the mountain."

Thomas saluted the Russian and rode around to the barn with Hamish, where they would wait for Diego and begin the journey to the mountain. They dismounted, tied their horses to a post, and filled their canteens from a small fountain.

"Where will you go when this is over?" Hamish asked.

He looked off into the distance before he answered. "I wish I knew," he began, but before he could continue, two horses shot around the back of the barn and galloped past them. The horses whirled around, and one sprinted at them while the other sat in wait. The dark-clad horseman raced to Hamish, swung his saber, and just missed the Scotsman's head. Thomas reached for his revolver, only to remember that he and Hamish had just given their guns to Major Rhine to check and clean before they left to go after Matthew Cord.

Thomas looked for something to use as a weapon, but Hamish beat him to it. He grabbed a ten-foot timber that was leaning against the barn, and when the rider flew back at them, he grasped the timber a few feet from the end, planted his feet, and swung with all his might. The log smashed the rider in the chest and sent him flying off his saddle and into a heap next to a water trough. The man lay still as his horse galloped away.

"Not quite a regulation caber," said Hamish, "but it will do in a pinch."

Thomas's smile disappeared when he saw movement at the other end of the barn; the second rider was coming their way. He scooped up the fallen rider's saber and held it behind his shoulder in a tight grip. As the horse got closer, he was able to make out the attacker's face; he would recognize those violet eyes and that black hair anywhere.

Hyacinth Claybourne was dressed all in black, from her boots to the ribbon holding her hair back. She reined her horse to a stop three feet from Hamish and Thomas and pulled her revolver. Her lips were drawn back, her eyes were moist, and her cheeks were flushed. It occurred to Thomas that this was exactly how she looked when she was riding him under the oak tree while the fireworks exploded above them.

Hamish was trying to make sense of what was happening when Hyacinth's Colt fired and struck him in the chest. A bewildered expression crossed his face as he looked down at the blood oozing from the wound, and then his knees turned to water, and he crashed to the ground.

Hyacinth trained her gun on Thomas and moved her horse two steps closer.

He gazed down at his friend and cursed the events that had led him to bring such a gentle soul to this place. Then he raised his head and looked up at Hyacinth. The sun was directly behind her, and he had to raise his palm above his brow to make out her face.

"For your father?" he asked her, looking at Hamish.

"Don't let the last words you will ever speak be those of a fool," Hyacinth said. Then she waved one hand in the direction of the compound and the prairie beyond and said, "All of this was going to be mine someday, you know. That time has merely come sooner than expected."

"And you think you can weather the storm that will come at you now? You think you will be allowed to keep your father's empire?"

"My father may have committed crimes, but the law does not allow for the sins of the father to be visited upon the child. It's the American way. Of course I will keep it all, and I will buy my own politicians and military men, ones who are far smarter and more capable than the idiots my father gathered around him."

He shook his head. "You are every bit as insane as he was. You've been in the house; you saw how he ended up. I promise you, Hyacinth, any victory you enjoy today will be short-lived."

She smiled. "No, my dearest Thomas, you are mistaken."

He heard the hammer on her Colt ratchet back. "It is you who are to be short-lived."

"I am so sorry, my friend," he said to Hamish. Then he raised his head and looked Hyacinth defiantly in the eyes.

"I almost regret this," she said as she stretched her arm forward to take the shot.

But, instead of the blast of the Colt, Thomas heard a swoosh, followed by a thumping sound, and Hyacinth pitched forward in her saddle with the shaft of a Cheyenne arrow protruding from her back. The revolver fell from her hand, and she slipped off her saddle and tumbled to the ground.

Before he could gather his wits, a pony emerged from out of the sun and swung to a stop in front of him. Dawn Pillow lowered her bow and smiled.

"You really should do a better job of choosing who you sleep with," she said.

He stepped up beside her horse and patted it on the neck. "You might want to think about that advice, given our own history," he said.

Then she saw Hamish lying motionless on the ground.

"Oh, Thomas, I am so very sorry."

"He saved my life. A lot of people have been doing that lately. I will never be able to repay him." He looked up at Dawn Pillow. "Or you."

She leaned down and ran her hand across his cheek. "I must go to my father. We have unfinished business with General Greer. Be well, my Thomas."

Dawn Pillow wheeled and galloped to the middle of the compound, where Sergey Baklanov was waiting on his horse. Thomas watched as the Cheyenne healer and the Cossack warrior briefly touched hands. Then they waved to him and galloped through the gate and out to the prairie where Red Elk and his warriors were waiting.

❋

SEVENTY TWO

Temptation Mountain

As soon as they began to pick their way up the well-marked mountain trail, the air began to cool, and by late afternoon it was quite pleasant. The barren, rocky glacial moraine at the base of the mountain yielded to stands of willow at the lower elevations, which were quickly supplanted by aspen groves and pockets of fir. Diego took a moment to pause beside a thicket of wild roses whose petals had been replaced by masses of bright red rose hips. Encountering roses like this, especially on the day he knew he was going to find Rosalilia, was a good omen.

Major Rhine had supplied them with a pack horse and an extra saddle mount for Rosalilia to ride on their return, and a half hour after Dawn Pillow and Sergey rode through the gate to join her father, Thomas and Diego were saying goodbye to Crane and Bat Masterson. As they prepared to ride out, a sergeant on the hill behind the smoke-house signaled that something was happening with General Greer's party, and the four men rode up the path together.

"I'm not sure what to make of it," said the sergeant as they rode up beside him, "but it don't look good."

He pointed to the east, where Greer's wagons were plodding slowly in the direction of the Denver road. No doubt they were taking it easy because of the busted wagon wheel, Crane thought as he reached for his binoculars. The other men took their field glasses out, and everyone focused on the prairie. Even from this distance it was easy to make out the three wagons and their escorts.

"Senator Mack is with them?" asked Masterson.

"Yes," replied Crane. "Along with Colonel Alphonse, and a US Congressman, an Assistant Secretary of State, and even a god-damned former Vice-President of Mexico. Every one of the bastards who approved the attack on Monteverde."

"You and Bat going to stop them here or pick them up in Denver?" asked Thomas.

"Denver would be my choice," said Masterson. "We'd have back up from the local federal magistrates, and a short distance to travel to put them in jail. I say we let them go."

The sergeant piped in. "But that's why I said this don't look good, gentlemen. Look there, about a quarter mile to the left, coming out of that stand of trees."

Thomas swung his head and looked where the sergeant was pointing. He focused his binoculars and almost immediately let out a soft whistle.

"Well, I'll be damned," he said.

"Sweet mother of mercy," added Crane.

Their astonishment was understandable: emerging from the thicket of trees were two mounted Cheyenne warriors. They wore feather headdresses and carried battle lances. As the men behind the smokehouse watched, another warrior came out of the trees, then another and another in a steady flow, until Thomas counted twenty-six fighting men. The Cheyenne lined up facing Langton Hall, almost as if they wanted to make sure that they were seen. Before Thomas could say anything to Crane, two more riders came out of the trees, and a moment later Dawn Pillow and Sergey had joined the battle line.

Then Captain Benjamin galloped up the hill to join Thomas and the others as they watched the gathering of the Cheyenne war party.

"What do we do about them, Major?" Benjamin asked.

"Well now, that would be the question, wouldn't it?" replied the major. "Damned if I wouldn't like to ride back down into the compound and pretend I never saw this."

"Why don't you?" said Diego.

"You mean let Red Elk and his people deliver whatever kind of justice they feel inclined to?" replied Crane. "That's crazy talk."

"Greer and the others deserve it," said Thomas. "You know it, and we know it, too." Then he turned to Bat Masterson and asked, "If those men are tried and convicted, what will their likely punishment be?"

"They'll hang, no question," replied the marshal.

"But the law will have been followed," said Crane. "We can't just let folks dole out whatever sentences they feel like. That's not justice, that's mob rule."

The men sat quietly on their horses, looking across at the Cheyenne, who were watching them in return.

"What in the hell are they waiting for?" asked Crane.

"For you to do the right thing," came a voice from behind them.

Thomas and the others turned to see Samuel Clemens, who had walked up the hill as they were talking.

"Doing the right thing as you call it, isn't my job, Mr. Clemens," said Crane. "My job is to follow orders and the rules of military justice."

"Justice?" said Clemens. "Do you really believe that a trial, no matter the outcome, will deliver justice to the families of those poor souls who were butchered at Monteverde? And didn't I hear both you and Marshal Masterson opine as to how it was quite possible that Greer and the others have enough political influence and money to buy their way out of this mess?"

"That's why we put the question of guilt or innocence before a jury," said Masterson. "They have the ultimate say. It's not a perfect, system, I agree, but I also know that the jury is the only thing standing between civilization and anarchy."

Clemens took a draw on his cigar. "A jury? Take a look, gentlemen." He pointed across the compound to the hill where Red Elk and his warriors sat stoically under the clear blue sky. "What do you think that is?" Then he dropped his cigar, stamped it out, and walked back down the hill.

Diego and Thomas sat motionless, waiting for the major to make his decision. Then Crane moved his horse over beside them and shook their hands. "Gentlemen," he said impassively, and then he and a smiling Captain Benjamin made their way down the hill and back into the compound.

"I can't be a part of what is going to happen now, Thomas," said Bat Masterson. "But from my heart, I tell you I agree." Then he rode away to join the others.

Thomas looked at Diego, who smiled and nodded. Thomas raised his rifle, and slowly waved it back and forth. A moment later, Red Elk raised his rifle and waved in return. Then the Cheyenne war party turned and trotted off to intercept the Monteverde conspirators. High above them, a red-tailed hawk led the way.

❖

Several hours later, Thomas and Diego were halfway up the rugged slope of Temptation Mountain. They had found Cord's man, Hayes, where Diego had left him bound and gagged that morning. When Hayes understood that Claybourne and most of the hired guns were dead, and that his only choice to avoid the same fate was to give them directions to the cabin where Rosalilia was being held, he drew a map in the dirt that showed the way to the to the trailhead and told them what markers to look for along the way. Then Thomas and Diego gave him a canteen of water and told him to go back to Langton Hall and surrender himself to Marshal Masterson.

When they stopped beside a mountain stream to eat and let the horses water, Thomas decided it was time to raise a difficult subject.

"She's been held by these bastards for over two months," he said to Diego.

Diego only nodded in reply.

"We don't know what to expect. No, I'm not talking about whoever is guarding her. I mean what to expect as far as how she has been treated."

Diego looked him hard in the eye. "You mean because she is a beautiful woman, and they are men," he finally answered.

"Yes, my friend. That is what I mean."

Diego leaned down and tightened the brace on his knee. Then he unholstered his Colt and spun the cylinder. "I am not the same man that I was three months ago, Tomás. I am a cripple. I have killed a dozen men. The only thing that has not changed about me is my love for her. So, the answer to your question is that I do not expect her to be the same person she was on the day of our engagement, either. I have no idea what she has had to do to survive."

He put his revolver back into the holster and swung up on his horse. "What I do know, Tomás, is that I am going to kill those who took her, and then we are going home. I will not ask her about these past months, and she will not ask me. It is enough that we find each other now and begin our lives from this day."

❖

The first purples and oranges of twilight were forming around the crest of the mountain when they rounded a bend on the trail and saw the cabin, less than a hundred yards ahead. It sat on a rocky outcropping, and the trees and bushes around it had been cleared to make it difficult for anyone to sneak up without being seen. Smoke from the cookstove was curling into the sky, and the oil lamps inside the cabin had already been lit.

They brought their horses to halt, spooking a deer that skittered across the trail ahead and disappeared into a thicket of aspens.

Diego started to get down from his horse, but Thomas reached over and laid a hand on his arm.

"I will hike up and try to look inside the cabin," Thomas said. "Then we can figure out how to do this."

Diego wanted to argue that he should be the one to go, but he knew Thomas was right. His leg injuries would slow him down, and he would be exhausted before the fight even began. He nodded and took the reins of Thomas's horse. Thomas untied the pack horse and extra saddle horse and moved them over between two pine trees before starting the hike up to the cabin.

The trail was heavily traveled and easy to navigate. When he was about fifty yards from the cabin, he moved off the trail and made a wide circle to the left. That meant making it through rows of thorny bushes and piles of sharp crushed rock, but it was the only way to approach the cabin without being seen.

He eased his way around the backside of the cabin and walked as quietly as he could past the privy and up to the porch. There was no door, but there was a small, curtainless window cut into in the center of the wall. He pressed himself flat against the boards, and slowly, slowly moved his head until he could see inside. A moment later, he turned away and silently wound his way back down the trail.

Diego was checking his revolver when Thomas stepped out from behind a line of trees. Even in the failing light he could see that Thomas was smiling.

"She is there?" Diego asked.

"Yes. She is sitting on the bed, reading."

"How does she look. Is she unharmed?"

"There is some bruising on one side of her face. Other than that, she seems well."

"Cabrones," muttered Diego. "Damn their souls to hell."

"That time will come soon enough, but first we need to get her out of there."

"What is the situation?"

"Two men are inside the cabin with her. They are sitting at a small table, drinking and playing cards."

"Is one of them Matthew Cord?"

Thomas nodded. "But Hayes told us there were three men up here. It's nearly dark, so I doubt the third man is out for a stroll."

"More likely he would be in the outhouse."

"If that's true I just this minute walked past him. Lucky for me he doesn't have good hearing."

"Lucky for you he was probably making loud music on the throne," smiled Diego.

"If he is in there, I've got to get back up there now. We can't let him return to the cabin. Handling Cord and the other man will be difficult enough. Fighting three of them in a space that small would be a nightmare."

With that, Thomas unsheathed his knife and trotted back up towards the cabin. When he came up behind the outhouse, he put his ear against the wood. Whoever was inside was not noisily passing gas, but they were humming. Thomas went around to the front and positioned himself beside the door. He gripped the knife tightly and waited.

Two minutes later, he heard rustling noises. The outhouse door opened, and a tall man stepped out into the cool night air. A cigarette dangled from his lip, and he was using both hands to button his fly. Thomas moved quickly; he took one step forward, grabbed the man's shoulder with his left hand and plunged his knife deep into the man's back. Then he withdrew the knife, slid his hand to the center of the man's back, and pushed hard. The man stumbled, coughing and gasping for breath as he collapsed to one knee. Thomas plunged the knife deep into his side two more times. The man coughed again, took a deep rasping breath, and then toppled to the ground. Thomas waited a moment and felt for a pulse at the neck. He was dead.

❖

Diego simply raised his eyebrows when Thomas stepped out of the darkness.

"Now we are fighting two," Thomas said.

Diego tied their horses to a bush and waited for Thomas to check his gear before they headed up the hill.

"We can't just go up and knock on the door," whispered Diego when they were fifty yards from the cabin.

"I've been thinking on that. I smelled liquor on the breath of the man in the outhouse. A lot of it. The way I see it, he is going to stumble going up the stairs, and then make a lot of noise falling onto the porch. One of his friends will open the door to give him a hand. We'll deal with that one fast, and then there will only be one left to fight."

Diego laid his hand on Thomas' forearm. "No matter who opens that door, Tomás, Matthew Cord is mine."

"No, Diego, Rosalilia is yours. When the tangle starts, we get who we get. One of us must get to her. Doesn't matter if it's you or me. We're past revenge now. Kill each one of them later, yes, I'm with you, but my job right now is to help you get her out safely."

Diego smiled. "And so now, *hermano*, you are also my conscience. I am blessed to have you as my friend."

They stopped before they got to the area that was illuminated by the door lantern. Thomas checked his knife and revolver and then rested his hand on Diego's shoulder. "Be well. Father a hundred children, and live forever," he whispered. Then he put his foot on the first porch step.

❖

Matthew Cord was just about to reach for another card when he and Spruce heard a crash on the porch, followed by a muffled "Damn it all to hell!"

"Reed, you dumb son of a bitch, I'm taking you off the sauce," Cord yelled. "The fool can't even take a leak by himself."

Rosalilia was used to exchanges like this and barely looked up from her book. Spruce took another shot of whiskey, and when Cord got up to go to the door, he reached across the table and took a quick peek at his boss's hand.

"This is the last time…" Cord laughed as he swung the door open. But his gap-toothed smile turned to shock when Colonel Thomas Scoundrel reached in and grabbed him by the front of his shirt and punched him in the face. Cord instinctively pulled back, but Thomas was expecting that and grabbed Cord by his hair and yanked him out onto the porch and into Diego's arms.

Thomas left Diego to sort things out with Cord and leapt into the small room. Spruce had just pushed the table away and was getting out of his chair to help Cord with whatever the hell was happening.

Rosalilia's eyes went wide with surprise and joy to see Thomas fly into the cabin, but she didn't let her excitement prevent her from acting. She pulled her dagger from her chemise, swung her legs off the bed, and got behind Spruce as he was pulling his own knife out. Before his blade slipped from its sheath, she stabbed him hard in the side of his neck and left her blade there.

Spruce put his hand up on the knife handle and Thomas saw a look of disappointment in his eyes. Did the man really expect that Rosalilia was going to come to his assistance? Thomas didn't wait for the answer. Spruce staggered forward two steps, and Thomas shot him through the heart. Spruce collapsed on the table and crashed to the floor.

"Diego," cried Rosalilia, and she jumped for the door.

Thomas grabbed her arm. "Not yet," he said. He stepped out onto the porch, but Cord and Diego were gone. It took a moment for his eyes to adjust to the dark, and then he saw them in a heap about fifty feet away, rolling down the hill. Thomas raced up to them just as Diego rolled on top and stopped their slide by pushing his boot into the dirt. He straddled Cord's chest and began to pummel him across the face with the butt of his revolver until Thomas heard Cord's nose break and saw blood gush from his nostrils and mouth. Diego held Cord's head back on the ground as he continued to batter the engineer's face over and over. Thomas watched in silence; he would intervene only if Diego needed help, but when Cord went limp, he knew there was no possibility of that happening.

Finally, exhausted, Diego lowered his arm, set his revolver on the ground and let Thomas help him to stand up.

Diego was breathing heavily as he brushed dirt from his shirt and pushed his hair back from his forehead. He wanted to look his best for his fiancée.

"He's still alive, you know," Thomas finally said.

Diego looked down at Cord, who was holding his head and moaning quietly. Then he wiped his sleeve across his mouth. "Do you suppose Red Elk and his men have killed Greer and the others?"

"That I do not know. Is it important?"

"If they are dead, who is left to face whatever justice may be left? I had no issue with Red Elk going after them; and I have no problem putting this dog down. But now, to my own surprise, I find I am weary of all this killing."

Thomas embraced his friend. "Go to her. I will tie him up and tomorrow we will take him to Bat Masterson."

Rosalilia stood motionless in the open doorway as Diego limped up to the cabin. He stopped at the bottom of the porch steps and smiled up at her. She brushed her hair off her face, smoothed her dress, and then rushed down the steps and leapt into his arms. "You are here," she sobbed.

"I have always been here, *mi amor*. Every minute of every day."

Thomas bound Cord's hands behind his back and led him a few yards down the trail, where he tied him to a tree in the darkness. The man would either survive the night or he wouldn't. In fact, if he knew what awaited him back at Langton Hall, he might prefer to have a cougar finish the job Diego started.

With Cord secured, he went into the cabin and drug Spruce's body out. Then he went down to retrieve the horses before coming back into the cabin to help Rosalilia clean up. Later they shared a drink as she tended to Diego's cuts and bruises, and then Thomas said goodnight and laid his bedroll in a thick patch of soft grass on a slope behind the cabin.

The half-moon shone like an alabaster stone in a sea of silver jewels as he lay his head down. He had never been so tired, or so happy.

⁂

Diego came out of the cabin at first light with a cup of coffee and a plate of buttered biscuits.

"Did you make these?" asked Thomas. "They're good."

"Apparently my Rosalilia taught herself to cook over these past months. Another miracle in the sea of miracles we have experienced."

"Do you want to rest here for a day before we go back?"

"She wants to leave as soon as possible, and what few things she has are already packed."

"That's fine with me. I'll need your help to get Cord on a horse, and then we can leave."

Diego looked disgusted.

"Are you sorry you let him live?"

"Perhaps. But it is far too beautiful a morning to be thinking about killing anyone."

Thomas smiled. They went down to the cabin, saddled the horses and slung Cord up on his mount. Then they bound Cord's wrists together and secured the other end of the rope to the stirrup. Cord tried to speak but his lips were too badly bruised and swollen to form words, so he simply shrugged his shoulders. Broken and bloody didn't matter; he wasn't done yet.

When Rosalilia came out on the porch and closed the door behind her for the last time, Diego said "Maybe we should burn the place down."

"Good idea, but Masterson is going to have to send someone up here to go through the place and bury the men I hauled into the brush," answered Thomas. "We'll have to leave the cabin as it is."

Diego nodded in agreement and then helped Rosalilia on to her horse. As he handed her the reins, Cord slammed his boot heels against his horse's flanks. It bolted away from the cabin and charged down the hill, but before Thomas could swing up on his horse and follow, Cord's horse hit a patch of loose rocks. With his hands bound behind him, Cord had no rein control, so when the horse stumbled and tried to right itself, the jarring motion sent him flying off the saddle. Unfortunately for him, the rope tying his wrists to the stirrup held tight. He fell down and to the right and his head slammed onto the ground. The horse raced forward, dragging him through dirt and rocks and brush with his head bouncing up and down like a child's spring-loaded toy.

The good news for Cord was that the horse only ran for about fifty feet before it realized something was wrong and came to a halt. Cord shook off the pain, struggled to his knees, and began working at the rope that bound his wrists.

Thomas started to ride down to him, but Diego took his arm. "You know," Diego said in a thoughtful tone, "I think your friend Mr. Clemens had it right; justice can come in many forms." Then he pulled his revolver and fired two shots over the head of Cord's horse.

The animal jerked back and shot off down the trail at a full gallop. They watched as Cord was bounced into the air, bashed against rocks, and dragged between downed tree limbs. The horse disappeared into the thick foliage a moment later, but the sound of Cord's body smashing into stumps and boulders continued for another twenty seconds.

"Wait here," Thomas said when the crashing noises stopped. He rode down the trail and returned a few minutes later with Cord's horse. "Masterson's men should have had three bodies to bury, but to tell you the truth, there isn't enough left of Mr. Cord for anybody but the buzzards to bother with," he told his friends.

❖

It was cool and sunny on the mountain top, and they could see for miles in all directions. Thomas adjusted his hat and scratched Ulysses behind the ear. Rosalila moved her horse close to his, took his hand, and kissed him on the cheek. Then she tied back her hair with a scarf and went over next to Diego.

"Let's go home," she said.

❖

EPILOGUE

Cuernavaca, Mexico, October 14,1882

Autumn light washed across the flower-strewn courtyard of the Verján residence and the soft breeze spilling off the lake gathered the scent of plumeria and roses in its breath as it passed through the garden. Two hundred guests were seated on chairs on the thick green lawn that curved around the patio, all under the watchful eyes of a detachment of soldiers from the city garrison on patrol around the villa. The presence of so many soldiers at the wedding of the town's most illustrious families was unusual, but, given the attack on Villa Verján last June after the engagement party, it was understandable.

Thomas stood by himself at the back of the garden next to a small table on which a bottle of mezcal and a cobalt-blue drinking glass had been placed. His hand rested on the back of an empty chair next to the sheath that held Itzcoatl's obsidian dagger.

Bishop Orozco and Diego were standing on a wooden dais at the front of the patio under a curtained arch capped with coral-colored bougainvillea vines. The bishop had just welcomed the assembled family and guests and now everyone was awaiting Rosalilia, who would be walking down the aisle on her uncle's arm.

In the front row alongside Rosalilia's mother were Diego's special guests; Katarina and Professor Von Sievers, Major T.R. Rhine and his wife, Anaya, and Mose and Calista Triplett. There was an empty seat up front reserved for Thomas, but he preferred to enjoy the event away from the press of the crowd.

When a solo piano began to play the opening notes of Mendelssohn's *Andante Con Moto* from the first book of *Song Without Words*, an expectant hush fell over the garden. Thomas knew that Rosalilia's first choice of music was the composer's more famous wedding march, but after the death of her father, she decided to go with the richer, more emotional *Andante.*

The piano played for a full minute before it was joined by a quartet of violins and cellos in an upwelling harmony that signaled that the bride was about to make her entrance, and then Rosalilia and her uncle appeared at the back of the garden and began their walk to the dais. Her simple ivory gown had a short train with an off the shoulder floral lace top that featured delicate bead work patterns. She wore her hair up with a pearl and diamond comb on either side, and Thomas was pleased to see that she was wearing the drop pearl earrings he had given her as a wedding gift.

Her uncle shook Diego's hand, kissed her, and then took a seat beside her mother. The bishop asked the couple to turn and greet their guests and then he, too, stepped down from the dais and sat down in the front row. The music died away and murmurs began to ripple through the crowd. It wasn't protocol for the priest officiating a wedding to leave his station before the ceremony had even begun.

Diego and Rosalilia did not seem concerned. They looked out across the sea of faces of friends and family and simply enjoyed the moment. Then they turned and faced the flower-draped arch. A moment later the curtain parted and Hamish Mackenzie stepped out onto the dais. His right arm was in a sling and he walked haltingly, but here he was, Bible in hand, ready to marry the couple for whom he and his friends had fought and sacrificed so much. Thomas could only smile and shake his head.

Everyone in the garden knew the story of Rosalilia's kidnapping and rescue, including the role played by the giant Scotsman. The guests began to applaud, and then they were on their feet clapping and cheering. Hamish, who had never known a bashful moment in his life, looked down at the ground and fought back tears.

Von Sievers, Mose, and Rhine turned in their chairs and raised their hands to Thomas. He returned their salutes and then, like Hamish, he struggled to stave off a flood of emotions. When the applause faded and the guests returned to their seats, Hamish opened his Bible, cleared his throat and prepared to speak. Before he began, he made eye contact with Thomas and nodded.

Then the breeze changed direction and the fragrance of night-blooming jasmine and lavender drifted his way. He turned around to identify the source of the perfume and saw that an extraordinarily beautiful woman had come quietly up behind him. Her raven hair was parted in the middle and arranged simply around her shoulders, and her steel-blue chiffon and lace dress magnified her olive complexion and deep emerald eyes. Her arms were crossed and she was tapping one foot impatiently.

Demetria Carnál smiled, stepped forward, and took his arm.

❖

Children's laughter floated up from the shore of the lake and a pair of collared doves swooped into the garden and lighted in an orange tree as Diego kissed his bride.

Hamish beamed and family, friends, and guests clapped when Rosalilia and Diego joined hands for the first time as man and wife.

As the applause continued, Demetria squeezed Thomas's arm and whispered, "I promise, *querida*, that I will never tie you up again."

He leaned over and kissed her on the lips. "Well," he answered, "maybe just now and again."

THE END

About the Author

B.R. O'Hagan completed undergraduate and graduate degrees at UCLA and wrote for film and television before turning to ghostwriting. He has written twenty-two books for Fortune 100 CEOs, national political figures and other prominent individuals.

He is also the author of the novel, *Martin's Way* and the family holiday book, *Jonathan Marvel's Christmas Pockets. Scoundrel in the Thick* is the first entry in his six-book Thomas Scoundrel series.

B.R. lives with his family in rural Oregon, surrounded by Douglas fir forests and the finest pinot noir vineyards on earth.

www.brohagan.com

ACKNOWLEDGMENTS

Writing a book, particularly an epic historical fiction like the *Scoundrel* series, is as much an exercise in accumulating debt as it is a process of research and creative thinking. I owe many for their support, encouragement and unwavering faith, beginning with my wife Lesli, who is keeper of the flame, guardian of the writing room door, and patient reader of each day's work product. I could not have finished this book, or, for that matter, any of my books, had she not walked the path alongside me.

To my daughter Natalie, who continues her amazing personal and professional journey, my love and thanks for the many gifts you have brought into my life.

I am also in debt to my friend and advisor Todd Rhine, whose steadfast belief in this endeavor has been nothing short of heroic. Todd moved mountains to help bring Thomas Scoundrel to life; if it is important, Todd will make it happen. I am blessed to have a man of his integrity and capability in my corner.

Thanks, too, to Brandon VanHeeswyk and Jon Starlight for their support. I feel better about the future knowing that young men of their caliber are stepping up to the plate.

To illustrator Tyler Jacobson, who brought my concept of Thomas Scoundrel to life brilliantly, I give my thanks and respect. At a time when art seems to be dying, his imagination and skill are helping to keep the barbarians from winning.

Thank you to copy editor extraordinaire Lori Szymanski for wielding the red pen authors fear the most with grace, professionalism and good humor, and to Carolyn Benjamin for listening, reading and offering honest commentary.

Finally, to young Mister Kai: it won't be long until you are in charge of the adventure. I can't wait.

COMING SOON!

Scoundrel in Paradise

Volume #2 in the Thomas Scoundrel Series

Winter 1872. Civil War hero and adventurer Thomas Scoundrel is working as a newspaper reporter in San Francisco. When he pens an exposé about a powerful politician and is marked for death, he stows away on a ship bound for Hawaii. Ten days later he is tossed ashore at Honolulu with just the clothes on his back, a finely honed sense of survival, and exceptional skills at cards. He bluffs his way into a high-stakes poker game and walks out of the saloon the next morning owning half of a pineapple plantation on the island of Lana'i.

When the politician discovers his whereabouts and sends a professional assassin after him, Thomas is on the run again, this time to Tahiti, where he befriends a French impressionist painter and lives quietly in a remote coastal village. During his absence from Hawaii, however, his partner in the plantation borrows money in Thomas's name and then disappears. Now he is being hunted by a ruthless killer and an equally remorseless Hawaiian banker. Forced to leave paradise, he strikes a deal with the artist to take his paintings to New York City in a bid to make the artist famous, and to clear his own name. But he won't be making the cross-country trip alone; the bank sends a pack of Tahitian warriors to collect the debt, and they join forces with the assassin to track him across the continent. Navigating the famously corrupt world of high-priced art soon becomes the least of his worries.

From a moonlight swim in a cobalt-blue lagoon with Hawaii's last royal princess to an epic fight in Hell's Kitchen against the leader of New York City's most notorious Irish gang, Thomas Scoundrel's sojourn to paradise is packed with action, compelling characters, humor and high adventure.

"Nanea i ka pihoihoi"

(Hawaiian: Enjoy the adventure!)

CPSIA information can be obtained
at www.ICGtesting.com
Printed in the USA
LVHW042216071221
705460LV00007B/20/J

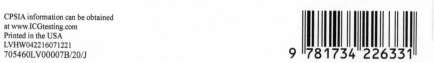